Dakwinsi Steppe

to Xanardwys

The Young Kingdor

Oma

Kwan

The Haghan'iin Host

SIGHING DESERT

Mordaga's Castle

The Ragged Pillars

The Teeth of Shenkh

Nishvalni-Oss

Valederia

Anakhazhan

Quarzhasaat

Bas'Uk

Elwher
ESHMIR

mar

WEEPING WASTE

to PHUM
Yeshpotoom-Kahlai

LMIORA Karlaak

ORG

Forest of Troos

Gorjhan

to OKARA
CHANG SHAI

Nadsokor Pignariom

Jadmar

Old Hrolmar

Uhaio

STRAITS of VILMIR

Ma-ha-kil-agra

Meni
Utkel

The Fortress of the Evening

ISLE of THE
PURPLE TOWNS

Oi Oi

Ufych-Sormeer

Chalal

THE
ROARING ROCKS

esaz

The River

Raschil

asaz

ILKHAR

saz ARGIMILIAR

Alorasaz

PIKARAYD

The Dead Hills

Ryfel

DOREL

For Jim Cawthorn-
The Master Cartographer
of Elric's World

THE
ELRIC
SAGA
VOLUME TWO

STORMBRINGER

THE ELRIC SAGA
VOLUME TWO

STORMBRINGER

Book 1: The Vanishing Tower

Book 2: The Revenge of the Rose

Book 3: The Bane of the Black Sword

Book 4: Stormbringer

BY MICHAEL MOORCOCK
WITH JOHN DAVEY, EDITOR AND BIBLIOGRAPHER

SAGA  PRESS

LONDON SYDNEY **NEW YORK** TORONTO NEW DELHI

SAGA ⟩⟩ PRESS

AN IMPRINT OF SIMON & SCHUSTER, INC.

1230 AVENUE OF THE AMERICAS, NEW YORK, NEW YORK 10020

First Saga Press hardcover edition April 2022

SAGA PRESS and colophon are trademarks of Simon & Schuster, Inc.

For information about special discounts for bulk purchases, please contact Simon & Schuster Special Sales at 1-866-506-1949 or business@simonandschuster.com

The Simon & Schuster Speakers Bureau can bring authors to your live event. For more information or to book an event, contact the Simon & Schuster Speakers Bureau at 1-866-248-3049 or visit our website at www.simonspeakers.com.

Interior design by Kathryn A. Kenney-Peterson

Manufactured in the United States of America

3   5   7   9   10   8   6   4   2

Library of Congress Cataloging-in-Publication Data is available.

ISBN 978-1-5344-4571-0
ISBN 978-1-5344-4573-4 (ebook)

CONTENTS

ART CREDITS

ENDPAPERS BY JOHN COLLIER

PAGE XI BY JOHN PICACIO

PAGE 822 BY ROBERT GOULD

INSERT ILLUSTRATIONS BY JOHN PICACIO, TYLER
JACOBSON, BROM, AND PIOTR JABLONSKI

FOREWORD

The minor masterpiece *The Sailor on the Seas of Fate*, like almost all of Michael Moorcock's efforts in the subgenre of heroic fantasy, is a complicated work, in the original sense of the term: that is, it folds together, with an insight both sophisticated and intuitive, 1) an apparently simple adventure story told in three episodes that are themselves interleaved in puzzling ways; 2) a sharp critique, of adventure stories generally (with their traditional freight of cruelty, wish-fulfillment, sexism, and violence), and of the heroic fantasy mode in particular; and 3) a remarkable working out (independently one feels of the work of Joseph Campbell) of the Transcendentalist premise that, as Emerson wrote, "one person wrote all the books." Moorcock took this literary universalism, with its implied corollary that one person reads all the books, and in *Sailor* began his career-long demonstration of the logical conclusion that all the books are one book, and all the heroes one hero (or antihero). From here it is only a short step, which the reader of heroic fantasy is eager to make, to the proposition that all readers and all writers are Odysseus, or Kull, or Elric of Melniboné, sharing through the acts of reading and writing a single essential, eternal heroic nature. This nature links us—all we heroes and Moorcocks—across all eras and lands. One might even attempt to chart these interconnections of story, hero, reader, and writer on a single map: Moorcock is such a cartographer. He called his map of our story-shaped world "the Multiverse."

It was Moorcock's insight, and it has been his remarkable artistic accomplishment, not just to complicate all this apparatus and insight and storytelling prowess, packing into one short novel such diverting fare as speculation on ontology and determinism, gory subterranean duels with giant killer baboons, literary criticism (the murmuring soul-vampiric sword Stormbringer offers what is essentially a running commentary on the equivocal nature of heroic swordsmen in fiction), buildings that are really alien beings, and ruminations on the self-similar or endlessly reflective interrelationship of hero, writer, and reader; but to do so with an almost offhanded ease, with a strong, plain, and unaffected English prose style that was nearing its peak in the mid-seventies.

That's part of what I would have liked to tell Michael Moorcock, when I recently had the good fortune to attend the Nebula Awards ceremony in Austin, Texas, and watch him receive a Grandmaster Award. I would have liked to tell him that when I was fourteen years old I found profound comfort in feeling that I shared in the nature of lost and wandering Elric, isolated but hungering for connection, heroically curious, apparently weak but capable of surprising power, unready and unwilling to sit on the moldering throne of his fathers but having nothing certain to offer in its stead. I would have liked to tell him that his work as a critic, as an editor, and as a writer has made it easier for me and a whole generation of us to roam the "moonbeam roads" of the literary multiverse. But as Mike rose to accept his award all I could do was sit there, next to him—marveling down to the deepest most twisted strands of my literary DNA—and applaud.

MICHAEL CHABON
MAY 2008

THE
ELRIC
SAGA

VOLUME TWO

STORMBRINGER

THE
VANISHING
TOWER

For Ken Bulmer, who, as editor of the magazine *Sword and Sorcery*, asked me to write this book as a serial for him. The magazine, which was to be a companion to *Vision of Tomorrow*, never appeared due to the backer withdrawing his support from both magazines.

THE VANISHING TOWER

CONTENTS

BOOK ONE

THE TORMENT OF THE LAST LORD

. . . and then did Elric leave Jharkor in pursuit
of a certain sorcerer who had, so Elric claimed,
caused him some inconvenience . . .

—The Chronicle of the Black Sword

I

Pale Prince on a Moonlit Shore

In the sky a cold moon, cloaked in clouds, sent down faint light that fell upon a sullen sea where a ship lay at anchor off an uninhabited coast.

From the ship a boat was being lowered. It swayed in its harness. Two figures, swathed in long capes, watched the seamen lowering the boat while they, themselves, tried to calm horses which stamped their hoofs on the unstable deck and snorted and rolled their eyes.

The shorter figure clung hard to his horse's bridle and grumbled.

"Why should this be necessary? Why could not we have disembarked at Trepesaz? Or at least some fishing harbour boasting an inn, however lowly . . ."

"Because, friend Moonglum, I wish our arrival in Lormyr to be secret. If Theleb K'aarna knew of my coming—as he soon would if we went to Trepesaz—then he would fly again and the chase would begin afresh. Would you welcome that?"

Moonglum shrugged. "I still feel that your pursuit of this sorcerer is no more than a surrogate for real activity. You seek him because you do not wish to seek your proper destiny . . ."

Elric turned his bone-white face in the moonlight and regarded Moonglum with crimson, moody eyes. "And what of it? You need not accompany me if you do not wish to . . ."

Again, Moonglum shrugged his shoulders. "Aye. I know. Perhaps I stay with you for the same reasons that you pursue the sorcerer of Pan Tang." He grinned. "So that's enough of debate, eh, Lord Elric?"

"Debate achieves nothing," Elric agreed. He patted his horse's nose as more seamen, clad in colourful Tarkeshite silks, came forward to take the horses and hoist them down to the waiting boat.

Struggling, whinnying through the bags muffling their heads, the horses were lowered, their hoofs thudding on the bottom of the boat as if they would stave it in. Then Elric and Moonglum, their bundles on their backs, swung down the ropes and jumped into the rocking craft. The sailors pushed off from the ship with their oars and then, bodies bending, began to row for the shore.

The late-autumn air was cold. Moonglum shivered as he stared towards the bleak cliffs ahead. "Winter is near and I'd rather be domiciled at some friendly tavern than roaming abroad. When this business is done with the sorcerer, what say we head for Jadmar or one of the other big Vilmirian cities and see what mood the warmer clime puts us in?"

But Elric did not reply. His strange eyes stared into the darkness and they seemed to be peering into the depths of his own soul and not liking what they saw.

Moonglum sighed and pursed his lips. He huddled deeper in his cloak and rubbed his hands to warm them. He was used to his friend's sudden lapses of silence, but familiarity did not make him enjoy them any better. From somewhere on the shore a nightbird shrieked and a small animal squealed. The sailors grunted as they pulled on their oars.

The moon came out from behind the clouds and it shone on Elric's grim, white face, made his crimson eyes seem to glow like the coals of hell, revealed the barren cliffs of the shore.

The sailors shipped their oars as the boat's bottom ground on shingle. The horses, smelling land, snorted and moved their hoofs. Elric and Moonglum rose to steady them.

Two seamen leapt into the cold water and brought the boat up higher. Another patted the neck of Elric's horse and did not look directly at the albino as he spoke. "The captain said you would pay me when we reached the Lormyrian shore, my lord."

Elric grunted and reached under his cloak. He drew out a jewel that shone brightly through the darkness of the night. The sailor gasped and stretched out his hand to take it. "Xiombarg's blood, I have never seen so fine a gem!"

Elric began to lead the horse into the shallows and Moonglum hastily followed him, cursing under his breath and shaking his head from side to side.

Laughing among themselves, the sailors shoved the boat back into deeper water.

As Elric and Moonglum mounted their horses and the boat pulled through the darkness towards the ship, Moonglum said: "That jewel was worth a hundred times the cost of our passage!"

"What of it?" Elric fitted his feet in his stirrups and made his horse walk towards a part of the cliff which was less steep than the rest. He stood up in his stirrups for a moment to adjust his cloak and settle himself more firmly in his saddle. "There is a path here, by the look of it. Much overgrown."

"I would point out," Moonglum said bitterly, "that if it were left to you, Lord Elric, we should have no means of livelihood at all. If I had not taken the precaution of retaining some of the profits made from the sale of that trireme we captured and auctioned in Dhakos, we should be paupers now."

"Aye," returned Elric carelessly, and he spurred his horse up the path that led to the top of the cliff.

In frustration Moonglum shook his head, but he followed the albino.

By dawn they were riding over the undulating landscape of small hills and valleys that made up the terrain of Lormyr's most northerly peninsula.

"Since Theleb K'aarna must needs live off rich patrons," Elric explained as they rode, "he will almost certainly go to the capital, Iosaz, where King Montan rules. He will seek service with some noble, perhaps King Montan himself."

"And how soon shall we see the capital, Lord Elric?" Moonglum looked up at the clouds.

"It is several days' ride, Master Moonglum."

Moonglum sighed. The sky bore signs of snow and the tent he carried rolled behind his saddle was of thin silk, suitable for the hotter lands of the East and West.

He thanked his gods that he wore a thick quilted jerkin beneath his breastplate and that before he had left the ship he had pulled on a pair of woollen breeks to go beneath the gaudier breeks of red silk that were his outer wear. His conical cap of fur, iron and leather had earflaps which were now drawn tightly and secured by a thong beneath his chin and his heavy deerskin cape was drawn closely around his shoulders.

Elric, for his part, seemed not to notice the chill weather. His own cape flapped behind him. He wore breeks of deep blue silk, a high-collared shirt of black silk, a steel breastplate lacquered a gleaming black, like his helmet, and embossed with patterns of delicate silverwork. Behind his saddle were deep panniers and across this was a bow and a quiver of arrows. At his side swung the huge runesword Stormbringer, the source of his strength and his misery, and on his right hip was a long dirk, presented him by Queen Yishana of Jharkor.

Moonglum bore a similar bow and quiver. On each hip was a sword, one short and straight, the other long and curved, after the fashion of the men of Elwher, his homeland. Both blades were in scabbards of beautifully worked Ilmioran leather, embellished with stitching of scarlet and gold thread.

Together the pair looked, to those who had not heard of them, like free-travelling mercenaries who had been more successful than most in their chosen careers.

Their horses bore them tirelessly through the countryside. These were tall Shazaarian steeds, known all over the Young Kingdoms for their stamina and intelligence. After several weeks cooped up in the hold of the Tarkeshite ship they were glad to be moving again.

Now small villages—squat houses of stone and thatch—came in sight, but Elric and Moonglum were careful to avoid them.

Lormyr was one of the oldest of the Young Kingdoms and much of the world's history had been made there. Even the Melnibonéans had heard the tales of Lormyr's hero of ancient times, Aubec of Malador of the province of Klant, who was said to have carved new lands from the stuff of Chaos that had once existed at World's Edge. But Lormyr had long since declined from her peak of power (though still a major nation of the south-west) and had mellowed into a nation that was at once picturesque and cultured. Elric and Moonglum passed pleasant farmsteads, well-nurtured fields, vineyards and orchards in which the golden-leaved trees were surrounded by time-worn, moss-grown walls. A sweet land and a peaceful land in contrast to the rawer, bustling north-western nations of Jharkor, Tarkesh and Dharijor which they had left behind.

Moonglum gazed around him as they slowed their horses to a trot. "Theleb K'aarna could work much mischief here, Elric. I am reminded of the peaceful hills and plains of Elwher, my own land."

Elric nodded. "Lormyr's years of turbulence ended when she cast off Melniboné's shackles and was first to proclaim herself a free nation. I have a liking for this restful landscape. It soothes me. Now we have another reason for finding the sorcerer before he begins to stir his brew of corruption."

Moonglum smiled quietly. "Be careful, my lord, for you are once again succumbing to those soft emotions you so despise . . ."

Elric straightened his back. "Come. Let's make haste for Iosaz."

"The sooner we reach a city with a decent tavern and a warm fire, the better." Moonglum drew his cape tighter about his thin body.

"Then pray that the sorcerer's soul is soon sent to limbo, Master Moonglum, for then I'll be content to sit before the fire all winter long if it suits you."

And Elric made his horse break into a sudden gallop as grey evening closed over the tranquil hills.

2

White Face Staring Through Snow

Lormyr was famous for her great rivers. It was her rivers that had helped make her rich and had kept her strong.

After three days' travelling, when a light snow had begun to drift from the sky, Elric and Moonglum rode out of the hills and saw before them the foaming waters of the Schlan River, tributary of the Zaphra-Trepek which flowed from beyond Iosaz down to the sea at Trepesaz.

No ships sailed the Schlan at this point, for there were rapids and huge waterfalls every few miles, but at the old town of Stagasaz, built where the Schlan joined the Zaphra-Trepek, Elric planned to send Moonglum into town and buy a small boat in which they could sail up the Zaphra-Trepek to Iosaz where Theleb K'aarna was almost certain to be.

They followed the banks of the Schlan now, riding hard and hoping to reach the outskirts of the town before nightfall. They rode past fishing villages and the houses of minor nobles, they were occasionally hailed by friendly fishermen who trawled the quieter reaches of the river, but they did not stop. The fishermen were typical of the area, with ruddy features and huge curling moustaches, dressed in heavily embroidered linen smocks and leather boots that reached almost to their thighs; men who in past times had been ever ready to lay down their nets, pick up swords and halberds and mount horses to go to the defence of their homeland.

"Could we not borrow one of their boats?" Moonglum suggested. But

Elric shook his head. "The fishermen of the Schlan are well known for their gossiping. The news of our presence might well precede us and warn Theleb K'aarna."

"You seem needlessly cautious . . ."

"I have lost him too often."

More rapids came in sight. Great black rocks glistened in the gloom and roaring water gushed over them, sending spray high into the air. There were no houses or villages here and the paths beside the banks were narrow and treacherous so that Elric and Moonglum were forced to slow their pace and make their way with caution.

Moonglum shouted over the noise of the water: "We'll not reach Stagasaz by nightfall now!"

Elric nodded. "We'll make camp below the rapids. There."

The snow was still falling and the wind drove it against their faces so that it became even more difficult to pick their way along the narrow track that now wound high above the river.

But at last the tumult began to die and the track widened out and the waters calmed and, with relief, they looked about them over the plain to find a likely camping place.

It was Moonglum who saw them first.

His finger was unsteady as he pointed into the sky towards the north.

"Elric. What make you of those?"

Elric peered up into the lowering sky, brushing snowflakes from his face.

His expression was at first puzzled. His brow furrowed and his eyes narrowed.

Black shapes against the sky.

Winged shapes.

It was impossible at this distance to judge their scale, but they did not fly the way birds fly. Elric was reminded of another flying creature—a creature he had last seen when he and the sea-lords fled burning Imrryr and the folk of Melniboné had released their vengeance upon the reavers.

That vengeance had taken two forms.

The first form had been the golden battle-barges which had waited for the attack as they left the Dreaming City.

The second form had been the great Phoorn, so-called dragons of the Bright Empire.

And these creatures in the distance had something of the look of dragons.

Had the Melnibonéans discovered a means of waking the Phoorn before the end of their normal sleeping time? Had they unleashed their dragons to seek out Elric, who had slain his own kin, betrayed his own unhuman kind in order to have revenge on his cousin Yyrkoon who had usurped Elric's place on the Ruby Throne of Imrryr?

Now Elric's expression hardened into a grim mask. His crimson eyes shone like polished rubies. His left hand fell upon the hilt of his great black battle-blade, the runesword Stormbringer, and he controlled a rising sense of horror.

For now, in mid-air, the shapes had changed. No longer did they have the appearance of dragons, but this time they seemed to be like multicoloured swans, whose gleaming feathers caught and diffracted the few remaining rays of light.

Moonglum gasped as they came nearer.

"They are huge!"

"Draw your swords, friend Moonglum. Draw them now and pray to whatever gods rule over Elwher. For these are creatures of sorcery and they are doubtless sent by Theleb K'aarna to destroy us. My respect for that conjuror increases."

"What are they, Elric?"

"Creatures of Chaos. In Melniboné they are called the Oonai. They can change shape at will. A sorcerer of great mental discipline, of superlative powers, who knows the apposite spells can master them and determine their appearance. Some of my ancestors could do such things, but I thought no mere conjuror of Pan Tang could master the chimerae!"

"Do you know no spell to counter them?"

"None comes readily to mind. Only a Lord of Chaos such as my patron demon Arioch could dismiss them."

Moonglum shuddered. "Then call your Arioch, I beg you!"

Elric darted a half-amused glance at Moonglum. "These creatures must fill you with great fear indeed if you are prepared to entertain the presence of Arioch, Master Moonglum."

Moonglum drew his long, curved sword. "Perhaps they have no business with us," he suggested. "But it is as well to be prepared."

Elric smiled. "Aye."

Then Moonglum drew his straight sword, curling his horse's reins around his arm.

A shrill, cackling sound from the skies.

The horses pawed at the ground.

The cackling grew louder. The creatures opened their beaks and called to one another and it was very plain now that they were indeed something other than gigantic swans, for they had curling tongues. And there were slim, sharp fangs bristling in those beaks. They changed direction slightly, winging straight for the two men.

Elric flung back his head and drew out his great sword and raised it skyward. It pulsed and moaned and a strange, black radiance poured from it, casting peculiar shadows over its owner's blanched features.

The Shazaarian horse screamed and reared and words began to pour from Elric's tormented face.

"Arioch! Arioch! Arioch! Lord of the Seven Darks, Duke of Chaos, aid me! Aid me now, Arioch!"

Moonglum's own horse had backed away in panic and the little man was having great difficulty in controlling it. His own features were almost as pale as Elric's.

"Arioch!"

Overhead the chimerae began to circle.

"Arioch! Blood and souls if you will aid me now!"

Then, some yards away, a dark mist seemed to well up from nowhere. It was a boiling mist that had strange, disgusting shapes in it.

"Arioch!"

The mist grew still thicker.

"Arioch! I beg you—aid me now!"

The horse pawed at the air, snorting and screaming, its eyes rolling, its nostrils flaring. Yet Elric, his lips curled back over his teeth so that he looked like a rabid wolf, continued to keep his seat as the dark mist quivered and a strange, unearthly face appeared in the upper part of the shifting column. It was a face of wonderful beauty, of absolute evil. Moonglum turned his head away, unable to regard it.

A sweet, sibilant voice issued from the beautiful mouth. The mist swirled languidly, becoming a mottled scarlet laced with emerald green.

"Greetings, Elric," said the face. "Greetings, most beloved of my children."

"Aid me, Arioch!"

"Ah," said the face, its tone full of rich regret. "Ah, that cannot be . . ."

"You must aid me!"

The chimerae had hesitated in their descent, sighting the peculiar mist.

"It is impossible, sweetest of my slaves. There are other matters afoot in the Realm of Chaos. Matters of enormous moment to which I have already referred. I offer only my blessing."

"Arioch—I beg thee!"

"Remember your oath to Chaos and remain loyal to us in spite of all. Farewell, Elric."

And the dark mist vanished.

And the chimerae came closer.

And Elric drew a racking breath while the runesword whined in his hand and quivered and its radiance dimmed a little.

Moonglum spat on the ground. "A powerful patron, Elric, but a damned inconstant one." Then he flung himself from his saddle as a creature which changed its shape a dozen times as it arrowed towards him reached out huge claws which clashed in the air where he had been. The riderless horse reared again, striking out at the beast of Chaos.

A fanged snout snapped.

Blood vomited from the place where the horse's head had been and the carcass kicked once more before falling to the ground to pour more gore into the greedy earth.

Bearing the remains of the head in what was first a scaled snout, then a beak, then a sharklike mouth, the Oonai thrashed back into the air.

Moonglum picked himself up. His eyes contemplated nothing but his own imminent destruction.

Elric, too, leapt from his horse and slapped its flank so that convulsively it began to gallop away towards the river. Another chimera followed it.

This time the flying thing seized the horse's body in claws which suddenly sprouted from its feet. The horse struggled to get free, threatening to break its own backbone in its struggles, but it could not. The chimera flapped towards the clouds with its catch.

Snow fell thicker now, but Elric and Moonglum were oblivious of it as they stood together and awaited the next attack of the Oonai.

Moonglum said quietly: "Is there no other spell you know, friend Elric?"

The albino shook his head. "Nothing specific to deal with these. The Oonai always served the folk of Melniboné. They never threatened us. So we needed no spell against them. I am trying to think . . ."

The chimerae cackled and yelled in the air above the two men's heads.

Then another broke away from the pack and dived to the earth.

"They attack individually," Elric said in a somewhat detached tone, as if studying insects in a bottle. "They never attack in a pack. I know not why."

The Oonai had settled on the ground and it had now assumed the shape of an elephant with the huge head of a crocodile.

"Not an aesthetic combination," said Elric.

The ground shook as it charged towards them.

They stood shoulder to shoulder as it approached. It was almost upon them—

—and at the last moment they divided, Elric throwing himself to one side and Moonglum to the other.

The chimera passed between them and Elric struck at the thing's side with his runesword.

The sword sang out almost lasciviously as it bit deep into the flesh which instantly changed and became a dragon dripping flaming venom from its fangs.

But it was badly wounded.

Blood ran from the deep wound and the chimera screamed and changed shape again and again as if seeking some form in which the wound could not exist.

Black blood now burst from its side as if the strain of the many changes had ruptured its body all the more.

It fell to its knees and the lustre faded from its feathers, died from its scales, disappeared from its skin. It kicked out once and then was still—a heavy, black, piglike creature whose lumpen body was the ugliest Elric and Moonglum had ever seen.

Moonglum grunted.

"It is not hard to understand why such a creature should want to change its form . . ."

He looked up.

Another was descending.

This had the appearance of a whale with wings, but with curved fangs, like those of a stomach fish, and a tail like an enormous corkscrew.

Even as it landed it changed shape again.

Now it had assumed human form. It was a huge, beautiful figure, twice as tall as Elric. It was naked and perfectly proportioned, but its stare was vacant and it had the drooling lips of an idiot child. Lithely it ran at them, its huge hands reaching out to grasp them as a child might reach for a toy.

This time Elric and Moonglum struck together, one at each hand.

Moonglum's sharp sword cut the knuckles deeply and Elric's lopped off two fingers before the Oonai altered its shape again and began first to be an octopus, then a monstrous tiger, then a combination of both, until at last it was a rock in which a fissure grew to reveal white, snapping teeth.

Gasping, the two men waited for it to resume the attack. At the base of the rock some blood was oozing. This put a thought into Elric's mind.

With a sudden yell he leapt forward, raised his sword over his head and brought it down on top of the rock, splitting it in twain.

Something like a laugh issued from the Black Sword then as the sundered shape flickered and became another of the piglike creatures. This was completely cut in two, its blood and its entrails spreading themselves upon the ground.

Then, through the snowy dusk, another of the Oonai came down, its body glowing orange, its shape that of a winged snake with a thousand rippling coils.

Elric struck at the coils, but they moved too rapidly.

The other chimerae had been watching his tactics with their dead companions and they had now gauged the skill of their victims. Almost immediately Elric's arms were pinned to his sides by the coils and he found himself being borne upward as a second chimera with the same shape rushed down on Moonglum to seize him in an identical way.

Elric prepared to die as the horses had died. He prayed that he would die swiftly and not slowly, at the hands of Theleb K'aarna, who had always promised him a slow death.

The scaly wings flapped powerfully. No snout came down to snap his head off.

He felt despair as he realised that he and Moonglum were being carried swiftly northward over the great Lormyrian steppe.

Doubtless Theleb K'aarna awaited them at the end of their journey.

3

Feathers Filling a Great Sky

Night fell and the chimerae flew on tirelessly, their shapes black against the falling snow.

The coils showed no signs of relaxing, though Elric strove to force them apart, keeping tight hold of his runesword and racking his brains for some means of defeating the monsters.

If only there were a spell . . .

He tried to keep his thoughts from what Theleb K'aarna would do if, indeed, it was that wizard who had set the Oonai upon them.

Elric's skill in sorcery lay chiefly in his command over the various elementals of air, fire, earth, water and ether, and also over the entities who had affinities with the flora and fauna of the Earth.

He had decided that his only hope lay in summoning the aid of Fileet, Lady of the Birds, who dwelt in a realm lying beyond the planes of Earth, but the invocation eluded him.

Even if he could remember it, the mind had to be adjusted in a certain way, the correct rhythms of the incantation remembered, the exact words and inflections recalled, before he could begin to summon Fileet's aid. For she, more than any other elemental, was as difficult to invoke as the fickle Arioch.

Through the drifting snow he heard Moonglum call out something indistinct.

"What was that, Moonglum?" he called back.

"I only—sought to learn—if you still—lived, friend Elric."

"Aye—barely . . ."

His face was chill and ice had formed on his helmet and breastplate. His whole body ached both from the crushing coils of the chimera and from the biting cold of the upper air.

On and on through the Southern night they flew while Elric forced himself to relax, to descend into a trance and to dredge from his mind the ancient knowledge of his forefathers.

At dawn the clouds had cleared and the sun's red rays spread over the snow like blood over damask. Everywhere stretched the steppe—a vast field of snow from horizon to horizon, while above it the sky was nothing but a blue sheet of ice in which sat the red pool of the sun.

And, tireless as ever, the chimerae flew on.

Elric brought himself slowly from his trance and prayed to his untrustworthy gods that he remembered the spell aright.

His lips were all but frozen together. He licked them and it was as if he licked snow. He opened them and bitter air coursed into his mouth. He coughed then, turning his head upwards, his crimson eyes glazing.

He forced his lips to frame strange syllables, to utter the old vowel-heavy words of the High Speech of Old Melniboné, a speech hardly suited to a human tongue at all.

"Fileet," he murmured. Then he began to chant the incantation. And as he chanted the sword grew warmer in his hand and supplied him with more energy so that the eldritch chant echoed through the icy sky.

Feathers fine our fates entwined
Bird and man and thine and mine,
Formed a pact that gods divine
Hallowed on an ancient shrine,
When kind swore service unto kind.

Fileet, fair feathered queen of flight
Remember now that fateful night
And help your brother in his plight.

There was more to the Summoning than the words of the invocation. There were the abstract thoughts in the head, the visual images which had to be retained in the mind the whole time, the emotions felt, the memories made sharp and true. Without everything being exactly right, the invocation would prove useless.

Centuries before, the Sorcerer Kings of Melniboné had struck this bargain with Fileet, Lady of the Birds: that any bird that settled in Imrryr's walls should be protected, that no bird would be shot by any of the Melnibonéan blood. This bargain had been kept and dreaming Imrryr had become a haven for all species of bird and at one time they had cloaked her towers in plumage.

Now Elric chanted his verses, recalling that bargain and begging Fileet to remember her part of it.

Brothers and sisters of the sky
Hear my voice where'er ye fly
And bring me aid from kingdoms high . . .

Not for the first time had he called upon the elementals and those akin to them. But lately he had summoned Haaashaastaak, Lord of the Lizards, in his fight against Theleb K'aarna and still earlier he had made use of the services of the wind elementals—the *sylphs*, the *sharnahs* and the *h'Haarshanns*—and the earth elementals.

Yet, Fileet was fickle.

And now that Imrryr was no more than quaking ruins, she could even choose to forget that ancient pact.

"Fileet . . ."

He was weak from the invoking. He would not have the strength to battle Theleb K'aarna even if he found the opportunity.

"Fileet . . ."

And then the air was stirring and a huge shadow fell across the chimerae bearing Elric and Moonglum northward.

Elric's voice faltered as he looked up. But he smiled and said:

"I thank you, Fileet."

For the sky was black with birds. There were eagles and robins and rooks and starlings and wrens and kites and crows and hawks and peacocks and flamingoes and pigeons and parrots and doves and magpies and ravens and owls. Their plumage flashed like steel and the air was full of their cries.

The Oonai raised its snake's head and hissed, its long tongue curling out between its front fangs, its coiled tail lashing. One of the chimerae not carrying Elric or Moonglum changed its shape into that of a gigantic condor and flapped up towards the vast array of birds.

But they were not deceived.

The chimera disappeared, submerged by birds. There was a frightful screaming and then something black and piglike spiralled to earth, blood and entrails streaming in its wake.

Another chimera—the last not bearing a burden—assumed its dragon shape, almost completely identical to those which Elric had once mastered as ruler of Melniboné, but larger and with not quite the same grace as Flamefang and the others.

There was a sickening smell of burning flesh and feathers as the flaming venom fell upon Elric's allies.

But now more and more birds were filling the air, shrieking and whistling and cawing and hooting, a million wings fluttering, and once again the Oonai was hidden from sight, once again a muffled scream sounded, once again a mangled, piglike corpse plummeted groundwards.

The birds divided into two masses, turning their attention to the chimerae bearing Elric and Moonglum. They sped down like two gigantic arrowheads, led, each group, by ten huge golden eagles which dived at the flashing eyes of the Oonai.

As the birds attacked, the chimerae were forced to change shape. Instantly Elric felt himself fall free. His body was numb and he fell like a stone, remembering only to keep his grip on Stormbringer, and as he fell he cursed at the irony. He had been saved from the beasts of Chaos only to hurtle to his death on the snow-covered ground below.

But then his cloak was caught from above and he hung swaying in the air. Looking up he saw that several eagles had grasped his clothing in their claws and beaks and were slowing his descent so that he struck the snow with little more than a painful bump.

The eagles flew back to the fray.

A few yards away Moonglum came down, deposited by another flight of eagles which immediately returned to where their comrades were fighting the remaining Oonai.

Moonglum picked up the sword which had fallen from his hand. He rubbed his right calf. "I'll do my best never to eat fowl again," he said feelingly. "So you remembered a spell, eh?"

"Aye."

Two more piglike corpses thudded down not far away.

For a few moments the birds performed a strange, wheeling dance in the sky, partly a salute to the two men, partly a dance of triumph, and then they divided into their groups of species and flew rapidly away. Soon there were no birds at all in the ice-blue sky.

Elric picked up his bruised body and stiffly he sheathed his sword Stormbringer. He drew a deep breath and peered upwards.

"Fileet, I thank thee again."

Moonglum still seemed dazed. "How did you summon them, Elric?"

Elric removed his helmet and wiped sweat from within the rim. In this clime that sweat would soon turn to ice. "An ancient bargain my ancestors made. I was hard pressed to remember the lines of the spell."

"I'm mightily pleased that you did remember!"

Absently, Elric nodded. He replaced his helmet on his head, staring about him as he did so.

Everywhere stretched the vast, snow-covered Lormyrian steppe.

Moonglum understood Elric's thoughts. He rubbed his chin.

"Aye. We are fairly lost, Lord Elric. Have you any idea where we may be?"

"I do not know, friend Moonglum. We have no means of guessing how far those beasts carried us, but I'm fairly sure it was well to the north of Iosaz. We are further away from the capital than we were . . ."

"But then so must Theleb K'aarna be! If we were, indeed, being borne to where he dwells . . ."

"It would be logical, I agree."

"So we continue north?"

"I think not."

"Why so?"

"For two reasons. It could be that Theleb K'aarna's idea was to take us to a place so far away from anywhere that we could not interfere with his plans. That might be considered a wiser action than confronting us and thus risking our turning the tables on him . . ."

"Aye, I'll grant you that. And what's the other reason?"

"We would do better to try to make for Iosaz where we can replenish both our gear and our provisions and enquire of Theleb K'aarna's whereabouts if he is not there. Also we would be foolish to strike further north without good horses and in Iosaz we shall find horses and perhaps a sleigh to carry us the faster across this snow."

"And I'll grant you the sense of that, too. But I do not think much of our chances in this snow, whichever way we go."

"We must begin walking and hope that we can find a river that has not yet frozen over—and that the river will have boats upon it which will bear us to Iosaz."

"A faint hope, Elric."

"Aye. A faint hope." Elric was already weakened from the energy spent in the invocation to Fileet. He knew that he must almost certainly die. He was not sure that he cared overmuch. It would be a cleaner death than some he had been offered of late—a less painful death than any he might expect at the hands of the sorcerer of Pan Tang.

They began to trudge through the snow. Slowly they headed south, two small figures in a frozen landscape, two tiny specks of warm flesh in a great waste of ice.

4

Old Castle Standing Alone

A day passed, a night passed.

Then the evening of the second day passed and the two men staggered on, for all that they had long since lost their sense of direction.

Night fell and they crawled.

They could not speak. Their bones were stiff, their flesh and their muscles numb.

Cold and exhaustion drove the very sentience from them so that when they fell in the snow and lay motionless they were scarcely aware that they had ceased to move. They understood no difference now between life and death, between existence and the cessation of existence.

And when the sun rose and warmed their flesh a little they stirred and raised their heads, perhaps in an effort to catch one last glimpse of the world they were leaving.

And they saw the castle.

It stood there in the middle of the steppe and it was ancient. Snow covered the moss and the lichen which grew on its worn, old stones. It seemed to have been there for eternity, yet neither Elric nor Moonglum had ever heard of such a castle standing alone in the steppe. It was hard to imagine how a castle so old could exist in the land once known as World's Edge.

Moonglum was the first to rise. He stumbled through the deep snow to where Elric lay. With chapped hands he tried to lift his friend.

The tide of Elric's thin blood had almost ceased to move in his body. He moaned as Moonglum helped him to his feet. He tried to speak, but his lips were frozen shut.

Clutching each other, sometimes walking, sometimes crawling, they progressed towards the castle.

Its entrance stood open. They fell through it and the warmth issuing from the interior revived them sufficiently to allow them to rise and stagger down a narrow passage into a great hall.

It was an empty hall.

It was completely bare of furnishings, save for a huge log fire that blazed in a hearth of granite and quartz built at the far end of the hall. They crossed flagstones of lapis lazuli to reach it.

"So the castle is inhabited."

Moonglum's voice was harsh and thick in his mouth. He stared around him at the basalt walls. He raised his voice as best he could and called:

"Greetings to whoever is the master of this hall. We are Moonglum of Elwher and Elric of Melniboné and we crave your hospitality, for we are lost in your land."

And then Elric's knees buckled and he fell to the floor.

Moonglum stumbled towards him as the echoes of his voice died in the hall. All was silent save for the crackling of the logs in the hearth.

Moonglum dragged Elric to the fire and lay him down near it.

"Warm your bones here, friend Elric. I'll seek the folk who live here."

Then he crossed the hall and ascended the stone stair leading to the next floor of the castle.

This floor was as bereft of furniture or decoration as the other. There were many rooms, but all of them were empty. Moonglum began to feel uneasy, scenting something of the supernatural here. Could this be Theleb K'aarna's castle?

For someone dwelt here, in truth. Someone had laid the fire and had opened the gates so that they might enter. And they had not left the castle in the ordinary way or he should have noticed the tracks in the snow outside.

Moonglum paused, then turned and slowly began to descend the stairs. Reaching the hall, he saw that Elric had revived enough to prop himself up against the chimneypiece.

"And—what—found you . . ." said Elric thickly.

Moonglum shrugged. "Nought. No servants. No master. If they have gone ahunting, then they hunt on flying beasts, for there are no signs of hoofprints in the snow outside. I am a little nervous, I must admit." He smiled slightly. "Aye—and a little hungry, too. I'll seek the pantry. If danger comes, we'd do as well to face it on full stomachs."

There was a door set back and to one side of the hearth. He tried the latch and it opened into a short passage at the end of which was another door. He went down the passage, hand on sword, and opened the door at the end. A parlour, as deserted as the rest of the castle. And beyond the parlour he saw the castle's kitchens. He went through the kitchens, noting that there were cooking things here, all polished and clean but none in use, and came finally to the pantry.

Here he found the best part of a large deer hanging and on the shelf above it were ranked many skins and jars of wine. Below this shelf were bread and some pasties and below that spices.

Moonglum's first action was to reach up on tiptoe and take down a jar of wine, removing the cork and sniffing the contents.

He had smelled nothing more delicate or delicious in his life.

He tasted the wine and he forgot his pain and his weariness. But he did not forget that Elric still waited in the hall.

With his short sword he cut off a haunch of venison and tucked it under his arm. He selected some spices and put them into his belt pouch. Under his other arm he put the bread and in both hands he carried a jar of wine.

He returned to the hall, put down his spoils and helped Elric drink from the jar.

The strange wine worked almost instantly and Elric offered Moonglum a smile that had gratitude in it.

"You are—a good friend—I wonder why . . ."

Moonglum turned away with an embarrassed grunt. He began to prepare the meat which he intended to roast over the fire.

He had never understood his friendship with the albino. It had always been a peculiar mixture of reserve and affection, a fine balance which both men were careful to maintain, even in situations of this kind.

Elric, since his passion for Cymoril had resulted in her death and the destruction of the city he loved, had at all times feared bestowing any tender emotion on those he fell in with.

He had run away from Rai-u Th'ee, the sculptress of Séred-Öma, and from Shaarilla of the Dancing Mist who had loved him dearly. He had fled from Queen Yishana of Jharkor who had offered him her kingdom to rule, in spite of her subjects' hatred of him. He disdained most company save Moonglum's, and Moonglum, too, became quickly bored by anyone other than the crimson-eyed prince of Imrryr. Moonglum would die for Elric and he knew that Elric would risk any danger to save his friend. But was not this an unhealthy relationship? Would it not be better if they went their different ways? He could not bear the thought. It was as if they were part of the same entity—different aspects of the character of the same man.

He could not understand why he should feel this. And he guessed that, if Elric had ever considered the question, the Melnibonéan would be equally hard put to find an answer.

He contemplated all this as he roasted the meat before the fire, using his long sword as a spit.

Meanwhile Elric took another draft of wine and began, almost visibly, to thaw out. His skin was still badly blistered by chilblains, but both men had escaped serious frostbite.

They ate the venison in silence, glancing around the hall, puzzling over the non-appearance of the owner, yet too tired to care greatly where he was.

Then they slept, having put fresh logs on the fire, and in the morning they were almost completely recovered from their ordeal in the snow.

They breakfasted on cold venison and pasties and wine.

Moonglum found a pot and heated water in it so that they might shave and wash and Elric found some salve in his pouch which they could put on their blisters.

"I looked in the stables," Moonglum said as he shaved with the razor he had taken from his own pouch. "But I found no horses. There are signs, however, that some beasts have been kept there recently."

"There is only one other way to travel," Elric said. "There might be skis somewhere in the castle. It is the sort of thing you might expect to find, for there is snow in these parts for at least half the year. Skis would speed our progress back towards Iosaz. As would a map and a lodestone if we could find one."

Moonglum agreed. "I'll search the upper levels." He finished his shaving, wiped his razor and replaced it in his pouch.

Elric got up. "I'll go with you."

Through the empty rooms they wandered, but they found nothing.

"No gear of any kind." Elric frowned. "And yet there is a strong sense that the castle *is* inhabited—and evidence, too, of course."

They searched two more floors and there was not even dust in the rooms.

"Well, perhaps we walk after all," Moonglum said in resignation. "Unless there was wood with which we could manufacture skis of some kind. I might have seen some in the stables . . ."

They had reached a narrow stair which wound up to the highest tower of the castle.

"We'll try this and then count our quest unsuccessful," Elric said.

And so they climbed the stair and came to a door at the top which was half-open. Elric pushed it back and then he hesitated.

"What is it?" Moonglum, who was below him, asked.

"This room is furnished," Elric said quietly.

Moonglum ascended two more steps and peered round Elric's shoulder. He gasped.

"And occupied!"

It was a beautiful room. Through crystal windows came pale light which sparkled and fell on hangings of many-coloured silk, on embroidered carpets and tapestries of hues so fresh they might have been made only a moment before.

In the centre of this room was a bed, draped in ermine, with a canopy of white silk.

And on the bed lay a young woman.

Her hair was black and it shone. Her gown was of the deepest scarlet. Her limbs were like rose-tinted ivory and her face was very fair, the lips slightly parted as she breathed.

She was asleep.

Elric took two steps towards the woman on the bed and then he stopped suddenly. He was shuddering. He turned away.

Moonglum was alarmed. He saw bright tears in Elric's crimson eyes.

"What is it, friend Elric?"

Elric moved his white lips but was incapable of speech. Something like a groan came from his throat.

"Elric . . ."

Moonglum placed a hand on his friend's arm. Elric shook it off.

Slowly the albino turned again towards the bed, as if forcing himself to behold an impossibly horrifying sight. He breathed deeply, straightening his back and resting his left hand on the pommel of his sorcerous blade.

"Moonglum . . ."

He was forcing himself to speak. Moonglum glanced at the woman on the bed, glanced at Elric. Did he recognise her?

"Moonglum—this is a sorcerous sleep . . ."

"How know you that?"

"It—it is a similar slumber to that in which my cousin Yyrkoon put my Cymoril . . ."

"Gods! Think you that . . . ?"

"I think nothing!"

"But it is not—"

"—it is not Cymoril. I know. I—she is like her—so like her. But unlike her, too . . . It is only that I could not have expected . . ."

Elric bowed his head.

He spoke in a low voice. "Come, let's be gone from here."

"But she must be the owner of this castle. If we awakened her we could—"

"She cannot be awakened by such as we. I told you, Moonglum . . ." Elric drew another deep breath. "It is an enchanted sleep she is in. I could not wake Cymoril from it, with all my powers of sorcery. Unless one has certain magical aids, some knowledge of the exact spell used, there is nothing that can be done. Quickly, Moonglum, let us depart."

There was an edge to Elric's voice which made Moonglum shiver.

"But . . ."

"Then I will go!"

Elric almost ran from the room. Moonglum heard his footsteps echoing rapidly down the long staircase.

He went up to the sleeping woman and stared down at her beauty.

He touched the skin. It was unnaturally cold. He shrugged and made to leave the chamber, pausing for a moment only to notice that a number of ancient battle-shields and weapons hung on one wall of the room, behind the bed. Strange trophies with which a beautiful woman should wish to decorate her bedroom, he thought. He saw the carved wooden table below the trophies. Something lay upon it. He stepped back into the room. A peculiar sensation filled him as he saw that it was a map. The castle was marked and so was the Zaphra-Trepek river.

Holding the map down to the table was a lodestone, set in silver on a long silver chain.

He grabbed the map in one hand and the lodestone in the other and ran from the room.

"Elric! Elric!"

He raced down the stairs and reached the hall. Elric had gone. The door of the hall was open.

He followed the albino out of the mysterious castle and into the snow.

"Elric!"

Elric turned, his face set and his eyes tormented.

Moonglum showed him the map and the lodestone.

"We are saved, after all, Elric!"

Elric looked down at the snow. "Aye. So we are."

5

Doomed Lord Dreaming

And two days later they reached the upper reaches of the Zaphra-Trepek and the trading town of Alorasaz with its towers of finely carved wood and its beautifully made timber houses.

To Alorasaz came the fur trappers and the miners, the merchants from Iosaz, downriver, or from afar as Trepesaz on the coast. A cheerful, bustling town with its streets lit and heated by great, red braziers at every corner. These were tended by citizens specially commissioned to keep them burning hot and bright. Wrapped in thick woollen clothing, they hailed Elric and Moonglum as they entered the city.

For all they had been sustained by the wine and meat Moonglum had thought to bring, they were weary from their walk across the steppe.

They made their way through the rumbustious crowd—laughing, red-cheeked women and burly, fur-swathed men whose breath steamed in the air, mingling with the smoke from the braziers, as they took huge swallows from gourds of beer or skins of wine, conducting their business with the slightly less bucolic merchants of the more sophisticated townships.

Elric was looking for news and he knew that if he found it anywhere it would be in the taverns. He waited while Moonglum followed his nose to the best of Alorasaz's inns and came back with the news of where it could be found.

They walked a short distance and entered a rowdy tavern crammed with big wooden tables and benches on which were jammed more traders and more merchants all arguing cheerfully, holding up furs to display their quality or to mock their worthlessness, depending on which point of view was taken.

Moonglum left Elric standing in the doorway and went to speak with the landlord, a hugely fat man with a glistening scarlet face.

Elric saw the landlord bend and listen to Moonglum. The man nodded and raised an arm to bellow at Elric to follow him and Moonglum.

Elric inched his way through the press and was knocked half off his feet by a gesticulating trader who apologised cheerfully and profusely and offered to buy him a drink.

"It is nothing," Elric said faintly.

The man got up. "Come on, sir, it was my fault . . ." His voice tailed off as he saw the albino's face. He mumbled something and sat down again, making a wry remark to one of his companions.

Elric followed Moonglum and the landlord up a flight of swaying wooden stairs, along a landing and into a private room which, the landlord told them, was all that was available.

"Such rooms as these are expensive during the winter market," the landlord said apologetically.

And Moonglum winced as, silently, Elric handed the man another precious ruby worth a small fortune.

The landlord looked at it carefully and then laughed. "This inn will have fallen down before your credit's up, master. I thank thee. Trading must be good this season! I'll have drink and viands sent up at once!"

"The finest you have, landlord," said Moonglum, trying to make the best of things.

"Aye—I wish I had better."

Elric sat down on one of the beds and removed his cloak and his sword belt. The chill had not left his bones.

"I wish you would give me charge of our wealth," Moonglum said as he removed his boots by the fire. "We might have need of it before this quest is ended."

But Elric seemed not to hear him.

After they had eaten and discovered from the landlord that a ship was leaving the day after tomorrow for Iosaz, Elric and Moonglum went to their separate beds to sleep.

Elric's dreams were troubled that night. More than usual did phantoms come to walk the dark corridors of his mind.

He saw Cymoril screaming as the Black Sword drank her soul. He saw Imrryr burning, her fine towers crumbling. He saw his cackling cousin Yyrkoon sprawling on the Ruby Throne. He saw other things which could not possibly be part of his past . . .

Never quite suited to be ruler of the cruel folk of Melniboné, Elric had wandered the lands of men only to discover that he had no place there, either. And in the meantime Yyrkoon had usurped the kingship, had tried to force Cymoril to be his and, when she refused, put her into a deep and sorcerous slumber from which only he could wake her.

Now Elric dreamed that he had found a Nanorion, the mystic gem which could awaken even the dead. He dreamed that Cymoril was still alive, but sleeping, and that he placed the Nanorion on her forehead and that she woke up and kissed him and left Imrryr with him, sailing through the skies on the Phoorn, Flamefang, the great Melnibonéan battle dragon, away to a peaceful castle in the snow.

He awoke with a start.

It was the dead of night.

Even the noise from the tavern below had subsided.

He opened his eyes and saw Moonglum fast asleep in the next bed.

He tried to return to sleep, but it was impossible. He was sure that he could sense another presence in the room. He reached out and gripped the hilt of Stormbringer, prepared to defend himself should any attackers strike at him. Perhaps it was thieves who had heard of his generosity towards the innkeeper?

He heard something move in the room and, again, he opened his eyes.

She was standing there, her black hair curling over her shoulders, her scarlet gown clinging to her body. Her lips curved in a smile of irony and her eyes regarded him steadily.

She was the woman he had seen in the castle. The sleeping woman. Was this part of the dream?

"Forgive me for thus intruding upon your slumber and your privacy, my lord, but my business is urgent and I have little time to spare."

Elric saw that Moonglum still slept as if in a drugged slumber.

He sat upright in his bed. Stormbringer moaned softly and then was silent.

"You seem to know me, my lady, but I do not—"

"I am called Myshella . . ."

"Empress of the Dawn?"

She smiled again. "Some have named me that. And others have called me the Dark Lady of Kaneloon."

"Whom Aubec loved? Then you must have preserved your youth carefully, Lady Myshella."

"No doing of mine. It is possible that I am immortal. I do not know. I know only one thing and that is that time is a deception . . ."

"Why do you come?"

"I cannot stay for long. I come to seek your aid."

"In what way?"

"We have an enemy in common, I believe."

"Theleb K'aarna?"

"The same."

"Did he place that enchantment upon you that made you sleep?"

"Aye."

"And he sent his Oonai against me. That is how—"

She raised her hand.

"I sent the chimerae to find you and bring you to me. They meant you no harm. But it was the only thing I could do, for Theleb K'aarna's spell was already beginning to work. I battle his sorcery, but it is strong and I am unable to revive myself for more than very short periods. This is one such period. Theleb K'aarna has joined forces with Prince Umbda, Lord of the Kelmain Host. Their plan is to conquer Lormyr and, ultimately, the entire Southern World!"

"Who is this Umbda? I have heard neither of him nor of the Kelmain Host. Some noble of Iosaz, perhaps, who . . ."

"Prince Umbda serves Chaos. He comes from the lands beyond World's Edge and his Kelmain are not men at all, though they have the appearance of men."

"So Theleb K'aarna was in the far south, after all."

"That is why I came to you tonight."

"You wish me to help you?"

"We both need Theleb K'aarna destroyed. His sorcery is what enabled Prince Umbda to cross World's Edge. Now that sorcery is strengthened by what Umbda brings—the friendship of Chaos. I protect Lormyr and I serve Law. I know that you serve Chaos, yet I hope your hatred of Theleb K'aarna overcomes that loyalty for the moment."

"Chaos has not served me, of late, lady, so I'll forget that loyalty. I would have my vengeance on Theleb K'aarna and if we can help each other in the matter, so much the better."

"Good."

She gasped then and her eyes glazed. When next she spoke it was with some difficulty.

"The enchantment is exerting its hold again. I have a steed for you near the town's north gate. It will bear you to an island in the Boiling Sea. On that island is a palace called Ashaneloon. It is there that I have dwelt of late, until I sensed Lormyr's danger . . ."

She pressed her hand to her brow and swayed.

". . . But Theleb K'aarna expected me to try to return there and he placed a guardian at the palace's gate. That guardian must be destroyed. When you have destroyed it you must go to the . . ."

Elric rose to help her, but she waved him away.

". . . to the eastern tower. In the tower's lower room is a chest. In the chest is a large pouch of cloth-of-gold. You must take that and—and bring it back to Kaneloon, for Umbda and his Kelmain now march against the castle. Theleb K'aarna will destroy the castle with their help—and destroy me, also. With the pouch, I may destroy them. But pray that I am able to wake, or the South is doomed and even you will not be able to go against the power that Theleb K'aarna will wield."

"What of Moonglum?" Elric glanced at his sleeping friend. "Can he accompany me?"

"Best not. Besides, he has a light enchantment upon him. There is no time to wake him . . ." She gasped again and flung her arms across her forehead. "No time . . ."

Elric leapt from the bed and began to pull on his breeks. He took his cloak from where it was draped across a stool and he buckled on his runesword. He went forward to help her, but she signalled him away.

"No . . . Go, please . . ."

And she vanished.

Still half asleep, Elric flung open the door and dashed down the stairs, out into the night, racing for the north gate of Alorasaz, passing through it and running on through the snow, looking this way and that. The cold flooded over him like a sudden wave. He was soon knee-deep in snow. Peering about him he carried on until he stopped in his tracks.

He gasped in astonishment when he saw the steed which Myshella had provided for him.

"What's this? Another chimera?"

He approached it cautiously.

6

Jewelled Bird Speaking

It was a bird, but it was not a bird of flesh and blood.

It was a bird of silver and of gold and of brass. Its wings clashed as he approached it and it moved its huge clawed feet impatiently, turning cold, emerald eyes to regard him.

On its back was a saddle of carved onyx chased in gold and copper and the saddle was empty, awaiting him.

"Well, I began all this unquestioningly," Elric said to himself. "I might as well complete it in the same manner."

And he went up to the bird and he climbed up its side and he lowered himself somewhat cautiously into the saddle.

The wings of gold and silver flapped with the sound of a hundred cymbals meeting and with three movements had taken the bird of metal and its rider high up into the night sky above Alorasaz. It turned its bright head on its neck of brass and it opened its curved beak of gem-studded steel.

"Well, master, I am commanded to take thee to Ashaneloon."

Elric waved a pale hand. "Wherever you will. I am at the mercy of you and your mistress."

And then he was jerked backward in the saddle as the bird's wings beat the stronger and it gathered speed and he was rushing through the freezing night, over snowy plains, over mountains, over rivers, until the coast came in sight and he saw the sea in the west which was called the Boiling Sea.

Down through the pitch blackness dropped the bird of gold and silver and now Elric felt damp heat strike his face and hands, heard a peculiar bubbling sound, and he knew they were flying over that strange sea said to be fed by volcanoes lying deep below its surface, a sea where few ships sailed.

Steam surrounded them now. Its heat was almost unbearable, but through it Elric began to make out the silhouette of a land mass, a small rocky island on which stood a single building with slender towers and turrets and domes.

"The palace of Ashaneloon," said the bird of silver and gold. "I will alight among the battlements, master, but I fear that thing you must meet before our errand is accomplished, so I will await you elsewhere. Then, if you live, I will return to take you back to Kaneloon. And, if you die, I will go back to tell my mistress of your failure."

Over the battlements the bird now hovered, its wings beating, and Elric reflected that there would be no advantage of surprise over whatever it was the bird feared so much.

He swung one leg from the saddle, paused, and then leapt down to the flat roof.

Hastily the bird retreated into the black sky.

Elric was alone.

All was silent, save for the drumming of warm waves on a distant shore.

He located the eastern tower and began to make his way towards the door. There was some chance, perhaps, that he could complete his quest without the necessity of facing the palace's guardian.

But then a monstrous bellow sounded behind him and he wheeled, knowing that this must be the guardian. A creature stood there, its red-rimmed eyes full of insensate malice.

"So you are Theleb K'aarna's slave," said Elric. He reached for Stormbringer and the sword seemed to spring into his hand at its own volition. "Must I kill you, or will you be gone now?"

The creature bellowed again, but it did not move.

THE VANISHING TOWER

The albino said: "I am Elric of Melniboné, last of a line of great Sorcerer Kings. This blade I wield will do more than kill you, friend demon. It will drink your soul and feed it to me. Perhaps you have heard of me by another name? By the name of the Soul Thief?"

The creature lashed its serrated tail and its bovine nostrils distended. The horned head swayed on the short neck and the long teeth gleamed in the darkness. It reached out scaly claws and began to lumber towards the prince of ruins.

Elric took the sword in both hands and spread his feet wide apart on the flagstones and prepared to meet the monster's charge. Foul breath struck his face. Another bellow and then it was upon him.

Stormbringer howled and spilled black radiance over both. The runes carved in the blade glowed with a greedy glow as the thing of hell slashed at Elric's body with its claws, ripping the shirt from him and baring his chest.

The sword came down.

The demon roared as the scales of its shoulder received the blow but did not part. It danced to one side and attacked again. Elric swayed back, but now a thin wound was opened in his arm from elbow to wrist.

Stormbringer struck for the second time and hit the demon's snout so that it shrieked and lashed out once more. Again its claws found Elric's body and blood smeared his chest from a shallow cut.

Elric fell back, losing his footing on the stones. He almost went down, but recovered his balance and defended himself as best he could. The claws slashed at him, but Stormbringer drove them to one side.

Elric began to pant and the sweat poured down his face and he felt desperation well in him and then that desperation took a different quality and his eyes glowed and his lips snarled.

"Know you that I am Elric!" he cried. "Elric!"

Still the creature attacked.

"I am Elric—more demon than man! Begone, you ill-shaped thing!"

The creature bellowed and pounced and this time Elric did not fall back,

* 45 *

but, his face writing in terrible rage, reversed his grip on the runesword and plunged it point first into the demon's open jaws.

He plunged the Black Sword down the stinking throat, down into the torso.

He wrenched the blade so that it split jaw, neck, chest and groin and the creature's life-force began to course along the length of the runesword. The claws lashed out at him, but the creature was weakening.

Then the life-force pulsed up the blade and reached Elric who gasped and screamed in dark ecstasy as the demon's energy poured into him. He withdrew the blade and hacked and hacked at the body and still the life-force flowed into him and gave greater power to his blows. The demon groaned and dropped to the flagstones.

And it was done.

And a white-faced demon stood over the dead thing of hell and its crimson eyes blazed and its pale mouth opened and it roared with wild laughter, flinging its arms upward, the runesword flaming with a black and horrid flame, and it howled a wordless, exultant song to the Lords of Chaos.

There was silence suddenly.

And then it bowed its head and it wept.

Now Elric opened the door to the eastern tower and stumbled through absolute blackness until he came to the lowest room. The door to the room was locked and barred, but Stormbringer smashed through it and the last lord of Melniboné entered a lighted room in which squatted a chest of iron.

His sword sundered the bands securing the chest and he flung open the lid and saw that there were many wonders in the chest, as well as the pouch made from cloth-of-gold, but he picked out only the pouch and tucked it into his belt as he raced from the room, back to the battlements where the bird of silver and gold stood pecking with its steel beak at the remnants of Theleb K'aarna's servant.

It looked up as Elric returned. In its eyes was an expression almost of humour.

"Well, master, we must make haste to Kaneloon."

"Aye."

Nausea had begun to fill Elric. His eyes were gloomy as he contemplated the corpse and that which he had stolen from it. Such life-force, whatever else it was, must surely be tainted. Did not he drink something of the demon's evil when his sword drank its soul?

He was about to climb back into the onyx saddle when he saw something gleaming amongst the black and yellow entrails he had spilled. It was the demon's heart—an irregularly shaped stone of deep blue and purple and green. It still pulsed, though its owner was dead.

Elric stooped and picked it up. It was wet and so hot that it almost burned his hand, but he tucked it into his pouch, then mounted the bird of silver and gold.

His bone-white face flickered with a dozen strange emotions as he let the bird bear him back over the Boiling Sea. His milk-white hair flew wildly behind him and he was oblivious of the wounds on his arm and chest.

He was thinking of other things. Some of his thoughts lay in the past and others were in the future. And he laughed bitterly twice and his eyes shed tears and he spoke once.

"Ah, what agony is this Life!"

7

Black Wizard Laughing

To Kaneloon they came in the early dawn and in the distance Elric saw a massive army darkening the snow and he knew it must be the Kelmain Host, led by Theleb K'aarna and Prince Umbda, marching against the lonely castle.

The bird of gold and silver flapped down in the snow outside the castle's entrance and Elric dismounted. Then the bird had risen into the air again and was gone.

The great gate of Castle Kaneloon was closed this time and he gathered his tattered cloak about his naked torso and he hammered on the gate with his fists and he forced a cry from his dry lips.

"Myshella! Myshella!"

There was no answer.

"Myshella! I have returned with that which you need!"

He feared she must have fallen into her enchanted slumber again. He looked towards the south and the dark tide had rolled a little closer to the castle.

"Myshella!"

Then he heard a bar being drawn and the gates groaned open and there stood Moonglum, his face strained and his eyes full of something of which he could not speak.

"Moonglum! How came you here?"

"I know not how, Elric." Moonglum stepped aside so that Elric could enter. He replaced the bar. "I lay in my bed last night when a woman came to me—the same woman we saw, sleeping, here. She said I must go with her. And somehow go I did. But I know not how, Elric. I know not how."

"And where is that woman?"

"Where we first saw her. She sleeps and I cannot wake her."

Elric drew a deep breath and told, briefly, what he knew of Myshella and the host that came against her Castle Kaneloon.

"Do you know the contents of that pouch?" Moonglum asked.

Elric shook his head and opened the pouch to peer inside. "It seems to be nothing but a pinkish dust. Yet it must be some powerful sorcery if Myshella believes it can defeat the entire Kelmain Host."

Moonglum frowned. "But surely Myshella must work the charm herself if only she knows what it is?"

"Aye."

"And Theleb K'aarna has enchanted her."

"Aye."

"And now it is too late, for Umbda—whoever he may be—nears the castle."

"Aye." Elric's hand trembled as he drew from his belt the thing he had taken from the demon just before he left the palace of Ashaneloon. "Unless this is the stone I think it is."

"What is that?"

"I know a legend. Some demons possess these stones as hearts." He held it to the light so that the blues and purples and greens writhed. "I have never seen one, but I believe it to be the thing I once sought for Cymoril when I tried to lift my cousin's charm from her. What I sought but never found was a Nanorion. A stone of magical powers said to be able to waken the dead—or those in deathlike sleep."

"And that is a Nanorion. It will awaken Myshella?"

"If anything can, then this will, for I took it from Theleb K'aarna's own demon and that must improve the efficaciousness of the magic. Come." Elric strode through the hall and up the stairs until he came to Myshella's room where she lay, as he had seen her before, on the bed hung with draperies, her wall hung with shields and weapons.

"Now I understand why these arms decorate her chamber," Moonglum said. "According to legend, these are the shields and weapons of all those who loved Myshella and championed her cause."

Elric nodded and said, as if to himself, "Aye, she was ever an enemy of Melniboné, was the Empress of the Dawn."

He held the pulsing stone delicately and reached out to place it on her forehead.

"It makes no difference," Moonglum said after a moment. "She does not stir."

"There is a rune, but I remember it not . . ." Elric pressed his fingers to his temples. "I remember it not . . ."

Moonglum went to the window. "We can ask Theleb K'aarna, perhaps," he said ironically. "He will be here soon enough."

Then Moonglum saw that there were tears again in Elric's eyes and that he had turned away, hoping Moonglum would not see. Moonglum cleared his throat. "I have some business below. Call me if you should require my help."

He left the room and closed the door and Elric was alone with the woman who seemed, increasingly, a dreadful phantom from his most frightful dreams.

He controlled his feverish mind and tried to discipline it, to remember the crucial runes in the High Speech of Old Melniboné.

"Gods!" he hissed. "Help me!"

But he knew that in this matter in particular the Lords of Chaos would not assist him—would hinder him if they could, for Myshella was one of the chief instruments of Law upon the Earth, had been responsible for driving Chaos from the world.

He fell to his knees beside her bed, his hands clenched, his face twisting with the effort.

And then it came back to him. His head still bent, he stretched out his right hand and touched the pulsing stone, stretched out his left hand and rested it upon Myshella's navel, and he began a chant in an ancient tongue that had been spoken before true men had ever walked the Earth . . .

"Elric!"

Moonglum burst into the room and Elric was wrenched from his trance.

"Elric! We are invaded! Their advance riders . . ."

"What?"

"They have broken into the castle—a dozen of them. I fought them off and barred the way up to this tower, but they are hacking at the door now. I think they have been sent to destroy Myshella if they could. They were surprised to discover me here."

Elric rose and looked carefully down at Myshella. The rune was finished and had been repeated almost through again when Moonglum had come in. She did not stir yet.

"Theleb K'aarna worked his sorcery from a distance," Moonglum said. "Ensuring that Myshella would not resist him. But he did not reckon with us."

He and Elric hurried from the room, down the steps to where a door was bulging and splintering beneath the weapons of those beyond.

"Stand back, Moonglum."

Elric drew the crooning runesword, lifted it high and brought it against the door.

The door split and two oddly shaped skulls were split with it.

The remainder of the attackers fell back with cries of astonishment and horror as the white-faced reaver fell upon them, his huge sword drinking their souls and singing its strange, undulating song.

Down the stairs Elric pursued them. Into the hall where they bunched together and prepared to defend themselves from this demon with his hell-forged blade.

And Elric laughed.

And they shuddered.

And their weapons trembled in their hands.

"So you are the mighty Kelmain," Elric sneered. "No wonder you needed sorcery to aid you if you are so cowardly. Have you not heard, beyond World's Edge, of Elric Kinslayer?"

But the Kelmain plainly did not understand his speech, which was strange enough in itself, for he had spoken in the common tongue, known to all men.

These people had golden skins and eye-sockets that were almost square. Their faces, in all, seemed crudely carved from rock, all sharp angles and planes, and their armour was not rounded, but angular.

Elric bared his teeth in a smile and the Kelmain drew closer together.

Then he screamed with dreadful laughter and Moonglum stepped back and did not look at what took place.

The runesword swung. Heads and limbs were chopped away. Blood gouted. Souls were taken. The Kelmain's dead faces bore expressions showing that before the life was drawn from them they had known the truth of their appalling fate.

And Stormbringer drank again, for Stormbringer was a thirsty hellsword.

And Elric felt his deficient veins swell with even more energy than that which he had taken earlier from Theleb K'aarna's demon.

The hall shook with Elric's insane mirth and he strode over the piled corpses and he went through the open gateway to where the great host waited.

And he shouted a name:

"Theleb K'aarna, Theleb K'aarna!"

Moonglum ran after him, calling for him to stop, but Elric did not heed him. Elric strode on through the snow, his sword dripping a red trail behind him.

Under a cold sun, the Kelmain were riding for the castle called Kaneloon and Elric went to meet them.

At their head, on slender horses, rode the dark-faced sorcerer of Pan Tang, dressed in flowing robes, and beside him was the prince of the Kelmain Host, Prince Umbda, in proud armour, bizarre plumes nodding on his helm, a triumphant smile on his strange, angular features.

Behind, the host dragged oddly fashioned war-gear which, for all its oddness, looked powerful—mightier than anything Lormyr could rally when the huge army fell upon her.

As the lone figure appeared and began to walk away from the walls of Castle Kaneloon Theleb K'aarna raised his hand and stopped the host's advance, reining in his own horse and laughing.

"Why, it is the jackal of Melniboné, by all the Gods of Chaos! He acknowledges his master at last and comes to deliver himself up to me!"

Elric came closer and Theleb K'aarna laughed on. "Here, Elric—kneel before me!"

Elric did not pause, seemed not to hear the Pan Tangian's words.

Prince Umbda's eyes were troubled and he said something in a strange tongue. Theleb K'aarna sniffed and replied in the same language.

And still the albino marched through the snow towards the huge host.

"By Chardros, Elric, stop!" cried Theleb K'aarna, his horse shifting nervously beneath him. "If you have come to bargain you are a fool. Kaneloon and her mistress must fall before Lormyr is ours—and Lormyr shall be ours, there's no doubting that!"

Then Elric did stop and he brought up his eyes to burn into those of the sorcerer and there was a still, cold smile upon his pale lips.

Theleb K'aarna tried to meet Elric's gaze but could not. His voice trembled when he next spoke.

"You cannot defeat the whole Kelmain Host!"

"I have no wish to, conjuror. Your life is all I desire."

The sorcerer's face twitched. "Well, you shall not have it! Hai, men of the Kelmain, take him!"

He wheeled his horse and rode into the protective ranks of his warriors, calling out his orders in their own tongue.

From the castle another figure burst, rushing to join Elric.

It was Moonglum of Elwher, a sword in either hand.

Elric half-turned.

"Elric! We'll die together!"

"Stay back, Moonglum!"

Moonglum hesitated.

"Stay back, if you love me!"

Moonglum reluctantly retreated to the castle.

The Kelmain horsemen swept in, broad-bladed straight swords raised, instantly surrounding the albino.

They threatened him, hoping that he would lay down his sword and let himself be captured. But Elric smiled.

Stormbringer began to sing. Elric grasped the sword in both hands, bent his elbows then suddenly held the blade straight out before him.

He began to whirl like a Tarkeshite dancer, round and round, and it was as if the sword dragged him faster and faster while it gouged and gashed and decapitated the Kelmain horsemen.

For a moment they fell back, leaving their dead comrades heaped about the albino, but Prince Umbda, after a hurried conference with Theleb K'aarna, urged them upon Elric again.

And Elric swung his blade once more, but not so many of the Kelmain perished this time.

Armoured body fell against armoured body, blood mingled with brother's blood, horses dragged corpses away with them across the snow and Elric did not fall, yet something was happening to him.

Then it dawned upon his berserker brain that, for some reason, his blade was sated. The energy still pulsed in its metal, but it transferred nothing more to its master. And his own stolen energy was beginning to wane.

"Damn you, Stormbringer! Give me your power!"

Swords rained down upon him as he fought and slew and parried and thrust.

"More power!"

He was still stronger than normal and much stronger than any ordinary mortal, but some of the wild anger was leaving him and he felt almost puzzled as more Kelmain came at him.

He was beginning to waken from the blood-dream.

He shook his head and drew deep breaths. His back was aching.

"Give me their strength, Black Sword!"

He struck at legs and arms and chests and faces and he was covered from head to foot in the blood of his attackers.

But the dead now hampered him worse than the living, for their corpses were everywhere and he almost lost his footing more than once.

"What ails you, runesword? Do you refuse to help me? Will you not fight these things because, like you, they are of Chaos?"

No, it could not be that. All that had happened was that the sword desired no more vitality and therefore gave Elric none.

He fought on for another hour before his grip on the sword weakened and a rider, half-mad with terror, struck a blow at his head, failed to split it but stunned him so that he fell upon the bodies of the slain, tried to rise, then was struck again and lost consciousness.

8

A Great Host Screaming

"It was more than I hoped," murmured Theleb K'aarna in satisfaction, "but we have taken him alive!"

Elric opened his eyes and looked with hatred on the sorcerer who was stroking his black forked beard as if to comfort himself.

Elric could barely remember the events which had brought him here and placed him in the sorcerer's power. He remembered much blood, much laughter, much dying, but it was all fading, like the memory of a dream.

"Well, renegade, your foolishness was unbelievable. I thought you must have an army behind you. But doubtless it was your fear which unbalanced your poor brain. Still, I'll not speculate upon the cause of my own good fortune. There's many a bargain I can strike with the denizens of other planes, were I to offer them your soul. And your body I will keep for myself—to show Queen Yishana what I did to her lover before he died . . ."

Elric laughed shortly and looked about him, ignoring Theleb K'aarna.

The Kelmain were awaiting orders. They had still not marched on Kaneloon. The sun was low in the sky. He saw the pile of corpses behind him. He saw the hatred and fear on the faces of the golden-skinned host and he smiled again.

"I do not love Yishana," he said distantly, as if scarcely aware of Theleb K'aarna's presence. "It is your jealous heart that makes you think so. I left Yishana's side to find you. It is never love that moves Elric of Melniboné, sorcerer, but always hatred."

"I do not believe you," Theleb K'aarna tittered. "When the whole South falls to me and my comrades, then will I court Yishana and offer to make her Queen of all the West as well as all the South. Our forces united, we shall dominate the Earth!"

"You Pan Tangians were ever an insecure breed, forever planning conquest for its own sake, forever seeking to destroy the equilibrium of the Young Kingdoms."

"One day," sneered Theleb K'aarna, "Pan Tang will have an empire that will make the Bright Empire seem a mere flickering ember in the fire of history. But it is not for the glory of Pan Tang that I do this . . ."

"It is for Yishana? By the gods, sorcerer, then I am glad I'm motivated by hatred and not by love, for I do not half the damage, it seems, done by those in love . . ."

"I will lay the South at Yishana's feet and she may use it as she pleases!"

"I am bored by this. What do you intend to do with me?"

"First I will hurt your body. I will hurt it delicately to begin with, building up the pain, until I have you in the proper frame of mind. Then I will consort with the Lords of the Higher Worlds to find which will give me most for your soul."

"And what of Kaneloon?"

"The Kelmain will deal with Kaneloon. One knife is all that's needed now to slit Myshella's throat as she sleeps."

"She is protected."

Theleb K'aarna's brow darkened. Then it cleared and he laughed again.

"Aye, but the gate will fall soon enough and your little red-haired friend will perish as Myshella perishes."

He ran his fingers through his oiled ringlets.

"I am allowing, at Prince Umbda's request, the Kelmain to rest a while before storming the castle. But Kaneloon will be burning by nightfall."

Elric looked towards the castle across the trampled snow. Plainly his runes had failed to counter Theleb K'aarna's spell.

"I would . . ." He began to speak when he paused.

He had seen a flash of gold and silver among the battlements and a thought without shape had entered his head and made him hesitate.

"What?" Theleb K'aarna asked him harshly.

"Nothing. I merely wondered where my sword was."

The sorcerer shrugged. "Nowhere you can reach it, reaver. We left it where you dropped it. The stinking hellblade is no use to us. And none to you, now . . ."

Elric wondered what would happen if he made a direct appeal to the sword. He could not get to it himself, for Theleb K'aarna had bound him tightly with ropes of silk, but he might *call* for it . . .

He lifted himself to his feet.

"Would you seek to run away, White Wolf?" Theleb K'aarna watched him nervously.

Elric smiled again. "I wished for a better view of the coming conquest of Kaneloon. Just that."

The sorcerer drew a curved knife.

Elric swayed, his eyes half-closed, and he began to murmur a name beneath his breath.

Theleb K'aarna leapt forward and his arm encircled Elric's head while the knife pricked into the albino's throat. "Be silent, jackal!"

But Elric knew that he had no other means of helping himself and, for all it was a desperate scheme, he murmured the words once more, praying that Theleb K'aarna's lust for a slow revenge would make the sorcerer hesitate before killing him.

Theleb K'aarna cursed, trying to prise Elric's mouth open.

"The first thing I'll do is cut out that damned tongue of yours!"

Elric bit the hand and tasted the sorcerer's blood. He spat it out.

Theleb K'aarna screamed. "By Chardros, if I did not wish to see you die over the months, I would . . ."

And then a sound came from the Kelmain.

It was a moan of surprise and it issued from every throat.

Theleb K'aarna turned and the breath hissed from between his clenched teeth.

Through the murky dusk a black shape moved. It was the sword, Stormbringer.

Elric had called it.

Now he cried aloud:

"Stormbringer! Stormbringer! To me!"

Theleb K'aarna flung Elric in the path of the sword and rushed into the security of the gathered ranks of Kelmain warriors.

"Stormbringer!"

The Black Sword hovered in the air near Elric.

Another shout went up from the Kelmain. A shape had left the battlements of Castle Kaneloon.

Theleb K'aarna shouted in hysteria. "Prince Umbda! Prepare your men for the attack! I sense danger to us!"

Umbda could not understand the sorcerer's words and Theleb K'aarna was forced to translate them.

"Do not let the sword reach him!" cried the sorcerer. Once more he shouted in the language of the Kelmain and several warriors ran forward to grasp the runesword before it could reach its albino master.

But the sword struck rapidly and the Kelmain died and none dared approach it after that.

Slowly Stormbringer moved towards Elric.

"Ah, Elric," cried Theleb K'aarna, "if you escape me this day, I swear that I shall find you."

"And if you escape me," Elric shouted back, "I will find you, Theleb K'aarna. Be sure of that."

The shape that had left Castle Kaneloon had feathers of silver and gold. It flew high above the host and hovered for a moment before moving to the outer edges of the gathering. Elric could not see it clearly, but he knew what it was. That was why he had summoned the sword, for he had an idea that Moonglum rode the giant bird of metal and that the Elwherite would try to rescue him.

"Do not let it land! It comes to save the albino!" screamed Theleb K'aarna.

But the Kelmain Host did not understand him. Under Prince Umbda's commands they were preparing themselves for the attack upon the castle.

Theleb K'aarna repeated his orders in their own tongue, but it was plain they were beginning not to trust him and could not see the need to bother themselves with one man and a strange bird of metal. It could not stop their engines of war. Neither could the man.

"Stormbringer," whispered Elric as the sword sliced through his bonds and gently settled in his hand. Elric was free, but the Kelmain, though not placing the same importance upon him as did Theleb K'aarna, showed that they were not prepared to let him escape now that the blade was in his grasp and not moving of its own volition.

Prince Umbda shouted something.

A huge mass of warriors rushed at Elric at once and he made no effort to take the attack to them this time for he was interested in fighting a defensive strategy until Moonglum could descend on the bird and help him.

But the bird was even further away. It appeared to be circling the outer perimeters of the host and showed no interest in his plight at all.

Had he been deceived?

He parried a dozen thrusts, letting the Kelmain warriors crowd in upon each other and thus hamper themselves. The bird of gold and silver was almost out of sight now.

And Theleb K'aarna—where was he?

Elric tried to find him, but the sorcerer was doubtless somewhere in the centre of the Kelmain ranks by now.

Elric killed a golden-skinned warrior, slitting his throat with the point of the runesword. More strength began to flow into him again. He killed another Kelmain with an overarm movement which split the man's shoulder. But nothing could be gained from this fight if Moonglum was not coming on the bird of silver and gold.

The bird seemed to change course and come back towards Kaneloon. Was it merely waiting for instructions from its sleeping mistress? Or was it refusing to obey Moonglum's commands?

Elric backed through the muddy, bloody snow so that the pile of corpses now lay behind him. He fought on, but with very little hope.

The bird went past, far to his right.

Elric thought ironically that he had completely mistaken the significance of the bird's leaving the castle battlements and by mistiming his decision had merely brought his death closer—perhaps Myshella's and Moonglum's deaths closer, too.

Kaneloon was doomed. Myshella was doomed. Lormyr and perhaps the whole of the Young Kingdoms were doomed.

And he was doomed.

It was then that a shadow passed across the battling men and the Kelmain screamed and fell back as a great din rent the air.

Elric looked up in relief, hearing the sound of the metal bird's clashing wings. He looked for Moonglum in the saddle and saw instead the tense face of Myshella herself, her hair blowing around her face as it was disturbed by the beating wings.

"Quickly, Lord Elric, before they close in again."

Elric sheathed the runesword and leapt towards the saddle, swinging himself behind the Dark Lady of Kaneloon. Then they rose into the air again, while arrows hurtled around their heads and bounced off the bird's metal feathers.

"One more circuit of the host and then we return to the castle," she said. "Your rune and the Nanorion worked to defeat Theleb K'aarna's enchantment, but they took longer than either of us would have liked. See, already Prince Umbda is ordering his men to mount and ride to Castle Kaneloon. And Kaneloon has only Moonglum to defend her now."

"Why this circuit of Umbda's army?"

"You will see. At least, I hope you will see, my lord."

She began to sing a song. It was a strange, disturbing chant in a language not dissimilar to the Melnibonéan High Speech, yet different enough for Elric to understand only a few words, for it was oddly accented.

Around the camp they flew. Elric saw the Kelmain form their ranks into battle order. Doubtless Umbda and Theleb K'aarna had by now decided on the best mode of attack.

Then back to the castle beat the great bird, settling on the battlements and allowing Elric and Myshella to dismount. Moonglum, his features taut, came running to meet them.

They went to look at the Kelmain.

And they saw that the Kelmain were on the move.

"What did you do to—" began Elric, but Myshella raised her hand.

"Perhaps I did nothing. Perhaps the sorcery will not work."

"What was it you . . . ?"

"I scattered the contents of the purse you brought. I scattered it around their whole army. Watch . . ."

"And if the spell has not worked—" Moonglum murmured. He paused, straining his eyes through the gloom. "What is that?"

Myshella's satisfied tone was almost ghoulish as she said: "It is the Noose of Flesh."

Something was growing out of the snow. Something pink that quivered. Something huge. A great mass that arose on all sides of the Kelmain and made their horses rear up and snort.

And it made the Kelmain shriek.

The stuff was like flesh and it had grown so high that the whole Kelmain Host was obscured from sight. There were noises as they tried to train their battle-engines upon the stuff and blast their way through. There were shouts. But not a single horseman broke out of the Noose of Flesh.

Then the substance began to fold in over the Kelmain and Elric heard a sound such as none he had heard before.

It was a voice.

A voice of a hundred thousand men all facing an identical terror, all dying an identical death.

It was a moan of desperation, of hopelessness, of fear.

But it was a moan so loud that it shook the walls of Castle Kaneloon.

"It is no death for a warrior," murmured Moonglum, turning away.

"But it was the only weapon we had," said Myshella. "I have possessed it for a good many years but never before did I feel the need to use it."

"Of them all, only Theleb K'aarna deserved that death," said Elric.

Night fell and the Noose of Flesh tightened around the Kelmain Host, crushing all but a few horses which had run free as the sorcery began to work.

It crushed Prince Umbda, who spoke no language known in the Young Kingdoms, who spoke no language known to the ancients, who had come to conquer from beyond World's Edge.

It crushed Theleb K'aarna, who had sought, for the sake of his love for a wanton queen, to conquer the world with the aid of Chaos.

It crushed all the warriors of that near-human race, the Kelmain. And it crushed all who could have told the watchers what the Kelmain had been or from where they had originated.

Then it absorbed them. Then it flickered and dissolved and was dust again.

No piece of flesh—man's nor beast's—remained. But over the snow was scattered clothing, arms, armour, siege engines, riding accoutrements, coins, belt-buckles, for as far as the eye could see.

Myshella nodded to herself. "That was the Noose of Flesh," she said. "I thank you for bringing it to me, Elric. I thank you, also, for finding the stone which revived me. I thank you for saving Lormyr."

"Aye," said Elric. "Thank me." There was a weariness on him now. He turned away, shivering.

Snow had begun to fall again.

"Thank me for nothing, Lady Myshella. What I did was to satisfy my own dark urges, to sate my thirst for vengeance. I have destroyed Theleb K'aarna.

The rest was incidental. I care nought for Lormyr, the Young Kingdoms, or any of your causes . . ."

Moonglum saw that Myshella had a sceptical look in her eyes and she smiled slightly.

Elric entered the castle and began to descend the steps to the hall.

"Wait," Myshella said. "This castle is magical. It reflects the desires of any who enter it—should I wish it."

Elric rubbed at his eyes. "Then plainly we have no desires. Mine are satisfied now that Theleb K'aarna is destroyed. I would leave this place now, my lady."

"You have none?" said she.

He looked at her directly. He frowned. "Regret breeds weakness which attacks the internal organs and at last destroys . . ."

"And you have no desires?"

He hesitated. "I understand you. Your own appearance, I'll admit . . ." He shrugged. "But are you—?"

She spread her hands. "Do not ask too many questions of me." She made another gesture. "Now. See. This castle becomes what you most desire. And in it, the things you most desire!"

And Elric looked about him, his eyes widening, and he began to scream.

He fell to his knees in terror. He turned pleadingly to her.

"No, Myshella! No. I do not desire this!"

Hastily she made yet another sign.

Moonglum helped his friend to his feet. "What was it? What did you see?"

Elric straightened his back and rested his hand on his sword and said grimly and quietly to Myshella:

"Lady, I would kill you for that if I did not understand you sought only to please me."

He studied the ground for a moment before continuing:

"Know this. Elric cannot have what he desires most. What he desires does not exist. What he desires is dead. All Elric has is sorrow, guilt, malice, hatred. This is all he deserves and all he will ever desire."

She put her hands to her own face and walked back to the room where he had first seen her. Elric followed.

Moonglum started after them but then he stopped and remained where he stood.

He watched them enter the room and saw the door close.

He walked back onto the battlements and stared into the darkness. He saw wings of silver and gold flashing in the moonlight and they became smaller and smaller until they had vanished.

He sighed. It was cold.

He went back into the castle and settled himself with his back against a pillar, preparing to sleep.

But a little while later he heard laughter come from the room in the highest tower.

And the laughter sent him running through the passages, through the great hall where the fire had died, out of the door, into the night to seek the stables where he could feel more secure.

But he could not sleep that night, for the distant laughter still pursued him.

And the laughter continued until morning.

BOOK TWO

TO SNARE THE PALE PRINCE

*. . . but it was in Nadsokor, City of Beggars,
that Elric found an old friend and learned
something concerning an old enemy . . .*

—The Chronicle of the Black Sword

I

The Beggar Court

Nadsokor, City of Beggars, was infamous throughout the Young Kingdoms. Lying near the shores of that ferocious river, the Varkalk, and not too far from the Kingdom of Org in which blossomed the frightful Forest of Troos, and exuding a stink which seemed thick enough ten miles distant, Nadsokor was plagued by few visitors.

From this unlovely place sallied out her citizens to beg their way about the world and steal what they could and bring it back to Nadsokor where half of their profits were handed over to their king in return for his protection.

Their king had ruled for many years. He was called Urish the Seven-fingered, for he had but four fingers on his right hand and three upon his left. Veins had burst all over his once handsome face and filthy, infested hair framed that seedy countenance upon which age and grime had traced a thousand lines. From out of all this ruin peered two bright, pale eyes.

As the symbol of his power Urish had a great cleaver called Hackmeat which was forever at his side. His throne was of crudely carved black oak, studded with bits of raw gold, bones and semi-precious gems. Beneath this throne was Urish's Hoard—a chest of treasure which he let none but himself look upon.

For the best part of every day Urish would lounge on his throne, presiding over a gloomy, festering hall thronged with his Court: a rabble of rascals too foul in appearance and disposition to be tolerated anywhere but here.

For heat and light there burned permanently braziers of garbage which gave out oily smoke and a stink which dominated all the other stinks in the hall.

And now there was a visitor at Urish's Court.

He stood before the dais on which the throne was mounted and from time to time he raised a heavily scented kerchief to his red, full lips.

His face, which was normally dark in complexion, was somewhat grey and his eyes had something of a haunted, tortured look in them as they glanced from begrimed beggar to pile of rubbish to guttering brazier. Dressed in the loose brocade robes of the folk of Pan Tang, the visitor had black eyes, a great hooked nose, blue-black ringlets and a curling beard. Kerchief to mouth, he bowed low when he reached Urish's throne.

As always, greed, weakness and malice mingled to form King Urish's expression as he regarded the stranger whom one of his courtiers had but lately announced.

Urish had recognised the name and he believed he could guess the Pan Tangian's business here.

"I heard you were dead, Theleb K'aarna—killed beyond Lormyr, near World's Edge." Urish grinned to display the black crags which were the rotting remains of his teeth.

Theleb K'aarna removed the kerchief from his lips and his voice was strangled at first, gaining strength as he remembered the wrongs recently done him. "My magic is not so weak I cannot escape a spell such as was woven that day. I conjured myself below the ground while Myshella's Noose of Flesh engulfed the Kelmain Host."

Urish's disgusting grin widened.

"You crept into a hole, is that it?"

The sorcerer's eyes burned fiercely. "I'll not dispute the strength of my powers with—"

He broke off and drew a deep breath which he at once regretted. He stared warily around him at the Beggar Court, all manged and maimed, which had deposited itself about the filthy hall, mocking him. The beggars of Nad-sokor knew the power of poverty and disease—knew how it terrified those who were not used to it. And thus their very squalor was their safeguard against intruders.

A repulsive cough which might have been a laugh now seized King Urish. "And was it your magic that brought you here?" As his whole body shook his bloodshot eyes continued, beadily, to regard the sorcerer.

"I have travelled across the seas and all across Vilmir to be here," Theleb K'aarna said, "because I had heard there was one you hated above all others . . ."

"And we hate *all* others—all who are not beggars," Urish reminded him. The king chuckled and the chuckle became, once more, a throaty, convulsive cough.

"But you hate Elric of Melniboné most."

"Aye. It would be fair to say that. Before he won fame as the Kinslayer, the traitor of Imrryr, he came to Nadsokor to deceive us, disguised as a leper who had begged his way from the Eastlands beyond Karlaak. He tricked me disgracefully and stole something from my Hoard. And my Hoard is sacred—I will not let another even glimpse it!"

"I heard he stole a scroll from you," Theleb K'aarna said. "A spell which had once belonged to his cousin Yyrkoon. Yyrkoon wished to be rid of Elric and let him believe that the spell would release the Princess Cymoril from her sorcerous slumber . . ."

"Aye. Yyrkoon had given the scroll to one of our citizens when he went abegging to the gates of Imrryr. He then told Elric what he had done. Elric disguised himself and came here. With the aid of sorcery he gained access to my Hoard—my Sacred Hoard—and plucked the scroll from it . . ."

Theleb K'aarna looked sideways at the Beggar King. "Some would say that it was not Elric's fault—that Yyrkoon was to blame. He deceived you both. The spell did not awaken Cymoril, did it?"

"No. But we have a Law in Nadsokor . . ." Urish raised the great cleaver Hackmeat and displayed its ragged, rusty blade. For all its battered appearance, it was a fearsome weapon. "That Law says that any man who looks upon the Sacred Hoard of King Urish must die and die most horribly—at the hands of the Burning God!"

"And none of your wandering citizens has yet managed to take this vengeance?"

"I must pass the sentence personally upon him before he dies. He must come again to Nadsokor, for it is only here that he may be acquainted with his doom."

Theleb K'aarna said: "I have no love for Elric."

Urish once more voiced the sound that was half laugh, half wheezing cough. "Aye—I have heard he has chased you all across the Young Kingdoms, that you have brought more and more powerful sorceries against him, yet every time he has defeated you."

Theleb K'aarna frowned. "Have a care, King Urish. I have had bad luck, yet I am still one of Pan Tang's greatest sorcerers."

"But you spend your powers freely and claim much from the Lords of Chaos. One day they will be tired of helping you and find another to do their work." King Urish closed soiled lips over black teeth. His pale eyes did not blink as he studied Theleb K'aarna.

There were stirrings in the hall, the Beggar Court moved in closer: the click of a crutch, the scrape of a staff, the shuffle of misshapen feet. Even the oily smoke from the braziers seemed to menace him as it drifted reluctantly into the darkness of the roof.

King Urish put one hand upon Hackmeat and the other upon his chin. Broken nails caressed stubble. From somewhere behind Theleb K'aarna a beggar woman let forth an obscene noise and then giggled.

Almost as if to comfort himself the sorcerer placed the scented kerchief firmly over his mouth and nostrils. He began to draw himself up, prepared to deal with an attack if it came.

"But you still have your powers now, I take it," said Urish suddenly, breaking the tension. "Or you would not be here."

"My powers increase . . ."

"For the moment, perhaps."

"My powers . . ."

"I take it you come with a scheme which you hope will result in Elric's destruction," continued Urish easily. The beggars relaxed. Only Theleb K'aarna now showed any signs of discomfort. Urish's bright, bloodshot eyes were sardonic. "And you desire our help because you know we hate the white-faced reaver of Melniboné."

Theleb K'aarna nodded. "Would you hear the details of my plan?"

Urish shrugged. "Why not? At least they may be entertaining."

Unhappily, Theleb K'aarna looked about him at the corrupt and tittering crew. He wished he knew a spell which would disperse the stink.

He took a deep breath through his kerchief and then began to speak . . .

2

The Stolen Ring

On the other side of the tavern the young dandy pretended to order another skin of wine while actually taking a sly look towards the corner where Elric sat.

Then the dandy leaned towards his compatriots—merchants and young nobles of several nations—and continued his murmured discourse.

The subject of that discourse, Elric knew, was Elric. Normally he was disdainful of such behaviour, but he was weary and he was impatient for Moonglum to return. He was almost tempted to order the young dandy to desist, if only to pass the time.

Elric was beginning to regret his decision to visit Old Hrolmar.

This rich city was a great meeting place for all the imaginative people of the Young Kingdoms. To it came explorers, adventurers, mercenaries, craftsmen, merchants, painters and poets for, under the rule of the famous Duke Avan Astran, this Vilmirian city-state had undergone a transformation in its character.

Duke Avan had been a man who had explored most of the world and had brought back great wealth and knowledge to Old Hrolmar. Its riches and its intellectual life attracted more riches, more intellectuals and so Old Hrolmar flourished.

But where riches are and where intellectuals are, then gossip also flourishes, for if there is any breed of man who gossips more than the merchant or the sailor then it is the poet and the painter. And, naturally enough, there was much gossip concerning the doom-driven albino, Elric, already a hero of several ballads by poets not over-talented.

Elric had allowed himself to be brought to the city because Moonglum had said it was the best place to find an income. Elric's carelessness with their wealth had made near-paupers of them, not for the first time, and they were in need of provisions and fresh steeds.

Elric had been for skirting Old Hrolmar and riding on towards Tanelorn, where they had decided to go, but Moonglum had argued reasonably that they would need better horses and more food and equipment for the long ride across the Vilmirian and Ilmioran plains to the edge of the Sighing Desert, where mysterious Tanelorn was situated. So Elric had at last agreed, though, after his encounter with Myshella and his witnessing of the destruction of the Noose of Flesh, he had become weary and craved for the peace which Tanelorn offered.

What made things worse was that this tavern was rather too well lit and catering too much to the better end of the trade for Elric's taste. He would have preferred a lowlier sort of inn which would have been cheaper and where men were used to holding back their questions and their gossip. But Moonglum had thought it wise to spend the last of their wealth on a good inn, in case they should need to entertain someone . . .

Elric left the business of raising treasure to Moonglum. Doubtless he intended to get it by thievery or trickery, but Elric did not care.

He sighed and suffered the sidelong looks of the other guests and tried not to overhear the young dandy. He sipped his cup of wine and picked at the flesh of the cold fowl Moonglum had ordered before he went off. He drew his head into the high collar of his black cloak, but succeeded only in emphasising the bone-white pallor of his face and the milky whiteness of his long hair. He looked around him at the silks and furs and tapestries swirling about the tavern as their owners moved from table to table and he longed with all his heart to be on his way to Tanelorn, where men spoke little because they had experienced so much.

"... killed mother and father, too—and the mother's lover, it is said ..."

"... and they say he lies with corpses for preference ..."

"... and because of that the Lords of the Higher Worlds cursed him with the face of a corpse ..."

"Incest, was it not? I got it from one who sailed with him that ..."

"... and his mother had congress with Arioch himself, thus producing ..."

"... shortly before he betrayed his own people to Smiorgan and the rest!"

"He looks a gloomy fellow, right enough. Not one to enjoy a jest ..."

Laughter.

Elric made himself relax in his chair and swallow more wine. But the gossip went on.

"They say also that he is an imposter. That the real Elric died at Imrryr ..."

"A true prince of Melniboné would dress in more lavish style. And he would ..."

More laughter.

Elric stood up, pushing back his cloak so that the great black broadsword at his hip was fully displayed. Most people in Old Hrolmar had heard of the runesword Stormbringer and its terrible power.

Elric crossed to the table where the young dandy sat.

"I pray you, gentlemen, to improve your sport! You can do much better now—for here is one who would offer you proof of certain things of which you speak. What of his penchant for vampirism of a particular sort? I did not hear you touch upon that in your conversation."

The young dandy cleared his throat and made a nervous little flirt of his shoulder.

"Well?" Elric feigned an innocent expression. "Cannot I be of assistance?"

The gossips had become dumb, pretending to be absorbed in their eating and drinking.

Elric smiled a smile which set their hands to shaking.

"I desire only to know what you wish to hear, gentlemen. Then I will demonstrate that I am truly the one you have called Elric Kinslayer."

The merchants and the nobles gathered their rich robes about them and, avoiding his eye, got up. The young dandy minced towards the exit—a parody of bravado.

But now Elric stood laughing in the doorway, his hand on the hilt of Stormbringer. "Will you not join me as my guests, gentlemen? Think how you could tell your friends of the meeting . . ."

"Gods, how boorish!" lisped the young dandy and then shivered.

"Sir, we meant no harm . . ." thickly said a fat Shazaarian herb trader.

"We spoke of another." A young noble with only the hint of a chin, but with an emphatic moustache, offered a feeble, placatory grin.

"We said how much we admired you . . ." stuttered a Vilmirian knight whose eyes appeared but recently to have crossed and whose face was now almost as pale as Elric's.

A merchant in the dark brocades of Tarkesh licked his red lips and attempted to conduct himself with more dignity than his friends. "Sir, Old Hrolmar is a civilised city. Gentlemen do not brawl amongst themselves here . . ."

"But like peasant women prefer to gossip," said Elric.

"Yes," said the youth with the abundance of moustache. "Ah—no . . ."

The dandy arranged his cloak about him and glowered at the floor.

Elric stepped aside. Uncertainly the Tarkeshite merchant moved forward and then ran for the darkness of the street, his companions tumbling behind him. Elric heard their footsteps running on the cobbles and he began to laugh. At the sound of his laugh the footfalls became a scamper and the party had soon reached the quayside where the water gleamed, turned a corner and disappeared.

Elric smiled and looked up beyond Old Hrolmar's baroque skyline at the stars. Now there were more footsteps coming from the other end of the street. He turned and saw the newcomers step into a pool of light thrown from the window of a nearby office.

It was Moonglum. The stocky Eastlander was returning in the company of two women who were scantily dressed and heavily painted and who were without doubt Vilmirian whores from the other side of city. Moonglum had an arm about each waist and he was singing some obscure but evidently disgraceful ballad, pausing frequently to have one of the laughing girls pour wine down his throat. Both the whores had large stone flasks in their free hands and they were matching Moonglum drink for drink.

As Moonglum stepped unsteadily nearer he recognised Elric and hailed him, winking. "You see I have not forgotten you, Prince of Melniboné. One of these beauties is for you."

Elric made an exaggerated bow. "You are very good to me. But I thought you planned to find some gold for us. Was that not the reason for coming to Old Hrolmar?"

"Aye!" Moonglum kissed the cheeks of the girls. They snorted with laughter. "Indeed! Gold it is—or something as good as gold. I have rescued these young ladies from a cruel whoremaster on the other side of town. I have promised to sell them to a kinder master and they are grateful to me!"

"You stole these slaves?"

"If you wish to say so—I 'stole' them. Aye, then, 'steal' I did. I stole in with my steel and I released them from a life of degradation. A humanitarian deed. Their miserable life is no more! They may look forward to . . ."

"Their miserable lives will be no more—as, indeed, will be ours when the whoremaster discovers the crime and alerts the watch. How found you these ladies?"

"They found me! I had made my swords available to an old merchant, a stranger to the city. I was to escort him about the murkier regions of Old Hrolmar in return for a good purse of gold (better, I think, than he expected to give me). While he whored above, as he could, I had a drink or two below in the public rooms. These two beauties took a liking to me and told me of their unhappiness. It was enough. I rescued them."

"A cunning plan," Elric said sardonically.

"'Twas theirs! They have brains as well as—"

"I'll help you carry them back to their master before the city guards descend upon us."

"But Elric!"

"But first . . ." Elric seized his friend and threw him over his shoulder, staggering with him to the quay at the end of the street, taking a good hold on his collar and lowering him suddenly into the reeking water. Then he hauled him up and stood him down. Moonglum shivered and looked sadly at Elric.

"I am prone to colds, as you know."

"And prone to drunken plans, too! We are not liked here, Moonglum. The watch needs only one excuse to set upon us. At best we should have to flee the city before our business was done. At worst we shall be disarmed, imprisoned, perhaps slain."

They began to walk back to where the two girls still stood. One of the girls ran forward and knelt to take Elric's hand and press her lips against his thigh. "Master, I have a message . . ."

Elric bent to raise her to her feet.

She screamed. Her painted eyes widened. He stared at her in astonishment and then, following her gaze, turned and saw the pack of bravos who had stolen round the corner and were now rushing at himself and Moonglum. Behind the bravos Elric thought he saw the young dandy he had earlier chased from the tavern. The dandy wished for revenge. Poignards glittered in the darkness and their owners wore the black hoods of professional assassins. There were at least a dozen of them. The young dandy must therefore be extremely rich, for assassins were expensive in Old Hrolmar.

Moonglum had already drawn both his swords and was engaging the leader. Elric pushed the frightened girl behind him and put his hand to Stormbringer's pommel. Almost at its own volition the huge runesword sprang from its scabbard and black light poured from its blade as it began to hum its own strange battle-cry.

He heard one of the assassins gasp "Elric!" and guessed that the dandy had not made it plain whom they were to slay. He blocked the thrust of the slim long-sword, turned it and chopped with a kind of delicacy at the owner's wrist. Wrist and sword flew into the shadows and the owner staggered back screaming.

More swords now and more cold eyes glittering from the black hoods. Stormbringer sang its peculiar song—half-lament, half-victory shout. Elric's own face was alive with battle-lust and his crimson eyes blazed from his bone-white face as he swung this way and that.

Shouts, curses, the screams of women and the groans of men, steel striking steel, boots on cobbles, the sounds of swords in flesh, of blades scraping bone. A confusion through which Elric fought, his broadsword clapped in both pale hands. He had lost sight of Moonglum and prayed that the Eastlander still stood. From time to time he glimpsed one of the girls and wondered why she had not run for safety.

Now the corpses of several hooded assassins lay upon the cobbles and the remainder were beginning to falter as Elric pressed them. They knew the power of his sword and what it did to those it struck. They had seen their comrades' faces as their souls were drawn from them by the hellblade. With every death Elric seemed to grow stronger and the black radiance from the blade seemed to burn fiercer. And now the albino was laughing.

His laughter rang over the rooftops of Old Hrolmar and those who were abed covered their ears, believing themselves in the grip of nightmares.

"Come, friends, my blade still hungers!"

An assassin made to stand his ground and Elric swept the Black Sword up. The man raised his blade to protect his head and Elric brought the Black Sword down. It sheared through the steel and cut down through the hood, through the neck, through the breastbone. It clove the assassin completely in two and it stayed in the flesh, feasting, drawing out the last traces of the man's dark soul. And then the rest were running.

Elric drew a deep breath, avoided looking at the man his sword had slain last, sheathed the blade and turned to look for Moonglum.

It was then that the blow came on the back of his neck. He felt nausea rise in him and tried to shake it off. He felt a prick in his wrist and through the haze he saw a figure he thought at first was Moonglum. But it was another—perhaps a woman. She was tugging at his left hand. Where did she want him to go?

His knees became weak, and he fell to the cobbles. He tried to call out, but failed. The woman was still tugging at his hand as if she sought to take him to safety. But he could not follow her. He fell on his shoulder, then on his back, glimpsed a swimming sky . . .

. . . and then the dawn was rising over the crazy spires of Old Hrolmar and he realised that several hours had passed since he had fought the assassins.

Moonglum's face appeared. It was full of concern.

"Moonglum?"

"Thank Elwher's gentle gods! I thought you slain by that poisoned blade."

Elric's head was clearing rapidly now. He rose to a sitting position. "The attacker came from behind. How . . . ?"

Moonglum looked embarrassed. "I fear those girls were not all they seemed."

Elric remembered the woman tugging at his left hand and he stretched out his fingers. "Moonglum! The Ring of Kings is gone from my hand! The Actorios has been stolen!"

The Ring of Kings had been worn by Elric's forefathers for centuries. It had been the symbol of their power, the source of much of their supernatural strength.

Moonglum's face clouded. "I thought I stole the girls. But they were thieves. They planned to rob us. An old trick."

"There's more to it, Moonglum. They stole nothing else. Just the Ring of Kings. There's still a little gold left in my purse." He jingled his belt pouch, climbing to his feet.

Moonglum jerked his thumb at the street's far wall. There lay one of the girls, her finery all smeared with mud and blood.

"She got in the way of one of the assassins as we fought. She's been dying all night—mumbling your name. I had not told it to her. Therefore I fear you're right. They were sent to steal that ring from you. I was duped by them."

Elric walked rapidly to where the girl lay and he knelt down beside her. Gently he touched her cheek. She opened her lids and stared at him from glazed eyes. Her lips formed his name.

"Why did you plan to rob me?" Elric asked. "Who is your master?"

"Urish . . ." she said in a voice that was a breeze passing through the grass. "Steal ring . . . take it to Nadsokor . . ."

Moonglum now stood on the other side of the dying girl. He had found one of the wine flasks and he bent to give her a drink. She tried to sip the wine but failed. It ran down her little chin, down her slim neck and onto her wounded breast.

"You are one of the beggars of Nadsokor?" Moonglum said.

Faintly, she nodded.

"Urish has always been my enemy," Elric told him. "I once recovered some property from him and he has never forgiven me. Perhaps he sought the Actorios ring in payment." He looked down at the girl. "Your companion—has she returned to Nadsokor?"

Again the girl seemed to nod. Then all intelligence left the eyes, the lids closed and she ceased to breathe.

Elric got up. He was frowning, rubbing at the hand on which the Ring of Kings had been.

"Let him keep the ring, then," said Moonglum hopefully. "He will be satisfied."

Elric shook his head.

Moonglum cleared his throat. "A caravan is leaving Jadmar in a week. It is commanded by Rackhir of Tanelorn and has been purchasing provisions for the city. If we took a ship round the coast we could soon be in Jadmar, join Rackhir's caravan and be on our way to Tanelorn in good company. As you know, it's rare for anyone of Tanelorn to make such a journey. We are lucky, for . . ."

"No," said Elric in a low voice. "We must forget Tanelorn for the moment, Moonglum. The Ring of Kings is my link with my fathers. More—it aids my conjurings and has saved our lives more than once. We ride for Nadsokor now. I must try to reach the girl before she gets to the City of Beggars. Failing that, I must enter the city and recover my ring."

Moonglum shuddered. "It would be more foolish than any plan of mine, Elric. Urish would destroy us."

"Nonetheless, to Nadsokor I must go."

Moonglum bent and began systematically to strip the girl's corpse of its jewellery. "We'll need every penny we can raise if we're to buy decent horses for our journey," he explained.

3

The Cold Ghouls

Framed against the scarlet sunset, Nadsokor looked from this distance more like a badly kept graveyard than a city. Towers tottered, houses were half-collapsed, the walls were broken.

Elric and Moonglum came up the peak of the hill on their fast Shazaarian horses (which had cost them all they had) and saw it. Worse—they smelled it. A thousand stinks issued from the festering city and both men gagged, turning their horses back down the hill to the valley.

"We'll camp here for a short while—until nightfall," Elric said. "Then we'll enter Nadsokor."

"Elric, I am not sure I could bear the stench. Whatever our disguise, our disgust would reveal us for strangers."

Elric smiled and reached into his pouch. He took out two small tablets and handed one to Moonglum.

The Eastlander regarded the thing suspiciously. "What's this?"

"A potion. I used it once before when I came to Nadsokor. It will kill your sense of smell completely—unfortunately your sense of taste as well . . ."

Moonglum laughed. "I did not plan to eat a gourmet meal while in the City of Beggars!" He swallowed the pill and Elric did likewise.

Almost instantly Moonglum remarked that the stink of the city was subsiding. Later, as they chewed the stale bread which was all that was left of their provisions, he said:

"I can taste nothing. The potion works."

Elric nodded. He was frowning, looking up the hill in the direction of the city as the night fell.

Moonglum took out his swords and began to hone them with the small stone he carried for the purpose. As he honed, he watched Elric's face, trying to see if he could guess Elric's thoughts.

At last the albino spoke. "We'll need to leave the horses here, of course, for most beggars disdain their use."

"They are proud in their perversity," Moonglum murmured.

"Aye. We'll need those rags we brought."

"Our swords will be noticed . . ."

"Not if we wear the loose robes over all. It will mean we'll walk stiff-legged, but that's not so strange in a beggar."

Reluctantly Moonglum got the bundles of rags from the saddle panniers.

So it was that a filthy pair, one stooped and limping, one short but with a twisted arm, crept through the débris which was ankle-deep around the whole city of Nadsokor. They made for one of the many gaps in the wall.

Nadsokor had been abandoned some centuries before by a people fleeing from the ravages of a particularly virulent pox which had struck down most of their number. Not long afterwards the first of the beggars had occupied it. Nothing had been done to preserve the city's defences and now the muck around the perimeters was as effective a protection as any wall.

No-one saw the two figures as they climbed over the messy rubble and entered the dark, festering streets of the City of Beggars. Huge rats raised themselves on their hind legs and watched them as they made their way to what had once been Nadsokor's senate building and which was now Urish's palace. Scrawny dogs with garbage dangling in their jaws warily slunk back into the shadows. Once a little column of blind men, each man with his right hand on the shoulder of the man in front, tapped their way through the night, passing directly across the street Elric and Moonglum were in. From some of the tumbledown buildings came cacklings and titterings as the maimed caroused with the crippled and the degenerate and corrupted coupled with their crones. As the disguised pair neared what had been Nadsokor's forum there came a scream from one shattered doorway and a young girl, barely over puberty, dashed out pursued by a monstrously fat beggar who propelled himself with astounding speed on his crutches, the livid stumps of his legs, which terminated at the knee, making the motions of running. Moonglum tensed, but Elric held him back as the fat cripple bore down on his prey, abandoned his crutches which rattled on the broken pavement, and flung himself on the child.

Moonglum tried to free himself from Elric's grasp but the albino whispered: "Let it happen. Those who are whole either in mind, body or spirit cannot be tolerated in Nadsokor."

There were tears in Moonglum's eyes as he looked at his friend.

"Your cynicism is as disgusting as anything they do!"

"I do not doubt it. But we are here for one purpose—to recover the stolen Ring of Kings. That, and nought else, is what we shall do."

"What matters that when . . . ?"

But Elric was continuing on his way to the forum and after hesitating for a moment Moonglum followed him.

Now they stood on the far side of the square looking at Urish's palace. Some of its columns had fallen, but on this building alone had there been some attempt at restoration and decoration. The archway of the main entrance was painted with crude representations of the Arts of Begging and Extortion. An example of the coinage of all the nations of the Young Kingdoms had been imbedded in the wooden door and above it had been nailed, perhaps ironically, a pair of wooden crutches, crossed as swords might be crossed, indicating that the weapons of the beggar were his power to horrify and disgust those luckier or better endowed than himself.

Elric stared through the murk at the building and he had a calculating frown on his face.

"There are no guards," he said to Moonglum.

"Why should there be? What have they to guard?"

"There were guards last time I came to Nadsokor. Urish protects his Hoard most assiduously. It is not outsiders he fears but his own despicable rabble."

"Perhaps he no longer fears them."

Elric smiled. "A creature like King Urish fears everything. We had best be wary when we enter the hall. Have your swords ready to draw at any hint that we have been lured into a trap."

"Surely Urish would not suspect we'd know where the girl came from?"

"Aye, it seemed good chance that one of them told us, but nonetheless we must make allowances for Urish's cunning."

"He would not willingly bring you here—not with the Black Sword at your side."

"Perhaps . . ."

They began to walk across the forum. It was very still, very dark. From far away came the occasional shout, a laugh or an obscene, indefinable sound.

Now they were at the door, standing beneath the crossed crutches.

Elric felt beneath his ragged robes for the hilt of his sword and with his left hand pushed at the door. It squeaked open a fraction. They looked about them to see if anyone had heard the sound, but the square was as still as it had been.

More pressure. Another squeak. And now they could squeeze their bodies through the aperture.

They stood in Urish's hall. Braziers of garbage gave off faint light. Oily smoke curled towards the rafters. They saw the dim outlines of the dais at the far end and on the dais stood Urish's huge, crude throne. The hall seemed deserted, but Elric's hand did not leave the hilt of the Black Sword.

He stopped as he heard a sound, but it was a great, black rat scuttling across the floor.

Silence again.

Elric moved forward, step by cautious step, along the length of the slimy hall, Moonglum behind him.

Elric's spirits began to rise, as they neared the throne. Perhaps Urish had, after all, grown complacent of his strength. He would open the trunk beneath the throne, remove his ring and then they would leave the city and be away before dawn, riding across country to join the caravan of Rackhir the Red Archer on its way to Tanelorn.

He began to relax but his step was just as cautious. Moonglum had paused, cocking his head to one side as if hearing something.

Elric turned. "What is it you hear?"

"Possibly nothing. Or maybe one of those great rats we saw earlier. It is just that—"

A silver-blue radiance burst out from behind the grotesque throne and Elric flung up his left hand to protect his eyes, trying to disentangle his sword from his rags.

Moonglum yelled and began to run for the door, but even when Elric put his back to the light he could not see. Stormbringer moaned in its scabbard as if in rage. Elric tugged at it, but felt his limbs grow weaker and weaker. From behind him came a laugh which he recognised. A second laugh—almost a throaty cough—joined it.

His sight came back but now he was held by clammy hands and when he saw his captors he shuddered. Shadowy creatures of limbo held him—ghouls summoned by sorcery. Their dead faces smiled but their dead eyes remained dead. Elric felt the heat and the strength leaving his body and it was as if the ghouls sucked it from him. He could almost feel his vitality travelling from his own body to theirs.

Again the laugh. He looked up at the throne and saw emerging from behind it the tall, saturnine figure of Theleb K'aarna, whom he had left for dead near the castle of Kaneloon a few months since.

Theleb K'aarna smiled in his curling beard as Elric struggled in the grasp of the ghouls. Now from the other side of the throne came the filthy carcass of Urish the Seven-fingered, the cleaver Hackmeat cradled in his left arm.

Elric could barely hold his head up as the ghouls' cold flesh absorbed his strength, but he smiled at his own foolishness. He had been right in suspecting a trap, but wrong in entering it so poorly prepared.

And where was Moonglum? Had he deserted him? The little Eastlander was nowhere to be seen.

Urish swaggered round the throne and sprawled his begrimed person in it, placing Hackmeat so that it lay across the arms. His pale, beady eyes stared hard at Elric.

Theleb K'aarna remained standing by the side of the throne, but triumph flamed in his eyes like Imrryr's own funeral fires.

"Welcome back to Nadsokor," wheezed Urish, scratching himself between the legs. "You have returned to make amends, I take it."

Elric shivered as the cold in his bones increased. Stormbringer stirred at his side but it could only help him if he drew it with his own hands. He knew he was dying.

"I have come to regain my property," he said through chattering teeth. "My ring."

"Ah! The Ring of Kings. It was yours, was it? My girl mentioned something of that."

"You sent her to steal it!"

Urish sniggered. "I'll not deny it. But I did not expect the White Wolf of Imrryr to step so easily into my trap."

"He would have stepped out again if you had not that amateur magic-maker's spells to help you!"

Theleb K'aarna glowered but then his face relaxed. "Are you not discomforted, then, by my ghouls?"

Elric was gasping as the last of the heat fled his bones. He now could not stand, but hung in the hands of the dead creatures. Theleb K'aarna must have planned this for weeks, for it took many spells and pacts with the guardians of limbo to bring such ghouls to Earth.

"And so I die," Elric murmured. "Well, I suppose I do not care . . ."

Urish raised his ruined features in what was a parody of pride. "You do not die yet, Elric of Melniboné. The sentence has yet to be passed. The formalities must be suffered! By my cleaver Hackmeat I must sentence you for your crimes against Nadsokor and against the Sacred Hoard of King Urish!"

Elric hardly heard him as his legs collapsed altogether and the ghouls tightened their grip on him.

Dimly he was aware of the beggar rabble shuffling into the hall.

Doubtless they had all been waiting for this. Had Moonglum died at their hands when he fled the hall?

"Put his head up!" Theleb K'aarna instructed his dead servants. "Let him see Urish, King of All Beggars, make his just decree!"

Elric felt a cold hand beneath his chin and his head was raised so he could watch, through misting eyes, as Urish stood up and grasped the cleaver Hackmeat in his four-fingered hand, stretching it towards the smoky ceiling.

"Elric of Melniboné, thou art convicted of many crimes against the Ignoblest of the Ignoble—myself, King Urish of Nadsokor. Thou has offended King Urish's friend, that most pleasingly degenerate villain Theleb K'aarna—"

At this Theleb K'aarna pursed his lips, but did not interrupt.

"—and, moreover, did come a second time to the City of Beggars to repeat thy crimes. By my great cleaver Hackmeat, the symbol of my dignity and power, I condemnest thee to the Punishment of the Burning God!"

From all sides of the hall came the foul applause of the Beggar Court. Elric remembered a legend of Nadsokor—that when the original population were first struck by the disease they summoned aid from Chaos—begging Chaos to cleanse the disease from the city—with fire if necessary. Chaos had played a joke upon these folk—sent their Burning God who had burned what was left of their possessions. A further summons to Law to help them had resulted in the Burning God's being imprisoned by Lord Donblas in the city. Having had enough of the Lords of the Higher Worlds the remnants of the citizens had abandoned their city. But was the Burning God still here in Nadsokor?

Faintly he still heard Urish's voice. "Take him to the labyrinth and give him to the Burning God!"

Theleb K'aarna spoke but Elric did not hear what he said, though he heard Urish's reply.

"His sword? How will that avail him against a Lord of Chaos? Besides, if the sword is released from the scabbard, who knows what will happen?"

Theleb K'aarna was evidently reluctant, by his tone, but at last agreed with Urish.

Now Theleb K'aarna's voice boomed commandingly.

"Things of limbo—release him! His vitality has been your reward! Now—begone!"

Elric fell to the muck on the flagstones but was now too weak to move as beggars came forward and lifted him up.

His eyes closed and his senses deserted him as he felt himself borne from the hall and heard the united voices of the wizard of Pan Tang and the King of the Beggars giving vent to their mocking triumph.

4

Punishment of the Burning God

"By Narjhan's droppings he's cold!"

Elric heard the rasping voice of one of the beggars who carried him. He was still weak but some of the beggars' body-heat had transferred itself to him and the chill of his bones was now by no means as intense.

"Here's the portal."

Elric forced his eyes open.

He was upside down but could see ahead of him through the gloom.

Something shimmered there.

It looked like the iridescent skin of some unearthly animal stretched across the arch of the tunnel.

He was jerked backwards as the beggars swung his body and hurled it towards the shimmering skin.

He struck it.

It was viscous.

It clung to him and he felt it was absorbing him. He tried to struggle but was still far too weak. He was sure that he was being killed.

But after long minutes he was through it and had struck stone and lay gasping in the blackness of the tunnel.

This must be the labyrinth of which Urish had spoken.

Trembling, he tried to rise, using his scabbarded sword as a support. It took him some time to get up but at last he could lean against the curving wall.

He was surprised. The stones seemed to be hot. Perhaps it was because he was so cold and in reality the stones were of normal heat.

Even this speculation seemed to weary him. Whatever the nature of the heat it was welcome. He pressed his back harder against the stones.

As their heat passed into his body he felt a sensation almost of ecstasy and he drew a deep breath. Strength was returning slowly.

"Gods," he murmured, "even the snows of the Lormyrian steppe could not compare with such a great cold."

He drew another deep breath and coughed.

Then he realised that the drug he had swallowed was beginning to wear off.

He wiped his mouth with the back of his hand and spat out saliva. Something of the stink of Nadsokor had entered his nostrils.

He stumbled back towards the portal. The peculiar stuff still shimmered there. He pressed his hand against it and it gave reluctantly but then held firm. He leaned his whole weight on it but it would still not give any further. It was like a particularly tough membrane but it was not flesh. Was this the stuff with which the Lords of Law had sealed off the tunnel, entrapping their enemy, the Lord of Chaos? The only light in the tunnel came from the membrane itself.

"By Arioch, I'll turn the tables on the Beggar King," Elric murmured. He threw back his rags and put his hand on Stormbringer's pommel. The blade purred as a cat might purr. He drew the sword from its scabbard and it began to sing a low, satisfied song. Now Elric hissed as its power flowed up his arm and into his body. Stormbringer was giving him the strength he needed—but he knew that Stormbringer must be paid soon, must taste blood and souls and thus replenish its energy. He aimed a great blow at the shimmering wall. "I'll hack down this portal and release the Burning God upon Nadsokor! Strike true, Stormbringer! Let flame come to devour the filth that is this city!"

But Stormbringer howled as it bit into the membrane and it was held fast. No rent appeared in the stuff. Instead Elric had to tug with all his might to get the sword free. He withdrew, panting.

"The portal was made to withstand the efforts of Chaos," Elric murmured. "My sword's useless against it. And so, unable to go back I must, perforce, go forward." Stormbringer in hand he turned and began to make his way along the passage. He took one turn and then another and then a third and the light had disappeared completely. He reached for his pouch where his flint and tinder were kept, but the beggars had cut that from his belt as they carried him. He decided to retrace his steps. But by now he was deeply within the labyrinth and he could not find the portal.

"No portal—but no god, it seems. Mayhap there's another exit from this place. If it's blocked by a door of wood, then Stormbringer will soon carve me a path to freedom."

And so he pressed further into the labyrinth, taking a hundred twists and turns in the darkness before he paused again.

He had noticed that he was growing warmer. Now, instead of feeling horribly cold, he felt uncomfortably hot. He was sweating. He removed some of the upper layers of his rags and stood in his own shirt and breeks. He had begun to thirst.

Another turning and he saw light ahead.

"Well, Stormbringer, perhaps we are free after all!"

He began to run towards the source of the light. But it was not daylight, neither was it the light from the portal. This was firelight—of brands, perhaps.

He could see the sides of the tunnel quite clearly in the firelight. Unlike the masonry in the rest of Nadsokor, this was free of filth—a plain, grey stone stained by the red light.

The source of the light was around the next bend. But the heat had grown greater and his flesh stung as the sweat sprang from his pores.

"AAH!"

A great voice suddenly filled the tunnel as Elric rounded the bend and saw the fire leaping not thirty yards distant.

"AAH! AT LAST!"

The voice came from the fire.

And Elric knew he had found the Burning God.

"I have no quarrel with you, my Lord of Chaos!" he called. "I, too, serve Chaos!"

"But I must eat," came the voice. "CHECKALAKH MUST EAT!"

"I am poor food for one such as you," Elric said reasonably, putting both his hands around Stormbringer's hilt and taking a step backward.

"Aye, beggar, that thou art—but thou art the only food they send!"

"I'm no beggar!"

"Beggar or not, Checkalakh will devour thee!"

The flames shook and a shape began to be made of them. It was a human shape but composed entirely of flame. Flickering hands of fire stretched out towards Elric.

And Elric turned.

And Elric ran.

And Checkalakh, the Burning God, came fast as a flash fire behind him.

Elric felt pain in his shoulder and he smelled burning cloth. He increased his speed, having no notion of where he ran.

And still the Burning God pursued him.

"Stop, mortal! It is futile! Thou canst not escape Checkalakh of Chaos!"

Elric shouted back in desperate humour. "I'll be no-one's roast pork!" His step began to falter. "Not—not even a god's!"

Like the roar of flames up a chimney, Checkalakh replied, "Do not defy me, mortal! It is an honour to feed a god!"

Both the heat and the effort of running were exhausting Elric. A plan of sorts had formed in his brain when he had first encountered the Burning God. That was why he had started to run.

But now, as Checkalakh came on, he was forced to turn.

"Thou art somewhat feeble for so mighty a Lord of Chaos," he panted, readying his sword.

"My long sojourn here has weakened me," Checkalakh replied, "else I would have caught thee ere now! But catch thee I will! And devour thee I must!"

Stormbringer whined its defiance at the enfeebled Chaos god and blade struck out at flaming head and gashed the god's right cheek so that paler fire flickered there and something ran up the black blade and into Elric's heart so that he trembled in a mixture of terror and joy as some of the Burning God's life-force entered him.

Eyes of flame stared at the Black Sword and then at Elric. Brows of flame furrowed and Checkalakh halted.

"Thou art no ordinary beggar, 'tis true!"

"I am Elric of Melniboné and I bear the Black Sword. Lord Arioch is my master—a more powerful entity than you, Lord Checkalakh."

Something akin to misery passed across the god's fiery countenance. "Aye—there are many more powerful than me, Elric of Melniboné."

Elric wiped sweat from his face. He drew in great gulps of burning air. "Then why—why not combine your strength with mine? Together we can tear down the portal and take vengeance on those who have conspired to bring us together."

Checkalakh shook his head and little tongues of fire fell from it. "The portal will only open when I am dead. So it was decreed when Lord Donblas of Law imprisoned me here. Even if we were successful in destroying the portal—it would result in my death. Therefore, most powerful of mortals, I must fight thee and eat thee."

And again Elric began to run, desperately seeking the portal, knowing that the only light he could hope to find in the labyrinth came from the Burning God himself. Even if he were to defeat the god, he would still be trapped in the complex maze.

And then he saw it. He was back at the place where he had been thrown through the membrane.

"It is only possible to enter my prison through the portal, not leave it!" called Checkalakh.

"I'm aware of that!" Elric took a firmer grip on Stormbringer and turned to face the thing of flame.

Even as his sword swung back and forth, parrying every attempt of the Burning God's to seize him, Elric felt sympathy for the creature. He had come in answer to the summonings of mortals and he had been imprisoned for his pains.

But Elric's clothes had begun to smoulder now and even though Stormbringer supplied him with energy every time it struck Checkalakh the heat itself was beginning to overwhelm him. He sweated no more. Instead his skin felt dry and about to split. Blisters were forming on his white hands. Soon he would be able to hold the blade no longer.

"Arioch!" he breathed. "Though this creature be a fellow Lord of Chaos, aid me to defeat him!"

But Arioch lent him no extra strength. He had already learned from his patron demon that greater things were being planned on and above the Earth and that Arioch had little time for even the most favourite of his mortal charges.

Yet, from habit, still Elric murmured Arioch's name as he swept the sword so that it struck first Checkalakh's burning hands and then his burning shoulder and more of the god's energy entered him.

It seemed to Elric that even Stormbringer was beginning to burn and the pain in his blistered hands grew so great that it was at last the only sensation of which he was aware. He staggered back against the iridescent membrane and felt its fleshlike texture on his back. The ends of his long hair were beginning to smoke and large areas of his clothes had completely charred.

Was Checkalakh failing, though? The flames burned less brightly and there was an expression of resignation beginning to form on the face of fire.

Elric drew on his pain as his only source of strength and he made the pain take the sword and bring it back over his head and he made the pain bring Stormbringer down in a massive blow aimed at the god's head.

And even as the blow descended the fire began to die. Then Stormbringer had struck and Elric yelled as an enormous wave of energy poured into his body and knocked him backwards so that the sword fell from his hand and he felt that his flesh could not contain what it now held. He rolled, moaning, on the floor and he kicked at the air, raising his twisted, blistered hands to the roof as if in supplication to some being who had the power to stop what was happening to him. There were no tears in his eyes, for it seemed that even his blood had begun to boil out of him.

"Arioch! Save me!" He was shuddering, screaming. "Arioch! Stop this thing happening to me!"

He was full of the energy of a god and the mortal frame was not meant to contain so much force.

"Aaaah! Take it from me!"

He became aware of a calm, beautiful face looking down upon him as he writhed. He saw a tall man—much taller than himself—and he knew that this was no mortal at all, but a god.

"It is over!" said a pure, sweet voice.

And, though the creature did not move, soft hands seemed to caress him and the pain began to diminish and the voice continued to speak.

"Long centuries ago, I, Lord Donblas the Justice Maker, came to Nadsokor to free it from the grip of Chaos. But I came too late. Evil brought more evil, as evil will, and I could not interfere too much with the affairs of mortals, for we of Law have sworn to let mankind make its own destiny if that is possible. Yet the Cosmic Balance swings now like the pendulum of a clock with a broken spring and terrible forces are at work on the Earth. Thou, Elric, art a servant of Chaos—yet thou hast served Law more than once. It has been said that the destiny of mankind rests within thee and that may be true. Thus, I aid thee—though I do so against mine own oath . . ."

And Elric closed his eyes and felt at peace for the first time that he remembered.

The pain had gone, but great energy still filled him. When he opened his eyes again there was no beautiful face looking down on him and the scintillating membrane which had covered the archway had disappeared. Nearby Stormbringer lay and he sprang up and seized the sword, returning it to his scabbard. He noticed that the blisters had left his hands and that even his clothes were no longer charred.

Had he dreamed it all—or most of it?

He shook his head. He was free. He was strong. He had his sword with him. Now he would return to the hall of King Urish and take his vengeance both on Nadsokor's ruler and Theleb K'aarna.

He heard a footfall and withdrew into the shadows. Light filtered into the tunnel from gaps in the roof and it was plain that at this point it was close to the surface. A figure appeared and he recognised it at once.

"Moonglum!"

The little Eastlander grinned in relief and sheathed his swords. "I came here to aid you if I could, but I see you need no aid from me!"

"Not here. The Burning God is no more. I'll tell you of that later. What became of you?"

"When I realised we were in a trap I ran for the door, deciding it would be best if one of us were free and I knew it was you they wanted. But then I saw the door opening and realised they had been waiting there all along." Moonglum wrinkled his nose and dusted at the rags he still wore. "Thus I came to find myself lying at the bottom of one of those heaps of garbage littered about Urish's hall. I dived into it and stayed there, listening to what passed. As soon as I could, I found this tunnel, planning to help you however I could."

"And where are Urish and Theleb K'aarna now?"

"It appears that they go to make good Theleb K'aarna's bargain with Urish. Urish was not altogether happy with the plan to lure you here for he fears your power—"

"He has reason to! Now!"

"Aye. Well, it seems that Urish had heard what we had heard, that the caravan for Tanelorn was on its way back to that city. Urish has knowledge of

Tanelorn—though not much, I gather—and fosters an unreasoning hatred for the place, perhaps because it is the opposite of what Nadsokor is."

"They plan to attack Rackhir's caravan?"

"Aye—and Theleb K'aarna is to summon creatures from hell to ensure that their attack is successful. Rackhir has no sorcery to speak of, I believe."

"He served Chaos once, but no more—those who dwell in Tanelorn can have no supernatural masters."

"I gathered as much from the conversation."

"When do they make this attack?"

"They have gone already—almost as soon as they had dealt with you. Urish is impatient."

"It is unlike the beggars to make a direct attack on a caravan."

"They do not always have a powerful wizard for an ally."

"True." Elric frowned. "My own powers of sorcery are limited without the Ring of Kings upon my hand. Its supernatural qualities identify me as a true member of the royal line of Melniboné—the line which made so many bargains with the elementals. First I must recover my ring and then we go at once to aid Rackhir."

Moonglum glanced at the floor. "They said something of protecting Urish's Hoard in his absence. There may be a few armed men in the hall."

Elric smiled. "Now that we are prepared and now I have the strength of the Burning God in me, I think we shall be able to deal with a whole army, Moonglum."

Moonglum brightened. "Then I'll lead the way back to the hall. Come. This passage will take us to a door which is let into the side of the hall, near the throne."

They began to run along the passage until they came at length to the door Moonglum had mentioned. Elric did not pause but drew his sword and flung the door open. It was only when he was in the hall that he stopped. Daylight now lit the gloomy place, but it was again deserted. No sword-bearing beggars awaited them.

Instead, there sat in Urish's throne a fat, scaly thing of yellow and green and black. Brown bile dripped from its grinning snout and it raised one of its many paws in a mockery of a salute.

"Greetings," it hissed, "and beware—for I am the guardian of Urish's treasure."

"A thing of hell," Elric said. "A demon raised by Theleb K'aarna. He has been brewing his spells for a long time, methinks, if he can command so many foul servants." He frowned and weighed Stormbringer in his hand but, oddly, the blade did not seem to hunger for battle.

"I warn thee," hissed the demon, "I cannot be slain by a sword—not even that sword. It is my wardpact . . ."

"What is that?" whispered Moonglum, eyeing the demon warily.

"He is of a race of demons used by all with sorcerous power. He is a guardian. He will not attack unless himself attacked. He is virtually invulnerable to mortal weapons and, in his case, he has a ward against swords—be they supernatural or no. If we attempted to slay him with our swords, we should be struck down by all the powers of hell. We could not possibly survive."

"But you have just destroyed a god! A demon is nothing compared with that!"

"A weak god," Elric reminded him. "And this is a strong demon—for he is a representative of all demons who would mass with him to preserve his wardpact."

"Is there no chance of defeating him?"

"If we are to help Rackhir, there is no reason for trying. We must get to our horses and try to warn the caravan. Later, perhaps, we can return and think of some sorcery which will aid us against the demon." Elric bowed sardonically to the demon and returned his salute. "Farewell, unlovely one. May your master not return to release you and thus ensure you squat in this filth for ever!"

The demon slobbered in rage. "My master is Theleb K'aarna—one of the most powerful sorcerers amongst your kind."

Elric shook his head. "Not my kind. I shall be slaying him soon and you will be left there until I discover the means of destroying you."

Somewhat pettishly, the demon folded its multitude of arms and closed its eyes.

Elric and Moonglum strode through the muck-strewn hall towards the door.

They were close to vomiting by the time they reached the steps leading into the forum. The rest of Elric's potions had been taken when his purse was taken and they had no protection now against the stink. Moonglum spat on the steps as they descended into the square and then he looked up and drew his two swords in a cross-arm motion.

"Elric!"

Some dozen beggars were rushing at them, bearing an array of clubs, axes and knives.

Elric laughed. "Here's a titbit for you, Stormbringer!" He drew his sword and began to swing the howling blade around his head, moving implacably towards the beggars. Almost immediately two of their number broke and ran, but the rest came in a rush at the pair.

Elric brought the sword lower and took a head from its shoulders and had bitten deep into the next man's shoulder before the first's blood had begun to spout.

Moonglum darted in with his two slim swords and engaged two of the beggars at the same time. Elric stabbed at another and the man screamed and danced, clutching at the blade which remorselessly drew out his soul and his life.

Stormbringer was singing a sardonic song now and three of the surviving beggars dropped their weapons and were off across the square as Moonglum neatly took both his opponents simultaneously in their hearts and Elric hacked down the rest of the rabble as they shouted and groaned for mercy.

Elric sheathed Stormbringer, looked down at the crimson ruin he had caused, wiped his lips as a man might who had just enjoyed a fine meal, caused Moonglum to shudder, and clapped his friend on the shoulder.

"Come—let's to Rackhir's aid!"

As Moonglum followed the albino, he reflected that Elric had absorbed more than just the Burning God's life-force in the encounter in the labyrinth. Much of the callousness of the Lords of Chaos was in him today.

Today Elric seemed a true warrior of ancient Melniboné.

5

Things Which are Not Women

The beggars had been too absorbed in their triumph over the albino and their plans for their attack on the caravan of Tanelorn to think to seek the mounts on which Elric and Moonglum had come to Nadsokor.

They found the horses where they had left them the previous night. The superb Shazaarian steeds were cropping the grass as if they had been waiting only a few minutes.

They climbed into their saddles and soon were riding as fast as the fleet horses could carry them—north-north-east to the point the caravan was logically due to reach.

Shortly after noon they had found it—a long sprawl of wagons and horses, awnings of gay, rich silks, brightly decorated harness, it stretched across the floor of a shallow valley. And surrounding it on all sides was the squalid and motley beggar army of King Urish of Nadsokor.

Elric and Moonglum reined in their horses when they reached the brow of the hill and they watched.

Theleb K'aarna and King Urish were not immediately visible and at last Elric saw them on the opposite hill. By the way in which the sorcerer was stretching out his arms to the deep blue sky Elric guessed he was already summoning the aid he had promised Urish.

Below Elric saw a flash of red and knew that it must be the scarlet garb of the Red Archer. Peering closer he saw one or two other shapes he recognised—

Brut of Lashmar with his blond hair and his huge, burly body almost dwarfing his warhorse; Carkan, once of Pan Tang himself, but now dressed in the chequered cloak and fur cap of the barbarians of Southern Ilmiora. All these men had forsworn their gods to go to live in peaceful Tanelorn where, it was said, even the greatest Lords of the Higher Worlds could not enter—Eternal Tanelorn, which had stood for uncountable cycles and would outlive the Earth herself.

Knowing nothing of Theleb K'aarna's plan Rackhir was plainly not too worried by the appearance of the beggar rabble which was as poorly armed as those Elric and Moonglum had fought in Nadsokor.

"We must ride through their army to reach Rackhir now," Moonglum said.

Elric nodded but he made no move. He was watching the distant hill where Theleb K'aarna continued his incantation, hoping that he might guess what kind of aid the sorcerer was summoning.

A moment later Elric yelled and spurred his horse down the hill at a gallop. Moonglum was almost as startled as the beggars as he followed his friend into the thick of the ragged horde, slashing this way and that with the longest of his swords.

Elric's Stormbringer emitted black radiance as it carved a bloody path through the beggar army, leaving in its wake a mess of dismembered bodies, entrails and dead, horrified eyes.

Moonglum's horse was splashed with blood to the shoulder and it snorted and baulked at following the white-skinned demon with the howling black blade, but Moonglum, afraid that the beggar ranks would close, forced it on until at last they were both riding towards the caravan and someone was yelling Elric's name.

It was Rackhir the Red Archer, clothed in scarlet from head to foot, with a red bone bow in his hand and a red quiver of crimson-fletched arrows on his back. On his head was a scarlet skull-cap decorated with a single scarlet feather. His face was weather-beaten and all but fleshless. He had fought with

Elric before the fall of Imrryr and together they had discovered the black swords. Rackhir had gone on to seek Tanelorn and find it at last.

Elric had not seen Rackhir since then. Now he noted an enviable look of peace in the archer's eyes. Rackhir had once been a Warrior Priest in the East-lands, serving Chaos, but now he served nothing but his tranquil Tanelorn.

"Elric! Have you come to help us send Urish and his beggars back to where they came from?" Rackhir was laughing, evidently pleased to see his old friend. "And Moonglum! When did you two meet? I have not seen thee since I left the Eastlands!"

Moonglum grinned. "Much has come to pass since those days, Rackhir."

Rackhir rubbed at his aquiline nose. "Aye—so I've heard."

Elric dismounted swiftly. "No time for reminiscence now, Rackhir. You're in greater danger than you know."

"What? When did the beggar rabble of Nadsokor offer anything to fear? Look how poorly armed they are!"

"They have a sorcerer with them—Theleb K'aarna of Pan Tang. See— that's him on yonder hill."

Rackhir frowned. "Sorcery. These days I've little guard against that. How good is the sorcerer, do you know?"

"He is one of the most powerful in Pan Tang."

"And the wizards of Pan Tang almost equal your folk, Elric, in their skills."

"I fear he more than equals me at present, for my Actorios ring has been stolen from me by Urish."

Rackhir looked strangely at Elric, noting something in the albino's face which he had evidently not seen there when they last parted. "Well," he said, "we shall have to defend ourselves as best we can . . ."

"If you cut loose your horses so that all your folk could be mounted we might be able to escape before Theleb K'aarna invokes whatever supernatural aid it is he seeks." Elric nodded as the giant, Brut of Lashmar, rode up grinning at him. Brut had been a hero in Lashmar before he had disgraced himself.

Rackhir shook his head. "Tanelorn needs the provisions we carry."

"Look," said Moonglum quietly.

On the hill where Theleb K'aarna had been standing there had now appeared a billowing cloud of redness, like blood in clear water.

"He is successful," Rackhir murmured. "Brut! Let all be mounted. We've no time to prepare further defences, but we'll have the advantage of being on horseback when they attack."

Brut thundered off, yelling at the men of Tanelorn. They began to unharness the wagon horses and ready their weapons.

The cloud of redness above was beginning to disperse and out of it shapes were emerging. Elric tried to distinguish the shapes but could not at that distance. He climbed back into his saddle as the horsemen of Tanelorn now formed themselves into groups which would, when the attack came, race through the unmounted beggars striking swiftly and passing on. Rackhir waved to Elric and went to join one of these divisions. Elric and Moonglum found themselves at the head of a dozen warriors armed with axes, pikes and lances.

Then Urish's voice cawed out over the waiting silence.

"Attack, my beggars! They are doomed!"

The beggar rabble began to move down the sides of the valley. Rackhir raised his sword as the signal to his men. Then the first groups of cavalry rode out from the caravan, straight at the advancing beggars.

Rackhir replaced his blade and took up his bow. From where he sat on his horse he began to send arrow after arrow into the beggar ranks.

There was shouting everywhere now as the warriors of Tanelorn met their foes, driving wedges everywhere in their mass.

Elric saw Carkan's chequered cape in the midst of a sea of rags, filthy limbs, clubs and knives. He saw Brut's great blond head towering over a cluster of human filth.

And Moonglum said: "Such creatures as these are unfit opponents for the warriors of Tanelorn."

Elric pointed firmly up the hill. "Perhaps they'll prefer their new foes."

Moonglum gasped. "They are women!"

Elric drew Stormbringer from its scabbard. "They are not women. They are Elenoin. They come from the Eighth Plane—and neither are they human. You will see."

"You recognise them?"

"My ancestors fought them once."

A strange, shrill ululation reached their ears now. It came from the hillside where Theleb K'aarna's figure could again be seen. It came from the shapes which Moonglum was sure were women. Red-haired women whose tresses fell almost to their knees and covered their otherwise completely naked bodies. They danced down the hill towards the besieged caravan and they whirled about their heads swords which must have been over five feet long.

"Theleb K'aarna is clever," Elric muttered. "The warriors of Tanelorn will hesitate before striking at women. And while they hesitate the Elenoin will rip and slash and slay them."

Rackhir had already seen the Elenoin and he, too, recognised them for what they were. "Do not be deceived, men!" he called. "These creatures are demons!" He glanced across at Elric and there was a look of resignation on his face. He knew the power of the Elenoin. He spurred his horse towards the albino. "What can we do, Elric?"

Elric sighed. "What can mortals do against the Elenoin?"

"Have you no sorcery?"

"With the Ring of Kings I could summon the Grahluk, perhaps. They are the ancient enemies of the Elenoin. Theleb K'aarna has already made a gateway from the Eighth Plane."

"Could you not try to call the Grahluk?" Rackhir begged.

"While I tried my sword would not be aiding you. I think Stormbringer is more use today than spells."

Rackhir shuddered and turned his horse away to order his men to re-form their ranks. He knew now that they were all to die.

And now the beggars fell back, as horrified by the Elenoin as were the men of Tanelorn.

Still singing their shrill, chill song, the Elenoin lowered their swords and spread out along the hill, each one smiling at them.

"How can they . . . ?" Then Moonglum saw their eyes. They were huge, orange, animal eyes. "Oh, by the gods!" And then he saw their teeth—long, pointed teeth which glinted like metal.

The horsemen of Tanelorn fell back to the wagons in a long, ragged line. Horror, despair, uncertainty was on every face save Elric's—and on his face was a look of grim anger. His crimson eyes smouldered as he held Stormbringer across his saddle pommel and regarded the demon women, the Elenoin.

The singing grew louder until it made their ears fill with sharp pain and made their stomachs turn. The Elenoin raised their slender arms and began to whirl their long swords about their heads again, staring at them all the while through beastlike, insensate eyes—malicious, unblinking eyes.

Then Carkan of Pan Tang, his fur cap askew, his chequered cloak billowing, gave a strangled yell and urged his heavy horse at them, his own sword waving.

"Back, demons! Back, spawn of hell!"

"Aaaaaaaah!" gasped the Elenoin in anticipation. "Eeeeeeeh!" they sang.

And Carkan was suddenly in the midst of a dozen slender, slashing swords and he and his horse were cut all to tiny morsels of flesh which lay in a heap at the feet of the Elenoin. And their laughter filled the valley as some of them bent to pop the flesh into their fanged mouths.

A groan of horror and hatred went up from the ranks of Tanelorn then and screaming men, hysterical with fear and disgust, began to fling themselves at the Elenoin who laughed the more and whirled their sharp swords.

Stormbringer murmured as it seemed to hear the sounds of battle, but Elric did not move as he stared at the scene. He knew that the Elenoin would kill all as they had killed Carkan.

Moonglum moaned. "Elric—there must be some sorcery against them!"

"There is! But I cannot summon the Grahluk!" Elric's chest was heaving and his brain was in turmoil. "I cannot, Moonglum!"

"For the sake of Tanelorn, you must try!"

Then Elric was riding forward, Stormbringer howling, riding at the Elenoin and screaming Arioch's name as his ancestors had screamed it since the founding of Imrryr!

"Arioch! Arioch! Blood and souls for my Lord Arioch!"

He parried the whirling blade of an Elenoin and glared into the bestial eyes as Stormbringer sent a shudder down his arm. He struck and his own blow was parried by the demon that was not a woman. Red hair swung and curled around his throat. He hacked at it and it loosened its grip. He thrust at the naked body and the Elenoin danced aside. Another whistling blow from the slim sword and he flung himself backwards to avoid it, toppling from his saddle and springing instantly to his feet to parry a second attack, gripped Stormbringer in both hands and stepped forward under the blade to plunge the Black Sword into the smooth belly. The Elenoin shouted with anger and green foulness billowed from the wound. The Elenoin fell, still glaring and snarling, still living. Elric chopped at the neck and the head sprang off, its hair thrashing at him. He dashed forward, picked up the head and began to run up the hill to where the beggars were gathered, watching the destruction of Tanelorn's warriors. As he approached the beggars broke and began to run, but he caught one in the back with his blade. The man fell, tried to crawl on, but his twisted knees would not support him and he collapsed into the stained grass. Elric picked the wretch up and flung him over his shoulder. Then he turned and began to run down the hill back to the camp. The warriors of Tanelorn were fighting well, but half their number had already been slain by the Elenoin. Almost unbelievably there were also several Elenoin corpses on the field.

Elric saw Moonglum defending himself with both swords. He saw Rackhir, still mounted, shouting orders to his men. He saw Brut of Lashmar in the thick of the fight. But he ran on until he stood behind one of the wagons and had dropped both his bloody bundles to the ground. With his sword he split open the twitching body of the beggar and he gathered up the hair of the Elenoin and soaked it in the man's blood.

Again he stood upright, looking towards the west, with the bloody hair in one hand and Stormbringer in the other. He raised both sword and head and began to speak in the ancient High Speech of Melniboné.

Held to the West and soaked in the blood of an enemy, the hair of an Elenoin must be used to summon the enemies of the Elenoin—the Grahluk. He remembered the words he had read in his father's ancient grimoire.

And now the invocation:

Grahluk come and Grahluk slay!
Come kill thine ancient enemy!
Make this thy victory day.

All the strength of the Burning God was leaving him as he used the energy to perform the invocation. And perhaps without the Ring of Kings he was wasting that strength for nothing.

Grahluk speed without delay!
Come kill thine ancient enemy!
Make this thy vengeance day.

The spell was far less complex than many he had used in the past. Yet it took as much from him as any spell ever had.

"Grahluk, I summon thee! Grahluk, here you may take vengeance on your foes!"

Many cycles since, the Elenoin were said to have driven the Grahluk from their lands in the Eighth Plane and the Grahluk sought revenge now at every opportunity.

All around Elric the air shivered and turned brown, then green, then black.

"Grahluk! Come destroy the Elenoin!" Elric's voice was weakening. "Grahluk—the gateway is made!"

And now the ground trembled and strange winds blew at the blood-soaked hair of the Elenoin and the air became thick and purple and Elric fell to his knees, still croaking the invocation.

"Grahluk . . ."

A shuffling sound. A grunting noise. The stink of something unnameable.

The Grahluk had come. They were apelike creatures as bestial as the Elenoin. They carried nets and ropes and shields. Once, it was said, both Grahluk and Elenoin had had intelligence—had been part of the same species which had devolved and divided.

They moved out of the purple mist in their scores and they stood looking at Elric who was still on his knees. Elric pointed at where the remaining warriors of Tanelorn were still fighting the Elenoin.

"There . . ."

The Grahluk snorted with battle-greed and shambled towards the Elenoin.

The Elenoin saw them and their shrill wailing voices changed in quality as they retreated a short distance up the hill.

Elric forced himself to his feet and gasped: "Rackhir! Withdraw your warriors. The Grahluk will do their work now . . ."

"You helped us after all!" Rackhir yelled, turning his horse. His clothes were all in tatters and there were a dozen wounds on his body.

They watched as the Grahluk's nets and nooses flashed towards the screaming Elenoin whose sword blows were stopped by the Grahluk shields. They watched as the Elenoin were crushed and throttled and parts of their entrails devoured by the grunting, apelike demons.

And when the last of the Elenoin was dead, the Grahluk picked up the fallen swords and reversed them and fell upon them.

Rackhir said: "They are killing themselves. Why?"

"They live only to destroy the Elenoin. Once that is done, they have nothing left for which to exist." Elric swayed and Rackhir and Moonglum caught him.

"See!" Moonglum laughed. "The beggars are running!"

"Theleb K'aarna," Elric muttered. "We must get Theleb K'aarna . . ."

"Doubtless he has gone back with Urish to Nadsokor," Moonglum said.

"I must—I must retrieve the Ring of Kings."

"Plainly you can work your sorcery without it," Rackhir said.

"Can I?" Elric looked up and showed his face to Rackhir who lowered his eyes and nodded.

"We will help you get back your ring," Rackhir said quietly. "There'll be no more trouble from the beggars. We'll ride with you to Nadsokor."

"I had hoped you would." Elric climbed with difficulty into the saddle of a surviving horse and jerked at its reins, turning it towards the City of Beggars. "Perhaps your arrows will slay what my sword cannot . . ."

"I do not understand you," Rackhir said.

Moonglum was mounting now. "We'll tell you on the way."

6

The Jesting Demon

Through the filth of Nadsokor now rode the warriors of Tanelorn.

Elric, Moonglum and Rackhir were at the head of the company but there
was no ostentatious triumph in their demeanour. The riders looked neither to
left nor to right and the beggars offered no threat now, not daring to attack
but instead cowering into the shadows.

A potion of Rackhir's had helped Elric recover some of his strength and
he no longer leaned over his horse's neck but sat upright as they crossed the
forum, came to the palace of the Beggar King.

Elric did not pause. He rode his horse up the steps and into the gloomy
hall.

"Theleb K'aarna!" Elric shouted.

His voice boomed through the hall, but Theleb K'aarna did not reply.

The braziers of garbage guttered in the wind from the opened door and
threw a little more light on the dais at the end.

"Theleb K'aarna!"

But it was not Theleb K'aarna who knelt there. It was a wretched, ragged
figure and it sprawled before the throne and it was sobbing, imploring, whining at something on the throne.

Elric walked his horse a little further into the hall and now he could see
what occupied the throne.

Squatting in the great chair of black oak was the demon which had been there earlier. Its arms were folded and its eyes were shut and it seemed, somewhat theatrically, to be ignoring the pleadings of the creature kneeling at its feet.

The others, also mounted, entered the hall now and together they rode up to the dais and stopped.

The kneeling figure turned its head and it was Urish. It gasped when it saw Elric and stretched out a maimed hand for its cleaver, abandoned some distance away.

Elric sighed.

"Do not fear me, Urish. I'm weary of bloodletting. I do not want your life."

The demon opened its eyes.

"Prince Elric, you have returned," it said. There seemed to be an indefinable difference in its tone.

"Aye. Where is your master?"

"I fear he has fled Nadsokor for ever."

"And left you to sit here for eternity."

The demon inclined its head.

Urish put a grimy hand on Elric's leg. "Elric—help me! I must have my Hoard. It is everything! Destroy the demon and I will give you back the Ring of Kings."

Elric smiled. "You are generous, King Urish."

Tears streamed down the filth on Urish's ruined face. "Please, Elric, I beg thee . . ."

"It is my intention to destroy the demon."

Urish looked nervously about him. "And aught else?"

"That decision lies with the men of Tanelorn whom you sought to rob and whose friends you caused to be slain in a most foul manner."

"It was Theleb K'aarna, not I!"

"And where is Theleb K'aarna now?"

"When you unleashed those ape things on our Elenoin he fled the field. He went towards the Varkalk River—towards Troos."

Without looking behind him Elric said, "Rackhir? Will you try the arrows now?"

There was the hum of a bowstring and an arrow struck the demon in the breast. It quivered there and the demon looked at it with mild interest, then breathed in deeply. As he breathed the arrow was drawn further into him and was eventually absorbed altogether.

"Aaah!" Urish scuttled for his cleaver. "It will not work!"

A second arrow sped from Rackhir's scarlet bow and it, too, was absorbed, as was the third.

Urish was gibbering now, waving his cleaver.

Elric warned him: "He has a wardpact against swords, King Urish!"

The demon rattled its scales. "Is that thing a sword, I wonder?"

Urish hesitated. Spittle ran down his chin and his red eyes rolled. "Demon—begone! I must have my Hoard—it is mine!"

The demon watched him sardonically.

With a yell of terror and anguish Urish flung himself at the demon, the cleaver Hackmeat swinging wildly. Its blade came down on the hell-thing's head, there was a sound like lightning striking metal and the cleaver shivered to pieces. Urish stood staring at the demon in quaking anticipation. Casually the demon reached out four of its hands and seized him. Its jaws opened wider than should have been possible, the bulk of the demon expanded until it was suddenly twice its original size. It brought the kicking Beggar King to its maw and suddenly there were only two legs waving from the mouth and then the demon gave a mighty swallow and there was nothing at all left of Urish of Nadsokor.

Elric shrugged. "Your wardpact is effective."

The demon smiled. "Aye, sweet Elric."

Now the tone of voice was very familiar. Elric looked narrowly at the demon. "You're no ordinary . . ."

"I hope not, most beloved of mortals."

Elric's horse reared and snorted as the demon's shape began to alter. There was a humming sound and black smoke coiled over the throne and then another figure was sitting there, its legs crossed. It had the shape of a man but it was more beautiful than any mortal. It was a being of intense and majestic beauty—unearthly beauty.

"Arioch!" Elric bowed his head before the Lord of Chaos.

"Aye, Elric. I took the demon's place while you were gone."

"But you have refused to aid me . . ."

"There are larger affairs afoot, as I've told you. Soon Chaos must engage with Law and such as Donblas will be dismissed to limbo for eternity."

"You knew Donblas spoke to me in the labyrinth of the Burning God?"

"Indeed I did. That was why I afforded myself the time to visit your plane. I cannot have you patronised by Donblas the Justice Maker and his humourless kind. I was offended. Now I have shown you that my power is greater than Law's." Arioch stared beyond Elric at Rackhir, Brut, Moonglum and the rest who were protecting their eyes from his beauty. "Perhaps you fools of Tanelorn now realise that it is better to serve Chaos!"

Rackhir said grimly: "I serve neither Chaos nor Law!"

"One day you will be taught that neutrality is more dangerous than side-taking, renegade!" The harmonious voice was now almost vicious.

"You cannot harm me," Rackhir said. "And if Elric returns with us to Tanelorn, then he, too, may rid himself of your evil yoke!"

"Elric is of Melniboné. The folk of Melniboné all serve Chaos—and are greatly rewarded. How else would you have rid this throne of Theleb K'aarna's demon?"

"Perhaps in Tanelorn Elric would have no need of his Ring of Kings," Rackhir replied levelly.

There was a sound like rushing water, the boom of thunder and Arioch's form began to grow larger. But as it grew it also began to fade until there was nothing left in the hall but the stench of its garbage.

Elric dismounted and ran to the throne. Reaching under it he drew out dead Urish's chest and hacked it open with Stormbringer. The sword murmured as if resenting the menial work. Gems, gold, artefacts scattered through the muck as Elric sought his ring.

And then at last he held it up in triumph, replacing it on his finger. His step was lighter as he returned to his horse.

Moonglum had in the meantime dismounted and was scooping the best of the jewels into his pouch. He winked at Rackhir, who smiled.

"And now," Elric said, "I go to Troos to seek Theleb K'aarna there. I have still to take my vengeance upon him."

"Let him rot in Troos's sickly forest," Moonglum said.

Rackhir placed a hand on Elric's shoulder. "If Theleb K'aarna hates you so, he will find you again. Why waste your own time in the pursuit?"

Elric smiled slightly at his old friend. "You were ever clear in your arguments, Rackhir. And it is true that I am weary—both gods and demons have fallen to my blade in the little while since I came to Nadsokor."

"Come, rest in Tanelorn—peaceful Tanelorn, where even the greatest Lords of the Higher Worlds cannot come without permission."

Elric looked down at the ring on his finger. "Yet I have sworn Theleb K'aarna shall perish . . ."

"There will be time yet to fulfil your oath."

Elric ran his hand through his milk-white hair and it seemed to his friends that there were tears in his crimson eyes.

"Aye," he said. "Aye. Time yet . . ."

And they rode away from Nadsokor, leaving the beggars to brood in the stink and the foulness and regret that they had aught to do with sorcery or with Elric of Melniboné.

They rode for Eternal Tanelorn. Tanelorn, which had welcomed and held all troubled wanderers who came upon it. All save one.

Doom-haunted, full of guilt, of sorrow, of despair, Elric of Melniboné prayed that this time Tanelorn might hold even him . . .

BOOK THREE

THREE HEROES WITH A SINGLE AIM

*... Elric, of all the manifestations of the Champion Eternal,
was to find Tanelorn without effort. And of all those
manifestations he was the only one to choose
to leave that city of myriad incarnations ...*

—The Chronicle of the Black Sword

I

Tanelorn Eternal

Tanelorn had taken many forms in her endless existence, but all those forms, save one, had been beautiful.

She was beautiful now, with the soft sunlight on her pastel towers and her curved turrets and domes. And banners flew from her spires, but they were not battle-banners, for the warriors who had found Tanelorn and had stayed there were weary of war.

She had been here always. None knew when Tanelorn had been built, but some knew that she had existed before time and would exist after the end of time and that was why she was known as Eternal Tanelorn.

She had played a significant role in the struggles of many heroes and many gods and because she existed beyond time she was hated by the Lords of Chaos who had more than once sought to destroy her. To the south of her lay the rolling plains of Ilmiora, a land where justice was known to prevail, and to the north of her lay the desolation which was the Sighing Desert, endless wasteland over which hissed a constant wind. If Ilmiora represented Law, then the Sighing Desert certainly mirrored something of the barrenness of Ultimate Chaos. Those who dwelt in Tanelorn had loyalty neither to Law nor to Chaos and they had chosen to have no part in the Cosmic Struggle which was waged continuously by the Lords of the Higher Worlds. There were no leaders and there were no followers in Tanelorn and her citizens lived in harmony with each other, even though many had been warriors of great reputation before they chose to stay there. But one of the most admired citizens of Tanelorn, one who was often consulted by the others, was Rackhir of the ascetic features who had once been a fierce Warrior Priest in the Eastlands where he had gained the name of the Red Archer because his skill with a bow was great and he dressed all in scarlet. His skill and his dress remained the same, but his urge to fight had left him since he had come to live in Tanelorn.

Close to the low west wall of the city lay a house of two storeys surrounded by a lawn in which grew all manner of wild flowers. The house was of pink and yellow marble and, unlike most of the other dwellings in Tanelorn, it had a tall, pointed roof. This was Rackhir's house and Rackhir sat outside it now, sprawled on a bench of plain wood while he watched his guest pace the lawn. The guest was his old friend the tormented albino prince of Melniboné.

Elric wore a simple white shirt and britches of heavy black silk. He had a band of the same black silk tied around his head to keep back the mane of milk-white hair which grew to his shoulders. His crimson eyes were downcast as he paced and he did not look at Rackhir at all.

Rackhir was unwilling to intrude upon his friend's reverie and yet he hated to see Elric as he was now. He had hoped that Tanelorn would comfort the albino, drive away the ghosts and the doubts inhabiting his skull, but it seemed that even Tanelorn could not bring Elric tranquillity.

At last Rackhir broke his silence. "It has been a month since you came to Tanelorn, my friend, yet still you pace, still you brood."

Elric looked up with a slight smile. "Aye—still I brood. Forgive me, Rackhir. I am a poor guest."

"What occupies your thoughts?"

"No particular subject. It seems that I cannot lose myself in all this peace. Only violent action helps me drive away my melancholy. I was not meant for Tanelorn, Rackhir."

"But violent action—or the results of it—produces further melancholy, does it not?"

"It is true. It is the dilemma with which I live constantly. It is a dilemma I have been in since the burning of Imrryr—perhaps before."

"It is a dilemma known to all men, perhaps," Rackhir said. "At least to some degree."

"Aye—to wonder what purpose there is to one's existence and what point there is to purpose, even if it should be discovered."

"Tanelorn makes such problems seem meaningless to me," Rackhir told him. "I had hoped that you, too, would be able to dismiss them from your thoughts. Will you stay on in Tanelorn?"

"I have no other plans. I still thirst for vengeance upon Theleb K'aarna, but I now have no idea of his whereabouts. And, as you or Moonglum told me, Theleb K'aarna is sure to seek me out sooner or later. I remember once, when you first found Tanelorn, you suggested that I bring Cymoril here and forget Melniboné. I wish I had listened to you then, Rackhir, for now, I think, I would know peace and Cymoril's dead face would not be infesting my nights."

"You mentioned this sorceress who, you said, resembled Cymoril . . . ?"

"Myshella? She who is called Empress of the Dawn? I first saw her in a dream and when I left her side it was I who was in a dream. We served each other to achieve a common purpose. I shall not see her again."

"But if she—"

"I shall not see her again, Rackhir."

"As you say."

Once more the two friends fell silent and there was only birdsong and the splash of fountains in the air as Elric continued his pacing of the garden.

Some while later Elric suddenly turned on his heel and went into the house followed by Rackhir's troubled gaze.

When Elric came out again he was wearing the great wide belt around his waist—the belt which supported the black scabbard containing his runesword Stormbringer. Over his shoulders was flung a cloak of white silk and he wore high boots.

"I go riding," he said. "I will go by myself into the Sighing Desert and I will ride until I am exhausted. Perhaps exercise is all I need."

"Be careful of the desert, my friend," Rackhir cautioned him. "It is a sinister and treacherous wilderness."

"I will be careful."

"Take the big golden mare. She is used to the desert and her stamina is legendary."

"Thank you. I will see you in the morning if I do not return earlier."

"Take care, Elric. I trust your remedy is successful and your melancholy disappears."

Rackhir's expression had little of relief in it as he watched his friend stride towards the nearby stables, his white cloak billowing behind him like a sea-fog suddenly risen.

Then he heard the sound of Elric's horse as its hoofs struck the cobbles of the street and Rackhir got to his feet to watch as the albino urged the golden mare into a canter and headed for the northern wall beyond which the great yellow waste of the Sighing Desert could be seen.

Moonglum came out of the house, a large apple in his hand, a scroll under his arm.

"Where goes Elric, Rackhir?"

"He looks for peace in the desert."

Moonglum frowned and bit thoughtfully into his apple. "He has sought peace in all other places and I fear he'll not find it there, either."

Rackhir nodded his agreement. "But it is my premonition he'll discover something else, for Elric is not always motivated by his own wishes. There are times when other forces work within him to make him take some fateful action."

"You think this is such a time?"

"It could be."

2

Return of a Sorceress

The sand rippled as the wind blew it so that the dunes seemed like waves in an almost petrified sea. Stark fangs of rock jutted here and there—the remains of mountain ranges which had been eroded by the wind. And a mournful sighing could just be heard, as if the sand remembered when it had been rock and the stones of cities and the bones of men and beasts and longed for its resurrection, sighed at the memory of its death.

Elric drew the cloak's cowl over his head to protect it from the fierce sun which hung in the steel-blue sky.

One day, he thought, I too shall know this peace of death and perhaps then I shall also regret it. He let the golden mare slow to a trot and took a sip of water from one of his canteens.

Now the desert surrounded him and it seemed infinite. Nothing grew. No animals lived there. There were no birds in the sky.

For some reason he shuddered and he had a presentiment of a moment in the future when he would be alone, as he was now, in a world even more barren than this desert, without even a horse for company. He shook off the thought, but it had left him so stunned that for a little while he achieved his ambition and did not brood upon his fate and his situation. The wind dropped slightly and the sighing became little more than a whisper.

Dazed, Elric fingered the pommel of his blade—Stormbringer, the Black Sword—for he associated his presentiment with the weapon but could not tell why. And it seemed to him that he heard an ironic note in the murmuring of the wind. Or did the sound emanate from his sword itself? He cocked his head, listening, but the sound became even less audible, as if aware that he listened.

The golden mare began to climb the gentle slope of a dune, stumbling once as her foot sank into deeper sand. Elric concentrated on guiding her to firmer ground.

Reaching the top of the dune he reined his horse in. The desert dunes rolled on, broken only by the occasional rock. He had it in mind then to ride on and on until it would be impossible to return to Tanelorn, until both he and his mount collapsed from exhaustion and were eventually swallowed by the sands. He pushed back his cowl and wiped sweat from his brow.

Why not? he thought. Life was not bearable. He would try death.

And yet would death deny him? Was he doomed to live? It sometimes seemed so.

Then he considered the horse. It would not be fair to sacrifice it to his desire. Slowly he dismounted.

The wind grew stronger and the sound of its sighing increased. Sand blew around Elric's booted feet. It was a hot wind and it tugged at his voluminous white cloak. The horse snorted nervously.

Elric looked towards the north-east, towards the edge of the world.

And he began to walk.

The horse whinnied enquiringly at him when he did not call it, but he ignored the sound and had soon left his mount behind him. He had not even bothered to bring water with him. He flung back his cowl so that the sun beat directly upon his head. His pace was even, purposeful, and he marched as if at the head of an army.

Perhaps he did sense an army behind him—the army of the dead, of all those friends and enemies whom he had slain in the course of his pointless search for a meaning to his existence.

And still one enemy remained alive. An enemy even stronger, even more malevolent than Theleb K'aarna—the enemy of his darker self, of that side of his nature which was symbolised by the sentient blade still resting at his hip. And when he died, then that enemy would also die. A force for evil would be removed from the world.

For several hours Elric of Melniboné tramped on through the Sighing Desert and gradually, as he had hoped, his sense of identity began to leave him so that it was almost as if he became one with the wind and the sand and, in so doing, was united at last with the world which had rejected him and which he had rejected.

Evening came, but he hardly noticed the sun's setting. Night fell, but he continued to march, unaware of the cold. Already he was weakening. He rejoiced in the weakness where previously he had fought to retain the strength he enjoyed only through the power of the Black Sword.

And sometime around midnight, beneath a pale moon, his legs buckled and he fell sprawling in the sand and lay there while the remains of his sensibilities left him.

"Prince Elric. My lord?"

The voice was rich, vibrant, almost amused. It was a woman's voice and Elric recognised it. He did not move.

"Elric of Melniboné."

He felt a hand on his arm. She was trying to pull him upright. Rather than be dragged he raised himself with some difficulty to a sitting position. He tried to speak, but at first no words would come from his mouth which was dry and full of sand. She stood there as the dawn rose behind her and brightened her long black hair framing her beautiful features. She was dressed in a flowing gown of blue, green and gold and she was smiling.

As he cleared the sand from his mouth he shook his head, saying at last: "If I am dead, then I am still plagued by phantoms and illusions."

"I am no more illusion than anything else in this world. You are not dead, my lord."

"You are, in that case, many leagues from Castle Kaneloon, my lady. You have come from the other side of the world—from edge to edge."

"I have been seeking you, Elric."

"Then you have broken your word, Myshella, for when we parted you said that you would not see me again, that our fates had ceased to be twined."

"I thought then that Theleb K'aarna was dead—that our mutual enemy had perished in the Noose of Flesh." The sorceress spread her arms wide and it was almost as if the gesture summoned the sun, for it appeared over the horizon, suddenly. "Why did you walk thus in the desert, my lord?"

"I sought death."

"Yet you know it is not your destiny to die in such a way."

"I have been told as much but I do not *know* it, Lady Myshella. However," he stumbled upright and stood swaying before her, "I am beginning to suspect that it is so."

She came forward, bringing a goblet from beneath her robes. It was full to the brim with a cool, silvery liquid. "Drink," she said.

He did not lift his hands towards the cup. "I am not pleased to see you, Lady Myshella."

"Why? Because you are afraid to love me?"

"If it flatters you to think that—aye."

"It does not flatter me. I know you are reminded of Cymoril and that I made the mistake of letting Kaneloon become that which you most desire—before I understood that it is also what you most fear."

He lowered his head. "Be silent!"

"I am sorry. I apologised then. We drove away the desire and terror together for a little while, did we not?"

He looked up and she was staring intently into his eyes. "Did we not?"

"We did." He took a deep breath and stretched out his hands for the goblet. "Is this some potion to sap my will and make me work for your interests?"

"No potion could do that. It will revive you, that is all."

He sipped the liquid and immediately his mouth was clean and his head clear. He drained the goblet and he felt a glow of strength in all his limbs and vitals.

"Do you still wish to die?" she asked as she received back the cup, replacing it beneath her robes.

"If death will bring me peace."

"It will not—not if you die now. That I know."

"How did you find me here?"

"Oh, by a variety of means, some of them sorcerous. But my bird brought me to you." She extended her right arm to point behind him.

He turned and there was the bird of gold and silver and brass which he himself had once ridden while in Myshella's service. Its great metallic wings were folded but there was intelligence in its emerald eyes as it waited for its mistress.

"Have you come, then, to return me to Tanelorn?"

She shook her head. "Not yet. I have come to tell you where you may discover our enemy Theleb K'aarna."

He smiled. "He threatens you again?"

"Not directly."

Elric shook sand from his cloak. "I know you well, Myshella. You would not interfere in my destiny unless it had again become in some way linked with your own. You have said that I am afraid to love you. That may be true, for I think I am afraid to love any woman. But you make use of love—the men to whom you give your love are men who will serve your purpose."

"I do not deny that. I love only heroes—and only heroes who work to ensure the presence of the power of Law upon this plane of our Earth . . ."

"I care not whether Law or Chaos gains predominance. Even my hatred of Theleb K'aarna has waned—and that was a personal hatred, nothing to do with any cause."

"What if you knew Theleb K'aarna once again threatens the folk of Tanelorn?"

"Impossible. Tanelorn is eternal."

"Tanelorn is eternal—but its citizens are not. I know. More than once has some catastrophe fallen upon those who dwell in Tanelorn. And the Lords of Chaos hate Tanelorn, though they cannot attack it directly. They would aid any mortal who thought he could destroy those whom the Chaos Lords regard as traitors."

Elric frowned. He knew of the enmity of the Lords of Chaos to Tanelorn. He had heard that on more than one occasion they had made use of mortals to attack the city.

"And you say Theleb K'aarna plans to destroy Tanelorn's citizens? With Chaos's aid?"

"Aye. Your thwarting of his schemes concerning Nadsokor and Rackhir's caravan made him extend his hatred to all dwelling in Tanelorn. In Troos he discovered some ancient grimoires—things which survived from the Age of the Doomed Folk."

"How can that be? They existed a whole time cycle before Melniboné!"

"True—but Troos itself has lasted since the Age of the Doomed Folk and these were people who had many great inventions, a means of preserving their wisdom . . ."

"Very well. I will accept that Theleb K'aarna found their grimoires. What did those grimoires tell him?"

"They showed him the means of causing a rupture in the division which separates one plane of Earth from another. This knowledge of the other planes is largely mysterious to us—even your ancestors only guessed at the variety of existences obtaining in what the ancients termed the 'multiverse'—and I know only a little more than do you. The Lords of the Higher Worlds can, at times, move freely between these temporal and spacial layers, but mortals cannot—at least not in this period of our being."

"And what has Theleb K'aarna done? Surely great power would be needed to cause this 'rupture' you describe? He does not have that power."

"True. But he has powerful allies in the Chaos Lords. The Lords of Entropy have leagued themselves with him as they would league themselves with anyone who was willing to be the means of destruction of those who dwell in

Tanelorn. He found more than manuscripts in the Forest of Troos. He discovered those buried devices which were the inventions of the Doomed Folk and which ultimately brought about their destruction. These devices, of course, were meaningless to him until the Lords of Chaos showed him how they could be activated using the very forces of creation for their energy."

"And he has activated them? Where?"

"He brought the device he wanted to these parts, for he needed space to work where he thought he could not be observed by such as myself."

"He is in the Sighing Desert?"

"Aye. If you had continued on your horse you would have found him by now—or he you. I believe that is what drove you into the desert—a compulsion to seek him out."

"I had no compulsion save a need to die!" Elric tried to control his anger.

She smiled again. "Have it thus if you will . . ."

"You mean I am so manipulated by Fate that I cannot choose to die if I wish?"

"Ask yourself for that answer."

Elric's face was clouded with puzzlement and despair. "What is it, then, which guides me? And to what end?"

"You must discover that for yourself."

"You want me to go against Chaos? Yet Chaos aids me and I am sworn to Arioch."

"But you are mortal—and Arioch is slow to aid you these days, perhaps because he guesses what lies in the future."

"What do you know of the future?"

"Little—and what I know I cannot speak of to you. A mortal may choose whom he serves, Elric."

"I have chosen. I chose Chaos."

"Yet much of your melancholy is because you are divided in your loyalties."

"That, too, is true."

"Besides, you would not fight for Law if you fought against Theleb K'aarna—you would merely be fighting against one aided by Chaos—and those of Chaos often fight among themselves do they not?"

"They do. It is also well known that I hate Theleb K'aarna and would destroy him whether he served Law or Chaos."

"Therefore you will not unduly anger those to whom you are loyal—though they may be reluctant to help you."

"Tell me more of Theleb K'aarna's plans."

"You must see for yourself. There is your horse." She pointed again and this time he saw the golden mare emerge from the other side of a dune. "Head north-east as you were heading, but move cautiously lest Theleb K'aarna becomes aware of your presence and traps you."

"Suppose I merely return to Tanelorn—or choose to try to die again?"

"But you will not, will you, Elric? You have loyalties to your friends, you wish in your heart to serve what I represent—and you hate Theleb K'aarna. I do not think you would wish to die for the moment."

He scowled. "Once more I am burdened with unwanted responsibilities, hedged by considerations other than my own desires, trapped by emotions which we of Melniboné have been taught to despise. Aye—I will go, Myshella. I will do what you wish."

"Be careful, Elric. Theleb K'aarna now has powers which are unfamiliar to you, which you will find difficult to combat." She gave him a lingering look and suddenly he had stepped forward and had seized her, kissed her while tears flowed down his white face and mingled with hers.

Later he watched as she climbed into the onyx saddle of the bird of silver and gold and called out a command. The metal wings beat with a great clashing, the emerald eyes turned and the gem-studded beak opened. "Farewell, Elric," said the bird.

But Myshella said nothing, did not look back.

Soon the metal bird was a speck of light in the blue sky and Elric had turned his horse towards the north-east.

3

The Barrier Broken

Elric reined in behind the cover of a crag. He had found the camp of Theleb
K'aarna. A large tent of yellow silk had been erected beneath the protection of
an overhang of rock which was part of a formation making a natural amphitheatre among the dunes of the desert. A wagon and two horses were close to
the tent, but all this was dominated by the thing of metal which reared in the
centre of the clearing. It was contained in an enormous bowl of clear crystal.
The bowl was almost globular with a narrow opening at the top. The device
itself was asymmetrical and strange, composed of many curved and angular
surfaces which seemed to contain myriad half-formed faces, shapes of beasts
and buildings, illusive designs coming and going even as Elric looked upon it.
An imagination even more grotesque than that of Elric's ancestors had fashioned the thing, amalgamating metals and other substances which logic denied
could ever be fused into one thing. A creation of Chaos which offered a clue
as to how the Doomed Folk had come to destroy themselves. And it was alive.
Deep within it something pulsed, as delicate and tentative as the heartbeat of a
dying wren. Elric had witnessed many obscenities in his life and was moved by
few of them, but this device, though superficially more innocuous than much
he had seen, brought bile into his mouth. Yet for all his disgust he remained
where he was, fascinated by the machine in the bowl, until the flap of the yellow tent was drawn back and Theleb K'aarna emerged.

The sorcerer of Pan Tang was paler and thinner than when Elric had last seen him, shortly before the battle between the beggars of Nadsokor and the warriors of Tanelorn. Yet unhealthy energy flushed the cheeks and burned in the dark eyes, gave a nervous swiftness to the movements. Theleb K'aarna approached the bowl.

As he came closer Elric could hear him muttering to himself.

"Now, now, now," murmured the sorcerer. "Soon, soon will die Elric and all who league with him. Ah, the albino will rue the day when he earned my vengeance and turned me from a scholar into what I am today. And when he is dead, then Queen Yishana will realise her mistake and give herself to me. How could she love that pale-faced anachronism more than a man of my great talents? How?"

Elric had almost forgotten Theleb K'aarna's obsession with Queen Yishana of Jharkor, the woman who had wielded a greater power over the sorcerer than could any magic. It had been Theleb K'aarna's jealousy of Elric which had turned him from a relatively peaceful student of the dark arts into a vengeful practitioner of the most frightful sorceries.

He watched as Theleb K'aarna began with his finger to trace complicated patterns upon the glass of the bowl. And with every completed rune the pulse within the machine grew stronger. Oddly coloured light began to flow through certain sections, bringing them to life. A steady thump issued from the neck of the bowl. A peculiar stink began to reach Elric's nostrils. The core of light became brighter and larger and the machine seemed to alter its shape, sometimes becoming apparently liquid and streaming around the inside of the bowl.

The golden mare snorted and began to shift uneasily. Elric automatically patted her neck and steadied her. Theleb K'aarna was now merely a silhouette against the swiftly changing light within the bowl. He continued to murmur to himself but his words were drowned by the heartbeats which now echoed among the surrounding rocks. His right hand drew still more invisible diagrams upon the glass.

The sky seemed to be darkening, though it was some hours to sunset. Elric looked up. Above his head the sky was still blue, the golden sun still strong, but the air around him had grown dark, as if a solitary cloud had come to cover the scene he witnessed.

Now Theleb K'aarna was stumbling back, his face stained by the strange light from the bowl, his eyes huge and mad.

"Come!" he screamed. "Come! The barrier is down!"

Elric saw a shadow then, behind the bowl. It was a shadow which dwarfed even the great machine. Something bellowed. It was scaly. It lumbered. It raised a huge and sinuous head. It reminded Elric of a dragon from one of his own caves, but it was bulkier and upon its enormous back were two rows of flapping ridges of bone. It opened its mouth to reveal row upon row of teeth and the ground shook as it walked from the other side of the bowl and stood staring down at the tiny figure of the sorcerer, its eyes stupid and angry. Another came pounding from behind the bowl, and another—great reptilian monsters from another Age of Earth. And following them came those who controlled them. The horse was snorting and prancing and desperately trying to escape, but Elric managed to calm her down again as he looked at the figures which now rested their hands on the obedient heads of the monsters. The figures were even more terrifying than the reptiles—for although they walked upon two legs and had hands of sorts they, too, were reptilian. They bore a peculiar resemblance to the dragon creatures and their size, also, was many times greater than a man's. In their hands they had ornate instruments which could only be weapons—instruments attached to their arms by spirals of golden metal. A hood of skin covered their black and green heads and red eyes glared from the shadows of their faces.

Theleb K'aarna laughed. "I have achieved it. I have destroyed the barrier between the planes and, thanks to the Lords of Chaos, have found allies which Elric's sorcery cannot destroy because they do not obey the sorcerous rules of this plane! They are invincible, invulnerable—and they obey only Theleb K'aarna!"

A huge snorting and screaming came from beasts and warriors alike.

"Now we shall go against Tanelorn!" Theleb K'aarna shouted. "And with this power I shall return to Jharkor, to make fickle Yishana my own!"

Elric felt a certain sympathy for Theleb K'aarna at that moment. Without the aid of the Lords of Chaos, his sorcery could not have achieved this. He had given himself up to them, had become one of their tools all because of his weak-minded love for Jharkor's ageing queen. Elric knew he could not go against the monsters and their monstrous riders. He must return to Tanelorn to warn his friends to leave the city, to hope that he might find a means of returning these frightful interlopers back to their own plane. But then the mare screamed suddenly and reared, maddened by the sights, the sounds and the smells she had been forced to witness. And the scream sounded in a sudden silence. The rearing horse revealed itself to Theleb K'aarna as he turned his mad eyes in Elric's direction.

Elric knew he could not outride the monsters. He knew those weapons could easily destroy him from a distance. He drew the black hellsword Stormbringer from its scabbard and it shouted as it came free. He drove his spurs into the horse and he rode directly down the rocks towards the bowl while Theleb K'aarna was still too startled to give orders to his new allies. His one hope was that he could destroy the device—or at least break some important part of it—and in so doing return the monsters to their own plane.

His white face ghastly in the sorcerous darkness, his sword raised high, he galloped past Theleb K'aarna and struck a mighty blow at the glass protecting the machine.

The Black Sword collided with the glass and sank into it. Carried on by the momentum, Elric was flung from his saddle and he, too, passed through the glass without apparently breaking it. He glimpsed the dreadful planes and curves of the Doomed Folk's device. His body struck them. He felt as if the fabric of his being was disintegrating . . .

. . . and then he lay sprawled upon sweet grass and there was nothing of the desert, of Theleb K'aarna, of the pulsing machine, of the horrible beasts and their dreadful masters, only waving foliage and warm sunshine. He heard birdsong and he heard a voice.

"The storm. It has gone. And you? Are you called Elric of Melniboné?"

He picked himself up and turned. A tall man stood before him. The man was clad in a conical silver helm and was encased to the knee in a byrnie also of silver. A scarlet, long-sleeved coat partly covered the byrnie. The man bore a scabbarded longsword at his side. His legs were encased in breeks of soft leather and there were boots of green-tinted doeskin on his feet. But Elric's attention was caught primarily by the man's features (which resembled those of a Melnibonéan much more than those of a true man) and the fact that he wore upon his left hand a six-fingered gauntlet encrusted with dark jewels, while over his right eye was a large patch which was also jewelled and matched the hand. The eye not covered by the patch was large and slanting and had a yellow centre and purple surrounds.

"I am Elric of Melniboné," the albino agreed. "Are you to thank for rescuing me from those creatures Theleb K'aarna summoned?"

The tall man shook his head. "'Twas I that summoned you, but I know of no Theleb K'aarna. I was told that I had only one opportunity to receive your aid and that I must take it in this particular place at this particular time. I am called Corum Jhaelen Irsei—the Prince in the Scarlet Robe—and I ride upon a quest of grave import."

Elric frowned. The name had a half-familiar ring, but he could not place it. He half-recalled an old dream . . .

"Where is this forest?" he asked, sheathing his sword.

"It is nowhere on your plane or in your time, Prince Elric. I summoned you to aid me in my battle against the Lords of Chaos. Already I have been instrumental in destroying two of the Sword Rulers—Arioch and Xiombarg—but the third, the most powerful, remains . . ."

"Arioch of Chaos—and Xiombarg? You have destroyed two of the most powerful members of the company of Chaos? Yet but a month since I spoke with Arioch. He is my patron. He . . ."

"There are many planes of existence," Prince Corum told him gently. "In some the Lords of Chaos are strong. In some they are weak. In some, I have heard, they do not exist at all. You must accept that here Arioch and Xiombarg have been banished so that effectively they no longer exist in my world. It is the third of the Sword Rulers who threatens us now—the strongest, King Mabelode."

Elric frowned. "In my—plane—Mabelode is no stronger than Arioch and Xiombarg. This makes a travesty of all my understanding . . ."

"I will explain as much as I can," said Prince Corum. "For some reason Fate has selected me to be the hero who must banish the domination of Chaos from the Fifteen Planes of Earth. I am at present travelling on my way to seek a city which we call Tanelorn, where I hope to find aid. But my guide is a prisoner in a castle close to here and before I can continue I must rescue him. I was told how I might summon aid to help me effect this rescue and I used the spell to bring you to me. I was to tell you that if you aided me, then you would aid yourself—that if I was successful then you would receive something which would make your task easier."

"Who told you this?"

"A wise man."

Elric sat down on a fallen tree trunk, his head in his hands. "I have been drawn away at an importunate time," he said. "I pray that you speak the truth to me, Prince Corum." He looked up suddenly. "It is a marvel that you speak at all—or at least that I understand you. How can this be?"

"I was informed that we should be able to communicate easily because 'we are part of the same thing.' Do not ask me to explain more, Prince Elric, for I know no more."

Elric shrugged. "Well this may be an illusion. I may have killed myself or become digested by that machine of Theleb K'aarna's, but plainly I have no choice but to agree to aid you in the hope that I am, in turn, aided."

Prince Corum left the clearing and returned with two horses, one white and one black. He offered the reins of the black horse to Elric.

Elric settled himself in the unfamiliar saddle. "You spoke of Tanelorn. It is for the sake of Tanelorn that I find myself in this dreamworld of yours."

Prince Corum's face was eager. "You know where Tanelorn lies?"

"In my own world, aye—but why should it lie in this one?"

"Tanelorn lies in all planes, though in different guises. There is one Tanelorn and it is eternal with many forms."

They were riding through the gentle forest along a narrow track.

Elric accepted what Corum said. There was a dreamlike quality about his presence here and he decided that he must regard all events here as he would regard the events in a dream. "Where go we now?" he asked casually. "To the castle?"

Corum shook his head. "First we must have the Third Hero—the Many-Named Hero."

"And will you summon him with sorcery, too?"

"I was told not. I was told that he would meet us—drawn from whichever age he exists in by the necessity to complete the Three Who Are One."

"And what mean these phrases? What is the Three Who Are One?"

"I know little more than you, friend Elric, save that it will need all three of us to defeat him who holds my guide prisoner."

"Aye," murmured Elric feelingly, "and it will need more than that to save my Tanelorn from Theleb K'aarna's reptiles. Even now they must march against the city."

4

The Vanishing Tower

The road widened and left the forest to wander among the heather of high and hilly moorland country. Far away to the west they could see cliffs, and beyond the cliffs was the deeper blue of the ocean. A few birds circled in the wide sky. It seemed a particularly peaceful world and Elric could hardly believe that it was under attack from the forces of Chaos. As they rode Corum explained that his gauntlet was not a gauntlet at all, but the hand of an alien being, grafted onto his arm, just as his eye was an alien eye which could see into a terrifying netherworld from which Corum could bring aid if he chose to do so.

"All you tell me makes the complicated sorceries and cosmologies of my world seem simple in comparison." Elric smiled as they crossed the peaceful landscape.

"It only seems complicated because it is strange," Corum said. "Your world would doubtless seem incomprehensible to me if I were suddenly flung into it. Besides," he laughed, "this particular plane is not my world, either, though it resembles it more than do many. We have one thing in common, Elric, and that is that we are both doomed to play a role in the constant struggle between the Lords of the Higher Worlds—and we shall never understand why that struggle takes place, why it is eternal. We fight, we suffer agonies of mind and soul, but we are never sure that our suffering is worthwhile."

"You are right," Elric said feelingly. "We have much in common, you and I, Corum."

Corum was about to reply when he saw something on the road ahead. It was a mounted warrior. He sat perfectly still as if he awaited them. "Perhaps this is the Third of whom Bolorhiag spoke."

Cautiously, they rode forward.

The man they approached stared at them from a brooding face. He was as tall as them, but bulkier. His skin was jet-black and he wore upon his head and shoulders the stuffed head and pelt of a snarling bear. His plate armour was also black, without insignia, and at his side was a great black-hilted sword in a black scabbard. He rode a massive roan stallion and there was a heavy round shield attached to the back of his saddle. As Elric and Corum came closer the man's handsome black features assumed an astonished expression and he gasped.

"I know you! I know you both!"

Elric, too, felt he recognised the man, just as he had noticed something familiar in Corum's features.

"How came you here to Balwyn Moor, friend?" Corum asked him.

The man looked about him as if in a daze. "Balwyn Moor? This is Balwyn Moor? I have been here but a few moments. Before that I was—I was . . . Ah! The memory starts to fade again." He pressed a large hand to his forehead. "A name—another name! No more! Elric! Corum! But I—I am now . . ."

"How do you know our names?" Elric asked him. A mood of dread had seized the albino. He felt that he should not ask these questions, that he should not know the answers.

"Because—don't you see?—I am Elric—I am Corum—oh, this is the worst agony . . . Or, at least, I have been or am to be Elric and Corum . . ."

"Your name, sir?" Corum said again.

"A thousand names are mine. A thousand heroes I have been. Ah! I am—I am—John Daker—Erekosë—Urlik—many, many, many more . . . The memories, the dreams, the existences." He stared at them suddenly through his pain-filled eyes. "Do you not understand? Am I the only one to be doomed to understand? I am he who has been called the Champion Eternal—I am the hero who has existed for ever—and, yes, I am Elric of Melniboné—Prince Corum Jhaelen Irsei—I am you, also. We three are the same creature and a myriad other creatures besides. We three are one thing—doomed to struggle for ever and never understand why. Oh! My head pounds. Who tortures me so? Who?"

Elric's throat was dry. "You say you are another incarnation of myself?"

"If you would phrase it so! You are both other incarnations of *myself!*"

"So," said Corum, "that is what Bolorhiag meant by the Three Who Are One. We are all aspects of the same man, yet we have tripled our strength because we have been drawn from three different ages. It is the only power which might successfully go against Voilodion Ghagnasdiak of the Vanishing Tower."

"Is that the castle wherein your guide is imprisoned?" Elric asked, casting a glance of sympathy at the groaning black man.

"Aye. The Vanishing Tower flickers from one plane to another, from one age to another, and exists in a single location only for a few moments at a time. But because we are three separate incarnations of a single hero it is possible that we form a sorcery of some kind which will enable us to follow the tower and attack it. Then, if we free my guide, we can continue on to Tanelorn . . ."

"Tanelorn?" The black man looked at Corum with hope suddenly flooding into his eyes. "I, too, seek Tanelorn. Only there may I discover some remedy to my dreadful fate—which is to know all previous incarnations and be hurled at random from one existence to another! Tanelorn—I must find her!"

"I, too, must discover Tanelorn," Elric told him, "for on my own plane her inhabitants are in great danger."

"So we have a common purpose as well as a common identity," Corum said. "Therefore we shall fight in concert, I pray. First we must free my guide, then go on to Tanelorn."

"I'll aid you willingly," said the black giant.

"And what shall we call you—you who are ourselves?" Corum asked him.

"Call me Erekosë—though another name suggests itself to me—for it was as Erekosë that I came closest to knowing forgetfulness and the fulfilment of love."

"Then you are to be envied, Erekosë," Elric said meaningly, "for at least you have come close to forgetfulness . . ."

"You have no inkling of what it is I must forget," the black giant told him. He shook his reins. "Now Corum—which way to the Vanishing Tower?"

"This road leads to it. We ride down now to Darkvale, I believe."

Elric's mind could hardly contain the significance of what he had heard. It suggested that the universe—or the multiverse, as Myshella had named it—was divided into infinite layers of existence, that time was virtually a meaningless concept save where it related to one man's life or one short period of history. And there were planes of existence where the Cosmic Balance was not known at all—or so Corum had suggested—and other planes where the Lords of the Higher Worlds had far greater powers than they had on his own world. He was tempted to consider the idea of forgetting Theleb K'aarna, Myshella, Tanelorn and the rest and devoting himself to the exploration of all these infinite worlds. But then he knew that this could not be for, if Erekosë spoke the truth, then he—or something which was essentially himself—existed in all these planes already. Whatever force it was which he named 'Fate' had admitted him to this plane to fulfil one purpose. An important purpose affecting the destinies of a thousand planes it must surely be if it brought him together in three separate incarnations. He glanced curiously at the black giant on his left, at the maimed man with the jewelled hand and eye on his right. Were they really himself?

Now he fancied he felt some of the desperation Erekosë must feel—to remember all those other incarnations, all those other mistakes, all that other pointless conflict—and never to know the purpose for it all, if purpose indeed there were.

"Darkvale," said Corum pointing down the hill.

The road ran steeply until it passed between two looming cliffs, disappearing in shadow. There was something particularly gloomy about the place.

"I am told there was a village here once," Corum said to them. "An uninviting spot, eh, brothers?"

"I have seen worse," murmured Erekosë. "Come, let's get all this done with . . ." He spurred his roan ahead of the others and galloped at great speed down the steep path. They followed his example and soon they had passed between the lowering cliffs and could barely see ahead of them as they continued to follow the road through the shadows.

And now Elric saw ruins huddled close to the foot of the cliffs on either side. Oddly twisted ruins which had not been the result of age or warfare— these ruins were warped, fused, as if Chaos had touched them while passing through the vale.

Corum had been studying the ruins carefully and at length he reined in. "There," he said. "That pit. Here is where we must wait."

Elric looked at the pit. It was ragged and deep and the earth in it seemed freshly turned as if it had been but lately dug. "What must we wait for, friend Corum?"

"For the tower," said Prince Corum. "I would guess that this is where it appears when it is in this plane."

"And when will it appear?"

"At no particular time. We must wait. And then, as soon as we see it, we must rush it and attempt to enter before it vanishes again, moving on to the next plane."

Erekosë's face was impassive. He dismounted and sat on the hard ground with his back against a slab of rock which had once belonged to a house.

"You seem more patient than I, Erekosë," said Elric.

"I have learned patience, for I have lived since time began and will live on at the end of time."

Elric got down from his own black horse and loosened its girth strap while Corum prowled about the edge of the pit. "Who told you that the tower would appear here?" Elric asked him.

"A sorcerer who doubtless serves Law as I do, for I am a mortal doomed to battle Chaos."

"As am I," said Erekosë the Champion Eternal.

"As am I," said Elric of Melniboné, "though I am sworn to serve it."

Elric looked at his two companions and it was possible to believe that these were two incarnations of himself. Certainly their lives, their struggles, their personalities, to some extent, were very similar.

"And why do you seek Tanelorn, Erekosë?" he asked.

"I have been told that I may find peace there—and wisdom—a means of returning to the world of the Eldren where dwells the woman I love, for it has been said that since Tanelorn exists in all planes at all times it is easier for a man who dwells there to pass between the planes, discover the particular one he seeks. What interest have you in Tanelorn, Lord Elric?"

"I know Tanelorn and I know that you are right to seek it. My mission seems to be the defence of that city upon my own plane—but even now my friends may be destroyed by that which has been brought against them. I pray Corum is right and that in the Vanishing Tower I shall find a means to defeat Theleb K'aarna's beasts and their masters."

Corum raised his jewelled hand to his jewelled eye. "I seek Tanelorn for I have heard the city can aid me in my struggle against Chaos."

"But Tanelorn will fight neither Law nor Chaos—that is why she exists for eternity," Elric said.

"Aye. Like Erekosë I do not seek swords but wisdom."

Night fell and Darkvale grew gloomier. While the others watched the pit Elric tried to sleep, but his fears for Tanelorn were too great. Would Myshella try to defend the city? Would Moonglum and Rackhir die? And what could he possibly find in the Vanishing Tower which would aid him? He heard the murmuring of conversation as his other selves discussed how Darkvale had come to exist.

"I heard that Chaos once attacked the town which at that time lay in a quiet valley," Corum told Erekosë. "The tower was then the property of a knight who gave shelter to one whom Chaos hated. They brought a huge force of creatures against Darkvale, raising and compressing the walls of the valley, but the knight sought the aid of Law which enabled him to shift his tower into another dimension. Then Chaos decreed that the tower should shift for ever, never being on one plane longer than a few moments. The knight and the fugitive went mad at last and killed each other. Then Voilodion Ghagnasdiak found the tower and became resident therein. Too late he realised his mistake as he was shifted from his own plane to an alien one. Since then he has been too fearful to leave the tower but desperate for company. He has taken to the habit of capturing whomever he can and forcing them to be his companions in the Vanishing Tower until they bore him. When they bore him, he slays them."

"And your guide may soon be slain? What manner of creature is this Voilodion Ghagnasdiak?"

"He is a monstrous evil creature commanding great powers of destruction, that is all I know."

"Which is why the gods have seen fit to call up three aspects of myself to attack the Vanishing Tower," said Erekosë. "It must be important to them."

"It is to me," said Corum, "for the guide is also my friend and the very existence of the Fifteen Planes is threatened if I cannot find Tanelorn soon."

Elric heard Erekosë laugh bitterly. "Why cannot I—we—ever be faced with a small problem, a domestic problem? Why are we forever involved with the destiny of the universe?"

Corum replied just as Elric began to nod into a half-doze. "Perhaps domestic problems are worse. Who knows?"

5

Jhary-a-Conel

"It is here! Hasten, Elric!"

Elric sprang up.

It was dawn. He had already stood watch once during the night.

He drew his black sword from its scabbard noticing with some astonishment that Erekosë had already drawn his own blade and that it was almost identical to his own.

There was the Vanishing Tower.

Corum was running towards it even now.

The tower was in fact a small castle of grey and solid stone, but about its battlements played lights and its outline was not altogether clear at certain sections of its walls.

Elric ran beside Erekosë.

"He keeps the door open to lure his 'guests' in," panted the black giant. "It is our only advantage, I think."

The tower flickered.

"Hasten!" Corum cried again and the Prince in the Scarlet Robe dashed into the darkness of the doorway.

"Hasten!"

They ran into a small antechamber which was lit by a great oil lamp hanging from the ceiling by chains.

The door closed suddenly behind them.

Elric glanced at Erekosë's tense black features, at Corum's blemished face. All had swords ready, but now a profound silence filled the hall. Without speaking Corum pointed through a window slit. The view beyond it had changed. They seemed now to be looking out over blue sea.

"Jhary!" Corum called. "Jhary-a-Conel!"

A faint sound came back. It might have been a reply or it might have been the squeak of a rat in the castle walls. "Jhary!" Corum cried again. "Voilodion Ghagnasdiak? Am I to be thwarted? Have you left this place?"

"I have not left it. What do you want with me?" The voice came from the next room. Warily the three heroes who were one hero went forward.

Something like lightning flickered in the room and in its ghastly glare Elric saw Voilodion Ghagnasdiak.

He was a dwarf clad all in puffed multicoloured silks, furs and satins, a tiny sword in his hand. His head was too large for his body, but it was a handsome head with thick black eyebrows which met in the middle. He smiled at them. "At last someone new to relieve my ennui. But lay down your swords, gentlemen, I beg you, for you are to be my guests."

"I know what fate your guests may expect," Corum said. "Know this, Voilodion Ghagnasdiak, we have come to release Jhary-a-Conel whom you hold prisoner. Give him up to us and we will not harm you."

The dwarf's handsome features grinned cheerfully at these words. "But I am very powerful. You cannot defeat me. Watch."

He waved his sword and more lightning lashed about the room. Elric half-raised his sword to ward it off, but it never quite touched him. He stepped angrily towards the dwarf. "Know this, Voilodion Ghagnasdiak, I am Elric of Melniboné and I have much power. I bear the Black Sword and it thirsts to drink your soul unless you release Prince Corum's friend!"

Again the dwarf laughed. "Swords? What power have they?"

"Our swords are not ordinary blades," Erekosë said. "And we have been brought here by forces you could not comprehend—wrenched from our own ages by the power of the gods themselves—specifically to demand that this Jhary-a-Conel be given up to us."

"You are deceived," said Voilodion Ghagnasdiak, "or you seek to deceive me. This Jhary is a witty fellow, I'd agree, but what interest could gods have in him?"

Elric raised Stormbringer. The Black Sword moaned in anticipation of a quenching.

Then the dwarf produced a tiny yellow ball from nowhere and flung it at Elric. It bounced on his forehead and he was flung backward across the room, Stormbringer clattering from his hand. Dizzily Elric tried to rise, reached out to take his sword, but he was too weak. On impulse he began to cry for the aid of Arioch, but then he remembered that Arioch had been banished from this world. There were no supernatural allies to call upon here—none but the sword and he could not reach the sword.

Erekosë leapt backward and kicked the Black Sword in Elric's direction. As the albino's hand encircled the hilt he felt strength come back to him, but it was no more than ordinary mortal strength. He climbed to his feet.

Corum remained where he was. The dwarf was still laughing. Another ball appeared in his hand. Again he flung it at Elric, but this time he brought up the Black Sword in time and deflected it. It bounced across the room and exploded against the far wall. Something black writhed from the fire.

"It is dangerous to destroy the globes," said Voilodion Ghagnasdiak equably, "for now what is in them will destroy you."

The black thing grew. The flames died.

"I am free," said a voice.

"Aye." Voilodion Ghagnasdiak was gleeful. "Free to kill these fools who reject my hospitality!"

"Free to be slain," Elric replied as he watched the thing take shape.

At first it seemed all made of flowing hair which gradually compressed until it formed the outline of a creature with the heavily muscled body of a gorilla, though the hide was thick and warted like that of a rhinoceros.

From behind the shoulders curved great black wings and on the neck was the snarling head of a tiger. It clutched a long, scythelike weapon in its hairy hands. The tiger head roared and the scythe swept out suddenly, barely missing Elric.

Erekosë and Corum began to move forward to Elric's aid. Elric heard Corum cry: "My eye—it will not see into the netherworld. I cannot summon help!" It seemed that Corum's sorcerous powers were also limited on this plane. Then Voilodion Ghagnasdiak threw a yellow ball at the black giant and the pale man with the jewelled hand. Both barely managed to deflect the missiles and, in so doing, caused them to burst. Immediately shapes emerged and became two more of the winged tiger-men, and Elric's allies were forced to defend themselves.

As he dodged another swing of the scythe Elric tried to think of some rune which would summon supernatural aid to him, but he could think of none which would work here. He thrust at the tiger-man but his blow was blocked by the scythe. His opponent was enormously strong and swift. The black wings began to beat and the snarling thing flapped upwards to the ceiling, hovered for a moment and then rushed down on Elric with its scythe whirling, a chilling scream coming from its fanged mouth, its yellow eyes glaring.

Elric felt something close to panic. Stormbringer was not supplying him with the strength he expected. Its powers were diminished on this plane. He barely managed to dodge the scythe again and lash at the creature's exposed thigh. The blade bit but no blood came. The tiger-man did not seem to notice the wound. Again it began to flap towards the ceiling.

Elric saw that his companions were experiencing a similar plight. Corum's face was full of consternation as if he had expected an easy victory and now foresaw defeat.

Meanwhile Voilodion Ghagnasdiak continued to scream his glee and flung more of the yellow balls about the room. As each one burst there emerged another snarling winged tiger-creature. The room was full of them. Elric, Erekosë and Corum backed to the far wall as the monsters bore down on them, their ears full of the fearful beating of the giant wings, the harsh screams of hatred.

"I fear I have summoned you two to your destruction," Corum panted. "I had no warning that our powers would be so limited here. The tower must shift so fast that even the ordinary laws of sorcery do not apply within its walls."

"They seem to work well enough for the dwarf," Elric said as he brought up his blade to block first one scythe and then another. "If I could slay but a single . . ."

His back was hard against the wall, a scythe nicked his cheek and drew blood, another tore his cloak, another slashed his arm. The tiger faces were grinning now as they closed in.

Elric aimed a blow at the head of the nearest creature, struck off its ear so that it howled. Stormbringer howled back and stabbed at the thing's throat.

But the sword hardly penetrated and served only to put the tiger-man slightly off balance.

As the thing staggered Elric wrenched the scythe from its hands and reversed the weapon, drawing the blade across the chest. The tiger-man screamed as blood spurted from the wound.

"I was right!" Elric shouted at the others. "Only their own weapons can harm them!" He moved forward with the scythe in one hand and Stormbringer in the other. The tiger-men backed off and then began to flap upwards to hover near the ceiling.

Elric ran towards Voilodion Ghagnasdiak. The dwarf gave a yell of terror and disappeared through a doorway too small easily to admit Elric.

Then, with thundering wings, the tiger-creatures descended again.

This time the other two strove to capture scythes from their enemies. Driving back those who attacked him, the albino prince took Corum's main assailant from behind and the thing fell with its head sliced off. Corum sheathed his longsword and plucked up the scythe, killing a third tiger-man almost immediately and kicking the fallen scythe towards Erekosë. Black feathers drifted in the stinking air. The flagstones of the floor were slippery with blood. The three heroes drove a path through their enemies into the smaller room they had lately left. Still the tiger-creatures came on, but now they had to pass through the door and this was more easily defended.

Glancing back Elric saw the window slit of the tower. Outside the scenery altered constantly as the Vanishing Tower continued its erratic progress through the planes of existence. But the three were wearying and all had lost some blood from minor wounds. Scythes clashed on scythes as the fight continued, wings beat loudly and the snarling faces spat at them and spoke words which could barely be understood. Without the strength supplied him by his hell-forged sword Elric was weakening rapidly. Twice he staggered and was borne up by the others. Was he to die in some alien world with his friends never knowing how he had perished? But then he remembered that his friends were even now under attack from the reptilian beasts Theleb K'aarna had sent against Tanelorn, that they, too, would soon be dead. This knowledge gave him a little more strength and enabled him to sweep his scythe deep into the belly of another tiger-creature.

This gap in the ranks of the sorcerous things enabled him to see the small doorway on the far side of the other room. Voilodion Ghagnasdiak was crouched there, hurling still more of the yellow globes. New winged tiger-men grew up to replace those who had fallen.

But then Elric heard Voilodion Ghagnasdiak give a yell and saw that something was covering his face. It was a black-and-white animal with small black wings which beat in the air. Some offspring of the beasts who attacked him? Elric could not tell. But Voilodion Ghagnasdiak was plainly terrified of it, trying to drag it from his face.

Another figure appeared behind the dwarf. Bright eyes peered from an intelligent face framed by long black hair. He was dressed as ostentatiously as the dwarf, but he was unarmed. He was calling to Elric and the albino strained to catch the words even as another tiger-creature came at him.

Corum saw the newcomer now. "Jhary!" he shouted.

"The one you came to save?" Elric asked.

"Aye."

Elric made to press forward into the room, but Jhary-a-Conel waved him back. "No! No! Stay there!"

Elric frowned, was about to ask why when he was attacked from two sides by the tiger-creatures and had to retreat, slashing his scythe this way and that.

"Link arms!" Jhary-a-Conel cried. "Corum in the centre—and you two draw your swords!"

Elric was panting. He slew another tiger-man and felt a new pain shoot through his leg. Blood gushed from his calf.

Voilodion Ghagnasdiak was still struggling with the thing which clung to his face.

"Hurry!" cried Jhary-a-Conel. "It is your only chance—and mine!"

Elric looked at Corum.

"He is wise, my friend," Corum said. "He knows many things which we do not. Here, I will stand in the centre."

Erekosë linked his brawny arm with Corum's and Elric did the same on the other side. Erekosë drew his sword in his left hand and Elric brought forth Stormbringer in his right.

And something began to happen. A sense of energy came back, then a sense of great physical well-being. Elric looked at his companions and laughed. It was almost as if by combining their powers they had made them four times stronger—as if they had become one entity.

A peculiar feeling of euphoria filled Elric and he knew that Erekosë had spoken the truth—that they were three aspects of the same being.

"Let us finish them!" he shouted—and he saw that they shouted the same. Laughing the linked three strode into the chamber and now the two swords wounded whenever they struck, slaying swiftly and bringing them more energy still.

The winged tiger-men became frantic, flapping about the room as the Three Who Were One pursued them. All three were drenched in their own blood and that of their enemies, all three were laughing, invulnerable, acting completely in unison.

And as they moved the room itself began to shake. They heard Voilodion Ghagnasdiak screaming.

"The tower! The tower! This will destroy the tower!"

Elric looked up from the last corpse. It was true that the tower was swaying wildly from side to side like a ship in a storm.

Jhary-a-Conel pushed past the dwarf and entered the room of death. The sight seemed obnoxious to him but he controlled his feelings. "It is true. The sorcery we have worked today must have its effect. Whiskers—to me!"

The thing on Voilodion Ghagnasdiak's face flew into the air and settled on Jhary's shoulder. Elric saw that it was a small black-and-white cat, ordinary in every detail save for its neat pair of wings which it was now folding.

Voilodion Ghagnasdiak sat crumpled in the doorway and he was weeping through sightless eyes. Tears of blood flowed down his handsome face.

Elric ran back into the other room, breaking his link with Corum. He peered through the window slit. But now there was nothing but a wild eruption of mauve and purple cloud.

He gasped. "We are in limbo!"

Silence fell. Still the tower swayed. The lights were extinguished by a strange wind blowing through the rooms and the only illumination came from outside where the mist still swirled.

Jhary-a-Conel was frowning to himself as he joined Elric at the window.

"How did you know what to do?" Elric asked him.

"I knew because I know you, Elric of Melniboné—just as I know Erekosë there—for I travel in many ages and on many planes. That is why I am sometimes called Companion to Champions. I must find my sword and my sack—also my hat. Doubtless all are in Voilodion's vault with his other loot."

"But the tower? If it is destroyed shall we, too, be destroyed?"

"A possibility. Come, friend Elric, help me seek my hat."

"At such a time, you look for a—hat?"

"Aye." Jhary-a-Conel returned to the larger room, stroking the black-and-white cat. Voilodion Ghagnasdiak was still there and he was still weeping. "Prince Corum—Lord Erekosë—will you come with me, too."

Corum and the black giant joined Elric and they squeezed into the narrow passage, inching their way along until it widened to reveal a flight of stairs leading downward. The tower shuddered again. Jhary lit a brand and removed it from its place in the wall. He began to descend the steps, the three heroes behind him.

A slab of masonry fell from the roof and crashed just in front of Elric. "I would prefer to seek a means of escape from the tower," he said to Jhary-a-Conel. "If it falls now, we shall be buried."

"Trust me, Prince Elric," was all that Jhary would say.

And because Jhary had already shown himself to possess great knowledge Elric allowed the dandy to lead him further into the bowels of the tower.

At last they reached a circular chamber and in it was set a huge metal door.

"Voilodion's vault," Jhary told them. "Here you will find all the things you seek. And I, I hope, will find my hat. The hat was specially made and is the only one which properly matches my other clothes . . ."

"How do we open a door like that?" Erekosë asked. "It is made of steel, surely!" He hefted the black blade he still bore in his left hand.

"If you link arms again, my friends," Jhary suggested with a kind of mocking deference, "I will show you how the door may be opened."

Once again Elric, Corum and Erekosë linked their arms together. Once again the supernatural strength seemed to flow through them and they laughed at each other, knowing that they were all part of the same creature.

Jhary's voice seemed to come faintly to Elric's ears. "And now, Prince Corum, if you would strike with your foot once upon the door . . ."

They moved until they were close to the door. That part of them which was Corum struck out with his foot at the slab of steel—and the door fell inward as if made of the lightest wood.

This time Elric was much more reluctant to break the link which held them. But he did so at last as Jhary stepped into the vault chuckling to himself.

The tower lurched. All three were flung after Jhary into Voilodion's vault. Elric fell heavily against a great golden chair of a kind he had once seen used as an elephant saddle. He looked around the vault. It was full of valuables, of clothes, shoes, weapons. He felt nauseated as he realised that these had been the possessions of all those Voilodion had chosen to call his guests.

Jhary pulled a bundle from under a pile of furs. "Look, Prince Elric. These are what you will need where Tanelorn is concerned." It seemed to be a bunch of long sticks rolled in thin sheets of metal.

Elric accepted the heavy bundle. "What is it?"

"They are the banners of bronze and the arrows of quartz. Useful weapons against the reptilian men of Pio and their mounts."

"You know of those reptiles? You know of Theleb K'aarna, too?"

"The sorcerer of Pan Tang? Aye."

Elric stared almost suspiciously at Jhary-a-Conel. "How can you know all this?"

"I have told you. I have lived many lives as a Friend of Heroes. Unwrap this bundle when you return to Tanelorn. Use the arrows of quartz like spears. To use the banners of bronze, merely unfurl them. Aha!" Jhary reached behind a sack of jewels and came up with a somewhat dusty hat. He smacked off the dust and placed it on his head. "Ah!" He bent again and displayed a goblet. He offered this to Prince Corum. "Take it. It will prove useful, I think."

From another corner Jhary took a small sack and put it on his shoulder. Almost as an afterthought he hunted about in a chest of jewels and found a gleaming ring of unnameable stones and peculiar metal. "This is your reward, Erekosë, in helping to free me from my captor."

Erekosë smiled. "I have the feeling you needed no help, young man."

"You are mistaken, friend Erekosë. I doubt if I have ever been in greater peril." He looked vaguely about the vault, staggering as the floor tilted alarmingly.

Elric said: "We should take steps to leave."

"Exactly." Jhary-a-Conel crossed swiftly to the far side of the vault. "The last thing. In his pride Voilodion showed me his possessions, but he did not know the value of all of them."

"What do you mean?" asked the Prince in the Scarlet Robe.

"He killed the traveller who brought this with him. The traveller was right in assuming he had the means to stop the tower from vanishing, but he did not have time to use it before Voilodion had slain him." Jhary picked up a small staff coloured a dull ochre. "Here it is. The Runestaff. Hawkmoon had this with him when I travelled with him to the Dark Empire . . ."

Noticing their puzzlement, Jhary-a-Conel, Companion to Champions, apologised. "I am sorry. I sometimes forget that not all of us have memories of other careers . . ."

"What is the Runestaff?" Corum asked.

"I remember one description—but I am poor at naming and explaining things . . ."

"That has not escaped my notice," Elric said, almost smiling.

"It is an object which can only exist under a certain set of spacial and temporal laws. In order to continue to exist, it must exert a field in which it can contain itself. That field must accord with those laws—the same laws under which we best survive."

More masonry fell.

"The tower is breaking up!" Erekosë growled.

Jhary stroked the dull ochre staff. "Please gather near me, my friends."

The three heroes stood around him. And then the roof of the tower fell in. But it did not fall on them for they stood suddenly on firm ground breathing fresh air. But there was blackness all around them. "Do not step outside this small area," Jhary warned, "or you will be doomed. Let the Runestaff seek what we seek."

They saw the ground change colour, breathed warmer, then colder, air. It was as if they moved from plane to plane of the multiverse, never seeing more than the few feet of ground upon which they stood.

And then there was harsh desert sand beneath their feet and Jhary shouted. "Now!" The four of them rushed out of the area and into the blackness to find themselves suddenly in sunlight beneath a sky like beaten metal.

"A desert," Erekosë murmured. "A vast desert . . ."

Jhary smiled. "Do you not recognise it, friend Elric?"

"Is it the Sighing Desert?"

"Listen."

And sure enough Elric heard the familiar sound of the wind as it made its mournful passage across the sands. A little way away he saw the Runestaff where they had left it. Then it was gone.

"Are you all to come with me to the defence of Tanelorn?" he asked Jhary.

Jhary shook his head. "No. We go the other way. We go to seek the device Theleb K'aarna activated with the help of the Lords of Chaos. Where lies it?"

Elric tried to get his bearings. He lifted a hesitant finger. "That way, I think."

"Then let us go to it now."

"But I must try to help Tanelorn."

"You must destroy the device after we have used it, friend Elric, lest Theleb K'aarna or his like try to activate it again."

"But Tanelorn . . ."

"I do not believe that Theleb K'aarna and his beasts have yet reached the city."

"Not reached it! So much time has passed!"

"Less than a day."

Elric rubbed at his face. He said reluctantly: "Very well. I will take you to the machine."

"But if Tanelorn lies so near," Corum said to Jhary, "why seek it elsewhere?"

"Because this is not the Tanelorn we wish to find," Jhary told him.

"It will suit me," Erekosë said. "I will remain with Elric. Then, perhaps . . ."

A look almost of terror spread over Jhary's features then. He said sadly: "My friend—already much of time and space is threatened with destruction. Eternal barriers could soon fall—the fabric of the multiverse could decay. You do not understand. Such a thing as has happened in the Vanishing Tower can only happen once or twice in an eternity and even then it is dangerous to all concerned. You must do as I say. I promise that you will have just as good a chance of finding Tanelorn where I take you. Your opportunity lies in Elric's future."

Erekosë bowed his head. "Very well."

"Come," Elric said impatiently, beginning to strike off to the north-east. "For all your talk of time, there is precious little left for me."

6

Pale Lord Shouting in Sunlight

The machine in the bowl was where Elric had last seen it, just before he had attacked it and found himself plunged into Corum's world.

Jhary seemed completely familiar with it and soon had its heart beating strongly. He shepherded the other two up to it and made them stand with their backs against the crystal. Then he handed something to Elric. It was a small vial.

"When we have departed," he said, "hurl this through the top of the bowl, then take your horse which I see is yonder and ride as fast as you can for Tanelorn. Follow these instructions perfectly and you will serve us all."

Elric accepted the vial. "Very well."

"And," Jhary said finally as he took his place with the others, "please give my compliments to my brother Moonglum."

"You know him? What—?"

"Farewell, Elric! We shall doubtless meet many times in the future, though we may not recognise each other."

Then the beating of the thing in the bowl grew louder and the ground shook and the strange darkness surrounded it—then the three figures had gone. Swiftly Elric hurled the vial upwards so that it fell through the opening of the bowl, then he ran to where his golden mare was tethered, leapt into the saddle with the bundle Jhary had given him under his arm, and galloped as fast as he could go towards Tanelorn.

Behind him the beating suddenly ceased. The darkness disappeared. A tense silence fell. Then Elric heard something like a giant's gasp and blinding blue light filled the desert. He looked back. Not only the bowl and the device had gone—so also had the rocks which had once surrounded it.

He came up behind them at last, just before they reached the walls of Tanelorn. Elric saw warriors on those walls.

The massive reptilian monsters bore their equally repulsive masters upon their backs, their feet leaving deep marks in the sand as they moved. And Theleb K'aarna rode at their head on a chestnut stallion—and there was something draped across his saddle.

Then a shadow passed over Elric's head and he looked up. It was the metal bird which had borne Myshella away. But it was riderless. It wheeled over the heads of the lumbering reptiles whose masters raised their strange weapons and sent hissing streams of fire in its direction, driving it higher into the sky. Why was the bird here and not Myshella? A peculiar cry came again and again from its metal throat and Elric realised what that cry resembled— the pathetic sound of a mother bird whose young is in danger.

He stared hard at the bundle over Theleb K'aarna's saddle and suddenly he knew what it must be. Myshella herself! Doubtless she had given Elric up for dead and had tried to go against Theleb K'aarna only to be beaten.

Anger boiled in the albino. All his intense hatred for the sorcerer revived and his hand went to his sword. But then he looked again at the vulnerable walls of Tanelorn, at his brave companions on the battlements, and he knew that his first duty was to help them.

But how was he to reach the walls without Theleb K'aarna seeing him and destroying him before he could bring the banners of bronze to his friends? He prepared to spur his horse forward and hope that he would be lucky. Then a shadow passed over his head again and he saw that it was the metal bird flying low, something like agony in its emerald eyes. He heard its voice. "Prince Elric! We must save her."

He shook his head as the bird settled in the sand. "First I must save Tanelorn."

"I will help you," said the bird of gold and silver and brass. "Climb up into my saddle."

Elric cast a glance towards the distant monsters. Their attention was now wholly upon the city they intended to destroy. He jumped from his horse and crossed the sand to clamber into the onyx saddle of the bird. The wings began to clash and with a rush they swept into the sky, turning towards Tanelorn.

More streaks of fire hissed around them as they neared the city, but the bird flew rapidly from side to side and avoided them. Down they drifted now to the gentle city, to land on the wall itself.

"Elric!" Moonglum came running along the defences. "We were told you were dead!"

"By whom?"

"By Myshella and by Theleb K'aarna when he demanded our surrender."

"I suppose they could only believe that," Elric said, separating the staffs around which were furled the thin sheets of bronze. "Here, you must take these. I am told that they will be useful against the reptiles of Pio. Unfurl them along the walls. Greetings, Rackhir." He handed the astounded Red Archer one of the banners.

"You do not stay to fight with us?" Rackhir asked.

Elric looked down at the twelve slender arrows in his hand. Each one was perfectly carved from multicoloured quartz so that even the fletchings seemed like real feathers. "No," he said. "I hope to rescue Myshella from Theleb K'aarna—and I can use these arrows better from the air, also."

"Myshella, thinking you dead, seemed to go mad," Rackhir told him. "She conjured up various sorceries against Theleb K'aarna—but he retaliated. At last she flung herself from the saddle of that bird you ride—flung herself upon him armed only with a knife. But he overpowered her and has threatened to slay her if we do not allow ourselves to be killed without retaliating. I know that he will kill Myshella anyway. I have been in something of a quandary of conscience . . ."

"I will resolve that quandary, I hope." Elric stroked the metallic neck of the bird. "Come, my friend, into the air again. Remember, Rackhir—unfurl the banners along the walls as soon as I have gained a good height."

The Red Archer nodded, his face puzzled, and once again Elric was rising into the air, the arrows of quartz clutched in his left hand.

He heard Theleb K'aarna's laughter from below. He saw the monstrous beasts moving inexorably towards the walls. The gates opened suddenly and a group of horsemen rode out. Plainly they had hoped to sacrifice themselves in order to save Tanelorn and Rackhir had not had time to warn them of Elric's message.

The riders galloped wildly towards the reptilian monsters of Pio, their swords and lances waving, their yells rising to where Elric drifted high above. The monsters roared and opened their huge jaws, their masters pointed their ornate weapons at the horsemen of Tanelorn. Flames burst from the muzzles, the riders shrieked as they were devoured by the dazzling heat.

In horror Elric directed the metal bird downwards. And at last Theleb K'aarna saw him and reined in his horse, his eyes wide with fear and rage. "You are dead! You are dead!"

The great wings beat at the air as the bird hovered over Theleb K'aarna's head. "I am alive, Theleb K'aarna—and I come to destroy you at long last! Give Myshella up to me."

A cunning expression came over the sorcerer's face. "No. Destroy me and she is also destroyed. Beings of Pio—turn your full strength against Tanelorn. Raze it utterly and show this fool what we can do!"

Each of the reptilian riders directed their oddly shaped weapons at Tanelorn where Rackhir, Moonglum and the rest waited on the battlements.

"No!" shouted Elric. "You cannot—"

There was something flashing on the battlements. They were unfurling at last the banners of bronze. And as each banner was unfurled a pure golden light blazed out from it until there was a vast wall of light stretching the whole length of the defences, making it impossible to see the banners themselves or the men who held them. The beings of Pio aimed their weapons and released streams of fire at the barrier of light which immediately repelled them.

Theleb K'aarna's face was suffused with anger. "What is this? Our earthly sorcery cannot stand against the power of Pio!"

Elric smiled savagely. "This is not our sorcery—it is another sorcery which *can* resist that of Pio! Now, Theleb K'aarna, give up Myshella!"

"No! You are not protected as Tanelorn is protected. Beings of Pio— destroy him!"

And, as the weapons began to be directed at him, Elric flung the first of the arrows of quartz. It flew true—directly into the face of the leading reptilian rider. A high whining escaped the rider's throat as it raised its webbed hands towards the arrow embedded in its eye. The beast the rider sat upon reared, for it was plain that it was only barely controlled. It turned away from the blinding light, from Tanelorn, and it galloped at earth-shaking speed away into the desert, the dead rider falling from its back. A streak of fire barely missed Elric and he was forced to take the bird up higher, flinging down another arrow and seeing it strike a rider's heart. Again the mount went out of control and followed its companion into the desert. But there were ten more of the riders and each now turned his weapon against Elric, though finding it hard to aim as all the mounts grew restive and sought to accompany the two who had fled. Elric left it to the metal bird to duck and to dive through the criss-cross of beams and he hurled down another arrow and another. His clothes and his hair were singed and he remembered another time when he had ridden the bird across the Boiling Sea. Part of the bird's right wing-tip had been melted and its flight was a little more erratic. But still it climbed and dived and still Elric threw the arrows of quartz into the ranks of the beings of Pio. Then, suddenly, there were only two left and they were turning to flee, for nearby a cloud of unpleasant blue smoke had begun to erupt where Theleb

K'aarna had been. Elric flung the last arrows after the reptiles of Pio and took each rider in the back. Now there were only corpses upon the sand.

The blue smoke cleared and Theleb K'aarna's horse stood there. And there was another corpse revealed. It was that of Myshella, Empress of the Dawn, and her throat had been cut. Theleb K'aarna had vanished, doubtless with the aid of sorcery.

Sickened, Elric descended on the bird of metal. On the walls of Tanelorn the light faded. He dismounted and he saw that the bird was weeping dark tears from its emerald eyes. He knelt beside Myshella.

An ordinary mortal could not have done it, but now she opened her lips and she spoke, though blood bubbled from her mouth and her words were hard to make out.

"Elric . . ."

"Can you live?" Elric asked her. "Have you some power to . . ."

"I cannot live. I am slain. Even now I am dead. But it will be some comfort to you to know that Theleb K'aarna has earned the disdain of the great Chaos Lords. They will never aid him again as they aided him this time, for in their eyes he has proved himself incompetent."

"Where has he gone? I will pursue him. I will slay him the next time, that I swear."

"I think that you will. But I do not know where he went. Elric—I am dead and my work is threatened. I have fought against Chaos for centuries and now, I think, Chaos will increase its power. Soon the great battle between the Lords of Law and the Lords of Entropy will take place. The threads of destiny become much tangled—the very structure of the multiverse seems about to transform itself. You have some part in this . . . some part . . . Farewell, Elric!"

"Oh, Myshella!"

"Is she dead now?" It was the sombre voice of the bird of metal.

"Aye." The word was forced from Elric's tight throat.

"Then I must take her back to Kaneloon."

Gently Elric picked up Myshella's bloody corpse, supporting the half-severed head on his arm. He placed the body in the onyx saddle.

The bird said: "We shall not see each other again, Prince Elric, for my death shall follow closely upon Lady Myshella's."

Elric bowed his head.

The shining wings spread and, with the sound of cymbals clashing, beat at the air.

Elric watched the beautiful creature circle in the sky and then turn and fly steadily towards the south and World's Edge.

He buried his face in his hands, but he was beyond weeping now. Was it the fate of all the women he loved to die? Would Myshella have lived if she had let him die when he had wanted to? There was no rage left in him, only a sense of impotent despair.

He felt a hand on his shoulder and he turned. Moonglum stood there, with Rackhir beside him. They had ridden out from Tanelorn to find him.

"The banners have vanished," Rackhir told him. "And the arrows, too. Only the corpses of those creatures remain and we shall bury them. Will you come back with us, now, to Tanelorn?"

"Tanelorn cannot give me peace, Rackhir."

"I believe that to be true. But I have a potion in my house which will deaden some of your memories, help you forget some of what has happened lately."

"I would be grateful for such a potion. Though I doubt . . ."

"It will work. I promise. Another would achieve complete forgetfulness from drinking this potion. But you may hope to forget a little."

Elric thought of Corum and Erekosë and Jhary-a-Conel and the implications of his experiences—that even if he were to die he would be reincarnated in some other form to fight again and to suffer again. An eternity of warfare and of pain. If he could forget that knowledge it would be enough. He had the impulse to ride far away from Tanelorn and concern himself as much as he could in the pettier affairs of men.

"I am so weary of gods and their struggles," he murmured as he mounted his golden mare.

Moonglum stared out into the desert.

"But when will the gods themselves weary of it, I wonder?" he said. "If they did, it would be a happy day for Man. Perhaps all our struggling, our suffering, our conflicts are merely to relieve the boredom of the Lords of the Higher Worlds. Perhaps that is why when they created us they made us imperfect."

They began to ride towards Tanelorn while the wind blew sadly across the desert. The sand was already beginning to cover up the corpses of those who had sought to wage war against eternity and had, inevitably, found that other eternity which was death.

For a while Elric walked his horse beside the others. His lips formed a name but did not speak it.

And then, suddenly, he was galloping towards Tanelorn dragging the screaming runesword from its scabbard and brandishing it at the impassive sky, making the horse rear up and lash its hoofs in the air, shouting over and over again in a voice full of roaring misery and bitter rage:

"Ah, damn you! Damn you! Damn you!"

But those who heard him—and some might have been the gods he addressed—knew that it was Elric of Melniboné himself who was truly damned.

THE REVENGE OF THE ROSE

For Christopher Lee—
Arioch awaits thee!

For Johnny and Edgar Winter—
rock on!

For Anthony Skene—
in gratitude.

THE REVENGE OF THE ROSE

CONTENTS

CONTENTS

Elric could enjoy the tranquillity of Tanelorn
only briefly and then must begin his restless
journeyings again. This time he headed eastward,
into the lands known as the Valederian Directorates,
where he had heard of a certain globe said to display
the nations of the future. In that globe he hoped
to learn something of his own fate, but in seeking it
he earned the enmity of that ferocious horde known
as the Haghan'iin Host, who captured and tortured him
a little before he escaped and joined forces with
the nobles of Anakhazhan to do battle with them . . .

—The Chronicle of the Black Sword

BOOK ONE

CONCERNING THE FATE OF EMPIRES

"What? Do you call us decadent, and
our whole nation, too?
My friend, you are too stern-hearted
for these times. These times are new.
Should you discern in us a selfish introspection;
a powerless pride:
In actuality, self-mockery and old age's wisdom
is all that you descry!"

—Wheldrake,
Byzantine Conversations

I

Of Love, Death, Battle & Exile; The White Wolf Encounters a Not Entirely Unwelcome Echo of the Past.

From the unlikely peace of Tanelorn, out of Bas'lk and Nish-valni-Oss, from Valederia, ever eastward runs the White Wolf of Melniboné, howling his red and hideous song, to relish the sweetness of a bloodletting . . .

. . . It is over. The albino prince sits bowed upon his horse, as if beneath the weight of his own exaggerated battle-lust; as if ashamed to look upon such profoundly unholy butchery.

Of the mighty Haghan'iin Host not a single soul survived an hour beyond the certain victory they had earlier celebrated. (How could they not win, when Lord Elric's army was a fragment of their own strength?)

Elric feels no further malice towards them, but he knows little pity, either. In their puissant arrogance, their blindness to the wealth of sorcery Elric commanded, they had been unimaginative. They had guffawed at his warnings. They had jeered at their former prisoner for a weakling freak of nature. Such violent, silly creatures deserved only the general grief reserved for all misshaped souls.

Now the White Wolf stretches his lean body, his pale arms. He pushes up his black helm. He rests, panting, in his great painted war-saddle, then takes the murmuring hellblade he carries and sheathes the sated iron into the softness of its velvet scabbard. There is a sound at his back. He turns brooding crimson eyes upon the face of the woman who reins up her horse beside him. Both woman and stallion have the same unruly pride, both seem excited by their unlooked-for victory; both are beautiful.

The albino reaches to take her ungloved hand and kiss it. "We share honours this day, Countess Guyë."

And his smile is a thing to fear and to adore.

"Indeed, Lord Elric!" She draws on her gauntlet and takes her prancing mount in check. "But for the fecundity of thy sorcery and the courage of my soldiery, we'd both be Chaos-meat tonight—and unlucky if still alive!"

He answers with a sigh and an affirmative gesture. She speaks with deep satisfaction.

"The Host shall waste no other lands, and its women in their home-trees shall bear no more brutes to bloody the world." Throwing back her heavy cloak, she slings her slender shield behind her. Her long hair catches the evening light, deep vermilion, restless as the ocean as she laughs, while her blue eyes weep; for she had begun the day in the fullest expectation that the best she could hope for was sudden death. "We are deeply in your debt, sir. We are obligated, all of us. You shall be known throughout Anakhazhan as a hero."

Elric's smile is ungrateful. "We came together for mutual needs, madam. I was but settling a small debt with my captors."

"There are other means of settling such debts, sir. We are still obliged."

"I would not take credit," he insists, "for altruism that is no part of my nature." He looks away into the horizon where a purple scar washed with red disguises the falling of the sun.

"I have a different sense of it." She speaks softly, for a hush is coming to the field, and a light breeze tugs at matted hair, bits of bloody fabric, torn skin. There are precious weapons and metals and jewels to be seen, especially where the Haghan'iin nobles had tried to make their escape, but not one of Countess Guyë's sworders, mercenary or free Anakhazhani, will approach the booty. There is a general tendency amongst these weary soldiers to drop back as far as possible from the field. Their captains neither question them on this nor do they try to stop them. "I have the sense, sir, that you serve some Cause or Principle, nonetheless."

He is quick to shake his head, his posture in the saddle one of growing impatience. "I am for no master nor moral persuasion. I am for myself. What your yearning soul, madam, might mistake for loyalty to person or Purpose is merely a firm and, aye, *principled* determination to accept responsibility only for myself and my own actions."

She offers him a quick, girlish look of puzzled disbelief, then turns away with a dawning, woman's grin. "There'll be no rain tonight," she observes, holding a dark, golden hand against the evening. "This mess'll be stinking and spreading fever in hours. We'd best move on, ahead of the flies." She hears the flapping even as he does and they both look back and watch the first gleeful ravens settling on flesh that has melted into one mile-wide mass of bloody meat, limbs and organs scattered at random, to hop upon and peck at half-destroyed faces still screaming for the mercy laughingly denied them as Elric's patron Duke of Hell, Lord Arioch, gave aid to his favourite son.

These were in the times when Elric left his friend Moonglum in Tanelorn and ranged the whole world to find a land which seemed enough like his own that he might wish to settle there, but no such land as Melniboné could be a tenth its rival in any place the new mortals might dwell. And all these lands were mortal now.

He had begun to learn that he had earned a loss which could never be assuaged and in losing the woman he loved, the nation he had betrayed, and the only kind of honour he had known he had also lost part of his own identity, some sense of his own purpose and reason upon the Earth.

Ironically, it was these very losses, these very dilemmas, which made him so unlike his Melnibonéan folk, for his people were cruel and embraced power for its own sake, which was how they had come to give up any softer virtues they might once have possessed, in their need to control not only their physical world but the supernatural world. They would have ruled the multiverse, had they any clear understanding how this might be achieved; but even a Melnibo-néan is not a god. There are some would argue they had not produced so much as a demigod. Their glory in earthly power had brought them to decadent ruin, as it brought down all empires who gloried in gold or conquest or those other ambitions which can never be satisfied but must forever be fed.

Yet even now Melniboné might, in her senility, live, had she not been be-trayed by her own exiled emperor.

And no matter how often Elric reminds himself that the Bright Empire was foredoomed to her unhappy end, he knows in his bones that it was his fierce need for vengeance, his deep love for Cymoril (his captive cousin); his own needs, in other words, which had brought down the towers of Imrryr and scattered her folk as hated wanderers upon the surface of the world they had once ruled.

It is part of his burden that Melniboné did not fall to a principle but to blind passion . . .

As Elric made to bid farewell to his temporary ally, he was attracted to some-thing in the countess's wicked eye, and he bowed in assent as she asked him to ride with her for a while; and then she suggested he might care to take wine with her in her tent.

"I would talk more of philosophy," she said. "I have longed so for the company of an intellectual equal."

And go with her he did, for that night and for many to come. These would be days he remembered as the days of laughter and green hills broken by lines of gentle cypress and poplar, on the estates of Guyë, in the Western Province of Anakhazhan in the lovely years of her hard-won peace.

Yet when they had both rested and both began to look to satisfy their unsleeping intelligences, it became clear that the countess and Lord Elric had very different needs and so Elric said his goodbyes to the countess and their friends at Guyë and took a good, well-furnished riding horse and two sturdy pack animals and rode on towards Elwher and the Unmapped East where he still hoped to find the peace of an untarnished familiarity.

He longed for the towers, sweet lullabies in stone, which stretched like guarding fingers into Imrryr's blazing skies; he missed the sharp wit and laughing ferocity of his kinfolk, the ready understanding and the casual cruelty that to him had seemed so ordinary in the time before he became a man.

No matter that his spirit had rebelled and made him question the Bright Empire's every assumption of its rights to rule over the demibrutes, the human creatures, who had spread so thoroughly across the great land masses of the North and West that were called now 'the Young Kingdoms' and dared, even with their puny wizardries and unskilled battlers, to challenge the power of the Sorcerer Emperors, of whom he was the last in direct line.

No matter that he had hated so much of his people's arrogance and unseemly pride, their easy resort to every unjust tyranny to maintain their power.

No matter that he had known shame—a new emotion to one of his kind. Still his blood yearned for home and all the things he had loved or, indeed, hated, for he had this in common with the humans amongst whom he now lived and travelled: he would sometimes rather hold close to what was familiar and encumbering than give it up for something new, though it offered freedom from the chains of heritage which bound him and must eventually destroy him.

And with this longing in him growing with his fresh loneliness, Elric took himself in charge and increased his pace and left Guyë far behind, a fading memory, while he pressed on in the general direction of unknown Elwher, his friend's homeland, which he had never seen.

He had come in sight of a range of hills the local people dignified as the Teeth of Shenkh, a provincial demon-god, and was following a caravan track down to a collection of shacks surrounded by a mud-and-timber wall that had been described to him as the great city of Toomoo-Kag-Sanapet-of-the-Invincible-

Temple, Capital of Iniquity and Unguessed-At Wealth, when he heard a pro-
testing cry at his back and saw a figure tumbling head over heels down the
hill towards him while overhead a previously unseen thundercloud sent silver
spears of light crashing to the earth, causing Elric's horses to rear and snort
in untypical nervousness. Then the world was washed with red-gold light, as
if in a sudden dawn, which turned to bruised blue and dark brown before
swirling like an angry current towards the horizon and vanishing to leave a
few disturbed clouds behind them in a drizzling and depressingly ordinary sky.

Deciding this event was sufficiently strange to merit more than his usually
brief attention, Elric turned towards the small, red-headed individual who was
picking himself out of a ditch at the edge of the silver-green cornfield, looking
nervously up at the sky and drawing a rather threadbare coat about his little
body. The coat would not meet at the front, not because it was too tight for
him, but because the pockets, inside and out, were crammed with small volumes. On his legs were a matching pair of trews, grey and shiny, a pair of laced
black boots which, as he lifted one knee to inspect a rent, revealed stockings
as bright as his hair. His face, adorned by an almost diseased-looking beard,
was freckled and pale, from which glared blue eyes as sharp and busy as a
bird's, above a pointed beak which gave him the appearance of an enormous
finch, enormously serious. He drew himself up at Elric's approach and began
to stroll casually down the hill. "D'ye think it will rain, sir? I thought I heard a
clap of thunder a moment ago. It set me off my balance." He paused, then cast
a look backward up the track. "I thought I had a pot of ale in my hand." He
scratched his wild head. "Come to think of it, I was sitting on a bench outside
the Green Man. Hold hard, sir, ye're an unlikely cove to be abroad on Putney
Common." Whereupon he sat down suddenly on a grassy hummock. "Good
lord! Am I transported yet again?" He appeared to recognise Elric. "I think
we've met, sir, somewhere. Or were you merely a subject?"

"You have the advantage of me, sir," said Elric, dismounting. He felt drawn
to this birdlike man. "I am called Elric of Melniboné and I am a wanderer."

"My name is Wheldrake, sir. Ernest Wheldrake. I have been travelling

THE REVENGE OF THE ROSE

somewhat reluctantly since I left Albion, first to Victoria's England, where I made something of a name, before being drawn on to Elizabeth's. I am growing used to sudden departures. What would your business be, Master Elric, if it is not theatrical?"

Elric, finding half what the man said nonsense, shook his head. "I have practised the trade of mercenary sword for some while. And you, sir?"

"I, sir, am a poet!" Master Wheldrake bristled and felt about his pockets for a certain volume, failed to find it, made a movement of the fingers as if to say he needed no affidavits, anyway, and settled his scrawny arms across his chest. "I have been a poet of the Court and of the Gutter, it's alleged. I should still be at Court had it not been for Doctor Dee's attempts to show me our Graecian past. Impossible, I have since learned."

"You do not know how you came here?"

"Only the vaguest notion, sir. Aha! But I have placed you." A snap of the long fingers. "A subject, I recall!"

Elric had lost interest in this vein of enquiry. "I am on my way to yonder metropolis, sir, and if you'd ride one of my pack animals, I'd be honoured to take you there. If you have no money, I'll buy you a room and a meal for the night."

"I would be glad of that, sir. Thanks." And the poet hopped nimbly up onto the furthest horse, settling himself amongst the packs and sacks with which Elric had equipped himself for a journey of indeterminate length. "I had feared it would rain and I am prone, these days, to chills . . ."

Elric continued down the long, winding track towards the churned mud streets and filthy log walls of Toomoo-Kag-Sanapet-of-the-Invincible-Temple while in a high-pitched yet oddly beautiful voice, reminiscent of a trilling bird, Wheldrake uttered some lines which Elric guessed were his own composition. "*With purpose fierce his heart was gripped, and blade gripped tighter, still. And honour struggling within, 'gainst vengeance, cold and cruel. Old Night and a New Age warred in him; all the ancient power, and all the new. Yet he did not stop his slaughtering.* And there is more, sir. He believes that he has conquered himself and his sword. He cries out: 'See, my masters! I force my moral will upon this hellblade and Chaos is no longer served by it! True Purpose shall triumph and Justice rule in Harmony with Romance in this most perfect of worlds.' And that, sir, was where my drama ended. Is your own story in any way the same, sir? Perhaps a little?"

"Perhaps a little, sir. I hope you will soon be taken back to whatever demon realm you've escaped from."

"You are offended, sir. In my verse you are a hero! I assure you I had the bones of the tale from a reliable source. A lady. And discretion demands I not reveal her name. Oh, sir! Oh, sir! What a magnificent moment this is for us, when metaphor becomes commonplace reality and the daily round runs into a thing of Fantasy and Myth . . ."

Scarcely hearing the little man's nonsense, Elric continued towards the town.

"Why, sir, what an extraordinary depression in yonder field," said Wheldrake suddenly, interrupting his own verse. "Do you see it, sir? That shape, as if some huge beast presses the corn? Is such a phenomenon common in these parts, sir?"

Elric glanced casually across the corn and was bound to agree that it had, indeed, been forced down across quite a broad area, and not by any obvious human agency. He reined in again, frowning. "I'm a stranger here, also. Perhaps some ceremony takes place, which causes the corn to bend so . . ."

At which there came a sudden snort, which shook the ground under their feet and half-deafened them. It was as if the field itself had discovered a voice.

"Is this odd to you, sir?" Wheldrake asked, his fingers upon his chin. "It's damned odd to me."

Elric found his hand straying towards the hilt of his runesword. There was a stink in the air which he recognised yet could not at that moment place.

Then there came a kind of crack, a roll like distant thunder, a sigh that filled the air and must have been heard by the whole town below, and then Elric knew suddenly how Wheldrake had entered this realm when he had no real business in it, for here was the creature who had actually created the lightning, bringing Wheldrake in its wake. Here was something supernatural broken through the dimensions to confront him.

The horses began to dance and scream. The mare carrying Wheldrake reared and tried to break from her harness, tangling with the reins of her partner and sending Wheldrake once more tumbling to the ground, while out of the unripe corn, like some sentient manifestation of the Earth herself, all tumbling stones and rich soil and clots of poppies and half the contents of the field, growing taller and taller and shaking itself free of what had buried it, rose an enormous reptile, with slender snout, gleaming greens and reds; razor teeth; saliva hissing as it struck the ground; faint smoky breath streaming from its flaring nostrils, while a long, thick scaly tail lashed behind it, uprooting shrubs and further ruining the crop upon which that metropolitan wealth was based. There came another clap like thunder and a leathery wing stretched upwards then descended with a noise only a little more bearable than the accompanying stink; then the other wing rose; then fell. It was as if the Phoorn dragon were being forced from some great, earthen womb—forced through the dimensions, through walls which were physical as well as supernatural; it struggled and raged to be free. It lifted its strangely beautiful head and it shrieked again and heaved again; and its slender claws, sharper and longer than any sword, clashed and flickered in the fading light.

Wheldrake, scrambling to his feet, began to run unceremoniously towards the town and Elric could do nothing else but let his pack animals run with him. The albino was left confronting a monster in no doubt on whom it wished to exercise its anger. Already its sinuous body moved with a kind of monumental grace as it turned to glare down at Elric. It snapped suddenly and Elric was crashing to the ground, blood pumping hugely from his horse's torso as the beast's remains collapsed onto the track. The albino rolled and came up quickly, Stormbringer growling and whispering in his hand, the black runes glowing the length of the blade and the black radiance flickering up and down its edges. And now the Phoorn hesitated, eyeing him almost warily as its jaws chewed for a few moments upon the horse's head and the throat made a single swallowing movement. Elric had no other course. He began running towards his massive adversary! The great eyes tried to follow him as he weaved in and out of the corn, and the jaws dripped, shaking their bloody ichor to sear and kill all it touched. But Elric had been raised among Phoorn and knew their vulnerability as well as their power. He knew, if he could come in close to the beast, there were points at which he might strike and at least wound it. It would be his only chance of survival.

As the monster's head turned, seeking him, the fangs clashing and the great breaths rushing from its throat and nostrils, Elric dashed under the neck and slashed once at the little spot about halfway up its length, where the scales were always soft, at least in Melnibonéan dragons; yet the dragon seemed to sense his stroke and reared back, claws slicing ground and crop like some monstrous scythe, and Elric was flung down by a great clot of earth, half-buried, so that *he* must now struggle to free himself.

It was at that moment some movement of the beast's head, some motion of the light upon its leathery lids, gave him pause and his heart leapt in sudden hope.

A memory teased at his lips but would not manifest itself as anything concrete. He found himself forming the Phoorn word, the same in the High Speech of old Melniboné, the word for "bondfriend." He was beginning to speak the ancient words of the dragon-calling, the cadences and tunes to which the Phoorn might, if they chose, respond.

There was a tune in his head, a way of speaking, and then came a single word again, but this was a sound like a breeze through willows, water through stones; a name.

At which the dragon brought her jaws together with a snap and sought the source of the voice. The iron-sharp wattles on the back of her neck and tail began to flatten and the corners of her mouth no longer boiled with poison.

Still deeply cautious, Elric got slowly to his feet and shook the damp earth from his flesh, Stormbringer as eager as always in his hand, and took a pace backward.

"Lady Scarsnout! I am your kin, I am Little Cat. I am your ward and your guider, Scarsnout lady, me!"

The green-gold muzzle, bearing a long-healed scar down the underside of the jaw, gave out an enquiring hiss.

Elric sheathed his grumbling hellblade and made the complicated and subtle gestures of kinship which he had been taught by his father for the day when he should be supreme Dragon Lord of Imrryr, Dragon Emperor of the World.

The Phoorn's brows drew together in something resembling a frown, the massive lids dropped, half-hiding the huge, cold eyes—the eyes of a beast more ancient than any mortal being; more ancient, perhaps, than the gods . . .

The nostrils, into which Elric could have crawled without much difficulty, quivered and sniffed—a tongue flickered—a great, wet leathery thing, long and slender and forked at the end. Once it almost touched Elric's face, then flickered over his body before the head was drawn back and the eyes stared down in fierce enquiry. For the moment, at least, the monster was calm.

Elric, virtually in a trance by now, as all the old incantations came flooding into his brain, stood swaying before the dragon. Soon her own head swayed, too, following the albino's movements.

And then, all at once, the dragon made a small noise deep in her belly and lowered her head to stretch her neck along the ground, down upon the torn and ruined corn. The eyes followed him as he stepped closer, murmuring the Song of Approach which his father had taught him when he was eleven and first taken to Melniboné's Dragon Caves. Her dragons slept there to this day. A dragon must sleep a hundred years for every day of activity, to regenerate that strange metabolism which could create fiery saliva strong enough to destroy cities.

How this jill-dragon had awakened and how she had come here was a mystery. Sorcery had brought her, without doubt. But had there been any reason for her arrival, or had it been, like Wheldrake's, a mere incidental to some other spell-working?

Elric had no time to debate that question now as he moved in gradual, ritualised steps towards the natural ridge just above the place where the leading part of her wing joined her shoulder. It was where the Dragon Masters of Melniboné had placed their *skeffla'an* and where, as a youth, he had ridden naked, with only his skill and the good will of the dragon to keep him safe.

It had been many years, and a shattering sequence of events, which had led him to this moment, when all the world was on the change, when he no longer trusted even his memories . . . The dragon almost called now, almost purred, awaiting his next command, as if a mother tolerated the games of her children.

"Scarsnout sister, Scarsnout kin, your Phoorn blood is mixed in ours and ours in yours and we are coupled, we are kind; we are one, the dragon rider and the dragon steed; one ambition, mutual need. Dragon sister, dragon matron, dragon honour, dragon pride . . ." The Old Speech rolled, trilled and clicked from his tongue; it came without conscious thought; it came without effort, without hesitation, for blood recalled blood and all else was natural. It was natural to climb upon the dragon's back and utter the ancient, joyful songs of command, the complex Phoorn Lays of his remote predecessors which combined their highest arts with their most practical needs. Elric was recollecting what was best and noblest in his own people and in himself, and even as he celebrated this he mourned the self-obsessed creatures they had become, using their power merely to preserve their power and that, he supposed, was true decay . . .

And now the Phoorn jill's slender neck rises, swaying like a mesmerised cobra, by degrees, and her snout tilts towards the sun, and her long tongue tastes the air and her saliva drips more slowly to devour the ground it touches and a great sigh, like a sigh of contentment, escapes her belly and she moves one hind leg, then the next, swaying and tilting like a storm-tossed ship, with Elric clinging on for his life, his body banged and rolled this way and that, until at last Scarsnout is poised, her claws folding tight as her hind legs rear. Yet still she seems to hesitate. Then she tucks her forelegs into the silk-soft leather of her stomach, and again she tests the air.

Her back legs give a kind of hop. The massive wings crack once, deafeningly. Her tail lashing out to steady her uneven weight, she has risen—she is aloft and mounting—mounting through those miserable clouds into blue perfection, a late-afternoon sky, with the clouds below now, like white and gentle hills and valleys where perhaps the harmless dead find peace; and Elric does not care where the dragon flies. He is glad to be flying as he flew as a boy—sharing his joy with his dragon-mate, sharing his senses and his emotions, for this is the true union between Elric's ancestors and the Phoorn—a union which had always existed and whose origins were explained only in unlikely legends—this was the symbiosis with which, natural and joyful at first, they had learned to defend themselves against would-be conquerors and later, turned conquerors, with which they had overwhelmed all victims. Having become greedy for even more conquests than were offered by the natural world, they sought supernatural conquests also and thus came to make their bond with Chaos, with Duke Arioch himself. And with Chaos to aid them they ruled ten thousand years; their cruelties refined but never abated.

Before then, thinks Elric—before then my people had never thought of war or power. And he knows that it was this respect for all life which must have brought about the original bond between Melnibonéan and dragon. And, as he lies along the natural pommel, the ridge above his jill's neck, he weeps with the wonder of suddenly recollected innocence, of something he believed lost as everything else is lost to him and which makes him believe, if only for this moment, that what he has lost might be, perhaps, restored . . .

Then he is free! Free in the air! Part of that impossible monster whose wings carry her as if she were a wind-dancing kestrel, light as down, through darkening skies, her skin giving off a sweetness like lavender and her head set in an expression which seems in a way to mirror Elric's own, and she turns and dives, she climbs and wheels while Elric clings without any seeming effort to her back and sings the wild old songs of his ancestors who had come as nomads of the worlds to settle here and had, some said, been welcomed by an even older race whom they superseded and with whom the royal line intermarried.

Up speeds Scarsnout, up she flies, and, when the air grows so thin it can no longer support her and Elric shivers in spite of his clothing and his mouth gasps at the atmosphere, down she goes in a mighty, rushing plummet until she brings herself up as if to land upon the cloud, then veers slowly away to where the clouds now break to reveal a moonlit tunnel in the surface and down this Scarsnout plunges while behind her lightning flashes once and a thunderclap seems to seal the tunnel as they descend into an unnatural coldness which makes Elric's whole skin writhe and his bones feel as if they must split and crack within him and yet still the albino does not fear, because the dragon does not fear.

Above them now the clouds have vanished. A blue velvet sky is further softened by a large yellow moon, whose light casts their long shadows upon the rushing meadowlands below, while the horizon shows a glint of the midnight sea and is filled with the emerald points of stars, and only as he begins to recognise the landscape below him does Elric know fear.

The dragon has carried him back to the ruins of his dreams, his past, his love, his ambitions, his hope.

She has brought him back to Melniboné.

She has brought him home.

2

Of Conflicting Loyalties and Unsummoned Ghosts; Of Bondage and Destiny.

Now Elric forgot his recent joy and remembered only his pain. He wondered wildly if this was mere coincidence or had the jill-Phoorn been sent to bring him here? Had his surviving kinfolk struck upon a means of capturing him so as to savour the slowness of his tortured passing? Or did the Phoorn themselves demand his presence?

Soon the familiar hills gave way to the Plain of Imrryr and Elric saw a city ahead—a ragged outline of burned and mutilated buildings. Was this the city of his birth, the Dreaming City he and his raiders had murdered?

As they flew closer Elric began to realise that he did not recognise the buildings. At first he thought they had been transformed by fire and siege, but they were not even, he noticed now, of the same materials. And he laughed at himself. He marvelled at his secret longings which had made him believe the dragon had brought him to Melniboné.

But then he knew he recognised the hills and woods, the line of the coast beyond the city. He knew that this was once, at least, where Imrryr stood. As Scarsnout sailed to a gentle landing, hopping once to steady herself, Elric looked across half a mile of familiar grassy ridges and knew that he looked not upon Imrryr the Beautiful, the greatest of all cities, but upon a city his people had called H'hui'shan, the City of the Island, in the High Melnibonéan tongue, and this was the city destroyed in one night in the only civil war Melniboné had ever known, when her lords quarrelled over whether to compact themselves with Chaos or remain loyal to the Balance. That war had lasted three days and left Melniboné hidden by oily black smoke for a month. When it had risen it had revealed ruins, but all who sought to attack her when she was weak were more than disappointed, for her pact was made and Arioch aided her, demonstrating the fearful variety of his mighty powers (there had been further suicides in Melniboné as her unhonourable victories rose, while others fled through the dimensions into foreign realms). The cruellest remained to relish an ever-tightening grip upon their world-encompassing empire.

At least, that was one of his people's legends, said to be drawn from the Dead Gods' Book.

Elric understood that Scarsnout had brought him to the remote past. But how had the dragon found the means of travelling so easily between the Spheres? And, again he wondered, why had he been transported here?

Hoping Scarsnout might choose some further action, Elric sat upon the monster's back for a while until it became obvious that the dragon had no intention of moving, so with some reluctance he dismounted, murmured the song of 'I-would-appreciate-your-continuing-concern-in-this-matter' and, there being nothing else for it, began to stride towards the desolate ruins of his people's earliest glories.

"Oh, H'hui'shan, City of the Island, if only I were here a week earlier, to warn thee of thy bond's consequences. But doubtless it would not suit my patron Arioch to let me thwart him so." And he smiled sardonically at this; smiled at his own aching need to make the past produce a finer present: one in which he did not bear such a burden of guilt.

"Perhaps our entire history is of Arioch's writing!" His bargain with the Duke of Hell was a pact of blood and human souls for aid—whatever the runesword did not feast upon belonged to Duke Arioch (though some old tales would have it that sword and patron demon were one and the same). And Elric rarely disguised his distaste for this tradition, which even he lacked the courage to break. It was immaterial to his patron what he thought so long as he continued to honour their bond. And this Elric understood profoundly.

The turf was still crossed by the trails he had known as a boy. He trod them as surely as he had done when, he recollected, his father—distant upon a charger—called to some servitor to take care with the child but to let him walk. He must grow up to remember every pathway that existed in Melniboné; for in those trails and tracks, those roads and highs, lay the configuration of their history, the geometry of their wisdom, the very key to their most secret understandings.

All these pathways, as well as the pathways to the otherworlds, Elric had memorised, together, where necessary, with their accompanying songs and gestures. He was a master sorcerer, of a line of master sorcerers, and he was proud of his calling, though disturbed by the uses to which he, as well as others, had put their powers. He could read a thousand meanings in a certain tree and its branches, but he still failed to understand his own torments of conscience, his moral crises, and that was why he wandered the world.

Dark sorceries and spells, images of horrific consequence, filled his head and threatened sometimes, when he dreamed, to seize control of him and plunge him into eternal madness. Dark memories. Dark cruelties. Elric shuddered as he drew close to the ruins, whose towers of wood and brick had collapsed and yet attained a picturesque and almost welcoming aspect, even in the moonlight.

He clambered over the burned rubble of a wall and entered a street which, at ground level, still bore some resemblance to the thing it had been. He sniffed sooty air and felt the ground still warm beneath his feet. Here and there, towards the centre of the city, a few fires still flickered like old rags in a wind and ash covered everything. Elric felt it clinging to his flesh. He felt it clogging his nostrils and drifting through his clothing—the ash of his distant ancestors, whose blackened corpses filled the houses in mimicry of life's activities, threatening to engulf him. But he walked on, fascinated by this glimpse into his past, at the very turning point in his race's destiny. He found himself wandering through rooms still occupied by the husks of their inhabitants, their pets, their playthings, their tools; through squares where fountains had once splashed, through temples and public buildings where his folk had met to debate and decide the issues of the day, before the emperors had taken all power to themselves and Melniboné had grown to depend upon her slaves, hidden away so that they should not make Imrryr ugly with their presence. He paused in a workshop, some shoe-seller's stall. He grieved for these dead, gone more than ten thousand years since.

The ruins touched something that was tender in him, and he found that he possessed a fresh longing, a longing for a past before Melniboné, out of fear, bargained for that power which conquered the world.

The turrets and gables, the blackened thatch and torn beams, the piles of broken stone and brick, the animal troughs and ordinary domestic implements abandoned outside the houses filled him with a melancholy he found almost sweet and he paused to inspect a cradle or a spinning wheel which showed an aspect of a proud Melnibonéan folk he had never known, but which he felt he understood.

There were tears in his eyes as he roamed those streets, desperately hoping to find just one living soul apart from himself, but he knew the city had stood unpopulated for at least a hundred years after her destruction.

"Oh, that I had destroyed Imrryr so that I might restore H'hui'shan!" He stood in a square of broken statues and fallen masonry looking up at the enormous moon which now rose directly above his head, sending his shadow to mingle with those of the ruins; and he dragged off his helmet and shook out his long, milk-white hair and turned yearning hands towards the city as if to beg forgiveness, and then he sat down upon a dusty slab carved with the delicacy and imagination of genius and over which blood had flowed, then baked, a coarse glaze; and he buried his crimson eyes in the sleeve of his ashy shirt and his shoulders shook and he groaned his complaint at whatever fate had led him to this ordeal . . .

There came a voice from behind him that seemed to echo from distant catacombs, across aeons of time, as resonant as the Dragon Falls where one of Elric's ancestors had died (in combat, it was said, with himself) and as commanding as the whole of Elric's long and binding royal history. It was a voice he recognised and had hoped, in so many ways, never to hear again.

Once more he wondered if he were mad. The voice was unmistakeably that of his dead father, Sadric the Eighty-Sixth, whose company in life he had so rarely shared.

"Ah, Elric, thou weepest, I see. Thou art thy mother's son and for that I love her memory, though thou kill'dst the only woman I shall ever truly love and for that I hate thee with an unjust hatred."

"Father?" Elric lowered his arm and turned his bone-white face behind him to where, leaning against a ruined pillar, stood the slender, frail presence of Sadric. Upon his lips was a smile that was terrible in its tranquillity.

Elric looked disbelievingly at the face which was exactly as it had been when he had last seen it as his father had lain in funeral state.

"For an unjust hatred there is no release, save the peace of death. And here, as you'll observe, I am denied the peace of death."

"I have dreamed of you, Father, and your disappointment with me. I would that I could have been all you desired in a son . . ."

"There was never a second, Elric, when you could have been that. The act of thy creation was the sealing of her doom. We had been warned of it in every omen but could do nothing to avert that hideous destiny—" and his eyes glared with a hatred only the unrested dead could know.

"How came you here, Father? I had thought you chosen by Chaos, gone to the service of our patron duke, Lord Arioch."

"Arioch could not claim me because of another pact I had made, with Count Mashabak. He is no longer my patron." And a kind of laugh escaped him.

"Your soul was claimed by Mashabak of Chaos?"

"But disputed by Arioch. My soul is hostage to their rivalries—or was. By some sorcery I still command, I betook myself here, to the very beginning of our true history. And here I have some short sanctuary."

"You are hiding, Father, from the Lords of Chaos?"

"I have gained some time while they dispute, for I have here a spell, my last great spell, which will free me to join your mother in the Forest of Souls where she awaits me."

"You have a passport to the Forest of Souls? I'd thought such things a myth." Elric wiped chilly sweat from his forehead.

"I sent thy mother there to remain until I joined her. I gave her the means, our Scroll of Dead-Speaking, and she is safe in that sweet eternity, which many souls seek and which few find. I swore an oath that I would do all I could to be reunited with her."

The shade stepped forward, as if entranced, and reached to touch Elric's face with something like affection. But when the hand fell away there was only torment in the old man's undead eyes.

Elric knew a certain sympathy. "Have you no companions here, Father?"

"Only thou, my son. Thee and I now haunt these ruins together."

An unwholesome frisson: "Am I, too, a prisoner here?" said the albino.

"At my humour, aye, my son. Now that I have touched thee we are bound together, whether thou leavest this place or no, for it is the fate of such as I to be linked always to the first living mortal his hand shall fall upon. We are one, now, Elric—or shall be."

And Elric shuddered at the hatred and the relish in his father's otherwise desolate voice.

"Can I not release you, Father? I have been to R'lin K'ren A'a, where our race began in this realm. I sought our past there. I could speak of it . . ."

"Our past is in our blood. It travels with us. Those degenerates of R'lin K'ren A'a, they were never our true kin. They bred with humans and vanished. It was not they who founded or preserved great Melniboné . . ."

"There are so many stories, Father. So many conflicting legends . . ." Elric was eager to continue the conversation with his father. Few such opportunities had existed while Sadric lived.

"The dead know truth from lies. They are privy to that understanding, at least. And I know the truth of it. We did not stem from R'lin K'ren A'a. Such questings and speculations are unnecessary. We are assured of our origins. Thou wouldst be a fool, my son, to question our histories, to dispute their truth. I had thee taught this."

Elric kept his own counsel.

"My magic called the jill-dragon from her cave. The one I had the strength to summon. But she came and I sent her to thee. This is the only sorcery I have left. It is the first significant sorcery of our race and the purest, the Phoorn-sorcery. But I could not instruct her. I sent her to thee knowing she would recognise thee or she would kill thee. Both actions would have brought us together, eventually, no doubt." The shade permitted itself a crooked smile.

"You cared no more than that, Father?"

"I could *do* no more than that. I long for thy mother. We were meant to be united for ever. Thou must help me reach her, Elric, and help me swiftly for my own energies and spells weaken—soon Arioch or Mashabak shall claim me. Or destroy me entirely in their struggle!"

"You have no further means of escaping them?" Elric felt his left leg shake uncontrollably for a few seconds before he forced it to obey his will. He realised it had been too long since he had last taken the infusion of herbs and drugs which allowed him the energy of a normal creature.

"In a way. If I remain attached to thee, my son, the object of my unjust hate, then my soul could hide with thine, occupying thy flesh and mine, disguised by blood that is my blood. *They would never sniff me out!*"

Again Elric was seized by a sensation of profound cold, as if death already claimed him; his head was a maelstrom of ungoverned emotions as he sought desperately to take a grip on himself, praying that with the sun's rising his father's ghost would vanish.

"The sun will not rise here, Elric. Not here. Not until the moment of our release or our destruction. That is *why* we are here."

"But does Arioch not object to this? He is my patron, still!" Elric looked for a new madness in his father's face but could find none.

"He is otherwise engaged and could not come to thee now, whether to aid or to punish. His dispute with Count Mashabak absorbs him. That is why thou canst serve me, to perform the task I did not know to perform when alive. Wouldst thou do this thing for me, my son? For a father who always hated thee but did his duty by thee?"

"If I performed this task for you, Father, would I be free of you?"

His father lowered his head in assent.

Elric put a trembling hand upon the pommel of his sword and flung back his head so that the long white hair filled the air like a halo in the moonlight and his uneasy eyes rose to stare into the face of the dead king.

He let out a sigh. In spite of all his horrors, there was some part of him which would be fulfilled if he achieved his father's desire. He wished, however, that he had been permitted the choice. But it was not the Melnibonéan way to permit choice. Even relatives had to be bonded by more than blood.

"Explain my task, Father."

"Thou must find my soul, Elric."

"Your *soul*—?"

"My soul is not with me." The shade itself seemed to make an effort to remain standing. "What animates me now is my will and old sorcery. My soul was hidden so that it might rejoin thy mother, but in avoiding Mashabak's and Arioch's wrath, I lost that which contained it. Find it for me, Elric."

"How shall I recognise it?"

"It resides in a box. No ordinary box, but a box of black rosewood carved all with roses and smelling always of roses. It was your mother's."

"How came you to lose such a valuable box, Father?"

"When Mashabak appeared to claim my soul, then Arioch, I drew up a false soul, which is the spell I taught thee in *Incantations After Death*, to deceive them. This quasi-soul became the object of their feuding for a while and my true soul fled to safety in the box which Diavon Slar, my old body-servant, was to keep safely for me on strictest instructions of secrecy."

"He maintained your secrecy, Father."

"Aye—and fled, believing he had a treasure, believing he could control me through his possession of that box! He fled to Pan Tang with what he understood to be my trapped spirit—some children's tale he had heard—and was disappointed to find no spirit obeyed him at his command. So he planned, instead, to sell his booty to the Theocrat. As it happened, he never reached Pan Tang but was seized by sea-raiders from the Purple Towns. They included the box in their casual booty. My soul was truly lost." And with this came a flicker of a former irony, the faintest of smiles.

"The pirates?"

"Of them, I know only what Diavon Slar told me as I was extracting the vengeance I had warned him I would take. The raiders probably returned to Menii, where they auctioned their booty. My soulbox left our world entirely." Sadric moved suddenly and it was as if an insubstantial shadow shifted in the moonlight. "I can still sense it. I know it travelled between the worlds and went where now only the jill-dragon can follow. That is what has thwarted me. For, until I called thee, I had no means of pursuit. I am bound to this place and now to thee. Thou must fetch back my soulbox, Elric, so that I can rejoin thy mother and rid myself of unjust hate. As thou wilt rid thyself of me."

Trembling with conflicting passions, Elric spoke at last:

"Father, I believe this to be an impossible quest. I cannot but suspect you send me upon it out of hatred alone."

"Hatred, aye, but more besides. *I must rejoin your mother, Elric! I must. I must.*"

Knowing his father's abiding obsession, that convinced Elric of the ghost's veracity.

"Do not fail me, my son."

"And should I succeed? What will happen to us, Father?"

"Bring back my soul and we are both released."

"But if I fail?"

"My soul will leave its prison and enter thee. We shall be united until thy death—I, with my unjust hatred, bonded to the object of my hatred, and thee burdened by all *thou* most hatest in proud Melniboné." He paused, almost to savour this. "That would be my consolation."

"Not mine."

Sadric nodded his corpse's head in silent understanding, and a soft, unlikely laugh escaped his throat. "Indeed!"

"And dost thou have other aid for me in this, Father? Some spell or charm?"

"Only what thou comest by on the way, my son. Bring back the rosewood box and we both can go our own ways. Fail, and our destinies and souls are linked for ever! Thou wilt never be free of me, thy past, or Melniboné! But thou wilt bring the old glories back, eh?"

Elric's drug-enlivened body began to tremble. The flight and this encounter had exhausted him, and there were no souls here on which his sword could feed.

"I am ailing, Father, and must soon return. The drugs that sustain me were lost with my pack animals."

Sadric shrugged. "As for that, thou hast merely to discover a source of souls on which thy blade might feed. There's killing aplenty ahead. And a little more that I perceive, but yet it does not come clear . . ." He frowned. "Go . . ."

Elric hesitated. Some ordinary impulse wanted him to tell his father that he no longer killed casually to further any whim. Like all Melnibonéans, Sadric had thought nothing of killing the human folk of their empire. To Sadric, the runesword was merely a useful tool, as a stick might be to a cripple. Supernatural schemer though his father was, player of complex games against the gods, he still unquestioningly assumed that one must pledge loyalty to one demon or another in order to survive.

Elric's vision, of universally held power, a place like Tanelorn, owing allegiance neither to Law nor to Chaos but only to itself, was anathema to his father who had made a religion and a philosophy of compromise, as had all his royal race for millennia, so that compromise itself was now raised over all other virtues and become the backbone of their beliefs. Elric wanted, again, to tell his father that there were other ideas, other ways to live, which involved neither excessive violence, nor cruelty, nor sorcery, nor conquest, that he had learned of these ideas not merely from the Young Kingdoms but also from his own folk's histories.

Yet he knew that it would be useless. Sadric was even now devoting all his considerable powers to restoring the past. He knew no other way of life or, indeed, of death.

The albino prince turned away, and it seemed to him at that moment that he had never experienced such grief, even when Cymoril had died on the blade of his runesword, even when Imrryr had blazed and he had known he was doomed to a rootless future, a lonely death.

"I shall seek your rosewood box, Father. But where can I begin?"

"The jill-dragon knows. She'll carry thee to the realm where the box was taken. Beyond that I cannot predict. Prediction grows difficult. All my powers weaken. Mayhap thou must kill to achieve the box. Kill many times." The voice was faint now, dry branches in the wind. "Or worse."

Elric found that he staggered. He was weakening by the moment. "Father, I have no strength."

"*The dragon venom . . .*" But his father was gone, leaving only a sense of his ghostly passing.

Elric forced himself to move. Now every fallen wall seemed an impossible obstacle. He picked his way slowly through the ruins, back over rubble and broken walls, over the little streams and coarse turf terraces of the hills, forcing himself with a will summoned from habit alone to climb the final hill where, outlined against the huge, sinking moon, Scarsnout awaited him, her wings folded, her long muzzle raised as her tongue tasted the wind.

He remembered his father's last words. They in turn made him recollect an old herbal which had spoken of the distillation of dragon venom; how it brought courage to the weak and skill to the strong, how a man might fight for five days and nights and feel no pain. And he remembered how the herbal had said to collect the venom, so before he clambered back upon the Phoorn he had reached up his helm and caught in hissing steel a small drop of venom which would cool and harden, he knew, into a pastille, a crumb or two of which might be taken cautiously with considerable liquid.

But now he must endure his pain and fight against his weakness as the dragon bears him up into the unwelcoming blackness which lies above the moon; and a single long, slow stroke of silver gashes the dark and a single sharp clap of thunder breaks the terrible silence of the sky, and the jill-dragon raises her head and beats her monstrous wings and roars a sudden challenge to those unlikely elements . . .

. . . While Elric howls the old wild songs of the Dragon Lords, and plunges, in sensuous symbiosis with the great reptile, out of the night and into the blinding glory of a summer afternoon.

3

Peculiar Geography of an Unknown Realm;
A Meeting of Travellers.
On the Meaning of Freedom.

As if aware of her rider's growing weakness, the Phoorn flew with long, deliberate strokes of her wings and banked with careful grace through the blue pallor of the sky until they flew over trees so close together, and with foliage so dense, that it seemed at first they crossed dark green clouds until the old forest gave way to grassy hills and fields through which a broad river ran, and again the gentle landscape had a familiarity to it, though this time Elric did not dread it.

Soon a sprawling city lay ahead, built on both banks and making the sky hazy with its smoke. Of stone and brick and wood, of slate and thatch and timber shingles, of a thousand blended stinks and noises, it was full of statues and markets and monuments over which the jill-dragon began slowly to circle while below, in panic and curiosity, the citizens ran to look or dashed for cover, depending upon their natures—but then Scarsnout had flapped her wings and taken them with stately authority back into the upper sky, as if she had investigated the place and found it unsuitable.

The summer day went on. More than once did the great dragon-she seem about to land—on scrubland, village, marsh, lake or elm-glade—but always Scarsnout rejected the place and flew on dissatisfied.

Though he had taken the precaution of tying himself by his long silk scarf to the dragon's spine-horn, Elric was losing strength with every moment. Now, moreover, he had no reason to welcome death. To be reunited with his father through eternity was perhaps the worst of all possible hells. It was only when the dragon flew through rainclouds and Elric was able to capture a little water in his helmet, crumbling into it the merest flake of dried venom and drinking the foul-tasting result off in a single draught, that he knew any hope. But when the liquid filled his every vein with fire whose stink made him loathe the flesh that harboured it and want to tear at offending arteries, muscles, skin, he wondered if he had not merely chosen an especially painful way of ensuring his eternal union with Sadric. With each nerve alight, he yearned for any death, any release from the agony.

But even as the pain filled him, the strength grew until soon it was possible to call on that strength and gradually abolish or ignore the pain until it was gone and he felt a cleaner, sweeter energy fill him, somehow purer than that he received from his runesword.

As the jill-dragon flew through evening skies, Elric felt himself grow whole again. A peculiar euphoria filled him. He sang out the ancient dragon-songs, the rich, silky, wicked songs of his folk who, for all their cruelty, had relished every experience that came their way and this relish for life and sensation came naturally to the albino, despite the weakness of his blood.

Indeed, it seemed to him that his blood was somehow touched by a compensatory quality, a world of almost unrelieved sensuality and vividness, so intense that it sometimes threatened to destroy not only him, but those around him. It was one of the reasons he was prepared to accept his loneliness.

Now it did not matter how far the jill-dragon flew. Her venom sustained him. The symbiosis was near-complete. On without rest beat Scarsnout until, beneath a golden late-afternoon sun which made the three-quarters ripened wheat glow and shimmer like burnished copper, where a startled figure in a pointed alabaster cap cried out in delight at the sight of them and a cloud of starlings rose suddenly to trace with their hurried flight some familiar hieroglyph in the delicate blue wash of the sky and leave a sudden silence behind them, Scarsnout extended her great ribbed wings in a sinuously elegant glide towards what seemed at first a road made of basalt or some other rock and then became a mile-wide long-healed scar through the wheatlands, too smooth, unpopulated and vast to be a road, yet with an unguessable purpose. It cut through the crops as if it had been laid that day, heaped on both sides by great unkempt banks on which a few weeds and wild flowers grew and over which hopped, flapped and crawled every kind of carrion vermin. As they dropped lower Elric could smell the vile stuff and almost gagged. His nose confirmed what he saw—piles of refuse, bones, human waste, bits of broken furniture and ruined pots—great continuous banks of detritus stretching on either side of the smoothly polished road from horizon to horizon, with no notion of where or from where it led . . . Elric sang to his jill to take him up and away from all this filth and into the sweet air of the high summer skies, but she ignored him, wheeling first to the north, then to the south, until she was swooping down the very middle of that great, smooth scar, which had something of the brownish-pink of sunned flesh, and she had landed, almost without any sensation, in the centre of it.

Now Scarsnout folded back her wings and settled her clawed feet upon the ground, clearly indicating that she intended to carry Elric no further. With some reluctance he climbed off her back, unravelling the ruined scarf and wrapping it around his waist, as if it would secure him from any dangers here-abouts, and sang the farewell chant of thanking and kinship and, as he called the last lines, the great jill-dragon lifted up her beautiful, reptilian head and joined, with sonorous gravity, in the final cadences. Her voice might have been the voice of Time itself.

Then her jaws snapped shut, her eyes turned once upon him, half-lidded, almost in affection, and, once her tongue had tasted the evening air, she had widened her wings, hopped twice, shaking the surface so that Elric thought it must crack, and was at last asky, mounting into the atmosphere again, her graceful body curling and twisting as her wings carried her up to the eastern horizon, the setting sun casting her long, terrible shadow across the fields, and then, near the horizon, a single flash of silver suggested to Elric that his jill-dragon had returned to her own dimension. He raised his helm in farewell, as grateful for her venom as her patience.

All Elric wished to do was to get free of this unnatural causeway. Though it gleamed like polished marble, he could see now that it was nothing more than beaten mud; earth piled on earth until it had almost the consistency of solid rock. Perhaps the whole thing was built of garbage? For some reason, this thought disturbed him and he began to walk rapidly towards the southern edge. Wiping sweat from his forehead, he wondered again what purpose the place had. Flies now surrounded him and buzzards regarded him as a possible contender for their sweetmeats. He coughed again at the stink but knew he must climb the stuff to get to the wholesome air of the wheatfields.

"Safe passage to your home-cave, sweet Lady Scarsnout," he murmured as he moved. "I owe you both life and death, it seems. But I bear you no ill will."

His scarf wrapped around his nose and mouth, the albino began to climb the yielding filth, disturbing bones and vermin with every movement and making slow progress, while around him birds and winged rats hissed and chittered at him. Again he wondered what kind of creature could have created such a path, if path it were. It could not, he felt sure, be the work of any human agency and this made him all the more anxious to return to the known qualities of the wheatfield.

He had reached the rim and was clambering along it to find a firmer foothold down. Scattering rotted matter and angry rodents as he went, he wondered what kind of culture brought its waste to line a track created by some supernatural being. Then he thought he saw something larger shift below, near where the wheat grew, but the light was bad and he put it down to his imagination. Was the refuse some kind of holy offering? Did this realm's people worship a god who patrolled from one habitation to another in the form of a gigantic snake?

There was another movement below him, as he slid down a few feet and came to rest on an old cistern, and he saw a soft felt hat rise above a pile of rags and an avian face stare up at him in astonished amusement. "Good heavens, sir. This cannot be coincidence! But what purpose has Fate for pairing we two, do you think?" It was Wheldrake, stumbling up from the wheatfield. "What lies behind you, sir, that's duller than this? More corn? Why, sir, this seems a world of corn!"

"Of corn and garbage and a somewhat idiosyncratic pathway of baffling purpose which slices through all, from east to west. It has a sinister air to it."

"So you go the other way, sir?"

"To avoid whichever unpleasant creation of Chaos has chosen to slither this route and take its choice of these offerings. My horses, I suppose, were not carried through the dimensions with you?"

"Not to my knowledge, sir. I'd guessed you eaten, by now. But the reptile was one of those with a sentimental weakness for heroes, I take it?"

"Something of the sort." Elric smiled, grateful in an odd way for the red-headed poet's ironies. They were preferable to his most recent conversation with his father. As he slid down some powdery and decomposing substance alive with maggots, he embraced the little man who almost chirped with pleasure at their reunion. "My dear sir!"

Whereupon, arm in arm they went, back to the bottom and the sweetening wheat, back in the direction of a river Elric had seen from his dragon steed. There had been a town upon that river which, he guessed, might be reached in less than a day. He spoke of this to Wheldrake, adding that they were sadly short of provisions or the means of obtaining any, unless they chewed the unripe wheat.

"I regret my poaching days in Northumberland are long behind me, sir. But as a lad I was apt enough with snare and a gun. It might be, since your scarf is rather badly the worse for wear, that you would not mind if I unravelled it a little more. It's just possible I might remember my old skills."

With an amiable shrug, Elric handed the birdlike poet his scarf and watched as the little fingers worked swiftly, unravelling and reknotting until he had a length of thin cord. "With evening drawing close, sir, I'd best get to work at once."

By now they were some distance from the wall of garbage and could smell only the rich, restful scents of the summer fields. Elric took his ease amongst the wheatstalks while Wheldrake went to work and within a short space of time, having cleared a wide area and dug a pit, they were able to enjoy a young rabbit while they speculated at such a strange world which grew such vast fields and yet seemed to have so few farmsteads or villages. Staring at the rabbit's carcass turning on a spit (also of Wheldrake's devising) Elric said that, for all his sorcerous education, he was not the familiar traveller through the realms that Wheldrake seemed to be.

"Not by choice, sir, I assure you. I blame a certain Doctor Dee, whom I consulted on the Greeks. It was to do with metre, sir. A metric question. I needed, I thought, to *hear* the language of Plato. Well, the story's long and not especially novel to those of us who travel, willy-nilly, through the multiverse, but I spent some while on one particular plane, shifting a little, I must admit, through time (but not the other dimensions) until I had come to rest, I was sure, in Putney."

"Would you return there, Master Wheldrake?"

"Indeed I would, sir. I'm growing a little long in the tooth for extra-dimensional adventuring, and I tend to form firm attachments, so it is rather hard on me, you know, to miss so many friends."

"Well, sir. I hope you will find them again."

"And you, sir. Good luck with whatever it is you hope to discover. Though I suspect you are the kind who's forever searching for the numinous."

"Perhaps," said Elric soberly, chewing upon a tender leg, "but I think the numinosity of what I presently seek would surprise you greatly . . ."

Wheldrake was about to ask more when he changed his mind and stared instead, with abiding pride, at his spit and his catch. Elric's own cares were considerably lightened by his relish for the little man's company and quirks of character.

And now Master Wheldrake has found his sought-for volume and has a handy candle to light at the fire so that he might read aloud to the last prince of Melniboné an account of some demigod of his own dimension and his challenge of a kingship, when there comes a sound of a horse walking slowly through the wheat—a horse which hesitates with every few steps as if controlled by a clever master. So Elric shouts out—

"Greetings, horseman. Would you share our meat?"

There's a pause, then the answering voice is muffled, distant, yet courteous: "I'd share your heat, sir, for a while. It's mighty cold just now, to me."

The horse continues towards them at the same pace, still pausing from time to time, still cautious, until at last they see its shadow against the firelight and a rider dismounts, walking softly towards them, a silhouette of alarming symmetry, a big man clad from head to foot in armour that flashes silver, gold, sometimes blue-grey. On his helm is a plume of dark yellow and his breastplate is etched with the yellow-and-black Arms of Chaos, the arms of a soul-bonded servant of the Lords of Unlikelihood, which are eight arrows radiating from a central hub, representing the variety and multiplicity of Chaos. Behind him his perfect war-stallion was furnished with a hood and surcoat of radiant black and silver silk, a high saddle of ornamental ivory and ebony, and silver harness bound with gold.

Elric got to his feet, ready for confrontation but chiefly puzzled by the stranger's appearance. The newcomer wore a helm apparently without a visor, but all of a piece from neck to crown. Only the eye slits relieved the smoothness of the coruscating steel, which seemed to contain living matter just below its polished surface: matter that flowed and stirred and threatened. Through those slits peered a pair of eyes displaying an angry pain which Elric understood. He was unable to identify a feeling of close affinity with the man as he came up to the fire and stretched gauntleted hands towards the flames. The firelight caught the metal and again suggested that something living was contained in it, trapped in it—some enormous energy, so powerful it could be observed *through* the steel. And yet the fingers stretched and curled like any fleshly finger warmed back to circulation, and the stranger's sigh was one of simple comfort.

"Will you take a little rabbit, sir?" Wheldrake gestured towards the roasting coney.

"Thank you, no, sir."

"Will you unburden yourself of your helm and sit with us? You're in no danger."

"I believe you, sir. But I am unable to remove this helm at present and have not, I'll be frank, fed upon commonplace sustenance for some while."

At this Wheldrake raised a ruddy eyebrow. "Does Chaos send her servants to become cannibals, these days, sir?"

"She's had servants aplenty who have been that," said the armoured man, turning his back now to the fire's heat, "but I am not of their number. I have not eaten flesh, fruit or vegetable, sir, for nigh on two thousand years. Or it could be more. I ceased attempting such a reckoning long ago. There are realms that are always Night and realms sweltering in perpetual Day and others where night and day fly by with a speed not of our usual perception."

"Some sort of vow, is it, sir?" says Wheldrake tentatively. "Some holy purpose?"

"A quest, aye, but for something simpler, sir, than you would believe."

"What are you seeking, sir? A particular lost bride?"

"You are perceptive, sir."

"Merely well-read, sir. But that is not all, eh?"

"I seek nothing less than death, sir. It is to that unhappy doom that the Balance did consign me when I betrayed her those numberless millennia since. It is also my doom to fight against those who serve the Balance, though I love the Balance with a ferocity, sir, that has never dissipated. It was ordained— though I have no reason to trust the oracle in question—that I should find peace at the hand of a servant of the Balance—one who was as I once was."

"And what were you once?" enquired Wheldrake, who had followed this last a little more swiftly than the albino.

"I was once a Prince of the Balance, a Servant and Confidant of that Unordinary Intelligence that tolerates, celebrates and loves all life throughout the multiverse and yet which both Law and Chaos would overthrow if they could. Discontented with multiplicity and massive adjustment in the multiverse, guessing something of a great conjunction which must come throughout the Key Planes and set the realities for countless aeons—realities where the Balance might no longer exist, I gave in to experiment. The notion was too strong for me. Curiosity and folly, self-importance and pride led me to convince myself that in doing what I attempted to do, I served the interests of the Balance. And for my failure, or my success, I would have paid an equal price. The price I now pay."

"That is not the whole of your story, sir." Wheldrake was enthralled. "You will not bore me, I know, if you wish to embroider it with more detail."

"I cannot, sir. I speak as I do because that is all I am allowed to unburden of my tale. The rest is for me alone to know until such time I shall be released and then it can be told."

"Released by death, sir? It would create some difficulties regarding the telling, I'd guess."

"The Balance doubtless will decide such things," said the stranger, without much humour.

"Is general death all you look for, sir? Or has death a name?" Elric spoke softly, with some sympathy.

"I am seeking three sisters. They came this way, I think, a few days since. Would you have seen three sisters? Riding together?"

"I regret, sir, that we are but recently transported to this realm, through no desire of our own, and thus are newly here without maps or directions." Elric shrugged. "I had hoped you would know a little of the place."

"It is in what they call the Nine Millionth Ring, the maguses here. It exists within what they have formalised as the Realms of Central Significance, and it is true there is an unusual quality to the plane which I have yet to identify. It is not a true Centre, for that is the Realm of the Balance, but it is what I would call a quasi-centre. You'll forgive the jargon, sir, I hope, of the philosopher. I was for some generations an alchemist in Prague."

"Prague!" cries Wheldrake with a caw of delighted recognition. "Those bells and towers, sir. And do you know Mirenburg, perhaps? Even more beautiful!"

"The memories are no doubt pleasant enough," says the armoured man, "since I do not recall them. I would take it that you, too, are upon a quest here?"

"Not I, sir," says Wheldrake, "unless it be for Putney Common and my lost half-pint."

"I am seeking something, aye," agreed Elric cautiously. He had hoped to learn a little of the geography rather than the mystical and astrological placing of this world. "I am Elric of Melniboné."

His name does not seem of any great significance to the armoured man. "And I am Gaynor, once a Prince of the Universal, now called the Damned. Perhaps we have met? Without these names or even faces? In some other incarnation?"

"It is not my misfortune to recall any other lives," says Elric softly, at last disturbed by Gaynor's enquiries. "I understand you only a little, sir. I am a mercenary soldier en route to a new location with a view to finding myself a fresh patron. To the supernatural, I am almost a stranger."

And he was grateful that Wheldrake's eyebrows were rising at that moment from behind Gaynor. Why he should decide upon such subterfuge he did not understand, only that, for all his being drawn to Gaynor, for all their mutual patronage under Chaos, he feared something in him. Gaynor had no reason to wish him harm and Elric guessed that Gaynor did not waste anything of himself in meaningless challenges or killings, yet still Elric grew more close-lipped, as if he, too, were fated by the Balance never to speak of his own story, and at length they settled down to sleep, three strange figures in what appeared to be an infinity of wheat.

Early the next morning, Gaynor resumed his saddle. "I was glad of the company, gentlemen. If you travel yonder, you'll find a pretty settlement. The people there are traders and welcome strangers. They treat us, indeed, with unusual respect. I go on my way. I have been informed that my sisters journeyed towards a place called the Gypsy Nation. Know you anything of that?"

"I regret, sir," said Wheldrake, wiping his hands upon an enormous red cotton handkerchief, "we are virgins in this world. Innocent as babes. We are wholly at a disadvantage, having but recently arrived in this realm and having no notion of its people or its gods. Perhaps, if I might be somewhat forward, I would suggest that you are yourself of divine or semi-divine origin?"

The answering laugh seemed to find an internal echo, as if the prince's helm disguised the entrance to some infinite chasm. It was far away, yet oddly intimate. "I told you, Master Wheldrake. I was a Prince of the Balance. But not now. Now, I assure you, sir, there is nothing divine about Gaynor the Damned."

Murmuring that he still did not understand the significance of the prince's title, Wheldrake subsided. "If we could help, sir, we would—"

"Who are these women you seek?" Elric asked.

"Three sisters, similar in looks and upon a quest or errand of some singular urgency to themselves. They are searching, I gather, for a lost countryman or perhaps even a brother and had asked hereabouts for the Gypsy Nation. When the people heard they sought the Nation they put them on their way but refused all further intercourse. My only advice to you would be to avoid the subject completely, unless it is raised by them! I have a suspicion, moreover, that once you encounter this band of nomads, you have precious little chance of leaving their ranks unscathed."

"I am grateful for your advice, Prince Gaynor," said Elric. "And did you learn who grows so much wheat, and why?"

"Fixed tenants they are called, and when I asked the same question I was told with a somewhat humourless laugh that it was to feed the locusts. I have heard of stranger practises. There is some tension with the gypsies, I gather. They will not speak much of any of this but become unsettled. The realm's called by them Salish-Kwoonn, which, you'll recall, is the name of the city in the Ivory Book. An odd irony, that. I was amused." And he turned his horse away from them as if he escaped wholly into the abstract, his natural environment, and rode slowly towards that distant depression, those hills of refuse, whose presence was already marked on the horizon by crows and kites, by masses of flies swarming like black smoke.

"A scholar," said Wheldrake, "if a little on the cryptic side. You understand him better than do I, Prince Elric. But I wish he had travelled our way. What do you make of the fellow?"

Elric paused, choosing his words, fiddling with the buckle of his belt. Then he said: "I am afraid of him. I fear him as I have never feared a human creature, mortal or immortal. His doom is terrible, indeed, for he has known the Sanctuary of the Balance, and that is what I yearn for. To have had it—and lost it . . ."

"Come, now, sir. You must exaggerate. Odd, he was, to be sure. But affable, I thought. Given his circumstances."

Elric shuddered, glad to see Prince Gaynor gone. "Yet I fear him as I fear nothing else."

"As you fear yourself, maybe, sir?" And then Wheldrake looked with regret upon the face of his new friend. "I beg you, sir, I did not wish to seem forward."

"You are too intelligent for me, Master Wheldrake. Your poet's eye is perhaps sharper than I would like."

"Random instinct, sir, I assure you. I understand nothing and say everything. That's *my* doom, sir! Not as grand as some, no doubt, but it gets me in and out of trouble in roughly equal proportions."

And with that Master Wheldrake assures himself of a dead fire, breaks down his spit and buries it with regret, keeps hold of his snare, which he tucks in his pocket with a volume which has lost its binding to reveal some vulgar marbling, throws his frock-coat over his shoulder and plunges through the wheat in Elric's wake. "Did I recite my verse epic, sir, concerning the love and death of Sir Tancred and Lady Mary? In the form of the Northumberland ballad, which was the first poetry I ever heard. The family estates were remote, but I was not lonely there."

His voice chirruping and trilling the cadences of a primitive dirge, the red-combed scrivener skipped and scampered to keep up with the tall albino.

Four hours later, they reached the broad, slow-flowing river and could see, rising on picturesque cliffs above the water, the town Elric sought. Meanwhile Wheldrake declaimed the ballad's last resounding couplets and seemed as relieved as Elric that his composition was concluded.

The town appeared to have been carved by fanciful master masons from the glinting limestone of the cliffs and was reached by a fairly narrow track, evidently of artificial construction in places, which wound above the rocks and white water some distance below, rising gradually before it blended with the town's chief street to wind again between tall, many-storeyed dwellings and warehouses, fanciful public buildings and statuary, topiary and elaborate flower gardens to become lost among a maze of other thoroughfares and alleys which lay below an ancient castle, itself covered in vines and flowering creepers, dominating both the town and the thirteen-arched bridge which spanned the river at its narrowest point and crossed to a smaller settlement beyond where, evidently, the wealthy citizens had built their pale villas.

The town had an air of contented prosperity and Elric became optimistic as he saw it lacked any real walls and clearly had not needed to defend itself against aggressors for many years. Now a few local people, in bright, much-embroidered clothing, very different in style from Elric's or, indeed, Wheldrake's, greeted them cheerfully and openly, like men and women who know considerable security and are used to strangers.

"If they welcomed Gaynor, Prince Elric," said Wheldrake, "then I would guess we would not seem especially alien to them! This place has a Frenchified air to it, reminding me of certain settlements along the Loire, though it lacks the characteristic cathedral. Is there any clue, do you perceive, to their form of religion?"

"Perhaps they have none," said Elric. "I have heard of such races." But clearly Wheldrake disbelieved him.

"Even the French have religion!"

The road took them past the first houses, perched on rocks and terraces above them and all displaying the richest flower gardens Elric remembered. A scent came off them, mingling with the faint smells of paint and cooking, and both travellers found themselves relaxing, smiling at those who hailed them, until Elric stopped for a moment and enquired of a young woman in a white-and-red smock the name of the town.

"Why, this is Agnesh-Val, sir. And across the river is Agnesh-Nal. How came you here, gentlemen? Was your boat wrecked at the Forli rapid? You should go to the Distressed Travellers House in Fivegroat Lane, just below Salt Pie Alley. They'll feed you there, at least. Do you carry the medal of the Insurers Guild?"

"I regret not, madam."

"Sadly, then, you will be entitled only to our hospitality."

"Which would seem more than generous, lady," said Wheldrake, offering her a rather inappropriate wink before skipping to catch up with his friend.

Eventually, through the twists and turns of the old, cobbled streets, they reached the Distressed Travellers House, a gabled building of considerable antiquity which leaned at all angles, as if too drunk to stand without the support of the houses on either side of it, and whose beams and walls bulged and warped in ways Elric would have thought impossible for natural matter not touched by Chaos.

Within the doorway of this establishment, seeming entirely of a piece with it, both in terms of posture and of age, leaned and sprawled, his limbs at every angle, his head this way, his hat that, a tooth jutting one direction, his pipe another, a creature of such profound thinness and gauntness and melancholy that Elric was moved, obscurely, to apologise and enquire if he had come to the right place.

"It's the place that you face, sir, by Our Watcher's Grace, my lord. Come for charity, have you? For charity and some smart advice?"

"Hospitality, sir, is what we were offered!" There was an edge to Wheldrake's outraged chirrup. "Not, sir, charity!" He resembled an angered grouse, his face almost as red as his hair.

"I care not what fancy words dress the action, my good lords," and the creature rose, folding and collapsing and extending itself in such a way as to bring itself upright, "I call it *charity*!" Tiny diamond-lights glittered from cavernous sockets and ill-fitting teeth clacked in flaccid lips. "I care not what dangers you have faced, what calamities have befallen you, what hideous losses you have sustained, what rich men you were, what poor men you have become. Had you not considered these risks, you would not have come this far and ventured across the Divide! Thus you have yourselves alone to blame for your misfortunes."

"We were told we might find food at this house," said Elric evenly. "Not ill-tempered crowfrighters and discourtesy."

"Hypocrites that they are, they lied. The House is closed for redecoration. It is being converted to a restaurant. With luck, it should soon turn a profit."

"Well, sir, we have put such narrow notions of accountability behind us in my world," said Wheldrake. "However, I apologise for disturbing you. We have been misinformed, as you say."

Elric, unused to such behaviour and still a Melnibonéan noble, found that he had gripped his sword hilt without his realising it. "Old man," he said, "I am discommoded by your insolence . . ." Then Wheldrake's warning hand fell upon the albino's arm and he collected himself.

"The old man lies! He lies! He lies!" From behind them, up the hill, a large key ready in his hand, bustled a stocky fellow of fifty or so, his grey hair bristling from beneath a velvet cap, his beard half-tangled, his robes and suitings all awry, as if he had dressed in a hurry from some half-remembered bed. "He lies, good sirs. He lies. (Be off with you, Reth'chat, to plague some other institution!) The man is a relic, gentlemen, from an age most of us have only read about. He would have us judged by our wealth and our martial glory rather than our good will and tranquillity of spirit. Good morrow, good morrow. You've come to dine, I hope."

MICHAEL MOORCOCK

"Cold and tasteless is the bread of charity," grumbled the Relic, scuttling down the street towards a group of playing children and failing to scatter them with his stick-insect arms. "Accountability and self-sufficiency! They will destroy the family. We shall all perish. We shall serve at the marching boards, mark my words!"

And with that he turned the corner into Old Museum Gate and disappeared with a final display of miraculous angularity into an arcade of shops.

The genial middle-aged man waved his key before inserting it in the ancient door. "He is an advertisement for himself only. You'll find such blowhards in every town. I take it that our gypsy friends exacted a 'tax' from you. What would you have been bringing us?"

"Gold, mostly," said Elric, understanding at last the manners and ready lies of a mercenary and a thief, "and precious jewels."

"You were brave to make the attempt. Did they find you this side of the Divide?"

"It would seem so."

"And stripped you of everything. You are lucky to have your clothing and weapons. And 'tis as well they did not catch you crossing the Divide."

"We waited a season before we were sure of our chance." This from Wheldrake, entering the spirit of it, as if in a childish game, a knowing grin upon his broad lips.

"Aye. Others have waited longer." The door opened silently and they entered a passage lit by glowing yellow lamps, its walls as twisted inside as they were without; its staircases rising in unlikely places and going where none could guess, its passages and chambers appearing suddenly and always of peculiar shapes and angles, sometimes brilliant with candles, sometimes gloomy and musty, as their host led them on, deeper and deeper into the house until they came at last to a large, cheerful hall in the centre of which was a great oaken table, lined with benches—enough space for two score of hungry travellers. There was, however, only one other guest, already helping herself to the rich stew steaming in a pot over the hearth. She was dressed in simple clothes of russet and green, a slender sword on her hip, a dagger to balance it, a muscular, full-hipped figure, broad shoulders and a face of brooding beauty beneath a mass of red-gold hair. She nodded to them as she swung her legs back over the bench and began to eat, clearly showing she did not wish to talk.

Their host dropped his voice. "I understand your fellow traveller to have experienced exceptional inconvenience to her person and her ambitions just recently. She has expressed some wish not to engage in conversation today. You will find all you need here, gentlemen. There is a servant about somewhere who will see to any particular needs, and I will return in a couple of hours to see what other aid we can supply. We do not discourage failed venturers in Agnesh-Val or we should never trade! It is our policy to help the failed ones just as we profit from the successful ones. This appears both fair and sane to us."

"And so it is, sir," said Wheldrake with approval. "You are of the Liberal persuasion, evidently. One hears so much Toryism as one travels throughout the rea . . . that is, the world."

"We believe in enlightened self-interest, sir, as I think do all civilised peoples. It is in the interest of the community and that larger community beyond to ensure that all are courteously and properly enabled to make what they wish of themselves. Will you eat, sir? Will you eat?"

Elric was aware of the woman's moody eyes regarding them as they spoke together and remarked to himself that he had not seen a face more lovely and more determined since Cymoril had lived. Her wide blue eyes were steady and unselfconscious as she chewed slowly, her thoughts unreadable. And then, suddenly, she smiled once before she gave her full attention to her food, leaving Elric with more of a mystery than before.

Having helped their deep plates to the stew, which gave off a delicious smell, they found themselves places at the table and ate for a while in silence until at last the woman spoke. There was unexpected warm humour in her voice and a certain heartiness which Elric found attractive. "What lie brought you this free meal, boys?"

"A misunderstanding, lady, rather than a lie," said Wheldrake diplomatically, licking his spoon and wondering whether to take a second trip to the cauldron.

"You are no more traders than am I," she said.

"That was the chief misunderstanding. Apparently they can imagine no other kind of traveller here."

"Apparently so. And you are recently here in this realm. By the river, no doubt."

"I do not understand the means," said Elric, still cautious.

"But you both seek the three sisters, of course."

"It seems that everyone does that," Elric told her, letting her believe whatever she wished. "I am Elric of Melniboné and this is my friend Master Wheldrake, the poet."

"Of Master Wheldrake I have heard." There was perhaps some admiration in the lady's voice. "But you, sir, I fear are unknown to me. I am called the Rose and my sword is called Swift Thorn while my dagger is called Little Thorn." She spoke with pride and defiance and it was clear that she uttered some kind of warning, though what she feared from them Elric could not guess. "I travel the time streams in search of my revenge." And she smiled down at her empty bowl, as if in self-mocking embarrassment at a shameful admission.

"And what do the three sisters mean to you, madam?" asked Wheldrake, his little voice now a charming trill.

"They mean everything. They have the means of leading me to the resolution of all I have lived for, since I swore my oath. They offer me the chance of satisfaction, Master Wheldrake. You are, are you not, that same Wheldrake who wrote *The Orientalist's Dream?*"

"Well, madam"—in some dismay—"I was but newly arrived in a new age. I needed to begin my reputation afresh. And the Orient was all the rage just then. However, as a mature work—"

"It is exceptionally sentimental, Master Wheldrake. But it helped me through a bad hour or two. And I still enjoy it for what it is. After that comes *The Song of Iananthe*, which is of course your finest."

"But Heavens, madam, I have not yet written the work! It is sketched, that's all, in Putney."

"It is excellent, sir. I'll say no more of it."

"I'm obliged for that, madam. And"—he recovered himself—"also for your praise. I, too, have some affection for my Oriental period. Did you read, perhaps, the novel which was just lately published—*Manfred; or, The Gentleman Houri?*"

"Not part of your canon when I last was settled anywhere, sir."

And while the pair of them talked of poetry, Elric found himself leaning his head upon his arms and dozing until suddenly he heard Wheldrake say:

"And how do these gypsies go about unpunished? Is there no authority to keep them in check?"

"I know only that they are a nation of travellers," said the Rose quietly, "perhaps a large nomad horde of some description. They call themselves the Free Travellers or the People of the Road and there is no doubt that they are powerful enough for the local folk to fear. I have some suggestion that the sisters rode to join the Gypsy Nation. So I would join it, too."

And Elric remembered the wide causeway of beaten mud and wondered if that had any connection with the Gypsy Nation. Yet they would not league themselves, surely, with the supernatural? He became increasingly curious.

"We are all three at a disadvantage," said the Rose, "since we allowed our hosts to assume we were victims of the gypsies. This means we cannot pursue any direct enquiries but must understand elliptically what we can. Unless we were to admit our deception."

"I have a feeling this would make us somewhat more unpopular. These people are proud of their treatment of traders. But of non-traders, we have not learned. Perhaps their fate is less pleasant." Elric sighed. "It matters not to me. But if you would have company, lady, we'll join forces to seek these sisters."

"Aye, for the moment I see no harm in such an alliance." She spoke sagely. "Have you heard anything of them?"

"As much as have you," said Elric, truthfully. Within him now a voice was speaking. He tried to quiet it but it would not be silent. It was his father's voice. *The sisters. Find them. They have the box. They have the box.* The voice was fading now. Was it false? Was he deceived? He had no other course to follow, he decided, so he might as well follow this one and hope, ultimately, it might lead him to the rosewood box and his father's stolen soul. Besides, there was something he enjoyed in this woman's company that he felt he might never find again, an easy, measured understanding which made him, in spite of his careful resolve, wish to tell her all the secrets of his life, all the hopes and fears and aspirations he had known, all the losses; not to burden her, but to offer her something she might wish to share. For they had other qualities in common, he could tell.

He felt, in short, that he had found a sister. And he knew that she, too, felt something of the same kinship, though he were Melnibonéan and she were not. And he wondered at all of this, for he had experienced kinship of a thoroughly different kind with Gaynor—yet kinship, nonetheless.

When the Rose had retired, saying she had not slept for some thirty-six hours, Wheldrake was full of enthusiasm for her. "She's as womanly a woman, sir, as I've ever seen. What a magnificent woman. A Juno in the flesh! A Diana!"

"I know nothing of your local divinities," said Elric gently, but he agreed with Wheldrake that they had met an exceptional individual that day. He had begun to speculate on this peculiar linking of fathers and sons, quasi-brothers and quasi-sisters. He wondered if he did not sense the presence of the Balance in this—or perhaps, more likely, the influence of the Lords of Chaos or of Law, for it had become obvious of late that the Dukes of Entropy and the Princes of Constancy were about to engage in a conflict of more than ordinary ferocity. Which went further to explaining the urgency that was in the air—the urgency his father had attempted to express, though dead and without his soul. Was there, in this slow-woven pattern that seemed to form about him, some reflection of a greater, cosmic configuration? And, for a second, he had a glimmering of the vastness of the multiverse, its complexity and variousness, its realities and its still-to-be-realised dreams; possibilities without end—wonders and horrors, beauty and ugliness—limitless and indefinable, full of the ultimate in everything.

And when the grey-haired man came back, a little better dressed, a little neater in his toilet, Elric asked him why they did not fear direct attack from the so-called Gypsy Nation.

"Oh, they have their own rules about such things, I understand. There is a status quo, you know. Not that it makes your circumstances any more fortunate . . ."

"You parley with them?"

"In a sense, sir. We have treaties and so forth. It is not Agnesh-Val we fear for, but those who would come to trade with us . . ." And again he made apologetic pantomime. "The gypsies have their ways, you know. Strange to us, and I would not serve them directly, I think, but we must see the positive as well as the negative side of their power."

"And they have their freedom, I suppose," said Wheldrake. "It is the great theme of *The Romany Rye*."

"Perhaps, sir." But their host seemed a trifle doubtful. "I am not aware of what you speak—a play?"

"An account, sir, of the joys of the open road."

"Ah, then it would be of gypsy origin. We do not buy their books, I fear. Now, gentlemen, I do not know if you would take advantage of what we offer distressed travellers by way of credit and cost-price equipment. If you have no money, we will take kind. Perhaps to be sure one of *those* books, if you like, Master Wheldrake, for a horse."

"A book for a horse, sir! Well, sir!"

"Two horses? I regret I have no notion of the market value. Book-reading is not a great habit among us. Perhaps we should feel ashamed, but we prefer the passive pleasures of the evening arena."

"As well as the horses, perhaps a few days' provisions?" suggested Elric.

"If that seems fair to you, sir."

"My books," pronounced Wheldrake through gritted teeth, his nose seeming more pointed than ever, "are my—my *self*, sir. They are my identity. I am their protector. Besides, though through the oddity of some telepathy we all enjoy, we can *understand* language, we cannot *read* it. Did you know that, sir? The ability does not extend to that. Logical, in one sense, I suppose. No, sir, I will not part with a page!"

But when Elric pointed out that Wheldrake had already explained that one of the volumes was in a language even he did not know and suggested that their lives might depend upon acquiring horses and throwing in with the Rose, who already had her horse, Wheldrake at last consented to part with the *Omar Khayyám* he had hoped one day to read.

So Elric, Wheldrake and the Rose all three rode back down the white road beside the river, back to where they had joined the trail on the previous day, but now they remained on the path, letting it carry them slowly and sinuously southward, following the lazy flow of the river. And Wheldrake sang his *Song of 'Rabia* to an entranced Rose, while Elric rode some distance ahead, wondering if he had entered a dream and fearing he would never find his father's soul.

They had reached a part of the river road Elric did not remember passing over and he was remarking to himself that this had been close to where the dragon had headed due south, away from the water's winding course, when his sensitive ears caught a distant noise he could not identify. He mentioned it to the others but neither could hear it. Only after another half-hour had passed did the Rose cup her hand to her ear and frown. "A kind of rushing. A sort of roar."

"I hear it now," said Wheldrake, rather obviously piqued that he, the poet, should be the least well-tuned. "I did not know you meant that rushing, roaring kind of noise. I had understood it to be a feature of the water." And then he had the grace to blush, shrug and take an interest in something at the end of his beaklike nose.

It was another two hours before they saw that the water was now gushing and leaping with enormous force, through rocks which even the most skilled navigator could not have negotiated, and sending up such a whistling and shouting and yelling it might have been a live thing, voicing its furious discontent. The roadway was slippery with spray and they could scarcely make themselves heard above the noise, could scarcely see more than a few paces in front of them, could smell only the angry water. And then the road had dropped away from the river and entered a hollow which made the noise suddenly distant.

The rocks around them still ran with water sprayed from above, but the near-silence was almost physically welcome to them and they breathed deep sighs of pleasure. Then Wheldrake rode a little ahead and came back to report that the road curved off, along what appeared to be a cliff. Perhaps they had reached the ocean.

They had left the hollow and were on the open road again where coarse grass stretched to an horizon which still roared, still sent up clouds of spray, like a silver wall. Now the road led them to the edge of a cliff and a chasm so deep the bottom was lost in blackness. It was into this abyss that water poured with such relentless celebration and when Elric looked up he gasped. Only at that moment had he seen the causeway overhead—a causeway that curved from the eastern cliff of a great bay to the western cliff—the same causeway, he was sure, that he had seen earlier. Yet this could not be made of beaten mud. The mighty curving span was woven of boughs and bones and strands of metal supporting a surface that seemed to be made of thousands of animal hides fixed one on top of another by layers of foul-smelling bone-glue—utterly primitive in one way, thought Elric, but otherwise a sturdy and sophisticated piece of engineering. His own people had once possessed similar ingenuity, before magic began to absorb them. He was admiring the extraordinary structure as they rode beside it, when Wheldrake spoke up.

"It's no wonder, friend Elric, nobody chooses to consider the river route below what is, I'm sure, the thing they call the Divide."

And Elric was forced to smile at this irony. "Does that strange causeway lead, do you think, to the Gypsy Nation?"

"Leads to death, disorder and dismay; leads to the craven Earl of Cray," intoned Wheldrake, the association sparking, as it did so often, snatches of self-quotation. *"Now Ulric takes the Urgent Brand and hand in hand they trembling stand, to bring the justice of the day, the terrible justice of the day, to evil Gwandyth, Earl of Cray."*

Even the admiring Rose did not applaud, nor think his verse appropriate to this somewhat astonishing moment, with the roaring river to one side, the cliffs and the chasm to another; above that a great causeway of primitive construction stretching for more than a mile from cliff to cliff, high over the water's spray—and some distance off the wide waters of a lake, blue-green and dreamy in the sun. Elric yearned for the peace it offered. Yet he guessed the peace might also be illusory.

"Look, gentlemen," says the Rose, letting her horse break into a bit of a canter, "there's a settlement ahead. Can it be an inn, by any happy chance?"

"It would seem an appropriate place for one, madam. They have a similar establishment at Land's End, in my last situation . . ." says Wheldrake, cheering.

The sky was overclouded now, dark and brooding, and the sun shone only upon the far-off lake, while from the chasm beside them came unpleasant booming noises, sounds like wailing human voices, savage and greedy. And all three joked nervously about this change in the landscape's mood and said how much they missed the easy boredom of the river and the wheat and would gladly return to it.

The unpainted, ramshackle collection of buildings—a two-storey house with crooked gables surrounded by about a dozen half-ruined outhouses—did, indeed, sport a sign—a crow's carcass nailed to a board. Presumably the indecipherable lettering gave a name to the place.

"'The Putrefied Crow' is good enough for me," says Wheldrake, seemingly in more need of this hostelry than the other two. "A place for pirate meetings and sinister executions. What think you?"

"I'm bound to agree." The Rose nods her pale red curls. "I would not choose to visit it, if there were any choice at all, but you'll note there's none. Let's see, at least, what information we can gain."

In the shadow of that causeway, on the edge of that abyss, the three unlikely companions gave their horses somewhat reluctantly up to an ostler of dirty, though genial, appearance, and stepped inside "the Putrefied Crow," to look with surprise upon the six burly men and women who were already enjoying such hospitality as the place offered.

"Greetings to you, gentlemen. My lady." One of them doffed a hat so trimmed in feathers, ribbons, jewels and other finery its outline was completely lost. All these folk were festooned in lace, velvet, satin, in the most vivid array, with caps and hats and helmets of every fanciful style, their dark curls oiled to mingle with the blue-black beards of the men or fall upon the olive shoulders of the women. All were armed to the teeth and clearly ready to address any argument with steel. "Have you travelled far?"

"Far enough for a day," said Elric, stripping off his gloves and cloak and taking them up to the fire. "And you, my friends. Do you come far?"

"Why," says one of the women, "we are the Companions of the Endless Way. We are travellers, always. Pledged to it. We follow the road. We are the free auxiliaries of the Gypsy Nation. Pure-bred Romans of the Southern Desert, with ancestors who travelled the world before there were nations of any sort!"

"Then I'm delighted to meet you, madam!" Wheldrake shook his hat into the fire, causing it to hiss and spit. "For it's the Gypsy Nation we seek."

"The Gypsy Nation requires no seeking," said the tallest man, in red and white velvet. "The gypsies will always come to you. All you must do is wait. Put a sign upon your door and wait. The season is near-ended. Soon begin the seasons of our passing. Then you shall see the crossing of the Treaty Bridge, by which we keep to our old trail, though the land has long since fallen away."

"The bridge is yours? And the road?" Wheldrake was puzzled. "Can gypsies own such things and still be gypsies?"

"I smell walkerspew!" One of the women rose, a threatening fist upon her dagger's hilt. "I smell the droppings of a professor-bird. There's nonsense in the air and the place for nonsense isn't here."

It was Elric who broke that specific tension, by moving easily between the two. "We are come to parley and perhaps to trade," he said, for he could think of no other excuse they might accept.

"Trade?" This caused a general grinning and muttering amongst the gypsies. "Well, gentlemen, everyone's welcome in the Gypsy Nation. Everyone who has the taste for wandering."

"You'll take us there?"

Again they seemed to find this amusing and Elric guessed few residents of this plane volunteered to travel with the gypsies.

It was clear to Elric that the Rose was deeply suspicious of this cut-throat half-dozen and not at all sure she wished to go with them, yet again she was determined to find the three sisters and would risk any danger to follow them.

"There are friends of ours gone ahead," said Wheldrake, ever the quickest wit in such situations. "Three young ladies, all very alike? Would you have made their acquaintance?"

"We are Romans of the Southern Desert and do not as a rule make small talk with the *diddicoyim.*"

"Ha!" exclaims Wheldrake. "Gypsy snobs! The multiverse reveals nothing but repetitions! And we continue to be surprised by them . . ."

"This is no time for social observation, Master Wheldrake," says the Rose severely.

"Madam, it is always time for that. Or what are we else, but beasts?" He's offended. He winks at the tall gypsy and raises his tiny voice in song. *"I'd rather go with the Gypsy Wild; And bear a Gypsy's nut-brown child!"* He hums the air. "Are you familiar with the ballad, good friends?"

And he charms them enough to make them ease their bodies more comfortably upon their benches and tell patronising jokes about a variety of non-gypsy peoples, including, of course, Wheldrake's own, while Elric's strange appearance soon gets him nicknamed "the Ermine," which he accepts with the equanimity with which he accepts all other names presented by those who find him unnatural and disturbing. He bides his time with a patience that has become almost physical, as if it is a shell he can strap around himself, to make himself wait. He knows he has but to draw Stormbringer for a minute and six gypsies would lie, drained of life and soul, upon the stained boards of the inn; but also, perhaps the Rose would die, or Wheldrake, for Stormbringer is not always satisfied merely with the lives of enemies. And because he is an adept, and no other person here, at the roaring edge of the world, has any inkling of his power, he smiles a little to himself. And if the gypsies take it for a placatory grin and tell him he's thin enough to wipe out a whole warren-full of rabbits, then he cares not. He is Elric of Melniboné, prince of ruins, last of his line, and he seeks the receptacle of his dead father's soul. He is a Melnibonéan and he draws upon this atavistic pride for all the strength it can give him, remembering the almost sensuous joy that came with the assumption of his superiority over all other creatures, natural and supernatural, and it armours him, though it brings back, too sharply, the pain in memory.

Meanwhile Wheldrake is teaching four of the gypsies a song with a noisy and vulgar chorus. The Rose engages the landlord in a discussion of the menu. He offers them rabbit couscous. It is all he has. She accepts it on their behalf, they eat as much of the food as they can bear, then retire to a mephitic loft where they sleep as best they can while a variety of bugs and small vermin search across their bodies for some worthwhile morsel, and find little. Elric's blood is never lusted after by insects.

Next morning, before the others wake, Elric creeps down to the kitchen and finds the water-tub, crumbling a little dragon's venom into a tankard, and muffling his own shrieks as the stuff punishes each corpuscle, each cell and atom of his being, and then his strength and arrogance return. He can almost feel the wings beating on his body, bearing him up into the skies where his Phoorn brothers wait for him. A dragon-song comes to his lips but he stifles that, too. He wishes to learn, not to draw attention to himself. It is the only way he can discover the whereabouts of his father's soul.

The other two find their travelling companion in jovial humour when they come down, already grinning at a joke concerning a famished ferret and a rabbit—the gypsies have a wealth of such bucolic reference, a constant source of amusement to them.

Elric's attempts at similar banter leave them puzzled, but when Wheldrake joins in with a string of stories concerning sheep and jackboots, the ice is thoroughly broken. By the time they ride towards the west cliff and the causeway, the gypsies have decided they are acceptable enough companions and assure them that they will be more than welcome in the Gypsy Nation.

"*Hark, hark, the dogs do bark*," warbles Wheldrake, still with his mug of breakfast porter in his hand as he leans upon his saddle and admires the grandeur of it all. "To tell you the truth of the matter, Prince Elric, I was growing a little bored with Putney. Though there was some talk of moving to Barnes."

"They are unsavoury places, then?" says Elric, happy to make ordinary conversation as they ride. "Full of sour magic and so forth?"

"Worse," says Wheldrake, "they are *South of the River*. I believe now I was writing too much. There is little else to do in Putney. Crisis is the true source of creativity, I think. And one thing, sir, that Putney promises is that you shall be free from Crisis."

Listening politely, as one does when a friend discusses the more abstruse or sticky points of their particular creed, Elric let the poet's words act as a lullaby to his still-tortured senses. It was clear that the venom's effect did not lessen with increasing use. But now, he knew, if their gypsy guides proved treacherous he would be able to kill them without much effort. He was a little contemptuous of local opinion. These ruffians might have terrorised the farmers of these parts, but they were clearly no match for trained fighters. And he knew he could rely on the Rose in any engagement, though Wheldrake would be next to useless. There was an air of awkwardness about him which made it clear that his use of a sword was more likely to confuse than threaten any opponent.

From time to time he shared glances with his friends, but it was clear neither had any idea of an alternative. Since the ones they sought had searched for the Gypsy Nation there could be no reason for not at least discovering what exactly the Gypsy Nation was.

Elric watched as the Rose, to release some of her anxiety no doubt, suddenly let her horse have free rein and went galloping along the narrow track beside the chasm while stones and tufts of clay and turf went tumbling down into the darkness and the roar of the unseen river. Then, one by one, the gypsies followed, galloping their horses with daredevil skill in the Rose's wake, yelling and hallooing, jumping up in their saddles, leaping and diving, as if all this were completely natural to them, and now Elric laughed joyously to see *their* joy, and Wheldrake clapped and hooted like a boy at the circus. And then they had come to the great wall of garbage, higher than anything Elric had seen earlier, where more gypsies waited at a passage they had made through the waste and they greeted their fellows with all manner of heartiness, while Elric, Wheldrake and the Rose were subjected to the same offhand contempt with which they treated all non-gypsies.

"They wish to join our free-roaming band," said the tall man in red and white. "As I told them, we never reject a recruit." And he guffawed as he accepted a somewhat over-ripe peach from one of the other gypsies' bags. "There's precious little to forage as usual. It's always thus at the end of the season, and at the beginning." He cocked his head suddenly. "But the season comes. Soon. We shall go to meet it."

Elric himself thought he felt the ground shivering slightly and heard something like a distant piping, a far-off drum, a drone. Was their god slithering along his causeway from one lair to the next? Were he and his companions to be sacrifices for that god? Was that what the gypsies found amusing?

"Which season?" asked the Rose, almost urgently, her long fingers combing at her curls.

"The Season of our Passing. Indeed, the *Seasons* of our Passing," said a woman spitting plum stones to the ashy filth of the ground. Then she had mounted her horse and was leading them through the passage, out onto the fleshy hardness of the great causeway, which trembled and shook as if from a distant earthquake and now, in the far distance, from the east, Elric looked down the mile-wide road and he saw movement, heard more noise, and he realised something was coming towards them even as they approached.

"Great Scott!" cried Wheldrake, lifting his hat in a gesture of amazement. "What can it be?"

It was a kind of darkness, a flickering of heavy shadows, of the occasional spark of light, of a constant and increasing shaking, which made the banks of garbage bounce and scatter and the carrion creatures rise in squawking flurries of flesh and feather. And it was still many miles off.

To the gypsies the phenomenon was so familiar they paid it not the slightest attention, but Elric, the Rose and Wheldrake could not keep their eyes away.

Now the rocking increased, a steady motion doubtless created partly by the free span of the road over the bay, until it was gentle but relentless, as if a giant's hand rocked them all in some bizarre cradle, and the shadow on the horizon grew larger and larger, filling the causeway from bank to bank.

"We are the free people. We follow the road and call no man our master!" sang out one of the women.

"Hear! Hear!" chirrups Wheldrake. "Hey-ho, for the open road!" But his voice falters a little as they draw nearer and see what now approaches, the first of many.

It is like a ship, but it is not a ship. It is a great wooden platform, as wide across as a good-sized village, with monstrous wheels on gigantic axles carrying it slowly forward. Around the bottom edge of the platform is a kind of leather curtain; around the top edge is built a stockade, and beyond that are the roofs and spires of a town, all moving on the platform, with slow, steady momentum, with dwellings for an entire tribe of settled folk.

It is only one of hundreds.

Behind that first comes another platform, with its own village, its own skyline, flying its own flags. Behind that is another. The causeway is crowded with these platforms, rumbling and creaking and, at turtle pace, ploughing steadily on, packing the refuse into the ground, making still smoother the smoothness of their road.

"My God!" whispers Wheldrake. "It is a nightmare by Brueghel! It is Blake's vision of Apocalypse!"

"It's an unnerving sight, right enough." The Rose tucks the tongue of her belt into its loop another notch and frowns. "A nomad nation, to be sure!"

"You are, it seems, pretty self-sufficient," says Wheldrake to one of the gypsies, who assents with proud gravity. "How many of those townships travel this way?"

The gypsy shakes his head and shrugs. He is not sure. "Some two thousand," he says, "but not all move as swiftly as these. There are cities of the Second Season following these, and cities of the Third Season following those."

"And the Fourth Season?"

"You know we have no fourth season. That we leave for you." The gypsy laughs as if at a simpleton. "Otherwise we should have no wheat."

Elric listens to the babble and the hullabaloo of the massive platforms, sees people climbing upon the walls, leaning over, shouting to one another. He smells all the stenches of any ordinary town, hears every ordinary sound, and he marvels at the things, all made of wood and iron rivets and bits bound together with brass or copper or steel, of wood so ancient it resembles rock, of wheels so huge they would crush a man as a dog-cart casually crushes an ant. He sees the washing fluttering on lines, makes out signs announcing various crafts and trades. Soon the travelling platforms are so close they dwarf him and he must look up to see the gleam of the greased axles, the old, metal-shod wheels, each spoke of which is almost as tall as one of Imrryr's towers, the smell, the deep smell of life in all its variety. And high above his head now geese shriek, dogs put their front paws upon the ramparts and bark and snarl for the pure pleasure of barking and snarling, while children peer down at them and try to spit on the heads of the strangers, shouting catcalls and infant witticisms to those below, to be cuffed by parents who in turn remark on the oddness of the strangers and do not seem over-enthusiastic that their ranks have grown. On both sides of them now the wheels creak by and from the sides are flung the pails of slops and ordure which form both banks, while here and there, walking behind the platforms, come men, women and children armed with brooms with which they whisk the refuse up onto the heaps, disturbing the irritated carrion eaters, creating clouds of dust and flies, or sometimes pausing to squabble and scrabble over a choice piece of detritus.

"Raggle-taggle, indeed," says Master Wheldrake, putting his huge red handkerchief to his face and coughing mightily. "Pray tell me, sir—where does this great road go?"

"Go, man?" The gypsy shakes his head in disbelief. "Why nowhere and everywhere. This is our road. The road of the Free Travellers. It follows itself, little poet! It winds around the world!"

4

On Joining the Gypsies.
Some Unusual Definitions
Concerning the Nature of Liberty.

And now, as Elric and his companions wandered in amazement amongst the advancing wheels, they saw that behind this first rank of moving villages came a vast mass of people; men, women and children of all ages, of all classes and in all conditions, talking and arguing and playing games as they went, some walking with an air of unconcerned familiarity in the wake of those pounding rims; others unaccountably miserable, hats in hands, weeping; their dogs and other domestic animals with them, like people on a pilgrimage. The mounted gypsies had disappeared by now, to join their own kind, and had no interest at all in the three they had found.

Wheldrake leaned down from his horse and addressed a genial matron, of the type which often took a fancy to him. His hat was swept from his red comb, his little bantam's eyes sparkled. "Forgive me for this interruption, madam. We are newcomers to your nation and thought perhaps we should seek out your authorities . . ."

"There are no authorities, little rooster, in the Gypsy Nation." She laughed at this absurdity. "We are all free here. We have a council, but it does not meet until the next season. If you would join us, as it seems you have already done, then you must find a village which will accept you. Failing that, you must walk." She pointed behind her without interrupting her stride. "Back there is best. The forward villages tend to be full of purebloods and they are never very welcoming. But someone there will be glad to take you in."

"We're obliged to you, ma'am."

"Many welcome the horseman," she said, as if quoting an old adage. "There is none more free than the gypsy rider."

On through this great march, which spanned the road from bank to squalid bank, rode Elric, Wheldrake and the Rose, sometimes greeting those who walked, sometimes being greeted in turn. There was in many parts a festive quality to the throng. There were snatches of song from here and there, a sudden merry barrel organ reel, the sound of a fiddle. And elsewhere, in rhythm with their stride, people joined in a popular chant.

"We have sworn the Gypsy Oath,
To uphold the Gypsy Law,
Death to all who disobey!
Death to all who disobey!"

Of which Wheldrake was disapproving on a number of moral, ethical, aesthetic and metrical counts. "I'm all for primitivism, friend Elric, but primitivism of the finer type. This is mere xenophobia. Scarcely a national epic . . ."

—But which the Rose found charming.

While Elric, lifting his head as a dragon might, to scent the wind, caught sight of a boy running at unseemly speed from beneath the wheels of one of the gigantic platforms and over to the banks of refuse (now being freshened by every settlement that rolled slowly by). The boy was trying to scramble up armed with pieces of board on hands and feet which were meant to aid his progress but actually only hampered him.

He was wild with terror now and screaming, but the chanting crowd marched by as if he did not exist. The boy tried to climb back to the road but the boards trapped him further. Again his cry was piteous over the confident chanting of the marching gypsies. Then, from somewhere, a black-fletched arrow flew, taking him in the throat to silence him. Blood ran from between his writhing lips. The boy was dying. Not a soul did more than flick a glance in his direction.

The Rose was forcing her horse through the people, shouting at them for their lack of concern, trying to reach the boy whose dying movements were burying him deeper in the filth. As Elric, Wheldrake and the Rose arrived it was clear that he was dead. Elric reached towards the corpse—and another black-fletched arrow came from above to bury itself squarely in the child's heart.

Elric looked back, enraged, and only Wheldrake and the Rose together stopped him from drawing his sword and seeking the source of the arrow.

"Foul cowardice! Foul cowardice!"

"Perhaps he committed a fouler crime," cautioned the Rose. She took hold of Elric's hand, leaning from her saddle to do so. "Be patient, albino. We are here to learn what these people can tell us, not challenge their customs."

Elric accepted her wisdom. He had witnessed far crueller actions amongst his own people and knew well enough how an outrageous deed of torture could seem like simple justice to some. So he controlled himself, but looked with even more wariness upon the crowd as the Rose led them on towards the next rank of moving villages, creaking with infinite slowness, no faster than an old man's pace, along the flesh-coloured highway, their long leather skirts brushing the ground as they advanced like so many massive dowagers out for an evening stroll.

"What sorcery powers those settlements," murmured the Rose as they moved, at last, through the stragglers, "and how can we get aboard one? These people won't chat. There is something they fear . . ."

"Clearly, madam." Elric looked back to where the boy had died, his sprawled corpse still visible upon the piled garbage.

"A free society such as this must pay no taxes, therefore can pay no-one to police it—therefore the family and the blood-feud become the chief instruments of justice and the law," said Wheldrake, still very distressed. "They are the only recourse. I would guess the boy paid for some relative's misdemeanour, if not his own. '*Blood for blood! groaned the Desert King, And an eye, I swear, for an eye. Ere this day's sun sets on Omdurman, the Nazarene must die!*' Not mine! Not mine!" he said hastily, "but a great favourite amongst the residents of Putney. M.C. O'Crook, the popular pantomime artist, wrote it, I was told . . ."

Believing the little poet merely babbled to comfort himself, Elric and the Rose paid him little attention, and now the Rose was hailing the nearest gigantic platform which approached, its skirts scraping and hissing, and from which, through a gap in the leather curtains, there strolled a man in bright green velvet with purple trimmings, a gold ring through his earlobe, more gold about his wrists and throat, a gold chain about his waist. His dark eyes looked them over, then he shook his head curtly and returned through the curtain. Wheldrake made to follow him, but hesitated. "For what, I wonder, are we being auditioned?"

"Let's discover that by trial," said the Rose, pushing her hair back from her face and flexing a strong hand as she rode towards the next slow-moving mass, to find a head poked out at her and a red-capped woman glancing at them without much curiosity before turning back in. Another and another followed. A fellow in a painted leather jerkin and a brass helmet was more interested in their horses than themselves, but eventually jerked his thumb to dismiss them, making Elric murmur that he would have no more to do with these barbarians but would find some other path and fulfil his quest that way.

The next village sent out a well-to-do old gypsy in a headscarf and embroidered waistcoat, his black velvet breeches tucked into white stockings. "We need the horses," he said, "but you seem like intellectuals to me. The last thing this village requires are troublemakers of that sort. So I'll bid thee fare-thee-well."

"We are valued neither for our looks nor our brains," said Wheldrake with a grin, "and only a little, it seems, for our horses."

"Persevere, Master Wheldrake"—the Rose was grim—"for we must find our sisters and it's my guess a village that will admit them will also have something in common with a village that will welcome us."

It was poor logic, reflected the albino, but logic, at least, of a sort, and he had nothing better to offer.

Five more villages inspected them and five more times they were rejected until out of a village that seemed smaller, and perhaps a little better-kept than most of the others, sauntered a tall man whose somewhat gaunt appearance was tempered by a pair of amused blue eyes, his attention to costume suggesting a pleasure in life belied by his features. "Good evening to you, gentlefolk," he said, his voice musical and a little affected, "I am Amarine Goodool. You have something interesting about you. Are you artists, by any chance? Or perhaps storytellers? Or you have, possibly, some affecting story of your own? As you see, we grow a trifle bored in Trollon."

"I am Wheldrake, the poet." The little coxcomb stepped forward without reference to his companions. "And I have written verse for kings, queens and commoners. I have published verse, moreover, in more than one century and have pursued the vocation of poet in more than one incarnation. I have a facility with metre, sir, which all envy—peers and my betters, sir, as a matter of fact. And I also have a certain gift for spontaneous versification, of sorts. *In Trollon, elegant and slow, dwelled Amarine Goodool, famed for his costume and his wit. To friends so valuable was he, they even saved his—*"

"And I am called the Rose and travel upon a quest for vengeance. My journey has taken me through more than one realm."

"Aha!" said Amarine Goodool. "You have followed the megaflow! You have broken down the walls between the realms! You have crossed the invisible barriers of the multiverse! And you, sir? You, my pale friend? What skills have you?"

"At home, in my own quiet town, I had some reputation as a conjuror and philosopher," said Elric meekly.

"Well, well, sir, but you would not be with this company if you had not something to offer. Your philosophy, perhaps, is of an unusual sort?"

"Fairly conventional, sir, I would say."

"Nonetheless, sir. Nonetheless. You have a horse. Please enter. And be welcome to Trollon. I think it very likely you will find yourselves amongst fellow spirits here. We are all a little odd in Trollon!" And he raised his head in a friendly bray.

Now he led them through the skirts of the village, into a musky darkness lit by dim lamps so that first it was possible to perceive only the vaguest of shapes. It was as if they had entered a vast stable, with row upon row of stalls disappearing into the distance. Elric smelled horses and human sweat and as they passed up a central aisle he could look down the rows and see the glistening backs of men, women and adolescents, leaning hard against poles reaching to their chests and pushing the huge edifice forward, inch by inch. Elsewhere horses were harnessed in ranks, also, trudging on heavy hoofs as they hauled at the thick ropes attached to the roof beams.

"Leave your horses with the lad," said Amarine Goodool, indicating a ragged youth who held out his hand for a small coin and grinned with pleasure at the value of what he received. "You'll be given receipts and so on. You'll be at ease for at least a couple of seasons to be sure. Or, if you are otherwise successful, for ever. Like myself. Of course"—he lowered his tone as he swung up a wooden stairway—"there are other responsibilities one must accept."

The long staircase led them, spiral by spiral, to the surface until they clambered out into a nondescript narrow side street from whose open windows people looked idly down without breaking their conversation. It was a picture of such ordinariness that it contrasted all the more with the scenes below.

"Are those people down there slaves, sir?" Wheldrake had to know.

"Slaves! By no means! They are free gypsy souls, like myself. Free to wander the great highway that spans the world, to breathe the air of liberty. They merely take their turn at the marching boards, as most of us must for some time in their lives. They perform a civic duty, sir."

"And should they not wish to perform such duty?" asked Elric quietly.

"Ah, well, sir, I can see that you are indeed a philosopher. Things so abstruse are beyond me, I fear, sir. But there are people in Trollon who would be only too pleased to debate such abstractions." He patted Elric amiably upon the shoulder. "Indeed, I can think of more than one friend of mine who will gladly welcome you."

"A prosperous place, this Trollon." The Rose looked through the gaps in the buildings to where similar villages moved at a similar pace.

"Well, we like to preserve certain standards, madam. I will arrange for your receipts."

"I do not think we plan to trade our horses here," said Elric. "We need to travel on as soon as possible."

"And travel you shall, sir. Travel, after all, is in our blood. But we must put your horses to work. Or, sir," he uttered a little snigger, "we shall not be travelling far at all, eh?"

Again a glance from the Rose stilled Elric's retort. But he was growing increasingly impatient as he thought of his dead father and the threat which hung over them both.

"We are only too happy to accept your hospitality," said the Rose diplomatically. "Are we the only people to join Trollon in recent days?"

"Did you have friends come ahead of you, lady?"

"Three sisters, perhaps?" suggested Wheldrake.

"Three sisters?" He shook his head. "I should have known if I had seen them, sir. But I will send enquiry of our neighbouring villages. Meanwhile, if you are hungry, I shall be only too happy to loan you a few credits. We have some wonderful restaurants in Trollon."

It was clear that there was little poverty in Trollon. The paint was fresh and the glass sparkling, while the streets were neat and clean as anything Elric had ever seen.

"It seems all the squalor and hardship is kept out of sight below," whispered Wheldrake. "I shall be glad to leave this place, Prince Elric."

"We might find ourselves in difficulties when we decide to end our stay." The Rose was careful not to be overheard. "Do they plan to make slaves of us, like those poor wretches down there?"

"I would guess they have no immediate intention of sending us to their marching boards," said Elric, "but I have no doubt they want us for our muscles and our horses as much as for our company. I do not intend to remain long in this place if I cannot quickly discover some clue to what I seek. I have little time." His old arrogance was returning. His old impatience.

He tried to quell them, as signs of the disease which had led to his present dilemma. He hated his own blood, his sorcery, his reliance upon his runesword, or other extraordinary means of sustenance. And when Amarine Goodool brought them into the village square (complete with shops and public buildings and houses of evident age) to meet a committee of welcome, Elric was less than warm, though he knew that lies, hypocrisy and deception were the order of the moment. His attempt to smile did not bring any answering gaiety.

"Gweetings, gweetings," cried an apparition in green, with a little pointed beard and a hat threatening to engulf his entire head and half his body. "On behalf of the Twollon weins-men and -morts, may we vawda yoah eeks with joy. Or, in the common speech, you must considah us all, now, your bwothahs and sistahs. My name is Filigwip Nant and I wun the theatwicals . . ." Whereupon he proceeded to introduce a miscellaneous group of people with odd-sounding names, peculiar accents and unnatural complexions whose appearance seemed to fill Wheldrake with horrified recognition. "It could be the Putney Fine Arts Society," he murmured, "or worse, the Surbiton Poetasters— I have been a reluctant guest of them both, and many more. Ilkley, as I recall, was the worst . . ." and he lapsed into his own gloomy contemplations as, with a smile no more convincing than the albino's, he suffered the roll-call of parochial fame, until he opened his little beak to a sky still filled with cloud and spray and began a kind of protective declamation which had him surrounded at once by green, black and purple velvet, by rustling brocade and romantic lace, by the scent of a hundred garden flowers and herbs, by the gypsy literati. And borne away.

The Rose and Elric also had their share of temporary acolytes. This was clearly a village of some wealth, which yearned for novelty.

"We're very cosmopolitan, you know, in Trollon. Like most of the 'diddi-coyim' (ha, ha) villages, we are now almost wholly made up from outsiders. I, myself, am an outsider. From another realm, you know. From Heeshigrowinaaz, actually. Are you familiar—?" A middle-aged woman with an elaborate wig and considerable paint linked her bangled arm in Elric's. "I'm Parapha Foz. My husband's Barraban Foz, of course. Isn't it boring?"

"I have the feeling," said the Rose in an undertone as she went by with her own burden of enthusiasts, "that this is to be the greatest ordeal of them all . . ."

But it seemed to Elric that she was also amused, especially by his own expression.

And he bowed, with graceful irony, to the inevitable.

There followed a number of initiating rituals with which Elric was unfamiliar, but which Wheldrake dreaded as being all too familiar, and the Rose accepted, as if she, too, had once known such experiences better.

There were meals and speeches and performances, tours of the oldest and quaintest parts of the village, small lectures on its history and its architecture and how wonderfully it had been restored until Elric, brooding always on his father's stolen soul, wished that they would turn into something with which he could more easily contend—like the hopping, slittering, drooling monsters of Chaos or some unreasonable demigod. He had rarely wished so longingly to draw his sword and let it silence this mélange of prejudice, semi-ignorance, snobbery and received opinion, of loud, superior voices so thoroughly reassured by all they met and read that they believed themselves confidently, un-vulnerably, totally in control of reality . . .

And all the while Elric thought of the poor souls below, pressing their bodies against the marching boards and sending this village, in concert with all the other free gypsy villages, in its relentless progress, inch by inch, around the world.

Unused to gaining the information he required by any means less direct than torture, Elric left it to the Rose to glean whatever she could and eventually, when they were alone together, Wheldrake having been taken as a trophy to sport at some dinner, she relaxed into a mood of satisfaction. They had been given adjoining rooms in what they were assured was the best inn of its sort in any of the second-rank villages. Tomorrow, they were told, they would be shown what apartments were available to them.

"We have survived this first day well, I think," she said, sitting on a chest to remove her doeskin boots. "We have proven interesting enough to them so that we still have our lives, relative liberty and, most important now, I think, our swords . . ."

"You mistrust them thoroughly, then?" The albino looked curiously at the Rose as she shook out her pale red-gold hair and peeled off her brown jerkin to reveal a blouse of dark yellow. "I have never encountered such folk before."

"Save that they are drawn from every part of the multiverse, they are very much of a type I left behind me long ago and like poor Wheldrake hoped never to encounter again. The sisters reached the Gypsy Nation less than a week before we did. The woman who told me this had it from a woman she knows in the next village. The sisters, however, were accepted by a village of the forward rank."

"And we can find them there?" Elric knew so much relief he only then realised how desperate he had become.

"Not so easily. We have no invitation to visit the village. There are forms to be observed before we can receive such an invitation. However, I also learned that Gaynor, of whom you spoke, is here, though he disappeared almost immediately and no-one has any notion of his whereabouts."

"He has not left the Nation?"

THE REVENGE OF THE ROSE

"I gather that is not easily done, even by the likes of Gaynor." There was suddenly an extra bitterness to her voice.

"It is forbidden?"

"Nothing," she echoed sardonically, "is forbidden in the Gypsy Nation. Unless," she added, "it is change of any kind!"

"Then why was the boy killed?"

"They tell me they know nothing about it. They told me they thought I was probably mistaken. They said they felt it was morbid to study the garbage heaps and think one saw things lurking in them. In short, as far as they are concerned, no boy was killed."

"He was trying to escape, however. We both saw that. From what, my lady?"

"They will not say, Prince Elric. There are subjects forbidden by good manners, it seems. As in many societies, I suppose, where the very fundamentals of their existence are the subject of the deepest taboos. What is this terror of reality, I wonder, which plagues the human spirit?"

"I am not, at present, looking for the answers to such questions, madam," said Elric, finding even the Rose's speculations irritating after so much babble. "My own view is that we should leave Trollon and head back to the village which accepted the three sisters. Did they know the name?"

"Duntrollin. Odd that they should accept the sisters at all. They are some kind of warrior-order, I understand, pledged to the defence of the road and its travellers. The Gypsy Nation is comprised of thousands of such mobile cantons, each with its peculiar contribution to the whole. A dream of democratic perfection, one might suppose."

"Were it not for the marching boards," said Elric, disturbed, even now, to know that as he prepared himself for rest, the great platform on which all this existed was being pushed gradually forward by emaciated men, women and children.

He slept badly that night, though he was not plagued by his usual nightmares. And for that small mercy he was grateful.

Breakfasting in a common hall, still hygienically free of any sign of a real commoner, served by young women in peasant frocks who found their work amusing rather than arduous, like children in a play, the three friends again shared what little they had discovered.

"They never stop moving," said Wheldrake. "The very thought is hideous to them. They believe their entire society will be destroyed if once they bring this vast caravan to a halt. So their *hoi polloi*, whatever their circumstances, push, with or without the help of horses, the villages on. And it is debtors and vagabonds and defaulters and creators of minor grievances who make up the throng walking on the road. These are, as it were, middle-class offenders of no great consequence. The fear of all is that they should join those at the marching boards and therefore lose their status and most chances of regaining it again. Their morals and their laws are based upon the rock, as it were, of perpetual motion. The boy wanted to stop walking, I gather, and there is only one rule where that is concerned—Move or Die. And Move Forward Always. I've lived in Gloriana's age, and Victoria's, and Elizabeth's, yet never have I encountered quite such fascinating and original hypocrisies."

"Are there no exceptions? Must everyone constantly move?" asked the Rose.

"There are no exceptions." Wheldrake helped himself to a dish of mixed meats and cheeses. "I must say that their standard of cuisine is excellent. One becomes so grateful for such things. If you were ever, for instance, in Ripon and had a positive dislike of the pie, you would starve." He poured himself a little light beer. "So we have our sisters. We believe Gaynor could be with them. We now need an invitation to Duntrollin, I take it. Which reminds me, why have they not asked you to give up your weapons? None here appears to sport a blade."

"I think they might be our next means of earning a season or two away from the boards," said Elric, who had also considered this. "They have no need to demand them. They will, they believe, possess them soon—for rent, or food or whatever it is they know people always prefer to liberty . . ." And he chewed moodily on his bread and stared into the middle distance, lost in some unhappy memory.

"Thus by deep injustice is that Unjust State upheld;
Thus by gags of deedless piety old Albion's voice is still'd."

intoned the little poet, rather mournful himself. "Is there no luxury that is not the creation of someone else's misery?" he wondered. "Was there ever a world where all were equal?"

"Oh, indeed," said the Rose with some alacrity. "Indeed, there was. My own!" And then she hesitated, thought better of her outburst, and fell silent over her porridge, leaving the others at something of a loss for conversation.

"Why, I wonder, are we discouraged from leaving this paradise?" said Elric at last. "How does the Gypsy Nation justify its strictures?"

"By one of a thousand similar arguments, friend Elric, I'm sure. Something circular, no doubt. And singularly apt, all in all. One is never short of metaphors as one travels the multiverse."

"I suppose not, Master Wheldrake. But perhaps that circular argument is the only means by which any of us rationalises their existence?"

"Indeed, sir. Quite likely."

And now the Rose was joining in with *sotto voce* reminders to Wheldrake that they were not here as Detectives of the Abstract but were searching with some urgency for the three sisters, who carried with them certain objects of power—or, at least, a key to the discovery of those objects. Wheldrake, knowing his own weakness for such tempting trains of thought, apologised. But before they could resume the subject of leaving Trollon and somehow gaining access to Duntrollin the outer doors of the room swung inwards to reveal a magnificent figure, all ballooning silks and lace, a mighty wig staggering on his head and his exquisite face painted with all the subtlety of a Jharkorian concubine.

"Forgive my interrupting your breakfast. My name is Vailadez Rench, at your service. I am here, dear friends, to offer you a choice of accommodation, so that you may begin to fit in with our community as quickly as possible. I gather you have the means of taking quarters of the better type?"

Having no choice for the moment, unless they were to arouse the Trollonian's suspicions, they followed meekly in Vailadez Rench's wake as the tall exquisite led them through the tidy and rather over-polished lanes of his picturesque little town. And still, inch by inch, the Gypsy Nation rolled on along the road it had beaten for centuries, creating a momentum that must be maintained above all other considerations. And forever returning to the identical point of arrival and departure.

They were shown a house upon the edge of the platform, looking out over the walls towards the distant walkers and the other snail-crawling settlements. They were shown apartments in quaint old gabled houses or converted from warehouses or stores, and eventually they were led by Vailadez Rench, whose sole conversation revolved, like some tight-wrought fugue, about the subject of Property, its desirability and its value, to a little house with a patch of garden outside it, the walls covered in climbing tea roses and brilliant nunshabit, all glowing purples and golds, the windows glittering and framed by lace, and smelling sweet and fresh as spring from the herb beds and the flowers; the Rose clapped her hands and for a moment it was clear she was tempted by the house, with its crooked roof and time-black gables. Something within her longed for such ordinary beauty and comfort. And Elric saw her expression change and she looked away. "It's pretty, this house," she said. "Perhaps it could be shared by all of us?"

"Oh, yes. It has a family, you see. Quite large. But they had their tragedies, you know, and must leave." Vailadez Rench sighed, then grinned and wagged a finger at her. "You've chosen the most expensive, yet! You have taste, dear lady."

Wheldrake, who had taken a gloomy dislike of this Paladin of Property, made some graceless remark which was ignored by everyone, for all their different reasons. He reached his nose towards a luscious paeony bush. "Is their scent here?"

Vailadez Rench rapped upon a door he could not open. "They were given their documents. They should be gone. There was some kind of disaster . . . Well, we must be merciful, I suppose, and thank the stars we are not ourselves sliding towards the board-hold and the eternal tramp."

The door was opened with a snap—wide—and there stood before them a dishevelled, round-eyed, red-faced fellow, almost as tall as Elric, with a quill in one hand and an inkpot in the other. "Dear sir! Dear sir! Bear with me, I beg you. I am at this very moment addressing a letter to a relative. There is no question of my credit. You know yourself what delays exist, these days, between the villages." He scratched his untidy, corn-coloured hair with the nib of his pen, causing dark green ink to run down his forehead and give him something of the appearance of a demented savage prepared for war. While his alert blue eyes went from face to face, his lips appealed. "I have such clients! Bills are not paid, you know, by dead people. Or by disappointed people. I am a clairvoyant. It is my vocation. My dear mother is a clairvoyant, and my brothers and sisters and, greatest of all, my noble son, Koropith. My Uncle Grett was famous across the Nation and beyond. Still more famous were we all before our fall."

"Your fall, sir?" asked Wheldrake, very curious and taking to the man at once. "Your debts?"

"Debt, sir, has pursued us across the multiverse. That is a constant, sir. It is *our* constant, at least. I speak of our fall from the king's favour, in the land my family had made its own and hoped to settle. Salgarafad, it was called, in a rim-sphere long forgotten by the Old Gardener, and why should it be otherwise? But death is not our fault, sir. It is not. We are friends to Death, but not His servants. And the king swore we had brought the plague by predicting it. And so we were forced to flee. Politics, in my view, had much to do with the matter. But we are not permitted to the counsels of the steersmen, let alone the Lords of the Higher Worlds, whom we serve, sir, in our own way, my family and myself."

This speech concluded, he drew breath, put one inky fist upon his right hip, the second, still holding the bottle, he rested across his chest. "The credits are," he insisted, "in the post."

"Then you can be found easily enough, dear sir, and reinstated here. Perhaps another house? But I would remind you, your credits were based upon certain services performed by your sister and your uncle on behalf of the community. And they are no longer resident here."

"You put them to the boards!" cried the threatened resident. "You gave them up to the marching boards. Admit it!"

"I am not privy to such matters. This property, sir, is required. Here are the new renters . . ."

"No," says the Rose, "not so. I will not be the cause of this man and his family losing their home!"

"Sentiment! Silly sentiment!" Vailadez Rench roared with laughter that held in it every kind of insult, every heartless mockery. "My dear madam, this family has rented property it cannot afford. You *can* afford it. That is a simple, natural rule, sir. That is a fact of the world, sir." (These last addressed to the offending debtor.) "Let us through, sir. Let us through. We uphold our time-honoured Right to View!" With which he pushed past the unfortunate letter-writer and drew the puzzled trio behind him into a dark passageway from which stairs led. From the landing peered bright button-eyes which might have belonged to a weasel, while from the stairs another pair of eyes regarded them with smouldering rage. They entered a large, untidy room, full of threadbare furnishings and old documents, where, in a wheeled chair made of ivory and boarwood, a tiny figure sat hunched. Again only the eyes seemed alive—black, penetrating eyes of no apparent intelligence. "Mother, they invade!" cried the besieged householder. "Oh, sir, you are cruel, to practise such fierce rectitude upon a frail old woman! How can she walk, sir? How can she move?

"She must be pushed, Master Fallogard! She will roll as we all roll. Forward, always forward. To a finer future, Master Fallogard. We work for that, you know." Vailadez Rench stooped to peer at the old woman. "Thus do we maintain the integrity of our great Nation."

"I had read somewhere," said Master Wheldrake quietly, stepping a little further into the room and inspecting it as if he truly intended to make it his home, "that a society dedicated solely to the preservation of her past, soon has only her past to sell. Why not stop the village, Master Rench, so that the old lady shall not have to move?"

"You enjoy these obscenities, I suppose, sir, in your own realm? They are not appreciated here." Vailadez Rench looked down his long nose—a stork offering a parakeet only disdain. "The platforms must *always* move. The Nation must *always* move. There can be no *pause* to the gypsy's way. And any who would *block* our way are our *enemies*! Any not invited to set foot on our road but who tread it in defiance of our laws—they are our *deadly* enemies, for they represent the many who would block our way and attempt to bring to a halt the Gypsy Nation, which has travelled, for more than a thousand times, the circumference of the world, over land and sea, along the road of their own making. The Free Road of the Free Gypsy People!"

"I, too, was taught schoolboy litanies to explain the follies of my own country," said Wheldrake, turning away. "I have no quarrel with such wounded, needy souls as yourself, who must chant a creed as some kind of primitive charm against the unknown. It seems to me, as I travel the multiverse, that reliance upon such insistencies is what all mortals have in common. Million upon million of different tribes, each with its own fiercely defended truth."

"Bravo, sir!" cries Fallogard Phatt with a wave of his generous quill (and ink goes flying over mother, books and papers), "but do not elaborate on such sentiments, I warn you! They are mine. They are my whole family's, yet they are forbidden here, as in so many worlds. Do not speak so frankly, sir, lest you'd follow my uncle and my sister to the boards and the Long Stroll to Oblivion."

"Heretic! You have no right to such fine property!" Vailadez Rench's lugubrious features twist with dismay, his delicate paint glowing from the heat of his own offended blood, as if some exotic fruit of Eden had bloomed and given voice simultaneously. "Evictors must be summoned and that will not be pleasant for Fallogard Phatt and the Family Phatt!"

"What remains of it," grumbles Phatt, suddenly downhearted, as if he had always anticipated his defeat. "I have a dozen futures. Which to pick?" And he closes his eyes and screws up his face as if he, too, has sipped a dragon's diluted venom, and he lets out a great keening noise, the cry of a wronged soul, the despairing voice of a creature which sees Justice suddenly as a Chimera and all displays of it a mere Charade. "A dozen futures, but still no fairness for the common folk! Where does this Tanelorn, this paradise, exist?"

And Elric, who is the only one Phatt is ever likely to meet who could supply him with anything but a metaphysical answer, remains silent, for in Tanelorn he took a vow as all do who receive her protection and her peace. Only true seekers after peace shall find Tanelorn, for Tanelorn is a secret carried by every mortal. And Tanelorn exists wherever mortals gather in mutual determination to serve the common good, creating as many paradises as there are human souls . . .

"I was told," he said, "that it exists within oneself."

At which Fallogard Phatt laid down his pen and ink, picked up a sack in which he had already, it appeared, packed his necessities, and began with downcast eyes to wheel his old mother from the room, calling out for the other members of his family as he did so.

Vailadez Rench watched them trail off with their bundles and their keepsakes and sniffed with considerable satisfaction as he looked around the house. "A lick of paint will soon brighten this property," he assured them, "and we will, of course, have all this clutter sent for salvage and put to efficient use. We are well rid, I'm sure you will agree, of the Family Phatt and that disgusting valetudinarian!"

By now Elric's self-control was growing weak and had it not been for the Rose's steady eyes upon him, for Wheldrake's grim and furious silence, he would have spoken his mind. As it was, the Rose approved the house, agreed the lease and accepted the keys from the fastidious fingers of that Sultan of

Sophistry, dismissed him swiftly and then led them in hurried pursuit of the exiled debtors, sighting them as they made their way slowly towards the nearest downside stairway.

Elric saw her catch up with Fallogard Phatt, place a comforting hand upon the shoulder of an adolescent girl, whisper a word in the ear of the mother, give a friendly tug to the hair of the boy, and bring them, bewildered, back with her. "They are to live with us—or at least upon our credit. That cannot, surely, be against even the Gypsy Nation's peculiar sense of security."

Elric regarded the threadbare group with some dismay, having no wish to burden himself with a family, especially one which seemed to him so feckless. He glanced at the girl, dark and petulant in her blossoming beauty, her expression one of almost permanent contempt for everything she looked upon, while the boy, aged about ten, had the black eyes he had noted on the stairs: the weasel's alert and eager eyes, and a narrow, pointed face to add to the effect, his long, blond hair slicked hard against his skull, his small-fingered hands twitching and eager, the nose questing, as if he already scented vermin. And when he grinned, in grateful understanding of the Rose's charity, he revealed sharp little teeth, white against the moist redness of his lips. "You shall see an end to your quest, lady," he said. "Blood and sap shall blend again—lest Chaos decide to challenge this prognosis. There is a road between the worlds that leads to a better place than the one on which we travel. You must take the Infinite Path, lady, and look at the end of it for the resolution to your troubles."

Instead of responding with puzzlement or fear to his strange words, the Rose smiled and bent to kiss him. "Clairvoyant, all of you?" she asked.

"It is the chief business of the Family Phatt," said Fallogard Phatt with some dignity. "It has always been our privilege to read the cards, see through the crystal's mist and know the future such as it ever can be foretold with any certainty. Which is why, of course, we were not unhappy when we found we must join the Gypsy Nation. But, we discovered, these folk have no true clairvoyance, merely a collection of tricks and illusions with which to impress or control others. Once their people had the richest powers of all. They dissipated, little by little, on their pointless march around the world. They gave them up for security you see, And now we, too, have no use for our powers . . ." He sighed and scratched rapidly at himself in several places, adjusting buttons and loops and ties as he did so, as if he only just realised his dishevelled condition. "What are we to do? Should we become walkers, we shall inevitably be doomed to end our days at the marching boards."

"We would join forces with you," Elric heard the Rose say, and he looked at her in surprise. "We have the power to help you against the jurisdiction of the Gypsy Nation. And you have the power to help us find what we seek here. There are three sisters we must discover. Perhaps they have another with them now, an armoured man whose face is never revealed."

"It is my mother you must ask in that respect," said Fallogard Phatt absently, as he considered her words. "And my niece. Charion has all her grandmother's skills, I think, though she must learn more wisdom yet . . ."

The girl glared at him, but she seemed flattered.

"It is my boy, Koropith Phatt, who is the greatest of all Phatts," said his father, laying a proud and perhaps proprietorial hand upon the infant, whose little black eyes regarded his father with amused affection and a certain knowing sympathy. "There has never *been* a Phatt as full of the gift as Koropith. He is *brimming* with psychic advantages!"

"Then he and we must come to our arrangements quickly," said the Rose. "For the time is here when we must seek a means of charting a specific course between the worlds. If we can free you, can you lead us where we must go?"

"I have that ability, at least," said Fallogard Phatt, "and will gladly aid you however I can. But the boy has found pathways through the realms I had not even heard rumoured. And the girl can seek out an individual through all the layers of the multiverse. She is a bloodhound, that child. She is a terrier. She is a spaniel . . ."

Interrupting this effusion of canine comparisons, Master Wheldrake found a book in one of his inner pockets and drew it forth with a flourish. "Here's what I remembered having! Here it is!"

They looked at him in polite expectation as he pulled his newly received credits from his waistcoat and pushed them into the hands of the baffled boy. "Here, young Master Koropith, go with your cousin to the market! I'll give you a list. Tonight I intend to make us all a meal substantial enough to help us through our coming adventure!"

He brandished the scarlet book. "Between Mrs Beeton and myself I think I can provide us with a supper the like of which you'll not have tasted in a twelvemonth!"

5

Conversations with Clairvoyants Concerning the Nature of the Multiverse &c. Dramatic Methods of Escape.

The elaborate and exquisite feast over, and soothed by a recitation of some excellent sonnets, even Elric was able to divert his attention, for a little while, away from the persistent memory of his dead father waiting for him in that dead city.

"We have lived by our wits, the Phatts, for generations." Fallogard Phatt was in his cups. Even his old mother put wine to her wizened lips and occasionally giggled. His son and niece were either in bed or hidden in the stairwell's shadows. Wheldrake refilled Mother Phatt's bumper while the Rose sat back in her chair, the only one determined to keep her mind upon the crucial issues of their circumstances. She drank no wine, but seemed content to let the others relax as they wished. Next to her around the table, Elric sipped the dark blue-black stuff and wished that it could have some effect upon him, reflecting sardonically to himself that after a draught of dragon's venom most drinks had something of an insipid quality . . .

"There are only a few adepts," Fallogard Phatt was saying, "who have ever explored even a fraction of the multiverse, but the Phatts, I must say, are as experienced as any. Mother here, for instance, has the routes of at least two thousand different pathways between some five thousand realms. Her instincts are occasionally a little dulled, these days, but our niece is learning well. She has the same talent."

"So you sought this plane deliberately?" said the Rose suddenly, as if his remarks coincided with her own thoughts.

This produced a wild peal of laughter in Fallogard Phatt, threatening to burst his thoroughly buttoned waistcoat while his hair sprang up around his head and his face grew red. "No, madam, that's the joke of it. Few here *ever* came because they had heard of the Gypsy Nation and wished to join it. But the Nation has set up its own peculiar field—a kind of psychic gravity—which draws many here who would otherwise be in limbo. It acts—in a psychic, but also in an oddly material way—as a kind of false limbo, a world of lost souls, indeed."

"Lost souls?" Elric now grew alert. "Lost souls, Master Phatt?"

"And bodies, too, of course. For the most part." Fallogard Phatt made a drunken movement with his hand then paused, as if he heard something, then peered with sudden intelligence into the albino's crimson eyes. "Aye, sir," he said in a quieter tone, "lost souls, indeed!" And Elric felt for a few seconds the sense of some benign presence within him, sympathetic and perhaps even protective. The sensation was quickly gone and Phatt was holding forth to Wheldrake on some jolly abstraction which seemed to excite them both, but the Rose was, if anything, more thoughtful as she glanced from Phatt to Elric and, frequently, at the busy head of little Mother Phatt, who sat with her two hands clutching her wine-cup, nodding and smiling and scarcely following, or caring to follow, the general drift, yet seemingly content and alert in her own mysterious way.

"I find it difficult to imagine, sir," Wheldrake was saying. "It is a trifle frightening, too, moreover, to contemplate such vastness. So many worlds, so many tribes, and each with a different understanding of the nature of reality! Billions of them, sir. Billions and billions—an infinity of possibilities and alternatives! And Law and Chaos fight to control all that?"

"The war is at present unadmitted," said Phatt. "Instead there are skirmishes here and there, battles for a world or two, or at best a realm. But a great conjunction is coming and it is then that the Lords of the Higher Worlds wish to establish their rule throughout the Spheres. Each Sphere contains a universe and there are thought to be at least a million of them. This is no ordinary cosmic event!"

"They fight to control infinity!" Wheldrake was impressed.

"The multiverse is not infinite in the strictest sense . . ." began Phatt, to be interrupted by his mother, suddenly shrill with irritability.

"Infinity? Loose talk! Infinity? The multiverse is *finite*. It has limits and dimensions which only a god may occasionally perceive—but they *are* limits and dimensions! Otherwise there would be no point in it!"

"In what, Mother?" Even Fallogard was surprised. "In what?"

"In the Family Phatt, of course. It is our firm belief that we shall one day—" And she left her son to recite the bulk of what was evidently the family creed . . .

"—learn the plan of the entire multiverse and travel at will from Sphere to Sphere, from realm to realm, from world to world, travel through the great clouds of shifting, multicoloured stars, the tumbling planets in all their millions, through galaxies that swarm like gnats in a summer garden, and rivers of light—glory beyond glory—pathways of moonbeams between the roaming stars.

"Why, sir, have you ever sometimes stood alone and seen visions? That moment, you recall, when you pause and are granted a glimpse of near-eternity, the multiverse? You might glance at a cloud or a burning log, you might notice a certain fold in a blanket, or the angle at which a blade of grass stands—it does not matter. You know what you have seen and it brings that larger vision. Yesterday, for instance—?" And he cocked an enquiring eye at the poet before receiving his new friend's approval to continue.

"—for instance, I look up at about noon. Silver light pours like water down the massed clouds, themselves vast floating asymmetric sea-beasts so large they are host to whole nations of other species, including, surely, Man? As if they entirely surfaced from their element, ready to plunge again into depths as mysterious to those below as oceans are to those above them." His face glowed a richer red with all this bright recollection, his eyes appeared to focus again upon those clouds, upon those monumental natural barges, like raised wrecks, alarmingly complete after millennia, alien beyond imagining, beyond any impulse of ordinary mortals to follow, which one's very soul yearned to forget, those obscenely ancient beast-ships grown insubstantial in their sudden element, this brilliancy of sun and sky, and gradually their outlines dim, turn grey and fade one into another until only the sun and the sky remain, witnesses of their unmourned passing. "Have they grown invisible or are they gone for ever, even from our blood's strange memory, that tiny speck of ancestral matter that informs our race's united soul? Would that be to say they never existed and never could exist? Many things existed before our ancestors ever lifted one webbed foot upon a steamy shore . . ."

And Elric smiled at this, for his race's memory went back before mankind's, at least in his own realm. His folk, older and unhuman settlers, pursued or banished or otherwise escaping through the realms, had been victims of a mighty catastrophe, perhaps of their own creation.

Memory follows memory, memory defeats memory; some things are banished only into the realms of our rich imaginings—but this does not mean that they do not or cannot or will not exist—they exist! They exist!

The last Melnibonéan thinks of his people's history and legends, and he tells his human friends some of what he knows and one day a human scribe will write these remembered words which will become in turn the foundation for whole cycles of myths, whole volumes of legend and superstition, so that a grain of a grain of pre-human memory is carried over to us, blood to blood, life to life. And the cycles turn and spin and intersect at unpredictable points in an eternity of possibilities, paradoxes and conjunctions, and one tale feeds another and one anecdote provides others with entire epics. Thus we influence past, present and future and all their possibilities. Thus are we all responsible for one another, through all the myriad dimensions of time and space that make up the multiverse . . .

"Human love," says Fallogard Phatt, turning his eyes from his vision, "it is finally our only real weapon against entropy . . ."

"Without Chaos and Law in balance," says Wheldrake, reaching for some cheese and wondering, idly, which terrorised region along the road provided that particular tribute, "we rob ourselves of the greatest possible number of choices. That is the singular paradox of this conflict between the Higher Worlds. Let one become dominant and half of what we have is lost. I cannot but sometimes feel that our fate is in the hands of creatures hardly more intelligent than a stoat!"

"Intelligence and power were never the same thing," murmurs the Rose, departing from her own train of thought for a moment. "Frequently a lust for power is nothing more than an impulse of the stupidly baffled who cannot understand why they have been treated so badly by Dame Fortune. Who can blame those brutes, sometimes? They are outraged by random Nature. Perhaps these gods feel the same? Perhaps they make us endure such awful trials because they know we are actually superior to them? Perhaps they have become senile and forget the point of their old truces?"

"You speak truth in one area, madam," said Elric. "Nature distributes power with about the same lack of discrimination as she distributes intelligence or beauty or wealth, indeed!"

"Which is why mankind," says Wheldrake, revealing a little of his own background, "has a duty to correct such mistakes of justice that Nature makes. That is why we must provide for those whom random Nature creates poor, or sick or otherwise distressed. If we do not do this, I think, then we are not fulfilling our own natural function. I speak," he said hastily, "as an agnostic. I am a thorough-going Radical, make no mistake. Yet it does seem to me that Paracelsus had it when he suggested . . ."

Whereupon the Rose, growing skilful at such things, halted his ascent into the realms of abstraction by enquiring loudly of Mother Phatt if she required more cheese.

"Cheese enough tonight," said the old woman mysteriously, but her smile was friendly. "Always moving. Always moving. Heel and toe, the walkers go. Heel and toe, heel and toe. All walking, my dear, in the hope of escaping their damnation. Unchanging; generation upon generation; injustice upon injustice; and sustained by further injustice. Heel and toe, the walkers go. Always moving. Always moving . . ." And she subsided almost gratefully into staring silence.

"Ah, such an infamous society, sir," says her son, with a sage nod, an approving wave of a biscuit. "Infamous. It is a lie, sir. A mighty deception, this 'free nation' that always seems to proceed, yet never changes! Is that not true decadence, sir?"

"Shall it be Engeland's fate, I wonder?" mused Wheldrake of some lost home. "Is it the fate of all unjust empires? Oh, I fear I see the future of my country!"

"Certainly it became the only future of my own," said Elric with a grin that revealed much more than it attempted to hide. "And that is why Melniboné collapsed like a worm-eaten husk, almost at a touch . . ."

"Now," says the Rose, "down to business." And she sketches a plan to move at night between the wheels and find Duntrollin, there to skulk amongst the marching boards until such time as they could gain the stairs—from there Fallogard Phatt would be their bloodhound, his clairvoyance focused to find the three sisters. "But we must discuss the details," she says, "there could be practicalities, Master Phatt, that I have overlooked."

"A few, ma'am, to be sure." Politely, he listed them. The flaps to the marching boards would be guarded. The warrior inhabitants of Duntrollin would almost certainly be prepared for such an attempt as theirs. He had never seen the sisters and therefore his gift would be unreliable. What was more, even when they had reached the sisters there was no certainty they would be welcomed by them. And then, how were they to leave the Gypsy Nation? The barriers of garbage were almost impossible to cross and the guardians always detected would-be escapers. Besides, it was useless for the Family Phatt to consider such things since they were trapped by that peculiar form of psychic gravity which brought so many poor souls to this road, to dwell upon it, or under it, for ever. "We are all of us trapped here by more than a few black-fletched arrows and a refuse heap," he said. "The Gypsy

Nation controls this world, my friends. It has gained a strange, dark power. It has struck bargains. It has harnessed something of Chaos to its own uses. That, I believe, is why they dare not stop. Everything depends on maintaining their momentum."

"Then *we* must stop the Nation moving," said the Rose simply.

"Nothing can do that, madam." Fallogard Phatt shook a sad and despairing head. "It exists to move. It moves to exist. That is why the road is never changed, but rebuilt, even when land has fallen away, as in the bay we shall soon be crossing. They *cannot* change the road. I put it to them, when we first arrived. They told me it was too expensive, that the community could not afford it. But the fact is they can no more break their orbit than can a planet change her course around the sun. And if we tried to escape it would be like a pebble attempting to escape gravity. We were told that our main concern here should be to stay in the villages but never *below* the villages!"

"This is a mere prison," says Wheldrake, still picking at the cheeses, "not a nation. It is a foul disturbance in the order of things. It is dead and maintained by death. Unjust and maintained by injustice. Cruel and sustained by cruelty. And yet, as we have seen, the folk of Trollon congratulate themselves upon their urbanity, their humanity, their kindness and their graceful manners: while the dead stagger under their feet, supporting them in all their self-deceiving folly! Producing this parody of progress!"

Mother Phatt's old head turned to regard Wheldrake. She chuckled at him, not mockingly but with affection. "My brother told them as much, and continued to tell them as much. But he died on the marching boards, nonetheless. I was with him. I felt him die."

"Ah!" said Wheldrake, as if he shared that death also. "This is an evil parody of freedom and justice! It is a lie of profound dishonesty! For while *one* soul in this world suffers what hundreds of thousands, perhaps millions, now suffer, they are culpable."

"They are fine fellows all, in Trollon," said Fallogard Phatt ironically.

"They are persons of good will and charity. They pride themselves on their wisdom and their equity . . ."

"No," says Wheldrake with an angry shake of his flaming comb, "they may accept that they are *lucky*, but cannot believe themselves either wise or good! For in the end such folk agree to any device which keeps them in privilege and ease, and so maintain their rulers, electing them with every show of democratic and republican zeal. It is the way of it, sir. And they do not ever address the injustice of it, sir. This makes them hypocrites through and through. If I had my way, sir, I would bring this whole miserable charade of progress to a halt!"

"Stop the progress of the Gypsy Nation!" Fallogard Phatt laughed with considerable glee, adding with pretended gravity, "Be careful, my dear sir. Here you are amongst friends—but in other circles such sentiments are the sheerest heresy! Be silent, sir. For your own sake!"

"Be silent! That is the perpetual admonition of Tyranny. Tyranny bellows 'Be silent!' even to the screams of its victims, the pathetic moans and groanings and supplications of its trampled millions. We are one, sir—or we are fragmented carrion which worms permit the false appearance of Life—corpses that twitch and tremble with their weight of maggots—the rotten carcass politic of an ideal freedom. The Free Gypsy Nation is an enormous falsehood! Movement, sir, is not Freedom!" Wheldrake drew furious breath.

From the corner of his eye, Elric saw the Rose get up from her chair and leave the room. He guessed that she had grown bored with the debate.

"The Wheel of Time groans and turns a million cogs which turn a million cogs again and so on, through infinity—or near infinity," said Phatt with a glance at his mother, who had closed her eyes again. "All mortals are its prisoners and its stewards. That is the inescapable truth."

"One may mirror the truth or seek to assuage it," said Elric. "Sometimes one can even try to change it . . ."

Wheldrake took a sudden pull on his bumper. "I was not raised to a world, sir, where truth was malleable and reality a question of what you made it. It is hard for me to hear such notions. Indeed, sir, I will admit to you that it alarms me. Not that I fail to appreciate the wonder of it, sir, or the optimism which you are, in your own way, expressing. It is just that I was born to trust and celebrate certain senses and accept that a great unchanging beauty was the order of the universe, a set of natural laws which, as it were, coincided in subtle ways with a mighty machine—intricate and complex but ultimately rational. This Nature, sir, was what I celebrated and worshipped, as others might celebrate and worship a Deity. What you suggest, sir, seems to me retrogressive. These, surely, are closer to the discredited notions of alchemy?"

And so the discussion continued until they all grew weary with the sound of their own voices and were not reluctant to seek their beds.

As Elric climbed the stairs, his lamp throwing enormous shadows on the lime-washed walls, he wondered at the Rose's sudden departure from the table and hoped that something had not offended her. Normally he would have cared little about such things, but he had a respect for the woman which went beyond mere appreciation of her intelligence and beauty. There was also an air of tranquillity about her which reminded him, in an odd way, of his time in Tanelorn. It was hard to believe that a woman of such evident integrity and wisdom was bent upon the resolution of a crude blood-feud.

In the narrow room he had chosen for himself, little more than a cupboard with a cot in it, he prepared himself for sleep. The Family Phatt had readily made them comfortable while involving themselves in only the minimum disruption, and had agreed to use their psychic powers in the service of the Rose's quest. Meanwhile, the albino would rest. He was weary and he was yearning deeply now for a world he could never know again. A world that he himself had destroyed.

Now the albino sleeps and his lean, pale body turns this way and that; a groan escapes the large, sensitive lips and once, even, the crimson eyes open wide and stare with terror into the darkness.

"Elric," says a voice, full of old rage and grief so great it has actually become a fixed aspect of the timbre, "my son. Hast thou found my soul? It is hard for me here. It is cold. It is lonely. Soon, whether I wish it or no, I must join thee. I must enter thy body and be forever part of thee . . ."

And Elric wakes with a scream that seems to fill the void in which he floats and his scream continues in his ears, finding an echo in another scream, until both are screaming in unison and he looks for his father's face, but it is not his father who screams . . .

It is an old woman—wise and tactful, full of extraordinary knowledge— who screams as if demented, as if in the grip of the most horrible torture, screams out "NO!"—screams "STOP!"—screams "THEY FALL—OH, DEAR ASTARTE, THEY FALL!"

Mother Phatt is screaming. Mother Phatt has a vision of such unbearable intensity her screaming cannot relieve the pain she experiences. And she becomes silent.

As the world is silent, save for the slow rumbling of the monstrous wheels, the steady, faraway sound of marching feet, never stopping, marching around the world . . .

"STOP!" cries the albino prince, but does not know what he commands. He has had just the merest glimpse of Mother Phatt's vision . . .

Now there are ordinary sounds outside his door. He hears Fallogard Phatt calling to his mother, hears Charion Phatt sobbing and realises there is uproar close to hand . . .

With his lamp relit and in his borrowed linen, Elric goes out upon the landing and sees through the open door Mother Phatt, bolt upright in her bed, her old lips flecked with foam, her eyes staring ahead of her, frightened and sightless. "They fall!" she moans. "Oh, how they fall. It should not come to this. Poor souls! Poor souls!"

Charion Phatt holds her grandmother in her arms and rocks her a little, as if she seeks to comfort a child wakened in a nightmare. *"No, Granny, no! No,*

Granny, no!" Yet it is evident from her own expression that she, too, has seen something utterly terrifying. And her uncle, beside himself—sweating, red, flustered, pleading, holding his own poor tangled head as if to shield it from bombardment, cries: "It is not! It cannot! Oh, and she has stolen the boy!"

"No, no," says Charion, shaking her head. "He went willingly. That was why you did not sense any danger. He did not believe there was any!"

"She plans this?" moans Fallogard Phatt in outraged disbelief. "She plans such *death*?"

"Bring him back," says Mother Phatt harshly, her eyes still blind to the world around her. "Get her back quickly. Find her and you shall save him."

"They went to Duntrollin to seek the sisters," Charion says. "They found them, but there was another . . . A battle? I cannot read in such confusion. Oh, Uncle Fallogard, they must be stopped." She grimaces in agony, clutching at her face. "Uncle! Such psychic disruptions!"

And Fallogard Phatt, too, is shaking with the pain of the experience while Elric, joined by Wheldrake, tries urgently to discover what it is they fear so much. "It is a wind howling through the multiverse," says Phatt. "A black wind howling through the multiverse! Oh, this is the work of Chaos. Who would have guessed it?"

"No," says Mother Phatt. "She does not serve Chaos, neither does she call on Chaos! Yet . . ."

"Stop them!" cries Charion.

And Fallogard Phatt raises long fingers in helpless despair. "It is too late. We are already witnessing the destruction!"

"Not yet," says Mother Phatt. "Not yet. There could be time . . . But it is so strong . . ."

Elric no longer bothered with thought. The Rose was in danger. Hurriedly the albino returned to his room and dressed, buckling on his blade. Wheldrake was with him as they left the house and ran through the wooden streets of Trollon, taking wrong directions in the unfamiliar darkness, until they found a stairway down to the marching boards and Elric, to whom caution was only ever a half-learned lesson, had drawn Stormbringer from its scabbard so that the black blade glowed with a formidable darkness and the runes writhed and twisted along its length, and suddenly was killing anyone with a weapon who sought to stop him.

Wheldrake, seeing the faces of the slain, shuddered and hardly knew whether to stay close to the albino or put a safe distance between them while Fallogard Phatt and what remained of the Family Phatt were themselves attempting to follow, carrying the old woman in her chair.

Elric knew only that the Rose was in certain danger. At last his patience had deserted him and it was almost with relief that he let the hellsword take its toll of blood and souls, while he felt a huge, thrilling vitality fill him and he cried out the impossible names of unlikely gods! He cut at the harnesses that held the horses, he struck at the chains which pegged the marchers to their boards, and then he had mounted a great black warhorse which whinnied with the sheer pleasure of its release and, with Elric clinging to its mane, reared, striking at the air with its massive hoofs, then galloped towards the opening.

From somewhere now could be heard a new sound—human voices yelling with mindless panic—and Mother Phatt sobbed still louder. "It is too late! It is too late!" Wheldrake took hold of one of the horses but it shook itself free and avoided him. He abandoned any further attempt to find himself a mount and instead ran in pursuit of the albino. Reaching the bottom of the staircase, Fallogard Phatt took hold of his mother's wheelchair while the old woman still opened her mouth in a wail of grieving terror. His niece covered her ears, running beside the chair.

Out into the night now—Elric a raging shadow ahead of them and the massive wheels of the ever-moving villages grinding inexorably forward—into a cold wind carrying rain—the wild night lit by the guttering fires and lamps of the walkers as they marched, of the distant villages of the first rank. There was a certain spring to the road now, which suggested they were approaching the bridge that spanned the bay.

Wheldrake heard snatches of song. He did not break his stride but forced himself to lengthen it, breathing expertly as he had once been taught. He heard laughter, casual conversation, and he wondered for a moment if this were merely a dream, with all the lack of consequence he associated with dreams. But there were other voices ahead—oaths and yells as Elric forced his horse between the walkers, hampered by so many bodies but refusing to use the runesword against this unarmed mass.

And behind him Mother Phatt grew quieter while her granddaughter's sobs grew louder.

Somehow Wheldrake and the Phatts were able to keep pace with Elric, even getting closer to him as he pushed on through the crowd and Mother Phatt cried "Stop! You must stop!" And all the folk of the Free Gypsy Nation who heard this obscenity upon an old woman's tongue drew away fastidiously, disgusted.

More confusion followed. Wheldrake began to wonder if they had not acted thoughtlessly, in response to a senile woman's nightmare. No wheel had stopped turning, no foot had ceased walking; everything was as it should be on the great road around the world. By the time they had made their way through the main mass and were able to move freely, Elric had slowed the horse to a canter, surprised not to be followed by the rest of Trollon's guard. Wheldrake, however, was prudent and waited until the albino had sheathed the great runesword before approaching him. "What did you see, Elric?"

"Only that the Rose was in danger. Perhaps something else. We must find Duntrollin swiftly. She was foolish to do what she did. I had thought her wiser than that. It was she, after all, who counselled us to caution!"

The wind blew harder and the flags of the Gypsy Nation cracked and snapped in the force of it.

"It will be dawn, soon," said Wheldrake. He turned to look back at the Family Phatt: three faces bearing the same stamp, of a fear so all-consuming it made them almost entirely blind to their surroundings. Imploring, wailing, shouting warnings, sobbing and shrieking, Mother Phatt led them in a hymn of unspeakable despair and pain. From which the free walkers discreetly removed themselves, casting the occasional disapproving glance.

Calmly onward moves the Gypsy Nation, wheels turning with steady slowness, propelled by her marching millions, making her perpetual progress around the world . . .

Yet there is something *wrong*—something profoundly alarming ahead—something which Mother Phatt can already see, which Charion can already hear and which Fallogard Phatt yearns with all his soul to avert!

It is only as the dawn comes up behind them, soaring pinks, blues and faint golds, washing the road ahead with pale, watery light, that Elric understands why Mother Phatt screams and Charion holds her hands over her ears, and why Fallogard Phatt's face is a tormented mask!

The light races forward over the great span of the causeway, revealing the lumbering settlements, the tramping thousands, the smoke and the dimming lamps, the ordinary domestic details of the day—but ahead—ahead is what the clairvoyants have foreseen . . .

The mile-wide span across the bay, that astonishing creation of an obsessively nomadic people, has been cut as if by a gigantic sword—sheared in a single blow!

Now the two halves rise and fall slowly with the shock of this catastrophe. That massive bridge of human bones and animal skins, of every kind of compacted ordure, trembles like a cut branch, lifting and dropping almost imperceptibly, with steady beats, while on the land-side the boiling waters release all their fury and the white spray makes rainbows high overhead.

One by one, with appalling deliberation, the villages of the Gypsy Nation crawl to the edge and plunge into the abyss.

To stop is obscene. They do not know how to stop. They can only die.

Elric, too, is screaming now, as he forces his horse forward. But he screams, he knows, at the apparent inevitability of human folly, of people who can destroy themselves to honour a principle and a habit that has long since ceased to have any practical function. They are dying because they would rather follow habit than alter their course.

As the villages crawl to the broken edge of the causeway and drop into oblivion, Elric thinks of Melniboné and his own race's refusals in the face of change. And he weeps for the Gypsy Nation, for Melniboné, and for himself.

They will not stop.

They cannot stop.

There is confusion. There is consternation. There is growing panic in the villages. But still they will not stop.

Through the falling mist rides Elric now, crying out for them to turn back. He rides almost to the edge of the causeway and his horse stamps and snorts in terror. The Gypsy Nation is dropping not into the distant ocean but into a great blossoming mass of reds and yellows, whose sides open like exotic petals and whose hot centre pulses as it swallows village after village. And it is then that Elric knows this is Chaos work!

He turns the black stallion away from the edge and gallops back through that doomed press to where Mother Phatt in her chair shrieks: "No! No! The Rose! Where is the Rose?"

Elric dismounts and seizes Fallogard Phatt by his lean, trembling shoulders. "Where is she? Do you know? Which village is Duntrollin?" But Fallogard Phatt shakes his head, his mouth moving dumbly, until at last all he can do is repeat her name. "The Rose!"

"She should not have done this," cries Charion. "It is wrong to do this!"

Even Elric could not condone what was happening, careless as he often was of human life, and he longed to call upon Chaos to bring a halt to the dreadful destruction. But Chaos had been summoned to perform this deed and he knew he would not be heeded. He had not believed the Rose capable of raising such formidable allies; he could scarcely accept that she would willingly permit such horror as thousands upon thousands of living creatures plunged into the abyss, their cries of terror now unified in the air, while overhead the white spray spumed and the rainbows glittered.

Then he had turned, hearing a familiar voice, and it was young Koropith Phatt, running towards them, his clothes in shreds and blood pouring from a score of minor cuts.

"Oh, what has she done!" cried Wheldrake. "The woman is a monster!"

But Koropith was panting, pointing backwards to where, as bloody and ragged as himself, her hair slick with sweat, her sword Swift Thorn in her right hand, her dagger Little Thorn in her left, staggered the Rose, with tears like diamonds upon her haggard face.

Wheldrake addressed her first. He, too, was crying. "Why did you do this? Nothing can justify such murder!"

She looked at him in exhausted puzzlement before his words made sense to her. Then she turned her back on him, sheathing her weapons. "You wrong me, sir. This is Chaos work. It could only be Chaos work. Prince Gaynor has an ally. He wreaks great sorcery. Greater than I could have guessed. It seems he does not care who or what or how many he kills in his desperate search for death . . ."

"Gaynor did this?" Wheldrake reached out to take her arm, but she resisted him. "Where is he now?"

"Where he believes I will not follow," she said. "But follow I must." There was an air of weary determination about the woman and Elric saw that Koropith Phatt, far from blaming her for his ordeal, had placed his hand in hers and was comforting her.

"We shall find him again, lady," said the child. He began to lead her back the way they had come.

But Fallogard Phatt intercepted them. "Is Duntrollin destroyed?"

The Rose shrugged. "No doubt."

"And the sisters?" Wheldrake wished to know. "Did Gaynor find them?"

"He found them. As did we—thanks to Koropith and his clairvoyance. But Gaynor—-Gaynor had possession of them in some way. We fought. He had already summoned aid from Chaos. He had doubtless planned everything in detail. He had waited until the Nation was approaching the bridge . . ."

"He has escaped? To where?" Elric already guessed some of the answer and she confirmed what he suspected.

She made a motion with her thumb towards the edge. "Down there," she said.

"He found his death then, after all." Wheldrake frowned. "But he wished to have as much company as possible, it seems, on his journey to oblivion."

"Who can say where he journeys?" The Rose had turned and was going slowly back towards the edge where now a village perched, half-toppled, her inhabitants wailing and scrambling, yet making no real attempt to escape. Then the whole thing had gone, tumbling down into that flaring manifestation of Chaos, to be swallowed, to be engulfed. "I would guess that only he knows that."

Leading his horse, Elric followed her. Her hand was still in Koropith's. Elric heard the boy say: "They are still there, lady. All of them. I can find them, lady. I can follow. Come." The boy was leading her now, leading her to the very lip of the broken causeway, to stand staring into the abyss.

"We shall find a way for you, lady," Fallogard Phatt promised, in sudden fear. "You cannot—"

But he was too late, for without warning both the woman and the boy had flung themselves into space, out over the pulsing, glowing maw that seemed so hungry, so eager for the souls which fell by their hundreds and thousands down. Down into the very stuff of Chaos!

Mother Phatt screamed again. It was one long, agonised scream that no longer mourned the general destruction. This time she voiced a thoroughly personal grief.

Elric ran to the edge, saw the two figures falling, dwindling, to be swiftly absorbed by the foul beauty of that voracious fundament.

Impressed by a courage, a desperation which seemed to him even greater than his own, he stepped backwards, speechless with astonishment—

—and was too late to anticipate Fallogard Phatt's single bellow of agonised outrage as the man pushed his mother to the lip of the broken causeway, hesitated for only a split second, then, with his niece clinging to his coat-tails, plunged after his disappearing child. Three more figures spun down through those pulsing, hungry colours, into the flames of Chaos.

Sickened, confused and attempting to control a fear he had never known before, Elric drew Stormbringer from its scabbard.

Wheldrake came to stand beside him. "She is gone, Elric. They are all gone. There is nothing you can fight here."

Elric nodded slowly in agreement. He stretched the blade before him then brought it up flat against his heaving chest, placing his other hand near the tip of the great broadsword on which runes flickered and glowed. "I have no choice," he said. "I would endure any danger rather than earn the fate my father has promised me . . ."

And with that he had screamed the name of his own patron Duke of Demons and had hurled his howling battle-blade, and his body with it, out over the Chaos pit, a wild, unlikely song upon his bloodless lips . . .

The last thing Wheldrake saw of his friend were crimson eyes glaring with a kind of terrible tranquillity as the Sorcerer Emperor was pulled remorselessly down into the flaming hub of that hellish abyss . . .

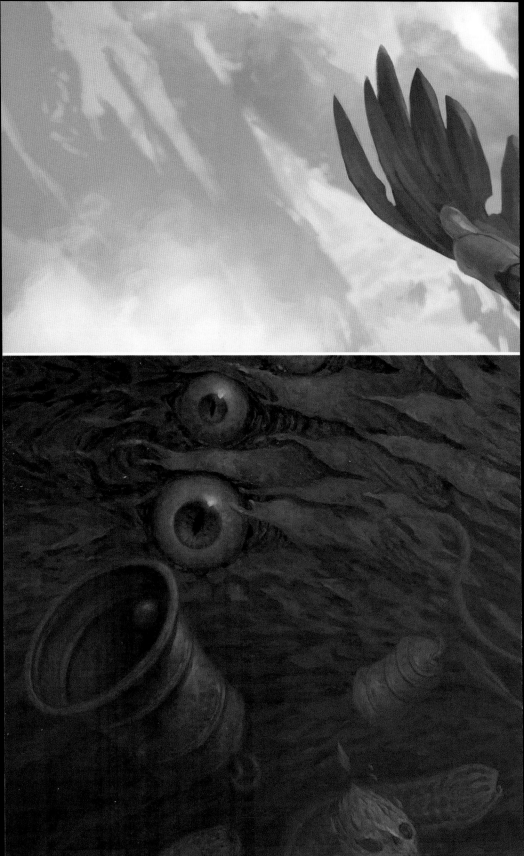

BOOK TWO

ESBERN SNARE;
THE NORTHERN WEREWOLF

Of the Troll of the Church they sing the rune
By the Northern Sea in the harvest moon;
And the fishers of Zealand hear him still
Scolding his wife in Ulshoi hill.

And seaward over its groves of birch
Still looks the tower of Kallundborg church,
Where, first at its altar, a wedded pair,
Stood Helva of Nesvek and Esbern Snare!

—Wheldrake,
Norwegian Songs

I

Consequences of Ill-Considered Dealings with the Supernatural; Something of the Discomforts of Unholy Compacts.

Elric fell through centuries of anguish, millennia of mortal misery and folly; he roared his defiance as he fell, his sword like a beacon and a challenge in his grip, down towards the luscious heart of Chaos while everywhere around him was confusion and cacophony, swift images of faces, cities, whole worlds, transmogrified and insane, warping and reshaping; for in unchecked Chaos everything was in perpetual change.

He was alone.

Very suddenly everything was still. His feet touched stable ground, though it was little more than a slab of rock floating in the flaming light of the quasi-infinite—universe upon universe blending one into the other, each ripple a different colour in a different spectrum, each facet a separate reality. It was as if he stood at the centre of a crystal of unimaginable complexity and his eyes, refusing the sights they were offered, somehow became blind to everything but the intense, shifting light, whose colours he could not identify, whose odours were full of hints of the familiar, whose voices offered every terror, every consolation and yet were not mortal. Which set the albino prince to sobbing, conquered and helpless as his strength drained from him, and his sword grew heavy in his hand, an ordinary piece of iron, and a soft, humorous song sounded from somewhere beyond the fires, becoming words:

"Thou hast such courage, sweetest of my slaves! Impetuous Champion of the Ever-Changing, where is thy father's soul?"

"I know not, Lord Arioch." Elric felt his own soul freeze on the very point of extermination, the imminent obliteration of everything he had ever been or would be—less than a memory. And Arioch knew he did not lie. He took away the chill. And Elric was soothed again . . .

He had never before experienced such a sense of impatience in his patron Lord of Hell. What emergency alarmed the gods? he wondered.

"Mortal morsel, thou art my darling and my dear one, pretty little sweet-meat . . ."

Elric, familiar with the cadences of his patron's moods, was both fascinated and afraid. Much that was in him wished for the approval of his patron at all costs. Much wished only to give itself up for ever to the mercies of Duke Arioch, whatever they might be, to suffer whatever agonies his lord decided, such was the power of that godling's presence, embracing him and coaxing him and praising him and blessed always with the absolute power of life or death over his eternal soul. Yet still, in the most profoundly secret part of his mind Elric kept a resolution to himself, that one day he would rid his world of gods entirely—should his life not be snuffed away the next second (such was his patron's present mood). Here, in his own true element, Arioch had his full power and any pact he had ever made with a mortal was meaningless; this was his own dukedom and here he required no allies, honoured no bargains and demanded instant compliance of all his slaves, mortal and supernatural, on pain of instant extinction.

"Speak, sweetmeat. What brought thee to my domain?"

"Mere chance, I think, Lord Arioch. I fell . . ."

"Ah, fell!" The word held considerable meaning, considerable understanding. "You *fell*."

"Into an abyss which only a Lord of the Higher Worlds could sink between the realms."

"Yes. You fell. IT WAS MASHABAK!"

Elric knew mindless relief that the rage was directed away from him. And he, too, understood what had occurred—that Gaynor the Damned had served Arioch's arch-rival, Count Mashabak of Chaos . . .

"You had servants in the Gypsy Nation, lord?"

"It was mine, that near-limbo. A useful device that many sought to control. And because he could not possess it for himself, Mashabak destroyed it . . ."

"Upon a whim, lord?"

"Oh, he served some creature's petty ends, I believe . . ."

"It was Gaynor, lord."

"Ah, Gaynor. He has become a politician, eh?"

Elric grew aware of his patron's brooding silence. After what might have been a year, the Duke of Hell murmured, with better humour, "Very well, sweetmeat, go upon thy way. But recollect that thou art mine and thy father's soul is mine. Both are mine. Both must be delivered up to me, for that is our ancient compact."

"Go where, patron?"

"Why, to Ulshinir, of course, where the three sisters have escaped their captor. And could be returning home."

"To Ulshinir, my lord?"

"Fear not, thou shalt travel like a gentleman. I shall send thy slave after thee." The Lord of the Higher Worlds had his attention upon other affairs now. It was not in the nature of a Duke of Chaos to dwell too long upon one matter, unless it was of monumental importance.

The fires went out.

Elric still stood upon that spur of rock, but now it was attached to a substantial hill, from which he could look down into a rugged valley, full of sparse grass and limestone crags across which a thin powder of snow blew. The air was cold and sharp and good to his senses and, though he was cold, he brushed vigorously at his naked arms and face as if to rid them of the grime of hell. At his feet something murmured. He looked down to see the runesword where he had dropped it during his audience with Arioch. He wondered at the power of his patron, that even Stormbringer felt compelled to acknowledge.

He raised the blade almost lovingly, cradling it like a child. "We have need of each other still, thee and I."

The blade was sheathed, the terrain inspected again, and he thought he saw a thread of smoke rising over the next hill. From there he might begin his search for Ulshinir.

He thanked chance that he had drawn on his boots before rushing in pursuit of the Rose, for he needed them now, against the jagged stones and treacherous turf down which he made his way. The cold was resisted with the expediency of dragon venom, again painfully absorbed, and in less than an hour he was striding down a narrow path to a stone cottage, thatched with peat and straw, which gave off the smell of earth, warmth and a wholesome fecundity, and was the first of several such dwellings, all as comfortably settled into the landscape as if they had grown naturally from it.

In answer to Elric's polite knock upon the gnarled oak door, a fair-skinned young woman opened it and smiled at him uncertainly, eyeing his appearance with a curiosity she attempted to disguise. She blushed as she pointed along the road to Ulshinir and told him it was less than three hours' easy walking from there, to the sea.

Gentle hills and shallow dales, a white limestone road through the mellow greens, coppers and purples of the grasses and heathers; Elric was glad to be walking. He wished to clear his head, to consider Arioch's demands, to wonder how Gaynor had come to lose the mysterious three sisters. And he wondered what he must find in Ulshinir.

And he wondered if the Rose still lived.

Indeed, he thought with some surprise, he cared if the Rose still lived. He was curious, he assured himself, to hear more of her story.

Ulshinir was a harbour town of steep-roofed houses and narrow spires, all with a scattering of early snow. The smell of wood-smoke, drifting through the autumnal air, somehow consoled him a little.

Within his belt he still had tucked a few gold coins which Moonglum had long ago insisted he carry and he hoped that gold was acceptable currency in

Ulshinir. The town certainly seemed of familiar appearance, very much like any town of the Northern Young Kingdoms, and he guessed this plane was close to his own part of the Sphere, at least, and possibly the realm. And this, too, gave him a little comfort. The few citizens he encountered upon the cobbled streets found his appearance strange, but they were friendly enough and were happy to point the way to the inn. The inn was spare, in the manner of such places in his own world, but warm and clean. He was glad of the nutty, full-bodied ale they brought him, of the broth and the pie. He paid for his bed in advance and, while his landlady was counting out considerable change in silver, he asked if she had heard of other visitors to the town—three sisters, in fact.

"Dark haired, pale beauties, with such wonderful eyes—not unlike your own in shape, sir, though theirs were of such a dense blue as to be almost black. And exquisite clothes and traps! There's not a woman in Ulshinir who did not turn out to get a glimpse of them. They took ship yesterday and their destination is the subject of considerable dispute amongst us, as you can imagine." She smiled tolerantly at her own weakness. "Legend says they're people from beyond our Heavy Sea. Were you a friend, perhaps? Or a relative?"

"They have a small thing that belonged to my father, that's all," said Elric casually. "They inadvertently took it with them. I doubt they know they have it! They had a boat, you say?"

"From the harbour yonder." She pointed through the window to the grey water enclosed by two long quays, each terminated by a tall lighthouse. There were only fishing boats moored there now. "The *Onna Peerthon*, she was. She calls here regularly with a cargo of haberdashery and needle-goods, usually, from Shamfird. Captain Gnarreh normally refuses passengers, but the sisters offered him a price, we heard, that he would have been a fool to refuse. But as to their destination . . ."

"Captain Gnarreh will return?"

"Next year, almost certainly."

"And what lies beyond your shores, lady?"

She shook her head and laughed as if she had never heard such a joke before. "First the island reefs and then the Heavy Sea. Should anything exist on the other side of the Heavy Sea—should it have a far side, indeed—then we have no knowledge of it. You are very ignorant, sir, if I may say so."

"You might say so, madam, and I apologise to you. I have been lately under some little enchantment and my mind is clouded."

"Then you should rest, sir, not be journeying towards the very edge of the world!"

"Which island might they have wished to visit?"

"Any one of a score, sir, would be my guess. If you like, I can find you an old map we have."

Gratefully Elric accepted her offer and took the map up to his room, poring over it in the hope that perhaps some instinct would direct his attention to the appropriate island. After half an hour of this, he was no wiser and was about to prepare for bed when he heard a sound below, a raised voice, that he thought he recognised.

It was with lifting heart that Elric, who had thought he would never see the man again, ran to the top of the stairs and looked down into the inn's main hall where a small red-headed poet, in frock-coat and trousers, waistcoat and cravat which looked as if they had come rather too close to a fire, declaimed some ode he hoped would buy him a bed—or at least a bowl of soup—for the night. "*Gold was the colour Gwyneth gave to Gwinefyr. And coral for cheeks, eyes blue as the sea. And bearing so perfect, so gracious, so fine. And lips red as Burgundy grapes, lush on the vine. These were the gifts she gave unto her tragic Queen. Her Queen of Caprice, by Tragedy Redeem'd.* Great Scott, sir! I thought you gone to perdition a year or more ago! It's good to see you, sir. You can help me with your Memoriam. I had so few particulars. I am afraid you will not like it. If I remember, it is not your preferred style. It tends, I will admit, to the Heroic. And the *ballade* form is considered merely quaint by many." He began to search his pockets for his manuscript. "It has gone, I fear, the way of the *triolet.* Or, indeed, the *rondel*—'*Lord Elric left his homeland weeping, For his dear young bride whom he loved of yore. We see him stand by the open door. While the sweet tears down her cheeks are creeping.'*—an attempt, dear friend, I must admit, to catch the popular taste. Such trifles have great general appeal and your subject, sir, I felt might attract public fancy. I had hoped to immortalise you, while at the same time—Aha! No, that is upon a Hugnit I met last week—and you will say that the *rondel* is inappropriate to epic form—but one has to *dress up* one's epics, these days—sweeten them in some way. And a few innocuous cadences do a great deal to achieve that end. I have no money, you see, sir . . ."

And the poor little fellow looked suddenly wan. He sat himself down upon a bench, his shoulders slumped, even his shock of red hair limp upon his avian head, his fingers screwing up miscellaneous pieces of paper in some unconscious pantomime of self-disgust.

"Why, then, I must commission a work from you," said Elric descending. He put a sympathetic hand upon his friend's shoulder. "After all, did you not tell me once that patronage of the artist was the only valuable vocation to which a prince might aspire?"

At which Wheldrake grinned, cheered by this confirmation of a friendship he believed gone for ever. "It has not been easy for me, sir, just lately, I must admit." There was a wealth of recent horror in the poet's eyes and Elric did not tax him on it. He knew himself that all Wheldrake wished to do at present was rid his mind of the memories. The poet had a momentary recollection and smoothed out the last piece of paper he had crumpled. "Yes, the *Ballade Memoriam*, I recall—I suppose it is a somewhat limited form. But for parody, sir—unexcelled! *A warrior rode death's lonely road, No lonelier road rode he* . . ." Again this brief revival of his old spark failed to ignite, as it were, the flashpan of his soul. "I am rather wanting, sir, I think, of food and drink. This is the first human settlement I have seen in several months."

And then Elric had the pleasure of ordering food and ale for his friend and watching him come slowly back to something like his old self. "Say what you will, sir, no poet ever did his best work starving, though he may have starved himself whilst doing the work, that I'll grant. They are different things, however." And he sat back from the bench, adjusting his bony bottom upon the boards, and belched discreetly before letting out a great sigh, as if only now could he afford to allow himself to believe that his fortunes had changed. "I am mighty glad to see you, Prince Elric. And glad, too, of your aristocratic conscience. I hope, however, you'll allow me to discuss the technicalities of the commission in the morning. As I remember, sir, you have only a passing interest in the profession of versification—questions of metre, rhyme—Licence, Poetic Combination, Mixed Metre—Orthometry in general—do not concern you."

"I'll take your advice on all of that, my friend." Elric wondered at his affection for the little man, his admiration for that strange, clever mind so thoroughly lost to its proper context that it must be forever grasping at the only constancies it had, those of the poetic craft. "And there is no haste. I would be glad of your company on a voyage I expect to be undertaking. As soon as a likely ship is free. Failing that, I might be forced to employ a little sorcery . . ."

"As a last resort, sir, I beg you. I've rather had my fill of wizardry and wild romance for the moment." Master Wheldrake took a conclusive pull upon his alepot. "But I seem to recall such stuff is as familiar to you, Prince Elric, as the Peckham Omnibus is to me, and I would rather link my fortune with one like yourself, who has at least some understanding of Chaos and her whimsical eruptions. So I shall be glad to accept both commission and companionship. I am mighty glad to see you again, sir." And with that he fell upon his own arm, snoring.

Then the albino prince took the little poet up and carried him, as if he were a child, to his room before returning to his own bed and his contemplation of the map—the islands of the great reef and, beyond it, darkness, an impossible ocean, unnavigable and unnatural, the Heavy Sea. Reconciled to hiring some fishing boat to visit the islands one by one, he fell into a deep sleep and was awakened by a scratching at his door and the bellow of some maid informing him that it was past the one thousand and fifteenth hour (their largest division of yearly time in Ulshinir) and there would be no breakfast for him if he did not rise at once.

He did not care for breakfast, but he was anxious to confer with Wheldrake on the subject of the three sisters and was somewhat surprised, once he had prepared himself for the day, to discover the poet declaiming on the very subject—or so it seemed . . .

"*Lord Soulis is a keen wizard,*
    A wizard mickle of lear:
Who cometh in bond of Lord Soulis,
    Thereof he hath little cheer.

"*He hath three braw castles to his hand,*
    That wizard mickle of age;
The first of Estness, the last of Westness,
    The middle of Hermitage.

"*He has three fair mays into his hand,*
    The least is good to see;
The first is Annet, the second is Janet,
    The third is Marjorie.

"*The firsten o' them has a gowden crown,*
    The neist has a gowden ring;
The third has sma' gowd her about,
    She has a sweeter thing.

"*The firsten o' them has a rose her on,*
    The neist has a marigold;
The third of them has a better flower,
    The best that springeth ower wold."

The inn's female servant, the landlady and her daughter, listened enraptured to Wheldrake's sing-song rendering. But it was the words that captured Elric's imagination . . .

"Good morning, Master Wheldrake. Is that a dialect of your own land?"

"It is, sir." Wheldrake kissed the hands of the ladies and strutted with all his old vigour across the room to greet his friend. "A border ballad, I believe, or something made very like one . . ."

"You did not write it?"

"I cannot answer you honestly, Prince Elric." Wheldrake sat down on the bench opposite the albino and watched him sip a dish of stewed herbs. "Have some honey in that." He pushed the pot forward. "It makes it palatable. There are some things I do not know if I wrote, if I heard, if I copied from another poet—though I doubt there's any can match Wheldrake's command of the poetic arts (I do not claim genius—but mere craft)—for I am prolific, you see. It is my nature, and perhaps my doom. Had I died after my first volume or two I should even now reside in Westminster Abbey."

Not wishing a lengthy and impossible-to-follow explanation on the nature of this particular Valhalla, Elric, as had become his habit, merely let the unfamiliar words roll by.

"But this Lord Soulis. Who is he?"

"A mere invention, for all I know, sir. I was reminded of the ballad by the three ladies here, but, of course, perhaps our three elusive sisters struck a memory, too. Certainly, if I remember further verses I'll speak up. But I believe it no more than a coincidence, Prince Elric. The multiverse is full of specific numbers of power and so on, and three is particularly popular with poets since three names are always excellent means of ringing changes on something long—which, of course, is the nature of narrative verse. Again, this slides from favour wherever I go. The artist is beyond fashion, but his purse, sir, is not. That's an odd ship, isn't it, sir, come into the harbour overnight?"

Elric had seen no ship. He put down his bowl and let Wheldrake lead him to the window where the landlady and her daughter still leaned, staring at a craft whose hull gleamed black and yellow and whose prow bore the marks of Chaos, while from her mast there flew a red-and-black flag centred with a sign in some unlikely alphabet. On her forecastle, weighting the ship oddly so that she was stern-light in the water and showing too much of her rudder, was a tall, square object swathed in black canvas and filling almost the whole deck. Occasionally the thing moved in a sudden convulsion and then was still again. There was no clue to what the canvas hid. But, as Elric watched, a figure strolled from the cabin under the forward deck, stood for a second on the polished planks and seemed to look directly at him. Elric could scarcely return the gaze, since the helmet had no eyes he could make out. It was Gaynor the Damned and the standard he flew was, Elric now recollected, that of Count Mashabak. They were fully rivals, it seemed, serving warring patrons.

Gaynor returned to his cabin and next a plank was lowered from the moored galley and laid onto the mole. The ship's hands moved with lithe speed, almost like monkeys, to secure the gangplank as there stepped onto it a lad of no more than fifteen, clad in all the vivid, pretty finery of a pirate lord, a cutlass in one side of his sash, a sabre in the other, to stride up towards the town with the confident swagger of a conqueror.

It was only as the figure drew close to the inn that Elric recognised who it was—and he wondered again at the turning Spheres of the multiverse, marvelled at the extraordinary combinations of events and worlds, both in and out of the dimensions of time, that were possible within the undiscoverable parameters of the quasi-infinite.

While, at the same moment something within him warned him that what he saw might be an illusion or worse: it could be someone whom illusion had consumed, who had given themselves up wholly to Chaos and was nothing more than Gaynor's marionette.

Yet, by her walk and the way she had of looking about her, alert and cheerful as she seemed, Elric could hardly believe she was unwillingly in Gaynor's service.

He left the window and went to greet her as the door was opened by Ernest Wheldrake, whose bright blue eyes went wide as he piped, with joyful surprise:

"Why, Charion Phatt, disguised as a boy! I am in love! You have grown up!"

2

In Which Old Acquaintanceships Are Resumed and New Agreements Reached.

Charion Phatt had reached womanhood since their last meeting and there was something about her which suggested her air of confidence was founded on faith in herself, rather than any artificial bravado. She was only a little surprised to see Wheldrake and even as she grinned a greeting at him her eyes searched inside the inn and found Elric.

"I bring an invitation from the ship's master for you—for you gentlemen—to join him this evening," she murmured.

"How long have you been in Prince Gaynor's service, Mistress Phatt?" asked Elric, with proper care to keep his tone neutral.

"Long enough, Prince Elric—more or less since I last saw you—that dawn on the gypsy bridge . . ."

"And your family?"

She smoothed chestnut hair against the lace and silk of her shirt. Her lids for a second hid her eyes. "They, sir? Why, I'm in alliance with Prince Gaynor on account of them. We are seeking them and have been seeking them since that great destruction."

And briefly she explained how Gaynor had found her imprisoned as a witch in a distant realm and had told her that he, too, sought her uncle and grandmother, since they alone, he believed, could tread with any certainty the pathways between the dimensions and lead him to the three sisters.

"You are certain they survived?" asked Wheldrake gently.

"Uncle and Grandma, at least," she said, "of those I'm certain. And I think little Koropith is further off—or veiled from me, perhaps. I'd guess something of him continues to exist—somewhere . . ." Then she took her leave of them and walked on into the town to buy, she said, a few luxuries.

"I am truly, truly in love," Wheldrake confided to his friend, who refrained from suggesting that there was a certain unsuitability in their ages. Wheldrake was approaching fifty, he would guess, and the young woman was not much more than eighteen.

"Such differences as exist between us mean nothing when two hearts beat in harmony," said Wheldrake rapturously, and it was not certain if he quoted himself or some admired peer.

Elric fell silent, ignoring his friend's effusions, and wondering at the ways of the multiverse, this environment which, as a sorcerer, he had until then only understood in terms of symbols.

He considers the symbol of the Balance, of that equilibrium which once all philosophers strove to achieve, until, by expediency or by threats to their lives and souls, they began to strike bargains, some with Law but mostly with Chaos, which is an element closer to the natures of most sorcerers. And so they ensured that they could never reach the goal for which they had been trained: for which some of them had been born: for which a few of them were fated. These last were the ones who understood the great perversion which had taken place, who understood all that they had given up.

Gaynor, ex-Prince of the Universal, understood better than any other, for he had known perfection and lost it.

It is at this moment, as he closes the door to an ordinary inn, that Elric re-alises his terror has turned to something else, a kind of determination. A kind of cold insanity. He gambles not only upon his own soul's fate, not only upon his father's—but far more. Rather than continue to be baffled by events, controlled by them, he makes up his mind to enter the game between the gods, and play it to the full, play it for himself and his mortal friends, the remaining creatures that he loves—for Tanelorn. This is no more than a promise he makes within himself, as yet scarcely coherent—but it will become the foundation of his future actions, this refusal to accept the Tyranny of Fate, to let his destiny be moved by every whim of some half-bestial divinity, whose only right over him is due to the superior power he wields. It is a reality his father accepted, even as he played the game, subtly and carefully, with his life and soul as the main stake—it is a reality, however, that Elric is beginning to refuse . . .

There is in him, too, another kind of coldness, the coldness of anger at any creature that can casually have so many of its fellows slain. It is an anger not only directed at Gaynor, but at himself. Perhaps that is why he fears Gaynor so much, because they are almost the same creature. If some philosophies were to be believed, they could indeed be aspects of a single creature. Deep memories stir in him but are unwelcome. He drives them down to where they lurk again, like the beasts of some impossible deep, terrifying all that encounter them, but themselves terrified by the light . . .

That other part of Elric, the part that is all Melnibonéan, chides him for a fool, wasting time with useless niceties of conscience and suggests that an alliance with Gaynor might give them, together, the power he desires to challenge—and perhaps even vanquish.

Or, even a temporary truce between the two would gain him, perhaps, his immediate needs—though what then? What would take place when Arioch demanded everything he had enjoined Elric to find? Could a Duke of Hell be tricked, even defeated, banished from a certain plane, by a mortal?

Elric realises that these are the ideas which brought his father to his present dilemma and, with a sardonic smile, he settles back behind his bench to enjoy his interrupted breakfast.

He will decide nothing until this evening, when he dines aboard Gaynor's ship.

Wheldrake looks once more after the departing beauty, takes parchment from one pocket, pen from another, a travelling inkwell from his top left waistcoat pocket, and begins first a sestina, *next a* roundelay, *then a* villanelle, *until settling again upon the* sestina . . .

> *This was the measure of my soul's delight;*
> *It had no power of joy to fly by day,*
> *Nor part in the large lordship of the light;*
> *But in a secret moon-beholden way*
> *Had all its will of dreams and pleasant night,*
> *And all the love and life that sleepers may.*

Whereupon the Prince of Ruins slips away, back to his maps and his particular problems, as Wheldrake pauses, sighs, and makes a stab this time at a sonnet . . .

"Or I had thought, perhaps, after all, an Ode. Along the lines, perhaps, of something I wrote in Putney.

> "*Golden eastern waters rocked the cradle where she slept*
> *Songless, crowned with bays to be of sovereign song,*
> *Breathed upon with balm and calm of bounteous seas that kept*
> *Secret all the blessing of her birthright, strong,*
> *Soft, severe, and sweet as dawn when first it laughed and leapt*
> *Forth of heaven, and clove the clouds that wrought it wrong!*

"Good evening, Prince Gaynor. I trust you have an explanation for your destruction of a nation? Your sophistries should, at least, be entertaining." The little poet looked up at the mysterious helm, his knuckles upon his hips, his beak flaring with disdain, unmoved by fear of Gaynor's power, nor of any social stricture to hold his tongue on the subject of his host's genocide as he stepped aboard the ship.

Elric, for his part, said little, keeping a distance between himself and the others, which he had once been taught to do as a matter of course, as a Melnibonéan princeling. This coolness was new to Wheldrake but would have been very familiar to Moonglum, were he here and not, perhaps, still in Tanelorn. Elric adopted the manner when circumstances led him once more towards a kind of cynicism, that cynicism oddly tinged with other qualities, harder to judge or to define. The long-fingered bone-white hand hung upon the pommel of the massive runesword and the head was set at a certain angle, as if further withdrawn, while the brooding crimson eyes held a humour which, on occasions, even the Lords of the Higher Worlds had considered dangerous. Yet he bowed. He made a movement with his free hand. He looked steadily into the eyes behind the helm, the eyes that smoked and glittered and writhed with the fires of hell.

"Good evening, Prince Gaynor." There was at once a softness and a steely sharpness to Elric's voice which reminded Wheldrake of a cat's claws sheathed in downy fur.

The ex-Prince of the Balance cocked his head a little to one side, perhaps in irony, and spoke with that musical voice which had served Chaos as a lure for so many centuries. "I am glad to see you, Master Wheldrake. I have only recently learned we should experience the privilege of your company. Though I was told by mutual friends that you, Elric, could be found in Ulshinir." He shrugged away the question. "We have, whatever you may call it, some kind of fresh luck forming, it seems. Or are we mere ingredients? Eggs in some mad god's omelette? My chef is excellent, by the way. Or so I'm told."

Then here came Mistress Charion Phatt, in black and white velvet and lace, her youthful beauty shining like a jewel from its box.

Half-swooning, Master Wheldrake made his elaborate courtesies, which she received with amused good will and drew him to her as they strolled towards the forward cabin where the looming shadow of that peculiar cargo rocked and shifted on the roof above and which Prince Gaynor and Charion Phatt both ignored as if they heard or saw nothing out of place.

Then came the dining. Elric, who frequently cared nothing for the refinements of appetite, found the food as delicious as Gaynor had promised. The damned prince told a tale of a voyage to Aramandy and the Mallow Country there to find Xermenif Blüche, the Master Chef of Volofar. And they might have been dining again amongst the wealthy intelligentsia of Trollon, heedless of any unusual circumstances—of warring gods, of stolen souls and lost clairvoyants and so on—and commenting on the delicacy of the mousse.

Prince Gaynor, in a carved black chair at the head of his table, which was swathed with a dark scarlet cloth, turned an enigmatic helm towards Elric and said that he had always preserved certain standards, even when in battle or in command of demibrutes, as one so frequently was, these days. One had after all, he added in some amusement, to control what one could, especially since one's fate grew so unmalleable as the Conjunction approached.

Elric had heard little of this and he moved impatiently in his seat, pushing away the plates and cutlery. "Will you tell us, Prince Gaynor, why you make us your guests here?"

"*If you will tell me, Elric, why you fear me!*" said Gaynor in a sudden whisper, the cold of limbo slicing into Elric's soul.

But Elric held his psychic ground, conscious of Gaynor's testing him.

"I fear you because you are prepared to go to any ends to achieve your own death. And since life has no value to you, you are to be feared as all such animals are feared. For you desire power only for that most selfish of all ends, and therefore you know no boundaries in the seeking and the gaining of it. That is why I fear you, Gaynor the Damned. And that is why you *are* damned."

The faceless creature flung back its steel-shod head, the colours behind the metal quivering and flaring, and laughed at this. "I fear *you*, Elric, because you are damned yet continue to behave as if you were not . . ."

"I have made no bargains such as yours, prince."

"Your whole race has made a bargain! And now it is paying the price—somewhere, not far from here, in a realm you will call home, the last of your people are being marshalled to march in the armies of Chaos. The time for that last great fight is not yet. But we are preparing for it. Would you survive it, Elric? Or would you be blasted to non-existence, not even your memory remaining—less enduring, say, than one of Master Wheldrake's verses—"

"I say, sir! You have already proved yourself an unmitigated villain! Pray, remember at least that you are a gentleman!" Then Wheldrake's eye returned to his beloved.

"Can you bear the prospect of everlasting death, Elric? You, who love life as much as I hate it. We could both have our deepest desire . . ."

"I think you fear me, Prince Gaynor, because I refuse that final compromise," said Elric. "I fear you because you belong wholly to Chaos. But you fear me because I do not."

A querulous noise issued from within the helm, almost like the snuffling of some cosmic pig. Then in came three sailors with a tambourine, a pipe and a musical sword, to play some mournful shanty, and who were swiftly dismissed by Gaynor, to the relief of all.

"Very well, sir," said Gaynor, all his equilibrium recovered, it seemed. "Then can I put a modest suggestion to you?"

"If you wish to join forces to seek the three sisters, I will consider your proposals," said Elric. "Otherwise I see little left to discuss between us."

"But that is just what I would discuss, Elric. We all desire something different, I suspect, of those sisters, and the reason why so much upheaval flings us this way and that through the multiverse is because there are several interests and several Lords of the Higher Worlds involved. You accept that, gentlemen?" Now he included Wheldrake. Charion Phatt sat back in her chair, evidently already privy to her ally's plan.

They nodded their agreement.

"In some ways we are all at odds," Gaynor continued, "but in others we have no battle between us. And I see you agree. Well, then, so let us search for the sisters, as well as the Family Phatt—or what remains of it—together. At least until such time as our interests are no longer the same."

And thus did Elric of Melniboné and Master Ernest Wheldrake accept the logic of the damned prince's compromise and agreed to sail with him when his ship left harbour the next morning, as soon as they had selected another sailor or two from the braver or more desperate seadogs of Ulshinir.

"But," said Elric, as they made to return ashore, while a scuffling and shifting went on, together with the occasional light pounding, overhead, "you have not yet discussed your destination, Prince Gaynor. Do we trust you in that or will you tell us the name of the island the three sisters have reached?"

"Island?" Gaynor's helm grew dark, almost in puzzlement, and blues and blacks swirled across its smooth, sometimes opaque, surface. "Island, sir? We do not go to any island."

"Then where are the three sisters?"

"Where *we* journey, sir, though they are lost to any immediate meeting between us, I fear."

"And where," said Wheldrake with a certain justified impatience, "do *we* journey, sir?"

Again the helm tilted a little as if in amusement and the musical voice sounded the words with considerable relish:

"Why, sir, I thought you'd guessed. Tomorrow we set sail into the Heavy Sea."

3

Unusual Methods of Sea Travel; Disappointments of Piracy. A Hellblade Misplaced.

It was not until Ulshinir was well below the horizon and the reefs still invisible ahead that Gaynor the Damned gave the order to "let some light on the poor toad" and the sailors obeyed with perhaps a touch of reluctance, drawing off and rolling up the black canvas to reveal the iron bars of a large cage from which, blinking, appeared two enormous green-lidded eyes set in a gnarled reptilian head whose nostrils flared and whose long scarlet mouth opened to reveal a pink, flickering tongue, while the extraordinarily dense weight of scaly flesh was supported on massive webbed feet, limbs as thick as elm-trunks, the whole thing shuddering and rippling with the effort of its breathing.

The eyes, like dark, semi-precious stones, sought Gaynor and fixed on him where he stood below, looking up at the cage. The red, spongey lips opened and closed and deep, groaning sounds issued from the monster. It was only after a moment of listening that Elric realised the reptile was speaking.

"*I am discontented, master. I am hungry.*"

"Soon you will be allowed to feed, my pretty one. Very soon." Gaynor chuckled as he climbed the companionway and gripped the bars of the cage with his gauntleted hands and peered at the gigantic toad which was five times his size and weight, at least.

Wheldrake had no wish, himself, to get closer. He hung back as Charion

Phatt, laughing at his hesitation, went to the toad which responded to her cluckings and cooings with more grumblings and shufflings.

"It's a self-pitying creature," said Elric, staring at the thing with a certain sympathy. "Where did you find it? Is it a gift of Count Mashabak's, something even Chaos will not suffer?"

"Khorghakh is a native of a nearby realm, Prince Elric." Gaynor was amused. "He will help us to cross the Heavy Sea."

"And what lies beyond?" Elric asked, watching as Charion Phatt took her sword and scratched the toad's belly, making him grunt with a certain pleasure and seem to relax a little, though he still insisted he was hungry.

"Khorghakh is a denizen of the Heavy Sea?"

"Not exactly," said Gaynor, "a denizen. But he is familiar with that singular ocean, or so I have been reassured. After three years of seeking him I acquired Khorghakh from some adventurers we encountered. They were coasting the islands looking for Ulshinir . . ."

"Looking for you," said Charion. "I knew you were here. It was only later that I sensed the presence of the three sisters. I had thought they were following you. Yet you sensed them, also. I did not know you were clairvoyant."

"I am not," said Elric. "At least, not in the way you imply. I had no choice in my destination. For you, as I can see, some years have passed. For me, very little has occurred since the moment I followed you all into the Chaos pit. Wheldrake has had at least a year of wandering. It suggests that even if we should find the three sisters or, indeed, your family, they could be children or wizened oldsters by the time we reach them."

"I like not this randomness at all," says Wheldrake. "Chaos was never to my taste, though my critics did not believe that. I was raised to accept that there were certain universal laws obeyed by all. To discover that this hyper-reality has only a few fundamental rules which, on occasions, may also be changed, is disturbing to me."

"It disturbed my uncle, also," said Charion. "It was why he elected to lead a life of quiet domesticity. Of course, he was not allowed that choice, after all.

He lost my mother, his brother and his wife to the machinations of Chaos. For my part, I have accepted the inevitable. I am aware that I live in the multiverse which, though it follows certain courses and measures, though, as I have been told, it obeys a great and inviolable logic, is so vast, so variable, so varied, that it appears to be ruled by Chance alone. So I will accept that my life is subject not to the consistency offered by Law but the uncertainty promised by Chaos."

"A pessimistic view, sweet lady." Wheldrake restrained his own feelings on the matter. "Is it not better to live as if there were some abiding logic to our existence?"

"Make no mistake, Master Wheldrake." She touched him with a certain affection. "I have accepted the abiding logic—and it is the logic of power and conquest . . ."

"So decided my own ancestors," said Elric quietly. "They perceived a multiverse that was all but random, and they conceived a philosophy to formalise what they saw. Since their world was controlled by the random whims of the Lords of the Higher Worlds, they argued, then the only way of ensuring their survival was to gain as much power as they could—power at least as great as that of certain minor deities. Power enough, at least, to make Chaos bargain with them, rather than threaten and destroy. But what did that power gain them in the end? Less, I suspect, than your uncle gained by his decision . . ."

"My uncle had no sense," said Charion, bringing an end to the conversation. She turned her attention back to the toad, who had settled again and, while she scratched its vast back with her blade, stared moodily towards the horizon where dark ridges had begun to appear, the first sight of the reefs separating, according to the folk of Ulshinir, the inhabitable world from the uninhabitable.

They could hear surf now, could see it spuming against the volcanic rocks so that they gleamed with an unwelcoming blackness.

"*I am discontented, mistress. I am hungry.*" The toad turned its eyes upon Charion, and Wheldrake understood that he had a rival. He enjoyed the peculiar experience of being amused, jealous and profoundly terrified all at the same time.

Elric, too, had witnessed the toad's expression when it looked at Charion and he frowned. Some instinct informed him but was not, as yet, a conscious thought. He was content to wait until the instinct had matured, found words, had confirmation and become an idea. Meanwhile he smiled at Wheldrake's discomfort. "Fear not, friend Wheldrake! If you lack that fellow's beauty and perhaps even his specific charm, you almost certainly have the superior wit."

"Oh, indeed, sir," said Wheldrake, mocking himself a little, "and I know that wit usually counts for nothing in the game of love! There is no verse form invented that could easily carry such a tale—of a poet whose rival is a reptile! The heartache of it! The uncertainty! The folly!"

And he paused suddenly, eyeing the monstrous toad as it returned his attention, glaring at him as if it had understood every word.

Then it opened its lips and spoke slowly.

"*Thou shalt not have mine egg . . .*"

"Exactly, sir. Exactly what I was remarking to my friend here." With a bow so theatrical and elaborate even Elric was unsure what, at certain times, the poet was performing, Wheldrake went off for a while to concern himself with some business in the stern.

From the crow's nest came the cry of the lookout and this brought Gaynor round from where he had been staring apparently out to sea, almost as if he slept, or as if his soul had left his body. "What? Ah, yes. The navigator. Fetch up the navigator!"

And now, up from the starboard lower deck, comes a grey man—a man whose skin has been tanned by rain and wind but never by the sun, a man whose eyes are hurt by the light, yet grateful for it, also. He rubs at wrists which, by the chafing on them, have lately been tied. He sniffs at the salty wind and he grins to himself, in memory.

"Navigator. Here's your means of earning your freedom," says Gaynor, signalling him up towards the prow which rises and falls with graceful speed as the wind takes the sail and the rocky shores of a dozen islands lie ahead—black, wicked teeth in mouths of roaring foam.

"Or killing us all and taking everyone to hell with me," says the navigator carelessly. He is a man of about forty-five, his light beard grey-brown as his shaggy hair and with grey-green eyes so piercing and strange that it is clear he has learned to keep them hooded, for now he squints as if against strong sun, though the sun lies behind him, and, with lithe movements of a man glad to be active again, he springs to the foredeck, squeezes around the toad's cage as though he encounters such beasts every day, and joins Gaynor in the prow. "You'd better haul in that sail as soon as you can," says the navigator, raising his voice above the gaining wind, "or turn about completely and take another approach. A couple of minutes and nothing will save us from those rocks!"

Gaynor turned shouting to his crew and Elric admired the skill with which the sailors went to their work, turning the ship just enough so that the sail hung limp on the mast, then hauling it in before the wind could find it again. The navigator shouted out encouragement, sending the men to their oars, for this was the only way to navigate the reefs at the edge of the world.

Slowly now the black-and-yellow ship moved through the tugging currents of the reef—a few inches this way, a few that, sometimes touching a rock so lightly there was the barest whisper of friction, sometimes seeming to squeeze between pillars of basalt and obsidian, while the wind yelled and the surf crashed and the whole world seemed once more to be given up to Chaos. It was noon before they had negotiated the first line of reefs and lay at anchor in the calm waters between themselves and the second line. Now the navigator gave instructions for the crew to eat well and to rest. They would not attempt the next line until the following day.

Next day they plunged again into cacophony and wave-tossed confusion as the navigator called out first one direction and then another, sometimes running back along the ship to take the wheel, sometimes clambering to the crow's nest to remind himself of what lay ahead, for it was clear he had navigated these reefs more than once.

Another river of clear, blue ocean running over pale sand; another patch of calm water—and the navigator made them rest another day.

Twelve days it took them to reach the farthest reef and look with unpleasant emotions upon the black surf pouring like oily smoke onto the massive natural barrier created by the last line of islands, onto beaches of smooth, fused obsidian. The Heavy Sea moved with extreme precision, the waves rising and falling with agonising slowness, and the deep sounds it made hinted at this sea having a voice largely inaudible to the human ear, for a peculiar silence existed over its dark, slow waters.

"It is like a sea of cold, liquefied lead," said Wheldrake. "It offends all natural laws!" At which remark of his own he shrugged, as if to say "What does not?" "How can any ship sail across that? The surface tension is rather more adequate than is needed, I would guess . . ."

The navigator lifted his head from where he had been resting it on the rail. "It can be crossed," he said. "It has been crossed. It is a sea that flows between the worlds, but there are folk for whom that ocean is as familiar as the one we have just left behind is to us. Mortal ingenuity can usually find a means of travelling through or over anything."

"But is it not a dangerous sea?" asked Wheldrake, looking upon it with considerable distaste.

"Oh, yes," agreed the navigator. "It is very dangerous." He spoke carelessly. "Although it could be argued, I suppose, that anything which becomes familiar is less dangerous . . ."

"Or more," said Elric with some feeling. He took one last look at the Heavy Sea and went below, to the cabin he shared with Wheldrake. That night he remained in his quarters, brooding on matters impossible to discuss with any other creature, while Wheldrake joined the navigator and the crew in cele-

bration of their successful crossing of the reefs and in the hope of gaining a little more courage for the voyage that remained. But if Wheldrake had planned
to learn more of the navigator, save that Gaynor had taken him aboard only
a couple of days before they came to Ulshinir, he was disappointed. Nor did
he see anything else of Charion, his beloved, that night. Something stopped
him from returning to the cabin—some sense of discretion—and he stayed,
instead, upon the deck for a while, listening to the sluggish breakers splashing
against the sea-smoothed obsidian and he thought of the Egyptian Book of the
Dead and the stories of the Boat of Souls, of Charon, Boatman to the Gods,
for to him this truly seemed like some netherworld ocean—perhaps the waters
which lapped the very shores of limbo.

And now Wheldrake found himself beside the cage where the monster
slept, its eyes tight shut as it snored and snuffled and smacked its loose,
spongey lips, and at that moment the poet felt a certain sympathy for the
creature, who was as surely trapped into compromise with Gaynor as almost
everyone else aboard the ship. He leaned his arm on the rail of black, carved
wood and watched as the moon emerged from behind a cloud and its light
fell upon the scales, the leathery folds of flesh, the almost translucent webbing
between the enormous fingers, and marvelled at such ugliness, enraptured of
such beauty. Whereupon he thought of himself, thought of a phrase, a certain
cadence, felt about his pockets for his ink, his quill and his parchment and set
to work in the moonlight to find romantic comparisons between Wheldrake
the Poet and Khorghakh the Toad which was, he felt with a certain degree
of self-satisfaction, all the more difficult if one attempted, for instance, some
version of trochaic dimeter . . .

> *Of this schism*
> *Occultism,*
> *Lately risen,*
> *(Euphemism)*
> *Calls for heroism rare.*

Which occupied him so successfully that it was not until dawn that he placed his pining head upon his pillow and fell into the sweetest dreams of love he had ever known . . .

Dawn found all but Wheldrake on deck, faces upturned towards a lowering sky from which fell a languorous rain. It had grown warmer overnight and the humidity was very high. Elric tugged at his clothes and wished that he were naked. He felt as if he walked through tepid mead. The navigator was up on the foredeck with the toad; they seemed to be in conference. Then the grey man straightened and came back to where Elric, Gaynor and Charion stood together under a rough awning upon which the rain drops thumped with deliberate rhythm. He brushed his own woollen sleeve. "It's like mercury, this stuff. You should try to swallow some. It won't harm you, but it's almost impossible—you have to chew it. Now, Prince Gaynor the Damned, you struck a bargain with me and I have fulfilled the first part. Whereupon you said you would return to me what was mine. Before, you agreed, we advance into the Heavy Sea."

The grey-green gaze was steady upon that shifting helm. They were eyes that feared almost nothing.

"True," says Gaynor, "such a bargain was made"—and he seems to hesitate, as if weighing the odds of breaking his oath, then deciding he would gain more by honouring it—"and I shall keep it, naturally. One moment." He leaves the quarter-deck to go below and re-emerge with a small bundle—perhaps a wrapped greatcoat—which he puts into the navigator's hands. For a second those strange eyes flare and the mouth grins oddly, then the grey man is impassive again. Carrying the bundle he returns to take a further word or two with the toad. Then it's "Get a man to the lookout" and "Oarsmen to their positions" and "Keep that sail down—'tis a slow wind that will fill her, but 'tis worth the attempt" and the navigator is moving about the black-and-yellow ship—a man of the wild sea, a man of well-garnered wisdom and natural intellect, everything that a ship's commander should be—encouraging, shouting, whistling, joking with all—even the great old toad that grumbled his way from the cage as Charion released him, to creep bit by bit to the prow, and lie along the creaking bowsprit, forcing the ship still further down into the sea—down now through a narrow channel (pointed out by the navigator hanging in the rigging above the toad's green head) where white water meets black, where airy foam meets leaden droplets, suspended in the thick air. The prow of the ship—sharp and honed like a razor in the manner of the *bakrasim* of the Vilmirian Peninsula—sliced into that sluggish mass, driven by the toad's weight, guided now by the toad's bellows translated by the navigator to the steersman, and they are entering the Heavy Sea, going into darkness, going into the place where the sky itself seems like a kind of skin off which all sounds echo and the fading echoes are themselves returned until it seems the voices of tormented mortals in all their billions are sounding in their agonised ears and it is impossible to hear anything but that. They are tempted to signal to Prince Gaynor, standing himself at the helm now, to turn the ship about, for they must all die of the noise.

But Gaynor the Damned would not heed them. His terrible helm is lifted against the elements, his armoured body challenges the multiverse, defiant of the natural or the supernatural, or any other form which might threaten him! For he is never alarmed by death.

The toad croaks and gestures, the navigator signs with his hands, and Gaynor turns the wheel a little this way, a little that, fine as a needlewoman at her stretcher, while Elric holds his hands against his ears, seeks for something to stuff into them, to stop the pain which must surely burst his brain. Up on deck, ghastly, comes Wheldrake—

—and then the sound is over. A silence encloses the ship.

"You too," says Wheldrake in some relief. "I thought it was last night's wine. Or possibly the poetry . . ."

He stares in dismay at the slow-moving darkness all around them, looks up at the bruised sky from which the leisurely rain still falls, and returns without further remark to his cabin for a moment.

The ship still moves, the Heavy Sea still heaves, and through this liquid

maze the craft of Chaos cleaves. The toad groans out his orders, the navigator shouts; and Gaynor on his quarter-deck turns the wheel a fraction south.
The toad's webbed hand makes urgent signs, the wheel is turned again, and
onward into laggard seas drive Gaynor and his men. And on every single face
of them, save Elric and his friend, is a wild, dark glee, and a sniffing at the sea
for the smell of purest fear. They sniffed for fear like hounds for blood; they
sniffed on that sluggish air; they sniffed for danger and scent of death and they
tasted the wind like bread. And the toad groans out his orders and his mouth
is wet with greed, and the toad's breath wheezes in the toad's dark maw, for
soon he must come to feed.

"*Master, I must feed!*"

The strange water rolls like mercury over the ship's decks as she plunges
on, sometimes threatening, it seems, to become stuck in a glutinous wave.
And at last the ship will not move at all. The toad takes ropes from the prow
and, its wide feet spread upon the water, long enough to break the surface
tension before treading on again at what is clearly a natural gait, hauls the
whole ship behind it. Behind him, momentarily, in the heavy water are the
toad's footprints and then the tension is broken by the prow until at last the
toad is swimming again, gasping with something akin to pleasure as the great
droplets roll over his scales. There is a noise from it; a noise of joy: a noise that
finds distant echo somewhere above, suggesting that they are in fact within a
vast cave, or perhaps some more organic manifestation of Chaos. Then the
booming song of the toad dies away and the creature comes paddling back to
the ship, to crawl slowly aboard, tipping down the prow again, and resume
its position along the bowsprit while the navigator climbs back overhead and
once more Gaynor takes up the wheel.

Elric, fascinated by these events, watches the drops of water roll from the
toad's glistening body and fall back into the sea. Above, in the rolling darkness, come sudden flashes of dusky scarlet and deep blue, as if whatever sun
burns on them is not like any they have seen before. Now even the air is so

thick that they must gulp at it like stranded fish and one man falls to the deck in a fit, but Gaynor does not lift a gauntleted hand from the wheel nor make any movement of his head to suggest that they must stop. And not one, now, asks him to stop. Elric realises they are like-minded nihilists who have suffered too much already to fear any pain that might lie ahead. Certainly they do not fear a clean death. Unlike Gaynor, these men are not questing for death with his desperation. These are men who would kill themselves if they did not believe that living was just a little more interesting than dying. Elric recognised in them something of what he frequently felt—a terrible, deep boredom with all the reminders one met of human venality and folly—yet there was also in him another feeling, a memory of his people before they founded Melniboné, when they were gentler and lived with the existing realities rather than attempt to force their own; a memory of justice and perfection. He went to the rail and looked out over the slow-heaving waters of the Heavy Sea and he wondered where, in all that sluggish darkness, were the three sisters to be found? And did they still have the box of black rosewood? And did that box still contain his father's soul?

Wheldrake appeared, with Charion Phatt, chanting some rhyme of almost mesmeric simplicity and then blushing suddenly and stopping.

"It would be useful, something like that," said Mistress Phatt, "for the rowers. They need a steady sort of rhythm. I have no intention, I assure you, Master Wheldrake, of marrying that toad. I have no intention of marrying at all. I believe you have heard my views on the perils of domesticity."

"Hopeless love!" wailed Wheldrake, with what was almost relish. He cast a scrap of paper over the side. It fell flat upon the water, undulating with it as if given a spark of life of its own.

"Whatever pleases you, sir." She winked at Elric cheerfully.

"You seem in excellent spirits," said the albino, "for one who is embarked upon such a voyage as this."

"I can sense the sisters," she said. "I told Prince Gaynor. I sensed them an hour ago. And I can sense them now. They have returned to this plane. And if they are here, then soon my uncle and my grandmother, and perhaps my cousin, will find them, too."

"You think the sisters will reunite you with your family? That's the only reason you seek them?"

"I believe that if they live it is inevitable that we shall meet, most probably through the sisters."

"But the Rose and the boy are dead."

"I said I did not know where they were, not that they were dead . . ." It was clear she feared the worst but was refusing to admit it.

Elric did not pursue the subject. He knew what it was like to live with grief.

And on sailed the Chaos ship, into the slow silence of the Heavy Sea, with the croaking of the great toad and the voice of the navigator the only sounds to cut through the swampy air.

That night they dropped anchor and all but Gaynor retired. The damned prince strode the deck with a steady pace, almost in rhythm with the languid waves, and occasionally Elric, who could not sleep but had no wish to join Gaynor on deck, heard the creature cry out as if startled. "Who's there?"

Elric wondered what kind of denizens occupied the Heavy Sea. Were there others, like the toad but of a more malevolent disposition?

At Gaynor's third cry, he got to his feet, pulling on some clothes, his scabbarded sword in his hand. Wheldrake, too, was disturbed, but merely raised himself up in his bunk and murmured a question.

Out into the salty miasma went Elric, seeking the source of Gaynor's shout. Then he saw, looming over the port rail, the bulk of what could only be some kind of ship. A tall, wooden construction—a kind of castellated tower from which were already swinging half a dozen figures, all of them armed with long, savage pikes and flenchers—brutal weapons, but effective in this kind of fighting.

But not, reflected Elric with a certain humour, as effective as a black runesword.

And with that he dragged the hellblade from its scabbard and ran on bare feet along the deck to greet the first of the pirates as they dropped aboard the ship.

Above them, on the foredeck, the navigator appeared for a moment, glaring upward and moving with an odd series of leaps back into the rigging. "Dramian Toad-hunters!" he cried to Elric. "They're after our guide! We are dead without it!"

Then the navigator had disappeared again and the first of the hunters stabbed at Elric with the jagged points of his pike—

—and died almost without realising it, wriggling like a speared fish as his soul was sucked into the blade . . .

Stormbringer seemed to purr with pleasure. The sword's song grew louder, greedier as one by one the hunters went down.

Elric, used to supernatural foes, stood amongst the growing pile of corpses like a farmer scything hay on a pleasant summer's day and it was left to Charion and the crew to finish off the few who now tried desperately to get back to their ship . . .

. . . But Elric was ahead of them, clambering up one of their own lines as a hunter desperately tried to saw at it with his pike. Elric reached the hunter before the rope was sheared and he drove the sword deep through the man's breastbone, watching him writhe. The hunter tried to keep his hold on the rope, then grasped the blade itself with both hands, as the sword relished its gradual feasting on the rich marrow of his soul. He tried to push himself off the sword, to cast himself into the dark water that now showed between the two ships, and on an impulse Elric released his grip on Stormbringer and watched with a sense of profound calm as sword and victim went plunging downwards. Weaponless, he continued his climb up the rope, swinging over the crenellations to discover that the bulky forward tower belonged to a vessel of singular slimness. It was a ship designed to race upon the surface of this peculiar ocean. Elric could see large outriggers, like the limbs of some huge water-insect, curving into the darkness.

And then, from a hatch in the deck, came more of the hunters, all armed with flenchers and grinning with the prospect of their butchery. Elric cursed himself for a fool and backed away from them, his eyes searching for some means of escape.

The hunters had the look of men who intended to enjoy their work. The first made an experimental swing with his flencher. The broad, curved blade whistled in the sultry air.

They were almost upon Elric when the albino heard a deep growling from somewhere over his head and thought the toad had climbed the tower undetected. But what he saw instead was a great snarling dog, silvery in the darkness, springing for the throat of the nearest hunter and tearing at it until it was nothing more than bloody meat, glaring up with a triumphant flaring of its nostrils as the other hunters fled. Elric did not care at that moment where his rescuer had come from. He merely thanked the animal and glanced down onto the deck to see how his companions fared. He saw Charion finishing off an adversary and lifting her lovely head in a high, ululating note.

The few hunters who still lived ran for the sides in blind panic; for now, over the starboard rail, its lips smacking and its eyes gleaming, breathing with wheezing slowness, crawled the toad they had sought to capture for themselves. The dog had vanished.

Khorghakh hesitated once he was aboard, his bulk enveloping parts of the rail and the hatches, and he cocked his head enquiringly.

From somewhere on the Chaos ship Elric heard Gaynor's voice crying out, exultant and full of an unusual excitement.

"*Now, toad! Now, my darling, now you can feed!*"

Later, when what was left of the hunters and their ship was burning in the darkness of the Heavy Sea and Khorghakh in his cage was snoring with monstrous hands upon a swollen belly, and Charion sat cross-legged beside him, as if comforted by the beast's enormous power, Elric walked slowly along the deck searching for his sword.

He had not for a moment believed that he had rid himself of the blade when he let it go with its victim. In the past whenever he had tried to abandon Stormbringer it had always returned to him. Now he regretted his folly. He was likely to need his sword. In trepidation, wondering if the blade had been stolen by some supernatural agency, he continued to search.

He searched again, in the shadows of the ship. He knew the blade refused to be separated from him. He had fully expected it to return. Yet the scabbard was gone, too, which suggested theft. He looked, also, for the dog which had appeared to help him and which had gone again so suddenly. Who, aboard, had owned such a dog? Or had it belonged to the hunters and, like the toad, taken vengeance on its oppressors?

As he passed the cabin under the foredeck, he heard a familiar sound. It came from Gaynor's berth—a low, peculiar moaning. He was astonished and further alarmed at the power commanded by the Prince of the Damned. No mortal could have taken up that naked sword and not been harmed, especially when it had so recently drawn enormous psychic force into itself!

Softly Elric moved to Gaynor's door. Now there was only silence on the other side.

The door was not locked. Gaynor was careless of any mortal attempt on his life or his person.

Elric paused for a second before flinging open the door, to reveal a sudden eruption of yelling light, a screeching and a hissing, and then Gaynor stood before him, adjusting his helm with one metal-shod hand, holding the runesword in the other. The runes along the blade juddered and whispered, as if the sword itself understood that the impossible had occurred. Yet Elric noticed that Gaynor trembled and that he had to put his other hand upon the runesword's hilt, to hold it steady, though his stance remained apparently casual.

Elric stretched his open palm towards the blade.

"Even you, Prince of the Damned, could not wield my runesword with impunity. Do you not understand that the blade and I are one? Do you not know that we are brothers, that sword and I? And that we have other kin who may be summoned to our aid when we require it? Know you nothing of that battle-blade's qualities, prince?"

"Only what I have heard of in legends." Gaynor sighed within his helm. "I would test it for myself. Will you lend me your sword, Prince Elric?"

"I could more easily lend you a limb." The albino gestured again for the return of his sword.

Prince Gaynor was reluctant. He studied the runes, he tested the balance. And then he returned the blade to both steel hands. "I do not fear your sword will kill me, Elric."

"I doubt it has the power to kill you, Gaynor. Is that what you desire of it? It might take your soul. It might transmogrify you. I doubt, however, if it will grant you your desire."

Before he gave it up, Gaynor laid one metal-clad finger upon the blade. "Is that the power of the anti-Balance, I wonder?"

"I have not heard of such a power," said Elric. He slid the scabbard back onto his belt.

"They say it is a power even more ambitious than the Lords of the Higher Worlds. More dangerous, more cruel, more effective than anything known to the multiverse. They say the power of the anti-Balance has the means of changing the whole nature of the multiverse in a single stroke."

"I know only that Fate has forged us together, that blade and I," said Elric. "Our destinies are the same." He glanced around Gaynor's sparely furnished cabin. "I have little interest in the broadly cosmic, Prince Gaynor. I have desires rather less exaggerated than most I have met of late. I seek only to find the answers to certain questions I have asked myself. I would gladly be free of all Lords of the Higher Worlds and their machinations. Even of the Balance itself."

Gaynor turned away from him. "You are an interesting creature, Elric of Melniboné. Ill-suited to serve Chaos, it would seem."

"Ill-suited for most things, sir," said Elric. "To serve Chaos is merely a family tradition with us."

Gaynor's helm came round again to stare broodingly at the albino. "You believe it is possible to banish Law and Chaos entirely—to banish them from the multiverse?"

"Of that I am not so sure. But I have heard of places where neither Law nor Chaos have jurisdiction." Elric was too cautious to mention Tanelorn. "I have heard of worlds where the Balance rules unchallenged, also . . ."

"I, too, have known such places. I dwelled in one . . ." There came a frightful chuckling from within the shifting steel helm and then a pause as the Prince of the Damned moved slowly to the far side of his cabin and appeared to be staring through the porthole.

His final words were uttered with such chilling ferocity that Elric, completely unprepared for them, felt he had been struck physically, to his vitals, by iron of such infinite coldness it reached to his soul . . .

"*Oh, Elric, I hate thee with such jealous hate! I hate thee for thine insistent relish of life! For what I once was and what I might have become, I hate thee! For what thou aspireth to, I hate thee most of all . . .*"

As he bent to close the door, the albino looked back at the figure of Gaynor and it seemed to him that the armour which enclosed the damned prince had long since ceased to protect him from any of the things he truly feared. Now the armour had become nothing more than a prison.

"And for my part, Gaynor the Damned," he said with gentle subtlety, "I pity thee with all my soul."

4

Land At Last!
A Certain Conflict of Interests.
Concerning the Anatomy of Lycanthropy.

"In my own world, sir, sad to say, human prejudice is matched only by human folly. Not a soul *claims* to be prejudiced, of course, as there are few who would describe themselves as fools . . ." Ernest Wheldrake addressed the grey navigator as they sat at breakfast on deck the next morning beneath a leaden sky upon the Heavy Sea and watched black waves rise and fall with what seemed unnatural slowness.

Elric, chewing on a piece of barely palatable salt beef, remarked that this seemed a quality of a good deal of society, throughout the multiverse.

The navigator turned his sharp green-grey eyes upon the albino and there was a certain restrained humour in his face when he spoke. "I have known whole Spheres where reason and gentleness, respect for self and for others, have existed together with vigorous intellectual and artistic pursuits—and where the supernatural world was merely a metaphor . . ."

At which Wheldrake smiled. "Even in my England, sir, such perfection was rarely found."

"I did not say perfection was common," murmured the grey man, and he curled his lithe old body off the bench and stood to peer into the green-black sky and stretch his long limbs and lick his thin lips and sniff at the wind and turn towards the prow and the toad, whose sleepy bellows had sounded like rage to the waking passengers. "There is a comet up there!" He pointed one tapering finger. "It means a prince has died." He listened for a moment until, mysteriously satisfied, he loped on about his duties.

"Where I once lived," came the sepulchral melody of Gaynor the Damned as he climbed up from his cabin, "they said that when a comet died a *poet* died." He clapped a shimmering gauntlet upon Wheldrake's resisting shoulder. "Do they say that, where you are from, Master Wheldrake?"

"You are in ungentle spirits, I see, this morning, sir." Wheldrake spoke gently, his cool anger overwhelming his fear. "Perhaps you have your toad's indigestion?"

Gaynor withdrew his hand and acknowledged the little man's admonishment. "Well, well, sir. Some princes are more eager for death than others. And poets, for life, we know. Lady Charion." A bow that set his whole helm to flowing with angry fire. "Prince Elric. Aha! And Master Snare—" for back from his post ran the grey navigator.

"I sought you earlier, Prince Gaynor. We had an agreement between us."

"There is no hope for you," said Gaynor the Damned, making a movement forward, perhaps of sympathy. "She is dead. She died when the church collapsed. You must seek your bride in limbo now, Esbern Snare."

"You promised you would tell me—"

"I promised I would tell thee the truth. And the truth is what I have told thee. She is dead. Her soul awaits thee."

The grey navigator bowed his shaggy head. "You know I cannot join her! I have forfeited my right to life after death! And in return, O, Heaven help me! I have joined with the Undead . . ." With that sudden statement of feeling, Esbern Snare rushed back to the forecastle and ran up into the rigging, to stare blindly into the seething horizon.

Whereupon Gaynor the Damned made a sound like a sigh, deep within his helm, and Elric understood how he had been rescued on the ship and why there was a fellow-feeling evident between the navigator and the deathless prince.

But Wheldrake was gasping with a kind of joy and clapping his hand upon the breakfast table, making the stewed herbs slop, unmourned, from cup to cloth. "By Heaven, sir, that's Esbjörn Snorrë, is it not? Now I have the trick of your pronunciation—and his, I note. I make no claims. We are, after all, rather grateful for that singular telepathy which provides us with the means, so frequently, of our survival in some highly inclement social weather—we should not begrudge benign Mother Nature a few regional accents—by way of a little light-hearted relief to her in her ever-vigilant concern for our continuing existence. Astonishing sir, when you think of it."

"You have heard of the navigator?" Lady Charion caught, as it were, at the coat-tails of his conversation's substance.

"I have heard of Esbern Snare. But the ending of his tale was a happy one. He tricked a troll into building a church for him and his bride to be married in. The troll's wife gave away the troll's name and so released Esbern Snare from his bargain. The troll's wife can still be heard wailing, they say, under Ulshoi hill. I wrote a kind of ballad about it in my *Norwegian Songs*. Pillaged, of course, by Whittier, but we'll say no more of that. No doubt he needed the money. Still, plagiarism's only dishonourable if the coin you earn with it is worth less than the coin you stole."

Again, Charion clutched bravely for the original substance:

"He married happily, you say? But you heard what Gaynor told him?"

"This is a sequel, it seems, to the original tale. I only know of the successful trickster. Any subsequent tragedy had been forgotten by the folklore of my day. Sometimes, you know, it occurs to me that I am in a dream in which all those heroes and heroines, villains and villainesses of my verses have come to life to haunt me, to befriend me, to make me one of themselves. A man, after all, could rarely hope to find such varied company in Putney . . ."

"So you do not know why Esbern Snare is aboard this ship, Master Wheldrake?"

"No better than you, my lady."

"And you, Prince Elric?" She attracted the albino's wandering attention. "Do you know this story?"

Elric shook his head.

"I only know," he said, "that he is a shape-changer and, that most cursed of souls, a person of rare goodness and sanity. Imagine such torment as is his!"

Even Wheldrake bowed his head, as if in respect. For there are few more terrible fates than that of the immortal separated, by force of the most profound natural logic, from those immortal souls it cherishes in life. It can know only the pain of death but never the ecstasy of everlasting life. Its pleasures and rewards are short-lived; its torment, eternal.

And this made Elric think of his father, lingering in that timeless destruction of Imrryr's ancestor; himself separated from his one abiding love by his willingness to bargain with his patron demon—even betray him—for a little more unearned power on Earth.

The albino found himself brooding upon the nature of all unholy bargains, of his own dependency upon the hellsword Stormbringer, of his willingness to summon supernatural aid without thought of any spiritual consequences to himself and, perhaps most significantly, of his *unwillingness* to find a way to cure himself of the occult's seductive attraction; for there was a part of his strange brain that was curious to follow its own fate; to learn whatever disastrous conclusion lay in store for it—it needed to know the end of the saga: the value, perhaps, of its torment.

Elric found that he had walked up the deck to the forecastle, past the reverberant toad, to put his back against the bowsprit's copper-shod knuckle and stare up at the navigator as he hung, still motionless, in the rigging.

"Where do you journey, Esbern Snare?" he asked.

The grey man cocked his head, as if hearing a distant but familiar whistle. Then his pale green-grey eyes stared down into the albino's crimson orbs and a great gust of air escaped him, and a tear appeared upon his cheek.

"Nowhere, now," said Esbern Snare. "Nowhere, now, sir."

"Would you continue in Gaynor's service?" Elric asked. "Even when land is sighted?"

"Until I choose to do otherwise, sir. As you shall yourself observe. There is land ahead, no more than a mile before us."

"You can see it?" Elric asked in surprise, attempting to peer into the swirling vapours of the Heavy Sea.

"No, sir," said Esbern Snare. "But I can smell it."

And land it soon was. Land rising up from the slow, awful waters of the Heavy Sea; land like a wakened monster, an angry shadow, all sharp ridges and jagged points; cliffs of black marble; beaches of carbon, and black breakers which poured like the smoke of hell upon that squealing shore . . .

Land so inhospitable the voyagers who looked at it now were all pretty much of the same accord, that the Heavy Sea was less daunting; and it was Wheldrake who suggested they sail on until they found a more accessible island.

But Gaynor shook his flickering helm and lifted up his glowing fist and put his steel palm upon the slender shoulders of Charion Phatt. "You told me, child, that the other Phatts are here. Have they found the sisters?"

The young woman shook her head slowly. Her face was grave and her eyes seemed to look into some different reality. "They have not found the sisters."

"Yet they—and the sisters—are here?"

"Beyond this—aye—in there . . ." Her mouth grew a little slack now as she lifted her head and pointed towards the massive cliffs dashed by that black foam. "Aye—there—and there, they go—yet—oh, Uncle! I see why! The sisters ride on. But Uncle? Where is Grandma? The sisters go towards the East. It is in their nature to bear always eastward, now. They are going home."

"Good," says Gaynor with deep satisfaction. "We must find a place to land."

And Wheldrake confided to Elric that he had the feeling Gaynor was prepared to wreck them all now, in order to make landfall and continue his pursuit.

And yet the ship was beached at last upon that black, salty shingle up which the gougy tide lazily rolled and as lazily retreated.

"It is like," said Wheldrake in distaste as, the skirts of his frock-coat wrapped around his narrow chest, he stepped gingerly through the shallows, "a form of molasses. What causes this, Master Snare?"

His bundle under his arm, Esbern Snare lifted his long legs through the liquid. "Nothing," he said, "save a minor distortion in the fabric of time. Such places are not uncommon in this particular Sphere. In my own they were rare. I came across a small one—a matter of a few feet—near the North Pole. That would have been around the turn of your century, Master Wheldrake, I think."

"Which one, sir? I am a native of several. I am, as it were, timeless. Perhaps I have been granted my own particular ironic doom, ha, ha!"

Now Esbern Snare loped ahead, up the beach to where a great crack had opened in the wall of marble and through the jagged opening poured a shaft of watery golden light. "I think we have our pathway to the cliff-top," he said.

His bundle between his teeth, he was already climbing—his long limbs perfect for the route he chose from jutting crag to jutting crag—a great, grey spider scuttling up the rock, finding first one ledge and then another, until he had marked a path for the others, an easy means of climbing from the beach to the surface of the cliff. They mounted this, one at a time, with Elric bringing up the rear. On Gaynor's orders the sailors were already letting down their sail and moving the ship back into the water while from the forecastle came the wailing and groanings of a recently awakened toad who only now realised that its beloved was departing, perhaps for ever.

Soon they all stood upon the cliff and tried to look back at the ocean, but already billowing black cloud buried the Heavy Sea from view, and all they could hear was the sinister tide scraping on the beaches, increasingly faint—as if the entire scene retreated downwards, away from them—or as if the cliff rose up.

Elric turned. They were above the cloud-line now and the air was easier to breathe. Stretching away from them was a flat plain of gleaming rock—an immense vista of marble in which, here and there, gleamed little lights, as if there were creatures so densely constituted that they lived in the marble as we might live in oxygen, and were occupied, domestically, below.

Esbern Snare voiced his own provincial fears. "This has the look of troll country," he said. "Have I travelled so far to endure the hospitality of Troll-heim? What an irony that would be."

Gaynor silenced him. "If we were all left to stand about bemoaning the particulars of our special dooms, gentlemen, we should be here for ever. Given that at least two of our company are immortal, this could prove singularly boring. I would beg of you, Esbern Snare, neither to keen nor to make any other vocal reminder of your soul's agony."

And the grey navigator frowned, perhaps a little surprised by an accusation which might have been better applied, he guessed, to the accuser himself. But Gaynor made no such acknowledgement. Of that socially misliked company he seemed the only one unwilling to extend to others the tolerance he longed for, the tolerance exemplified by the sublime justice of the Cosmic Balance which he had forsaken. Increasingly, it seemed, he grew both frightened and impatient, perhaps because he had secrets from them—a prior knowledge of this land and its inhabitants? He fell silent now and spoke no more to them until at last the uncompromising hardness of the marble gave way to earth and then to grass and the land began to slope downwards towards a surprisingly lovely valley through which a stream meandered and whose hills were clad with all kinds of thickly growing winter trees. Yet there was no sign of habitation and the air grew steadily colder as they descended the trackless slopes towards the valley floor until they were glad of the extra garments they had brought in their packs.

Only Esbern Snare refused to put his bundled apparel about his shoulders. Instead he hugged the parcel tighter to his chest, as if threatened. And again Elric felt a frisson of understanding for the grey man who only today had lost the last of his hope.

They camped that night in a pine-spinney, with a big fire roaring against the bitter cold and a moon appearing, almost unexpectedly overhead in the clear winter sky, huge and silver and casting deep shadows amongst the trees—shadows which were calm contrast to the leaping, unsettled shadows made by the great fire.

Soon the fire had grown so hot, fed by a lucky find of dead wood, that Elric, Charion and Wheldrake were forced to move a little further away, lest they be scorched in their sleep. Only Esbern Snare and Gaynor the Damned were left in the blaze of firelight, the grey, sad man, and the supernatural prince in his unstable armour—two doomed immortals attempting to warm their souls against the chill of eternal night; creatures who would have chosen the flames of hell rather than endure their present suffering, who longed for another reality, such as once they had both known, where pain was banished, and men and women were rarely tempted to give up the peace of their souls in return for the gaudy treasures, the greedy pleasures of the occult.

"What a beautiful thing," said Charion, almost in echo of these thoughts, "is a butterfly's wing. The bounty of nature bestow'd on a rose. Do you know that one, Master Wheldrake?"

The poet admitted that it was not in his repertoire. He considered the metre. He wondered if it were the best choice for the sentiment.

"I think I am ready for sleep now," she said, a hint of regret in her tone.

"Sleep is a preferred theme in my own work," he agreed. "Daniel's sonnet on the subject is excellent. At least, academically speaking. Do you know it?

"*Care-charmer Sleep, son of the sable Night,*
Brother to Death, in silent darkness born,
Relieve my languish, and restore the light;
With dark forgetting of my care return,
And let the day be time enough to mourn
The shipwreck of my ill-adventured youth."

He quoted on, while a thin, cold breeze ran amongst the trees and soon his snores had gently and unostentatiously joined the rest . . .

Dawn had brought some snow. While most of the party shivered against it and cursed their bad luck, Esbern Snare opened his mouth and drew in the smell of it, licked his lips at the taste of it; a spring in his gait as he performed his tasks in the making of the morning meal. But already there was conflict as Gaynor cried: "Do you not recall a bargain made between us, my lady? A bargain which you yourself proposed!"

"A bargain which is now ended, sir. You have had your several uses of me. I become my own woman again. I brought you here and you shall seek your sisters here, but with no help from me!"

"Our interests are the same! It is folly to separate." Prince Gaynor's hand was upon the pommel of his broadsword as if he would threaten her had his pride permitted it. He had thought his native power was enough to persuade her and this was evident in every thwarted movement of his body, his frustrated tones. "Your family will find the sisters. They are bound to. We are upon the same quest!"

"No," said Charion. "For whatever reason—and I cannot detect one—the sisters go that way, but my uncle goes yonder—and to my uncle, sir, I must follow!"

"You agreed we should seek the sisters together."

"That was until I knew my uncle and grandma were in danger. I go to them. I go, sir, unquestionably, to them!"

And with that she was off through the trees, bidding farewell to no-one, dashing the snow from the branches she bent in her progress, her breath steaming and her wiry body gathering speed, as if she had no more time to lose.

Wheldrake was picking up his books and his miscellaneous possessions shouting out for her to pause. He would go with her! She needed a man, he said, upon her adventure. His own farewells were rapid and half-ended as he fled upon his beloved's trail leaving a cold and sudden silence behind him as, over the ashes of the guttering fire, the three doomed men regarded one another in uncertain camaraderie.

"Will you seek the sisters with me, Elric?" Gaynor asked at last. His voice was calmer now, almost chastened.

"The sisters have what I require, so I must find them in order to ask them for it," said Elric.

"And you, Esbern Snare?" Gaynor asked. "Are you with us, still?"

"I have no interest in your elusive sisters," said Esbern Snare, "unless they have the key to my release."

"They carry two keys, it seems," said Elric, putting a friendly hand on the grey man's shoulder, "so perhaps they have a third for you."

"Very well," said Esbern Snare. "I will join you. Do you go towards the East?"

"Always east, we've learned, for our sisters," said Gaynor.

So the three of them—tall figures, lean as winter weasels—began their journey eastward, up the steep slopes of the valley, through frozen foothills, to a range of ancient mountains, whose rotting granite threatened to collapse with every foot they set upon it, while the snow came thicker now and they must break ice to get their water, save at noon, when the thin sun warmed the world enough to make it run; wide ribbons of silver racing through the glittering white shards.

Gaynor continued to brood in silence while Esbern Snare, loping ahead much of the time, grew increasingly alert as if he had found his native element. And all the while his bundle never left him, whether he slept or ate, so that one day, as they made cautious progress above a deep gorge which had filled with snow to make a sort of glacier, below which a fierce torrent could be heard rushing through caverns and tunnels it had carved through the ice, Elric asked him why he valued the thing so greatly. Was it some keepsake, perhaps?

They had paused for breath upon the narrow path, their feet hardly as long as the track was wide, but Gaynor had marched tirelessly on, apparently oblivious of the depth and steepness of the gorge.

"It is a treasure in a sense, sir!" Esbern Snare uttered a humourless laugh.

"For I must value it as I value nothing else. As I value, if you like, my very life. My soul, I fear, has modest worth now, or I would name that, also."

"So it is precious to you, indeed," said Elric. He talked chiefly to rid himself of the grief he felt for losing Wheldrake's company, as if part of him—that part which relished life and human love—was forbidden to him, banished. He felt as frozen as the glacier below, with a torrent bursting within him, unable to find expression in the ways he most valued—the ordinary ways of loving the world and the friends it offered. Perhaps he lacked the refinements of language required to adapt and modify his sentiments and yet he understood, better than anyone, how language itself was the perfect and perhaps the only honourable way of earning his right to respect among those denizens of the natural world whom he, in turn, respected. Yet still it was through action, rather than words, that he tried to accomplish his unvoiced ambitions. Thoughtless action, blind romance, had led him to destroy everything he cherished and he had sought understanding in taking only the action suggested by others, by following the trade of other impoverished Melnibonéan nobles, of mercenary—and a mercenary of exceptional accomplishments and gifts. Even now his quest was not of his own devising. In his heart of hearts he knew he must soon begin to look for some more positive means of achieving what he had hoped to achieve with the sack of the Dreaming City and the destruction of the Bright Empire of Melniboné. Thus far he had looked chiefly at the past. But there were no answers there. Only examples which scarcely suited his present condition.

There was a long silence as the two men stood together on the narrow ridge, staring across the gorge at the far banks, at the lifeless landscape, where not a bird or a rabbit could be seen, as if time, already slowing in the Heavy Sea, had come almost to a stop, and the crashing of the water underneath the ice seemed to fade away to leave only the steady sound of their breathing.

"I loved her," said the grey man suddenly, his breast convulsing, almost as if struck by something heavy. Another pause, as if he drowned, and then his manner was steady again. "Her name was Helva of Nesvek, daughter of the

Lord of Nesvek, and the finest and most womanly of mortals, in all her wit and art, her grace and her charity; there was none saintlier, nor more natural (in natural matters), than my Helva. Well, I was of good family but not wealthy in the way that Lord Nesvek was wealthy and it had been pronounced by the great lord himself that his daughter's hand should go to the man worthiest of God. I understood that in Lord Nesvek's judgement God was inclined to bless those worthiest of Him with worldly riches and this, to Nesvek's lord, was the true and proper order of things. So I knew I could not win my Helva's hand, though she had already chosen me. I conceived the notion of seeking supernatural aid and, in short, made a bargain with a troll, by which the troll should build me a fine cathedral church—the finest in the Northlands—whereupon, when the building was completed, I was to have discovered the name of the architect or forfeit my eyes and heart to him. Well, by happy chance, I overheard the troll's wife singing to her infant child, telling him that he should not cry, for soon Fine, his father, would be home with a human's eyes and heart for him to feast upon.

"Thus did I achieve my end and Lord Nesvek found it impossible, of course, to refuse a suitor who could build such a magnificent monument to God, and at monumental cost, quite evidently.

"Meanwhile, of course, the poor troll-wife, the source of my salvation, was beaten regularly by her infuriated spouse and I began the building of our estate, about a mile from Kallundborg, where I had built the church and would be able to see the spire from my new house's tower. The building went well, even without trollish labour, and soon the hall was raised, with good outhouses and cottages for the servants, on prime land, thanks to my Helva's dowry. Thus were we all accommodated, it seemed. Until the coming of the wolf to our land that next winter, when we settled to enjoy the long nights with merriment and stories and all manner of festivity, as well as the hard work of winter stock-caring. Made harder, now, because of our wolf. A huge beast, twice the weight and bulk of a tall man, the wolf had killed dogs, cattle, sheep and a child in its search for food. Few bones had been found, and those gnawed through for the marrow, as if the wolf fed cubs as well as itself. Which we found strange for dead of winter, though it has been known for wolves to bear more than one litter in a year, especially after a mild previous winter and an early spring. Then the wolf killed the pregnant wife of my steward and carried off what remains we did not find in the shallow hole it had rested in while it devoured the flesh it needed to continue its rapid escape from us. For, of course, we pursued it.

"One by one the other men gave up, for a variety of reasons which the steward and I accepted with good grace, and then there were only the two of us following the wolf's trail into a deep, wooded ravine, until one night the wolf leapt over the fires we had built, believing ourselves safe, and took my steward—killing him before he dragged him off through the fires as if they did not exist.

"I will admit, Prince Elric, that I was near-frozen with terror! Though I had shot arrows at the beast and cut at it with my sword, I had not harmed it. The wounds I made healed immediately. I knew then—and only then, sir— that I was dealing with no natural animal."

For a little while Esbern Snare inched his way along the path, to keep circulation and in the hope of reaching a better thoroughfare before nightfall. When next they took breath, he concluded his story.

"I continued to track the beast, though I believe it thought itself free of pursuit—perhaps deliberately killing my steward, not because it was hungry, but because it wished to be rid of our company. Indeed, I found most of his remains a day later and was surprised to discover that what I assumed to be some human traveller had helped itself to the dead man's effects, though the clothes, of course, were too bloody and torn to be of use.

"I grew so angry and greedy for revenge that I could no longer sleep. Un-rested and yet untired now, I kept up a steady pursuit until one night, under a three-quarter moon, I came upon a human camp. It was a woman who camped there. I watched her through the trees, too cautious to announce myself, yet ready to defend her if the wolf attacked. Now, to my concern, I saw that she had two small children with her, a boy and a girl, both clad in a mixture of animal hides and a miscellany of other garments, who were eating soup from a pot she had built over her fire. The woman looked weary and I assumed she was fleeing from some brutish husband, or that her village had been destroyed by raiders—for we were now on the borderland between the Northern people and the Easterners, those cruel nomads who are without Christian religion nor any pagan honesty. Yet something in me still kept me back. I realised at length that I was using her as a lure—as bait for the wolf. Well, the wolf did not come, and as I watched I took note of everything within that camp, until I saw the great wolfskin which hung upon the tree under which she slept with her children, and I took it for some kind of charm, some way in which the wolf could be resisted. So I watched another day and another night, following the woman up towards the far mountains, where the savage Eastern nomads roamed, and I thought to warn her of her danger, yet it was becoming gradually clear to me that she was not the one who was in danger. Her movements were sure, and she cared for her children with the air of someone who had long lived a wild life beyond the very outposts of civilisation. I admired her. She was a good-looking woman and the way she moved made me forget my marriage oath. Perhaps, too, I watched her for that reason. I began to feel a sense of power in this observation, this secret knowledge of her. I know now that I did, indeed, possess a kind of power which only those of her like might possess and those were the only creatures whose presence she could not detect. Had another been with me, she would have known at once.

"It was on the night of the full moon that I saw her take out the folded wolfskin and drape it around her shoulders, saw her drop to all fours and in a bewildering instant stand, growling faintly at the children to stay close to the fire, looking out into the night, an enormous wolf. Yet still she did not see me, did not scent me. I was invisible to her supernatural senses. She moved off towards the mountains and was back at noon that next day with a kill, some nomad boy, probably a herder, and two lambs, which she had dragged, using the boy's body as a kind of sledge. The human remains she left for herself, but assumed her woman form once she had brought the lambs into camp. These she prepared for her children. Later that evening, as they ate the rich-smelling stew she had cooked, she returned to her human kill and devoured a good deal of him, almost certainly in wolf shape. I was too cautious to get closer to her.

"By now, of course, I understood that the woman was a werewolf. A werewolf of special ferocity, since she had two human cubs to feed. These little creatures were innocent children and had no lycanthropic taint. My guess was that she had taken to this life from desperation, in order that her children should not starve. Yet this had meant other children would starve and more would die, merely to sustain her brood, so my sympathy was limited. As soon as she slept that night, glutted with food, I gathered the courage to sneak into the camp, tear the wolfskin from the tree and make my way back into the forest.

"She awakened almost immediately, but now that I possessed the skin, with which she transformed herself into an invincible beast, I knew I was safe. From the shadows I spoke to her. 'Madam, I have the frightful thing you have used to kill my friends and their families. It will be burned outside the church of Kallundborg when I return! I would not kill a mother before her own children, so while you are with them you are safe from my vengeance. I bid thee farewell.'

"At which the poor creature began to wail and scream—quite unlike the self-possessed mother who had cared for her young in the wild. But I would not listen to her. I knew she must be punished. What I did not know then, of course, was how cruel her punishment would be. 'Do you understand how I must survive if you take away my skin?' she asked. 'Aye, madam, I do,' said I. 'But you must suffer those consequences now. There is meat enough for several days in your pot—and a little meat left outside your camp, which I do not think you are too squeamish to use. So farewell again, madam. This evil thing will be burning soon upon a Christian pyre.'

"'You must have pity,' she said, 'for you are of my blood. Few can change as I can change—as you can change. Only you could steal that skin. I knew that I should fear you more. Yet I spared you, for I recognised my kindred. Would you not, sir, show loyalty to our common blood and spare my children their unthinkable fate?'

"But I listened no more and I left. As I went away she set up a terrible wailing and howling—a screaming and begging—a bestial, horrible whining—as she called out for her only means of any dignity, any vestige of humanity. That is the final irony of the Undead—that they cling to such shreds of human pride—cling to the memory of the very thing they have bartered in order to become what they have become! Surely the worst fate, I thought, that a werewolf could know. But there are worse fates than that, sir—or at least refinements on them. I left that wolf-woman howling and slavering—already a maddened wretch. It was almost impossible to imagine such agony as she already expressed, let alone imagine the pain to come.

"Oh, well, sir, the story's the usual miserable tale of folly and expediency you know so well. Trapped by the winter of the Eastern wastes, I resorted to using the skin myself. By the time I returned to Kallundborg I was wedded to it more powerfully than I was wedded to my sweetheart and my wife, Helva of Nesvek. I sought religious help and found only horror at my tale. Thus I left to wander the world, seeking some salvation, some means of returning to the past I had known, of being reunited with my darling. More unearthly adventures befell me, sir, from Sphere to Sphere, and then I learned that the troll itself sought vengeance and tricked some cleric, some visiting bishop, into a bargain that brought down the whole cathedral while the larger part of the population, my wife among them, prayed for my lost soul . . .

"That is what Gaynor promised to tell me—the fate of my wife. And that is why I weep now, sir, so long after the event."

Elric could find no words of reply and none of consolation for this good man cursed to rely for his only existence upon that horrible skin, forced to perform the most inhuman acts of evil savagery or go for ever into nothingness, never to be united with his lost love, even in death.

Perhaps it was not therefore surprising that Elric fingered the pommel of his hellsword and thought deeply upon his own relationship with the blade and saw in poor Esbern Snare a fate more terrible than his own.

The next time he extended a generous hand to the grey man as he stumbled through the twilight, there was a peculiar sense of kinship in the gesture. Slowly, the two whose stories were so different, and whose fates were so similar, continued their progress along that narrow ridge of rock above the sinister whisper of water as it cut its way through the snows of the ravine.

5

Detecting Certain Hints of the Higher Worlds;
A Convention of the Patrons and the Patronised;
Sacrifice of the Sane and Good.

Prince Gaynor the Damned paused upon the rocky slopes of the last mountain and peered across a waste of scrub grass towards a far distant range. "This land seems all mountains," he said. "Perhaps, however, that is the rim of the far shore? The sisters must be close. We could scarcely miss them on this barren plain."

They had eaten the last of their food and still had seen no signs of animals on earth or in the sky.

"It's as if it never had inhabitants," said Esbern Snare. "As if life has been exiled from this plain completely."

"I've seen such sights before," Elric told him. "They make me uncomfortable—for it can be a sign that Law has conquered everything or that Chaos rules, as yet unmanifested . . ."

They agreed that they had all shared such experiences, but now Gaynor grew even more impatient, exhorting them to make better speed towards the mountains, "lest the sisters take ship from the farther shore," but Esbern Snare, sustained neither by whatever hellish force fed Gaynor nor by the dragon venom which Elric used, grew hungry and began to fall back, fingering the bundle he carried, and sometimes Elric thought he heard him slavering and growling to himself and when he turned once to enquire, he looked into eyes of purest suffering.

When they broke camp next morning, Esbern Snare, the Northern Were-wolf, was gone, succumbing to the temptation which had already destroyed any hope that was ever in him. Twice, Elric thought he heard a mournful howling which was echoed by the mountains and so impossible to trace. Then, once more, there was nothing but silence.

For a day and a night, Elric and Gaynor exchanged not one word but marched in a kind of dogged trance towards the mountains. With the follow-ing dawn, however, they found that the plain was rising slightly, in a gentle hill, beyond which they thought they could detect the faintest sounds of a settlement, perhaps even a large town.

Gaynor, in good spirits, clapped Elric upon the back and said, almost jauntily, "Soon, friend Elric, we shall both have what we seek!"

And Elric said nothing, wondering what Gaynor would do if, by some strange chance, they both sought the same thing—or, at least, the same container. And this made him think of the Rose again and he mourned the loss of her.

"Perhaps we should determine the exact nature of our quest," he said, "lest we are unprepared when we eventually meet the sisters."

Gaynor shrugged. He turned his helm towards Elric and his eyes seemed less troubled than they had been of late. "We do not seek the same thing, Elric of Melniboné, of that you can be assured."

"I seek a rosewood box," said Elric bluntly.

"And I seek a flower," said Gaynor carelessly, "that has bloomed since time began."

They were close to the brow of the hill now and had almost reached it when the earth was suddenly shaken by an enormous booming which threat-ened to throw them off their balance. Again came the great reverberant noise. Seemingly some vast gong was being struck, and struck again, until Elric was covering his ears, while Gaynor had fallen to one knee, as if pressed to the ground by a gigantic hand.

Ten times in all the great gong sounded, but its reverberations continued, almost endlessly, to shake the crags of the surrounding mountains.

Able to move forward again, Elric and Gaynor reached the top of the hill to stare upwards at the enormous construction which, both could have sworn, had not been there even a moment before. Yet here it was in all its solid and complicated detail, a network of wooden gantries and monstrous cogs, all creaking and groaning and turning with slow precision, while metal whirled and flashed within—copper and bronze and silver wires and levers and balances, forming impossible patterns, peculiar diffractions—revealing the thousands of human figures toiling upon this vast framework, turning the handles, walking the treadmills, carrying the sand or the pails of water up and down the walkways, balancing between pegs which were carefully placed to maintain some delicate internal equilibrium, and the whole thing shuddering as if it must fall at any moment and send every naked man, woman and child who worked perpetually upon it to their immediate destruction. At the very top of this tower was a large globe which Elric thought at first must be of crystal but then he realised it consisted entirely of the strongest ectoplasmic membrane he had ever seen—and he guessed at once what the membrane imprisoned, for there was scarcely a sorcerer on Earth who had not sought its secret . . .

Gaynor, too, understood what the membrane contained and it was clear he feared what must soon be revealed as that vast, unearthly skeleton-clock measured off the moments and a humorous voice spoke casually from nowhere.

"See, my little treasures, how Arioch brings time to a timeless world? Merely one of the small benefits of Chaos. It is my homage to the Cosmic Balance."

And his laughter was hideous in its easy cruelty.

The immense clock clicked and clattered, whirred and grunted, and the structure trembled, shivering with every movement, while from within the globular membrane at the very top, which turned and shook with the passing of each second, an angry eye occasionally appeared, while a fanged mouth raged in supernatural silence and claws, fiercer than any dragon's, flashed and scratched and tore, but never with effect, for the entity was trapped within the most powerful prison known in, below or beyond the Higher Worlds. The only entity Elric knew which required such bonds to hold it was a Lord of the Higher Worlds!

Now Gaynor, realising the same thing at the same time, took steps backwards and looked about him, as if he might find some sudden refuge, but there was none and Arioch laughed the louder at his dismay. "Aye, little Gaynor, your silly strategies have gained you nothing. When will you all learn that you have neither the resources nor, indeed, the character required to gamble against the gods, even such petty gods as myself and Count Mashabak here?" The laughter was richer now.

This was what Gaynor had feared. His master, the only creature capable of protecting him against Arioch, had lost whatever engagement had taken place between them. And this meant, too, that Sadric's attempt to cheat his patrons of their tribute might also have failed.

Yet Gaynor had lost too much already, faced too much horror, contemplated too many repellent fates, caused and observed too much suffering, to show any distress of his own. He drew himself up, his hands folded before him, and lowered his helmeted head in the slightest of acknowledgements. "Then I must call thee master now, Lord Arioch," he said.

"Aye. Always thy true master. Always the master concerned for his slaves. I take a great interest in the activities of my little humans, for in so many ways their ambitions and dreams mirror those of the gods. Arioch was ever the Duke of Hell most mortals turn to when they have need of Chaos's ministrations. And I love thee. But I love the folk of Melniboné most, and of these I love Sadric and Elric most of all."

And Gaynor waited, his helm still slightly bowed, as if expecting some doom of singular and exquisite savagery.

"See how I protect my slaves," Arioch continued, still invisible, his voice moving from one part of the valley to the next, yet always intimate, always amused. "The clock sustains their lives. Should any one of them, old or young, for a moment fail in their specific function, the whole structure will collapse.

Thus do my creatures learn the true nature of interdependence. One peg in the wrong socket, one pail of water in the wrong sluice, one false step upon a treadmill, one hesitant hand upon a lever, and all are destroyed. To continue to live, they must work the clock, and each creature is responsible for the lives of all the rest. While my friend Count Mashabak up there would not, of course, be greatly harmed, there would be a certain pleasure for me in watching his little prison rolling about at random amongst the ruins. Do you see your ex-master, Gaynor? What was it he told you to seek?"

"A flower, master. A flower that has lived for thousands of years, since it was first plucked."

"I wonder why Mashabak would not tell me that himself. I am pleased with thee, Gaynor. Wouldst thou serve me?"

"As thou wishest, master."

"Sweet slave, I love thee again! Sweet, sweet, obedient slave! Oh, how I love thee!"

"And I love thee, master," came Gaynor's bitter response—a voice that had known millennia of defeat and frustrated longing. "I am thy slave."

"My slave! My lovely slave! Wouldst thou not remove thine helm and reveal thy face to me?"

"I cannot, master. There is nothing to reveal."

"As thou art nothing, Gaynor, save for the life I permit in thee. Save for the forces of the pit which empower thee. Save for the all-consuming greed which informs thee. Wouldst thou have me destroy thee, Gaynor?"

"If it pleases thee, master."

"I think you should work for a while upon the clock. Would you serve me there, Gaynor? Or would you continue your quest?"

"As it pleases thee, Lord Arioch."

Elric, sickened by this, found himself full of a peculiar self-loathing. Was it his fate, also, to serve Chaos as thoroughly as Gaynor served it—without even the remains of self-respect or will? Was this the final price one paid for all bargains with Chaos? And yet he knew his own doom was not the same, that he was still cursed with a degree of free will. Or was that merely an illusion with which Arioch softened the truth? He shuddered.

"And Elric, would you work upon the clock?"

"I would destroy thee first, Lord Arioch," said the albino coolly, his hand upon the hilt of his hellsword. "My compacts with thee are of blood and ancient inheritance. I made no special bargain of my soul. 'Tis others' souls, my lord, I dedicate to thee."

He sensed within himself now some strength which even the Duke of Hell could not annihilate—some small part of his soul which remained his own. Yet, also, he saw a future where that tiny fragment of integrity could dissipate and leave him as empty of hope and self-respect as Gaynor the Damned . . .

His glance at the ex-Prince of the Universal held no contempt—only a certain understanding and affinity with the wretched creature Gaynor had become. He was but a step away from that ultimate indignity.

There came a kind of thin screech from the ectoplasmic prison and Count Mashabak seemed to take some small pleasure in his rival's discomfort.

"Thou art my slave, Elric, make no mistake," purred the Chaos Lord. "And will ever remain so, as all your ancestors were mine . . ."

"Save one before me," Elric said firmly. "The bargain was broken by another, Lord Arioch. I have inherited no such thing. I told thee, my lord—when thou aidest me, I giveth thee the immortal plundering to thyself—souls like these, who worketh thine clock. These, great Duke of Hell, I do not begrudge thee, neither am I sparing in the numbers I allot thee. Without my summoning, as thou knowest, it is all but impossible for any Lord of the Higher Worlds to get to *my* world and upon that world I am the most powerful of all mortal sorcerers. Only I have the native powers to call to thee across the dimensions of the multiverse and provide a psychic path which thou canst follow. That thou knowest. That is why I live. That is why thou aideth me. I am the key which one day Chaos hopes to turn and open wide all the doors throughout the unconquered multiverse. That is my greatest power. And, Lord Arioch, it is mine to use as I desire, to bargain with as I choose and with whom I choose. It is my strength and my shield against all supernatural fierceness and threatening demands. I accept thee as my patron, Noble Demon, but not as my master."

"These are just silly words, little Elric. Wisps of dandelion on the summer breeze. Yet here you are, through no decision of your own. And here I am, by determined effort, exactly where I wish to be. Which freedom seems the best to you, my poorly pigmented pet?"

"If you are saying, Lord Arioch, would I rather be myself or thyself, I must still say that I would be myself; for perpetual Chaos must be as tedious as perpetual Law, or any other constant. A kind of death. I believe I still have more to relish of the multiverse than hast thou, Sir Demon. I still live. I am still of the living."

And from within the helm of Prince Gaynor the Damned came a great groan of anguish, for he, like Esbern Snare, was neither of the living nor the dead.

Then, sitting astride the ectoplasmic ball in which Count Mashabak squatted and glared, there appeared the naked, golden image of a handsome youth, a dream of fair Arcadia, whose goodness was sweeter than honey, whose beauty was richer than cream, and whose wicked eyes, delirious with cruelty, flashed the appalling lie for everything unholy and perverse that it was.

It giggled.

Arioch giggled. Then grinned. Then made water over the bulging membrane, as his helpless rival, engorged with the psychic energies of a hundred suns, raged and shouted from within, as helpless as a weasel in a snare.

"*Mad Jack Porker ran the cripple down again; seized him by the brain, they said; didn't stop till he was dead . . . Greedy Porker, Greedy Porker, hung him by his humpo-storker . . . Sit still, my dear count, while I take my comforts, sir, I pray you. You are an ill-mannered demon, sir. I always said so . . . Hee, hee, hee . . . Do you smell cheese, sir? Would you have a piece of ice about you, Jim? Hee, hee, hee . . .*"

"As I believe I observed earlier," said the albino prince to the still-cowed Gaynor, "the most powerful of beings are not necessarily the most intelligent, nor, indeed, sane, nor well-mannered. The more one knows of the gods, the more one learns this fundamental lesson . . ." He turned his back upon Arioch and his clock, trusting that his patron demon did not decide, upon a whim, to extinguish him. He knew that while he protected that tiny spark of self-respect within him, nothing could destroy him in spirit. It was his own thing; what some would have called his immortal soul.

Yet with every movement and every word he trembled and weakened, wanting to cry out that he was no more than Arioch's creature, to do his master's every bidding and be rewarded by his master's every bounty: and, even so, be struck down, as he might be struck now, on a chance change of his master's mood.

For this was the other thing that Elric knew; that to compromise with Tyranny is always to be destroyed by it. The sanest and most logical choice lay always in resistance. This knowledge gave Elric his strength—his profound anger at injustice and inequality—his belief, now that he had visited Tanelorn, that it was possible to live in harmony with mortals of all persuasions and remain vital and engaged with the world. These things he would neither sell nor offer for sale and, in refusing to give himself up wholly to Chaos, it meant he bore his weight of crimes upon his own conscience and must live, night and day, with the knowledge of what and whom he had killed or ruined. This, he guessed, was a weight that Gaynor had been unable to bear. For his part, he would rather bear the weight of his own guilt than the weight that Gaynor had chosen.

He turned again to look up at that obscene clock, Arioch's cruel joke upon his slaves, upon his conquered rival, and every atom of his deficient blood cried out against such casual injustice, such delight in the terror and misery of others, such contempt for everything that lived within the multiverse, including itself; such cosmic cynicism!

"Have you brought me thy father's soul, Elric? Where is that which I told thee to find, my sweet?"

"I seek it still, Lord Arioch." Elric knew that Arioch had not yet established his rule across this whole realm and that his hold upon his new territory must still be tenuous. This meant that Arioch had nothing like the power he possessed in his own domain, where only the most crazed sorcerer would ever consider venturing. "And when I find it, I shall give it up to my father. Then, I would say, the rest is between yourself and him."

"You are a brave little stoat, my darling, now that you are no longer in my kingdom. But this one shall soon be mine. All of it. Do not anger me, darling pale one. *Soon the time will come when thou shalt serve mine every command!*"

"Possibly, great Lord of Hell, but meanwhile that time is not here. I make no further bargains. And I believe that thou wouldst as readily keep our old bargain as have none at all."

A growl of rage escaped Lord Arioch as he pummelled at the ectoplasmic prison with his fists, while Count Mashabak screamed with insane laughter from within. The Duke of Hell looked down upon the labouring thousands, each one of whom maintained, only by the most accurate and mechanical rhythms, the lives of its fellows, and he smirked, threatening with a pointed, golden finger to poke at one of the little figures and so bring the whole complicated structure to collapse.

Then he looked up at where Gaynor the Damned stood, unmoving, as he had been for some time. "Find me that flower and I will make you a Knight of Chaos, immortal nobility, ruling in our name a thousand kingdoms!"

"I will find the flower, great duke," said Gaynor.

"We shall make an example of thee, Elric," said Arioch. "Even now. By conquering thee, I shall establish Chaos fully upon this plane." And one golden hand stretched suddenly, longer and longer, larger and larger, towards Elric's face. But the albino had drawn his runesword with all the rapid skill of years and the great battle-blade roared out a challenge and a threat to all the myriad denizens of the Lower, Middle and Higher Worlds, to come to it, to cast themselves upon it, to feed it and its master, for this thing was not an owned thing at all, but had become, if it had not always been, an independent force

whose sole loyalty was to its own existence, yet was as dependent upon Elric's
wielding it as Elric was dependent upon its energy for his own survival. This
unholy symbiosis, more profoundly mysterious than the wisest philosophers
could fathom, was what made Elric the chosen child of Fate and it was what
had, in the end, robbed him of his happiness.

"This must not be!" Arioch pulled back in thwarted anger. "Force must
not fight force! Not yet. Not yet."

"There is more than Law and Chaos at work in the multiverse, my lord,"
said Elric calmly, the sword still held before him, "and more than one of these
is thine enemy. Do not anger me too much."

"Ah, most dangerous and courageous of my souls, thou art truly fitted to
be my chosen mortal above all the others, ruling in my name, with my power.
Whole worlds would be thine, Elric—whole Spheres to mould to thy every
whim. All pleasure can be thine. All experience. And unendingly. Without price
or consequence. Eternal pleasure, Elric!"

"I have made myself clear, already, Lord Duke, on the subject of perpetu-
ality. It could be that one day in the future I shall determine that my fate lies
wholly with thee. But until that time . . ."

"I shall attack thy memory. That I *can* do!"

"Only in some ways, Lord Arioch. Never in dreams. In my dreams, I recall
everything. But with this pell-mell twirling from plane to plane and Sphere to
Sphere, the worlds of memory and dreams become confused with the worlds
of reality and immediacy. Aye, you can attack my mind, my lord. But not my
soul's memory."

Which set insane Count Mashabak to cackling again. "*Gaynor!*" His wild
eyes caught sight of his former servant. "*Free me from this and thy reward will
be tenfold what I promised.*"

"Death," said Gaynor suddenly. "Death, death, death is all I'm greedy for.
And that you all deny me!"

"Because we value thee, dear one . . ." said the honey-sweet boy, lifting its
head and chittering, like a startled wren. "I am Chaos. I am everything. I am

the Lord of the Non-Linear, Captain of the *Random Particle* and Entropy's greatest celebrant! I am the wind from nowhere and I am the drowner of worlds; I am the Prince of Infinite Possibility! What glorious changes shall bloom upon the face of the multiverse, what unlikely and perverse marriages shall be sanctified by hell's priesthood, and what wonders and pleasures there will be, Elric! Nothing predictable. The only true justice in the multiverse— where all, even the gods, are subject to random birth and random annihilation! To banish Resolution and have instead eternal Revolution. A multiverse in permanent, gorgeous Crisis!"

"I fear I have spent too long with the gentler folk of the Young Kingdoms," said Elric softly, "to be much tempted by thy promises, my lord. Nor can I say I am much feared of thy threats. Prince Gaynor and myself are upon a quest. If we are to be of service to one another, sir, then I propose you let us continue upon that quest."

At which Arioch shifted his beautiful rump upon the yielding globe and said pettishly, "The damned one can go on his way. As for thee, recalcitrant servant, I cannot punish thee directly, but I can hamper thy quest until this more trustworthy servant achieves his end—whereupon I shall promise him far more than Mashabak promised him. I shall promise him a true death."

There came a sob from within Gaynor's peculiar helm and he fell to his knees, perhaps in gratitude.

Now Arioch raised a golden hammer in either fist and his youthful features were ablaze with glee as he brought first one hammer and then another down upon the yielding surface of the ectoplasmic womb, and with each blow came an unlikely booming, like that of a great gong, while within the prison Count Mashabak clapped scaly claws to his asymmetrical ears and howled in fearsome silence, as if whole universes were in anguish.

"It is the Time," cried Arioch. "It is the Time!"

Down falls Elric, screaming, with his hands, too, upon his ears. And Gaynor goes down, crawling and shrieking in a voice so high-pitched it sounds above the booming of the hammers.

And then there is a low whistling and Elric feels his substance being sucked away, bit by bit, from this plane to another. And he tries to fight against that force which only a Duke of Hell would use, since it damages whole histories and peoples with the violence of the dimensional rupturing, but he is helpless and his runesword will not help him. Stormbringer seems glad to leave that lifeless plane; it needs to feed on living souls and Arioch had offered it not a morsel from his store.

Yet, even as he watches the monstrous clock shimmer and grow misty to his sight, even as Gaynor's mysterious armour becomes faintly outlined against a fainter landscape, the albino sees a huge grey shape loping towards him, the red tongue lolling, the grey-green eyes glaring, the white fangs clashing in its ferocious head, and he knows that it is the hungered werewolf, become so maddened by its lack of food that it is ready to risk even Stormbringer's edge!

But then it has turned, sniffing, its savage mouth grinning and the hot saliva showering from its jaws, the ears laid first forward, then laid back, and it seems to curve in mid-air, a single fluid motion, and direct its great body straight upwards to where Lord Arioch giggles, then squeals in genuine surprise as Esbern Snare buries his fangs in the throat of one he recognises as his true tormentor.

So startled was Arioch, and so sparing now of his remaining powers upon this plane, that he could neither change his shape nor did he wish to flee—for by fleeing he would leave his captured rival, who might then be freed, and that he could not bear. So he struggled upon the swaying clock while the damned souls below worked frantically to correct every unpredictable motion of the thing, and the last Elric saw of Esbern Snare was his wolf body burning with a fierce, red-gold light as if he gave up, with selfless joy, his last few embers of life.

Then Elric saw the ectoplasmic sphere topple and fall towards the earth, with Arioch and Esbern Snare still locked together in conflict, and something flared and a darkness poured in upon him and swallowed him up and carried him relentlessly through the broken walls of a thousand dimensions, every one of which lifted a separate voice in protest; every one of which exploded with a different angry colour. He was propelled through the multiverse with almost the last remaining energy Arioch had been able to summon upon that plane.

That was what Esbern Snare had known and that was why he had awaited this opportunity to help his companions.

For Esbern Snare was, indeed, a man of rare goodness and sanity. He had lived too long in thrall to an evil power. He had seen all that he valued destroyed because of it. So, though he could not reclaim his immortal soul, he could ensure himself at least an immortal memorial, some action to ensure that his name, and the name of the love he could never find again, would be forever linked in the tales told amongst the realms, in all the various futures which lay ahead.

Thus did Esbern Snare the Northern Werewolf redeem his honour, if not his soul.

BOOK THREE

A ROSE REDEEMED; A ROSE REVIVED

Three swift swords for the sisters three;
* The first shall be of ivory;*
The second sword's forged of rarest gold;
* The third shall be cut from a granite fold.*

The first sword's name is "Just Old Man";
* And the second is called "The Urgent Brand";*
While the third thirsty sword of that glamour'd three
* Is the hungry blade named "Liberty."*

—Wheldrake,
Border Ballads

I

Of Weapons Possessed of Will;
A Family Reunion; Old Friends Found;
A Quest Resumed.

Now Elric fought to resist the force of Arioch's rage; stretching out his left hand as if to grasp at the fabric of time and space and slow his rush through the dimensions; clinging to his runesword while it howled and gibbered in his right hand, itself insane with mysterious supernatural anger at the Lord of Hell who had expended the last of his temporal energy on this plane in one final act of petty, and passing, vengeance. For Arioch had proved himself as whimsical as any other denizen of Chaos, willing to destroy all hoped-for futures in order to satisfy a momentary irritation. Which was why Chaos could be trusted no better than Law (which was inclined to permit similar actions, but in the name of principles whose purpose and point were frequently long-forgotten, creating as much mortal misery in the name of Intellect as Chaos wrought in the name of Sensibility).

Such thoughts were available to the albino, as he was flung through the radiantly pierced barriers of the multiverse—*for almost an eternity*—because, when eternity eludes the consciousness, then soon all which that consciousness knows is the singular agony of an expectation never *quite* fulfilled. Eternity is the end to time; the end to the suffering of anticipation; it is the beginning of life, of life unbounded! And thus Elric sought to embrace the beauty and the psychic grace of that perfect promised multiverse, perpetually in a state of transformation, between Life and Death, between Law and Chaos—accepting all, loving all, protecting all—that state of forever-changing societies, natural intelligences, benign supernature, evolving realities, forever relishing their own and others' differences, all in harmonious anarchy—that natural state, the wise ones knew, of each and every creature in each and every world, and which some imagined as a single omniscient entity, as the perfect Sum of Entirety.

Human love, thought the albino, as universe upon universe engulfed and expelled him, is our only constancy, the only quality with which we may conquer the inescapable logic of Entropy. And at that the sword trembled in his hand and seemed to be trying to twist free, almost as if it were disgusted by such sentimental altruism. But Elric clung to the blade as his only reality, his only security in this wildness of ruptured time and space, where the meaning of colour became profound and the meaning of sound unfathomable.

Again it wrenched at his grasp so that he must hold tighter to the quillons as the hellsword began to take its own determined course through the dimensions. It was at this point that Elric grew to respect the extraordinary power which dwelled within the black blade, of a power which seemed born of Chaos yet which had loyalty neither to Chaos nor to Law—yet neither did it serve the Balance—of a power so thoroughly a thing of itself that it required few outward manifestations and yet which might be the profound opposite of everything Elric valued and fought to create—as if some warring force were symbolised by this ironic bond between yearning idealist and cynical solipsist, a force, perhaps, which might be discovered in most thinking creatures, and which found over-dramatic resolution in the symbiosis between Stormbringer and the last lord of Melniboné . . .

Now the albino flew behind the runesword as it carved a path for itself—almost as if it drove back against Arioch's power, refusing the consequences not from any emotion Elric could understand, but to prove some principle as thoroughly upheld as any perhaps less mysterious principles of Law, almost as if it sought to correct some obscene malformation in the fabric of the cosmos, some event which it refused to permit . . .

Now Elric was caught up in a kind of intradimensional hurricane, in which a thousand reverses occurred within his brain at once and he became a thousand other creatures for an instant, and where he lived through more than ten other lives; a fate only minimally different from the one that was familiar to him and so vast did the multiverse become, so unthinkable, that he began to go mad as he attempted to make sense of just a fraction of what laid siege to his sanity and he begged the sword to rest, to pause in its complex flight, to spare him.

But he knew that the sword considered him secondary to its chief concern, which was to re-establish itself at the point it felt was *right* for it in the multiverse . . . Perhaps it was an impulse no more conscious than instinct . . .

Elric's senses multiplied and became changed.

There was a sweet, calm sound of roses while his father's music flooded his arteries with bewildered sadness . . . with excruciating anxiety . . . as if to let him know that the time was almost over when Sadric had any choice but to seek out his son's soul and join it with his own . . .

At which the howling runesword gave up a bellow of resistance, as if this, too, attacked its own ambitions and the logic of its own unreasoning determination to survive without compromise with any other entity in the multiverse—even, ultimately, Elric who must be extinguished, as soon as he had fulfilled his final destiny, which at present was known to no-one, even the runesword, which did not live in any past, present or future understood by creatures of the Lower, Middle or Higher Worlds; yet it wove a pattern of its own, calling upon vaster energies than any Elric had witnessed, than any it had ever been required to utilise in giving aid to him in return for the souls not apportioned to Arioch . . .

"Elric!"

"Father, I fear I have lost thy soul . . . !"

"My soul shall never be lost to thee, my son . . ."

A bright and sudden gleam of hard, pink-gold light, like a weapon against his eyes, and a smack of freezing air against his flesh, and a rhythmic sound, so familiar, so wonderful to him, that he felt the hot tears fall once, then twice, upon his chilled cheeks . . .

> "*So Gaynor rode to* The Ship That Was,
>   *And made of it his own,*
> *And three sisters rare he did ensnare,*
>   *To ensure the Chaos Throne.*

> *The first of these sisters was The Unfolded Flower,*
>   *The second was Duty's Bud,*
> *While the third-born they christened Secret Thorn*
>   *And her bower was built of blood.*"

And, sobbing, Elric fell into the welcoming arms of that great-hearted, if dwarfish, poet, Master Ernest Wheldrake. "My dear, good, sir! My good, old friend! Greetings to thee, Prince Elric. Does something pursue thee?" And he pointed back up through the deep snowbanks terracing the valley wall, where a fresh-ploughed furrow ran, as if Elric had slid from the top of the cliff to the bottom.

"I am glad to see thee, Master Wheldrake." He brushed caked snow from his clothing, wondering, not for the first time, if he had dreamed his journey through the multiverse or if the dragon venom, perhaps, possessed more than restorative qualities. He glanced across the fresh-trod snow of a small clearing in the winter birchwood and saw Stormbringer leaning, almost casually, against a tree, and for a pure, clear moment, he knew absolute hatred of the blade, that part of himself he could no longer exist without or (as some small voice continued to tell him) that part, perhaps, that he wished to keep alive, since only in the rage of supernatural battle did he ever know any true relief from the burden of his conscience.

With deliberate slowness he strolled to the tree, picked up the blade and sheathed it as a man might sheath any ordinary weapon, his attention still upon his friend's dishevelled features. "How came you here, Master Wheldrake? Is it a plane familiar to you?"

"Familiar enough, Prince Elric. And to yourself, I should think. We have not left the realm where flows the Heavy Sea."

And now Elric realised exactly what the Black Sword had done, dragging them both back to the very world from which Arioch had sought to banish them. And this suggested that the hellblade had motives of its own for ensuring his remaining here. He said none of this to Wheldrake but listened while his friend explained how Charion Phatt was at last reunited with her Uncle Fallogard and her grandmother.

"But Koropith remains lost to us at present," the poet concluded. "Fallogard, however, has a close sense of his son's presence. So we are hopeful, dear prince, that soon all surviving Phatts shall know again the pleasures of family security." He lowered his voice to a kind of conspiratorial squeak. "There is some talk of marriage between myself and my beloved Charion."

And, before he could burst into verse, the snowy branches of a forest path parted and here came the confident Charion, carrying the handles of a litter on which Mother Phatt sat, smiling and nodding, like a queen in a procession, the other end borne by her tall, untidy son who flashed a smile of jolly recognition towards the albino, as one might greet a familiar face at a local tavern. Only Charion seemed a little disturbed to discover the newcomer. "I sensed your destruction a year ago," she said quietly, after she had lowered her grandmother's litter to the ground. "I sensed you blasted out of any recognisable form of existence. How could you have survived that? Are you Gaynor or some shape-changer in Elric's guise?"

"I assure you, Mistress Phatt," said Elric, also disturbed, "I am only the one you know. For some reason, Fate does not want me annihilated as yet. It seems, indeed, that I am surviving annihilation rather successfully."

It was this last little irony that seemed to convince her and she relaxed.

But it was clear every psychic sense in her was probing his being for signs of imposture. "You are indeed a remarkable creature, Elric of Melniboné," said Charion Phatt as she turned away to attend to her grandmother.

"I am glad you found us, sir. We ourselves have some rather excellent intimations concerning my missing son," called out Fallogard Phatt cheerfully, oblivious of his niece's suspicions. "So, gradually, we become, as it were, concrete again. You already know, I believe, my niece's intended?"

At which Charion Phatt blushed girlishly, to her own furious embarrassment, yet the eye she cast upon the little coxcomb was not unlike that which a certain toad had once cast upon her: for there is never anything but apparent paradox in the choices made by lovers.

And Mother Phatt opened her merry red mouth in which a few fangs still glittered and cried: "Ding dong, for the six sad drabs! Ding dong for the dilly-o!" As if, in senility, she had become possessed by a mad parrot. Yet she waved an approving hand upon her granddaughter's choice and her wink at Elric was full of knowing wit and, when he returned it, he was sure she smiled. "Dark days for the lily-white boy; bright days for the darkling joy! Feast of evil, feast of good, feasting fine the Chaos brood. Feast the devil, feast the Son; dark days for the shining one. For the flowers of the forest are blooming at night, and the ships of the ocean are sailing on land. Ding dong for the lily-white lad, ding dong for the good and the bad; sail through the wildwood, sow grain on the sea; Chaos has come to the Land of the Three."

But when they taxed her on the meaning, if any, of her rhymes, she merely chuckled and called for her tea. "Mother Phatt is a greedy old woman," she confided to Elric. "But she's done her bit in the past, vicar, I think you'll agree. Mother Phatt sat under a tree; bore five strong sons to Eternity."

"Koropith, then, is not far from here?" Elric spoke to Fallogard Phatt. "You can sense him, you said, sir."

"Too much Chaos, you see," exclaimed the tall clairvoyant with a vigorous nod. "Hard to part it—hard to look through. Hard to call. Hard to hear an answer. Fuzzy, sir. The cosmos is always fuzzy when Chaos goes to work. This world is threatened, sir, you see. The first invaders have long since gained their foothold. Yet something holds them back, it seems."

Elric thought again of the runesword, yet had the notion that his blade was neither helping nor resisting the complicated flow of events; it had merely fought to return to the plane on which it must be at a certain time, during a certain movement of the multiverse. Some other power fought Chaos here, of that he was sure. And he wondered about the three sisters and their part in this. That they possessed certain treasures, which both he and Gaynor coveted, was almost all he knew—save for Wheldrake's ballad, which was mostly the poet's own invention and therefore of little use as an objective oracle. Did the sisters exist at all? Were they wholly the creation of the Bard of Putney? Was everyone pursuing a chimera—the invention of a highly romantic and over-coloured imagination?

"In the third grey month on the third grey day,
Three sistren rode to Radinglay,
Seeking three treasures they had lost,
To the laughing lord of The Ship That Was."

"Well, sir," says Elric, helping with the fire they are building, for they had planned to make camp here, even before his sudden arrival, "do those old rhymes of yours give you any clue to the whereabouts of the sisters?"

"I must admit, sir, that I have modified the verses a little, to allow for the new things I have learned, so I am an unreliable source of truth, sir, save in its most fundamental sense. Like a majority of poets, sir. Speaking of Gaynor, we have intimations of him, but none of Master Snare. We were wondering what had become of him."

"He sacrificed himself," said Elric bluntly. "I think he saved me, also, from Arioch's full fury. To the best of my knowledge Arioch was driven from this plane by him—and he died in that act of banishing the Lord of Hell."

"You have lost your ally, then?"

"I have lost an ally, Master Wheldrake, as much as I have lost an enemy. I also appear to have lost a year in this realm. However, I do not mourn the loss of my patron Duke of Entropy . . ."

"Yet Chaos still threatens," said Fallogard Phatt. "This plane stinks of it. Hovering, as it were, before it devours the entire world!"

"Is it ourselves that Chaos desires?" Charion Phatt wished to know. Her uncle shook his head. "Not us, child. It is not *greedy* for us. We are merely, at present, an irritant to it, I think. No longer useful. But it would be rid of us." He closed his heavily lidded eyes. "It grows angry, I know. There is Gaynor now . . . See—smell—taste him—Gaynor—feel his presence—see him riding . . . gone, gone . . . There he is—riding—I think he seeks the sisters still. And is close to discovering them! Gaynor serves it and himself. A subtle power. They desire to possess it. Without it they can never fully conquer this plane. The sisters—at last—I can sense the sisters. They seek another. Gaynor? Chaos? What is this? An alliance? They seek—not Gaynor, I think . . . Ah! The Chaos-stuff, it is too strong . . . Mist again. Uncertain mist . . ." He lifted his head and gasped at the cold twilight air as if he had been close to drowning in that psychic sea on which he was, often, the only voyager . . .

"Gaynor rode to the eastern mountains," said Elric. "Are the sisters still there?"

"No," said Fallogard Phatt, frowning. "They have long since left the Mynce and yet—time—Gaynor has gained time—he has been aided in this—is there a trap? What? What? I cannot see him!"

"We must break camp early," said Charion with all her usual practicality, "and try to reach the sisters before Gaynor. Yet our first duty is to family. Koropith is here."

"On this plane?" Elric asked.

"Or one that presently intersects this realm." She broke off a piece of candied leather and offered it to the albino who shook his head, having no love for the sweetmeats of her world where, Wheldrake swore, the taste in food was even worse than in his own. "I wonder," she added, "if anyone but me has any notion of Gaynor's positive will to evil?" And when she looked into the fire, her eyes were hidden from them all.

The snow came softly in the morning, covering the scars they had made behind them, covering the paths ahead, and the world was bitter with cold and silence as they trudged on through the forest, following the line of the cliff-top above and guessing, from thin sunlight, the direction in which they walked—yet they moved without hesitation, doggedly onward, following a psychic scent through this world where they appeared to be the only living creatures. They paused briefly to rest, to tend to Mother Phatt's needs, to boil her warming drinks of the herbs she herself had told them to pick and which were chiefly what they now lived on, together with the sweet jerky Charion carried. Then they were up again and marching where the snow was shallow and Mother Phatt inspected the moss and the bark they brought her and she told them that the realm had been in the grip of winter for more than a year and that this was Chaos work without doubt, and she murmured of old Ice Giants and the Cold Folk and the legends of her mother's people, who had been of the race, she claimed, that came before Man, that had ruled Cornwall before it was named by human tongues. There had been one, then, she said, that was also a prince, and that prince was of the old race, while the woman he married was of the new. They were her mother's ancestors. "It is why we have so great a gift of the Second Sight," she said to Elric intimately, patting his shoulder as he knelt beside her during one of their brief rests. She spoke to him as she might a favourite grandchild. "And they were not unlike you in appearance, save for the pigment, those folk."

"They were of Melniboné?"

"No, no, no! The word is meaningless. These were the great Vadhagh people who came before the Mabden. So, we are related, perhaps, you and I, Prince Elric?" Her intelligence was undisguised for a moment and complemented her humour. And Elric, looking into that face, thought that he looked into the face of Time itself.

"Are we," she asked him, "both of that Heroic blood?"

"It seems likely, madam," said Elric gently, scarcely aware of what she spoke, but glad to help her ease the burden she carried and which in some ways she appeared to resent.

"And born to bear a greater share of the world's grief, I fear," she said.

At which she began to cackle again, and to sing. "Dingly-dongly-bongly! Old Pim's adabblingo! Ring the rich and lively boy to bleed his heart for May to bloom!" Whereupon she began to beat a kind of savage dirge with her spoon and plate. "Up from the blood and into the brain jumps that memory of pain!"

"O, Ma! O, Loins of my Creation! When Chaos mists so much, your recollection of ancient savageries does further encloud my sight!" Fallogard Phatt spoke with nervous grace and entreating hands.

"They'll gnaw and pick at poor old Ma's few remaining bits of brain." The ancient matron drew upon her store of pathos to charm her son, but he was adamant.

"Ma, we're almost onto Koropith and the going looks to get hard from now on. We must save our energies, Ma! We must hold our tongues and stop the scattering of random charms and jingles or you'll leave a witch-trail behind us to march an army up. Which is never prudent, Ma."

"Prudence never pickled no rats," said Ma Phatt with a reminiscent chuckle, but she obeyed her son. She accepted his logic.

Elric had begun to notice that the air grew warmer and the ice was melting in the trees, while snow fell heavily to mushy ground and was quickly absorbed. By that afternoon, under an intense sun, they had crossed a line of grotesquely armoured beast-men tortured into even stranger shapes and enshrouded in ice which was burning hot to the touch but through which the travellers saw eyes moving, lips straining to speak, limbs frozen in attitudes of perpetual agony. A small Chaos army, Fallogard Phatt had agreed with Elric, defeated by some unknown sorcery, perhaps an effort of Law? Now they rode across a desert through which ran what was almost certainly an artificial watercourse and from which they could drink.

The desert ended by the next day and they saw ahead of them the immense foliage of a dark, lush forest, whose trees bore leaves as long as a man, with trunks as slender and sinewy as human bodies, whose gorgeous foliage was deep scarlets and deep yellows, dusty browns and clouded blues, while mingling with these rich, threatening colours were strands of pale pink and veins of purple or grey, as if the forest was fed by blood.

"It is there, I think, we shall find our missing prodigal!" announced Fallogard Phatt heartily, though even his mother looked doubtfully at that menacing tangle of massive blooms and sinuous branches. There seemed to be no hint of a pathway through it.

But Fallogard Phatt, now at the head of the litter, trotted forward, causing his shorter niece to take quicker steps to maintain the balance and momentum of their progress, until she cried out for her uncle to stop as he plunged forward into the sticky, almost reptilian forest.

Glad to be in the shade, Elric leaned against a yielding trunk. It was as if he sank into soft flesh. He straightened his back and shifted his weight to his feet. "This is without doubt Chaos work," he said. "I am familiar with these creations, half-animal, half-vegetable, which are usually the first growths Chaos achieves on any world. They are essentially the detritus of unskilled sorceries and no self-respecting emperor of Melniboné would have wasted time on such stuff. But Chaos, as you no doubt have already learned, has very little taste—whereas Law, of course, has rather too much."

They found the forest easier going than they had imagined, for the fleshy branches parted easily and only occasionally did a pod cling sensually to an arm or part of a face, while a glossy green tentacle embraced the body like the arms of a lover. Yet the things were not greatly animated by Chaos-energy and Fallogard Phatt's progress was scarcely ever blocked for long.

Until, without warning, the jungle was no longer organic.

It became crystalline.

Pale light of a thousand shades fell through the prisms of the forest roof, flashed and skipped from branch to crystal leaf, flooded down trunks and across canopies—and still Fallogard Phatt continued his relentless advance through the jungle, for the crystals yielded as easily as had the branches.

"And this is Law's work, surely?" said Charion Phatt to Elric. "This sterile beauty?"

"I would admit—" said Elric studying the way the light fell in multicoloured slabs one upon the other until the forest floor ran with flooding light, like rubies and emeralds and dark amethysts, until they were knee-deep in it, wading on through this wealth of pigment which was also reflected in their skins so that Elric himself was at last one with his friends, for all looked in wondering pleasure at their swirling motley flesh which seemed to glint and dance with the crystals all around them. Then they had reached and entered a mighty cavern of cool, silver radiance—where distant water lapped gentle banks and they knew an intense peace, such as Elric had only known before in Tanelorn.

And it was here that Fallogard Phatt stopped and signed for his niece to lower the litter to the sweet-smelling moss of the cavern floor. "We have entered a zone where neither Law nor Chaos rules—where the Rule of the Balance is undertaken, perhaps. Here we shall find Koropith. Here we shall seek the three sisters."

Then, from somewhere above them, where the cavern roof caught the light of a setting sun and reflected it down to them, they heard a thin, angry shout and a voice calling from a distant gallery:

"Hurry, you idiots! Come up! Come up! Gaynor is here! He has captured the sisters!"

2

A Rose Rejoined; Further Familial Joy;
Gaynor's Rape Thwarted and
the Sisters Found At Last—
Still Another Strange Turn of Fate's Wheel.

"Koropith, my heartsease! Oh, my beauty! Oh, my fruit!" Fallogard Phatt peered up through the shafts of intersecting light, through the galleries of green foliage and dark rock, through the richly scented blooms, and stretched slender fingers out for his son.

"Quick, Pa! All of you! Up here! We must not let him succeed!" The boy's voice was clear as a mountain spring. His tone was desperate.

Elric had found steps cut into the cave wall, winding up towards the roof. Without further thought he began to climb these, followed by Fallogard and Charion Phatt who left Wheldrake to protect Mother Phatt.

Through the cool tranquillity of that tall cave they climbed and Fallogard Phatt, panting, observed that the place was like a natural cathedral, "as if God had placed it here as an example to us" (by disposition and background he was a monotheist) and had it not been for his son's urgent cries from above he would have paused to observe the beauty and the wonder of it.

"There he is! There's two of 'em, now!" cries Wheldrake cryptically from below. "You're almost there! Carefully, my delicacy! Look out for her, Pa!"

Charion needed help from no-one. Sure-footed, her sword already in her hand, she followed quickly behind Elric and would have passed him had there been room on the narrow steps.

They came to a gallery whose wall was made of a kind of hedge, growing thickly from the side of the cliff and clearly designed to protect anyone who used the path. Elric wondered at the artistry of the people who had lived here and if any of them had survived the coming of Chaos to their world. If so, where were they?

The gallery widened and became the entrance to a large tunnel.

And there stood Koropith Phatt, gasping with the burning immediacy of his predicament yet weeping to see his father and cousin again. "Quick, Pa! Gaynor will destroy her if we do not hurry! There is some chance he will destroy them all—destroy everyone!"

And he was dashing ahead of them, pausing to make sure they followed, dashing on again, calling. He had gained height and seemed to have lost weight; was turning into a skinny youth, as angular and gangling as his father. Dashing through galleries of green light, through peaceful chambers, through suites of rooms which looked out over the vastness of the cave itself, from windows set cunningly near the roof, and none of them occupied, all of them with a faint air of desolation. Dashing up curving stairways and gracefully sinuous corridors, through a city that was a palace or a palace that was large as a city, where a gentle people had lived in civilised harmony—

—and then comes the sounding of a pair in psychic, supernatural and physical combat—an explosion of orange light, a collapsing of a certain kind of darkness, the swirl of unnatural colours, followed by sounds, as if of a deep, irregular heartbeat—

—and Elric leads the others into a hall that, in its artfulness and delicate architectural intelligence, rivals the great cave below—almost an homage to it . . .

—and lying upon a floor of pale blue marble shot through with veins of the most subtle silver is the body of a young woman in brown and green, a great shock of pink-gold hair identifying her at once. There is a sword near her unmoving right hand, a dagger still in her left.

"Ah! No!" cries Koropith Phatt in anguish. "She cannot be dead!"

Elric, sheathing Stormbringer, knelt beside her, feeling for a pulse and finding one, faint, steady, in her cool throat just at the moment she opened her lovely hazel eyes and frowned at him. "Gaynor?" she murmured.

"Gone, it seems," said Elric. "And the sisters with him, I think."

"No! I was sure I had protected them!" The Rose made a weak movement of her arms, tried to rise and failed. Koropith Phatt hovered at Elric's shoulder, murmuring and crooning with helpless concern. She gave him a reassuring smile. "I am unharmed," she said. "Merely exhausted . . ." She drew two quick breaths. "Gaynor has a Lord of Chaos to help him in this, I think. It took all the spells I bought in Oio to resist him. I have little left."

"I did not understand you to be a sorceress as well as a swordswoman," Elric said, helping her to sit.

"Our magic is of a natural order," she said, "but not all of us chose to practise it. Chaos has fewer weapons against it, which proved an advantage to me, though I had hoped to imprison him and learn more from him."

"He is in Count Mashabak's employ still, I think," said Elric.

"That much, sir, I know," said the Rose softly and with a significance only clear to herself.

Soon they had her seated on a cushioned settle, her skin pale pink in the gentle light of the blue hall, her hair folding about her delicate skull like petals.

It was some while, after Koropith had returned with Wheldrake and Mother Phatt, through tunnels easier to climb than the outer steps, before the Rose was ready to tell them what had occurred after she had reached this cave ("slithering through the dimensions like sneak-thieves"). She had found the sisters hidden, having failed in a quest of their own, which had taken them so far afield. Not for the first time she had offered them her aid, and they had been glad to accept it, but some rupturing of the cosmic fabric had been detected by Gaynor, whose own stronghold lay not fifty miles from here, and he had arrived with a small army to seize the sisters and their treasure. He had not expected to be resisted, especially by the singular magic commanded by the Rose, which was of a nature too subtle for Chaos easily to understand.

"My magic draws neither from Law nor from Chaos," she said, "but from the natural world. Sometimes it takes a century for one of our spells to stifle the roots of some spectacular tyranny, but when it is dead, it is thoroughly dead. It was our vocation to seek out tyranny and destroy it. So successful were we that we began to anger certain Lords of the Higher Worlds, who ruled through such people."

"You are the Daughters of the Garden," said Wheldrake, breaking in and then stopping apologetically. "There is an old Persian tale which speaks of you, I think. Or perhaps it is from Baghdad. The Daughters of Justice was another name . . . But you were Martyred . . . Forgive me, madam. There was a tale . . .

"*Came cruel Count Malcolm to that land,*
  With fire and steel in either hand,
And a curse which fouled his breath;
  I seek the Flowers of Bannon Brae;
I bring them pain and death.

"Good heavens, madam, sometimes I feel I am trapped in some vast, un-ending epic of my own invention!"

"You recall the old ballad's ending, Master Wheldrake?"

"There are one or two," said Wheldrake diplomatically.

"You recall a certain ending, however, do you not?"

"I recall it, madam," said Wheldrake in dawning horror. "Oh, madam! No!"

"Aye," said the Rose. And she spoke slowly, with great, weary strength . . .

"Each brand that burn'd in Bannon Brae,
  Was a soul in cruel torment.
Count Malcolm who cut the bright flowers down,
  Left but one to sing Lament.

"I," said the Rose, "was the only flower not, eventually, cut down by him whom the ballad calls 'Count Malcolm.' The one whom Gaynor had preceded, with his lies to us concerning his own heroic struggles against the forces of the Dark." And she paused, as if she stilled a tear. "That was how we were caught unawares of the invasion. We trusted Gaynor. Indeed, I spoke for him! He is economical in his methods, I learned. He deceives us all with the same few tales. Our valley was a wasteland within hours. You can imagine the up-heavals, for we were unprepared for Chaos, which could only enter our realm through mortal agency. Through Gaynor's agency. And that of the unwitting fools he deceived . . ."

"Oh, madam!" says Wheldrake again. At which she reaches out a friendly hand to comfort him. But he would comfort her. "The only flower . . ."

"Save one," she said, "but she resorted to desperate sorcery and died an unholy death . . ."

"The sisters are not your kinswomen, then?" murmured Fallogard Phatt. "I had assumed . . ."

"Sisters in spirit, perhaps, though they are not of my vocation. They seek to resist a common enemy, which is why I have aided them until now. For they, among others, possess the key to my own particular goal."

"But where has Gaynor taken them?" Charion Phatt wished to know. "His stronghold is only fifty miles from here, you say?"

"And it is surrounded by a Chaos army awaiting only his order to march against us. But I do not know yet if he has the sisters."

"He took them, surely?" Charion Phatt said.

But the Rose shook her head. Gradually, she was restoring herself and was now able to walk unaided. "I had to hide them from him. There was so little time. I could not hide their treasures with them. But I do not know if I acted swiftly enough."

It was evident she did not want to be asked further questions about that incident, so they asked her and Koropith what had happened on the Gypsy causeway. She told them how she had found Gaynor and the sisters at the very moment Mashabak was about to cut the bridge. He had been summoned, of course, by Gaynor. "I sought to stop Mashabak and save as many lives as I could. But in so doing I allowed Gaynor to escape—though not with the sisters, who had managed to free themselves from him. I had tried to warn the gypsies and when that failed I went in search of Gaynor—or Mashabak. We have come close, Koropith and I, to finding them at different times, but now we know they have returned here, as have the sisters. Chaos gathers strength. This realm is almost theirs, save for the resistance provided by ourselves, and the sisters."

"I have little stomach for a journey to a Court of Chaos, madam," said Wheldrake slowly, "but if I can be of any assistance to you in this matter, please feel free to make use of me however you wish." He offered her a grave little bow.

And Charion, at her intended's side, donated her own sword and wits in the Rose's service.

All of which was accepted graciously but with lifted hand. "We do not yet know what we must do," she said and then she raised herself to her feet, the velvet robe falling in folds upon the marble couch, and, lifting her marvellous head, pursed her lips in a whistle.

There came the sound of padded feet upon those marble floors and a hot panting, as if the Rose had summoned the Hounds of Hell to aid them; then into the hall bounded three huge dogs—great wolfhounds with lolling red tongues and fangs of pre-human heritage—a white hound, a blue-grey hound and a pale golden hound, ready, it seemed, to do battle with any enemy, pursue any prey. And they grouped at the Rose's side and looked up into her face as if ready to obey her slightest order.

But then one of the dogs glanced to one side and saw Elric. Immediately it became agitated, growling softly and attracting the attention of the other two hounds, until Elric began to wonder if these were not some close relatives of Esbern Snare who did not approve of the werewolf's act of sacrifice on Elric's behalf.

Next they were up and moving towards the albino while the Rose cried out in surprise; cried for them to return to heel.

But they would not.

Elric did not fear the great hounds as they approached him. Indeed, there was something about them which reassured him. But he was deeply puzzled.

Now they came closer, prowling around him, sniffing, quizzing, with the soft growls forever being exchanged between them until at last they seemed satisfied and returned, passively, to the Rose's side.

The Rose was mystified. "I was about to explain," she said, "why we must wait before we take further action. These hounds are the three sisters. I put a glamour on them to protect them from Gaynor's sorcery, as well as to give them a means of defending themselves, for they are spent, you see, of magic and all ingenuity. They have failed in their quest."

"What was that quest?" asked Elric softly, stepping from behind the others and looking with a new curiosity at the dogs, who returned his gaze with a kind of abstracted longing.

"It was for thee," said the golden hound as she rose from all fours and in a single flowing motion became a woman clad in silk the colour that her fur had been, and her face was of that long, refined sort which Elric recognised at once as belonging to his own people. Grey-blue fur turned to grey-blue silk, white to white, until all three sisters were standing there before him, tiny figures, yet unmistakeably of Melnibonéan stock. "It was for thee, Elric of Melniboné, that we sought," they said again.

They had black hair framing their exquisite features like helmets, large slanting violet eyes, fair skin like the palest brass, their lips were perfect bows—

—and they had spoken to him alone. They had used the old High Speech of Melniboné which even Wheldrake found hard to understand.

Confronted by this unexpected turn of events, Elric had taken an unwitting step backward. Then he steadied himself, bowed briefly and discovered himself, in spite of all he'd ever sworn, making the old blood greeting of the Bright Empire's ruling families. "I am bonded to thee and thine interests . . ."

". . . and we to thine, Elric of Melniboné," said the golden woman. "I am the Princess Tayaratuka and these are my sisters, also of the Caste, Princess Mishiguya and Princess Shanug'a. Prince Elric, we have hunted thee through millennia and across a thousand Spheres!"

"I have hunted thee only a few hundred years and perhaps five hundred Spheres," said Elric modestly, "but it seems I am the tail that chases the weasel . . ."

"When Mad Jack Porker staked his leg!" cried Ma Phatt from where she enjoyed the luxury of a fresh couch and luxurious linen. "We have been chasing one another in circles, then? See! I knew there was a pattern to it! Somewhere, there is always a pattern to it. Dongle-my-dingle, the lad's lost his jingle. It's the famous race, you know. Porker's Trial by Accident. His last dash was pure heroism. Everyone said so. Ladies and gentlemen, they are nailing our feet to the ground. That is not fair play!" And she relapsed into some comic dialogue with herself in which she relived her girlhood on the boards. "Buffalo Bill and the Wandering Jew! It was our grand finale. The last touch."

To which the three sisters listened with perfect patience before continuing . . .

"We sought thee to ask of thee a boon," said Princess Tayaratuka, "and to offer thee in exchange for that boon a gift."

"I am bound to thee as if I were thine own hands," said Elric automatically.

"And we to thee," replied the sisters, equally familiar with the ritual.

Then Princess Tayaratuka dropped to one knee, raising her hands to place them on his arms and bring him down to her so that he, too, was kneeling as she kneeled. "My lord, good power to thee," she said, and offered her forehead for his kiss. This ritual was performed until all had spoken and been kissed in turn.

"How may I help thee, sisters?" said Elric when they had next kissed the triple kiss of kinship. All his old Melnibonéan blood stirred in him and he grew chill with a longing for his homeland and the speech and customs of his own unhuman folk. These women were his peers; already a deep understanding existed between them, stronger than blood, stronger than love, yet in no way encumbering or demanding. Elric knew in his bones that their command of sorcery might well have been the match of his own, before they exhausted all their strength in their search for him. He had known and loved many powerful women, including his lost betrothed Cymoril, and Myshella, the Dark Lady of Kaneloon, the sorceress he had but lately served, but, save for the Rose, the three princesses were the most striking of all the living women he had yet encountered, since he had left Imrryr as the pyre for his beloved's corpse.

"I am flattered that you should have sought me, your majesties," he said, relaxing for good manners' sake into the common tongue. "How may I be of service to you?"

"We would borrow your sword, Elric," said Princess Shanug'a.

"Borrow it you shall, madam. And myself to wield it for you." He spoke gallantly, as honour bade him do, but he still feared the threat of his father's ghost hovering somewhere not too far off, ready to flee at the first threat of extinction and pour his soul into Elric's being, to blend for ever . . . And had not Gaynor coveted the Black Sword?

"You do not ask why we would borrow the blade," said Princess Mishiguya, seating herself beside the Rose and helping herself to the small fruits which had been placed on the arm of the couch. "You would not bargain with us?"

"I would expect you to help me as I help you," said Elric in a matter-of-fact tone, "but I have sworn the blood oath, as have you. It is done. We are the same. Our interests are the same."

"Yet you have a deep fear in you, Elric," said Charion Phatt suddenly. "You have not told these women what you fear if you allow yourself to aid them!" She spoke out as a child might, for justice, without understanding why the albino did not wish to betray his own anxieties.

"And they have not told me of what *they* fear if I agree to aid them," said Elric quietly to the young woman. "We are riding the stallions of terror, every one of us at present, Mistress Phatt, and the best we can hope to do is to keep some kind of grip upon the reins."

Charion Phatt accepted this and subsided, though she glanced furiously at Wheldrake, as if she wished him to speak on her behalf. But the poet remained a diplomat, unsure of the game he witnessed or of the stakes, but willing to go wherever his almost-betrothed determined.

"Where would you have me bear this blade?" Elric asked again.

Princess Tayaratuka glanced at her sisters before getting their unspoken assent to continue. "We do not need you to bear the blade," she said gently. "We spoke quite literally. We wish to borrow your runesword, Prince Elric. I will explain."

And she told a tale of a world where all lived in harmony with nature. This world had possessed few cities in the usual sense and its settlements were built to conform with the contours of the hills and valleys, the mountains and the streams, to blend with the forest but not to encroach upon it, so that anyone visiting their plane would have seen virtually no signs of habitation upon the continent where they lived. But Chaos came, led by Gaynor the Damned, who sought their hospitality and betrayed it, as he had betrayed so many other souls through the centuries, summoning in his patron lord who had immediately put the marks of Chaos upon their land.

"Few of our habitations were ever visible to potential enemies from other continents, so well-protected were we by the Heavy Sea, which encircles us.

So dense were our forests and wide and winding our rivers that no-one cared to risk their lives on seeking after any legends which might have crept to other parts of the world. It is true we lived in paradise. But it was a paradise achieved at the expense of no other creature, including those of the wild, with whom we lived. Yet within a day or two all that had gone and we were left with a few barricaded outposts like this one, where our sorcery was used to maintain our world as it had been before Chaos came."

"And Chaos has laid siege here for a long while, madam?" asked Fallogard Phatt sympathetically, and raised his eyebrows at her answer.

"For something over a thousand years there has been a sort of stalemate. Most of our people left this world to found new settlements in other planes, but some of us felt duty-bound to stay and fight Chaos. We are the last of those. While we sought Elric, many of our kinfolk were killed in forays with Chaos attempting to attack the main stronghold."

"But what achieved the amnesty?" Elric asked.

"A feud between two Dukes of Hell took up their attention, especially after Arioch, employing some complicated strategy which involved Mashabak's cutting of the gypsy bridge and various other machinations and manipulations of the multiverse, was able to capture Mashabak in the territory he considered his own—our realm. Without demonic aid, Gaynor had to hope that we sisters would lead him back here. However, all that is altered. Some event occurred recently which ended the truce, such as it was. Mashabak has returned here and must soon send all his forces against us. Whoever broke that cosmic stalemate robbed us of whatever time we thought we had left . . ."

And Elric said nothing, remembering Esbern Snare and his leap at the Duke of Hell; remembering the courage of the Northern Werewolf as he had sought to save his friend—and had unwittingly broken the balance of power which had allowed the sisters some respite in their own palace.

Gaynor, insanely determined, abandoned by Mashabak, battled his own way through the dimensions, sworn to reclaim his conquests not in Mash-abak's name, but his own! He challenged Chaos as he had once challenged the Balance! To him, no master was tolerable! The ex-Prince of the Universal had been lost, forced to spend years of subjective time searching for a way back to this realm. He had employed every strategy, every trick—furious that his cosmic ally had, apparently, deserted him, but determined to establish his rule here! Eventually he decided that he would follow the sisters, since they must eventually return to their own realm. Originally Mashabak had sent him on a quest—to follow the escaping sisters through the dimensions and bring back the living rose. But when Mashabak no longer aided him, the rose had become secondary to Gaynor. He desired Elric's sword rather more urgently.

Now he had returned, and demonstrated that the palace was no longer proof against him. He had entered and threatened the sisters at sword point, demanding their now-legendary Three Treasures which they had carried back with them to return to the one who had loaned them. Gaynor's plan was to force the sisters out of the palace and into the cavern, at the eastern entrance of which his Chaos pack waited, unable themselves to enter that unlikely place.

With Koropith Phatt's skills stretched to snapping, and almost over-whelmed by a desperate urgency as the young Phatt sensed the sisters' danger, the Rose at last broke through into this realm—barely in time to place a pro-tective glamour on the sisters and challenge Gaynor, whom she drove back into the palace by her swordplay and her witchcraft. But he, in turn, had found a source of sorcery and had eventually left her for dead, escaping back to his stronghold as Elric and the others arrived.

"We were prepared for nothing but death," said Princess Shanug'a, "until this moment. I wonder what has brought us together now? And *why* should it bring us together at this moment? Do you have a hint of that, Master Phatt? Are we all moved by the hand of some manipulative Destiny?"

"It can only be the Balance," said Fallogard Phatt with nodding certainty.

But Elric said nothing. He knew that Stormbringer did not serve the Balance, and, were it not for the runesword, he would not now be here—ready to help the sisters. But did the sword know what they required of it?

Then, suddenly, Elric was struck by a terrifying thought. What if he had already served the sword's purpose so that Stormbringer no longer had use of the symbiosis on which the albino had come to rely? While this notion filled him with panic, he also loathed himself for his dependency upon the blade. He unhooked its scabbard from his belt and, volunteering what he had earlier refused Gaynor, offered it to the sisters.

"Here is the sword you sought, my kinswomen." He offered it without question, either in expression or gesture, without hesitation or any sign of reluctance. Honour required nothing else.

Princess Tayaratuka stepped forward and, bowing, received the sword in both her little hands. Her muscles flexed with the blade's weight, but she did not flinch. She was considerably stronger than she appeared to be.

"We have our Rune," she said. "We have always had it. Since our people first came here and made this world their own. Even when the dragons left, we were not afraid, for we had our Rune. The Rune of Final Resort, it was called by some. But we had no sword. For the Rune of Final Resort must be spoken in conjunction with a ritual and a certain object. First it is required that the Black Sword be present: then he who wields the Sword must join us in the rune-calling. Then we must know the names of certain entities which must be summoned. All these things must come together at the same time. This is the pattern we must make, to mirror that which already exists and so create a duality which, in turn, releases the raw life-force of the multiverse. And only then, if we are accurate in our delicate weaving, will we revive the allies we seek against Chaos—the power to drive Mashabak and Gaynor and all their minions from our realm! If we are successful in this, Prince Elric, we are prepared to offer you one of three reclaimed treasures . . ." She glanced towards the Rose, but Wheldrake was quoting excitedly—

"*The first of these treasures of Radinglay,*
    Was a rosewood box with roses 'graved,
While the second was that maiden's dower,
    A fresh-pick'd summer rose in flower.
The third of these treasures were briar rings three,
    To make fast the Kind of the Cold Country."

"Exactly," said Princess Mishiguya with something of a lifted eyebrow, as if she had scarcely expected her tale to be the subject of a minstrel's repertoire.

"He has," said Charion Phatt by way of apology for her near-betrothed, "something of a memory for verse . . ."

"Especially," said Wheldrake, bridling at what he interpreted as snobbery, "my own! Disapprove, if you like. I'm adrift in my own rhymes and rhythms." And he mumbled another stanza or two to himself.

Princess Mishiguya was gracious. The Rose also came to the poet's defence. "Without Master Wheldrake's cadences and remembered names we should even now be separated," she said. "His talents have proved of subtle usefulness to us all."

"Should we succeed," said Elric, replying, "I would accept your promise of a gift. For, I must admit, my own fate is somewhat bound up with one of those objects of power you have carried so long . . ."

"Not knowing which of the three you would accept. We did not even know you to be our kin—though it should have occurred to us. Sadly, of course, we no longer have those borrowed gifts in our possession . . ."

"The gifts are not redeemed!" said the Rose in sudden agitation. "We hid them from Gaynor . . ."

"You were able to protect us," said Princess Tayaratuka, "but not your treasures. Gaynor raped them from their hiding place before he fled back to

The Ship That Was. Those objects of power, lady, are already in the hands of Chaos. I thought you understood that."

The Rose sat slowly down upon a bench. Something like a groan escaped her. She waved them on. "Which makes your ritual all the more important to us . . ."

And Elric, following behind the women as they bore his sword into the depths of the palace where the ritual must take place, knew that both his own and his father's soul must now be truly doomed.

3

Rituals of Blood; Rituals of Iron.
Three Sisters of the Sword.
Six Swords Against Chaos.

Through cloisters of pink-and-red mosaic, down avenues of flowering bushes lit by glowing, refracted sunshine from hidden skylights, past galleries of paintings and sculpture, the four moved steadily. "This has a hint of Melniboné and yet is not Melniboné," said Elric thoughtfully.

Princess Tayaratuka was almost offended. "There is nothing of your Melniboné here, I hope. We have no strain in us of that warlike line. We are of those Vadhagh who fled the Mabden when Chaos aided them . . ."

"We of Melniboné determined we should flee no more," said Elric quietly. He had no quarrel with his ancestors' determined learning of the arts of battle lest they be scattered again. It was what such easy logic led to that he feared.

"I intended no criticism," said the princess. "We prefer, if necessary, to wander, rather than imitate the ways of those who would destroy us . . ."

"But now," said Princess Shanug'a, "we must do battle with Chaos, to defend what is ours."

"I did not say that we would not fight," her sister said firmly, "I said that we would not resort to the building of empires. These are two distinct things."

"I understand you, my lady," said the albino, "and I accept that difference. I have no liking for my people's penchant for empire-building."

"Well, my lord, there are many other ways to achieve security," said Princess Mishiguya a little mysteriously, even sharply, as they continued their way through the lovely apartments and galleries of this most civilised of settlements.

Princess Tayaratuka still carried the great sword, though with a certain effort. Even when Elric offered to take the weight for a while she refused, as if this were her duty.

Now a corridor widened into another triangular cloister which surrounded a cool rose garden open to the dark-blue sky above. At the centre of the garden was a fountain. The base of the fountain was carved with all manner of odd and grotesque creatures, somewhat out of keeping with the general style, and the plinth rose up in a three-sided column to where it widened into a large bowl around which were carved the sinuous shapes of dragons and maidens engaged in some cryptic dance. Silvery water still sprayed from the fountain and Elric felt that it was a kind of blasphemy to bring the Black Sword to a place of such peace.

"This is the Garden of the Rune," said the Princess Mishiguya. "It lies at the very centre of our realm, our land; at the centre of this palace. This was the first garden built by the Vadhagh when they came here." She took a deep breath of the ancient rosy scent. She held it as if it might be her last.

Princess Tayaratuka set the scabbarded runesword upon a bench and went to put her hands in the cool water, pouring it over her head almost as if she sought a blessing. Princess Shanug'a walked to the far end of the first of the three galleries and returned almost immediately bearing a cylinder of pale gold set with rubies which she handed now to Princess Mishiguya who drew from the cylinder another tube, of finely carved ivory bound with gold, and this tube she handed to Princess Tayaratuka who, in turn, drew from that a rod of engraved grey stone whose dark-blue runes twisted and writhed as if alive and were like those same runes Stormbringer bore. Elric had seen such things on only one other object, the sword Mournblade, which his cousin had sought to bear against him, the sister sword to Stormbringer. Dimly, he recalled other tales of runic objects, but he had studied little in such areas. Did they have qualities in common?

Princess Tayaratuka was holding up the stone cylinder now, wondering at the shifting runes as if she had never seen them alive before, and her lips moved as she read them, forming words she had been taught in a time before she had learned to read any ordinary alphabet. This was her inheritance, this Rune of Power . . .

"Only three virgins born of the same mother and the same father at the same time may know the Ritual of the Rune," said Shanug'a in a whisper. "But the Rune cannot be completed until we have seen the Black Sword's runes and read those aloud in the Garden of the Rune. All these things must happen at once. Then, if we have spoken the Rune correctly, and if the magic has not faded in the centuries since it was distilled, then perhaps we shall regain those things with which our ancestors brought us to this realm."

Princess Mishiguya went to the bench where the hellsword rested, almost passively, and she picked it up and took it to the fountain where her sister, Shanug'a, waited, the water flowing over her and seeming to merge with the silken gown she wore, and Shanug'a took the sword's grip in both her little hands and pulled deliberately so that bit by bit the blade emerged from the scabbard, the angry scarlet runes glowing already along the black metal, and a song escaped the sword that was unlike anything Elric had heard before. In all other hands, even perhaps Gaynor's, the unscabbarded hellsword would have resisted, turned upon the one who sought to hold it and almost certainly killed them. Important sorcery was needed to hold the Black Sword even for a short while. Yet now it sang a song so strange and so sweet, high and unhappy, full of longing and unfulfilled hungers, that Elric was momentarily terrified. He had never suspected such qualities in the sword.

Even as Stormbringer continued its strange, unlikely song, Princess Shanug'a raised it high in the air and brought the tip down into the centre of the oddly carved bowl so that suddenly the fountain ceased to gush and at once there was a silence in the rose garden.

A stillness came to the sky above, as if the dark-blue light froze; a stillness in the garden, as if every flower and bud waited; a stillness in that triangular cloister, as if the very stones held themselves in readiness for some momentous event.

Even the three sisters seemed frozen in the attitudes of their ritual.

Awed by the scene, Elric felt he intruded and it occurred to him to withdraw, as if he were not required here, but Princess Tayaratuka was turning to him, smiling—offering him the runestone as it writhed and glowed in her palm.

"It is for you to read," she said. "Only you, of all the creatures in the multiverse, have this power. That is why we sought you so eagerly. You must read our Rune—as we read the Black Sword's. Thus shall we begin the weaving of this powerful magic. This is what we have been trained to do, almost since birth. You must believe us and trust us, Prince Elric."

"I have sworn the blood-bond," said Elric simply. He would do whatever they required of him, even if it meant his death, the enslavement of his immortal soul, the prospect of a hellish eternity. He would trust them without question.

The monstrous battle-blade stood upright in the bowl, the song still escaping it, the runes still flickering up and down its radiant black metal. It was almost as if it were about to speak, to transform itself into another shape, possibly its true shape. And Elric felt a chill in his soul and it seemed for a second that he looked into his future, to some predetermined doom for which this was a kind of rehearsal. Then he disciplined his mind and contemplated the task at hand.

One sister now stood on each side of the column, looking up at the sword. Their voices began to chant in unison, until it was no longer possible to distinguish their cadences from the sword's . . .

. . . Then Elric found that he was lifting up the runestone in his two hands stretched before him and his lips began to form wordless, beautiful sounds . . .

They had sought him for his sword; but they had sought him also for this unique gift. Only Elric of Melniboné, of all living mortals, had the power and the skills to read such potent symbols, to voice them as they must be voiced, matching each part of a note to each nuance of the rune. This rune, the sisters knew by heart, but the rune that blazed upon the Black Sword they themselves had to read. Thus they combined all their resources, all their talents, into the reading of a double rune, the mightiest of all Runes of Power.

The runesong rose in volume and became increasingly complicated—

—for now the four adepts were rune-weaving—folding their spells in and out of time, moving their voices beyond the audible range, making the air crease and shiver into thousands of strands which they wove and threaded—

—weaving the runes into a thing of impossible strength, making the very atmosphere bubble and dance, while all around now the shrubs and flowers swayed, as if adding their own rhythms and cadences to the runesong.

Everything was alive with a thousand different qualities, blending and separating, changing and transforming. Colours ran through the air like rivers. Eruptions of nameless forces came and went around them, while the bowl and the sword and the runestone seemed to become the only constancies in that double triangle.

Elric now understood how this was a place of enormously concentrated psychic energy. From this source, he guessed, they had drawn the power with which they had so far resisted Chaos—enough at least to protect a few settlements like these. But with the power of the Black Sword combined, the Garden of the Rune was becoming something infinitely mightier than anything it could have become on its own.

. . . to shatter the Sword of Alchemy and make the One power Three . . .

Elric realised he was hearing a story woven in amongst the runes, almost an incidental to the ritual they performed. It was a story of how these people were led by a dragon through the dimensions—a dragon which had dwelled once within a sword. Such legends were common to his folk and doubtless referred to some long-forgotten part of their wandering history. At last they had come to this land, which was uninhabited by human folk. So they made it their own, building to follow the existing contours of the earth, its forests and rivers. But first they had built the Garden of the Rune. For through their considerable sorcery they had changed and hidden the power which, they believed, was the result of their salvation and any future salvation for their descendants.

The runesong went on. The story continued. Into the fountain were built what the song called "the tools of last resort." The princesses' ancestors passed the runestone down from mother to daughter since they believed no man capable of carrying the secret.

Only against Chaos could these tools of last resort be used, and only then when all else had failed them. They could only be used in combination with another great object of power. The borrowed objects of power which the sisters had held, and with which they had intended to bargain for Elric's help, ignorant of how close a kinsman he was, were not strong enough for the work.

Gaynor had stolen those Objects, knowing that Chaos feared them and desired them. One such Object had already been stolen from the Rose and returned to her possession by a surprising and circuitous means. The others she had guarded better. But none had been powerful enough to use in the Ritual of the Garden.

Yet while the three sisters sought Elric and the Black Sword, others, like Elric, had sought what the sisters carried. Now the circle was completed. Now every proper element in the psychic model was in place, giving the four of them the astral means to range free, to let their minds and souls roam beyond the dimensions, beyond the Spheres, even beyond the multiverse; to re-enter it with a fresh knowledge, a deeper understanding of that complex geometry whose secrets were the basis for all sorcery; whose forms were the basis for all poetry and all song; whose language was the basis of all thought and whose shapes were the basis for all aesthetics, for all beauty; all ugliness . . . Into this the four plunged, weaving with their runesongs fresh and original psychic patterns which had the effect of healing wounds and ruptures in the walls of time and space, while at the same time creating an enormous force with which to reanimate three other ancient objects of power.

More urgent and more complex were the runes now as they sang with their bodies and swam with their minds through near-infinities of screaming rainbows; sailing through their own bodies and out again into worlds and worlds of desolation, millennia of unchecked joy and a hint of that seductive ordinariness where so much of the human heart must always lie but which it so rarely celebrates . . .

So those old unhuman folk wove their spell, making manifest the promise of the runes, controlling the potency of unmoral magic which knew no loyalty save to itself.

The spell grew upon its own volition now, as it was meant to do, twisting and curling and creeping like the supple boughs of the yew hedge which clung together to create so much modest strength, and then they began to fashion what they had woven, forming it and re-forming it over and over again between them, twisting it and turning it, throwing it one to the other, touching it and tasting it and sniffing it and stroking it, until the force they now balanced between them, which hovered over the Black Sword itself, was of the perfect supernatural shape and almost ready for release . . .

Yet still the songs must be sung, to hold the force, to channel it; to bridle it and saddle it; to charge it with a moral will, to force it to make a *choice*—for this *stuff*, this prime matter, was constitutionally incapable of choice, of moral direction or persuasion. And so *must* be forced . . .

Forced by a concentration of psychic energy, of disciplined will and moral strength which resisted all attack upon it, either from without or within, and which refused to be deflected from its purpose by an argument, example or threat . . .

Forced by four creatures so similar that they were almost one flesh and, at this moment, essentially one mind . . .

Forced downwards through the Black Sword which was not itself the receptacle of that power but merely the final and much-needed conductor . . .

Forced through the living stone, into the slab of rock from which the bowl, column and plinth had been carved, thousands of years before . . .

To transform it—to alter it entirely from any kind of material remotely akin to stone—a living form of energy so immense it was impossible, even for the adepts themselves, to imagine the fullness of its power, or how such power could possibly be contained.

Now this energy, coruscating, swirling, dancing, celebrating its own incredible being, joined in the song of the sisters, the albino and the runesword, until they formed a choir which could be heard throughout the multiverse, in every Sphere, upon every part of every planet; echoing for ever throughout the multitude of planes and dimensions of the quasi-infinite. To be heard always, now, somewhere, while the multiverse existed. It was a song of promise, of responsibility and of celebration. A promise of harmony; the triumph of love; a celebration of the multiverse in balance. It was through an exquisite metaphysical harmony that they controlled this force and made it obey them, releasing it once more . . .

. . . Releasing it into three great objects of power which, as the fountain faded away, were revealed, grouped around the Black Sword standing in the centre of the small pool . . .

. . . Three swords, the weight and length of Stormbringer, but otherwise very different in appearance:

The first sword was made of ivory, with an ivory blade that looked oddly sharp and an ivory hilt and an ivory grip, bound about with bands of gold which seemed to have grown into the ivory.

The second sword was made of gold, yet was as sharp as its companion, and it was bound with ebony.

The third sword was of blue-grey granite furnished in silver.

These were the swords the Rune had hidden so well and which were now infused with a power to match that of Stormbringer itself . . .

Princess Tayaratuka, all in flowing gold, reached a golden hand towards the golden sword and took it to her breast with a deep sigh . . .

Her sister Mishiguya, in grey-blue silks, stretched out her own hand to the granite sword, seized it and gasped, grinning with the ecstasy and triumph of their success . . .

. . . and Princess Shanug'a, very grave in white robes, took down the ivory sword and kissed it. "Now," she said, turning to the others, "we are ready to do battle with a Lord of Chaos."

Elric, still weak from the rune-weaving, staggered to take hold of his own sword. Out of some sense of respect, or some unremembered ritual, he replaced it with the runestone, from which he had read the beginning of that great Casting . . .

Elric, my son—hast thou my soulbox? Did the sisters give it thee?

His father's voice. Some intimation of what he would know for always should he fail. And it seemed that he had certainly failed . . .

Elric, the time is almost here. My sorcery cannot hold me much longer . . . I must come to thee, my son . . . I must come to the one I hate most in the entire multiverse . . . To live with him for ever . . .

"I have not found your soulbox, Father," he murmured and then looked up to see the sisters watching him curiously when, all of a sudden, into the cloister came a breathless Koropith Phatt.

"Oh, thank heaven! I thought you all destroyed! There was a—a kind of storm. But you are here! They did not attack from within as we had feared."

"Gaynor?" said Elric, rescabbarding the oddly quiescent runeblade. "Has he returned?"

"Not Gaynor—at least, I think not—but a Chaos army—coming against us. Oh, prince, dear princesses, we are upon the point of our extinguishment!"

Which had them running as fast as they could go in the wake of the youth as he took them up to join the others in a room formed from a ledge of rock and disguised by foliage; this formed a natural balcony from which they could look out over the surrounding countryside and see the crystalline trees shattering and smashing as a great river of armoured semi-humanity pressed towards their retreat.

An army of bestial men and manlike beasts, some with natural carapaces, like gigantic beetles, all armed with pikes and morningstars and maces and broadswords and meat cleavers of every description, some riding one upon the other, some dragging snoring companions, some in mysterious congress, some pausing to throw dice or settle a quarrel before being beaten back into line by their officers, whose helms sported the yellow blazon of eight-arrowed Chaos.

Snorting and wheezing, whiffling and sneezing; grunting and squealing and yelping; bellowing like bulls in a slaughterhouse, the Chaos army advanced: a single appetite.

The Rose turned frightened eyes to greet her friends. "There is nothing we have can withstand that army," she said. "It is retreat again, then . . . ?"

"No," said Princess Tayaratuka. "This time we do not need to retreat." She was leaning on a sword almost as tall as herself but which she carried with considerable panache, as if she and the blade had always been one.

Her sisters, too, bore their swords as casually, and with fresh confidence.

"These swords are powerful enough to challenge Chaos?" Wheldrake was the first to voice the question. "Good heavens, your majesties! See how the old rhyme does poor justice to the true value of the epic! It is what I always tell them when they accuse me of being over-imaginative! I cannot *begin* to describe what is really out there! What I *actually* see!" He virtually crowed with excitement. "What, indeed, the world around them is *really* like! Are we to do battle with Chaos at last?"

"You must stay here with Mother Phatt," said Charion. "It is your duty, my dear."

"You must stay, too, dear child!" cried Fallogard Phatt in great dismay. "You are not a warrior! You are a clairvoyant!"

"I am both now, Uncle," she said firmly. "I have no special blade to aid me, but I have my special wit, which gives me considerable advantage of most opponents. I learned much, Uncle, in the service of Gaynor the Damned! Let me go with you, ladies, I beg."

"Aye," said Princess Mishiguya, "you are well-fitted to battle Chaos. You may go with us."

"And I would go with you, also," said the Rose. "My magic is exhausted, but I have fought Chaos many times and survived, as you know. Let me bear my Swift Thorn and my Little Thorn into battle beside you. For if we are to die at this time, I would rather die fulfilling my vocation."

"Then so be it," said Princess Shanug'a and looked enquiringly towards her kinsman. "Five swords against Chaos—or six?"

Elric was still staring at that horrific army which looked as if everything obscene and evil and brutish and greedy in the human race had been given features. He turned back with a shrug. "Six, of course. But they will require our every resource to defeat them. I suspect that we do not see all that Chaos sends against us. Yet I, too, have not made use of everything . . ."

He raised his gauntleted hand to his lips, brooding on a matter which had just entered his mind.

Then he said: "The others must stay here, to make their escape if need be. I charge you, Master Wheldrake, with the well-being of Mother Phatt and Koropith Phatt, as well as Fallogard . . ."

"Really, sir. I am capable . . ." said that untidy idealist.

"I have every respect for your capabilities, sir," said Elric, "but you are not experienced in these matters. You must be ready to flee, since you have no means of defending yourself or your people. Your psychic gifts might help you find a means of escape before Chaos discovers you. Believe me, Master Phatt, if it seems we are about to be defeated you must flee this realm! Use whatever powers you still possess to find a means of escape—and take the others with you."

"I will not leave while Charion is here," said Wheldrake firmly.

"You must, for everyone's sake," Charion said. "Uncle Fallogard will have need of you."

But it was fairly clear from Wheldrake's manner that he had made up his own mind on the matter.

"The horses are ready for us in the stables below," said Princess Tayaratuka. "Six horses of copper and silver, as the weaving demands."

Wheldrake watched his friends leave. Something he disliked in himself was grateful that he did not have to go with them and face such disgusting foes; something else yearned to go with them, yearned to be part of their epic fight, rather than its mere recorder . . .

A little later, as he leaned upon the balcony and watched the slow, sickening advance of that evil, brutified pack, crushing all it encountered and taking only absent-minded pleasure in the destruction it caused, the poet saw six figures leave the shadows of the cliff and ride on chestnut, silver-maned horses without hesitating into the clashing crystals of the forest. Elric, the three sisters, Charion Phatt and the Rose—side by side they cantered—straight-backed in their saddles—to do battle with that manifestation of perverse evil and greedy cruelty—to fight for their very future: for their history; for the merest memory of their ever having existed somewhere in the vast multiverse . . .

At this sight, Wheldrake laid down his expectant pen and, instead of concocting some glorious Romance from the action of those six brave riders, he offered up an impassioned prayer in respect of the lives and the souls of his cherished friends.

Pride in his companions, together with his fears for their well-being, had struck the little man speechless.

Now he watched as the Rose broke away from her fellows and rode a little way ahead until she was only a few yards from the first swaying howdahs of the massive war-beasts, part mammal, part reptile, which Chaos habitually used in its attacks. Already the stupid heads, lips and nostrils glistening with ichor which hung like dirty ropes from their orifices and left a trail of slime for the others to follow, were turning to sniff some alien scent, some body not yet touched and warped by the limitless, cruel and casual creativity of Chaos.

Then, from the leading howdah, all hung with human skins and other savageries, poked out a head to peer down at the Rose as she advanced upon the throng.

The helmet was immediately recognised by Wheldrake.

It belonged to Gaynor, ex-Prince of the Universal.

The death-seeker had come personally to savour the final agonies of these most irritating of his enemies.

4

The Fight in the Crystalline Wood:
Chaos Regenerated. The Tangled Woman.
To *The Ship That Was*.

"Prince Gaynor," said the Rose, "you and your warriors have invaded this land." She spoke with angry formality. "And we now order you to leave. We are here to banish Chaos from this realm."

Gaynor said coolly: "Sweet Rose, you have been driven mad by your knowledge of our power. You should not resist us further, lady. We ourselves are here to establish Gaynor's rule once and for all upon your realm. We offer you the mercy of immediate death."

"That mercy is a lie!" said Charion Phatt from where she sat on her silver-maned horse beside the others. "All that you say is a lie. And what is not a lie is mere vainglory!"

Gaynor's mysterious helm turned slowly to regard the young woman and a deep, assured chuckle escaped the Prince of the Damned. "You have a naïve courage, child, but it is by no means sufficient to offer resistance to the power Chaos commands. Which *I* command."

There was a fresh note in Gaynor's voice, a new kind of confidence, and Elric wondered, with some unease, how the Prince of the Damned had come by it. Gaynor seemed to believe his position was, if anything, stronger. Did more Chaos Lords group behind him? Was this to be the beginning of the great battle between Law and Chaos which so many oracles had predicted in recent centuries?

As he watched the Rose raise herself in her saddle and draw her sword Swift Thorn, Elric marvelled at the woman's self-control; for she faced the creature that had betrayed her and caused the agonised deaths of all her people. She faced him and did not reveal in any way her contempt and hatred of him. Yet twice he had bested her in a struggle without beating her and this he must know. Perhaps that was the reason for his new-found braggadocio? Perhaps he sought to deceive them into believing he had more power than was apparent?

Now the Rose was riding back to rejoin her friends crying: "Know this, Gaynor the Damned, whatever is the worst thing you fear, *that* shall be your fate after this day! This I promise you!"

Gaynor's answering laughter had little humour, merely threat. "There is no punishment I fear, madam. Do you not know that yet? Since I am not permitted the luxury of death, then I shall find it for myself—and make millions seek it with me! Each death I cause, lady, consoles me for an instant. You die in my place. All of you shall die in my place. For me." His tone became a lover's and his words caressed her retreating back like the foul coaxing hand of Vice personified. "For *me*, lady."

When she took her place again with the others, the Rose looked steadily into Gaynor's helm, which squirmed with the flames and smoke of his own myriad torments, and she said: "None of us shall die, Prince Gaynor. Least of all, on your behalf!"

"My surrogates!" called Gaynor, laughing again. "My sacrifices! Go to find death! Go! You do not realise I am your benefactor!"

But already the six of them, Elric and the Rose slightly ahead of their companions, were cantering through the shimmering, jangling forest, their swords drawn, their chestnut, silver-maned horses, bred in a distant age only for war and brought here by the sisters from some more barbaric realm, lifting their hoofs in sprightly anticipation of battle, their heavy harness clattering in unison with the broken branches of the crystal trees, their great heads nodding in impatience, their nostrils flaring as they anticipated the stink of blood, snorting and gnashing their teeth, rolling their eyes and glorying in the anticipation of the coming fight, for this was what they had been bred to do; becoming only fully alive when in the thick of violent destruction.

Elric, glad to feel such a fine war-stallion under him, understood how these horses looked forward to the ecstatic oblivion of battle. He too knew that singular joy, when every sense was alert and at its sharpest, when life never seemed sweeter or death more fearsome—and yet he knew what a false lure it was to lose himself in such mindless struggle. He wondered, not for the first time, if he was fated always to seek such struggles out, as if he, like the horses, had been bred for one special task? Hating it, he swiftly gave himself up to the thrilling delight of his battle-lust, and soon, as the first of Chaos's creatures came against him, he knew nothing but that lust . . .

Wheldrake, watching from the bower far above, saw the six riders converge upon the forces of Chaos and it seemed that they must be immediately swallowed. The very size of the Chaos beasts, the weight and grotesque power of the Chaos army, was more than enough, surely, to crush them in an instant?

Now a great shaft of scintillating light illuminated the riders as they merged with the colossal war-beasts who rumbled relentlessly on through the coruscating forest. Wheldrake saw six points flickering in that generality of lumbering limbs and widening jaws—one was a dark radiance he recognised as Stormbringer's—two were of ordinary, metallic glint—one more was a creamy white light, another the grey hard gleam of granite, and the last was the warm glow of ancient gold. Half-blinded by the crystal's shattered brightness, Wheldrake lost sight of the swords again and, when he could see clearly once more, he was astonished!

Four half-reptilian monsters lay in agony upon the radiant crystals, their howdahs crushed as they rolled and bellowed.

Wheldrake saw Gaynor's agitated figure, all angry, living metal, running back into the heart of his army, seeking a fresh mount. There was a sword in his gauntleted fist now—a sword that forked black and yellow—a sword whose blade seemed to twist in and out of the dimensions even as the damned one wielded it . . .

And Wheldrake guessed that the three sisters were not the only adepts who had sung a great rune or cast some other potent spell, for the sword in Gaynor's hand was unlike any he had borne before.

Yet elsewhere, still, the Chaos creatures fell before a kind of thin ribbon of glittering light which carved into their ranks as surely as a scythe through wheat . . .

Hand raised against his eyes to see through the blinding crystalline multicoloured rays that mirrored in some terrible way the beauty of the multiverse, Elric swung his great black blade this way and that, feeling only the faintest of resistance as, with thirsty ease, Stormbringer feasted upon the lives and souls of the warped half-beasts who had once been men and women before they pledged their miserable lives to Chaos . . .

There was no satisfaction at this killing, even though there was joy in the act of battle. Each fighter at Elric's side knew that, but for chance and a certain firmness of purpose, they, too, might be part of this army of damned souls . . . for Chaos was not the master most readily chosen by the majority of mortals . . .

Yet kill them they must—or be killed. Or see whole realms perish as Chaos gathered momentum, drawing upon the power of the conquered worlds to accomplish further conquests . . .

With the grace of dancers, with the precision of surgeons, with the sorrowing eyes of unwilling slaughterers, the three sisters joined in battle with those who had already destroyed most of their kinfolk.

Charion Phatt, dismounted from a horse she found too unresponsive, darted here and there with her sword, cutting swiftly at a Chaos creature's vitals and slipping in to cut again, using her psychic gifts to anticipate attack from any quarter and never being present when the attack came. Like the sisters, her movements were efficient and she took no pleasure in the destruction . . .

. . . Only the Rose shared some of Elric's joy, for she, like him, had been trained to battle—even if her enemies were somewhat different—and Swift Thorn struck with expert skill at exposed organs and vulnerable places on the malformed half-men, using subtlety and speed as her chief defence—guiding her chestnut-and-silver warhorse into the densest parts of the Chaos pack's ranks and slicing so accurately at a chosen target that she brought one monster tumbling down upon another, a churning of heavy paws and legs which killed more of their own kind even as they, themselves, perished.

The wild exultant battle-song of his ancestors came to Elric's lips as he followed the Rose into the heart of the enemy and the sword fed him the energy it did not take itself until his eyes glowed almost as hotly as Gaynor's, so that it seemed he, too, was filled to bursting with the fires of hell . . .

Now Wheldrake began to gasp as he saw that the six thin needles of radiance still flickered amongst all that slaughter—and already more than half the apparently invincible Chaos army was destroyed, a mass of torn and crushed flesh, of grotesque limbs and even more grotesque heads lifted in the final torments of unholy death . . .

. . . while clambering through this carnage, pushing aside imploring claws and pleading faces, plunging his steel heels into screaming mouths or agonised eyes, using for leverage any limb or organ or foothold in bone or flesh he could find, his flaring Chaos-blazoned armour all spotted with the blood and offal of his ruined army, came Gaynor the Damned, the black-and-yellow sword forking and fluttering in his hand like some living flag, and now there were names on his lips—names which became curses—names which became the synonyms for everything he hated, feared and most longingly desired . . .

. . . but this was a hatred expressed through random, disruptive violence and destruction; a fear which found its swiftest form in raging aggression; a desire so intense and so eternally frustrated that this had become the thing in himself Gaynor hated worst of all and hated in every creature he encountered . . .

. . . and it was upon Elric of Melniboné, who might have been his alter ego, some cosmic opposite, who had chosen the hardest of roads to follow rather than the easiest, that Gaynor the Damned concentrated the greatest volume of his enraged hatred. For Elric might yet become what Gaynor the Damned had been and which he could never be again . . .

. . . so thoroughly saturated with the air of Chaos was Gaynor that at this moment he was little more than a half-beast himself. He growled and he shrieked as he crawled over the corpses of his slain warriors, he made hideous, wordless noises, he slobbered as if he already tasted Elric's deficient blood . . .

"*Elric! Elric of Melniboné! Now I shall send thee to do eternal service with thy banished master! Elric! Arioch awaits thee. I offer up to him in friendly reconciliation the soul of his recalcitrant servitor . . .*"

But Elric did not hear his enemy. His own ears were full of ancient battle-songs, his concentration was upon his immediate opponents as, one by one, he cut them down and took their souls for himself.

These souls he did not dedicate to Arioch, for Arioch had proved himself too fickle a patron and, as was clear, had no power in this realm. Whatever was left of Esbern Snare had carried Arioch back through the dimensions to his own domain, where he must recoup his strength and make fresh plots in his eternal rivalry with his fellow lords.

Elsewhere Charion Phatt and the Rose continued their delicate butchery, while Stormbringer's sister swords rose and fell and made their own sweet, eery music, as subtle and as dangerous as the three sisters who wielded them. Elric had never known such mortal peers. The knowledge that they were nearby filled him with a kind of pride and made his battle-joy the greater as he continued his sorcerous slaughter while, dimly now, through all that din of outraged militancy, he thought he heard his own name being called.

Two Chaos warriors, with spiked armour half-hiding skin like barnacles, struck at him together but were too slow for Elric and his hellblade—their heads flew like buckets at a sideshow and one spiked an eye in a second pair who came against him, confusing them both so that they slew each other, but meanwhile Elric galloped beside a wading half-reptile as it clambered over the ruined flesh towards the Rose and with two quick strokes had severed secret tendons and brought the Chaos beast crashing upon the bodies of its fallen fellows, roaring out its impotent anger, its stupefied astonishment at this discovery of its own mortality . . .

Yet more insistent now was that faint, familiar sound . . .

"*Elric! Elric! Chaos awaits thee, Elric!*" A high, keening sound; a vengeful wind.

"*Elric! Soon we shall see an end to all thine optimism!*"

Up a mound of Chaos carrion rode Elric on his war-trained steed, to take stock of their battle . . .

Wheldrake on his balcony saw Elric's horse climb that rise in the carpet of the conquered, saw the Black Sword raised in the albino's black-gauntleted right hand, saw the left hand lifted against the blazoning rays which still sprang from every direction, wherever the crystal trees were broken. That dazzling intermixture of colour and light gave still more distance to the scene and Wheldrake, seeing what Elric did not yet see, offered up another prayer . . .

. . . Gaynor, carving his way through a pile of already rotting corpses, his armour now almost wholly encrusted with the remains of his warriors, plunged forward, still snarling Elric's name, still obsessed with nothing but vengeance . . .

"*Elric!*"

A thin sound, like the warning cry of a faraway bird, and Elric recognised the voice as Charion Phatt's.

"*Elric! He is close to you. I can sense him. He has more power than we suspected. You must destroy him somehow . . . Or he will destroy us all!*"

"ELRIC!" This last a great grunt of satisfaction as, through the piled corpses, Gaynor broke at last, to stand with his horrid eyes trained upon the face of his greatest enemy, the black-and-yellow sword, the ragged sword, flickering in his hand like lava fresh from some volcanic maw. "I did not think I would have need of this new power of mine, as yet. But here you are. And here am I!"

With that Gaynor lunged at Elric and the albino brought up Stormbringer easily to block him. At which Gaynor, surprisingly, laughed and lingered in the attitude of his failed stroke until, suddenly, the albino realised what was happening and tried to pull back, dragging Stormbringer free of the leechblade now seeking to suck all life from it. Elric had heard of blades which fed, in some strange manner, on the energies of such as Stormbringer—a parasite on whatever occult force emanated from the alien iron out of which these swords were forged.

"You resort to some ungentlemanly sorcery, it seems, Prince Gaynor." Elric knew that much of the power still remained in his blade, but could not risk further leeching of that energy.

"Honour has no place in my catalogue of useful qualities!" Gaynor spoke almost lightly, feinting with the black-and-yellow leechblade. "But if it did, I would say, Prince Elric, that you lack courage to face a foe, man to man—each with a singular sword to aid his work. Are we not fairly matched, Prince of Ruins?"

"Well enough, well enough, I suppose, sir," said Elric, hoping that the sisters would understand the urgency of their joint predicament. And, expertly, he made his horse sidestep another almost playful feint.

"You fear me, Elric, eh? You fear death, do you?"

"Not death," said Elric. "Not that ordinary death which is a transition . . ."

"What of that death which is sudden and everlasting oblivion?"

"I do not fear it," said the albino. "Though I do not desire it, either."

"As you know I desire it!"

"Aye, Prince Gaynor. But you are not permitted to possess it. You never shall suffer such easy release."

"Maybe." Gaynor the Damned became almost secretive at this and he turned to look over his shoulder to chuckle as he saw Princess Tayaratuka riding back towards them while her sisters and the other two women continued their fierce advance. "Are there, I wonder, any constants at all in the multiverse? Is the Balance no more than a pleasant invention with which mortals reassure themselves that there is some kind of order? What evidence do we observe of this?"

"We can *create* the evidence," said Elric quietly. "It is within our power to do that. To create order, justice, harmony . . ."

"You moralise too much, my lord. It is the sign of a morbid mind, sir. An overburdened conscience, perhaps."

"I will not be condescended to by such as yourself, Gaynor." Elric let his body appear to relax, his expression become casual. "A conscience is not always a burden."

"O, murderer of kin and betrothed! What else but loathing can ye feel for your deficient character?" Gaynor feinted with words even as he feinted with the leechsword, and both were designed to deprive the albino of his faith in his own skills, his will to survive.

"I have killed more villains than I have killed innocents," said Elric firmly, though it was clear Gaynor knew how to strike at the very vitals of his being. "And I regret only that I cannot have the pleasure of slaying thee, failed Servant of the Balance."

"Make no mistake, my lord, it would be a pleasure for us both," said Gaynor—and now he lunged—now Elric must block the blow. And again the energy from the sword was drained in a great gobbling up of cosmic force, and the black-and-yellow leechsword began to pulse with dirty light.

Elric, unprepared for the power of Gaynor's sword, fell backwards and almost lost his seat, the runesword hanging uselessly from its wrist thong. The albino, slumping forward in his saddle, gasping for air, saw all they had lately won about to be taken back in moments . . . He croaked for Princess Tayaratuka, riding close now, to flee—to avoid the leechsword at any cost, for now it was twice as powerful as it had been . . .

But the princess could not hear him. Even now, with a grace that made her seem almost weightless, she was bearing down upon Gaynor the Damned, the golden sword whistling and ululating in her right hand, her black hair whipped behind her, her violet eyes alight with the prospect of Gaynor's doom . . .

. . . and again Gaynor blocked her blow. Again he laughed. And again, in astonishment, Princess Tayaratuka felt the energy draining from herself and her blade . . .

. . . then, almost casually, Gaynor had knocked her from her saddle with the butt of his sword, leaving her to lie helplessly amongst the mangled flesh and bone of the field, and on her horse was riding to where the others fought, still oblivious of the danger he brought . . .

Princess Tayaratuka lifted her eyes to Elric's as the albino strove to drag himself upright. "Elric, have you no other sorcery to help us?"

Elric racked his brains, considering all the grimoires and charts and words he had memorised as a child, and could put himself in tune with no psychic power at all . . .

"Elric," came Tayaratuka's hoarse whisper, "see—Gaynor has downed Shanug'a—the horse races with her, beyond control . . . and now Mishiguya is fallen from her horse . . . Elric, we are lost! We are lost in spite of all our sorceries!"

And Elric began dimly to recollect an old alliance his folk had had with some near-supernatural creatures who had helped them in the early days of the founding of Melniboné, but he could remember only a name . . .

"*Tangled Woman*," he murmured, his lips dry and cracking. It was as if his whole body were drained of substance and that any movement would snap it in a dozen places. "The Rose will know . . ."

"Come," said Tayaratuka, getting to her feet and grabbing hold of his horse's bridle, "we must tell them . . ."

But Elric had nothing to tell; merely the memory of a memory, of an old tryst with some natural spirit which owed no loyalty to Law or Chaos; of a nagging hint of a spell—some chant he had been taught as a boy, as an exercise in summoning . . .

The Tangled Woman.

He could not remember who she was.

Gaynor was disappeared again, into his own ranks, seeking out Charion

Phatt and the Rose, for now he was armed with a sword four times more powerful than those which had come against him and he wished to test the blade
on ordinary, mortal flesh . . .

Wheldrake, still watching, still praying, saw everything from his balcony.
He saw Princess Tayaratuka sheath her golden sword and lead Elric's horse
to where her sisters stood, also in attitudes of exhaustion. Their horses had
bolted in Gaynor's wake.

Yet still Gaynor had not found the Rose, and Charion Phatt evaded him
as easily as an urchin in a market, returning to the others and speaking with
some heat to the prone albino . . .

. . . When, round a pile of corpses, rode the Rose, dismounting in a single
movement as she saw the predicament of her friends . . .

Then she, too, kneeled beside the fallen albino and she took his hand . . .

"There is one spell," said Elric. "I am trying to recall it. There is, perhaps, a
memory. Concerning you, Rose, or some folk of your own . . ."

"All my folk are dead, save me," said the Rose, her soft, pink skin flushed
with the work of battle. "And it seems I, too, am to die."

"No!" Elric struggled to his feet. He held tight to his pommel while the
horse shifted nervously, not knowing why it could not continue with its battle.
"You must help me, lady. There is something about a woman, the Tangled
Woman . . ."

The name was familiar to her.

"All I know is this," she said, and, with furrowed brow, she recalled some
lines of verse . . .

"*In the first creative weaving of a world,*
In the time before the time of long ago,
When neither haughty Law nor fractured Chaos rules,
Lives a creature born of foliage and flesh,

Who seeks to weave her world a-fresh,
And weaves one fine, a woven womb,
A womb of bramble flowers strong,
In which to sing her briar-song,
And bear her thorny child, who grows
Into a perfect rose.

"They are Wheldrake's. From his youth, he says."

But then she saw that she had, in a way she might never understand, communicated something to the pale lord, for Elric's lips were moving and his eyes were raised to look into worlds the others could not see. Strange musical sounds came out of his lips, and even the three sisters could not understand what he said, for he spoke no earthly tongue. He spoke a tongue of the dark clay and the winding roots, of the old bramble-nests where the wild Vadhagh once, legend had it, played and spawned their strange offspring, part flesh, part leafy wood, a people of the forest and forgotten gardens, and, when he hesitated, it was the Rose who joined him in his song, in the language of a folk who were not her own, but whose ancestors had mingled with her own and whose blood flowed in her to this day.

They sang together, sending their song through all the dimensions of the multiverse, to where a dreaming creature stirred and lifted up arms made of a million woven brambles and turned faces which, too, were of knotted rose-wood, in the direction of the song it had not heard for a hundred thousand years. And it was as if the song brought her to life, gave her some meaning at a moment when she had been about to die, so that, almost upon a whim, from something like curiosity, the Tangled Woman shifted her brambly body, arm by arm and leg by leg, then head by head, and, with a rustling movement which made all her foliage shudder, she formed herself into a shape very like a human shape, though somewhat larger.

And with that, she took a casual step through time and space which had not been in existence when she had first decided to sleep, and which she therefore ignored, and found herself standing in an ill-smelling morass of corrupt flesh and rotting bone which displeased her. But through all this she sensed another scent, something of herself in it, and she lowered her massive, woven head, a head of thick thorn branches whose eyes were not eyes at all, but flowers and leaves, and then she opened her briar lips and asked, in a voice so low it shook the ground, why her daughter had summoned her?

To which the Rose replied, in similar speech, while Elric sang his own tale to her, in a melody she found tolerable. It seemed that she concentrated her woven branches more thickly about her and looked with a certain sternness towards Gaynor and the remains of the Chaos army which had come full stop to stare at her before, at Gaynor's lifting of his black-and-yellow sword, a shard of raging energy, they began to race to the attack!

And the sisters clutched hands, linked with Charion and Elric and the Rose, and they held tight for security and power, for they somehow informed the Tangled Woman in her primitive soul—they directed her as she bent and reached a many-branched hand towards Gaynor, who barely yanked his horse aside in time and rode beneath her, slashing at the wood which, because the energy which enlivened it was of a kind that no power could suck out nor any mortal weapon damage, was scarcely marked and, where it was marked, healed immediately.

With calm deliberation now, as if she performed some unwelcome household task, the Tangled Woman stretched her long fingers through the attacking ranks of Chaos, oblivious to their hacking swords and jabbing pikes, their bitings and their clawings, and wove her fingers thoroughly amongst them, twining and twisting and bending and entangling them until every Chaos warrior and every Chaos beast still living was embraced and fixed by her bramble fingers.

Only one figure escaped, riding like fury from the bloody crystals of that battlefield, slashing at the horse's rump with the satiated leechsword.

Tangled Woman reached thin tentacles out towards the disappearing Gaynor but had little strength left; just enough to flick, with a thin, green branch, the sword from his flailing hand and bear it triumphantly up, to fling it away, deep into the forest where a black pool began to spread, turning all the surrounding crystal to the consistency of coal.

Then the leechsword vanished and they heard Gaynor's furious yell as he forced the sweating stallion up out of the valley and rode, without looking back, down the other side, to vanish.

Tangled Woman had lost interest in Gaynor. Slowly she withdrew her brambly fingers from the field, from the bloody corpses her thorns had pierced, from the flesh from which life had been crushed, her victims knowing a cleaner death than any Elric offered.

But now Elric pulled himself into his saddle and, while the others refused to look, he went about the business of slaughtering the wounded, letting the sword feast and renew his energy. He was determined to find and punish Gaynor for the evil he had done. And as he passed among what remained of the living, their imploring wails were ignored. "I must steal from you what your master would have stolen from us," he explained. And that killing had neither honour nor satisfaction in it. He did only what was necessary.

When he returned to his companions the Tangled Woman had gone, taking whatever payment she required, and all that were left were the dead.

"The Chaos army is defeated," said Princess Shanug'a. "But Chaos still dwells within our realm. Gaynor still has power here. He will soon come against us again." She had recaptured her horse.

"We must not *let* him come again," said the Rose, cleaning Swift Thorn upon a scrap of satin surcoat. "We must drive him back to hell and ensure he nevermore threatens your realm!"

"It is true," said Elric, moody with his own unquiet thoughts, "we must track the beast back to its lair and it must be confined, even if we cannot kill it. Can you find the way, Charion Phatt?"

"I can find it," she said. She had several minor wounds, which the others had helped her dress, but there was a kind of breathless pleasure in the way she moved, as if she were still exulting in her unexpected salvation. "He has returned, without doubt, to *The Ship That Was*."

"His stronghold . . ." murmured the Rose.

"Where," said Princess Mishiguya, settling herself in her saddle, "his power must be greatest."

"There is a power there, to be sure," agreed Charion drawing her brows together—"a mightier power than any he commanded on this field. Yet I cannot completely understand why he did not use it against us here."

"Perhaps he awaits us," said Elric. "Perhaps he knows we will come . . ."

"We must go to reclaim the Rose's treasures," said Princess Tayaratuka. "We cannot allow Prince Gaynor to hold them."

"Indeed," agreed Elric with some feeling and a renewing sense of urgency. He had remembered that his father's soul remained in Gaynor's keeping and that very soon Arioch or some other Duke of Hell would try to claim it, whereupon it would flee to him and hide within his own being, forever united, father and son.

Elric drew off his black gauntlets and put his hands upon his horse's muscular flanks, but nothing would take away the chill that gripped his being. No ordinary warmth could comfort him.

"What of the others?" said Charion. "What of my uncle and my grandma, my cousin and my betrothed? I think they must be reassured."

They rode slowly back towards the cavern city, stabling their horses before beginning the long climb up the steps and walkways hidden within the walls, and when they finally reached the balcony where they had left the others, they found only Wheldrake.

He was distraught. His eyes were full of tears. He embraced Charion Phatt but his gesture was one of consolation rather than joy. "They have gone," he said. "They saw that you were losing the battle. Or thought they saw that.

Fallogard had to consider his son and his mother. He did not want to leave, but I made him. He had the power to do it. He could have taken me, but there was no time and I would not go."

"Gone?" said Charion, holding him at arm's length now. "Gone, my love?"

"Mother Phatt opened what she called a 'tuck' and they crawled under it, to disappear—at the very moment when that vast thicket materialised. It was too late. They have escaped!"

"From what?" yelled Charion Phatt, enraged. "To what? Oh, must we begin this search all over again?"

"It seems so, my dear," said Wheldrake meekly, "if we are to have your uncle's blessing, as we had hoped."

"We must follow them," she said firmly.

"Not yet," said the Rose softly. "First we must ride to *The Ship That Was*. I have a small reckoning to extract from Gaynor the Damned—and from the company I suspect he keeps."

5

Concerning the Capturing and the Auctioning of Certain Occult Artefacts: Reverses in the Higher Worlds; The Rose Exacts Her Revenge; Resolving a Cosmic Compromise.

The little caravan came to a ragged halt as the cliffs were reached at last. Their remaining horses, sometimes carrying double, were almost completely exhausted. But they had found the Heavy Sea; dragging its dark and weighty waves upon the shore, then dragging them back again, all beneath a slow, morbid sky. They looked down now at the narrow entrance of a bay, where the sea seemed calmer. Its high, obsidian walls enclosed a beach of oddly co-loured shingle, of bits of quartz and shards of limestone, of semi-precious stones and glaring flint.

Anchored in the bay was a ship which Elric recognised at once. Her sail was furled, but the great covered cage in the forecastle made her prow-heavy. Gaynor's ship and her crew had rejoined their master. On the far side of a spur of rock, which obscured their sight of the rest of the beach, there seemed to be activity—perhaps a figure or two—and now they must allow their horses to pick their way slowly down the narrow track from cliff to beach, threatening to slip on the shiny rock. Then at last the hoofs were grinding down upon the gleaming shingle, making a sound like ice being crushed, and the companions could see that the beach extended beyond the spur and that it was possible to ride along it.

Princess Tayaratuka rode a little ahead; then came her sisters (sharing a horse). Then came the Rose, followed by Elric and Charion Phatt, with Wheldrake's tiny hands about her waist. A strangely disparate party, but with many shared ambitions . . .

Then they had rounded the point and they looked upon *The Ship That Was*. Before them stood one of the most grotesque settlements Elric had ever seen.

Once it had, indeed, been a ship. A ship whose score of decks rose higher and higher to form what had been a vast, floating ziggurat crewed by huge, unhuman creatures; a ship worthy of Chaos herself. Her lines had the appearance of something organic which had petrified suddenly after being tortured into unnatural forms. Here and there were suggestions of faces, limbs, torsos, of otherworldly beasts and birds, of gigantic fish and creatures which were combinations of all these things. And the ship seemed to Elric to be of a piece with the Heavy Sea which, like green quartz turned viscous and sluggish now, flung its spume upon that gloomy strand where men, women and children, in every variety of clothing, in rags and silks and shoes which rarely matched, in the filthy sables of some slaughtered king, in the jerkins and breeks of a nameless sailor, in the dresses and undergarments of the drowned, in the hats and jewels and embroidery with which the dead had once celebrated their vanity, moved backwards and forwards amongst those dreadful breakers, amongst carrion and flotsam brought here on the morose tide, the detritus of centuries, to scuttle with any treasure they might discover back to the warren of the ship, which lay at a slight angle on the beach, its starboard buried, its port atilt, where perhaps a mast had halted its complete upending.

A dead husk, the ship was infested with its human inhabitants much as the body of some slain sea-giant might be infested with worms. They stained it with their very presence, dishonoured it by their squalor, as the bones of the fallen are stained and dishonoured by the droppings and the débris of the crows which feed upon their putrefying flesh. Within the ship was constant movement, an impression of one writhing mass of life without individual identity or concerns, without dignity, respect or shame—wriggling, scampering, quarrelling, fighting, squealing, roaring, whining and hissing, as if in imitation of that horrible sea itself, these were those humans pledged to Chaos but not yet transformed by Chaos; creatures who doubtless had had little choice in their masters as Gaynor carried the banner of Count Mashabak out into this world. They were wretches now, however, and they had only their shame. They would not look up as Elric and his companions rode towards the looming shadow of *The Ship That Was*.

They would not answer the albino's questions. They would not listen when the sisters tried to speak to them. Terror and shame consumed them. They had already given up hope, even of an afterlife, for they reasoned that the misery they suffered surely proved that the entire multiverse had been conquered by their tormentors.

"We are here," said Elric at last, "to take prisoner Prince Gaynor the Damned and to hold him to account!"

Yet even this did not move them. They were used to Gaynor's deceptions, the games he had, in his moments of boredom, played with their lives and their emotions. To them, all speech had become a lie.

The seven rode to where a kind of drawbridge had been built into the body of the upturned ship and, without hesitation, they cantered inside, to discover a nightmare of murky galleries and ragged holes, where crude doors had been carved between bulkheads, all strung with shreds of net and rope and various roughly made implements, drying bits of cloth and rag, of tattered clothing and ill-washed linen, where lean-to shacks and teetering shanties were erected, often on the very brink of an injured deck. Something large and strong had pierced this ship and brought her to her end, rupturing her innards.

Through the portholes from deck to deck poured a foggy, unpleasant light, creating a lattice of pale and dark shadows within the ship's serpentine bowels, making the shapes of the inhabitants equally shadowy, like ghosts, crouching, skulking, coughing, wheezing, tittering, too despairing to look upon the living without increasing their already unbearable misery. The floor of *The Ship That Was* was deep with human ordure, with discarded litter even they did not value. Wheldrake put a hand to his mouth and dropped down from Charion's horse. "Ugh, this is worse than the Stepney warrens. I'll let you go about your business. I have nothing useful to do here." And somewhat to Charion's surprise he returned to the comparative wholesomeness of that dark beach.

"It is true," said the Rose, "that he can do little that is practical. But his poetic inspiration is without parallel when it comes to tuning oneself to the harmony of the multiverse . . ."

"It is his most delightful quality," agreed Charion with a lover's enthusiasm, glad that what she admired in her beau was reflected in another's opinion—which went a short distance to disproving what lovers always suspect of themselves; that they have gone entirely mad.

Now Elric was losing patience with that conspiracy of the desperate and the dumb. As his warhorse stamped upon the filthy shingle, he drew the runesword out of its scabbard so Stormbringer's black radiance poured into that great, ruined space, and a dangerous murmuring song came out of it, as if it lusted for the soul of he who had tried to steal its energy.

And the warhorse reared up, pawing at the murky air; and the albino's scarlet eyes blazed through all that layered darkness, and he cried out the name of the one who had wronged them, who had created all this, who had abused every power, every responsibility, every duty, every treaty, every trust ever placed in him.

"Gaynor! Gaynor the Damned! Gaynor, thou foulest hellspawn! We have come to be revenged on thee!"

From somewhere high above, in what had once been the deepest and strongest parts of the ship, where the darkness was complete, came a distant chuckling that could only emanate from that faceless helm.

"Such rhetoric, my dear prince! Such bluster!"

Then Elric was finding a way for himself and his horse, crashing upwards into the shadows, through the trellises of misty light, up companionways which had once felt the feet of massive sailors and which were now all crowded and cluttered with the débris of these human inhabitants, knocking aside steaming pots and scattering fires, heedless of any damage, knowing that whatever materials constituted this hull it could not burn from mortal flames, the Rose close at his heels, shouting for the sisters and Charion to follow.

Riding through galleries of filthy darkness, where startled eyes stared for a second from a cranny or hunched figures skittered into ill-smelling holes; riding through this collection of hopeless souls, to seek their master and (all manner of entities and forces willing) free them from his tyranny! It was the Rose who now threw up her head in a clear, sweet song—a song which spoke, through its melodies, of lost love, lost lands and frustrated revenge—of a dedication to make an end to this particular injustice, this obscene perversion in the order of the multiverse; the Rose who drew out her sword Swift Thorn and brandished it like a banner. Then the sisters, too, had drawn their blades—one of ivory, one of granite, one of gold—and were joining in with their own harmonies of outrage, determined that the cause of their despair should perpetrate no further harm. Only Charion Phatt sang no song. She was an inexpert rider and had fallen behind the others. Sometimes she looked back, perhaps hoping that Wheldrake had decided to follow after all.

They reached at last a pair of massive doors, their carvings so alien that they were, right or wrong way up, indecipherable to the mortals. Once these doors had guarded the quarters of whatever beast had ruled the ship and had been deep at the vessel's heart, but now they lay close to the roof from beyond which could be heard the slow booming of the heavy breakers.

"Perhaps," came Gaynor's amused tones again, "I should reward such folly. I sought to bring you here, sweet princesses, to show off my little kingdom to you, but you refused to come! Now curiosity brings you here, anyway."

"It is not curiosity, Prince Gaynor, which brings us to *The Ship That Was*." Princess Shanug'a dropped from the horse she shared with her sister and went to push at one of the heavy doors, forcing it back a fraction—enough for them to pass through after they had all dismounted. "It is our intention to end your rule in this realm!"

"Brave words now, madam. Were it not for primitive earth-magic, you would be my slaves at this moment. Just as you shall be my slaves very soon."

The foggy air was thick with hot, unnatural odours and brands burned in it, scarcely casting better light than the flickering candles whose huge yellow stems dripped hissing wax upon what had once been an intricately carved roof but which was now covered in matted straw and rags. Webs were silhouetted in the air, hinting at the workings of enormous spiders, and from the deeper shadows came a scuttling that could only be of rats. Yet it seemed to Elric that all this was merely an illusion, a curtain which was being parted, for into view—and he was never sure how—came the fierce, rich, roiling colours of Chaos—a great sphere whose contents were in constant movement—and this displayed the dark outline of Gaynor the Damned, standing before it as if at some kind of altar on which he had placed some few small objects . . .

"Oh, you are most welcome," he said. He was half-crazed with delight at what he was sure must soon be their acceptance of his sovereignty. "There is little need for this display of challenges and insults, my friends, for I can surely solve our differences!" The helm pulsed now with a scarlet fire, shot through with veins of black. "Let us put an end to exuberant violence and settle these matters as wiser folk should."

"I have heard your reasoning tone before, Gaynor," said the Rose contemptuously, "when you tried to make my sisters bargain for their honour or their lives. I do not bargain with you, any more than did they!"

"Long memories, sweet lady. I had forgotten such a trifle and so should you. It was yesterday. I promise you a glorious rule in tomorrow!"

"What can you promise that we could possibly value?" said Charion Phatt. "Your mind is chiefly mysterious to me, but I know that you lie to us. You have all but lost your grip upon this realm. The power which aided thee, aids thee no longer! But you would make it aid thee, again . . ."

At this the great pulsing ectoplasmic sphere behind Gaynor flared and shivered and revealed, for an instant, three glaring eyes, tusks, drooling jaws and furious claws, and Elric realised to his horror that Mashabak was *not* free, that

Gaynor had somehow kept control of the prison, appearing to do Count Mash-abak's bidding while scheming to take the power of a Chaos Lord for himself!

Arioch had been banished from this plane, dragged through the dimensions by the last brave action of Esbern Snare, and Gaynor had been more audacious than any of them could imagine—he had determined that *he* should take the place of Arioch, rather than freeing his master! But though he held the Chaos Lord prisoner, he had no means of harnessing his power, of using it for his own ends. Was this why, with his leechblade, he had sought to steal the energy of Stormbringer and its sister swords?

"Aye," said Gaynor, reading his enemy's expression. "I had planned to gain the necessary power by other means. But I am a practical immortal, as thou must understand by now, and if I must bargain—why I shall happily go to market with thee!"

"You have nothing I need, Gaynor," said Elric coldly.

But the ex-Prince of the Universal was already mocking him, holding up one of the objects he had placed there and jeering softly. "Do you not want this, Prince Elric? Is this not what you have sought for so long? Across the realms, sir? With such considerable impatience, sir?"

And Elric saw that it was the box of black rosewood, its gnarled surfaces all carved with black roses. Even from here he could smell its wonderful perfume. His father's soulbox.

And again Gaynor jeered, louder now. "It was stolen by one of your sorcerer ancestors, given to your mother, then your father (who conceived his extraordinary deception once he understood what it was!), whose servant lost it! It was purchased, I believe, for a few groats by its owner in Menii. A pirate auction. Some small irony is to be enjoyed, I'd say . . ."

The Rose shouted suddenly, "You shall not bargain with us for that box, Gaynor!"

And Elric wondered why she had grown subtly more aggressive since they had entered those doors, as if she had rehearsed this moment, as if she knew exactly what she had to say and do.

"But I must, madam. I must!" Gaynor opened the box and drew out of it, between flickering blue finger and thumb, a great, lush crimson rose. He held it up by its dewy stem. It seemed to have been fresh-picked a moment earlier. A perfect rose. "The last living thing in your land, madam! Save yourself, of course. The only other survivor of that particularly enjoyable victory. Like you, madam, it has survived all that Chaos could do to it. Up to now . . ."

"It is not yours," said Princess Tayaratuka. "It is what the Rose gave us when she first knew of our plight. It was hers to give us. And ours to return to her. The Eternal Rose."

"Well, madam, it is mine now. To bargain with as *I* choose," said Gaynor with a hint of arrogant impatience, as if to a child who has not understood what has been explained.

"You have no right to those treasures," said Princess Mishiguya. "Give me back the briar rings, which are my part of our charge."

"But the briar rings are not your property," said Gaynor, "as well you know, madam. All these treasures were loaned to you, so that you could go onto the paths between the realms and seek Elric."

"Then give them back to me," said the Rose, stepping forward. "For they were, indeed, my treasures to loan or to bestow as I chose. They are the last treasures of my forgotten land. I brought them here, hoping to find peace from my tormented cravings. And then came Chaos and my hostesses' need was greater than my own. But now they have the swords they sought. They did not have to bargain, after all, with Elric. There's another sweet irony, prince. And we are here to reclaim those treasures. Give them up to us, Prince Gaynor, or we must take them by force."

"By force, madam?" Gaynor's laughter grew louder at this, and coarser, too. "You have no force to use against me! To use against Mashabak! I cannot yet control him, perhaps. But I can *release* him! I can release him into your realm, madam, and have him gobble it up in an instant, and all of us with it. Aye, and it would delight me to do so, madam, almost as much as it delights me to control such power. For would it not be *my* decision which brought about the conquests of unbridled Chaos? This blackthorn wand will set him free—with one tiny tap of its tip." And he revealed the thin, black branch that was bound with brass and elinfleur. "I repeat, madam, you have no force to use against me. While I remain here and my wand remains there, we are all of us safe as Arioch himself was safe when he made this cage . . ."

And suddenly there came a squawling and a roiling and a braying from the sphere and Count Mashabak's unlovely features were pressed there for a moment as he raved in response to his captor's name, at his absolute loss of honour in becoming the prisoner of a mere demi-demon. So vast and angry was the life-force imprisoned there that Elric and his companions felt driven back by it; felt as if they might be snuffed into non-existence by the very sight of it.

"And you, Prince Elric," yelled Gaynor the Damned above the cacophony of his recklessly captured prize, "you, too, have come to trade, no doubt. What? Will you have this? The skin your fierce friend left behind?" And he brandished the grey wolf's pelt that was all that remained of the tormented Northerner.

But to Elric it was no trophy Gaynor held. The abandoned wolfskin meant that Esbern Snare had died a free mortal. "I echo all the sentiments expressed by my friends," said Elric. "I do not trade with such as thee, Gaynor the Damned. There is no virtue left in thee."

"Vice alone, Prince Elric. Vice alone, I must admit. But such creative, *imaginative* vice, eh? You have yet to hear your choices. I want your swords, you see."

"They are our bond-blades," said Princess Mishiguya. "They are ours by blood and by right. They are ours to conquer thee and drive thee from our realm. Never shalt thou take them, Gaynor the Damned!"

"But I offer you those treasures you borrowed and lost, madam. I'll speak plain. I want four swords such as the four you have between you. I have here *six* objects of power. I will trade them all for the swords! Is that not generous? Even foolish?"

"You are insane, Gaynor," said Princess Shanug'a. "The swords are our inheritance. They are our duty."

"But it's *your* duty, madam, surely, to give back what you have borrowed? However, think upon that for a little. Now I am going to offer Elric his sweet old father's soul!" And he laid caressing steel upon the rosewood.

Angry at Arioch's betrayal of his secret, Elric could scarcely speak. Gaynor knew the true value of the soulbox and what it meant to Sadric's son!

"Would you be united—or would you be free?" Gaynor asked him, savouring every syllable of this temptation; understanding exactly what he offered the albino.

With a wordless oath, Elric lunged towards the altar but Gaynor motioned edgily with his wand and almost touched the ectoplasmic membrane where Count Mashabak roared and flexed his claws, his eyes seeming fierce enough to burn through those mystic walls and let him come rushing out, to devour, to warp, to make of this realm one screaming extrusion of tormented life.

"Your father's soul, Prince Elric, in return for that sword of yours. You know which you would rather have, surely? Come, Prince Elric, that's not a decision you must brood upon. Take the bargain. It releases you. It will free you from all thy dooms, sweet prince . . ."

And Elric felt the lure of it, the tempting prospect of being free for ever from his hellblade, from that unwanted symbiosis upon which he had grown to rely, of being free from the threat of his father's soul eternally merging with his own, of being able to help his father reach his mother in the Forest of Souls, where neither Law, nor Chaos, nor the Cosmic Balance had dominion.

"Your father's soul, Elric, for you to set free. The ending of his suffering and your own. You do not need the sword to live. You did not need its power to find it, to brave those ordeals, and others. Let me have the sword, Elric. And I shall give you all these treasures . . ."

"You want the sword so that you can control the demon with it," said Elric. "Do you have a spell which will give you such power? Perhaps you do, Prince Gaynor. But the spell alone is not sufficient. You must be able to frighten Count Mashabak—"

Again that raging din, that squawling and screeching and threatening . . .

"—and you think you can do that with Stormbringer. But you would need more than Stormbringer, Prince Gaynor, to achieve such control!" And again Elric reflected on the wild audacity of Gaynor the Damned, who sought to tame a Lord of Hell to his own bidding!

"True, sweet prince." Prince Gaynor's tone was softer again, and amused. "But happily I have more than your sword. The Rose knows of the spell I mean . . ."

And the Rose lifted her head and she spat at him, which made him laugh all the more merrily. "Ah, how lovers learn to regret those little confidences . . ."

Which brought a sudden understanding to Elric and a fresh sympathy for the woman, the last of her kind, and the particular nature of her moral burden.

"Give me the blade, Prince Elric." Gaynor stretched out the gauntleted left hand in which he held the soulbox. In his right hand, the blackthorn wand hovered near the ectoplasmic membrane. "There is nought to lose."

"I would only gain, I think," said Elric, "if you were to let me go free with that thing."

"Of course. Who would be harmed?"

But Elric knew the answer to the question. His companions would be harmed. This realm would be harmed. Many more would be harmed once Gaynor controlled Count Mashabak. He did not know exactly how the Prince of the Damned intended to use the weapon to control the Lord of Chaos, but it was clear there was such a means. Once, long ago, the Rose had confided her secret, her knowledge of such a powerful old sorcery.

"Or would you join your sire for ever, Elric of Melniboné?" The tone from within the helm was cooler now, more evidently threatening. "I would even share my new power with you. Your sword shall be the stick I'll use to goad Mashabak to my bidding . . ."

Elric yearned to agree with Gaynor the Damned. If he had been a true

Melnibonéan, even one like his father, he would have thought no more of the matter and given up the sword in return for the soulbox. But through whatever ties of character, blood and disposition they were, his loyalty was for his fellows and he would not consign one more human creature to the mercies of Chaos.

And so he refused.

Which brought a yell of rage from the ex-Prince of the Universal and he cried out that Elric was a fool, that he might have saved something from these realms, but now they would be entirely devoured by angry Mashabak . . .

. . . when there came a creaking and a groaning and a scattering of plaster and bits of stone, of candle-wax and falling flambeaux, as some ancient bilge-system, some trapdoor in the hull, began to creak open from above and through the gap came a questioning croak.

It was Khorghakh the toad. It was the navigating monster from the ship, pushing its way through. It sniffed and turned its head. It saw Charion. Whereupon it gave a grunt of satisfaction and began swiftly to clamber down the carved walls while Elric, taking advantage of Gaynor's inattention, chopped suddenly across the makeshift altar and struck the wand from the prince's hand, then thrust at him again, while Gaynor grabbed for his own sword and flung a blow at the albino's head.

But now Stormbringer sent up such a fearful keening, a sharp, specific utterance of rage, that there came a gasp of pain from within the helm—a helm that had not known pain for millennia. Gaynor brought up his sword to try to block the runeblade, but staggered.

Then Elric drew back the point of his hellsword and drove it directly at that place in Gaynor's armour which would have hidden his heart—and the Prince of the Damned howled with sudden agony as he was lifted upward, like a lobster on a spike, his arms and legs flailing, roaring his rage as Count Mashabak still roared his—suspended, helpless upon Stormbringer's point—

"Where is there a hell that could effect thy just punishment, Gaynor the Damned?" said Elric through clenching teeth.

And the Rose said softly:

"I know of such a place, Elric. You must summon your patron demon. Summon Arioch to this realm!"

"Madam, you are mad!"

"You must trust me here. Arioch's power will be weak. It has not had time to build. But you must speak to him."

"What good can Arioch do us in this? Will you return his prisoner to him?"

"Call him," she said. "This is the way that it should be. You must call him, Elric. Only by doing that can any harmony be achieved again."

And so Elric, with his enemy Prince Gaynor squirming like a spider on a stick in front of him, called out the name of his patron Duke of Hell, a creature who had betrayed him, who had attempted to extinguish him for ever.

"Arioch! Arioch! Come to thy servant, Lord Arioch. I beg thee."

Meanwhile the toad had reached the floor and was lumbering towards Charion, towards its lost love, and there was a kind of soft affection in its face as Mistress Phatt approached it, stroking its huge hands, patting its scales, while from above came a thin voice:

"We were in time, it seems! The toad found this entrance for us." And through the ruptured trapdoor came Ernest Wheldrake's head, looking down at them with some concern. "I was afraid we should be late."

Charion Phatt was patting the toad's enraptured head and laughing. "You did not tell us you had gone to bring extra help, my love!"

"I thought it best to make no promises. But I bring further good news." He looked at the route by which the toad had clambered, from carving to carving, to the floor and he shook his head. "I'll rejoin you as soon as I can." And he was gone.

"Arioch!" cried Elric. "Come to me, my patron!" But he could not offer blood and souls today.

"Arioch!"

And there, in one corner of this makeshift hall, a dark, smoky thing curled and shook itself and grumbled and then it had become a handsome youth, wonderful in his grace, but still not quite substantial. And the smile had all the sweetness of the hive. "What is it, my pet, my savoury . . . ?"

The Rose said: "Here is your chance to bargain, now, Elric. What does this demon own that you would have from him?"

Elric, his eyes moving from Gaynor to Arioch, saw his patron peering, almost as if he were purblind, at the leaping ectoplasmic sphere, at the writhing Gaynor.

"Only his lease," said Elric, "upon my father's soul."

"Then ask him for it," said the Rose. Her voice was vibrant with controlled urgency. "Ask him to give up his claim on that soul!"

"He will not agree," said Elric. Even with the sword's mighty energy, he was beginning to tire.

"Ask him for it," she said.

So Elric called over his shoulder. "My Lord Arioch. My patron Duke of Hell. Will you give up your claim on my father's soul?"

"I will not," said Arioch, his voice sly and puzzled. "Why should I? He was mine, as thou art mine."

"We shall neither be thine, if Mashabak is freed," said Elric. "And that you know, my patron."

"Give him to me," said Arioch thinly, "give me my prisoner, who is mine by right, whom I ensnared with the power of my occult subtleties. Give me Mashabak, and I will give up my claim."

"Mashabak is not mine to give you, Lord Arioch," said Elric, understanding at last. "But I will give thee Gaynor to make that exchange!"

"No!" cried the Prince of the Damned. "I could not bear such ignominy!"

Arioch was already smiling. "Oh, indeed, sweet immortal traitor, you shall bear it and much else besides. I know fresh torments that are presently inconceivable to you but which you will look back upon with nostalgia, as a time before your agony really began. I shall bestow upon thee all the tortures I had reserved for Mashabak—"

Then the golden body had streaked towards the bellowing Gaynor, who begged Elric in the name of everything he held holy, not to give him up to the Duke of Hell.

"You cannot be slain, Gaynor the Damned," said the Rose, her face flushed with triumph, "but you can still be punished! Arioch will punish you and, as he punishes you, you will remember that you were brought to this by the Rose and that this is the revenge of the Rose upon you, for the doom you brought to our paradise!"

Elric began to realise that not all had been coincidence, that much of what had happened was the result of some long-nurtured plan of the Rose to ensure that Gaynor would betray no others as he had betrayed her and her kin. That was why she had come back here. It was why she had loaned the sisters the treasures of her own lost land.

"Go now, Gaynor!" She watched as the golden shadow embraced the writhing prince . . . seemed to absorb the whole armoured creature into itself, before flowing back again into its corner, and thence down whatever narrow tunnel through the multiverse Elric had created with his Summoning.

"Go now, Prince Gaynor, to your unsleeping eternal consciousness, to all those horrors you had thought familiar . . ." She spoke with considerable satisfaction, while the face of Count Mashabak pressed for a moment against the membrane and the fangs clashed and drooled as he sought a glimpse of his rival, bearing back, with something close to gratitude, his small prize to his own dimension.

"*I have no claim now, Elric, to your father's soul . . .*"

"But Mashabak?" said Elric as it dawned on him the responsibility they had brought upon themselves. "What shall we do with Mashabak?"

The Rose smiled at him, a gentle smile that was full of wisdom. "There is something yet we have to do," she said, and she turned to murmur to the three sisters, who took their swords—one of ivory, one of gold and one of granite—and with slow care placed a black briar ring upon the tip of each blade so that suddenly the swords were alive with glowing, flowery light—a calm energy—Nature's energy balanced against the raging power of Chaos. Then they lifted these swords in unison beneath the heaving membrane of that cosmic prison, so that each tip stood lightly upon the skin.

And Count Mashabak growled and threatened and spoke some words in a language known only to himself; made helpless by the very act of being captured, for he was a creature that had known almost limitless power and had no means of existing with the shock of its own enforced impotence. He knew not how to beg or bargain or even to coax, as Arioch coaxed, for his nature was more direct. He had revelled in the unchecked force of his power. He had grown used to creating whatever he desired, of destroying whatever displeased him. He screamed at them to release him, he grumbled, he subsided, as the tips of the swords continued to support the ectoplasmic sphere. He was a crude, brutish sort of demigod and knew only how to threaten.

The Rose smiled. It was as if she were achieving everything she had dreamed of over the years. "He will take some taming, that demon," she said.

If Elric had been disbelieving of Gaynor's audacity, he was admiring of the Rose's. "You knew all along how Mashabak could be controlled," he said. "You manipulated events so that we should be here at the same time . . ." It was not an accusation, merely a statement of his understanding.

"I took the events that existed," said the Rose simply. "I did what I could in my weaving. But I was never certain, even as Gaynor bargained with you for your father's soul, what the outcome would be. I still do not know, Elric. Watch!"

She went to the table where Gaynor had placed his stolen treasures and she took the sweet-smelling rosewood box, advancing towards where the sisters held the sphere upon the tips of their swords, as delicately as if they balanced a soap-bubble, each woman concentrating upon her task while a strange, bubbling energy began to pulse along the blades. Down the ivory poured a smoky whiteness and down the granite a grey, curling substance; while the golden blade shook with light the colour of fresh-cut broom, all these colours spinning together and forming a kind of spiral which wound upwards again and back into the sphere.

Led by the Rose, the sisters began a chant, harnessing streamers of multiversal life-force and bringing them together in a shimmering net of pale cerise light which surrounded them as they worked.

Then the Rose cried out to Elric. "Bring your sword now. Bring it quickly. It must be the conductor once more, of all this energy!" She opened the lid of the box.

The albino moved forward, his body making strange ritualistic gestures whose meaning was unknown to him.

He lifted the Black Sword even as it uttered a moan of protest, and he placed it between the other swords, at the very apex.

Carefully and slowly the Rose moved until she held the opened soulbox directly under the pommel of the runesword and cried: "Strike! Strike upwards, Elric, into the demon's heart—!"

And the albino yelled in terrifying anguish as the hellforce poured from the Chaos Lord in response to his single thrust. And Mashabak's unholy demon's soul poured with a gush of dark radiance which sent Stormbringer to shivering and howling again, down the blade and into the soulbox the Rose held ready for it.

And it was only at that moment that Elric realised what, under the Rose's direction, he had done!

"My father's soul," he said, "You have wed it to that demon's! You have destroyed it!"

"Now we control him!" The Rose's subtle pink skin glowed with her pleasure. "Now we have Mashabak. No mortal has the power to destroy him, but he is our prisoner. He will remain so for ever! While we can destroy his soul. He is forced to obey. Through him we shall re-create the worlds he crushed." She closed the lid.

"How can you control him, when Gaynor could not?" Elric looked up to where, oddly passive, the demon count peered from his prison.

"Because now we possess his soul," said the Rose. "This is my satisfaction and my revenge."

Wheldrake emerged from beyond the scaly back of his rival in love. "It is not a very dramatic vengeance, madam."

"I sought resolution to my grief," said the Rose. "And we learned, my sisters and I, that such resolution is rarely achieved by further destruction. These two, besides, could never be destroyed. Yet, living, we have seen to it that they have served some useful purpose, the pair of them, and that is all I wished to bring about. To do positive good where positive harm had been done. It is the only possible form of revenge for such as myself."

And Elric, staring with growing horror at the soulbox, could not respond to her. He had been through all this, he thought, to fail to the very moment when he thought he had succeeded.

The Rose was smiling at him still. Her warm fingers were gentle on his face. He glanced at her, but he could not speak.

The sisters were lowering their swords. They looked drained and could barely replace the weapons in their scabbards. Charion Phatt, leaving the toad and Wheldrake, went to tend to them.

"Here." The Rose strode to the table and picked up the living bloom from where it lay upon the rosewood box which contained those three briar rings of power which had helped chain a demon's soul. She handed him the flower. There was dew upon the leaves as if it still grew in a country garden.

"I thank you for the keepsake, lady," he said quietly, but his mind was still full of the horror to come.

"You must take it to your father," she said. "He will be awaiting you in those ruins. The ruins where your people made their final pact with Chaos."

Elric did not find her humour amusing. "I shall be speaking to my father soon enough, lady," he said. With a deep sigh he sheathed his battle-blade. And he did not look into the future with any pleasure . . .

She was laughing. "Elric! Your father's soul was never in that box! At least, not trapped by it as the demon's is. The briar rings are for the bonding of a demon's soul. The box was built to *hold* a demon's soul. But the Eternal Rose is too delicate a thing to contain such a soul. It can only hold the soul of a mortal who has loved another better than itself. This flower protects and is nourished by your father's soul, Elric. That is why it lives. It is informed by all that is good in Sadric. Take it to your father. Once he has that, he can rejoin your mother as he longed to do. Arioch has forsworn all claim on him—and Mashabak has no power over him. *We* shall use the power of Mashabak. We shall force the Count of Hell to restore everything we loved. And so, by turning this evil into good, we redeem the past! And that is the *only* way by which we mortals may ever redeem our pasts! It is the only positive revenge. Take the flower."

"I will take it to my father, lady," said Elric.

"And then," she said, "you may bring me back with you to Tanelorn."

He looked into her quiet, hazel eyes and he hesitated for a moment. "I would be honoured, lady," he said.

Suddenly Wheldrake's yelling: "The toad! The toad!" And the creature is crawling, on massive hands and feet, through the door of the chamber and out into the galleries, the ruined decks, where all the wretches released from their servitude to Chaos are running and scampering and fleeing—out of the great hull, flushed rabbits from a warren, and Wheldrake runs behind him calling "Stop, dear toad. Sweet rival! For the sake of our mutual love, stop, I beg thee!"

But the toad has turned now, at the entrance to *The Ship That Was*, and looks back at Wheldrake, looks back at Charion Phatt who also follows, and pauses, as if awaiting them. As they come closer, it waddles out of the hull and into the light, the humans running like lice around it, escaping back into the land no longer ruled by Chaos. And then it squats, waiting for them . . .

. . . Where Ma Phatt, unsteady in her swaying chair, is borne along the beach by her son and grandson, the pair of them sweating and exhausted as she yells at them to increase their speed, then sees her granddaughter and Wheldrake and shrieks for them to stop. "My dolly-joys, my sweety-hearts, my jammy, juicy jolly-boy!" She discards the tattered parasol with which she has protected her wise old head and licks her lips at him; she ogles him. "My rock, my tasty wordsmith! Oh, how happy my Charion will be! How happy I would have been, had I but known you were in Putney! Put me down! Put me down, boys! We have arrived. I told you they were safe! I told you she had a machination or two, a twist in the cosmic fabric, a little smoothing out of the tangled sleeves. Sweet-rumped little coxcomb! Tiny reveller in rhyme! Come with me. We'll seek the End of Time!"

"A confusing place, as I recall," says Wheldrake, but he basks in her approval, her celebration of him, her pleasure at his joining her family.

"I told you we did not go far, Father!" declared Koropith Phatt a little too triumphantly, so that Fallogard Phatt caught his eye in a stern glare. "Although you, too, were right, of course, when you recognised this beach."

The Rose and the three sisters were emerging now, to greet their friends, but they carried only the soulbox. The metaphysically filleted Count of Hell was left within, to think for a little upon the nature of his fate, in which he would be forced to create everything that was anathema to him. In her left hand the Rose carried, so that it hung loose and dragged upon the shingle, the grey wolf pelt which Gaynor had sported, not knowing that it was a sign that, in some manner at least, Esbern Snare had been released from his particular burden.

"What?" said Wheldrake, a trifle surprised. "Do you take that as a trophy, madam?"

But the Rose shook her head gently. "It belonged once," she said, "to a sister of mine. The only other survivor of Gaynor's treachery . . ."

And only then did Elric understand the full import of the Rose's fate-weaving, of her astonishing manipulation of the fabric of the multiverse.

Ma Phatt was looking at her quizzically. "You have your satisfaction then, my dear?"

"As much as is possible," agreed the Rose.

"You serve a powerful thing," added the old woman, clambering down from her rickety litter and hobbling across the shingle, her red face alive with a variety of pleasures. "Do you call that thing the Balance, by any chance?"

But the Rose linked an arm in Ma Phatt's and helped her to sit upon an upturned bucket and she said: "Let us simply agree that I am opposed to all forms of tyranny, whether of Law or of Chaos or any other power . . ."

"Then it is Fate itself you serve," said the old woman firmly. "For this was a powerful weaving, child. It has made fresh reality in the multiverse. It has corrected the disruptions which upset us so badly. Now we can continue on our journey."

"Where do you go, Mother Phatt?" asked Elric. "Where will you find the security you seek?"

"My niece's future husband has convinced us that we should discover the kind of domestic peace we value in the place he knows called 'Putney,'" said Fallogard Phatt with a kind of hesitant heartiness. "And so we shall all seek this place with him. He has, he said, an unfinished epic, in two volumes, concerning some local champion of his people. Which he left in Putney, do you see. So we must begin there, at least. We are all one united family now and do not intend to be further separated."

"I go with them, lady," said Koropith Phatt, grasping the Rose's hand quickly and kissing it, almost as if embarrassed. "We'll take the ship and the toad and cross the Heavy Sea again. From there we shall follow the pathways through the realms until, no doubt, we shall come inevitably to Putney."

"I wish you a safe and direct journey," she said. Then she too kissed his hands. "I will miss you, Master Phatt, and your expert tracking through the multiverse. There was never a better psychic bloodhound!"

> *"Prince Elric fled from that fateful strand,*
> *Great hope had he in his heart,*
> *From the sweet rose blooming in his hand,*
> *No mortal could dispart . . ."*

intoned the red-headed poet and then shrugged by way of apology. "I was not prepared, today, for epilogues. I had hoped only for a noble end. Come toad! Come Charion! Come family all! We sail again upon the Heavy Sea! For far-flung Putney and the golden bliss of happy domesticity!"

And there was something in the proud prince of ruins that yearned, as he waved farewell, for the less dramatic adventures of the hearth.

Then he turned towards the Rose, that mysterious manipulator of destinies, and he bowed. "Come, madam," he said, "we have a dragon to summon and a journey to make! My father is doubtless a trifle concerned for the well-being of his much-bartered soul."

EPILOGUE

In Which the Prince of Ruins Honours a Vow.

Against the full heat of a harvest moon, Lady Scarsnout lifted her magnificent head to taste the wind, flapped her wings once to set her course and lifted away from that perpetuity of night where Sadric's ghost had hidden.

Elric had put the living rose into his father's pale hand. He had watched as the rose faded and died at last, no longer kept alive by the thing which had been hidden in it. And then Sadric had sighed. "I can hate thee no longer, son of thy mother," he said. "I had not hoped for so much as the gifts thou broughtest me."

And his father had kissed him with lips suddenly warm upon his cheek, with a momentary gesture of affection such as he had never made in life. "I will await thee, my son, where thy mother awaits me now, in the Forest of Souls."

Elric had watched the ghost fade away, like a whisper on the wind, and, looking up, he had realised that time was no longer stilled, and that Melniboné's bloody history, her ten thousand years of dominance, of cruelty and heartless conquest, was at the point of its beginning.

For a brief instant he had considered taking some new action—some action to change the course of the Bright Empire's progress down the centuries—to make of his race a gentler, nobler people—but then he had shaken his head and turned his back on H'hui'shan, on his past and on all brooding about what might have been, and he had settled himself into that natural *skeffla'a* behind the Phoorn's shoulders and was calling confidently, with a new hope in his voice, for his mount to bear him skyward.

Then up they went together, dragon-leather slapping against the swirling clouds, up into the starry languor of a Melnibonéan night, into a future where, by a certain crossroads at the edge of time, the Rose awaited him.

For he had promised her that, when she first saw Tanelorn, she would be riding upon a dragon.

THE BANE OF THE BLACK SWORD

To the memory of Hans Stefan Santesson, an editor of great patience and kindness who, with L. Sprague de Camp, encouraged me in the late 1950s to write heroic fantasy. His magazine, *Fantastic Universe*, ceased publication before I could contribute, much to my regret, for it was, in my opinion, one of the best fantasy magazines ever produced.

THE BANE OF THE BLACK SWORD

CONTENTS

BOOK ONE

THE STEALER OF SOULS

*In which Elric once again makes the acquaintance of
Queen Yishana of Jharkor and Theleb K'aarna of
Pan Tang and receives satisfaction at last.*

I

In a city called Bakshaan, which was rich enough to make all other cities of the north-east seem poor, in a tall-towered tavern one night, Elric, Lord of the smoking ruins of Melniboné, smiled like a shark and dryly jested with four powerful merchant princes whom, in a day or so, he intended to pauperise.

Moonglum the Outlander, Elric's companion, viewed the tall albino with admiration and concern. For Elric to laugh and joke was rare—but that he should share his good humour with men of the merchant stamp, that was unprecedented. Moonglum congratulated himself that he was Elric's friend and wondered upon the outcome of the meeting. Elric had, as usual, elaborated little of his plan to Moonglum.

"We need your particular qualities as swordsman and sorcerer, Lord Elric, and will, of course, pay well for them." Pilarmo, overdressed, intense and scrawny, was main spokesman for the four.

"And how shall you pay, gentlemen?" enquired Elric politely, still smiling.

Pilarmo's colleagues raised their eyebrows and even their spokesman was slightly taken aback. He waved his hand through the smoky air of the tavern room which was occupied only by the six men.

"In gold—in gems," answered Pilarmo.

"In chains," said Elric. "We free travellers need no chains of that sort."

Moonglum bent forward out of the shadows where he sat, his expression showing that he strongly disapproved of Elric's statement.

Pilarmo and the other merchants were plainly astonished, too. "Then how shall we pay you?"

"I will decide that later," Elric smiled. "But why talk of such things until the time—what do you wish me to do?"

Pilarmo coughed and exchanged glances with his peers. They nodded. Pilarmo dropped his tone and spoke slowly:

"You are aware that trade is highly competitive in this city, Lord Elric. Many merchants vie with one another to secure the custom of the people. Bakshaan is a rich city and its populace is comfortably off, in the main."

"This is well known," Elric agreed; he was privately likening the well-to-do citizens of Bakshaan to sheep and himself to the wolf who would rob the fold. Because of these thoughts, his scarlet eyes were full of a humour which Moonglum knew to be malevolent and ironic.

"There is one merchant in this city who controls more warehouses and shops than any other," Pilarmo continued. "Because of the size and strength of his caravans, he can afford to import greater quantities of goods into Bakshaan and thus sell them for lower prices. He is virtually a thief—he will ruin us with his unfair methods." Pilarmo was genuinely hurt and aggrieved.

"You refer to Nikorn of Ilmar?" Moonglum spoke from behind Elric.

Pilarmo nodded mutely.

Elric frowned. "This man heads his own caravans—braves the dangers of the desert, forest and mountain. He has earned his position."

"That is hardly the point," snapped fat Tormiel, beringed and powdered, his flesh aquiver.

"No, of course not." Smooth-tongued Kelos patted his colleague's arm consolingly. "But we all admire bravery, I hope." His friends nodded. Silent Deinstaf, the last of the four, also coughed and wagged his hairy head. He put his unhealthy fingers on the jewelled hilt of an ornate but virtually useless poignard and squared his shoulders. "But," Kelos went on, glancing at Deinstaf with approval, "Nikorn takes no risks selling his goods cheaply—he's killing us with his low prices."

"Nikorn is a thorn in our flesh," Pilarmo elaborated unnecessarily.

"And you gentlemen require myself and my companion to remove this thorn," Elric stated.

"In a nutshell, yes." Pilarmo was sweating. He seemed more than a trifle wary of the smiling albino. Legends referring to Elric and his dreadful, doom-filled exploits were many and elaborately detailed. It was only because of their desperation that they had sought his help in this matter. They needed one who could deal in the nigromantic arts as well as wield a useful blade. Elric's arrival in Bakshaan was potential salvation for them.

"We wish to destroy Nikorn's power," Pilarmo continued. "And if this means destroying Nikorn, then—" He shrugged and half-smiled, watching Elric's face.

"Common assassins are easily employed, particularly in Bakshaan," Elric pointed out softly.

"Uh—true," Pilarmo agreed. "But Nikorn employs a sorcerer—and a private army. The sorcerer protects him and his palace by means of magic. And a guard of desert men serve to ensure that if magic fails, then natural methods can be used for the purpose. Assassins have attempted to eliminate the trader, but unfortunately, they were not lucky."

Elric laughed. "How disappointing, my friends. Still, assassins are the most dispensable members of the community—are they not? And their souls probably went to placate some demon who would otherwise have plagued more honest folk."

The merchants laughed half-heartedly and, at this, Moonglum grinned, enjoying himself from his seat in the shadows.

Elric poured wine for the other five. It was of a vintage which the law in Bakshaan forbade the populace to drink. Too much drove the imbiber mad, yet Elric had already quaffed great quantities and showed no ill effects. He raised a cup of the yellow wine to his lips and drained it, breathing deeply and with satisfaction as the stuff entered his system. The others sipped theirs cautiously. The merchants were already regretting their haste in contacting the albino. They had a feeling that not only were the legends true—but they did not do justice to the strange-eyed man they wished to employ.

Elric poured more yellow wine into his goblet and his hand trembled slightly and his dry tongue moved over his lips quickly. His breathing increased as he allowed the beverage to trickle down his throat. He had taken more than enough to make other men into mewling idiots, but those few signs were the only indication that the wine had any effect upon him at all.

This was a wine for those who wished to dream of different and less tangible worlds. Elric drank it in the hope that he would, for a night or so, cease to dream.

Now he asked: "And who is this mighty sorcerer, Master Pilarmo?"

"His name is Theleb K'aarna," Pilarmo answered nervously.

Elric's scarlet eyes narrowed. "The sorcerer of Pan Tang?"

"Aye—he comes from that island."

Elric put his cup down upon the table and rose, fingering his blade of black iron, the runesword Stormbringer.

He said with conviction: "I will help you, gentlemen." He had made up his mind not to rob them, after all. A new and more important plan was forming in his brain.

Theleb K'aarna, he thought. *So you have made Bakshaan your bolt-hole, eh?*

Theleb K'aarna tittered. It was an obscene sound, coming as it did from the throat of a sorcerer of no mean skill. It did not fit with his sombre, black-bearded countenance, his tall, scarlet-robed frame. It was not a sound suited to one of his extreme wisdom.

Theleb K'aarna tittered and stared with dreamy eyes at the woman who lolled on the couch beside him. He whispered clumsy words of endearment into her ear and she smiled indulgently, stroking his long, black hair as she would stroke the coat of a dog.

"You're a fool, for all your learning, Theleb K'aarna," she murmured, her hooded eyes staring beyond him at the bright green and orange tapestries which decorated the stone walls of her bedchamber. She reflected lazily that a woman could not but help take advantage of any man who put himself so fully into her power.

"Yishana, you are a bitch," Theleb K'aarna breathed foolishly, "and all the learning in the world cannot combat love. I love you." He spoke simply, directly, not understanding the woman who lay beside him. He had seen into the black bowels of hell and had returned sane, he knew secrets which would turn any ordinary man's mind into quivering, jumbled jelly. But in certain arts he was as unversed as his youngest acolyte. The art of love was one of those. "I love you," he repeated, and wondered why she ignored him.

Yishana, Queen of Jharkor, pushed the sorcerer away from her and rose abruptly, swinging bare, well-formed legs off the divan. She was a handsome woman, with hair as black as her soul; though her youth was fading, she had a strange quality about her which both repelled and attracted men. She wore her multicoloured silks well and they swirled about her as, with light grace, she strode to the barred window of the chamber and stared out into the dark and turbulent night. The sorcerer watched her through narrow, puzzled eyes, disappointed at this halt to their love-making.

"What's wrong?"

The queen continued to stare out at the night. Great banks of black cloud moved like predatory monsters, swiftly across the wind-torn sky. The night was raucous and angry about Bakshaan; full of ominous portent.

Theleb K'aarna repeated his question and again received no answer. He stood up angrily, then, and joined her at the window.

"Let us leave now, Yishana, before it is too late. If Elric learns of our presence in Bakshaan, we shall both suffer." She did not reply, but her breasts heaved beneath the flimsy fabric and her mouth tightened.

The sorcerer growled, gripping her arm. "Forget your renegade freebooter, Elric—you have me now, and I can do much more for you than any sword-swinging medicine-man from a broken and senile empire!"

Yishana laughed unpleasantly and turned on her lover. "You are a fool, Theleb K'aarna, and you're much less of a man than Elric. Three aching years have passed since he deserted me, skulking off into the night on your trail and leaving me to pine for him! But I still remember his savage kisses and his wild love-making. Gods! I wish he had an equal. Since he left, I've never found one to match him—though many have tried and proved better than you—until you came skulking back and your spells drove them off or destroyed them." She sneered, mocking and taunting him. "You've been too long among your parchments to be much good to me!"

The sorcerer's face muscles tautened beneath his tanned skin and he scowled. "Then why do you let me remain? I could make you my slave with a potion—you know that!"

"But you wouldn't—and are thus *my* slave, mighty wizard. When Elric threatened to displace you in my affections, you conjured that demon and Elric was forced to fight it. He won, you'll remember—but in his pride refused to compromise. You fled into hiding and he went in search of you—leaving me! That is what you did. You're in *love*, Theleb K'aarna . . ." she laughed in his face. "And your love won't let you use your arts against me—only my other lovers. I put up with you because you are often useful, but if Elric were to return . . ."

Theleb K'aarna turned away, pettishly picking at his long black beard. Yishana said: "I half hate Elric, aye! But that is better than half loving you!"

The sorcerer snarled: "Then why did you join me in Bakshaan? Why did you leave your brother's son upon your throne as regent and come here? I sent word and you came—you must have some affection for me to do that!"

Yishana laughed again. "I heard that a pale-faced sorcerer with crimson eyes and a howling runesword was travelling in the north-east. That is why I came, Theleb K'aarna."

Theleb K'aarna's face twisted with anger as he bent forward and gripped the woman's shoulder in his taloned hand.

"You'll remember that this same pale-faced sorcerer was responsible for your own brother's death," he spat. "You lay with a man who was a slayer of his kin and yours. He deserted the fleet, which he had led to pillage in his own land, when the Dragon Masters retaliated. Dharmit, your brother, was aboard one of those ships and he now lies scorched and rotting on the ocean bed."

Yishana shook her head wearily. "You always mention this and hope to shame me. Yes, I entertained one who was virtually my brother's murderer— but Elric had ghastlier crimes on his conscience and I still loved him, in spite or because of them. Your words do not have the effect you require, Theleb K'aarna. Now leave me, I wish to sleep alone."

The sorcerer's nails were still biting into Yishana's cool flesh. He relaxed his grip. "I am sorry," he said, his voice breaking. "Let me stay."

"Go," she said softly. And, tortured by his own weakness, Theleb K'aarna, sorcerer of Pan Tang, left. Elric of Melniboné was in Bakshaan—and Elric had sworn several oaths of vengeance upon Theleb K'aarna on several separate occasions—in Lormyr, Nadsokor and Tanelorn, as well as in Jharkor. In his heart, the black-bearded sorcerer knew who would win any duel which might take place.

2

The four merchants had left swathed in dark cloaks. They had not deemed it wise for anyone to be aware of their association with Elric. Now, Elric brooded over a fresh cup of yellow wine. He knew that he would need help of a particular and powerful kind, if he were going to capture Nikorn's castle. It was virtually unstormable and, with Theleb K'aarna's nigromantic protection, a particularly potent sorcery would have to be used. He knew that he was Theleb K'aarna's match and more when it came to wizardry, but if all his energy were expended on fighting the other magician, he would have none left to effect an entry past the crack guard of desert warriors employed by the merchant prince.

He needed help. In the forests which lay to the south of Bakshaan, he knew he would find men whose aid would be useful. But would they help him? He discussed the problem with Moonglum.

"I have heard that a band of my countrymen have recently come north from Vilmir where they have pillaged several large towns," he informed the Eastlander. "Since the great battle of Imrryr four years ago, the men of Melniboné have spread outwards from the Dragon Isle, becoming mercenaries and freebooters. It was because of me that Imrryr fell—and this they know, but if I offer them rich loot, they might aid me."

Moonglum smiled wryly. "I would not count on it, Elric," he said. "Such an act as yours can hardly be forgotten, if you'll forgive my frankness. Your countrymen are now unwilling wanderers, citizens of a razed city—the oldest and greatest the world has known. When Imrryr the Beautiful fell, there must have been many who wished great suffering upon you."

Elric emitted a short laugh. "Possibly," he agreed, "but these *are* my people and I know them. We Melnibonéans are an old and sophisticated race—we rarely allow emotions to interfere with our general well-being."

Moonglum raised his eyebrows in an ironic grimace and Elric interpreted the expression rightly. "I was an exception for a short while," he said. "But now Cymoril and my cousin lie in the ruins of Imrryr and my own torment will avenge any ill I have done. I think my countrymen will realise this."

Moonglum sighed. "I hope you are right, Elric. Who leads this band?"

"An old friend," Elric answered. "He was Dragon Master and led the attack upon the reaver ships after they had looted Imrryr. His name is Dyvim Tvar, once Lord of the Dragon Caves."

"And what of his beasts, where are they?"

"Asleep in the caves again. They can be roused only rarely—they need years to recuperate while their venom is re-distilled and their energy revitalised. If it were not for this, the Dragon Masters would rule the world."

"Lucky for you that they don't," Moonglum commented.

Elric said slowly, ironically: "Who knows? With me to lead them, they might yet. At least, we could carve a new empire from this world, just as our forefathers did."

Moonglum said nothing. He thought, privately, that the Young Kingdoms would not be so easily vanquished. Melniboné and her people were ancient, cruel and wise—but even their cruelty was tempered with the soft disease which comes with age. They lacked the vitality of the barbarian race who had been the ancestors of the builders of Imrryr and her long-forgotten sister cities. Vitality was often replaced by tolerance—the tolerance of the aged, the ones who have known past glory but whose day is done.

"In the morning," said Elric, "we will make contact with Dyvim Tvar and hope that what he did to the reaver fleet, coupled with the conscience-pangs which I have personally suffered, will serve to give him a properly objective attitude to my scheme."

"And now, sleep, I think," Moonglum said. "I need it, anyway—and the wench who awaits me might be growing impatient."

Elric shrugged. "As you will. I'll drink a little more wine and seek my bed later."

The black clouds which had huddled over Bakshaan on the previous night were still there in the morning. The sun rose behind them, but the inhabitants were unaware of it. It rose unheralded, but in the fresh, rain-splashed dawn, Elric and Moonglum rode the narrow streets of the city, heading for the south gate and the forests beyond.

Elric had discarded his usual garb for a simple jerkin of green-dyed leather which bore the insignia of the royal line of Melniboné: a scarlet Phoorn dragon, rampant on a gold field. On his finger was the Ring of Kings, the single rare Actorios stone set in a ring of runecarved silver. This was the ring that Elric's mighty forefathers had worn; it was many centuries old. A short cloak hung from his shoulders and his hose was blue, tucked into high black riding boots. At his side hung Stormbringer.

A symbiosis existed between man and sword. The man without the sword could become a cripple, lacking sight and energy—the sword without the man could not drink the blood and the souls it needed for its existence. They rode together, sword and man, and none could tell which was master.

Moonglum, more conscious of the inclement weather than his friend, hugged a high-collared cloak around him and cursed the elements occasionally.

It took them an hour's hard riding to reach the outskirts of the forest. As yet, in Bakshaan, there were only rumours of the Imrryrian freebooters' coming. Once or twice, a tall stranger had been seen in obscure taverns near the southern wall, and this had been remarked upon but the citizens of Bakshaan felt secure in their wealth and power and had reasoned, with a certain truth in their conviction, that Bakshaan could withstand a raid far more ferocious than those raids which had taken weaker Vilmirian towns. Elric had no idea why his countrymen had driven northwards to Bakshaan. Possibly they had come only to rest and turn their loot into food supplies in the bazaars.

The smoke of several large campfires told Elric and Moonglum where the Melnibonéans were entrenched. With a slackening of pace, they guided their horses in that direction while wet branches brushed their faces and the scents of the forest, released by the life-bringing rain, impinged sweetly upon their nostrils. It was with a feeling akin to relaxation that Elric met the outguard who suddenly appeared from the undergrowth to bar their way along the forest trail.

The Imrryrian guard was swathed in furs and steel. Beneath the visor of an intricately worked helmet he peered at Elric with wary eyes. His vision was slightly impaired by the visor and the rain which dripped from it so that he did not immediately recognise Elric.

"Halt. What do you in these parts?"

Elric said impatiently, "Let me pass—it is Elric, your lord and your emperor."

The guard gasped and lowered the long-bladed spear he carried. He pushed back his helmet and gazed at the man before him with a myriad of different emotions passing across his face. Among these were amazement, reverence and hate.

He bowed stiffly. "This is no place for you, my liege. You renounced and betrayed your people four years ago and while I acknowledge the blood of kings which flows in your veins, I cannot obey you or do you the homage which it would otherwise be your right to expect."

"Of course," said Elric proudly, sitting his horse straight-backed. "But let your leader—my boyhood friend Dyvim Tvar—be the judge of how to deal with me. Take me to him at once and remember that my companion has done you no ill, but treat him with respect as befits the chosen friend of an emperor of Melniboné."

The guard bowed again and took hold of the reins of Elric's mount. He led the pair down the trail and into a large clearing wherein were pitched the tents of the men of Imrryr. Cooking fires flared in the centre of the great circle of pavilions and the fine-featured warriors of Melniboné sat talking softly around them. Even in the light of the gloomy day, the fabrics of the tents were bright and gay. The soft tones were wholly Melnibonéan in texture. Deep, smoky greens, azure, ochre, gold, dark blue. The colours did not clash—they blended. Elric felt sad nostalgia for the sundered, multicoloured towers of Imrryr the Beautiful.

As the two companions and their guide drew nearer, men looked up in astonishment and a low muttering replaced the sounds of ordinary conversation.

"Please remain here," the guard said to Elric. "I will inform Lord Dyvim Tvar of your coming." Elric nodded his acquiescence and sat firmly in his saddle conscious of the gaze of the gathered warriors. None approached him and some, whom Elric had known personally in the old days, were openly embarrassed. They were the ones who did not stare but rather averted their eyes, tending to the cooking fires or taking a sudden interest in the polish of their finely wrought longswords and dirks. A few growled angrily, but they were in a definite minority. Most of the men were simply shocked—and also inquisitive. Why had this man, their king and their betrayer, come to their camp?

The largest pavilion, of gold and scarlet, had at its peak a banner upon which was emblazoned a dormant dragon, blue upon white. This was the tent of Dyvim Tvar and from it the Dragon Master hurried, buckling on his sword belt, his intelligent eyes puzzled and wary.

Dyvim Tvar was a man a little older than Elric and he bore the stamp of Melnibonéan nobility. His mother had been a princess, a cousin to Elric's own mother. His cheekbones were high and delicate, his eyes slightly slanting while his skull was narrow, tapering at the jaw. Like Elric, his ears were thin, near lobeless and coming almost to a point. His hands, the left one now folded around the hilt of his sword, were long-fingered and, like the rest of his skin, pale, though not nearly so pale as the dead white of the albino's. He strode towards the mounted emperor of Melniboné and now his emotions were controlled. When he was five feet away from Elric, Dyvim Tvar bowed slowly, his head bent and his face hidden. When he looked up again, his eyes met those of Elric and remained fixed.

"Dyvim Tvar, Lord of the Dragon Caves, greets Elric, Master of Melniboné, Exponent of her Secret Arts." The Dragon Master spoke gravely the age-old ritual greeting.

Elric was not as confident as he seemed as he replied: "Elric, Master of Melniboné, greets his loyal subject and demands that he give audience to Dyvim Tvar." It was not fitting, by ancient Melnibonéan standards, that the emperor should *request* an audience with one of his subjects and the Dragon Master understood this. He now said:

"I would be honoured if my liege would allow me to accompany him to my pavilion."

Elric dismounted and led the way towards Dyvim Tvar's pavilion. Moonglum also dismounted and made to follow, but Elric waved him back. The two Imrryrian noblemen entered the tent.

Inside, the small oil lamp augmented the gloomy daylight which filtered through the colourful fabric. The tent was simply furnished, possessing only a soldier's hard bed, a table and several carved wooden stools. Dyvim Tvar bowed and silently indicated one of these stools. Elric sat down.

For several moments, the two men said nothing. Neither allowed emotion to register on their controlled features. They simply sat and stared at one another. Eventually Elric said:

"You know me for a betrayer, a thief, a murderer of my own kin and a slayer of my countrymen, Dragon Master."

Dyvim Tvar nodded. "With my liege's permission, I will agree with him."

"We were never so formal in the old days, when alone," Elric said. "Let us forget ritual and tradition—Melniboné is broken and her sons are wanderers. We meet, as we used to, as equals—only, now, this is wholly true. We *are* equals. The Ruby Throne crashed in the ashes of Imrryr and now no emperor may sit in state."

Dyvim Tvar sighed. "This is true, Elric—but why have you come here? We were content to forget you. Even while thoughts of vengeance were fresh, we made no move to seek you out. Have you come to mock?"

"You know I would never do that, Dyvim Tvar. I rarely sleep, in these days, and when I do I have such dreams that I would rather be awake. You know that Yyrkoon forced me to do what I did when he usurped the throne for the second time, after I had trusted him as regent, when, again for the second time, he put his sister, whom I loved, into a sorcerous slumber. To aid that reaver fleet was my only hope of forcing him to undo his work and release Cymoril from the spell. I was moved by vengeance but it was Stormbringer, my sword, which slew Cymoril, not I."

"Of this, I am aware." Dyvim Tvar sighed again and rubbed one jewelled hand across his face. "But it does not explain why you came here. There should be no contact between you and your people. We are wary of you, Elric. Even if we allowed you to lead us again you would take your own doomed path and us with you. There is no future here for myself and my men."

"Agreed. But I need your help for this one time—then our ways can part again."

"We should kill you, Elric. But which would be the greater crime? Failure to do justice and slay our betrayer—or regicide? You have given me a problem at a time when there are too many problems already. Should I attempt to solve it?"

"I but played a part in history," Elric said earnestly. "Time would have done what I did, eventually. I but brought the day nearer—and brought it when you and our people were still resilient enough to combat it and turn to a new way of life."

Dyvim Tvar smiled ironically. "That is one point of view, Elric—and it has truth in it, I grant you. But tell it to the men who lost their kin and their homes because of you. Tell it to warriors who had to tend maimed comrades, to brothers, fathers and husbands whose wives, daughters and sisters—proud Melnibonéan women—were used to pleasure the barbarian pillagers."

"Aye," Elric dropped his eyes. When he next spoke it was quietly. "I can do nothing to replace what our people have lost—would that I could. I yearn for Imrryr often, and her women, and her wines and entertainments. But I can offer plunder. I can offer you the richest palace in Bakshaan. Forget the old wounds and follow me this once."

"Do you seek the riches of Bakshaan, Elric? You were never one for jewels and precious metal! Why, Elric?"

Elric ran his hands through his white hair. His red eyes were troubled. "For vengeance, once again, Dyvim Tvar. I owe a debt to a sorcerer from Pan Tang—Theleb K'aarna. You may have heard of him—he is fairly powerful for one of a comparatively young race."

"Then we're joined in this, Elric," Dyvim Tvar spoke grimly. "You are not the only Melnibonéan who owes Theleb K'aarna a debt! Because of that bitch-queen Yishana of Jharkor, one of our men was done to death a year ago in a most foul and horrible manner. Killed by Theleb K'aarna because he gave his embraces to Yishana who sought a substitute for you. We can unite to avenge that blood, King Elric, and it will be a fitting excuse for those who would rather have your blood on their knives."

Elric was not glad. He had a sudden premonition that this fortunate coincidence was to have grave and unpredictable outcomings. But he smiled.

3

In a smoking pit, somewhere beyond the limitations of space and time, a creature stirred. All around it, shadows moved. They were the shadows of the souls of men and these shadows which moved through the bright darkness were the masters of the creature. It allowed them to master it—so long as they paid its price. In the speech of men, this creature had a name. It was called Quaolnargn and would answer to this name if called.

Now it stirred. It heard its name carrying over the barriers which normally blocked its way to the Earth. The calling of the name effected a temporary pathway through those intangible barriers. It stirred again, as its name was called for the second time. It was unaware of why it was called or to what it was called. It was only muzzily conscious of one fact. When the pathway was opened to it, it could *feed*. It did not eat flesh and it did not drink blood. It fed on the minds and the souls of adult men and women. Occasionally, as an appetiser, it enjoyed the morsels, the sweetmeats as it were, of the innocent life-force which it sucked from children. It ignored animals since there was not enough *awareness* in an animal to savour. The creature was, for all its alien stupidity, a gourmet and a connoisseur.

Now its name was called for the third time. It stirred again and flowed forward. The time was approaching when it could, once again, *feed* . . .

Theleb K'aarna shuddered. He was, basically, he felt, a man of peace. It was not his fault that his avaricious love for Yishana had turned him mad. It was not his fault that, because of her, he now controlled several powerful and malevolent demons who, in return for the slaves and enemies he fed them, protected the palace of Nikorn the merchant. He felt, very strongly, that none of it was his fault. It was circumstance which had damned him. He wished sadly that he had never met Yishana, never returned to her after that unfortunate episode outside the walls of Tanelorn. He shuddered again as he stood within the pentacle and summoned Quaolnargn. His embryonic talent for precognition had shown him a little of the near-future and he knew that Elric was preparing to do battle with him. Theleb K'aarna was taking the opportunity of summoning all the aid he could control. Quaolnargn must be sent to destroy Elric, if it could, before the albino reached the castle. Theleb K'aarna congratulated himself that he still retained the lock of white hair which had enabled him, in the past, to send another, now deceased, demon against Elric.

Quaolnargn knew that it was reaching its master. It propelled itself sluggishly forward and felt a stinging pain as it entered the alien continuum. It knew that its master's soul hovered before it but, for some reason, was disappointingly unattainable. Something was dropped in front of it. Quaolnargn scented at it and knew what it must do. This was part of its new *feed*. It flowed gratefully away, intent on finding its prey before the pain which was endemic of a prolonged stay in the strange place grew too much.

Elric rode at the head of his countrymen. On his right was Dyvim Tvar, the Dragon Master, on his left, Moonglum of Elwher. Behind him rode two hundred fighting men and behind them the wagons containing their loot, their war machines and their slaves.

The caravan was resplendent with proud banners and the gleaming, long-bladed lances of Imrryr. They were clad in steel, with tapering greaves, helmets and shoulder pieces. Their breastplates were polished and glinted where their long fur jerkins were open. Over the jerkins were flung bright cloaks of Imrryrian fabrics, scintillating in the watery sunshine. The archers were immediately close to Elric and his companions. They carried unstrung bone bows of tremendous power, which only they could use. On their backs were quivers crammed with black-fletched arrows. Then came the lancers, with their shining lances at a tilt to avoid the low branches of the trees. Behind these rode the main strength—the Imrryrian swordsmen carrying longswords and shorter stabbing weapons which were too short to be real swords and too long to be named as knives. They rode, skirting Bakshaan, for the palace of Nikorn which lay to the north of Bakshaan. They rode, these men, in silence. They could think of nothing to say while Elric, their liege, led them to battle for the first time in five years.

Stormbringer, the black hellblade, tingled under Elric's hand, anticipating a new sword-quenching. Moonglum fidgeted in his saddle, nervous of the forthcoming fight which he knew would involve dark sorcery. Moonglum had no liking for the sorcerous arts or for the creatures they spawned. To his mind, men should fight their own battles without help. They rode on, nervous and tense.

Stormbringer shook against Elric's side. A faint moan emanated from the metal and the tone was one of warning. Elric raised a hand and the cavalcade reined to a halt.

"There is something coming near which only I can deal with," he informed the men. "I will ride on ahead."

He spurred his horse into a wary canter, keeping his eyes before him. Stormbringer's voice was louder, sharper—a muted shriek. The horse trembled and Elric's own nerves were tense. He had not expected trouble so soon and he prayed that whatever evil was lurking in the forest was not directed against him.

"Arioch, be with me," he breathed. "Aid me now, and I'll dedicate a score of warriors to you. Aid me, Arioch."

A foul odour forced itself into Elric's nostrils. He coughed and covered his mouth with his hands, his eyes seeking the source of the stink. The horse whinnied. Elric jumped from the saddle and slapped his mount on the rump, sending it back along the trail. He crouched warily, Stormbringer now in his grasp, the black metal quivering from point to pommel.

He sensed it with the witch-sight of his forefathers before he saw it with his eyes. And he recognised its shape. He, himself, was one of its masters. But this time he had no control over Quaolnargn—he was standing in no pentacle and his only protection was his blade and his wits. He knew, also, of the power of Quaolnargn and shuddered. Could he overcome such a horror single-handedly?

"*Arioch! Arioch! Aid me!*" It was a scream, high and desperate.

"*Arioch!*"

There was no time to conjure a spell. Quaolnargn was before him, a great green reptilian thing which hopped along the trail obscenely, moaning to itself in its Earth-fostered pain. It towered over Elric so that the albino was in its shadow before it was ten feet away from him. Elric breathed quickly and screamed once more: "*Arioch! Blood and souls, if you aid me, now!*"

Suddenly, the reptile-demon leapt.

Elric sprang to one side, but was caught by a long-nailed foot which sent him flying into the undergrowth. Quaolnargn turned clumsily and its filthy mouth opened hungrily, displaying a deep toothless cavity from which a foul odour poured.

"*Arioch!*"

In its evil and alien insensitivity, the reptile-thing did not even recognise the name of so powerful a demon-god. It could not be frightened—it had to be fought.

And as it approached Elric for the second time, the clouds belched rain from their bowels and a downpour lashed the forest.

Half-blinded by the rain smashing against his face, Elric backed behind a tree, his runesword ready. In ordinary terms, Quaolnargn was blind. It could not see Elric or the forest. It could not feel the rain. It could only see and smell men's souls—its *feed*. The reptile-demon blundered past him and, as it did so, Elric leapt high, holding his blade with both hands, and plunged it to the hilt into the demon's soft and quivering back. Flesh—or whatever Earth-bound stuff formed the demon's body—squelched nauseatingly. Elric pulled at Stormbringer's hilt as the sorcerous sword seared into the hell-beast's back, cutting down where the spine should be but where no spine was. Quaolnargn piped its pain. Its voice was thin and reedy, even in such extreme agony. It retaliated.

Elric felt his mind go numb and then his head was filled with a pain which was not natural in any sense. He could not even shriek. His eyes widened in horror as he realised what was happening to him. His soul was being drawn from his body. He knew it. He felt no physical weakness, he was only aware of looking out into . . .

But even that awareness was fading. Everything was fading, even the pain, even the dreadful hell-spawned pain.

"Arioch!" he croaked.

Savagely, he summoned strength from somewhere. Not from himself, not even from Stormbringer—from somewhere. Something was aiding him at last, giving him strength—enough strength to do what he must.

He wrenched the blade from the demon's back. He stood over Quaolnargn. Above him. He was floating somewhere, not in the air of Earth. Just floating over the demon. With thoughtful deliberation he selected a spot on the demon's skull which he somehow knew to be the only spot on his body where Stormbringer might slay. Slowly and carefully, he lowered Stormbringer and twisted the runesword through Quaolnargn's skull.

The reptilian thing whimpered, dropped—and vanished.

Elric lay sprawled in the undergrowth, trembling the length of his aching body. He picked himself up slowly. All his energy had been drained from him. Stormbringer, too, seemed to have lost its vitality, but that, Elric knew, would return and, in returning, bring him new strength.

But then he felt his whole frame tugged rigid. He was astounded. What was happening? His senses began to blank out. He had the feeling that he was staring down a long, black tunnel which stretched into nowhere. Everything was vague. He was aware of motion. He was travelling. How—or where, he could not tell.

For brief seconds he travelled, conscious only of an unearthly feeling of motion and the fact that Stormbringer, his life, was clutched in his right hand.

Then he felt hard stone beneath him and he opened his eyes—or was it, he wondered, that his vision returned?—and looked up at the gloating face above him.

"Theleb K'aarna," he whispered hoarsely, "how did you effect this?"

The sorcerer bent down and, with gloved hands, tugged Stormbringer from Elric's enfeebled grasp. He sneered. "I followed your commendable battle with my messenger, Lord Elric. When it was obvious that somehow you had summoned aid—I quickly conjured another spell and brought you here. Now I have your sword and your strength. I know that without it you are nothing. You are in my power, Elric of Melniboné."

Elric gasped air into his lungs. His whole body was pain-racked. He tried to smile, but he could not. It was not in his nature to smile when he was beaten. "Give me back my sword."

Theleb K'aarna gave a self-satisfied smirk. He chuckled. "Who talks of vengeance, now, Elric?"

"Give me my sword!" Elric tried to rise but he was too weak. His vision blurred until he could hardly see the gloating sorcerer.

"And what kind of bargain do you offer?" Theleb K'aarna asked. "You are not a well man, Lord Elric—and sick men do not bargain. They beg."

Elric trembled in impotent anger. He tightened his mouth. He would not beg—neither would he bargain. In silence, he glowered at the sorcerer.

"I think that first," Theleb K'aarna said smiling, "I shall lock this away. He hefted Stormbringer, which he had now sheathed, in his hand and turned towards a cupboard behind him. From his robes he produced a key with which he unlocked the cupboard and placed the runesword inside, carefully locking the door again when he had done so. "Then, I think, I'll show our virile hero to his ex-mistress—the sister of the man he betrayed four years ago."

Elric said nothing.

"After that," Theleb K'aarna continued, "my employer Nikorn shall be shown the assassin who thought he could do what others failed to achieve." He smiled. "What a day," he chuckled. "What a day! So full. So rich with pleasure."

Theleb K'aarna tittered and picked up a hand-bell. He rang it. A door behind Elric opened and two tall desert warriors strode in. They glanced at Elric and then at Theleb K'aarna. They were evidently amazed.

"No questions," Theleb K'aarna snapped. "Take this refuse to the chambers of Queen Yishana."

Elric fumed as he was hefted up between the two. The men were dark-skinned, bearded and their eyes were deep-set beneath shaggy brows. They wore the heavy wool-trimmed metal caps of their race, and their armour was not of iron but of thick, leather-covered wood. Down a long corridor they lugged Elric's weakened body and one of them rapped sharply on a door.

Elric recognised Yishana's voice bid them enter. Behind the desert men and their burden came the tittering, fussing sorcerer. "A present for you, Yishana," he called.

The desert men entered. Elric could not see Yishana but he heard her gasp. "On the couch," directed the sorcerer. Elric was deposited on yielding fabric. He lay completely exhausted on the couch, staring up at a bright, lewd mural which had been painted on the ceiling.

Yishana bent over him. Elric could smell her erotic perfume. He said hoarsely: "An unprecedented reunion, queen." Yishana's eyes were, for a moment, concerned, then they hardened and she laughed cynically.

"Oh—my hero has returned to me at last. But I'd rather he'd come at his own volition, not dragged here by the back of his neck like a puppy. The wolf's teeth have all been drawn and there's no-one to savage me at nights." She turned away, disgust on her painted face. "Take him away, Theleb K'aarna. You have proved your point."

The sorcerer nodded.

"And now," he said, "to visit Nikorn—I think he should be expecting us by this time . . ."

4

Nikorn of Ilmar was not a young man. He was well past fifty but had pre-served his youth. His face was that of a peasant, firm-boned but not fleshy. His eyes were keen and hard as he stared at Elric who had been mockingly propped in a chair.

"So you are Elric of Melniboné, the Wolf of the Snarling Sea, spoiler, reaver and womanslayer. I think that you could hardly slay a child now. How-ever, I will say that it discomforts me to see any man in such a position—particularly one who has been so active as you. Is it true what the spell-maker says? Were you sent here by my enemies to assassinate me?"

Elric was concerned for his men. What would they do? Wait—or go on. If they stormed the palace now they were doomed—and so was he.

"Is it true?" Nikorn was insistent.

"No," whispered Elric. "My quarrel was with Theleb K'aarna. I have an old score to settle with him."

"I am not interested in old scores, my friend," Nikorn said, not unkindly. "I *am* interested in preserving my life. Who sent you here?"

"Theleb K'aarna speaks falsely if he told you I was sent," Elric lied. "I was interested only in paying my debt."

"It is not only the sorcerer who told me, I'm afraid," Nikorn said. "I have many spies in the city and two of them independently informed me of a plot by local merchants to employ you to kill me."

Elric smiled faintly. "Very well," he agreed. "It was true, but I had no in-tention of doing what they asked."

Nikorn said: "I might believe you, Elric of Melniboné. But now I do not know what to do with you. I would not turn anyone over to Theleb K'aarna's mercies. May I have your word that you will not make an attempt on my life again?"

"Are we bargaining, Master Nikorn?" Elric said faintly.

"We are."

"Then what do I give my word in return for, sir?"

"Your life and freedom, Lord Elric."

"And my sword?"

Nikorn shrugged regretfully. "I'm sorry—not your sword."

"Then take my life," said Elric brokenly.

"Come now—my bargain's good. Have your life and freedom and give your word that you will not plague me again."

Elric breathed deeply. "Very well."

Nikorn moved away. Theleb K'aarna who had been standing in the shadows put a hand on the merchant's arm. "You're going to release him?"

"Aye," Nikorn said. "He's no threat to either of us now."

Elric was aware of a certain feeling of friendship in Nikorn's attitude towards him. He, too, felt something of the same. Here was a man both courageous and clever. But—Elric fought madness—without Stormbringer, what could he do to fight back?

The two hundred Imrryrian warriors lay hidden in the undergrowth as dusk gave way to night. They watched and wondered. What had happened to Elric? Was he now in the castle as Dyvim Tvar thought? The Dragon Master knew something of the art of divining, as did all members of the royal line of Melniboné. From what small spells he had conjured, it seemed that Elric now lay within the castle walls.

But without Elric to battle Theleb K'aarna's power, how could they take it?

Nikorn's palace was also a fortress, bleak and unlovely. It was surrounded by a deep moat of dark, stagnant water. It stood high above the surrounding forest, built into rather than onto the rock. Much of it had been carved out of the living stone. It was sprawling and rambling and covered a large area, surrounded by natural buttresses. The rock was porous in places, and slimy water ran down the walls of the lower parts, spreading through dark moss. It was not a pleasant place, judging from the outside, but it was almost certainly impregnable. Two hundred men could not take it, without the aid of magic.

Some of the Melnibonéan warriors were becoming impatient. There were a few who muttered that Elric had, once again, betrayed them. Dyvim Tvar and Moonglum did not believe this. They had seen the signs of conflict—and heard them—in the forest.

They waited, hoping for a signal from the castle itself.

They watched the castle's great main gate—and their patience at last proved of value. The huge wood-and-metal gate swung inwards on chains and a white-faced man in the tattered regalia of Melniboné appeared between two desert warriors. They were supporting him, it seemed. They pushed him forward—he staggered a few yards along the causeway of slimy stone which bridged the moat.

Then he fell. He began to crawl wearily, painfully, forward.

Moonglum growled. "What have they done to him? I must help him." But Dyvim Tvar held him back.

"No—it would not do to betray our presence here. Let him reach the forest first, then we can help him."

Even those who had cursed Elric now felt pity for the albino as, staggering and crawling alternately, he dragged his body slowly towards them. From the battlements of the fortress a tittering laugh was borne down to the ears of those below. They also caught a few words.

"*What now, wolf?*" said the voice. "*What now?*"

Moonglum clenched his hands and trembled with rage, hating to see his proud friend so mocked in his weakness. "What's happened to him? What have they done?"

"Patience," Dyvim Tvar said. "We'll find out in a short while."

It was an agony to wait until Elric finally crawled on his knees into the undergrowth.

Moonglum went forward to aid his friend. He put a supporting arm around Elric's shoulders but the albino snarled and shook it off, his whole countenance aflame with terrible hate—made more terrible because it was impotent. Elric could do nothing to destroy that which he hated. Nothing.

Dyvim Tvar said urgently: "Elric, you must tell us what happened. If we're to help you—we must know what happened."

Elric breathed heavily and nodded his agreement. His face partially cleared of the emotion he felt and weakly he stuttered out the story.

"So," Moonglum growled, "our plans come to nothing—and you have lost your strength for ever."

Elric shook his head. "There must be a way," he gasped. "There must!"

"What? How? If you have a plan, Elric—let me hear it now."

Elric swallowed thickly and mumbled. "Very well, Moonglum, you shall hear it. But listen carefully, for I have not the strength to repeat it."

Moonglum was a lover of the night, but only when it was lit by the torches found in cities. He did not like the night when it came to open countryside and he was not fond of it when it surrounded a castle such as Nikorn's, but he pressed on and hoped for the best.

If Elric had been right in his interpretation, then the battle might yet be won and Nikorn's palace taken. But it still meant danger for Moonglum and he was not one deliberately to put himself into danger.

As he viewed the stagnant waters of the moat with distaste he reflected that this was enough to test any friendship to the utmost. Philosophically, he lowered himself down into the water and began to swim across it.

The moss on the fortress offered a flimsy handhold, but it led to ivy which gave a better grip. Moonglum slowly clambered up the wall. He hoped that Elric had been right and that Theleb K'aarna would need to rest for a while before he could work more sorcery. That was why Elric had suggested he make haste. Moonglum clambered on, and eventually reached the small unbarred window he sought. A normal-size man could not have entered, but Moonglum's small frame was proving useful.

He wriggled through the gap, shivering with cold, and landed on the hard stone of a narrow staircase which ran both up and down the interior wall of the fortress. Moonglum frowned, and then took the steps leading upwards. Elric had given him a rough idea of how to reach his destination.

Expecting the worst, he went soft-footed up the stone steps. He went towards the chambers of Yishana, Queen of Jharkor.

In an hour, Moonglum was back, shivering with cold and dripping with water. In his hands he carried Stormbringer. He carried the runesword with cautious care—nervous of its sentient evil. It was alive again; alive with black, pulsating life.

"Thank the gods I was right," Elric murmured weakly from where he lay surrounded by two or three Imrryrians, including Dyvim Tvar who was staring at the albino with concern. "I prayed that I was correct in my assumption and Theleb K'aarna was resting after his earlier exertions on my behalf . . ."

He stirred, and Dyvim Tvar helped him to sit upright. Elric reached out a long white hand—reached like an addict of some terrible drug towards the sword. "Did you give her my message?" he asked as he gratefully seized the pommel.

"Aye," Moonglum said shakily, "and she agreed. You were also right in your other interpretation, Elric. It did not take her long to inveigle the key out of a weary Theleb K'aarna. The sorcerer was tremendously tired and Nikorn was becoming nervous wondering if an attack of any kind would take place while Theleb K'aarna was incapable of action. She went herself to the cupboard and got me the blade."

"Women can sometimes be useful," said Dyvim Tvar dryly. "Though usually, in matters like these, they're a hindrance." It was possible to see that something other than immediate problems of taking the castle was worrying

Dyvim Tvar, but no-one thought to ask him what it was that bothered him. It seemed a personal thing.

"I agree, Dragon Master," Elric said, almost gaily. The gathered men were aware of the strength which poured swiftly back into the albino's deficient veins, imbuing him with a new hellborn vitality. "It is time for our vengeance. But remember—no harm to Nikorn. I gave him my word."

He folded his right hand firmly around Stormbringer's hilt. "Now for a sword-quenching. I believe I can obtain the help of just the allies we need to keep the sorcerer occupied while we storm the castle. I'll need no pentacle to summon my friends of the air!"

Moonglum licked his long lips. "So it's sorcery again. In truth, Elric, this whole country is beginning to stink of wizardry and the minions of hell."

Elric murmured for his friend's ears: "No hell-beings these—but honest elementals, equally powerful in many ways. Curb your belly-fear, Moonglum—a little more simple conjuring and Theleb K'aarna will have no desire to retaliate."

The albino frowned, remembering the secret pacts of his forefathers. He took a deep breath and closed his pain-filled scarlet eyes. He swayed, the runesword half-loose in his grip. His chant was low, like the far-off moaning of the wind itself. His chest moved quickly up and down, and some of the younger warriors, those who had never been fully initiated into the ancient lore of Melniboné, stirred with discomfort. Elric's voice was not addressing human folk—his words were for the invisible, the intangible—the supernatural. An old and ancient rhyme began the casting of word-runes . . .

"*Hear the doomed one's dark decision,*
Let the Wind Giant's wail be heard,
Graoll and Misha's mighty moaning
Send my enemy like a bird.

"*By the sultry scarlet stones,*
By the bane of my black blade,

By the Lasshaar's lonely mewling,
Let a mighty wind be made.

"Speed of sunbeams from their homeland,
Swifter than the sundering storm,
Speed of arrow deerwards shooting,
Let the sorcerer so be borne."

His voice broke and he called high and clear:

"*Misha! Misha! In the name of my fathers I summon thee, Lord of the Winds!*"

Almost at once, the trees of the forest suddenly bent as if some great hand had brushed them aside. A terrible soughing voice swam from nowhere. And all but Elric, deep in his trance, shivered.

"ELRIC OF MELNIBONÉ," the voice roared like a distant storm, "WE KNEW YOUR FATHERS. I KNOW THEE. THE DEBT WE OWE THE LINE OF ELRIC IS FORGOTTEN BY MORTALS BUT GRAOLL AND MISHA, KINGS OF THE WIND, REMEMBER. HOW MAY THE LASSHAAR AID THEE?"

The voice seemed almost friendly—but proud and aloof and awe-inspiring.

Elric, completely in a state of trance now, jerked his whole body in convulsions. His voice shrieked piercingly from his throat—and the words were alien, unhuman, violently disturbing to the ears and nerves of the human listeners. Elric spoke briefly and then the invisible Wind Giant's great voice roared and sighed:

"I WILL DO AS YOU DESIRE." Then the trees bent once more and the forest was still and muted.

Somewhere in the gathered ranks, a man sneezed sharply and this was a sign for others to start talking—speculating.

For many moments, Elric remained in his trance and then, quite suddenly, he opened his enigmatic eyes and looked gravely around him, puzzled for a second. Then he clasped Stormbringer more firmly and leaned forward, speaking to the men of Imrryr. "Soon Theleb K'aarna will be in our power, my friends, and so also will we possess the loot of Nikorn's palace!"

But Dyvim Tvar shuddered then. "I'm not so skilled in the esoteric arts as you, Elric," he said quietly. "But in my soul I see three wolves leading a pack to slaughter and one of those wolves must die. My doom is near me, I think."

Elric said uncomfortably: "Worry not, Dragon Master. You'll live to mock the ravens and spend the spoils of Bakshaan." But his voice was not convincing.

5

In his bed of silk and ermine, Theleb K'aarna stirred and awoke. He had a brooding inkling of coming trouble and he remembered that earlier in his tiredness he had given more to Yishana than had been wise. He could not remember what it was and now he had a presentiment of danger—the closeness of which overshadowed thoughts of any past indiscretion. He arose hurriedly and pulled his robe over his head, shrugging into it as he walked towards a strangely silvered mirror which was set on one wall of his chamber and reflected no image.

With bleary eyes and trembling hands he began preparations. From one of the many earthenware jars resting on a bench near the window, he poured a substance which seemed like dried blood mottled with the hardened blue venom of the black serpent whose homeland was in far Dorel which lay on the edge of the world. Over this, he muttered a swift incantation, scooped the stuff into a crucible and hurled it at the mirror, one arm shielding his eyes. A crack sounded, hard and sharp to his ears, and bright green light erupted suddenly and was gone. The mirror flickered deep within itself, the silvering seemed to undulate and flicker and flash and then a picture began to form.

Theleb K'aarna knew that the sight he witnessed had taken place in the recent past. It showed him Elric's summoning of the Wind Giants.

Theleb K'aarna's dark features grinned with a terrible fear. His hands jerked as spasms shook him. Half-gibbering, he rushed back to his bench and, leaning his hands upon it, stared out of the window into the deep night. He knew what to expect.

A great and dreadful storm was blowing—and he was the object of the Lasshaar's attack. He *had* to retaliate, else his own soul would be wrenched from him by the Giants of the Wind and flung to the air spirits, to be borne for eternity on the winds of the world. Then his voice would moan like a banshee around the cold peaks of high ice-clothed mountains for ever—lost and lonely. His soul would be damned to travel with the four winds wherever their caprice might bear it, knowing no rest.

Theleb K'aarna had a respect born of fear for the powers of the aeromancer, the rare wizard who could control the wind elementals—and aeromancy was only one of the arts which Elric and his ancestors possessed. Then Theleb K'aarna realised what he was battling—ten thousand years and hundreds of generations of sorcerers who had gleaned knowledge from the Earth and beyond it and passed it down to the albino whom he, Theleb K'aarna, had sought to destroy. Then Theleb K'aarna fully regretted his actions. Then—it was too late.

The sorcerer had no control over the powerful Wind Giants as Elric had. His only hope was to combat one element with another. The fire-spirits must be summoned, and quickly. All of Theleb K'aarna's pyromantic powers would be required to hold off the ravening supernatural winds which were soon to shake the air and the earth. Even hell would shake to the sound and the thunder of the Wind Giants' wrath.

Quickly, Theleb K'aarna marshalled his thoughts and, with trembling hands, began to make strange passes in the air and promise unhealthy pacts with whichever of the powerful fire elementals would help him this once. He promised himself to eternal death for the sake of a few more years of life.

With the gathering of the Wind Giants came the thunder and the rain. The lightning flashed sporadically, but not lethally. It never touched the earth. Elric, Moonglum, and the men of Imrryr were aware of disturbing movements in the atmosphere, but only Elric with his witch-sight could see a little of what was happening. The Lasshaar Giants were invisible to other eyes.

The war-engines which the Imrryrians were even now constructing from pre-fashioned parts were puny things compared to the Wind Giants' might. But victory depended upon these engines since the Lasshaar's fight would be with the supernatural not the natural.

Battle-rams and siege ladders were slowly taking shape as the warriors worked with frantic speed. The hour of the storming came closer as the wind rose and thunder rattled. The moon was blanked out by huge billowings of black cloud, and the men worked by the light of torches. Surprise was no great asset in an attack of the kind planned.

Two hours before dawn, they were ready.

At last the men of Imrryr, Elric, Dyvim Tvar and Moonglum riding high at their head, moved towards the castle of Nikorn. As they did so, Elric raised his voice in an unholy shout—and thunder rumbled in answer to him. A great gout of lightning seared out of the sky towards the palace and the whole place shook and trembled as a ball of mauve and orange fire suddenly appeared over the castle and *absorbed* the lightning! The battle between fire and air had begun.

The surrounding countryside was alive with a weird and malignant shrieking and moaning, deafening to the ears of the marching men. They sensed conflict all round them, and only a little was visible.

Over most of the castle an unearthly glow hung, waxing and waning, defending a gibbering wretch of a sorcerer who knew that he was doomed if once the Lords of the Flame gave way to the roaring Wind Giants.

Elric smiled without humour as he observed the war. On the supernatural plane, he now had little to fear. But there was still the castle and he had no extra supernatural aid to help him take that. Swordplay and skill in battle were the only hope against the ferocious desert warriors who now crowded the battlements, preparing to destroy the two hundred men who came against them.

Up rose the Dragon Standards, their cloth-of-gold fabric flashing in the eery glow. Spread out, walking slowly, the sons of Imrryr moved forward to do battle. Up, also, rose the siege ladders as captains directed warriors to begin the assault. The defenders' faces were pale spots against the dark stone and thin shouts came from them; but it was impossible to catch their words.

Two great battle-rams, fashioned the day before, were brought to the vanguard of the approaching warriors. The narrow causeway was a dangerous one to pass over, but it was the only means of crossing the moat at ground level. Twenty men carried each of the great iron-tipped rams and now they began to run forward while arrows hailed downwards. Their shields protecting them from most of the shafts, the warriors reached the causeway and rushed across it. Now the first ram connected with the gate. It seemed to Elric as he watched this operation that nothing of wood and iron could withstand the vicious impact of the ram, but the gates shivered almost imperceptibly—and held!

Like vampires, hungry for blood, the men howled and staggered aside crabwise to let pass the log held by their comrades. Again the gates shivered, more easily noticed this time, but they yet held.

Dyvim Tvar roared encouragement to those now scaling the siege ladders. These were brave, almost desperate men, for few of the first climbers would reach the top and even if they were successful, they would be hard-pressed to stay alive until their comrades arrived.

Boiling lead hissed from great cauldrons set on spindles so that they could be easily emptied and filled quickly. Many a brave Imrryrian warrior fell earthwards, dead from the searing metal before he reached the sharp rocks beneath. Large stones were released out of leather bags hanging from rotating pulleys which could swing out beyond the battlements and rain bone-crushing death on the besiegers. But still the invaders advanced, voicing half a hundred war-shouts and steadily scaling their long ladders, whilst their comrades, using a shield barrier still, to protect their heads, concentrated on breaking down the gates.

Elric and his two companions could do little to help the scalers or the rammers at that stage. All three were hand-to-hand fighters, leaving even the archery to their rear ranks of bowmen who stood in rows and shot their shafts high into the castle defenders.

The gates were beginning to give. Cracks and splits appeared in them, ever widening. Then, all at once, when hardly expected, the right gate creaked on tortured hinges and fell. A triumphant roar erupted from the throats of the invaders and, dropping their hold on the logs, they led their companions through the breach, axes and maces swinging like scythes and flails before them—and enemy heads springing from necks like wheat from the stalk.

"The castle is ours!" shouted Moonglum, running forward and upward towards the gap in the archway. "The castle's taken."

"Speak not too hastily of victory," replied Dyvim Tvar, but he laughed as he spoke and ran as fast as the others to reach the castle.

"And where is your doom, now?" Elric called to his fellow Melnibonéan, then broke off sharply when Dyvim Tvar's face clouded and his mouth set grimly. For a moment there was tension between them, even as they ran, then Dyvim Tvar laughed loud and made a joke of it. "It lies somewhere, Elric, it lies somewhere—but let us not worry about such things, for if my doom hangs over me, I cannot stop its descent when my hour arrives!" He slapped Elric's shoulder, feeling for the albino's uncharacteristic confusion.

Then they were under the mighty archway and in the courtyard of the castle where savage fighting had developed almost into single duels, enemy choosing enemy and fighting him to the death.

Stormbringer was the first of the three men's blades to take blood and send a desert man's soul to hell. The song it sang as it was lashed through the air in strong strokes was an evil one—evil and triumphant.

The dark-faced desert warriors were famous for their courage and skill with swords. Their curved blades were reaping havoc in the Imrryrian ranks for, at that stage, the desert men far outnumbered the Melnibonéan force.

Somewhere above, the inspired scalers had got a firm foothold on the battlements and were closing with the men of Nikorn, driving them back, forcing many over the unrailed edges of the parapets. A falling, still-screaming warrior plummeted down, to land almost on Elric, knocking his shoulder and causing him to fall heavily to the blood- and rain-slick cobbles. A badly scarred desert man, quick to see his chance, moved forward with a gloating look on his travesty of a face. His scimitar moved up, poised to hack Elric's neck from his shoulders, and then his helmet split open and his forehead spurted a sudden gout of blood.

Dyvim Tvar wrenched a captured axe from the skull of the slain warrior and grinned at Elric as the albino rose.

"We'll both live to see victory, yet," he shouted over the din of the warring elementals above them and the sound of clashing arms. "My doom, I will escape until—" He broke off, a look of surprise on his fine-boned face, and Elric's stomach twisted inside him as he saw a steel point appear in Dyvim Tvar's right side. Behind the Dragon Master, a maliciously smiling desert warrior pulled his blade from Dyvim Tvar's body. Elric cursed and rushed forward. The man put up his blade to defend himself, backing hurriedly away from the infuriated albino. Stormbringer swung up and then down, it howled a death song and sheared right through the curved steel of Elric's opponent—and it kept on going, straight through the man's shoulder blade, splitting him half in two. Elric turned back to Dyvim Tvar who was still standing up, but was pale and strained. His blood dripped from his wound and seeped through his garments.

"How badly are you hurt?" Elric said anxiously. "Can you tell?"

"That trollspawn's sword passed through my ribs, I think—no vitals were harmed." Dyvim Tvar gasped and tried to smile. "I'm sure I'd know if he'd made more of the wound."

Then he fell. And when Elric turned him, he looked into a dead and staring face. The Dragon Master, Lord of the Dragon Caves, would never tend his beasts again.

Elric felt sick and weary as he got up, standing over the body of his kinsman. Because of me, he thought, another fine man has died. But this was the only conscious thought he allowed himself for the meantime. He was forced to defend himself from the slashing swords of a couple of desert men who came at him in a rush.

The archers, their work done outside, came running through the breach in the gate and their arrows poured into the enemy ranks.

Elric shouted loudly: "My kinsman Dyvim Tvar lies dead, stabbed in the back by a desert warrior—avenge him, brethren. Avenge the Dragon Master of Imrryr!"

A low moaning came from the throats of the Melnibonéans and their attack was even more ferocious than before. Elric called to a bunch of axemen who ran down from the battlements, their victory assured.

"You men, follow me. We can avenge the blood that Theleb K'aarna took!" He had a good idea of the geography of the castle.

Moonglum shouted from somewhere. "One moment, Elric, and I'll join you!" A desert warrior fell, his back to Elric, and from behind him emerged a grinning Moonglum, his sword covered in blood from point to pommel.

Elric led the way to a small door, set into the main tower of the castle. He pointed at it and spoke to the axemen. "Set to with your axes, lads, and hurry!"

Grimly, the axemen began to hack at the tough timber. Impatiently, Elric watched as the wood chips started to fly.

The conflict was appalling. Theleb K'aarna sobbed in frustration. Kakatal, the Fire Lord, and his minions were having little effect on the Wind Giants. Their power appeared to be increasing if anything. The sorcerer gnawed his knuckles and quaked in his chamber while below him the human warriors fought, bled and died. Theleb K'aarna made himself concentrate on one thing only—total destruction of the Lasshaar forces. But he knew, somehow, even then, that sooner or later, in one way or another, he was doomed.

The axes drove deeper and deeper into the stout timber. At last it gave. "We're through, my lord," one of the axemen indicated the gaping hole they'd made.

Elric reached his arm through the gap and prised up the bar which secured the door. The bar moved upwards and then fell with a clatter to the stone flagging. Elric put his shoulder to the door and pushed.

Above them, now, two huge, almost-human figures had appeared in the sky, outlined against the night. One was golden and glowing like the sun and seemed to wield a great sword of fire. The other was dark blue and silver, writhing, smokelike, with a flickering spear of restless orange in his hand.

Misha and Kakatal clashed. The outcome of their mighty struggle might well decide Theleb K'aarna's fate.

"Quickly," Elric said. "Upwards!"

They ran up the stairs. The stairs which led to Theleb K'aarna's chamber.

Suddenly the men were forced to stop as they came to a door of jet-black, studded with crimson iron. It had no keyhole, no bolts, no bars, but it was quite secure. Elric directed the axemen to begin hewing at it. All six struck at the door in unison.

In unison, they screamed and vanished. Not even a wisp of smoke remained to mark where they had disappeared.

Moonglum staggered backwards, eyes wide in fear. He was backing away from Elric who remained firmly by the door, Stormbringer throbbing in his hand. "Get out, Elric—this is a sorcery of terrible power. Let your friends of the air finish the wizard!"

Elric shouted half-hysterically: "Magic is best fought by magic!" He hurled his whole body behind the blow which he struck at the black door. Stormbringer whined into it, shrieked as if in victory and howled like a soul-hungry demon. There was a blinding flash, a roaring in Elric's ears, a sense of weightlessness; and then the door had crashed inwards. Moonglum witnessed this—he had remained against his will.

"Stormbringer has rarely failed me, Moonglum," cried Elric as he leapt through the aperture. "Come, we have reached Theleb K'aarna's den—" He broke off, staring at the gibbering thing on the floor. It had been a man. It had been Theleb K'aarna. Now it was hunched and twisted—sitting in the middle of a broken pentacle and tittering to itself.

Suddenly, intelligence came into its eyes. "Too late for vengeance, Lord Elric," it said. "I have won, you see—I have claimed your vengeance as my own."

Grim-faced and speechless, Elric stepped forward, lifted Stormbringer and brought the moaning runesword down into the sorcerer's skull. He left it there for several moments.

"Drink your fill, hellblade," he murmured. "We have earned it, you and I."

Overhead, there was a sudden silence.

6

"It's untrue! You lie!" screamed the frightened man. "We were not responsible." Pilarmo faced the group of leading citizens. Behind the overdressed merchant were his three colleagues—those who had earlier met Elric and Moonglum in the tavern.

One of the accusing citizens pointed a chubby finger towards the north and Nikorn's palace.

"So—Nikorn was an enemy of all other traders in Bakshaan. That I accept. But now a horde of bloody-handed reavers attacks his castle with the aid of demons—and Elric of Melniboné leads them! You know that you are responsible—the gossip's all over the city. You employed Elric—and this is what's happened!"

"But we didn't know he would go to such lengths to kill Nikorn!" Fat Tormiel wrung his hands, his face aggrieved and afraid. "You are wronging us. We only . . ."

"We're wronging *you*!" Faratt, spokesman for his fellow citizens, was thick-lipped and florid. He waved his hands in angry exasperation. "When Elric and his jackals have done with Nikorn—they'll come to the city. Fool! That is what the albino sorcerer planned to begin with. He was only mocking you—for you provided him with an excuse. Armed men we can fight—but not foul sorcery!"

"What shall we do? What shall we do? Bakshaan will be razed within the day!" Tormiel turned on Pilarmo. "This was your idea—you think of a plan!"

Pilarmo stuttered: "We could pay a ransom—bribe them—give them enough money to satisfy them."

"And who shall give this money?" asked Faratt.

Again the argument began.

Elric looked with distaste at Theleb K'aarna's broken corpse. He turned away and faced a blanch-featured Moonglum who said hoarsely: "Let's away, now, Elric. Yishana awaits you in Bakshaan as she promised. You must keep your end of the bargain I made for you."

Elric nodded wearily. "Aye—the Imrryrians seem to have taken the castle by the sound of it. We'll leave them to their spoiling and get out while we may. Will you allow me a few moments here, alone? The sword rejects the soul."

Moonglum sighed thankfully. "I'll join you in the courtyard within the quarter hour. I wish to claim some measure of the spoils." He left clattering down the stairs while Elric remained standing over his enemy's body. He spread out his arms, the sword, dripping blood, still in his hand.

"Dyvim Tvar," he cried, "You and our countrymen have been avenged. Let any evil one who holds the soul of Dyvim Tvar release it now and take instead the soul of Theleb K'aarna."

Within the room something invisible and intangible—but sensed all the same—flowed and hovered over the sprawled body of Theleb K'aarna. Elric looked out of the window and thought he heard the beating of dragon wings—smelled the acrid breath of Phoorn—saw a shape winging across the dawn sky bearing Dyvim Tvar the Dragon Master away.

Elric half-smiled. "The gods of Melniboné protect thee wherever thou art," he said quietly and turned away from the carnage, leaving the room.

On the stairway, he met Nikorn of Ilmar.

The merchant's rugged face was full of anger. He trembled with rage. There was a big sword in his hand.

"So I've found you, wolf," he said. "I gave you your life—and you have done this to me!"

Elric said tiredly: "It was to be. But I gave my word that I would not take your life and, believe me, I would not, Nikorn, even had I not pledged my word."

Nikorn stood two steps from the door blocking the exit. "Then I'll take yours. Come—engage!" He moved out into the courtyard, half-stumbled over an Imrryrian corpse, righted himself and waited, glowering, for Elric to emerge. Elric did so, his runesword sheathed.

"No."

"Defend yourself, wolf!"

Automatically, the albino's right hand crossed to his sword hilt, but he still did not unsheathe it. Nikorn cursed and aimed a well-timed blow which barely missed the white-faced sorcerer. He skipped back and now he tugged out Stormbringer, still reluctant, and stood poised and wary, waiting for the Bakshaanite's next move.

Elric intended simply to disarm Nikorn. He did not want to kill or maim this brave man who had spared him when he had been entirely at the other's mercy.

Nikorn swung another powerful stroke at Elric and the albino parried. Stormbringer was moaning softly, shuddering and pulsating. Metal clanged and then the fight was on in full earnest as Nikorn's rage turned to calm, possessed fury. Elric was forced to defend himself with all his skill and power. Though older than the albino, and a city merchant, Nikorn was a superb swordsman. His speed was fantastic and, at times, Elric was not on the defensive only because he desired it.

But something was happening to the runeblade. It was twisting in Elric's hand and forcing him to make a counter-attack. Nikorn backed away—a light akin to fear in his eyes as he realised the potency of Elric's hell-forged steel. The merchant fought grimly—and Elric did not fight at all. He felt entirely in the power of the whining sword which hacked and cut at Nikorn's guard.

Stormbringer suddenly shifted in Elric's hand. Nikorn screamed. The runesword left Elric's grasp and plunged on its own accord towards the heart of his opponent.

"No!" Elric tried to catch hold of his blade but could not. Stormbringer plunged into Nikorn's great heart and wailed in demoniac triumph. "No!" Elric got hold of the hilt and tried to pull it from Nikorn. The merchant shrieked in hell-brought agony. He should have been dead.

He still half-lived.

"It's taking me—the thrice-damned thing is taking me!" Nikorn gurgled horribly, clutching at the black steel with hands turned to claws. "Stop it, Elric—I beg you, stop it! *Please*!"

Elric tried again to tug the blade from Nikorn's heart. He could not. It was rooted in flesh, sinew and vitals. It moaned greedily, drinking into it all that was the being of Nikorn of Ilmar. It sucked the life-force from the dying man and all the while its voice was soft and disgustingly sensuous. Still Elric struggled to pull the sword free. It was impossible. "Damn you!" he moaned. "This man was almost my friend—I gave him my word not to kill him." But Stormbringer, though sentient, could not hear its master.

Nikorn shrieked once more, the shriek dying to a low, lost whimper. And then his body died.

It died—and the soul-stuff of Nikorn joined the souls of the countless others, friends, kin and enemies who had gone to feed that which fed Elric of Melniboné.

Elric sobbed.

"Why is this curse upon me? Why?"

He collapsed to the ground in the dirt and the blood.

Minutes later, Moonglum came upon his friend lying face downward. He grasped Elric by his shoulder and turned him. He shuddered when he saw the albino's agony-racked face.

"What happened?"

Elric raised himself on one elbow and pointed to where Nikorn's body lay a few feet away. "Another, Moonglum. Oh, curse this blade!"

Moonglum said uncomfortably: "He would have killed you, no doubt. Do not think about it. Many a word's been broken through no fault of he who gave it. Come, my friend, Yishana awaits us in the Tavern of the Purple Dove."

Elric struggled upright and began to walk slowly towards the battered gates of the castle where horses awaited them.

As they rode for Bakshaan, not knowing what was troubling the people of that city, Elric tapped Stormbringer which hung, once more, at his side. His eyes were hard and moody, turned inwards on his own feelings.

"Be wary of this devil-blade, Moonglum. It kills the foe—but savours the blood of friends and kinfolk most."

Moonglum shook his head quickly, as if to clear it, and looked away. He said nothing.

Elric made as if to speak again but then changed his mind. He needed to talk, then. He needed to—but there was nothing to say at all.

Pilarmo scowled. He stared, hurt-faced, as his slaves struggled with his chests of treasure, lugging them out to pile them in the street beside his great house. In other parts of the city, Pilarmo's three colleagues were also in various stages of heartbreak. Their treasure, too, was being dealt with in a like manner. The burghers of Bakshaan had decided who was to pay any possible ransom.

And then a ragged citizen was shambling down the street, pointing behind him and shouting.

"The albino and his companion—at the north gate!"

The burghers who stood near to Pilarmo exchanged glances. Faratt swallowed.

He said: "Elric comes to bargain. Quick. Open the treasure chests and tell the city guard to admit him." One of the citizens scurried off.

Within a few minutes, while Faratt and the rest worked frantically to expose Pilarmo's treasure to the gaze of the approaching albino, Elric was galloping up the street, Moonglum beside him. Both men were expressionless. They knew enough not to show their puzzlement.

"What's this?" Elric said, casting a look at Pilarmo.

Faratt cringed. "Treasure," he whined. "Yours, Lord Elric—for you and your men. There's much more. There is no need to use sorcery. No need for your men to attack us. The treasure here is fabulous—its value is enormous. Will you take it and leave the city in peace?"

Moonglum almost smiled, but he controlled his features.

Elric said coolly: "It will do. I accept it. Make sure this and the rest is delivered to my men at Nikorn's castle or we'll be roasting you and your friends over open fires by the morrow."

Faratt coughed suddenly, trembling. "As you say, Lord Elric. It shall be delivered."

The two men wheeled their horses in the direction of the Tavern of the Purple Dove. When they were out of earshot Moonglum said: "From what I gathered, back there, it's Master Pilarmo and his friends who are paying that unasked-for toll."

Elric was incapable of any real humour, but he half-chuckled. "Aye. I'd planned to rob them from the start—and now their own fellows have done it for us. On our way back, we shall take our pick of the spoils."

He rode on and reached the tavern. Yishana was waiting there, nervously, dressed for travelling.

When she saw Elric's face she sighed with satisfaction and smiled silkily. "So Theleb K'aarna is dead," she said. "Now we can resume our interrupted relationship, Elric."

The albino nodded. "That was my part of the bargain—you kept yours when you helped Moonglum to get my sword back for me." He showed no emotion.

She embraced him, but he drew back. "Later," he murmured. "But this is one promise I shall not break, Yishana."

He helped the puzzled woman mount her waiting horse. They rode back towards Pilarmo's house.

She asked: "And what of Nikorn—is he safe? I liked that man."

"He died," Elric's voice was strained.

"How?" she asked.

"Because, like all merchants," Elric answered, "he bargained too hard."

There was an unnatural silence among the three as they made their horses speed faster towards the gates of Bakshaan, and Elric did not stop when the others did, to take their pick of Pilarmo's riches. He rode on, unseeing, and the others had to spur their steeds in order to catch up with him, two miles beyond the city.

Over Bakshaan, no breeze stirred in the gardens of the rich. No winds came to blow cool on the sweating faces of the poor. Only the sun blazed in the heavens, round and red, and a shadow, shaped like a dragon, moved across it once, and then was gone.

BOOK TWO

KINGS IN DARKNESS

Three Kings in Darkness lie,
Gutheran of Org, and I,
Under a bleak and sunless sky—
The third Beneath the Hill.

—Song of Veerkad
by James Cawthorn

I

Elric, Lord of the lost and sundered Empire of Melniboné, rode like a fanged wolf from a trap—all slavering madness and mirth. He rode from Nadsokor, City of Beggars, and there was hate in his wake for he had been recognised as their old enemy before he could obtain the secret he had sought there. Now they hounded him and the grotesque little man who rode laughing at Elric's side; Moonglum the Outlander, from Elwher and the Unmapped East.

The flames of brands devoured the velvet of the night as the yelling, ragged throng pushed their bony nags in pursuit of the pair.

Starvelings and tattered jackals that they were, there was strength in their gaudy numbers, and long knives and bone bows glinted in the brandlight. They were too strong for a couple of men to fight, too few to represent serious danger in a hunt, so Elric and Moonglum had chosen to leave the city without dispute and now sped towards the setting full moon which stabbed its sickly beams through the darkness to show them the disturbing waters of the Varkalk River and a chance of escape from the incensed mob.

They had half a mind to stand and face the mob, since the Varkalk was their only alternative. But they knew well what the beggars would do to them, whereas they were uncertain what would become of them once they had entered the river. The horses reached the sloping banks of the Varkalk and reared, with hoofs lashing.

Cursing, the two men spurred the steeds and forced them down towards the water. Into the river the horses plunged, snorting and spluttering. Into the river which led a roaring course towards the hell-spawned Forest of Troos which lay within the borders of Org, country of necromancy and rotting, ancient evil.

Elric blew water away from his mouth and coughed. "They'll not follow us to Troos, I think," he shouted at his companion.

Moonglum said nothing. He only grinned, showing his white teeth and the unhidden fear in his eyes. The horses swam strongly with the current and behind them the ragged mob shrieked in frustrated bloodlust while some of their number laughed and jeered.

"Let the forest do our work for us!"

Elric laughed back at them, wildly, as the horses swam on down the dark, straight river, wide and deep, towards a sun-starved morning, cold and spikey with ice. Scattered, slim-peaked crags loomed on either side of the flat plain, through which the river ran swiftly. Green-tinted masses of jutting blacks and browns spread colour through the rocks, and the grass was waving on the plain as if for some purpose. Through the dawnlight, the beggar crew chased along the banks, but eventually gave up their quarry to return, shuddering, to Nadsokor.

When they had gone, Elric and Moonglum made their mounts swim towards the banks and climb them, stumbling, to the top where rocks and grass had already given way to sparse forest land which rose starkly on all sides, staining the earth with sombre shades. The foliage waved jerkily, as if alive—sentient.

It was a forest of malignantly erupting blooms, blood-coloured and sickly-mottled. A forest of bending, sinuously smooth trunks, black and shiny; a forest of spiked leaves of murky purples and gleaming greens—certainly an unhealthy place if judged only by the odour of rotting vegetation which was almost unbearable, impinging as it did upon the fastidious nostrils of Elric and Moonglum.

Moonglum wrinkled his nose and jerked his head in the direction they had come. "Back now?" he enquired. "We can avoid Troos and cut swiftly across a corner of Org to be in Bakshaan in just over a day. What say you, Elric?"

Elric frowned. "I don't doubt they'd welcome us in Bakshaan with the same warmth we received in Nadsokor. They'll not have forgotten the destruction we wrought there—and the wealth we acquired from their merchants. No, I have a fancy to explore the forest a little. I have heard tales of Org and its unnatural forest and should like to investigate the truth of them. My blade and sorcery will protect us, if necessary."

Moonglum sighed. "Elric—this once, let us not court the danger."

Elric smiled icily. His scarlet eyes blazed out of his dead white skin with peculiar intensity. "Danger? It can bring only death."

"Death is not to my liking, just yet," Moonglum said. "The fleshpots of Bakshaan, or if you prefer—Jadmar—on the other hand . . ."

But Elric was already urging his horse onward, heading for the forest. Moonglum sighed and followed.

Soon dark blossoms hid most of the sky, which was dark enough, and they could see only a little way in all directions. The rest of the forest seemed vast and sprawling; they could sense this, though sight of most of it was lost in the depressing gloom.

Moonglum recognised the forest from descriptions he had heard from mad-eyed travellers who drank purposefully in the shadows of Nadsokor's taverns.

"This is the Forest of Troos, sure enough," he said to Elric. "It's told of how the Doomed Folk released tremendous forces upon the Earth and caused terrible changes among men, beasts and vegetation. This forest is the last they created, and the last to perish."

"A child will always hate its parents at certain times," Elric said mysteriously.

"Children of whom to be extremely wary, I should think," Moonglum retorted. "Some say that when they were at the peak of their power, they had no gods to frighten them."

"A daring people, indeed," Elric replied, with a faint smile. "They have my respect. Now fear and the gods are back and that, at least, is comforting."

Moonglum puzzled over this for a short time, and then, eventually, said nothing.

He was beginning to feel uneasy.

The place was full of malicious rustlings and whispers, though no living animal inhabited it, as far as they could tell. There was a discomforting absence of birds, rodents or insects and, though they normally had no love for such creatures, they would have appreciated their company in the disconcerting forest.

In a quavering voice, Moonglum began to sing a song in the hope that it would keep his spirits up and his thoughts off the lurking forest.

"A grin and a word is my trade;
From these, my profit is made.
Though my body's not tall and my courage is small,
My fame will take longer to fade."

So singing, with his natural amiability returning, Moonglum rode after the man he regarded as a friend—a friend who possessed something akin to mastery over him, though neither admitted it.

Elric smiled at Moonglum's song. "To sing of one's own lack of size and absence of courage is not an action designed to ward off one's enemies, Moonglum."

"But this way I offer no provocation," Moonglum replied glibly. "If I sing of my shortcomings, I am safe. If I were to boast of my talents, then someone might consider this to be a challenge and decide to teach me a lesson."

"True," Elric assented gravely, "and well spoken."

He began pointing at certain blossoms and leaves, remarking upon their alien tint and texture, referring to them in words which Moonglum could not understand, though he knew the words to be part of a sorcerer's vocabulary. The albino seemed to be untroubled by the fears which beset the Eastlander, but often, Moonglum knew, appearances with Elric could hide the opposite of what they indicated.

They stopped for a short break while Elric sifted through some of the samples he had torn from trees and plants. He carefully placed his prizes in his belt pouch but would say nothing of why he did so to Moonglum.

"Come," he said, "Troos's mysteries await us."

But then a new voice, a woman's, said softly from the gloom: "Save the excursion for another day, strangers."

Elric reined his horse, one hand at Stormbringer's hilt. The voice had had an unusual effect upon him. It had been low, deep and had, for a moment, sent the pulse in his throat throbbing. Incredibly, he sensed that he was suddenly standing on one of Fate's roads, but where the road would take him, he did not know. Quickly, he controlled his mind and then his body and looked towards the shadows from where the voice had come.

"You are very kind to offer us advice, madam," he said sternly. "Come, show yourself and give explanation . . ."

She rode then, very slowly, on a black-coated gelding that pranced with a power she could barely restrain. Moonglum drew an appreciative breath for although heavy-featured, she was incredibly beautiful. Her face and bearing was patrician, her eyes were grey-green, combining enigma and innocence. She was very young. For all her obvious womanhood and beauty, Moonglum aged her at seventeen or little more.

Elric frowned: "Do you ride alone?"

"I do now," she replied, trying to hide her obvious astonishment at the albino's colouring. "I need aid—protection. Men who will escort me safely to Karlaak. There, they will be paid."

"Karlaak, by the Weeping Waste? It lies the other side of Ilmiora, a hundred leagues away and a week's travelling at speed." Elric did not wait for her to reply to this statement. "We are not hirelings, madam."

"Then you are bound by the vows of chivalry, sir, and cannot refuse my request."

Elric laughed shortly. "Chivalry, madam? We come not from the upstart nations of the South with their strange codes and rules of behaviour. We are nobles of older stock whose actions are governed by our own desires. You would not ask what you do, if you knew our names."

She wetted her full lips with her tongue and said almost timidly: "You are . . . ?"

"Elric of Melniboné, madam, called Elric Womanslayer in the West, and this is Moonglum of Elwher; he has no conscience."

She said: "There are legends—the white-faced reaver, the hell-driven sorcerer with a blade that drinks the souls of men . . ."

"Aye, that's true. And however magnified they are with the retelling, they cannot hint, those tales, at the darker truths which lie in their origin. Now, madam, do you still seek our aid?" Elric's voice was gentle, without menace, as he saw that she was very much afraid, although she had managed to control the signs of fear and her lips were tight with determination.

"I have no choice. I am at your mercy. My father, the Senior Senator of Karlaak, is very rich. Karlaak is called the City of the Jade Towers, as you will know, and such rare jades and ambers we have. Many could be yours."

"Be careful, madam, lest you anger me," warned Elric, although Moonglum's bright eyes lighted with avarice. "We are not nags to be hired or goods to be bought. Besides which," he smiled disdainfully, "I am from crumbling Imrryr, the Dreaming City, from the Isle of the Dragon, hub of ancient Melniboné, and I know what beauty really is. Your baubles cannot tempt one who has looked upon the milky Heart of Arioch, upon the blinding iridescence that throbs from the Ruby Throne, of the languorous and unnameable colours in the Actorios stone of the Ring of Kings. These are more than jewels, madam— they contain the lifestuff of the universe."

"I apologise, Lord Elric, and to you, Sir Moonglum."

Elric laughed, almost with affection. "We are grim clowns, lady, but the Gods of Luck aided our escape from Nadsokor and we owe them a debt. We'll escort you to Karlaak, City of the Jade Towers, and explore the Forest of Troos another time."

Her thanks were tempered by the wary look in her eyes.

"And now we have made introductions," said Elric, "perhaps you would be good enough to give your name and tell us your story."

"I am Zarozinia from Karlaak, a daughter of the Voashoon, the most powerful clan in south-eastern Ilmiora. We have kinsmen in the trading cities on the coasts of Pikarayd and I went with two cousins and my uncle to visit them."

"A perilous journey, Lady Zarozinia."

"Aye and there are not only natural dangers, sir. Two weeks ago we made our goodbyes and began the journey home. Safely we crossed the Straits of Vilmir and there employed men-at-arms, forming a strong caravan to journey through Vilmir and so to Ilmiora. We skirted Nadsokor since we had heard that the City of Beggars is inhospitable to honest travellers . . ."

Here, Elric smiled: "And sometimes to dishonest travellers, as we can appreciate."

Again the expression on her face showed that she had some difficulty in equating his obvious good humour with his evil reputation. "Having skirted Nadsokor," she continued, "we came this way and reached the borders of Org wherein, of course, Troos lies. Very warily we travelled, knowing dark Org's reputation, along the fringes of the forest. And then we were ambushed and our hired men-at-arms deserted us."

"Ambushed, eh?" broke in Moonglum. "By whom, madam, did you know?"

"By their unsavoury looks and squat shapes they seemed natives. They fell upon the caravan and my uncle and cousins fought bravely but were slain. One of my cousins slapped the rump of my gelding and sent it galloping so that I could not control it. I heard—terrible screams—mad, giggling shouts— and when I at last brought my horse to a halt, I was lost. Later I heard you approach and waited in fear for you to pass, thinking you also were of Org, but when I heard your accents and some of your speech, I thought that you might help me."

"And help you we shall, madam," said Moonglum bowing gallantly from the saddle. "And I am indebted to you for convincing Lord Elric here of your need. But for you, we should be deep in this awful forest by now and experiencing strange terrors no doubt. I offer my sorrow for your dead kinfolk and assure you that you will be protected from now onwards by more than swords and brave hearts, for sorcery can be called up if needs be."

"Let's hope there'll be no need," frowned Elric. "You talk blithely of sorcery, friend Moonglum—you who hate the art."

Moonglum grinned.

"I was consoling the young lady, Elric. And I've had occasion to be grateful for your horrid powers, I'll admit. Now I suggest that we make camp for the night and so refreshed be on our way at dawn."

"I'll agree to that," said Elric, glancing almost with embarrassment at the girl. Again he felt the pulse in his throat and this time he had more difficulty in controlling it.

The girl also seemed fascinated by the albino. There was an attraction between them which might be strong enough to throw both their destinies along wildly different paths than any they had guessed.

Night came again quickly, for the days were short in those parts. While Moonglum tended the fire, nervously peering around him, Zarozinia, her richly embroidered cloth-of-gold gown shimmering in the firelight, walked gracefully to where Elric sat sorting the herbs he had collected. She glanced at him cautiously and then seeing that he was absorbed, stared at him with open curiosity.

He looked up and smiled faintly, his eyes for once unprotected, his strange face frank and pleasant. "Some of these are healing herbs," he said, "and others are used in summoning spirits. Yet others give unnatural strength to the imbiber and some turn men mad. They will be useful to me."

She sat down beside him, her thick-fingered hands pushing her black hair back. Her small breasts lifted and fell rapidly.

"Are you really the terrible evil-bringer of the legends, Lord Elric? I find it hard to credit."

"I have brought evil to many places," he said, "but usually there has already been evil to match mine. I seek no excuses, for I know what I am and I know what I have done. I have slain malignant sorcerers and destroyed oppressors, but I have also been responsible for slaying fine men, and a woman, my cousin, whom I loved, I killed—or my sword did."

"And you are master of your sword?"

"I often wonder. Without it, I am helpless." He put his hand around Stormbringer's hilt. "I should be grateful to it." Once again his red eyes seemed to become deeper, protecting some bitter emotion rooted at the core of his soul.

"I'm sorry if I revived unpleasant recollection . . ."

"Do not feel sorry, Lady Zarozinia. The pain is within me—you did not put it there. In fact I'd say you relieve it greatly by your presence."

Half-startled, she glanced at him and smiled. "I am no wanton, sir," she said, "but . . ."

He got up quickly.

"Moonglum, is the fire going well?"

"Aye, Elric. She'll stay in for the night." Moonglum cocked his head on one side. It was unlike Elric to make such empty queries, but Elric said nothing further so the Eastlander shrugged, turned away to check his gear.

Since he could think of little else to say, Elric turned and said quietly, urgently: "I'm a killer and a thief, not fit to . . ."

"Lord Elric, I am . . ."

"You are infatuated by a legend, that is all."

"No! If you feel what I feel, then you'll know it's more."

"You are young."

"Old enough."

"Beware. I must fulfil my destiny."

"Your destiny?"

"It is no destiny at all, but an awful thing called doom. And I have no pity except when I see something in my own soul. Then I have pity—and I pity. But I hate to look and this is part of the doom which drives me. Not Fate, nor the Stars, nor Men, nor Demons, nor Gods. Look at me, Zarozinia—it is Elric, poor white chosen plaything of the Gods of Time—Elric of Melniboné who causes his own gradual and terrible destruction."

"It is suicide!"

"Aye. I drive myself to slow death. And those who go with me suffer also."

"You speak falsely, Lord Elric—from guilt-madness."

"Because I am guilty, lady."

"And does Sir Moonglum go to doom with you?"

"He is unlike others—he is indestructible in his own self-assurance."

"I am confident, also, Lord Elric."

"But your confidence is that of youth, it is different."

"Need I lose it with my youth?"

"You have strength. You are as strong as we are. I'll grant you that."

She opened her arms, rising. "Then be reconciled, Elric of Melniboné."

And he was. He seized her, kissing her with a deeper need than that of passion. For the first time Cymoril of Imrryr was forgotten as they lay down, together on the soft turf, oblivious of Moonglum who polished away at his curved sword with wry jealousy.

They all slept and the fire waned.

Elric, in his joy, had forgotten, or not heeded, that he had a watch to take and Moonglum, who had no source of strength by himself, stayed awake for as long as he could but sleep overcame him.

In the shadows of the awful trees, figures moved with shambling caution.

The misshapen men of Org began to creep inwards towards the sleepers.

Then Elric opened his eyes, aroused by instinct, stared at Zarozinia's peaceful face beside him, moved his eyes without turning his head and saw the danger. He rolled over, grasped Stormbringer and tugged the runeblade from its sheath. The sword hummed, as if in anger at being awakened.

"Moonglum! Danger!" Elric bellowed in fear, for he had more to protect than his own life. The little man's head jerked up. His curved sabre was already across his knees and he jumped to his feet, ran towards Elric as the men of Org closed in.

"I apologise," he said.

"My fault, I . . ."

And then the men of Org were at them. Elric and Moonglum stood over the girl as she came awake, saw the situation and did not scream. Instead she looked around for a weapon but found none. She remained still, where she was, the only thing to do.

Smelling like offal, the gibbering creatures, some dozen of them, slashed at Elric and Moonglum with heavy blades like cleavers, long and dangerous.

Stormbringer whined and smote through a cleaver, cut into a neck and beheaded the owner. Blood gurgled from the corpse as it slumped back across the fire. Moonglum ducked beneath a howling cleaver, lost his balance, fell, slashed at his opponent's legs and hamstrung him so that he collapsed shrieking. Moonglum stayed on the ground and lunged upwards, taking another in the heart. Then he sprang to his feet and stood shoulder to shoulder with Elric while Zarozinia got up behind them.

"The horses," grunted Elric. "If it's safe, try to get them."

There were still seven natives standing and Moonglum groaned as a cleaver sliced flesh from his left arm, retaliated, pierced the man's throat, turned slightly and sheared off another's face. They pressed forward, taking the attack to the incensed foe. His left hand covered with his own blood, Moonglum painfully pulled his long poignard from its sheath and held it with his thumb along the handle, blocked an opponent's swing, closed in and killed him with a ripping upward thrust of the dagger, the action of which caused his wound to pound with agony.

Elric held his great runesword in both hands and swung it in a semicircle, hacking down the howling misshapen things. Zarozinia darted towards the horses, leapt onto her own and led the other two towards the fighting men. Elric smote at another and got into his saddle, thanking his own forethought to leave the equipment on the horses in case of danger. Moonglum quickly joined him and they thundered out of the clearing.

"The saddlebags," Moonglum called in greater agony than that created by his wound. "We've left the saddlebags!"

"What of it? Don't press your luck, my friend."

"But all our treasure's in them!"

Elric laughed, partly in relief, partly from real humour. "We'll retrieve them, friend, never fear."

"I know you, Elric. You've no value for the realities."

But even Moonglum was laughing as they left the enraged men of Org behind them and slowed to a canter.

Elric reached and hugged Zarozinia. "You have the courage of your noble clan in your veins," he said.

"Thank you," she replied, pleased with the compliment, "but we cannot match such swordmanship as that displayed by you and Moonglum. It was fantastic."

"Thank the blade," he said shortly.

"No. I will thank you. I think you place too much reliance upon that hell weapon, however powerful it is."

"I need it."

"For what?"

"For my own strength and, now, to give strength to you."

"I'm no vampire," she smiled, "and need no such fearful strength as that supplies."

"Then be assured that I do," he told her gravely. "You would not love me if the blade did not give me what I need. I am like a spineless sea-thing without it."

"I do not believe that, but will not dispute with you now."

They rode for a while without speaking.

Later, they stopped, dismounted, and Zarozinia put herbs that Elric had given her upon Moonglum's wounded arm and began to bind it.

Elric was thinking deeply. The forest rustled with macabre, sensuous sounds. "We're in the heart of Troos," he said, "and our intention to skirt the forest has been forestalled. I have it in mind to call on the King of Org and so round off our visit."

Moonglum laughed. "Shall we send our swords along first? And bind our own hands?" His pain was already eased by the herbs which were having quick effect.

"I mean it. We owe, all of us, much to the men of Org. They slew Zarozinia's uncle and cousins, they wounded you and they now have our treasure. We have many reasons for asking the king for recompense. Also, they seem stupid and should be easy to trick."

"Aye. The king will pay us back for our lack of common sense by tearing our limbs off."

"I'm in earnest. I think we should go."

"I'll agree that I'd like our wealth returned to us. But we cannot risk the lady's safety, Elric."

"I am to be Elric's wife, Moonglum. Therefore if he visits the King of Org, I shall come too."

Moonglum lifted an eyebrow. "A quick courtship."

"She speaks the truth, however. We shall all go to Org—and sorcery will protect us from the king's uncalled-for wrath."

"And still you wish for death and vengeance, Elric," shrugged Moonglum mounting. "Well, it's all the same to me since your roads, whatever else, are profitable ones. You may be the Lord of Bad Luck by your own reckoning, but you bring good luck to me, I'll say that."

"No more courting death," smiled Elric, "but we'll have some revenge, I hope."

"Dawn will be with us soon," Moonglum said. "The Orgian citadel lies six hours' ride from here by my working, south-south-east by the Ancient Star, if the map I memorised in Nadsokor was correct."

"You have an instinct for direction that never fails, Moonglum. Every caravan should have such a man as you."

"We base an entire philosophy on the stars in Elwher," Moonglum replied. "We regard them as the master plan for everything that happens on Earth. As they revolve around the planet they see all things, past, present and future. They are our gods."

"Predictable gods, at least," said Elric and they rode off towards Org with light hearts considering the enormity of their risk.

2

Little was known of the tiny kingdom of Org save that the Forest of Troos lay within its boundaries and to that, other nations felt, it was welcome. The people were unpleasant to look upon, for the most part, and their bodies were stunted and strangely altered. Legend had it that they were the descendants of the Doomed Folk. Their rulers, it was said, were shaped like normal men in so far as their outward bodily appearance went, but their minds were warped more horribly than the limbs of their subjects.

The inhabitants were few and were generally scattered, ruled by their king from his citadel which was also called Org.

It was for this citadel that Elric and his companions rode and, as they did so, Elric explained how he planned to protect them all from the natives of Org.

In the forest he had found a particular leaf which, when used with certain invocations (which were harmless in that the invoker was in little danger of being harmed by the spirits he marshalled) would invest that person, and anyone else to whom he gave the drug distilled from the leaf, with temporary invulnerability.

The spell somehow reknitted the skin and flesh structure so that it could withstand any edge and almost any blow. Elric explained, in a rare garrulous mood, how the drug and spell combined to achieve the effect, but his archaicisms and esoteric words meant little to the other two.

They stopped an hour's ride from where Moonglum expected to find the citadel so that Elric could prepare the drug and invoke the spell.

He worked swiftly over a small fire, using an alchemist's pestle and mortar, mixing the shredded leaf with a little water. As the brew bubbled on the fire, he drew peculiar runes on the ground, some of which were twisted into such alien forms that they seemed to disappear into a different dimension and reappear beyond it.

"Bone and blood and flesh and sinew,
Spell and spirit bind anew;
Potent potion work the life charm,
Keep its takers safe from harm."

So Elric chanted as a small pink cloud formed in the air over the fire, wavered, re-formed into a spiral shape which curled downwards into the bowl. The brew spluttered and then was still. The albino sorcerer said: "An old boyhood spell, so simple that I'd near forgotten it. The leaf for the potion grows only in Troos and therefore it is rarely possible to perform."

The brew, which had been liquid, had now solidified and Elric broke it into small pellets. "Too much," he warned, "taken at one time is poison, and yet the effect can last for several hours. Not always, though, but we must accept that small risk." He handed both of them a pellet which they received dubiously. "Swallow them just before we reach the citadel," he told them, "or in the event of the men of Org finding us first."

Then they mounted and rode on again.

Some miles to the south-east of Troos, a blind man sang a grim song in his sleep and so woke himself . . .

They reached the brooding citadel of Org at dusk. Guttural voices shouted at them from the battlements of the square-cut ancient dwelling place of the Kings of Org. The thick rock oozed moisture and was corroded by lichen and sickly, mottled moss. The only entrance large enough for a mounted man to pass through was reached by a path almost a foot deep in evil-smelling black mud.

"What's your business at the Royal Court of Gutheran the Mighty?"

They could not see who asked the question.

"We seek hospitality and an audience with your liege," called Moonglum cheerfully, successfully hiding his nervousness. "We bring important news to Org."

A twisted face peered down from the battlements. "Enter, strangers, and be welcome," it said unwelcomingly.

The heavy wooden drawgate shifted upwards to allow them entrance and the horses pushed their way slowly through the mud and so into the courtyard of the citadel.

Overhead, the grey sky was a racing field of black tattered clouds which streamed towards the horizon as if to escape the horrid boundaries of Org and the disgusting Forest of Troos.

The courtyard was covered, though not so deeply, with the same foul mud as had impaired their progress to the citadel. It was full of heavy, unmoving shadow. On Elric's right, a flight of steps went up to an arched entrance which was hung, partially, with the same unhealthy lichen he had seen on the outer walls and, also, in the Forest of Troos.

Through this archway, brushing at the lichen with a pale, beringed hand, a tall man came and stood on the top step, regarding the visitors through heavy-lidded eyes. He was, in contrast to the others, handsome, with a massive, leonine head and long hair as white as Elric's; although the hair on the head of this great, solid man was somewhat dirty, tangled, unbrushed. He was dressed in a heavy jerkin of quilted, embossed leather, a yellow kilt which reached to his ankles and he carried a wide-bladed dagger, naked in his belt. He was older than Elric, aged between forty and fifty and his powerful if somewhat decadent face was seamed and pock-marked.

He stared at them in silence and did not welcome them; instead he signed to one of the battlement guards who caused the drawgate to be lowered. It came down with a crash, blocking off their way of escape.

"Kill the men and keep the woman," said the massive man in a low monotone. Elric had heard dead men speak in that manner.

As planned, Elric and Moonglum stood either side of Zarozinia and remained where they were, arms folded.

Puzzled, shambling creatures came warily at them, their loose trousers dragging in the mud, their hands hidden by the long shapeless sleeves of their filthy garments. They swung their cleavers. Elric felt a faint shock as the blade thudded onto his arm, but that was all. Moonglum's experience was similar.

The men fell back, amazement and confusion on their bestial faces.

The tall man's eyes widened. He put one ring-covered hand to his thick lips, chewing at a nail.

"Our swords have no effect upon them, king! They do not cut and they do not bleed. What are these folk?"

Elric laughed theatrically. "We are not common folk, little human, be assured. We are the messengers of the gods and come to your king with a message from our great masters. Do not worry, we shall not harm you since we are in no danger of being harmed. Stand aside and make us welcome."

Elric could see that King Gutheran was puzzled and not absolutely taken in by his words. Elric cursed to himself. He had measured their intelligence by those he had seen. This king, mad or not, was much more intelligent, was going to be harder to deceive. He led the way up the steps towards glowering Gutheran.

"Greetings, King Gutheran. The gods have, at last, returned to Org and wish you to know this."

"Org has had no gods to worship for an eternity," said Gutheran hollowly, turning back into the citadel. "Why should we accept them now?"

"You are impertinent, king."

"And you are audacious. How do I know you come from the gods?" He walked ahead of them, leading them through the low-roofed halls.

"You saw that the swords of your subjects had no effect upon us."

"True. I'll take that incident as proof for the moment. I suppose there must be a banquet in your—honour—I shall order it. Be welcome, messengers." His words were ungracious but it was virtually impossible to detect anything from Gutheran's tone, since the man's voice stayed at the same pitch.

Elric pushed his heavy riding cloak back from his shoulders and said lightly: "We shall mention your kindness to our masters."

The Court was a place of gloomy halls and false laughter and although Elric put many questions to Gutheran, the king would not answer them, or did so by means of ambiguous phrases which meant nothing. They were not given chambers wherein they could refresh themselves but instead stood about for several hours in the main hall of the citadel and Gutheran, while he was with them and not giving orders for the banquet, sat slumped on his throne and chewed at his nails, ignoring them.

"Pleasant hospitality," whispered Moonglum.

"Elric—how long will the effects of the drug last?" Zarozinia had remained close to him. He put his arm around her shoulders. "I do not know. Not much longer. But it has served its purpose. I doubt if they will try to attack us a second time. However, beware of other attempts, subtler ones, upon our lives."

The main hall, which had a higher roof than the others and was completely surrounded by a gallery which ran around it well above the floor, fairly close to the roof, was chilly and unwarmed. No fires burned in the several hearths, which were open and let into the floor, and the walls dripped moisture and were undecorated; damp, solid stone, time-worn and gaunt. There were not even rushes upon the floor which was strewn with old bones and pieces of decaying food.

"Hardly house-proud, are they?" commented Moonglum looking around him with distaste and glancing at brooding Gutheran who was seemingly oblivious of their presence.

A servitor shambled into the hall and whispered a few words to the king. He nodded and arose, leaving the Great Hall.

Soon men came in, carrying benches and tables and began to place them about the hall.

The banquet was, at last, due to commence. And the air had menace in it.

The three visitors sat together on the right of the king who had donned a richly jewelled chain of kingship, whilst his son and several pale-faced female members of the royal line sat on the left, unspeaking even among themselves.

Prince Hurd, a sullen-faced youth who seemed to bear a resentment against his father, picked at the unappetising food which was served them all.

He drank heavily of the wine which had little flavour but was strong, fiery stuff and this seemed to warm the company a little.

"And what do the gods want of us poor folk of Org?" Hurd said, staring hard at Zarozinia with more than friendly interest.

Elric answered: "They ask nothing of you but your recognition. In return they will, on occasions, help you."

"That is all?" Hurd laughed. "That is more than those from the Hill can offer, eh, Father?"

Gutheran turned his great head slowly to regard his son.

"Yes," he murmured, and the word seemed to carry warning.

Moonglum said: "The Hill—what is that?"

He got no reply. Instead a high-pitched laugh came from the entrance to the Great Hall. A thin, gaunt man stood there staring ahead with a fixed gaze. His features, though emaciated, strongly resembled Gutheran's. He carried a stringed instrument and plucked at the gut so that it wailed and moaned with melancholy insistence.

Hurd said savagely: "Look, Father, 'tis blind Veerkad, the minstrel, your brother. Shall he sing for us?"

"Sing?"

"Shall he sing his songs, Father?"

Gutheran's mouth trembled and twisted and he said after a moment: "He may entertain our guests with an heroic ballad if he wishes, but . . ."

"But certain other songs he shall not sing . . ." Hurd grinned maliciously. He seemed to be tormenting his father deliberately in some way which Elric could not guess. Hurd shouted at the blind man: "Come, Uncle Veerkad—sing!"

"There are strangers present," said Veerkad hollowly above the wail of his own music. "Strangers in Org."

Hurd giggled and drank more wine. Gutheran scowled and continued to tremble, gnawing at his nails.

Elric called: "We'd appreciate a song, minstrel."

"Then you'll have the song of the Three Kings in Darkness, strangers, and hear the ghastly story of the Kings of Org."

"No!" shouted Gutheran, leaping from his place, but Veerkad was already singing:

"*Three Kings in Darkness lie,*
Gutheran of Org, and I,
Under a bleak and sunless sky—
The third Beneath the Hill.
When shall the third arise?
Only when another dies . . ."

"Stop!" Gutheran got up in an obviously insane rage and stumbled across the table, trembling in terror, his face blanched, striking at the blind man, his brother. Two blows and the minstrel fell, slumping to the floor and not moving. "Take him out! Do not let him enter again." The king shrieked and foam flecked his lips.

Hurd, sober for a moment, jumped across the table, scattering dishes and cups and took his father's arm.

"Be calm, Father. I have a new plan for our entertainment."

"You! You seek my throne. 'Twas you who goaded Veerkad to sing his dreadful song. You know I cannot listen without . . ." He stared at the door. "One day the legend shall be realised and the Hill-King shall come. Then shall I, you and Org perish."

"Father," Hurd was smiling horribly, "let the female visitor dance for us a dance of the gods."

"What?"

"Let the woman dance for us, Father."

Elric heard him. By now the drug must have worn off. He could not afford to show his hand by offering his companions further doses. He got to his feet.

"What sacrilege do you speak, prince?"

"We have given you entertainment. It is the custom in Org for our visitors to give us entertainment also."

The hall was filled with menace. Elric regretted his plan to trick the men of Org. But there was nothing he could do. He had intended to exact tribute from them in the name of the gods, but obviously these mad men feared more immediate and tangible dangers than any the gods might represent.

He had made a mistake, put the lives of his friends in danger as well as his own. What should he do? Zarozinia murmured: "I have learned dances in Ilmiora where all ladies are taught the art. Let me dance for them. It might placate them and bedazzle them to make our work easier."

"Arioch knows our work is hard enough now. I was a fool to have conceived this plan. Very well, Zarozinia, dance for them, but with caution." He shouted at Hurd: "Our companion will dance for you, to show you the beauty that the gods create. Then you must pay the tribute, for our masters grow impatient."

"The tribute?" Gutheran looked up. "You mentioned nothing of tribute."

"Your recognition of the gods must take the form of precious stones and metals, King Gutheran. I thought you to understand that."

"You seem more like common thieves than uncommon messengers, my friends. We are poor in Org and have nothing to give away to charlatans."

"Beware of your words, king!" Elric's clear voice echoed warningly through the hall.

"We'll see the dance and then judge the truth of what you've told us."

Elric seated himself, grasped Zarozinia's hand beneath the table as she arose, giving her comfort.

She walked gracefully and confidently into the centre of the hall and there began to dance. Elric, who loved her, was amazed at her splendid grace and artistry. She danced the old, beautiful dances of Ilmiora, entrancing even the thick-skulled men of Org and, as she danced, a great golden Guest Cup was brought in.

Hurd leaned across his father and said to Elric: "The Guest Cup, lord. It is our custom that our guests drink from it in friendship."

Elric nodded, annoyed at being disturbed in his watching of the wonderful dance, his eyes fixed on Zarozinia as she postured and glided. There was silence in the hall.

Hurd handed him the cup and absently he put it to his lips; seeing this Zarozinia danced onto the table and began to weave along it to where Elric sat. As he took the first sip, Zarozinia cried out and, with her foot, knocked the cup from his hand. The wine splashed onto Gutheran and Hurd who half rose, startled. "It was drugged, Elric. They drugged it!"

Hurd lashed at her with his hand, striking her across the face. She fell from the table and lay moaning slightly on the filthy floor. "Bitch! Would the messengers of the gods be harmed by a little drugged wine?"

Enraged, Elric pushed aside Gutheran and struck savagely at Hurd so that the young man's mouth gushed blood. But the drug was already having effect. Gutheran shouted something and Moonglum drew his sabre, glancing upwards. Elric was swaying, his senses were jumbled and the scene had an unreal quality. He saw servants grasp Zarozinia but could not see how Moonglum was faring. He felt sick and dizzy, could hardly control his limbs.

Summoning up his last remaining strength, Elric clubbed Hurd down with one tremendous blow. Then he collapsed into unconsciousness.

3

There was the cold clutch of chains about his wrists and a thin drizzle was falling directly onto his face which stung where Hurd's nails had ripped it.

He looked about him. He was chained between two stone menhirs upon an obvious burial barrow of gigantic size. It was night and a pale moon hovered in the heavens above him. He looked down at the group of men below. Hurd and Gutheran were among them. They grinned at him mockingly.

"Farewell, messenger. You will serve us a good purpose and placate the Ones from the Hill!" Hurd called as he and the others scurried back towards the citadel which lay, silhouetted, a short distance away.

Where was he? What had happened to Zarozinia—and Moonglum? Why had he been chained thus upon—realisation and remembrance came—*the Hill*!

He shuddered, helpless in the strong chains which held him. Desperately he began to tug at them, but they would not yield. He searched his brain for a plan, but he was confused by torment and worry for his friends' safety. He heard a dreadful scuttling sound from below and saw a ghastly white shape dart into the gloom. Wildly he struggled in the rattling iron which held him.

In the Great Hall of the citadel, a riotous celebration was now reaching the state of an ecstatic orgy. Gutheran and Hurd were totally drunk, laughing insanely at their victory.

Outside the hall, Veerkad listened and hated. Particularly he hated his brother, the man who had deposed and blinded him to prevent his study of sorcery by means of which he had planned to raise the King from Beneath the Hill.

"The time has come, at last," he whispered to himself and stopped a passing servant.

"Tell me—where is the girl kept?"

"In Gutheran's chamber, master."

Veerkad released the man and began to grope his way through the gloomy corridors up twisting steps, until he reached the room he sought. Here he produced a key, one of many he'd had made without Gutheran's knowing, and unlocked the door.

Zarozinia saw the blind man enter and could do nothing. She was gagged and bound with her own dress and still dazed from the blow Hurd had given her. They had told her of Elric's fate, but Moonglum had so far escaped them, guards hunted him now in the stinking corridors of Org.

"I've come to take you to your companion, lady," smiled blind Veerkad, grasping her roughly with strength that his insanity had given him. Picking her up, he fumbled his way towards the door. He knew the passages of Org perfectly, for he had been born and had grown up among them.

But two men were in the corridor outside Gutheran's chambers. One of them was Hurd, Prince of Org, who resented his father's appropriation of the girl and desired her for himself. He saw Veerkad bearing the girl away and stood silent while his uncle passed.

The other man was Moonglum, who observed what was happening from the shadows where he had hidden from the searching guards. As Hurd followed Veerkad, on cautious feet, Moonglum followed him.

Veerkad went out of the citadel by a small side door and carried his living burden towards the looming Burial Hill.

All about the foot of the monstrous barrow swarmed the leprous-white ghouls who sensed the presence of Elric, the folk of Org's sacrifice to them.

Now Elric understood.

These were the things that Org feared more than the gods. These were the living-dead ancestors of those who now revelled in the Great Hall. Perhaps these were actually the Doomed Folk. Was that their doom? Never to rest? Never to die? Just to degenerate into mindless ghouls? Elric shuddered.

Now desperation brought back his memory. His voice was an agonised wail to the brooding sky and the pulsing earth.

"Arioch! Destroy the stones. Save your servant! Arioch—master—aid me!"

It was not enough. The ghouls gathered together and began to scuttle, gibbering up the barrow towards the helpless albino.

"Arioch! These are the things that would forsake your memory! Aid me to destroy them!"

The earth trembled and the sky became overcast, hiding the moon but not the white-faced, bloodless ghouls who were now almost upon him.

And then a ball of fire formed in the sky above him and the very sky seemed to shake and sway around it. Then, with a roaring crash two bolts of lightning slashed down, pulverising the stones and releasing Elric.

He got to his feet, knowing that Arioch would demand his price, as the first ghouls reached him.

He did not retreat, but in his rage and desperation leapt among them, smashing and flailing with the lengths of chain. The ghouls fell back and fled, gibbering in fear and anger, down the Hill and into the barrow.

Elric could now see that there was a gaping entrance to the barrow below him, black against the blackness. Breathing heavily, he found that his belt pouch had been left him. From it he took a length of slim, gold wire and began frantically to pick at the locks of the manacles.

Veerkad chuckled to himself and Zarozinia hearing him was almost mad with terror. He kept drooling the words into her ear: "When shall the third arise? Only when another dies. When that other's blood flows red—we'll hear the footfalls of the dead. You and I, we shall resurrect him and such vengeance will he wreak upon my cursed brother. Your blood, my dear, it will be that released him." He felt that the ghouls were gone and judged them placated by their feast. "Your lover has been useful to me," he laughed as he began to enter the barrow. The smell of death almost overpowered the girl as the blind madman bore her downwards into the heart of the Hill.

Hurd, sobered after his walk in the colder air, was horrified when he saw where Veerkad was going; the barrow, the Hill of the King, was the most feared spot in the land of Org. Hurd paused before the black entrance and turned to run. Then, suddenly, he saw the form of Elric, looming huge and bloody, descending the barrow slope, cutting off his escape.

With a wild yell he fled into the Hill passage.

Elric had not previously noticed the prince, but the yell startled him and he tried to see who had given it but was too late. He began to run down the steep incline towards the entrance of the barrow. Another figure came scampering out of the darkness.

"Elric! Thank the stars and all the gods of Earth! You live!"

"Thank Arioch, Moonglum. Where's Zarozinia?"

"In there—the mad minstrel took her with him and Hurd followed. They are all insane, these kings and princes, I see no sense to their actions."

"I have an idea that the minstrel means Zarozinia no good. Quickly, we must follow."

"By the stars, the stench of death! I have breathed nothing like it—not even at the great battle of the Eshmir Valley where the armies of Elwher met those of Kaleg Vogun, usurper prince of the Tanghensi, and half a million corpses strewed the valley from end to end."

"If you've no stomach . . ."

"I wish I had none. It would not be so bad. Come . . ."

They rushed into the passage, led by the faraway sounds of Veerkad's maniacal laughter and the somewhat nearer movements of a fear-maddened Hurd who was now trapped between two enemies and yet more afraid of a third.

Hurd blundered along in the blackness, sobbing to himself in his terror.

In the phosphorescent Central Tomb, surrounded by the mummified corpses of his ancestors, Veerkad chanted the resurrection ritual before the great coffin of the Hill-King—a giant thing, half as tall again as Veerkad who was tall enough. Veerkad was forgetful for his own safety and thinking only of vengeance upon his brother Gutheran. He held a long dagger over Zarozinia who lay huddled and terrified upon the ground near the coffin.

The spilling of Zarozinia's blood would be the culmination of the ritual and then—

Then hell would, quite literally, be let loose. Or so Veerkad planned. He finished his chanting and raised the knife just as Hurd came screeching into the Central Tomb with his own sword drawn. Veerkad swung round, his blind face working in thwarted rage.

Savagely, without stopping for a moment, Hurd ran his sword into Veerkad's body, plunging the blade in up to the hilt so that its bloody point appeared sticking from his back. But the other, in his groaning death spasms, locked his hands about the prince's throat. Locked them immovably.

Somehow, the two men retained a semblance of life and, struggling with each other in a macabre death dance, swayed about the glowing chamber. The coffin of the Hill-King began to tremble and shake slightly, the movement hardly perceptible.

So Elric and Moonglum found Veerkad and Hurd. Seeing that both were near dead, Elric raced across the Central Tomb to where Zarozinia lay, unconscious, mercifully, from her ordeal. Elric picked her up and made to return.

He glanced at the throbbing coffin.

"Quickly, Moonglum. That blind fool has invoked the dead, I can tell. Hurry, my friend, before the hosts of hell are upon us."

Moonglum gasped and followed Elric as he ran back towards the cleaner air of night.

"Where to now, Elric?"

"We'll have to risk going back to the citadel. Our horses are there and our goods. We need the horses to take us quickly away, for I fear there's going to be a terrible bloodletting soon if my instinct is right."

"There should not be too much opposition, Elric. They were all drunk when I left. That was how I managed to evade them so easily. By now, if they continued drinking as heavily as when last I saw them, they'll be unable to move at all."

"Then let's make haste."

They left the Hill behind them and began to run towards the citadel.

4

Moonglum had spoken truth. Everyone was lying about the Great Hall in drunken sleep. Open fires had been lit in the hearths and they blazed, sending shadows skipping around the hall. Elric said softly:

"Moonglum, go with Zarozinia to the stables and prepare our horses. I will settle our debt with Gutheran first." He pointed. "See, they have heaped their booty upon the table, gloating in their apparent victory."

Stormbringer lay upon a pile of burst sacks and saddlebags which contained the loot stolen from Zarozinia's uncle and cousins and from Elric and Moonglum.

Zarozinia, now conscious but confused, left with Moonglum to locate the stables and Elric picked his way towards the table, across the sprawled shapes of drunken men of Org, around the blazing fires and caught up, thankfully, his hell-forged runeblade.

Then he leapt over the table and was about to grasp Gutheran, who still had his fabulously gemmed chain of kingship around his neck, when the great doors of the hall crashed open and a howling blast of icy air sent the torches dancing and leaping. Elric turned, Gutheran forgotten, and his eyes widened.

Framed in the doorway stood the King from Beneath the Hill.

The long-dead monarch had been raised by Veerkad whose own blood had completed the work of resurrection. He stood in rotting robes, his near-fleshless bones covered by tight, tattered skin. His heart did not beat, for he had none; he drew no breath, for his lungs had been eaten by the creatures which feasted on such things. But, horribly, he lived . . .

The King from the Hill. He had been the last great ruler of the Doomed Folk who had, in their fury, destroyed half the Earth and created the Forest of Troos. Behind the dead king crowded the ghastly hosts who had been buried with him in a legendary past.

The massacre began!

What secret vengeance was being reaped, Elric could only guess at—but whatever the reason, the danger was still very real.

Elric pulled out Stormbringer as the awakened horde vented their anger upon the living. The hall became filled with the shrieking, horrified screams of the unfortunate men of Org. Elric remained, half-paralysed in his horror, beside the throne. Aroused, Gutheran woke up and saw the King from the Hill and his host. He screamed, almost thankfully:

"At last I can rest!"

And fell dying in a seizure, robbing Elric of his vengeance.

Veerkad's grim song echoed in Elric's memory. The Three Kings in Darkness—Gutheran, Veerkad and the King from Beneath the Hill. Now only the last lived—and he had been dead for millennia.

The King's cold, dead eyes roved the hall and saw Gutheran sprawled upon his throne, the ancient chain of office still about his throat. Elric wrenched it off the body and backed away as the King from Beneath the Hill advanced. And then his back was against a pillar and there were feasting ghouls everywhere else.

The dead King came nearer and then, with a whistling moan which came from the depths of his decaying body, launched himself at Elric who found himself fighting desperately against the Hill-King's clawing, abnormal strength, cutting at flesh that neither bled nor suffered pain. Even the sorcerous runeblade could do nothing against this horror that had no soul to take and no blood to let.

Frantically, Elric slashed and hacked at the Hill-King but ragged nails raked his flesh and teeth snapped at his throat. And above everything came the almost overpowering stench of death as the ghouls, packing the Great Hall with their horrible shapes, feasted on the living and the dead.

Then Elric heard Moonglum's voice calling and saw him upon the gallery which ran around the hall. He held a great oil jar.

"Lure him close to the central fire, Elric. There may be a way to vanquish him. Quickly man, or you're finished!"

In a frantic burst of energy, the Melnibonéan forced the giant king towards the flames. Around them, the ghouls fed off the remains of their victims, some of whom still lived, their screams calling hopelessly over the sound of carnage.

The Hill-King now stood, unfeeling, with his back to the leaping central fire. He still slashed at Elric. Moonglum hurled the jar.

It shattered upon the stone hearth, spraying the King with blazing oil. He staggered, and Elric struck with his full power, the man and the blade combining to push the Hill-King backwards. Down went the King into the flames and the flames began to devour him.

A dreadful, lost howling came from the burning giant as he perished.

Flames licked everywhere throughout the Great Hall and soon the place was like hell itself, an inferno of licking fire through which the ghouls ran about, still feasting, unaware of their destruction. The way to the door was blocked.

Elric stared around him and saw no way of escape—save one.

Sheathing Stormbringer, he ran a few paces and leapt upwards, just grasping the rail of the gallery as flames engulfed the spot where he had been standing.

Moonglum reached down and helped him to clamber across the rail.

"I'm disappointed, Elric," he grinned, "you forgot to bring the treasure."

Elric showed him what he grasped in his left hand—the jewel-encrusted chain of kingship.

"This bauble is some reward for our hardships," he smiled, holding up the glittering chain. "I stole nothing, by Arioch! There are no kings left in Org to wear it! Come let's join Zarozinia and get our horses."

They ran from the gallery as masonry began to crash downwards into the Great Hall.

They rode fast away from the halls of Org and looking back saw great fissures appear in the walls and heard the roar of destruction as the flames consumed everything that had been Org. They destroyed the seat of the monarchy, the remains of the Three Kings in Darkness, the present and the past. Nothing would be left of Org save an empty burial mound and two corpses, locked together, lying where their ancestors had lain for centuries in the Central Tomb. They destroyed the last link with the previous age and cleansed the Earth of an ancient evil. Only the dreadful Forest of Troos remained to mark the coming and the passing of the Doomed Folk.

And the Forest of Troos was a warning.

Weary and yet relieved, the three saw the outlines of Troos in the distance, behind the blazing funeral pyre.

And yet, in his happiness, Elric had a fresh problem on his mind now that danger was past.

"Why do you frown now, love?" asked Zarozinia.

"Because I think you spoke the truth. Remember you said I placed too much reliance on my runeblade here?"

"Yes—and I said I would not dispute with you."

"Agreed. But I have a feeling that you were partially right. On the burial mound and in it I did not have Stormbringer with me—and yet I fought and won, because I feared for your safety." His voice was quiet. "Perhaps, in time, I can keep my strength by means of certain herbs I found in Troos and dispense with the blade for ever?"

Moonglum shouted with laughter hearing these words.

"Elric—I never thought I'd witness this. You daring to think of dispensing with that foul weapon of yours. I don't know if you ever shall, but the thought is comforting."

"It is, my friend, it is." He leaned in his saddle and grasped Zarozinia's shoulders, pulling her dangerously towards him as they galloped without slackening speed. And as they rode he kissed her, heedless of their pace.

"A new beginning!" he shouted above the wind. "A new beginning, my love!"

And then they all rode laughing towards Karlaak by the Weeping Waste, to present themselves, to enrich themselves, and to begin planning for the strangest wedding the Northern lands would ever have witnessed.

BOOK THREE

THE FLAME BRINGERS

*In which Moonglum returns from
the Eastlands with disturbing news . . .*

I

Bloody-beaked hawks soared on the frigid wind. They soared high above a mounted horde inexorably moving across the Weeping Waste.

The horde had crossed two deserts and three mountain ranges to be there and hunger drove them onwards. They were spurred on by remembrances of stories heard from travellers who had come to their Eastern homeland, by the encouragements of their thin-lipped leader who swaggered in his saddle ahead of them, one arm wrapped around a ten-foot lance decorated with the gory trophies of his pillaging campaigns.

The riders moved slowly and wearily, unaware that they were nearing their goal.

Far behind the horde, a stocky rider left Elwher, the singing, boisterous capital of the Eastern World, and came soon to a valley.

The hard skeletons of trees had a blighted look and the horse kicked earth the colour of ashes as its rider drove it fiercely through the sick wasteland that had once been gentle Eshmir, the golden garden of the East.

A plague had smitten Eshmir and the locust had stripped her of her beauty. Both plague and locust went by the same name—Terarn Gashtek, Lord of the Mounted Hordes, sunken-faced carrier of destruction; Terarn Gashtek, insane blood-drawer, the shrieking flame bringer. And that was his other name—Flame Bringer.

The rider who witnessed the evil that Terarn Gashtek had brought to gentle Eshmir was named Moonglum. Moonglum was riding, now, for Karlaak by the Weeping Waste, the last outpost of the Western civilisation of which those in the Eastlands knew little. In Karlaak, Moonglum knew he would find Elric of Melniboné who now dwelt permanently in his wife's graceful city. Moonglum was desperate to reach Karlaak quickly, to warn Elric and to solicit his help.

He was small and cocky, with a broad mouth and a shock of red hair, but now his mouth did not grin and his body was bent over the horse as he pushed it on towards Karlaak. For Eshmir, gentle Eshmir, had been Moonglum's home province, and with his ancestors had formed him into what he was.

So, cursing, Moonglum rode for Karlaak.

But so did Terarn Gashtek. And already the Flame Bringer had reached the Weeping Waste. The horde moved slowly, for they had wagons with them which had at one time dropped far behind but now the supplies they carried were needed. As well as provisions, one of the wagons carried a bound prisoner who lay on his back cursing Terarn Gashtek and his slant-eyed battlemongers.

Drinij Bara was bound by more than strips of leather, that was why he cursed, for Drinij Bara was a sorcerer who could not normally be held in such a manner. If he had not succumbed to his weakness for wine and women just before the Flame Bringer had come down on the town in which he was staying, he would not have been trussed so, and Terarn Gashtek would not now have Drinij Bara's soul.

Drinij Bara's soul reposed in the body of a small black-and-white cat—the cat which Terarn Gashtek had caught and carried with him always, for, as was the habit of Eastern sorcerers, Drinij Bara had hidden his soul in the body of the cat for protection. Because of this he was now slave to the Lord of the Mounted Hordes, and had to obey him lest the man slay the cat and so send his soul to hell.

It was not a pleasant situation for the proud sorcerer, but he did not deserve less.

There was on the pale face of Elric of Melniboné some slight trace of an earlier haunting, but his mouth smiled and his crimson eyes were at peace as he looked down at the young, black-haired woman with whom he walked in the terraced gardens of Karlaak.

"Elric," said Zarozinia, "have you found your happiness?"

He nodded. "I think so. Stormbringer now hangs amid cobwebs in your father's armoury. The drugs I discovered in Troos keep me strong, my eyesight clear, and need to be taken only occasionally. I need never think of travelling or fighting again. I am content, here, to spend my time with you and study the books in Karlaak's library. What more would I require?"

"You compliment me overmuch, my lord. I would become complacent."

He laughed. "Rather that than you were doubting. Do not fear, Zarozinia, I possess no reason, now, to journey on. Moonglum, I miss, but it was natural that he should become restless of residence in a city and wish to revisit his homeland."

"I am glad you are at peace, Elric. My father was at first reluctant to let you live here, fearing the black evil that once accompanied you, but three months have proved to him that the evil has gone and left no fuming berserker behind it."

Suddenly there came a shouting from below them, in the street a man's voice was raised and he banged at the gates of the house.

"Let me in, damn you, I must speak with your master."

A servant came running: "Lord Elric—there is a man at the gates with a message. He pretends friendship with you."

"His name?"

"An alien one—Moonglum, he says."

"Moonglum! His stay in Elwher has been short. Let him in!"

Zarozinia's eyes held a trace of fear and she held Elric's arm fiercely. "Elric—pray he does not bring news to take you hence."

"No news could do that. Fear not, Zarozinia." He hurried out of the garden and into the courtyard of the house. Moonglum rode hurriedly through the gates, dismounting as he did so.

"Moonglum, my friend! Why the haste? Naturally, I am pleased to see you after such a short time, but you have been riding hastily—why?"

The little Eastlander's face was grim beneath its coating of dust and his clothes were filthy from hard riding.

"The Flame Bringer comes with sorcery to aid him," he panted. "You must warn the city."

"The Flame Bringer? The name means nothing—you sound delirious, my friend."

"Aye, that's true, I am. Delirious with hate. He destroyed my homeland, killed my family, my friends and now plans conquests in the West. Two years ago he was little more than an ordinary desert raider but then he began to gather a great horde of barbarians around him and has been looting and slaying his way across the Eastern lands. Only Elwher has not suffered from his attacks, for the city was too great for even him to take. But he has turned two thousand miles of pleasant country into a burning waste. He plans world conquest, rides westwards with five hundred thousand warriors!"

"You mentioned sorcery—what does this barbarian know of such sophisticated arts?"

"Little himself, but he has one of our greatest wizards in his power—Drinij Bara. The man was captured as he lay drunk between two wenches in a tavern in Phum. He had put his soul into the body of a cat so that no rival sorcerer might steal it while he slept. But Terarn Gashtek, the Flame Bringer, knew of this trick, seized the cat and bound its legs, eyes and mouth, so imprisoning Drinij Bara's soul. Now the sorcerer is his slave—if he does not obey the barbarian, the cat will be killed by an iron blade and Drinij Bara's soul will go to hell."

"These are unfamiliar sorceries to me," said Elric. "They seem little more than superstitions."

"Who knows that they may be—but so long as Drinij Bara believes what he believes, he will do as Terarn Gashtek dictates. Several proud cities have been destroyed with the aid of his magic."

"How far away is this Flame Bringer?"

"Three days' ride at most. I was forced to come hence by a longer route, to avoid his outriders."

"Then we must prepare for a siege."

"No, Elric—you must prepare to flee!"

"To flee—should I request the citizens of Karlaak to leave their beautiful city unprotected, to leave their homes?"

"If they will not—you must, and take your bride with you. None can stand against such a foe."

"My own sorcery is no mean thing."

"But one man's sorcery is not enough to hold back half a million men also aided by sorcery."

"And Karlaak is a trading city—not a warrior's fortress. Very well, I will speak to the Council of Elders and try to convince them."

"You must convince them quickly, Elric, for if you do not Karlaak will not stand half a day before Terarn Gashtek's howling bloodletters."

"They are stubborn," said Elric as the two sat in his private study later that night. "They refuse to realise the magnitude of the danger. They refuse to leave and I cannot leave them for they have welcomed me and made me a citizen of Karlaak."

"Then we must stay here and die?"

"Perhaps. There seems to be no choice. But I have another plan. You say that this sorcerer is a prisoner of Terarn Gashtek. What would he do if he regained his soul?"

"Why he would take vengeance upon his captor. But Terarn Gashtek would not be so foolish as to give him the chance. There is no help for us there."

"What if we managed to aid Drinij Bara?"

"How? It would be impossible."

"It seems our only chance. Does this barbarian know of me or my history?"

"Not as far as I know."

"Would he recognise you?"

"Why should he?"

"Then I suggest we join him."

"Join him—Elric you are no more sane than when we rode as free travellers together!"

"I know what I am doing. It would be the only way to get close to him and discover a subtle way to defeat him. We will set off at dawn, there is no time to waste."

"Very well. Let's hope your old luck is good, but I doubt it now, for you've forsaken your old ways and the luck went with them."

"Let us find out."

"Will you take Stormbringer?"

"I had hoped never to have to make use of that hell-forged blade again. She's a treacherous sword at best."

"Aye—but I think you'll need her in this business."

"Yes, you're right. I'll take her."

Elric frowned, his hands clenched. "It will mean breaking my word to Zarozinia."

"Better break it—than give her up to the Mounted Hordes."

Elric unlocked the door to the armoury, a pitch torch flaring in one hand. He felt sick as he strode down the narrow passage lined with dulled weapons which had not been used for a century.

His heart pounded heavily as he came to another door and flung off the bar to enter the little room in which lay the disused regalia of Karlaak's long-dead War Chieftains—and Stormbringer. The black blade began to moan as if welcoming him as he took a deep breath of the musty air and reached for the sword. He clutched the hilt and his body was racked by an unholy sensation of awful ecstasy. His face twisted as he sheathed the blade and he almost ran from the armoury towards cleaner air.

Elric and Moonglum mounted their plainly equipped horses and, garbed like common mercenaries, bade urgent farewell to the Councillors of Karlaak.

Zarozinia kissed Elric's pale hand.

"I realise the need for this," she said, her eyes full of tears, "but take care, my love."

"I shall. And pray that we are successful in whatever we decide to do."

"The White Gods be with you."

"No—pray to the Lords of the Darks, for it is their evil help I'll need in this work. And forget not my words to the messenger who is to ride to the south-west and find Dyvim Slorm."

"I'll not forget," she said, "though I worry lest you succumb again to your old black ways."

"Fear for the moment—I'll worry about my own fate later."

"Then farewell, my lord, and be lucky."

"Farewell, Zarozinia. My love for you will give me more power even than this foul blade here." He spurred his horse through the gates and then they were riding for the Weeping Waste and a troubled future.

2

Dwarfed by the vastness of the softly turfed plateau which was the Weeping Waste, the place of eternal rains, the two horsemen drove their hard-pressed steeds through the drizzle.

A shivering desert warrior, huddled against the weather, saw them come towards him. He stared through the rain trying to make out details of the riders, then wheeled his stocky pony and rode swiftly back in the direction he had come. Within minutes he had reached a large group of warriors attired like himself in furs and tasselled iron helmets. They carried short bone bows and quivers of long arrows fletched with hawk feathers. There were curved scimitars at their sides.

He exchanged a few words with his fellows and soon they were all lashing their horses towards the two riders.

"How much further lies the camp of Terarn Gashtek, Moonglum?" Elric's words were breathless, for both men had ridden for a day without halt.

"Not much further, Elric. We should be—look!"

Moonglum pointed ahead. About ten riders came swiftly towards them. "Desert barbarians—the Flame Bringer's men. Prepare for a fight—they won't waste time parleying."

Stormbringer scraped from the scabbard and the heavy blade seemed to aid Elric's wrist as he raised it, so that it felt almost weightless.

Moonglum drew both his swords, holding the short one with the same hand with which he grasped his horse's reins.

The Eastern warriors spread out in a half-circle as they rode down on the companions, yelling wild war-shouts. Elric reared his mount to a savage stand-still and met the first rider with Stormbringer's point full in the man's throat. There was a stink like brimstone as it pierced flesh and the warrior drew a ghastly choking breath as he died, his eyes staring out in full realisation of his terrible fate—that Stormbringer drank souls as well as blood.

Elric cut savagely at another desert man, lopping off his sword-arm and splitting his crested helmet and the skull beneath. Rain and sweat ran down his white, taut features and into his glowing crimson eyes, but he blinked it aside, half-fell in his saddle as he turned to defend himself against another howling scimitar, parried the sweep, slid his own runeblade down its length, turned the blade with a movement of his wrist and disarmed the warrior. Then he plunged his sword into the man's heart and the desert warrior yelled like a wolf at the moon, a long baying shout before Stormbringer took his soul.

Elric's face was twisted in self-loathing as he fought intently with super-human strength. Moonglum stayed clear of the albino's sword for he knew its liking for the lives of Elric's friends.

Soon only one opponent was left. Elric disarmed him and had to hold his own greedy sword back from the man's throat.

Reconciled to the horror of his death, the man said something in a guttural tongue which Elric half-recognised. He searched his memory and realised that it was a language close to one of the many ancient tongues which, as a sorcerer, he had been required to learn years before.

He said in the same language: "Thou art one of the warriors of Terarn Gashtek the Flame Bringer."

"That is true. And you must be the White-faced Evil One of legends. I beg you to slay me with a cleaner weapon than that which you hold."

"I do not wish to kill thee at all. We were coming hence to join Terarn Gashtek. Take us to him."

The man nodded hastily and clambered back on his horse.

"Who are you who speaks the High Tongue of our people?"

"I am called Elric of Melniboné—dost thou know the name?"

The warrior shook his head. "No, but the High Tongue has not been spoken for generations, save by shamans—yet you're no shaman but, by your dress, seem a warrior."

"We are both mercenaries. But speak no more. I will explain the rest to thy leader."

They left a jackal's feast behind them and followed the quaking Easterner in the direction he led them.

Fairly soon, the low-lying smoke of many campfires could be observed and at length they saw the sprawling camp of the barbarian warlord's mighty army.

The camp encompassed over a mile of the great plateau. The barbarians had erected skin tents on rounded frames and the camp had the aspect of a large primitive town. Roughly in the centre was a much larger construction, decorated with a motley assortment of gaudy silks and brocades.

Moonglum said in the Western tongue: "That must be Terarn Gashtek's dwelling. See, he has covered its half-cured hides with a score of Eastern battle flags." His face grew grimmer as he noted the torn standard of Eshmir, the lion-flag of Okara and the blood-soaked pennants of sorrowing Chang Shai.

The captured warrior led them through the squatting ranks of barbarians who stared at them impassively and muttered to one another. Outside Terarn Gashtek's tasteless dwelling was his great war-lance decorated with more trophies of his conquests—the skulls and bones of Eastern princes and kings.

Elric said: "Such a one as this must not be allowed to destroy the reborn civilisation of the Young Kingdoms."

"Young kingdoms are resilient," remarked Moonglum, "but it is when they are old that they fall—and it is often Terarn Gashtek's kind that tear them down."

"While I live he shall not destroy Karlaak—nor reach as far as Bakshaan."

Moonglum said: "Though, in my opinion, he'd be welcome to Nadsokor. The City of Beggars deserves such visitors as the Flame Bringer. If we fail, Elric, only the sea will stop him—and perhaps not that."

"With Dyvim Slorm's aid—we shall stop him. Let us hope Karlaak's messenger finds my kinsman soon."

"If he does not we shall be hard put to fight off half a million warriors, my friend."

The barbarian shouted: "Oh, Conqueror—mighty Flame Bringer—there are men here who wish to speak with you."

A slurred voice snarled: "Bring them in."

They entered the badly smelling tent which was lighted by a fire flickering in a circle of stones. A gaunt man, carelessly dressed in bright captured clothing, lounged on a wooden bench. There were several women in the tent, one of whom poured wine into a heavy golden goblet which he held out.

Terarn Gashtek pushed the woman aside, knocking her sprawling and regarded the newcomers. His face was almost as fleshless as the skulls hanging outside his tent. His cheeks were sunken and his slanting eyes narrow beneath thick brows.

"Who are these?"

"Lord, I know not—but between them they slew ten of our men and would have slain me."

"You deserved no more than death if you let yourself be disarmed. Get out—and find a new sword quickly or I'll let the shamans have your vitals for divination." The man slunk away.

Terarn Gashtek seated himself upon the bench once more.

"So, you slew ten of my bloodletters, did you, and came here to boast to me about it? What's the explanation?"

"We but defended ourselves against your warriors—we sought no quarrel with them." Elric now spoke the cruder tongue as best he could.

"You defended yourselves fairly well, I grant you. We reckon three soft-living house-dwellers to one of us. You are a Westerner, I can tell that, though your silent friend has the face of an Elwherite. Have you come from the East or the West?"

"The West," Elric said, "we are free-travelling warriors, hiring our swords to those who'll pay or promise us good booty."

"Are all Western warriors as skilful as you?" Terarn Gashtek could not hide his sudden realisation that he might have underestimated the men he hoped to conquer.

"We are a little better than most," lied Moonglum, "but not much."

"What of sorcery—is there much strong magic here?"

"No," said Elric, "the art has been lost to most."

The barbarian's thin mouth twisted into a grin, half of relief, half of triumph. He nodded his head, reached into his gaudy silks and produced a small black-and-white bound cat. He began to stroke its back. It wriggled but could do no more than hiss at its captor. "Then we need not worry," he said.

"Now, why did you come here? I could have you tortured for days for what you did, slaying ten of my best outriders."

"We recognised the chance of enriching ourselves by aiding you, Lord Flame Bringer," said Elric. "We could show you the richest towns, lead you to ill-defended cities that would take little time to fall. Will you enlist us?"

"I've need of such men as you, true enough. I'll enlist you readily—but mark this, I'll not trust you until you've proved loyal to me. Find yourselves quarters now—and come to the feast, tonight. There I'll be able to show you something of the power I hold. The power which will smash the strength of the West and lay it waste for ten thousand miles."

"Thanks," said Elric. "I'll look forward to tonight."

They left the tent and wandered through the haphazard collection of tents and cooking fires, wagons and animals. There seemed little food, but wine was in abundance and the taut, hungry stomachs of the barbarians were placated with that.

They stopped a warrior and told him of Terarn Gashtek's orders to them. The warrior sullenly led them to a tent.

"Here—it was shared by three of the men you slew. It is yours by right of battle, as are the weapons and booty inside."

"We're richer already," grinned Elric with feigned delight.

In the privacy of the tent, which was less clean than Terarn Gashtek's, they debated.

"I feel uncommonly uncomfortable," said Moonglum, "surrounded by this treacherous horde. And every time I think of what they made of Eshmir, I itch to slay more of them. What now?"

"We can do nothing now—let us wait until tonight and see what develops." Elric sighed. "Our task seems impossible—I have never seen so great a horde as this."

"They are invincible as they are," said Moonglum. "Even without Drinij Bara's sorcery to tumble down the walls of cities, no single nation could withstand them and, with the Western nations squabbling among themselves, they could never unite in time. Civilisation itself is threatened. Let us pray for inspiration—your dark gods are at least sophisticated, Elric, and we must hope that they'll resent the barbarian's intrusion as much as we do."

"They play strange games with their human pawns," Elric replied, "and who knows what they plan?"

Terarn Gashtek's smoke-wreathed tent had been further lighted by rush torches when Elric and Moonglum swaggered in, and the feast, consisting primarily of wine, was already in progress.

"Welcome, my friends," shouted the Flame Bringer, waving his goblet. "These are my captains—come, join them!"

Elric had never seen such an evil-looking group of barbarians. They were all half-drunk and, like their leader, had draped a variety of looted articles of clothing about themselves. But their swords were their own.

Room was made on one of the benches and they accepted wine which they drank sparingly.

"Bring in our slave!" yelled Terarn Gashtek. "Bring in Drinij Bara our pet sorcerer." Before him on the table lay the bound and struggling cat and beside it an iron blade.

Grinning warriors dragged a morose-faced man close to the fire and forced him to kneel before the barbarian chief. He was a lean man and he glowered at Terarn Gashtek and the little cat. Then his eyes saw the iron blade and his gaze faltered.

"What do you want with me now?" he said sullenly.

"Is that the way to address your master, spell-maker? Still, no matter. We have guests to entertain—men who have promised to lead us to fat merchant cities. We require you to do a few minor tricks for them."

"I'm no petty conjuror. You cannot ask this of one of the greatest sorcerers in the world!"

"We do not ask—we order. Come, make the evening lively. What do you need for your magic-making? A few slaves—the blood of virgins? We shall arrange it."

"I'm no mumbling shaman—I need no such trappings."

Suddenly the sorcerer saw Elric. The albino felt the man's powerful mind tentatively probing his own. He had been recognised as a fellow sorcerer. Would Drinij Bara betray him?

Elric was tense, waiting to be denounced. He leaned back in his chair and, as he did so, made a sign with his hand which would be recognised by Western sorcerers—would the Easterner know it?

He did. For a moment he faltered, glancing at the barbarian leader. Then he turned away and began to make new passes in the air, muttering to himself.

The beholders gasped as a cloud of golden smoke formed near the roof and began to metamorphose into the shape of a great horse bearing a rider which all recognised as Terarn Gashtek. The barbarian leader leaned forward, glaring at the image.

"What's this?"

A map showing great land areas and seas seemed to unroll beneath the horse's hoofs. "The Western lands," cried Drinij Bara. "I make a prophecy."

"What is it?"

The ghostly horse began to trample the map. It split and flew into a thousand smoky pieces. Then the image of the horseman faded, also, into fragments.

"Thus will the mighty Flame Bringer rend the bountiful nations of the West," shouted Drinij Bara.

The barbarians cheered exultantly, but Elric smiled thinly. The Eastern wizard was mocking Terarn Gashtek and his men.

The smoke formed into a golden globe which seemed to blaze and vanish.

Terarn Gashtek laughed. "A good trick, magic-maker—and a true prophecy. You have done your work well. Take him back to his kennel!"

As Drinij Bara was dragged away, he glanced questioningly at Elric but said nothing.

Later that night, as the barbarians drank themselves into a stupor, Elric and Moonglum slipped out of the tent and made their way to the place where Drinij Bara was imprisoned.

They reached the small hut and saw that a warrior stood guard at the entrance. Moonglum produced a skin of wine and, pretending drunkenness, staggered towards the man. Elric stayed where he was.

"What do you want, Outlander?" growled the guard.

"Nothing my friend, we are trying to get back to our own tent, that's all. Do you know where it is?"

"How should I know?"

"True—how should you? Have some wine—it's good—from Terarn Gashtek's own supply."

The man extended a hand. "Let's have it."

Moonglum took a swig of the wine. "No, I've changed my mind. It's too good to waste on common warriors."

"Is that so?" The warrior took several paces towards Moonglum. "We'll find out, won't we? And maybe we'll mix some of your blood with it to give it flavour, my little friend."

Moonglum backed away. The warrior followed.

Elric ran softly towards the tent and ducked into it to find Drinij Bara, wrists bound, lying on a pile of uncured hides. The sorcerer looked up.

"You—what do you want?"

"We've come to aid you, Drinij Bara."

"Aid me? But why? You're no friend of mine. What would you gain? You risk too much."

"As a fellow sorcerer, I thought I'd help you," Elric said.

"I thought you were that. But, in my land, sorcerers are not so friendly to one another—the opposite, in fact."

"I'll tell you the truth—we need your aid to halt the barbarian's bloody progress. We have a common enemy. If we can help you regain your soul, will you help?"

"Help—of course. All I do is plan the way I'll avenge myself. But for my sake be careful—if he suspects that you're here to aid me, he'll slay the cat and slay us, too."

"We'll try to bring the cat to you. Will that be what you need?"

"Yes. We must exchange blood, the cat and I, and my soul will then pass back into my own body."

"Very well, I'll try to—" Elric turned, hearing voices outside. "What's that?"

The sorcerer replied fearfully. "It must be Terarn Gashtek—he comes every night to taunt me."

"Where's the guard?" The barbarian's harsh voice came closer as he entered the little tent. "What's . . . ?" He saw Elric standing above the sorcerer.

His eyes were puzzled and wary. "What are you doing here, Westerner—and what have you done with the guard?"

"Guard?" said Elric, "I saw no guard. I was looking for my own tent and heard this cur cry out, so I entered. I was curious, anyway, to see such a great sorcerer clad in filthy rags and bound so."

Terarn Gashtek scowled. "Any more of such unwary curiosity my friend, and you'll be discovering what your own heart looks like. Now, get hence—we ride on in the morning."

Elric pretended to flinch and stumbled hurriedly from the tent.

A lone man in the livery of an Official Messenger of Karlaak goaded his horse southwards. The mount galloped over the crest of a hill and the messenger saw a village ahead. Hurriedly he rode into it, shouting at the first man he saw.

"Quickly, tell me—know you aught of Dyvim Slorm and his Imrryrian mercenaries? Have they passed this way?"

"Aye—a week ago. They went towards Rignariom by Vilmir's border, to offer their services to the Ilmioran Pretender."

"Were they mounted or on foot?"

"Both."

"Thanks, friend," cried the messenger behind him and galloped out of the village in the direction of Rignariom.

The messenger from Karlaak rode through the night—rode along a recently made trail. A large force had passed that way. He prayed that it had been Dyvim Slorm and his Imrryrian warriors.

In the sweet-smelling garden city of Karlaak, the atmosphere was tense as the citizens waited for news they knew they could not expect for some time. They were relying on both Elric and on the messenger. If only one were successful, there would be no hope for them. Both had to be successful. Both.

3

The tumbling sound of moving men cut through the weeping morning and the hungry voice of Terarn Gashtek lashed at them to hurry.

Slaves packed up his tent and threw it into a wagon. He rode forward and wrenched his tall war-lance from the soft earth, wheeled his horse and rode westwards, his captains, Elric and Moonglum among them, behind him.

Speaking the Western tongue, Elric and Moonglum debated their problem. The barbarian was expecting them to lead him to his prey, his outriders were covering wide distances so that it would be impossible to lead him past a settlement. They were in a quandary for it would be disgraceful to sacrifice another township to give Karlaak a few days' grace, yet . . .

A little later two whooping outriders came galloping up to Terarn Gashtek.

"A town, lord! A small one and easy to take!"

"At last—this will do to test our blades and see how easy Western flesh is to pierce. Then we'll aim at a bigger target." He turned to Elric: "Do you know this town?"

"Where does it lie?" asked Elric thickly.

"A dozen miles to the south-west," replied the outrider.

In spite of the fact that the town was doomed, Elric felt almost relieved. They spoke of the town of Gorjhan.

"I know it," he said.

Cavim the Saddler, riding to deliver a new set of horse furniture to an outlying farm, saw the distant riders, their bright helmets caught by a sudden beam of sunlight. That the riders came from off the Weeping Waste was undoubtable—and he recognised menace in their massed progress.

He turned his mount about and rode with the speed of fear, back the way he had come to the town of Gorjhan.

The flat, hard mud of the street trembled beneath the thudding hoofs of Cavim's horse and his high, excited shout knifed through shuttered windows.

"*Raiders come! 'Ware the raiders!*"

Within a quarter of an hour, the head-men of the town had met in hasty conference and debated whether to run or to fight. The older men advised their neighbours to flee the raiders, other younger men preferred to stay ready, armed to meet a possible attack. Some argued that their town was too poor to attract any raider.

The townspeople of Gorjhan debated and quarrelled and the first wave of raiders came screaming to their walls.

With the realisation that there was no time for further argument came the realisation of their doom, and they ran to the ramparts with their pitiful weapons.

Terarn Gashtek roared through the milling barbarians who churned the mud around Gorjhan: "Let's waste no time in siege. Fetch the sorcerer!"

They dragged Drinij Bara forward. From his garments, Terarn Gashtek produced the small black-and-white cat and held an iron blade at its throat.

"Work your spell, sorcerer, and tumble the walls quickly."

The sorcerer scowled, his eyes seeking Elric, but the albino averted his own eyes and turned his horse away.

The sorcerer produced a handful of powder from his belt pouch and hurled it into the air where it became first a gas, then a flickering ball of flame and finally a face, a dreadful unhuman face, formed in the flame.

"Dag-Gadden the Destroyer," intoned Drinij Bara, "you are sworn to our ancient pact—will you obey me?"

"I must, therefore I will. What do you command?"

"That you obliterate the walls of this town and so leave the men inside naked, like crabs without their shells."

"My pleasure is to destroy and destroy I shall." The flaming face faded, altered, shrieked a searing course upward and became a blossoming scarlet canopy which hid the sky.

Then it swept down over the town and, in the instant of its passing, the walls of Gorjhan groaned, crumbled and vanished.

Elric shuddered—if Dag-Gadden came to Karlaak, such would be their fate.

Triumphant, the barbarian battlemongers swept into the defenceless town.

Careful to take no part in the massacre, Elric and Moonglum were also helpless to aid the slaughtered townspeople. The sight of the senseless, savage bloodshed around them enervated them. They ducked into a small house which seemed so far untouched by the pillaging barbarians. Inside they found three cowering children huddled around an older girl who clutched an old scythe in her soft hands. Shaking with fear, she prepared to stand them off.

"Do not waste our time, girl," Elric said, "or you'll be wasting your lives. Does this house have a loft?"

She nodded.

"Then get to it quickly. We'll make sure you're unharmed."

They stayed in the house, hating to observe the slaughter-madness which had come upon the howling barbarians. They heard the dreadful sounds of carnage and smelled the stench of dead flesh and running blood.

A barbarian, covered in blood which was not his own, dragged a woman into the house by her hair. She made no attempt to resist, her face stunned by the horror she had witnessed.

Elric growled: "Find another nest, hawk—we've made this our own."

The man said: "There's room enough here for what I want."

Then, at last, Elric's clenched muscles reacted almost in spite of him. His right hand swung over to his left hip and the long fingers locked around Stormbringer's black hilt. The blade leapt from the scabbard as Elric stepped forward and, his crimson eyes blazing his sickened hatred, he smashed his sword down through the man's body. Unnecessarily, he clove again, hacking the barbarian in two. The woman remained where she lay, conscious but unmoving.

Elric picked up her inert body and passed it gently to Moonglum. "Take her upstairs with the others," he said brusquely.

The barbarians had begun to fire part of the town, their slaying all but done. Now they looted. Elric stepped out of the doorway.

There was precious little for them to loot but, still hungry for violence, they spent their energy on smashing inanimate things and setting fire to the broken, pillaged dwellings.

Stormbringer dangled loosely in Elric's hand as he looked at the blazing town. His face was a mask of shadow and frisking light as the fire threw up still longer tongues of flames to the misty sky.

Around him, barbarians squabbled over the pitiful booty; and occasionally a woman's scream cut above the other sounds, intermingled with rough shouts and the clash of metal.

Then he heard voices which were pitched differently to those in the immediate vicinity. The accents of the reavers mingled with a new tone—a whining, pleading tone. A group led by Terarn Gashtek came into view through the smoke.

Terarn Gashtek held something bloody in his hand—a human hand, severed at the wrist—and behind him swaggered several of his captains holding a naked old man between them. Blood ran over his body and gushed from his ruined arm, spurting sluggishly.

Terarn Gashtek frowned when he saw Elric. Then he shouted: "Now, Westerner, you shall see how we placate our gods with better gifts than meal and sour milk as this swine once did. He'll soon be dancing a pretty measure, I'll warrant—won't you, Lord Priest?"

The whining note went out of the old man's voice then and he stared with fever-bright eyes at Elric. His voice rose to a frenzied and high-pitched shriek which was curiously repellent.

"You dogs can howl over me!" he spat, "but Mirath and T'aargano will be revenged for the ruin of their priest and their temple—you have brought flame here and you shall die by flame." He pointed the bleeding stump of his arm at Elric—"And you—you are a traitor and have been one in many causes, I can see it written in you. Though now . . . You are—" the priest drew breath . . .

Elric licked his lips.

"I am what I am," he said, "and you are nothing but an old man soon to die. Your gods cannot harm us, for we do not pay them any respect. I'll listen no more to your senile meanderings!"

There was in the old priest's face all the knowledge of his past torment and the torment which was to come. He seemed to consider this and then was silent.

"Save your breath for screaming," said Terarn Gashtek to the uncomprehending priest.

And then Elric said: "It's bad luck to kill a priest, Flame Bringer!"

"You seem weak of stomach, my friend. His sacrifice to our own gods will bring us good luck, fear not."

Elric turned away. As he entered the house again, a wild shriek of agony seared out of the night and the laughter which followed was not pleasant.

Later, as the still-burning houses lit the night, Elric and Moonglum, carrying heavy sacks on their shoulders, clasping a woman each, moved with a simulation of drunkenness to the edge of the camp. Moonglum left the sacks and the women with Elric and went back, returning soon with three horses.

They opened the sacks to allow the children to climb out and watched the silent women mount the horses, aiding the children to clamber up.

Then they galloped away.

"Now," said Elric savagely, "we must work our plan tonight, whether the messenger reached Dyvim Slorm or not. I could not bear to witness another such sword-quenching."

Terarn Gashtek had drunk himself insensible. He lay sprawled in an upper room of one of the unburned houses.

Elric and Moonglum crept towards him. While Elric watched to see that he was undisturbed, Moonglum knelt beside the barbarian leader and, light-fingered, cautiously reached inside the man's garments. He smiled in self-approval as he lifted out the squirming cat and replaced it with a stuffed rabbitskin he had earlier prepared for the purpose. Holding the animal tight, he arose and nodded to Elric. Together, warily, they left the house and made their way through the chaos of the camp.

"I ascertained that Drinij Bara lies in the large wagon," Elric told his friend. "Quickly, now, the main danger's over."

Moonglum said: "When the cat and Drinij Bara have exchanged blood and the sorcerer's soul is back in his body—what then, Elric?"

"Together, our powers may serve at least to hold the barbarians back, but—" he broke off as a large group of warriors came weaving towards them.

"It's the Westerner and his little friend," laughed one. "Where are you off to, comrades?"

Elric sensed their mood. The slaughter of the day had not completely satiated their bloodlust. They were looking for trouble.

"Nowhere in particular," he replied. The barbarians lurched around them, encircling them.

"We've heard much of your straight blade, stranger," grinned their spokesman, "and I'd a mind to test it against a real weapon." He grabbed his own scimitar out of his belt. "What do you say?"

"I'd spare you that," said Elric coolly.

"You are generous—but I'd rather you accepted my invitation."

"Let us pass," said Moonglum.

The barbarians' faces hardened. "Speak you so to the conquerors of the world?" said the leader.

Moonglum took a step back and drew his sword, the cat squirming in his left hand.

"We'd best get this done," said Elric to his friend. He tugged his runeblade from its scabbard. The sword sang a soft and mocking tune and the barbarians heard it. They were disconcerted.

"Well?" said Elric, holding the half-sentient blade out.

The barbarian who had challenged him looked uncertain of what to do. Then he forced himself to shout: "Clean iron can withstand any sorcery," and launched himself forward.

Elric, grateful for the chance to take further vengeance, blocked his swing, forced the scimitar back and aimed a blow which sliced the man's torso just above the hip. The barbarian screamed and died. Moonglum, dealing with a couple more, killed one but another came in swiftly and his sweeping sword sliced the little Eastlander's left shoulder. He howled—and dropped the cat. Elric stepped in, slew Moonglum's opponent, Stormbringer wailing a triumphant dirge. The rest of the barbarians turned and ran off.

"How bad is your wound?" gasped Elric, but Moonglum was on his knees staring through the gloom.

"Quick, Elric—can you see the cat? I dropped it in the struggle. If we lose it—we too are lost."

Frantically, they began to hunt through the camp.

But they were unsuccessful, for the cat, with the dexterity of its kind, had wriggled free of its bindings and hidden itself.

A few moments later they heard the sounds of uproar coming from the house which Terarn Gashtek had commandeered.

"He's discovered that the cat's been stolen!" exclaimed Moonglum. "What do we do now?"

"I don't know—keep searching and hope he does not suspect us."

They continued to hunt, but with no result. While they searched, several barbarians came up to them. One of them said:

"Our leader wishes to speak with you."

"Why?"

"He'll inform you of that. Come on."

Reluctantly, they went with the barbarians to be confronted by a raging Terarn Gashtek. He clutched the stuffed rabbitskin in one clawlike hand and his face was warped with fury.

"My hold over the sorcerer has been stolen from me," he roared. "What do you know of it?"

"I don't understand," said Elric.

"The cat is missing—I found this rag in its place. You were caught talking to Drinij Bara recently, I think you were responsible."

"We know nothing of this," said Moonglum.

Terarn Gashtek growled: "The camp's in disorder, it will take a day to reorganise my men—once loosed like this they will obey no-one. But when I've restored order, I shall question the whole camp. If you tell the truth, then you will be released, but meanwhile you will be given all the time you need to speak with the sorcerer." He jerked his head. "Take them away, disarm them, bind them and throw them in Drinij Bara's kennel."

As they were led away, Elric muttered: "We must escape and find that cat, but meanwhile we need not waste this opportunity to confer with Drinij Bara."

Drinij Bara said in the darkness: "No, Brother Sorcerer, I will not aid you. I will risk nothing until the cat and I are united."

"But Terarn Gashtek cannot threaten you any more."

"What if he recaptures the cat—what then?"

Elric was silent. He shifted his bound body uncomfortably on the hard boards of the wagon. He was about to continue his attempts at persuasion when the awning was thrown aside and he saw another trussed figure thrown towards them. Through the blackness he said in the Eastern tongue: "Who are you?"

The man replied in the language of the West: "I do not understand you."

"Are you, then, a Westerner?" asked Elric in the common speech.

"Yes—I am an Official Messenger from Karlaak. I was captured by these odorous jackals as I returned to the city."

"What? Are you the man we sent to Dyvim Slorm, my kinsman? I am Elric of Melniboné."

"My lord, are we all, then, prisoners? Oh, gods—Karlaak is truly lost."

"Did you get to Dyvim Slorm?"

"Aye—I caught up with him and his band. Luckily they were nearer to Karlaak than we suspected."

"And what was his answer to my request?"

"He said that a few young ones might be ready, but even with sorcery to aid him it would take some time to get to the Dragon Isle. There is a chance."

"A chance is all we need—but it will be no good unless we accomplish the rest of our plan. Somehow Drinij Bara's soul must be regained so that Terarn Gashtek cannot force him to defend the barbarians. There is one idea I have—a memory of an ancient kinship that we of Melniboné had for a being called Meerclar. Thank the gods that I discovered those drugs in Troos and I still have my strength. Now, I must call my sword to me."

He closed his eyes and allowed his mind and body first to relax completely and then concentrate on one single thing—the sword Stormbringer.

For years the evil symbiosis had existed between man and sword and the old attachments lingered.

He cried: "Stormbringer! Stormbringer, unite with your brother! Come, sweet runeblade, come hell-forged kinslayer, your master needs thee . . ."

Outside, it seemed that a wailing wind had suddenly sprung up. Elric heard shouts of fear and a whistling sound. Then the covering of the wagon was sliced apart to let in the starlight and the moaning blade quivered in the air over his head. He struggled upwards, already feeling nauseated at what he was about to do, but he was reconciled that he was not, this time, guided by self-interest but by the necessity to save the world from the barbarian menace.

"Give me thy strength, my sword," he groaned as his bound hands grasped the hilt. "Give me thy strength and let us hope it is for the last time."

The blade writhed in his hands and he felt an awful sensation as its power, the power stolen vampirelike, from a hundred brave men, flowed into his shuddering body.

He became possessed of a peculiar strength which was not by any means wholly physical. His white face twisted as he concentrated on controlling the new power and the blade, both of which threatened to possess him entirely. He snapped his bonds and stood up.

Barbarians were even now running towards the wagon. Swiftly he cut the leather ropes binding the others and, unconscious of the nearing warriors, called a different name.

He spoke a new tongue, an alien tongue which normally he could not remember. It was a language taught to the Sorcerer Kings of Melniboné, Elric's ancestors, even before the building of Imrryr, the Dreaming City, over ten thousand years previously.

"Meerclar of the Cats, it is I, your kinsman, Elric of Melniboné, last of the line that made vows of friendship with you and your people. Do you hear me, Lord of the Cats?"

Far beyond the Earth, dwelling within a world set apart from the physical laws of space and time which governed the planet, glowing in a deep warmth of blue and amber, a manlike creature stretched itself and yawned, displaying tiny, pointed teeth. It pressed its head languidly against its furry shoulder—and listened.

The voice it heard was not that of one of its people, the kind he loved and protected. But he recognised the language. He smiled to himself as remembrance came and he felt the pleasant sensation of fellowship. He remembered a race which, unlike other humans (whom he disdained), had shared his qualities—a race which, like him, loved pleasure, cruelty and sophistication for its own sake. The race of Melnibonéans.

Meerclar, Lord of the Cats, Protector of the Feline Kind, projected himself gracefully towards the source of the voice.

"How may I aid thee?" he purred.

"We seek one of your folk, Meerclar, who is somewhere close to here."

"Yes, I sense him. What do you want of him?"

"Nothing which is his—but he has two souls, one of them not his own."

"That is so—his name is Fiarshern of the great family of Trrrechoww. I will call him. He will come to me."

MICHAEL MOORCOCK

Outside, the barbarians were striving to conquer their fear of the supernatural events taking place in the wagon. Terarn Gashtek cursed them: "There are five hundred thousand of us and a few of them. Take them now!"

His warriors began to move cautiously forward.

Fiarshern, the cat, heard a voice which it knew instinctively to be that of one which it would be foolish to disobey. It ran swiftly towards the source of that voice.

"Look—the cat—there it is. Seize it quickly."

Two of Terarn Gashtek's men jumped forward to do his bidding, but the little cat eluded them and leapt lightly into the wagon.

"*Give the human back its soul, Fiarshern,*" said Meerclar softly. The cat moved towards its human master and dug its delicate teeth into the sorcerer's veins.

A moment later Drinij Bara laughed wildly. "My soul is mine again. Thank you, great Cat Lord. Let me repay you!"

"*There is no need,*" smiled Meerclar mockingly, "*and, anyway, I perceive that your soul is already bartered. Goodbye, Elric of Melniboné. I was pleased to answer your call, though I see that you no longer follow the ancient pursuits of your fathers. Still, for the sake of old loyalties I do not begrudge you this service. Farewell, I go back to a warmer place than this inhospitable one.*"

The Lord of the Cats faded and returned to the world of blue and amber warmth where he once more resumed his interrupted sleep.

"Come, Brother Sorcerer," cried Drinij Bara exultantly. "Let us take the vengeance which is ours."

He and Elric sprang from the wagon, but the two others were not quite so quick to respond.

Terarn Gashtek and his men confronted them. Many had bows with long arrows fitted to them.

"Shoot them down swiftly," yelled the Flame Bringer. "Shoot them now before they have time to summon further demons!"

A shower of arrows whistled towards them. Drinij Bara smiled, spoke a

* 548 *

few words as he moved his hands almost carelessly. The arrows stopped in mid-flight, turned back and each uncannily found the throat of the man who had shot it. Terarn Gashtek gasped and wheeled back, pushing past his men and, as he retreated, shouted for them to attack the four.

Driven by the knowledge that if they fled they would be doomed, the great mass of barbarians closed in.

Dawn was bringing light to the cloud-ripped sky as Moonglum looked upwards. "Look, Elric," he shouted pointing.

"Only five," said the albino. "Only five—but perhaps enough."

He parried several lashing blades on his own sword and, although he was possessed of superhuman strength, all the power seemed to have left the sword so that it was only as useful as an ordinary blade. Still fighting, he relaxed his body and felt the power leave him, flowing back into Stormbringer.

Again the runeblade began to whine and thirstily sought the throats and hearts of the savage barbarians.

Drinij Bara had no sword, but he did not need one, he was using subtler means to defend himself. All around him were the gruesome results, boneless masses of flesh and sinew.

The two sorcerers and Moonglum and the messenger forced their way through the half-insane barbarians who were desperately attempting to overcome them. In the confusion it was impossible to work out a coherent plan of action. Moonglum and the messenger grabbed scimitars from the corpses of the barbarians and joined in the battle.

Eventually, they had reached the outer limits of the camp. A whole mass of barbarians had fled, spurring their mounts westwards. Then Elric saw Terarn Gashtek, holding a bow. He saw the Flame Bringer's intention and shouted a warning to his fellow sorcerer who had his back to the barbarian. Drinij Bara, yelling some disturbing incantation, half-turned, broke off, attempted to begin another spell, but the arrow pierced his eye.

He screamed: "*No!*"

Then he died.

Seeing his ally slain, Elric paused and stared at the sky and the great wheeling beasts which he recognised.

Dyvim Slorm, son of Elric's cousin Dyvim Tvar the Dragon Master, had brought the legendary dragons of Imrryr to aid his kinsman. But most of the huge beasts slept, and would sleep for another century—only five dragons had been aroused. As yet, Dyvim Slorm could do nothing for fear of harming Elric and his comrades.

Terarn Gashtek, too, had seen the magnificent beasts. His grandiose plans of conquest were already fading and, thwarted, he ran towards Elric.

"You white-faced filth," he howled, "you have been responsible for all this—and you will pay the Flame Bringer's price!"

Elric laughed as he brought up Stormbringer to protect himself from the incensed barbarian. He pointed to the sky: "These, too, can be called Flame Bringers, Terarn Gashtek—and are better named than thou!"

Then he plunged the evil blade full into Terarn Gashtek's body and the barbarian gave a choking moan as his soul was drawn from him.

"Destroyer, I may be, Elric of Melniboné," he gasped, "but my way was cleaner than yours. May you and all you hold dear be cursed for eternity!"

Elric laughed, but his voice shook slightly as he stared at the barbarian's corpse. "I've rid myself of such curses once before, my friend. Yours will have little effect, I think." He paused. "By Arioch, I hope I'm right. I'd thought my fate cleansed of doom and curses, but perhaps I was wrong . . ."

The huge horde of barbarians was nearly all mounted now and fleeing westwards. They had to be stopped for, at the pace they were travelling, they would soon reach Karlaak and only the gods knew what they would do when they got to the unprotected city.

Above him, he heard the flapping of thirty-foot wings and scented the familiar smell of the great flying reptiles which had pursued him years before when he had led a reaver fleet on the attack of his home city. Then he heard the curious notes of the Dragon Horn and saw that Dyvim Slorm was seated on the back of the leading beast, a long spearlike goad in his gauntleted right hand.

The dragon spiralled downward and its great bulk came to rest on the ground thirty feet away, its leathery wings folding back along its length. The Dragon Master waved to Elric.

"Greetings, King Elric, we barely managed to arrive in time I see."

"Time enough, kinsman," smiled Elric. "It is good to see the son of Dyvim Tvar again. I was afraid you might not answer my plea."

"Old scores were forgotten at the Battle of Bakshaan when my father Dyvim Tvar died aiding you in the siege of Nikorn's fortress. I regret only the younger beasts were ready to be awakened. You'll remember the others were used but a few years past."

"I remember," said Elric. "May I beg another favour, Dyvim Slorm?"

"What is that?"

"Let me ride the chief Phoorn. I am trained in the arts of the Dragon Master and have good reason for riding against the barbarians—we were forced to witness insensate carnage a while ago and may, perhaps, pay them back in their own coin."

Dyvim Slorm nodded and swung off his mount. The beast stirred restlessly and drew back the lips of its tapering snout to reveal teeth as thick as a man's arm, as long as a sword. Its forked tongue flickered and it turned its huge, cold eyes to regard Elric.

Elric sang to it in the old Melnibonéan speech, took the goad and the Dragon Horn from Dyvim Slorm and carefully climbed into the *skeffla'a* at the base of the dragon's neck. He placed his booted feet into the great silver stirrups.

"Now, fly, dragon brother," he sang, "up, up and have your venom ready."

He heard the snap of displaced air as the wings began to beat and then the great beast was clear of the ground and soaring upwards into the grey and brooding sky.

The other four dragons followed the first and, as he gained height, sounding specific notes on the horn to give them directions, he drew his sword from its scabbard.

Centuries before, Elric's ancestors had ridden their dragon steeds to conquer the whole of the Western World. There had been many more dragons in the Dragon Caves in those days. Now only a handful remained, and of those only the youngest had slept sufficiently long to be awakened.

High in the wintry sky climbed the huge reptiles and Elric's long white hair and stained black cloak flew behind him as he sang the exultant Song of the Phoorn and urged his charges westwards.

> Wild wind-horses soar the cloud-trails,
> Unholy horn doth sound its blast,
> You and we were first to conquer,
> You and we shall be the last!

Thoughts of love, of peace, of vengeance even were lost in that reckless sweeping across the glowering skies which hung over that ancient Age of the Young Kingdoms. Elric, archetypal, proud and disdainful in his knowledge that even his deficient blood was the blood of the Sorcerer Kings of Melniboné, became detached.

He had no loyalties then, no friends and, if evil possessed him, then it was a pure, brilliant evil, untainted by human drivings.

High soared the dragons until below them was the heaving black mass, marring the landscape, the fear-driven horde of barbarians who, in their ignorance, had sought to conquer the lands beloved of Elric of Melniboné.

"Ho, dragon brothers—loose your venom—burn—burn! And in your burning cleanse the world!"

Stormbringer joined in the wild shout and, diving, the Phoorn swept across the sky, down upon the crazed barbarians, shooting streams of combustible venom which water could not extinguish, and the stink of charred flesh drifted upwards through the smoke and flame so that the scene became a scene of hell—and proud Elric was a Lord of Demons reaping awful vengeance.

He did not gloat, for he had done only what was needed, that was all. He shouted no more but turned his dragon mount back and upward, sounding his horn and summoning the other reptiles to him. And as he climbed, the exultation left him and was replaced by cold horror.

I am still a Melnibonéan, he thought, and cannot rid myself of that whatever else I do. And, in my strength I am still weak, ready to use this cursed blade in any small emergency. With a shout of loathing, he flung the sword away, flung it into space. It screamed like a woman and went plummeting downwards towards the distant earth.

"There," he said, "it is done at last." Then, in calmer mood, he returned to where he had left his friends and guided his reptilian mount to the ground.

Dyvim Slorm said: "Where is the sword of your forefathers, King Elric?" But the albino did not answer, just thanked his kinsman for the loan of the Phoorn leader. Then they all remounted the dragons and flew back towards Karlaak to tell them the news.

Zarozinia saw her lord riding the first dragon and knew that Karlaak and the Western World were saved, the Eastern World avenged. His stance was proud but his face was grave as he went to meet her outside the city. She saw in him a return of an earlier sorrow which he had thought forgotten. She ran to him and he caught her in his arms, holding her close but saying nothing.

He bade farewell to Dyvim Slorm and his fellow Imrryrians and, with Moonglum and the messenger following at a distance, went into the city and thence to his house, impatient of the congratulations which the citizens showered upon him.

"What is it, my lord?" Zarozinia said as, with a sigh, he sprawled wearily upon the great bed. "Can speaking help?"

"I'm tired of swords and sorcery, Zarozinia, that is all. But at last I have rid myself once and for all of that hellblade which I had thought my destiny to carry always."

"Stormbringer you mean?"

"What else?"

She said nothing. She did not tell him, then, of the sword which, apparently of its own volition, had come screaming into Karlaak and passed into the armoury to hang, in its old place, in darkness there.

He closed his eyes and drew a long, sighing breath.

"Sleep well, my lord," she said softly. With tearful eyes and a sad mouth she lay herself down beside him.

She did not welcome the morning.

EPILOGUE

To Rescue Tanelorn . . .

*In which we learn of the further adventures of Rackhir
the Red Archer and other heroes and places Elric
has hitherto encountered only in what he chooses to
consider his dreams . . .*

Beyond the tall and ominous glass-green Forest of Troos, well to the north and
unheard of in Bakshaan, Elwher or any other city of the Young Kingdoms, on
the shifting shores of the Sighing Desert lay Tanelorn, a lonely, long-ago city,
loved by those it sheltered.

Tanelorn had a peculiar nature in that it welcomed and held the wanderer.
To its peaceful streets and low houses came the gaunt, the savage, the brutal-
ised, the tormented, and in Tanelorn they found rest.

Now, most of these troubled travellers who dwelt in peaceful Tanelorn
had thrown off earlier allegiances to the Lords of Chaos who, as gods, took
more than a mild interest in the affairs of men. It happened, therefore, that
these same lords grew to resent the unlikely city of Tanelorn and, not for the
first time, decided to act against it.

They instructed one of their number (more they could not, then, send)
Lord Narjhan, to journey to Nadsokor, the City of Beggars, which had an old
grudge against Tanelorn, and raise an army that would attack undefended

Tanelorn and destroy it and its inhabitants. So he did this, arming his ragged army and promising them many things.

Then, like a ferocious tide, did the beggar rabble set off to tear down Tanelorn and slay its residents. A great torrent of men and women in rags, on crutches, blind, maimed, but moving steadily, ominously, implacably northwards towards the Sighing Desert.

In Tanelorn dwelt the Red Archer, Rackhir, from the Eastlands beyond the Sighing Desert, beyond the Weeping Waste. Rackhir had been born a Warrior Priest, a servant of the Lords of Chaos, but had forsaken this life for the quieter pursuits of thievery and learning. A man with harsh features slashed from the bone of his skull, strong, fleshless nose, deep eye-cavities, a thin mouth and a thin beard. He wore a red skull-cap, decorated with a hawk's feather, a red jerkin, tight-fitting and belted at the waist, red breeks and red boots. It was as if all the blood in him had transferred itself to his gear and left him drained. He was happy, however, in Tanelorn, the city which made all such men happy, and felt he would die there if men died there. He did not know if they did.

One day he saw Brut of Lashmar, a great, blond-headed noble of shamed name, ride wearily, yet urgently, through the low wall-gate of the city of peace. Brut's silver harness and trappings were begrimed, his yellow cloak torn and his broad-brimmed hat battered. A small crowd collected around him as he rode into the city square and halted. Then he gave his news.

"Beggars from Nadsokor, many thousands, move against our Tanelorn," he said, "and they are led by Narjhan of Chaos."

Now, all the men in there were soldiers of some kind, good ones for the most part, and they were confident warriors, but few in number. A horde of beggars, led by such a being as Narjhan, could destroy Tanelorn, they knew.

"Should we, then, leave Tanelorn?" said Uroch of Nieva, a young, wasted man who had been a drunkard.

"We owe this city too much to desert her," Rackhir said. "We should defend her—for her sake and ours. There will never be such a city again."

Brut leaned forward in his saddle and said: "In principle, Red Archer, I am in agreement with you. But principle is not enough without deeds. How would you suggest we defend this low-walled city against siege and the powers of Chaos?"

"We should need help," Rackhir replied, "supernatural help if need be."

"Would the Grey Lords help us?" Zas the One-handed asked the question. He was an old, torn wanderer who had once gained a throne and lost it again.

"Aye—the Grey Lords!" Several voices chorused this hopefully.

"Who are the Grey Lords?" said Uroch, but no-one heard him.

"They are not inclined to aid anyone at all," Zas the One-handed pointed out, "but surely Tanelorn, coming as it does under neither the Forces of Law nor the Lords of Chaos, would be worth their while preserving. After all, they have no loyalties either."

"I'm for seeking the Grey Lords' aid," Brut nodded. "What of the rest of us?" There was general agreement, then silence when they realised that they knew of no means of contacting the mysterious and insouciant beings. At last Zas pointed this out.

Rackhir said: "I know a seer—a hermit who lives in the Sighing Desert. Perhaps he can help?"

"I think that, after all, we should not waste time looking for supernatural assistance against this beggar rabble," Uroch said. "Let us prepare, instead, to meet the attack with physical means."

"You forget," Brut said wearily, "that they are led by Narjhan of Chaos. He is not human and has the whole strength of Chaos behind him. We know that the Grey Lords are pledged neither to Law nor to Chaos but will sometimes help either side if the whim takes them. They are our only chance."

"Why not seek the aid of the forces of Law, sworn enemies of Chaos and mightier than the Grey Lords?" Uroch said.

"Because Tanelorn is a city owing allegiance to neither side. We are all of us men and women who have broken our pledge to Chaos but have made no new one to Law. The forces of Law, in matters of this kind, will help only those sworn to them. The Grey Lords only may protect us, if they would." So said Zas.

"I will go to find my seer," Rackhir the Red Archer said, "and if he knows how I may reach the Domain of the Grey Lords, then I'll continue straight on, for there is so little time. If I reach them and solicit their help you will soon know I have done so. If not, you must die in Tanelorn's defence and, if I live, I will join you in that last battle."

"Very well," Brut agreed, "go quickly, Red Archer. Let one of your own arrows be the measure of your speed."

And taking little with him save his bone bow and quiver of scarlet-fletched arrows, Rackhir set off for the Sighing Desert.

From Nadsokor, south-west through the land of Vilmir, even through the squalid country of Org which has in it the dreadful Forest of Troos, there was flame and black horror in the wake of the beggar horde, and insolent, disdainful of them though he led them, rode a being completely clad in black armour with a voice that rang hollow in the helm. People fled away at their approach and the land was made barren by their passing. Most knew what had happened, that the beggar citizens of Nadsokor had, contrary to their traditions of centuries, vomited from their city in a wild, menacing horde. Someone had armed them—someone had made them go northwards and westwards towards the Sighing Desert. But who was the one who led them? Ordinary folk did not know. And why did they head for the Sighing Desert? There was no city beyond Karlaak, which they had skirted, only the Sighing Desert—and beyond that the edge of the world. Was that their destination? Were they heading, lemminglike, to their destruction? Everyone hoped so, in their hate for the horrible horde.

Rackhir rode through the mournful wind of the Sighing Desert, his face and eyes protected against the particles of sand which flew about. He was thirsty and had been riding a day. Ahead of him at last were the rocks he sought.

He reached the rocks and called above the wind.

"Lamsar!"

The hermit came out in answer to Rackhir's shout. He was dressed in oiled leather to which sand clung. His beard, too, was encrusted with sand and his skin seemed to have taken on the colour and texture of the desert. He recognised Rackhir immediately, by his dress, beckoned him into the cave and disappeared back inside. Rackhir dismounted and led his horse to the cave entrance and went in.

Lamsar was seated on a smooth rock. "You are welcome, Red Archer," he said, "and I perceive by your manner that you wish information from me and that your mission is urgent."

"I seek the help of the Grey Lords, Lamsar," said Rackhir.

The old hermit smiled. It was as if a fissure had suddenly appeared in a rock. "To risk the journey through the Five Gates, your mission must be important. I will tell you how to reach the Grey Lords, but the road is a difficult one."

"I'm willing to take it," Rackhir replied, "for Tanelorn is threatened and the Grey Lords could help her."

"Then you must pass through the First Gate, which lies in our own dimension. I will help you find it."

"And what must I do then?"

"You must pass through all five gates. Each gateway leads to a realm which lies beyond and within our own dimension. In each realm you must speak with the dwellers there. Some are friendly to men, some are not, but all must answer your question: 'Where lies the next Gate?' though some may seek to stop you passing. The last gate leads to the Grey Lords' Domain."

"And the first gate?"

"That lies anywhere in this realm. I will find it for you now." Lamsar composed himself to meditate and Rackhir, who had expected some sort of gaudy miracle-working from the old man, was disappointed.

Several hours went by until Lamsar said: "The gate is outside. Memorise the following: If X is equal to the spirit of humanity, then the combination of the two must be of double power, therefore the spirit of humanity always contains the power to dominate itself."

"A strange equation," said Rackhir.

"Aye—but memorise it, meditate upon it and then we will leave."

"We—you as well?"

"I think so."

The hermit was old. Rackhir did not want him on the journey. But then he realised that the hermit's knowledge could be of use to him, so did not object. He thought upon the equation and, as he thought, his mind seemed to glitter and become diffused until he was in a strange trance and all his powers felt greater, both those of mind and body. The hermit got up and Rackhir followed him. They went out of the cave mouth but, instead of the Sighing Desert, there was a hazy cloud of blue shimmering light ahead and when they had passed through this, in a second, they found themselves in the foothills of a low mountain range and below them, in a valley, were villages. The villages were strangely laid out, all the houses in a wide circle about a huge amphitheatre containing, at its centre, a circular dais.

"It will be interesting to learn the reason why these villages are so arranged," Lamsar said, and they began to move down into the valley.

As they reached the bottom and came close to one of the villages, people came gaily out and danced joyfully towards them. They stopped in front of Rackhir and Lamsar and, jumping from foot to foot as he greeted them, the leader spoke.

"You are strangers, we can tell—and you are welcome to all we have, food, accommodation and entertainment."

The two men thanked them graciously and accompanied them back to the circular village. The amphitheatre was made of mud and seemed to have been stamped out, hollowed into the ground encompassed by the houses. The leader of the villagers took them to his house and offered them food.

"You have come to us at a Rest Time," he said, "but do not worry, things will soon commence again. My name is Yerleroo."

"We seek the next Gate," Lamsar said politely, "and our mission is urgent. You will forgive us if we do not stay long?"

"Come," said Yerleroo, "things are about to commence. You will see us at our best, and must join us."

All the villagers had assembled in the amphitheatre, surrounding the platform in the centre. Most of them were light-skinned and light-haired, gay and smiling, excited—but a few were evidently of a different race, dark, black-haired, and these were sullen.

Sensing something ominous in what he saw, Rackhir asked the question directly: "Where is the next Gate?"

Yerleroo hesitated, his mouth worked and then he smiled. "Where the winds meet," he said.

Rackhir declared angrily: "That's no answer."

"Yes it is," said Lamsar softly behind him. "A fair answer."

"Now we shall dance," Yerleroo said. "First you shall watch our dance and then you shall join in."

"Dance?" said Rackhir, wishing he had brought a sword, or at least a dagger.

"Yes—you will like it. Everyone likes it. You will find it will do you good."

"What if we do not wish to dance?"

"You must—it is for your own good, be assured."

"And he—" Rackhir pointed at one of the sullen men. "Does he enjoy it?"

"It is for his own good."

Yerleroo clapped his hands and at once the fair-haired people leapt into a frenetic, senseless dance. Some of them sang. The sullen people did not sing. After a little hesitation, they began to prance dully about, their frowning fea-

tures contrasting with their jerking bodies. Soon the whole village was dancing, whirling, singing a monotonous song.

Yerleroo flashed by, whirling. "Come, join in now."

"We had better leave," Lamsar said with a faint smile. They backed away.

Yerleroo saw them. "No—you must not leave—you must dance."

They turned and ran as fast as the old man could go. The dancing villagers
changed the direction of their dance and began to whirl menacingly towards
them in a horrible semblance of gaiety.

"There's nothing for it," Lamsar said and stood his ground, observing
them through ironic eyes. "The mountain gods must be invoked. A pity, for
sorcery wearies me. Let us hope their magic extends to this plane. *Gordar!*"

Words in an unusually harsh language issued from Lamsar's old mouth.
The whirling villagers came on.

Lamsar pointed at them.

The villagers became suddenly petrified and slowly, disturbingly, their
bodies caught in a hundred positions, turned to smooth, black basalt.

"It was for their own good," Lamsar smiled grimly. "Come, to the place
where the winds meet," and he took Rackhir there quite swiftly.

At the place where the winds met they found the second gateway, a column
of amber-coloured flame, shot through with streaks of green. They entered
it and, instantly, were in a world of dark seething colour. Above them was a
sky of murky red in which other colours shifted, agitated, changing. Ahead
of them lay a forest, dark, blue, black, heavy, mottled green, the tops of
its trees moving like a wild tide. It was a howling land of unnatural phe-
nomena.

Lamsar pursed his lips. "On this plane Chaos rules, we must get to the
next gate swiftly for obviously the Lords of Chaos will seek to stop us."

"Is it always like this?" Rackhir gasped.

"It is always boiling midnight—but the rest, it changes with the moods of
the lords. There are no rules at all."

They pressed on through the bounding, blossoming scenery as it erupted and changed around them. Once they saw a huge winged figure in the sky, smoky yellow and roughly man-shaped.

"Vezhan," Lamsar said, "let's hope he did not see us."

"Vezhan!" Rackhir whispered the name—for it was to Vezhan that he had once been loyal.

They crept on, uncertain of their direction or even of their speed in that disturbing land.

At length, they came to the shores of a peculiar ocean.

It was a grey, heaving, timeless sea, a mysterious sea which stretched into infinity. There could be no other shores beyond this rolling plain of water. No other lands or rivers or dark, cool woods, no other men or women or ships. It was a sea which led to nowhere. It was complete to itself—a sea.

Over this timeless ocean hovered a brooding ochre sun which cast moody shadows of black and green across the water, giving the whole scene something of the look of being enclosed in a vast cavern, for the sky above was gnarled and black with ancient clouds. And all the while the doom-carried crash of breakers, the lonely, fated monotony of the ever-rearing white-topped waves; the sound which portended neither death nor life nor war nor peace—simply existence and shifting inharmony. They could go no further.

"This has the air of our death about it," Rackhir said shivering.

The sea roared and tumbled, the sound of it increasing to a fury, daring them to go on towards it, welcoming them with wild temptation—offering them nothing but achievement—the achievement of death.

Lamsar said: "It is not my fate wholly to perish." But then they were running back towards the forest, feeling that the strange sea was pouring up the beach towards them. They looked back and saw that it had gone no further, that the breakers were less wild, the sea more calm. Lamsar was a little way behind Rackhir.

The Red Archer gripped his hand and hauled him towards him as if he had rescued the old man from a whirlpool. They remained there, mesmerised, for a long time, while the sea called to them and the wind was a cold caress on their flesh.

In the bleak brightness of the alien shore, under a sun which gave no heat, their bodies shone like stars in the night and they turned towards the forest, quietly.

"Are we trapped, then, in this realm of Chaos?" Rackhir said at length. "If we meet someone, they will offer us harm—how can we ask our question?"

Then there emerged from the huge forest a great figure, naked and gnarled like the trunk of a tree, green as lime, but the face was jovial.

"Greetings, unhappy renegades," it said.

"Where is the next Gate?" said Lamsar quickly.

"You almost entered it, but turned away," laughed the giant. "That sea does not exist—it is there to stop travellers from passing through the gate."

"It exists here, in the Realm of Chaos," Rackhir said thickly.

"You could say so—but what exists in Chaos save the disorders of the minds of gods gone mad?"

Rackhir had strung his bone bow and fitted an arrow to the string, but he did it in the knowledge of his own hopelessness.

"Do not shoot the arrow," said Lamsar softly. "Not yet." And he stared at the arrow and muttered.

The giant advanced carelessly towards them, unhurried. "It will please me to exact the price of your crimes from you," it said, "for I am Hionhurn the Executioner. You will find your death pleasant—but your fate unbearable." And he came closer, his clawed hands outstretched.

"Shoot!" croaked Lamsar and Rackhir brought the bowstring to his cheek, pulled it back with might and released the arrow at the giant's heart. "Run!" cried Lamsar, and in spite of their forebodings they ran back down the shore towards the frightful sea. They heard the giant groan behind them as they reached the edge of the sea and, instead of running into water, found themselves in a range of stark mountains.

"No mortal arrow could have delayed him," Rackhir said. "How did you stop him?"

"I used an old charm—the Charm of Justice, which, when applied to any weapon, makes it strike at the unjust."

"But why did it hurt Hionhurn, an immortal?" Rackhir asked.

"There is no justice in the world of Chaos—something constant and inflexible, whatever its nature, must harm any servant of the Lords of Chaos."

"We have passed through the Third Gate," Rackhir said, unstringing his bow, "and have the fourth and fifth to find. Two dangers have been avoided—but what new ones will we encounter now?"

"Who knows?" said Lamsar, and they walked on through the rocky mountain pass and entered a forest that was cool, even though the sun had reached its zenith and was glaring down through parts of the thick foliage. There was an air of ancient calm about the place. They heard unfamiliar bird calls and saw tiny golden birds which were also new to them.

"There is something calm and peaceful about this place—I almost distrust it," Rackhir said, but Lamsar pointed ahead silently.

Rackhir saw a large domed building, magnificent in marble and blue mosaic. It stood in a clearing of yellow grass and the marble caught the sun, flashing like fire.

They neared the domed construction and saw that it was supported by big marble columns set into a platform of milky jade. In the centre of the platform, a stairway of bluestone curved upwards and disappeared into a circular aperture. There were wide windows set into the sides of the raised building but they could not see inside. There were no inhabitants visible and it would have seemed strange to the pair if there had been. They crossed the yellow glade and stepped onto the jade platform. It was warm, as if it had been exposed to the sun. They almost slipped on the smooth stone.

They reached the blue steps and mounted them, staring upwards, but they could still see nothing. They did not attempt to ask themselves why they were so assuredly invading the building; it seemed quite natural that they should do what they were doing. There was no alternative. There was an air of familiarity about the place. Rackhir felt it but did not know why. Inside was a cool, shadowy hall, a blend of soft darkness and bright sunlight which entered by the windows. The floor was pearl-pink and the ceiling deep scarlet. The hall reminded Rackhir of a womb.

Partially hidden by deep shadow was a small doorway and beyond it, steps. Rackhir looked questioningly at Lamsar. "Do we proceed in our exploration?"

"We must—to have our question answered, if possible."

They climbed the steps and found themselves in a smaller hall similar to the one beneath them. This hall, however, was furnished with twelve wide thrones placed in a semicircle in the centre. Against the wall, near the door, were several chairs, upholstered in purple fabric. The thrones were of gold, decorated with fine silver, padded with white cloth.

A door behind the thrones opened and a tall, fragile-looking man appeared, followed by others whose faces were almost identical. Only their robes were noticeably different. Their faces were pale, almost white, their noses straight, their lips thin but not cruel. Their eyes were unhuman—green-flecked eyes which stared outwards with sad composure. The leader of the tall men looked at Rackhir and Lamsar. He nodded and waved a pale, long-fingered hand gracefully. "Welcome," he said. His voice was high and frail, like a girl's, but beautiful in its modulation. The other eleven men seated themselves in the thrones but the first man, who had spoken, remained standing. "Sit down, please," he said.

Rackhir and Lamsar sat down on two of the purple chairs.

"How did you come here?" enquired the man.

"Through the gates from Chaos," Lamsar replied.

"And were you seeking our realm?"

"No—we travel towards the Domain of the Grey Lords."

"I thought so, for your people rarely visit us save by accident."

"Where are we?" asked Rackhir as the man seated himself in the remaining throne.

"In a place beyond time. Once our land was part of the Earth you know, but in the dim past it became separated from it. Our bodies, unlike yours, are immortal. We choose this, but we are not bound to our flesh, as you are."

"I don't understand," frowned Rackhir. "What are you saying?"

"I have said what I can in the simplest terms understandable to you. If you do not know what I say then I can explain no further. We are called the Guardians—though we guard nothing. We are warriors, but we fight nothing."

"What else do you do?" enquired Rackhir.

"We exist. You will want to know where the next gateway lies?"

"Yes."

"Refresh yourselves here, and then we shall show you the gateway."

"What is your function?" asked Rackhir.

"To function," said the man.

"You are unhuman!"

"We are human. *You* spend your lives chasing that which is within you and that which you can find in any other human being—but you will not look for it there—you must follow more glamorous paths—to waste your time in order to discover that you wasted your time. I am glad that we are no longer like you— but I wish that it were lawful to help you further. This, however, we may not do."

"Ours is no meaningless quest," said Lamsar quietly, with respect. "We go to rescue Tanelorn."

"Tanelorn?" the man said softly. "Does Tanelorn still remain?"

"Aye," said Rackhir, "and shelters tired men who are grateful for the rest she offers." Now he realised why the building had been familiar—it had the same quality, but intensified, as Tanelorn.

"Tanelorn was the last of our cities," said the Guardian. "Forgive us for judging you—most of the travellers who pass through this plane are searchers, restless, with no real purpose, only excuses, imaginary reasons for journeying on. You must love Tanelorn to brave the dangers of the gateways?"

"We do," said Rackhir, "and I am grateful that you built her."

"We built her for ourselves, but it is good that others have used her well—and she them."

"Will you help us?" Rackhir said. "For Tanelorn?"

"We cannot—it is not lawful. Now, refresh yourselves and be welcome."

The two travellers were given foods, both soft and brittle, sweet and sour, and drink which seemed to enter the pores of their skin as they quaffed it, and then the Guardian said: "We have caused a road to be made. Follow it and enter the next realm. But we warn you, it is the most dangerous of all."

And they set off down the road that the Guardians had caused to be made and passed through the fourth gateway into a dreadful realm—the Realm of Law.

Nothing shone in the grey-lit sky, nothing moved, nothing marred the grey.

Nothing interrupted the bleak grey plain stretching on all sides of them, for ever. There was no horizon. It was a bright, clean wasteland. But there was a sense about the air, a presence of something past, something which had gone but left a faint aura of its passing.

"What dangers could be here?" said Rackhir shuddering, "here where there is nothing?"

"The danger of the loneliest madness," Lamsar replied. Their voices were swallowed in the grey expanse.

"When the Earth was very young," Lamsar continued, his words trailing away across the wilderness, "things were like this—but there were seas, there were seas. Here there is nothing."

"You are wrong," Rackhir said with a faint smile. "I have thought—here there is Law."

"That is true—but what is Law without something to decide between? Here is Law—bereft of justice."

They walked on, all about them an air of something intangible that had once been tangible. On they walked through this barren world of Absolute Law.

Eventually, Rackhir spied something. Something that flickered, faded, appeared again until, as they neared it, they saw that it was a man. His great head was noble, firm, and his body was massively built, but the face was twisted in a tortured frown and he did not see them as they approached him.

They stopped before him and Lamsar coughed to attract his attention. The man turned that great head and regarded them abstractedly, the frown clearing at length, to be replaced by a calmer, thoughtful expression.

"Who are you?" asked Rackhir.

The man sighed. "Not yet," he said, "not yet, it seems. More phantoms."

"Are *we* the phantoms?" smiled Rackhir. "That seems to be more your own nature." He watched as the man began slowly to fade again, his form less definite, melting. The body seemed to make a great heave, like a salmon attempting to leap a dam, then it was back again in a more solid form.

"I had thought myself rid of all that was superfluous, save my own obstinate shape," the man said tiredly, "but here is something, back again. Is my reason failing—is my logic no longer what it was?"

"Do not fear," said Rackhir, "we are material beings."

"That is *what* I feared. For an eternity I have been stripping away the layers of unreality which obscure the truth. I have almost succeeded in the final act, and now you begin to creep back. My mind is not what it was, I think."

"Perhaps you worry lest we do not exist?" Lamsar said slowly, with a clever smile.

"You know that is not so—you do not exist, just as I do not exist." The frown returned, the features twisted, the body began, again, to fade, only to resume, once more, its earlier nature. The man sighed. "Even to reply to you is betraying myself, but I suppose a little relaxation will serve to rest my powers and equip me for the final effort of will which will bring me to the ultimate truth—the truth of non-being."

"But non-being involves non-thought, non-will, non-action," Lamsar said. "Surely you would not submit yourself to such a fate?"

"There is no such thing as self. I am the only reasoning thing in creation—I am almost pure reason. A little more effort and I shall be what I desire to be—the one truth in this non-existent universe. That requires first ridding myself of anything extraneous around me—such as yourselves—and then making the final plunge into the only reality."

"What is that?"

"The state of absolute nothingness where there is nothing to disturb the order of things because there is no order of things."

"Scarcely a constructive ambition," Rackhir said.

"Construction is a meaningless word—like all words, like all so-called existence. Everything means nothing—that is the only truth."

"But what of this realm? Barren as it is, it still has light and firm rock. You have not succeeded in reasoning that out of existence," Lamsar said.

"That will cease when I cease," the man said slowly, "just as you will cease to be. Then there can be nothing but nothing and Law will reign unchallenged."

"But Law cannot reign—it will not exist either, according to your logic."

"You are wrong—nothingness is the Law. Nothingness is the object of Law. Law is the way to its ultimate state, the state of non-being."

"Well," said Lamsar musingly, "then you had better tell us where we may find the next Gate."

"There is no gate."

"If there were, where would we find it?" Rackhir said.

"If a gate existed, and it does not, it would have been inside the mountain, close to what was once called the Sea of Peace."

"And where was that?" Rackhir asked, conscious now of their terrible predicament. There were no landmarks, no sun, no stars—nothing by which they could determine direction.

"Close to the Mountain of Severity."

"Which way do you go?" Lamsar enquired of the man.

"Out—beyond—to nowhere."

"And where, if you succeed in your object, will we be consigned?"

"To some other nowhere. I cannot truthfully answer. But since you have never existed in reality, therefore you can go on to no non-reality. Only I am real—and I do not exist."

"We are getting nowhere," said Rackhir with a smirk which changed to a frown.

"It is only my mind which holds the non-reality at bay," the man said, "and I must concentrate or else it will all come flooding back and I shall have to start from the beginning again. In the beginning, there was everything—Chaos. I *created* nothing."

With resignation, Rackhir strung his bow, fitted an arrow to the string and aimed at the frowning man.

"You wish for non-being?" he said.

"I have told you so." Rackhir's arrow pierced his heart, his body faded, became solid and slumped to the grass as mountains, forests and rivers appeared around them. It was still a peaceful, well-ordered realm and Rackhir and Lamsar, as they strode on in search of the Mountain of Severity, savoured it. There seemed to be no animal life here and they talked, in puzzled terms, about the man they had been forced to kill, until, at length, they reached a great smooth pyramid which seemed, though it was of natural origin, to have been carved into this form. They walked around its base until they discovered an opening.

There could be no doubt that this was the Mountain of Severity, and a calm ocean lay some distance away. They went into the opening and emerged into a delicate landscape. They were now through the last gateway and in the Domain of the Grey Lords.

There were trees like stiffened spiderwebs.

Here and there were blue pools, shallow, with shining water and graceful rocks balanced in them and around their shores. Above them and beyond them the light hills swept away towards a pastel yellow horizon which was tinted with red, orange and blue, deep blue.

They felt overlarge, clumsy, like crude, gross giants treading on the fine, short grass. They felt as if they were destroying the sanctity of the place.

Then they saw a girl come walking towards them.

She stopped as they came closer to her. She was dressed in loose black robes which flowed about her as if in a wind, but there was no wind. Her face was pale and pointed, her black eyes large and enigmatic. At her long throat was a jewel.

"Sorana," said Rackhir thickly, "you died."

"I disappeared," said she, "and this is where I came. I was told that you would come to this place and decided that I would meet you."

"But this is the Domain of the Grey Lords—and you serve Chaos."

"I do—but many are welcome at the Grey Lords' Court, whether they be of Law, Chaos or neither. Come, I will escort you there."

Bewildered, now, Rackhir let her lead the way across the strange terrain and Lamsar followed him.

Sorana and Rackhir had been lovers once, in Yeshpotoom-Kahlai, the Unholy Fortress, where evil blossomed and was beautiful. Sorana, sorceress, adventuress, was without conscience but had high regard for the Red Archer since he had come to Yeshpotoom-Kahlai one evening, covered in his own blood, survivor of a bizarre battle between the Knights of Tumbru and Loheb Bakra's brigand-engineers. Seven years ago, that had been, and he had heard her scream when the Blue Assassins had crept into the Unholy Fortress, pledged to murder evil-makers. Even then he had been in the process of hurriedly leaving Yeshpotoom-Kahlai and had considered it unwise to investigate what was obviously a death-scream. Now she was here—and if she was here, then it was for a strong reason and for her own convenience. On the other hand, it was in her interests to serve Chaos and he must be suspicious of her.

Ahead of them now they saw many great tents of shimmering grey which, in the light, seemed composed of all colours. People moved slowly among the tents and there was an air of leisure about the place.

"Here," Sorana said, smiling at him and taking his hand, "the Grey Lords hold impermanent court. They wander about their land and have few artefacts and only temporary houses which you see. They'll make you welcome if you interest them."

"But will they help us?"

"You must ask them."

"You are pledged to Eequor of Chaos," Rackhir observed, "and must aid her against us, is that not so?"

"Here," she smiled, "is a truce. I can only inform Chaos of what I learn of your plans and, if the Grey Lords aid you, must tell them how, if I can find out."

"You are frank, Sorana."

"Here there are subtler hypocrisies—and the subtlest lie of all is the full truth," she said, as they entered the area of tall tents and made their way towards a certain one.

In a different realm of the Earth, the huge horde careered across the grasslands of the North, screaming and singing behind the black-armoured horseman, their leader. Nearer and nearer they came to lonely Tanelorn, their motley weapons shining through the evening mists. Like a boiling tidal wave of insensate flesh, the mob drove on, hysterical with the hate for Tanelorn which Narjhan had placed in their thin hearts. Thieves, murderers, jackals, scavengers—a scrawny horde, but huge . . .

And in Tanelorn the warriors were grim-faced as their outriders and scouts flowed into the city with messages and estimates of the beggar army's strength.

Brut, in the silver armour of his rank, knew that two full days had passed since Rackhir had left for the Sighing Desert. Three more days and the city would be engulfed by Narjhan's mighty rabble—and they knew there was no chance of halting their advance. They might have left Tanelorn to its fate, but they would not. Even weak Uroch would not. For Tanelorn the Mysterious had given them all a secret power which each believed to be his only, a strength which filled them where before they had been hollow men. Selfishly, they stayed—for to leave Tanelorn to her fate would be to become hollow again, and that they all dreaded.

Brut was the leader and he prepared the defence of Tanelorn—a defence which might just have held against the beggar army—but not against it and Chaos. Brut shuddered when he thought that if Chaos had directed its full force against Tanelorn, they would be sobbing in hell at that moment.

Dust rose high above Tanelorn, sent flying by the hoofs of the scouts' and messengers' horses. One came through the gate as Brut watched. He pulled his mount to a stop before the nobleman. He was the messenger from Karlaak, by the Weeping Waste, one of the nearest major cities to Tanelorn.

The messenger gasped: "I asked Karlaak for aid but, as we supposed, they had never heard of Tanelorn and suspected that I was an emissary from the beggar army sent to lead their few forces into a trap. I pleaded with the Senators, but they would do nothing."

"Was not Elric there—he knows Tanelorn?"

"No, he was not there. There is a rumour which says that he himself fights Chaos now, for the minions of Chaos captured his wife Zarozinia and he rides in pursuit of them. Chaos, it seems, gains strength everywhere in our realm."

Brut was pale.

"What of Jadmar—will Jadmar send warriors?" The messenger spoke urgently, for many had been sent to the nearer cities to solicit aid.

"I do not know," replied Brut, "and it does not matter now—for the beggar army is not three days' march from Tanelorn and it would take two weeks for a Jadmarian force to reach us."

"And Rackhir?"

"I have heard nothing and he has not returned. I have the feeling he'll not return. Tanelorn is doomed."

Rackhir and Lamsar bowed before the small men who sat in the tent, but one of them said impatiently: "Do not humble yourselves before us, friends—we who are humbler than any." So they straightened their backs and waited to be further addressed.

The Grey Lords assumed humility, but this, it seemed, was their greatest ostentation, for it was a pride that they had. Rackhir realised that he would need to use subtle flattery and was not sure that he could, for he was a warrior, not a courtier or a diplomat. Lamsar, too, realised the situation and he said:

"In our pride, lords, we have come to learn the simpler truths which are only truths—the truths which you can teach us."

The speaker gave a self-deprecating smile and replied: "Truth is not for us to define, guest, we can but offer our incomplete thoughts. They might interest you or help you to find your own truths."

"Indeed, that is so," Rackhir said, not wholly sure with what he was agreeing, but judging it best to agree. "And we wondered if you had any suggestions on a matter which concerns us—the protection of our Tanelorn."

"We would not be so prideful as to interfere with our own comments. We are not mighty intellects," the speaker replied blandly, "and we have no confidence in our own decisions, for who knows that they may be wrong and based on wrongly assessed information?"

"Indeed," said Lamsar, judging that he must flatter them with their own assumed humility, "and it is lucky for us, lords, that we do not confuse pride with learning—for it is the quiet man who observes and says little who sees the most. Therefore, though we realise that you are not confident that your suggestions or help would be useful, nonetheless we, taking example from your own demeanour, humbly ask if you know of any way in which we might rescue Tanelorn?"

Rackhir had hardly been able to follow the complexities of Lamsar's seemingly unsophisticated argument, but he saw that the Grey Lords were pleased.

Out of the corner of his eye he observed Sorana. She was smiling to herself and it seemed evident, by the characteristics of that smile, that they had behaved in the right way. Now Sorana was listening intently and Rackhir cursed to himself that the Lords of Chaos would know of everything and might, even if they did gain the Grey Lords' aid, still be able to anticipate and stop any action they took to save Tanelorn.

The speaker conferred in a liquid speech with his fellows and said finally: "Rarely do we have the privilege to entertain such brave and intelligent men. How may our insignificant minds be put to your advantage?"

Rackhir realised quite suddenly, and almost laughed, that the Grey Lords were not very clever after all. Their flattery had got them the help they required. He said:

"Narjhan of Chaos heads a huge army of human scum—a beggar army—and is sworn to tear down Tanelorn and kill her inhabitants. We need magical aid of some kind to combat one so powerful as Narjhan *and* defeat the beggars."

"But Tanelorn cannot be destroyed . . ." said a Grey Lord. "She is Eternal . . ." said another. "But this manifestation . . ." murmured the third. "Ah, yes . . ."

"There are beetles in Kaleef," said a Grey Lord who had not spoken before, "which emit a peculiar venom."

"Beetles, lord?" said Rackhir.

"They are the size of mammoths," said the third Lord, "but can change their size—and change the size of their prey if it is too large for their gullets."

"As for that matter," the first speaker said, "there is a chimera which dwells in mountains south of here—it can change its shape and contains hate for Chaos since Chaos bred it and abandoned it with no real shape of its own.

"Then there are four brothers of Himerscahl who are endowed with sorcerous power," said the second lord, but the first interrupted him:

"Their magic is no good outside our own dimension," he said. "I had thought, however, of reviving the Blue Wizard."

"Too dangerous and, anyway, beyond our powers," said his companion.

They continued to debate for a while, and Rackhir and Lamsar said nothing, but waited.

Eventually the first speaker said:

"The Boatmen of Xerlerenes, we have decided, will probably be best equipped to aid you in defence of Tanelorn. You must go to the mountains of Xerlerenes and find their lake."

"A lake," said Lamsar, "in a range of mountains, I see."

"No," the lord said, "their lake lies above the mountains. We will find someone to take you there. Perhaps they will aid you."

"You can guarantee nothing else?"

"Nothing—it is not our business to interfere. It is up to them to decide whether they will aid you or not."

"I see," said Rackhir, "thank you."

How much time had passed since he had left Tanelorn? How much time before Narjhan's beggar army reached the city? Or had it already done so?

Suddenly he thought of something, looked for Sorana, but she had left the tent.

"Where lies Xerlerenes?" Lamsar was asking.

"Not in our realm," one of the Grey Lords replied, "come we will find you a guide."

Sorana spoke the necessary word which took her immediately into the blue half-world with which she was so familiar. There were no other colours in it, but many, many shades of blue. Here she waited until Eequor noticed her presence. In the timelessness, she could not tell how long she had waited.

The beggar horde came to an undisciplined and slow halt at a sign from its leader. A voice rang hollowly from the helm that was always closed.

"Tomorrow, we march against Tanelorn—the time we have anticipated is almost upon us. Make camp now. Tomorrow shall Tanelorn be punished and the stones of her little houses will be dust on the wind."

The million beggars cackled their glee and wetted their scrawny lips. Not one of them asked why they had marched so far, and this was because of Narjhan's power.

In Tanelorn, Brut and Zas the One-handed discussed the nature of death in quiet, over-controlled tones. Both were filled with sadness, less for themselves than for Tanelorn, soon to perish. Outside, a pitiful army tried to place a cordon around the town but failed to fill the gaps between men, there were so few of them. Lights in the houses burned as if for the last time, and candles guttered moodily.

Sorana, sweating as she always did after such an episode, returned to the plane occupied by the Grey Lords and discovered that Rackhir, Lamsar and their guide were preparing to leave. Eequor had told her what to do—it was for her to contact Narjhan. The rest the Lords of Chaos would accomplish. She blew her ex-lover a kiss as he rode from the camp into the night. He grinned at her defiantly, but when his face was turned from her he frowned and they went in silence into the Valley of the Currents where they entered the realm where lay the Mountains of Xerlerenes. Almost as soon as they arrived, danger presented itself.

Their guide, a wanderer called Timeras, pointed into the night sky which was spiked by the outlines of crags.

"This is a world where the air elementals are dominant," he said. "Look!"

Flowing downwards in an ominous sweep they saw a flight of owls, great eyes gleaming. Only as they came nearer did the men realise that these owls were huge, almost as large as a man. In the saddle Rackhir strung his bow. Timeras said:

"How could they have learned of our presence so soon?"

"Sorana," Rackhir said, busy with the bow, "she must have warned the Lords of Chaos and they have sent these dreadful birds." As the first one homed in, great claws grasping, great beak gaping, he shot it in its feathery

throat and it shrieked and swept upwards. Many arrows fled from his humming bowstring to find a mark while Timeras drew his sword and slashed at
them, ducking as they whistled downwards.

Lamsar watched the battle but took no part, seemed thoughtful at a time when
action was desired of him.

He mused: "If the spirits of air are dominant in this realm, then they will
resent a stronger force of other elementals," and he racked his brain to remember a spell.

Rackhir had but two arrows left in his quiver by the time they had driven
the owls off. The birds had not been used, evidently, to a prey which fought
back and had put up a poor fight considering their superiority.

"We can expect more danger," said Rackhir somewhat shakily, "for the
Lords of Chaos will use other means to try and stop us. How far to Xerlerenes?"

"Not far," said Timeras, "but it's a hard road."

They rode on, and Lamsar rode behind them, lost in his own thoughts.

Now they urged their horses up a steep mountain path and a chasm lay
below them, dropping, dropping, dropping. Rackhir, who had no love for
heights, kept as close to the mountainside as was possible. If he had had gods
to whom he could pray, he would have prayed for their help then.

The huge fish came flying—or swimming—at them as they rounded a bend.
They were semi-luminous, big as sharks but with enlarged fins with which
they planed through the air like rays. They were quite evidently fish. Timeras
drew his sword, but Rackhir had only two arrows left and it would have been
useless against the airfish to have shot them, for there were many of them.

But Lamsar laughed and spoke in a high-pitched, staccato speech.
"*Crackhor—pishtasta salaflar!*"

Huge balls of flame materialised against the black sky—flaring balls of
multicoloured fire which shaped themselves into strange, warlike forms and
streamed towards the unnatural fish.

The flame-shapes seared into the big fish and they shrieked, struck at the fireballs, burned, and fell flaming down the deep gorge.

"Fire elementals!" Rackhir exclaimed.

"The spirits of the air fear such beings," Lamsar said calmly.

The flame-beings accompanied them the rest of the way to Xerlerenes and were with them when dawn came, having frightened away many other dangers which the Lords of Chaos had evidently sent against them.

They saw the boats of Xerlerenes in the dawn, at anchor on a calm sky, fluffy clouds playing around their slender keels, their huge sails furled.

"The boatmen live aboard their vessels," Timeras said, "for it is only their ships which deny the laws of nature, not they."

Timeras cupped his hands about his mouth and called through the still mountain air: "Boatmen of Xerlerenes, freemen of the air, guests come with a request for aid!"

A black and bearded face appeared over the side of one of the red-gold vessels. The man shielded his eyes against the rising sun and stared down at them. Then he disappeared again.

At length a ladder of slim thongs came snaking down to where they sat their horses on the tops of the mountains. Timeras grasped it, tested it and began to climb. Rackhir reached out and steadied the ladder for him. It seemed too thin to support a man but when he had it in his hands he knew that it was the strongest he had ever known.

Lamsar grumbled as Rackhir signalled for him to climb, but he did so and quite nimbly. Rackhir was the last, following his companions, climbing up through the sky high above the crags, towards the ship that sailed on the air.

The fleet comprised some twenty or thirty ships and Rackhir felt that with these to aid him, there was good chance to rescue Tanelorn—if Tanelorn survived. Narjhan would, anyway, be aware of the nature of the aid he sought.

Starved dogs barked the morning in and the beggar horde, waking from where they had sprawled on the ground, saw Narjhan already mounted, but talking to a newcomer, a girl in black robes that moved as if in a wind—but there was no wind. There was a jewel at her long throat.

When he had finished conversing with the newcomer, Narjhan ordered a horse be brought for her and she rode slightly behind him when the beggar army moved on—the last stage of their hateful journey to Tanelorn.

When they saw lovely Tanelorn and how it was so poorly guarded, the beggars laughed, but Narjhan and his new companion looked up into the sky.

"*There may be time,*" said the hollow voice, and gave the order to attack.

Howling, the beggars broke into a run towards Tanelorn. The attack had started.

Brut rose in his saddle and there were tears flowing down his face and glistening in his beard. His huge war-axe was in one gauntleted hand and the other held a spiked mace across the saddle before him.

Zas the One-handed gripped the long and heavy broadsword with its pommel of a rampant golden lion pointed downwards. This blade had won him a crown in Andlermaigne, but he doubted whether it would successfully defend his peace in Tanelorn. Beside him stood Uroch of Nieva, pale-faced but angry as he watched the ragged horde's implacable approach.

Then, yelling, the beggars met with the warriors of Tanelorn and, although greatly outnumbered, the warriors fought desperately for they were defending more than life or love—they were defending that which had told them of a reason for living.

Narjhan sat his horse aside from the battle, Sorana next to him, for Narjhan could take no active part in the battle, could only watch and, if necessary, use magic to aid his human pawns or defend his person.

The warriors of Tanelorn, incredibly, held back the roaring beggar horde, their weapons drenched with blood, rising and falling in that sea of moving flesh, flashing in the light of the red dawn.

Sweat now mingled with the salt tears in Brut's bristling beard and with agility he leapt clear of his black horse as the screaming beast was cut from under him. The noble war-cry of his forefathers sang on his breath and, although in his shame he had no business to use it, he let it roar from him as he slashed about him with biting war-axe and rending mace. But he fought hopelessly for Rackhir had not come and Tanelorn was soon to die. His one fierce consolation was that he would die with the city, his blood mingling with its ashes.

Zas, also, acquitted himself very well before he died of a smashed skull. His old body twitched as trampling feet stumbled over it as the beggars made for Uroch of Nieva. The gold-pommelled sword was still gripped in his single hand and his soul was fleeing for limbo as Uroch, too, was slain fighting.

Then the Ships of Xerlerenes suddenly materialised in the sky and Brut, looking upward for an instant, knew that Rackhir had come at last—though it might be too late.

Narjhan, also, saw the ships and was prepared for them.

They skimmed through the sky, the fire elementals which Lamsar had summoned flying with them. The spirits of air and flame had been called to rescue weakening Tanelorn . . .

The Boatmen prepared their weapons and made themselves ready for war. Their black faces had a concentrated look and they grinned in their bushy beards. War-harness clothed them and they bristled with weapons—long, barbed tridents, nets of steel mesh, curved swords, long harpoons. Rackhir stood in the prow of the leading ship, his quiver packed with slim arrows loaned him by the Boatmen. Below him he saw Tanelorn and was relieved that the city still stood.

He could see the milling warriors below, but it was hard to tell, from the air, which were friends and which were foes. Lamsar called to the frisking fire elementals, instructing them. Timeras grinned and held his sword ready as the ships rocked on the wind and dropped lower.

Now Rackhir observed Narjhan with Sorana beside him.

"The bitch has warned him—he is ready for us," Rackhir said, wetting his lips and drawing an arrow from his quiver.

Down the Ships of Xerlerenes dropped, coursing downwards on the currents of air, their golden sails billowing, the warrior crews straining over the side and keen for battle.

Then Narjhan summoned the *Kyrenee.*

Huge as a storm cloud, black as its native hell, the *Kyrenee* grew from the surrounding air and moved its shapeless bulk forward towards the Ships of Xerlerenes, sending out flowing tendrils of poison towards them. Boatmen groaned as the coils curled around their naked bodies and crushed them.

Lamsar called urgently to his fire elementals and they rose again from where they had been devouring beggars, came together in one great blossoming of flame which moved to do battle with the *Kyrenee.*

The two masses met and there was an explosion which blinded the Red Archer with multicoloured light and sent the ships rocking and shaking so that several capsized and sent their crews hurtling downwards to death.

Blotches of flame flew everywhere and patches of poison blackness from the body of the *Kyrenee* were flung about, slaying those they touched before disappearing.

There was a terrible stink in the air—a smell of burning, a smell of outraged elements which had never been meant to meet.

The *Kyrenee* died, lashing about and wailing, while the flame elementals, dying or returning to their own sphere, faded and vanished. The remaining bulk of the great *Kyrenee* billowed slowly down to the earth where it fell upon the scrabbling beggars and killed them, leaving nothing but a wet patch on the ground for yards around, a patch glistening with the bones of beggars.

Now Rackhir cried: "Quickly—finish the fight before Narjhan summons more horrors!"

And the boats sailed downwards while the Boatmen cast their steel nets, pulling large catches of beggars aboard their ships and finishing the wriggling starvelings with their tridents or spears.

Rackhir shot arrow after arrow and had the satisfaction of seeing each one take a beggar just where he had aimed it. The remaining warriors of Tanelorn, led by Brut who was covered in sticky blood but grinning in his victory, charged towards the unnerved beggars.

Narjhan stood his ground, while the beggars, fleeing, streamed past him and the girl. Sorana seemed frightened, looked up and her eyes met Rackhir's. The Red Archer aimed an arrow at her, thought better of it and shot instead at Narjhan. The arrow went into the black armour but had no effect upon the Lord of Chaos.

Then the Boatmen of Xerlerenes flung down their largest net from the vessel in which Rackhir sailed and they caught Lord Narjhan in its coils and caught Sorana, too.

Shouting their exhilaration, they pulled the struggling bodies aboard and Rackhir ran forward to inspect their catch. Sorana had received a scratch across her face from the net's wire, but the body of Narjhan lay still and dreadful in the mesh.

Rackhir grabbed an axe from a Boatman and knocked back the helm, his foot upon the chest.

"Yield, Narjhan of Chaos!" he cried in mindless merriment. He was near hysterical with victory, for this was the first time a mortal had ever bested a Lord of Chaos.

But the armour was empty, if it had ever been occupied by flesh, and Narjhan was gone.

Calm settled aboard the Ships of Xerlerenes and over the city of Tanelorn. The remnants of the warriors had gathered in the city's square and were cheering their victory.

Friagho, the Captain of Xerlerenes, came up to Rackhir and shrugged.

"We did not get the catch we came for—but these will do. Thanks for the fishing, friend."

Rackhir smiled and gripped Friagho's black shoulder. "Thanks for the aid—you have done us all a great service." Friagho shrugged again and turned back to his nets, his trident poised. Suddenly Rackhir shouted: "No, Friagho—let that one be. Let me have the contents of that net."

Sorana, the contents to which he'd referred, looked anxious as if she had rather been transfixed on the prongs of Friagho's trident. Friagho said: "Very well, Red Archer—there are plenty more people on the land." He pulled at the net to release her.

She stood up shakily, looking at Rackhir apprehensively.

Rackhir smiled quite softly and said: "Come here, Sorana." She went to him and stood staring up at his bony hawk's face, her eyes wide. With a laugh he picked her up and flung her over his shoulder.

"Tanelorn is safe!" he shouted. "You shall learn to love its peace with me!" And he began to clamber down the trailing ladders that the Boatmen had dropped over the side.

Lamsar waited for him below. "I go now, to my hermitage again."

"I thank you for your aid," said Rackhir. "Without it Tanelorn would no longer exist."

"Tanelorn will always exist while men exist," said the hermit. "It was not a city you defended today. It was an ideal. That is Tanelorn."

And Lamsar smiled.

STORMBRINGER

For J.G. Ballard, whose enthusiasm for Elric gave me encouragement to begin this particular book, my first attempt at a full-length novel, and for Jim Cawthorn, whose illustrations based on my ideas in turn gave me inspiration for certain scenes in this book, and for Dave Britton, who kept the magazines in which the serial first appeared and who kindly loaned them to me so that I could restore this novel to its original shape and length.

STORMBRINGER

CONTENTS

BOOK FOUR: DOOMED LORD'S PASSING

PROLOGUE

There came a time when there was great movement upon the Earth and above it, when the destiny of Men and Gods was hammered out upon the forge of Fate, when monstrous wars were brewed and mighty deeds were designed. And there rose up in this time, which was called the Age of the Young Kingdoms, heroes. Greatest of these heroes was a doom-driven adventurer who bore a crooning runeblade that he loathed.

His name was Elric of Melniboné, king of ruins, lord of a scattered race that had once ruled the ancient world. Elric, sorcerer and swordsman, slayer of kin, despoiler of his homeland, white-faced albino, last of his line.

Elric, who had come to Karlaak by the Weeping Waste and had married a wife in whom he found some peace, some surcease from the torment in him.

And Elric, who had within him a greater destiny than he knew, now dwelt in Karlaak with Zarozinia, his wife, and his sleep was troubled, his dream dark, one brooding night in the Month of Anemone . . .

BOOK ONE

DEAD GOD'S HOMECOMING

In which, at long last, Elric's fate begins to be revealed to him as the forces of Law and Chaos gather strength for the final battle which will decide the future of Elric's world . . .

I

Above the rolling Earth great clouds tumbled down and bolts of lightning charged groundwards to slash the midnight black, split trees in twain and sear through roofs that cracked and broke.

The dark mass of forest trembled with the shock and out of it crept six hunched, unhuman figures who paused to stare beyond the low hills towards the outline of a city. It was a city of squat walls and slender spires, of graceful towers and domes; and it had a name which the leader of the creatures knew. Karlaak by the Weeping Waste it was called.

Not of natural origin, the storm was ominous. It groaned around the city of Karlaak as the creatures skulked past the open gates and made their way through shadows towards the elegant palace where Elric slept. The leader raised an axe of black iron in its clawed hand. The group came to a stealthy halt and regarded the sprawling palace which lay on a hill surrounded by languorously scented gardens. The earth shook as lightning lashed it and thunder prowled across the turbulent sky.

"Chaos has aided us in this matter," the leader grunted. "See—already the guards fall in magic slumber and our entrance is thus made simple. The Lords of Chaos are good to their servants."

He spoke the truth. Some supernatural force had been at work and the warriors guarding Elric's palace had dropped to the ground, their snores echoing the thunder. The servants of Chaos crept past the prone guards, into the main courtyard and from there into the darkened palace. Unerringly they climbed twisting staircases, moved softly along gloomy corridors, to arrive at length outside the room where Elric and his wife lay in uneasy sleep.

As the leader laid a hand upon the door, a voice cried out from within the room: "*What's this? What things of hell disrupt my rest?*"

"He sees us!" sharply whispered one of the creatures.

"No," the leader said, "he sleeps—but such a sorcerer as this Elric is not so easily lulled into a stupor. We had best make speed and do our work, for if he wakes it will be the harder!"

He twisted the handle and eased the door open, his axe half raised. Beyond the bed, heaped with tumbled furs and silks, lightning gashed the night again, showing the white face of the albino close to that of his dark-haired wife.

Even as they entered, he rose stiffly in the bed and his crimson eyes opened, staring out at them. For a moment the eyes were glazed and then the albino forced himself awake, shouting: "Begone, you creatures of my dreams!"

The leader cursed and leapt forward, but he had been instructed not to slay this man. He raised the axe threateningly.

"Silence—your guards cannot aid you!"

Elric jumped from the bed and grasped the thing's wrist, his face close to the fanged muzzle. Because of his albinism he was physically weak and required magic to give him strength. But so quickly did he move that he had wrested the axe from the creature's hand and smashed the shaft between its eyes. Snarling, it fell back, but its comrades jumped forward. There were five of them, huge muscles moving beneath their furred skins.

Elric clove the skull of the first as others grappled with him. His body was spattered with the thing's blood and brains and he gasped in disgust at the foetid stuff. He managed to wrench his arm away and bring the axe up and down into the collarbone of another. But then he felt his legs gripped and he fell, confused but still battling. Then there came a great blow on his head and pain blazed through him. He made an effort to rise, failed and fell back insensible.

Thunder and lightning still disturbed the night when, with throbbing head, he awoke and got slowly to his feet using a bedpost as support. He stared dazedly around him.

Zarozinia was gone. The only other figure in the room was the stiff corpse of the beast he had killed. His black-haired girl-wife had been abducted.

Shaking, he went to the door and flung it open, calling for his guards, but none answered him.

His runesword Stormbringer hung in the city's armoury and would take time to get. His throat tight with pain and anger, he ran down the corridors and stairways, dazed with anxiety, trying to grasp the implications of his wife's disappearance.

Above the palace, thunder still crashed, eddying about in the noisy night. The palace seemed deserted and he had the sudden feeling that he was completely alone, that he had been abandoned. But as he ran out into the main courtyard and saw the insensible guards he realised at once that their slumber could not be natural. Realisation was coming even as he ran through the gardens, through the gates and down to the city, but there was no sign of his wife's abductors.

Where had they gone?

He raised his eyes to the shouting sky, his white face stark and twisted with frustrated anger. There was no sense to it. Why had they taken her? He had enemies, he knew, but none who could summon such supernatural help. Who, apart from himself, could work this mighty sorcery that made the skies themselves shake and a city sleep?

To the house of Lord Voashoon, Chief Senator of Karlaak and father of Zarozinia, Elric ran panting like a wolf. He banged with his fists upon the door, yelling at the astonished servants within.

"Open! It is Elric. Hurry!"

The doors gaped back and he was through them. Lord Voashoon came stumbling down the stairs into the chamber, his face heavy with sleep.

"What is it, Elric?"

"Summon your warriors. Zarozinia has been abducted. Those who took her were demons and may be far from here by now—but we must search in case they escaped by land."

Lord Voashoon's face became instantly alert and he shouted terse orders to his servants between listening to Elric's explanation of what had happened.

"And I must have entrance into the armoury," Elric concluded. "I must have Stormbringer!"

"But you renounced the blade for fear of its evil power over you!" Lord Voashoon reminded him quietly.

Elric replied impatiently. "Aye—but I renounced the blade for Zarozinia's sake, too. I must have Stormbringer if I am to bring her back. The logic is simple. Quickly, give me the key."

In silence Lord Voashoon fetched the key and led Elric to the armoury where the weapons and armour of his ancestors were held, unused for centuries. Through the dusty place strode Elric to a dark alcove that seemed to contain something which lived.

He heard a soft moaning from the great black battle-blade as he reached out a slim-fingered white hand to take it. It was heavy, yet perfectly balanced, a two-handed broadsword of prodigious size, with its wide crosspiece and its blade smooth and broad, stretching for over five feet from the hilt. Near the hilt, mystic runes were engraved and even Elric did not know what they fully signified.

"Again I must make use of you, Stormbringer," he said as he buckled the sheath about his waist, "and I must conclude that we are too closely linked now for less than death to separate us."

With that he was striding from the armoury and back to the courtyard where mounted guards were already sitting nervous steeds, awaiting his instructions.

Standing before them, he drew Stormbringer so that the sword's strange, black radiance flickered around him, his white face, as pallid as bleached bone, staring out of it at the horsemen.

"You go to chase demons this night. Search the countryside, scour forest and plain for those who have done this thing to our princess! Though it's likely that her abductors used supernatural means to make their escape, we cannot be sure. So search—and search well!"

All through the raging night they searched but could find no trace of either the creatures or Elric's wife. And when dawn came, a smear of blood in the morning sky, his men returned to Karlaak where Elric awaited them, now filled with the nigromantic vitality which his sword supplied.

"Lord Elric—shall we retrace our trail and see if daylight yields a clue?" cried one.

"He does not hear you," another murmured as Elric gave no sign.

But then Elric turned his pain-racked head and he said bleakly, "Search no more. I have had time to meditate and must seek my wife with the aid of sorcery. Disperse. You can do nothing further."

Then he left them and went back towards his palace, knowing that there was still one way of learning where Zarozinia had been taken. It was a method which he ill-liked, yet it would have to be employed.

Curtly, upon returning, Elric ordered everyone from his chamber, barred the door and stared down at the dead thing. Its congealed blood was still on him, but the axe with which he had slain it had been taken away by its comrades.

Elric prepared the body, stretching out its limbs on the floor. He drew the shutters of the windows so that no light filtered into the room, and lit a brazier in one corner. It swayed on its chains as the oil-soaked rushes flared. He went to a small chest by the window and took out a pouch. From this he removed a bunch of dried herbs and with a hasty gesture flung them on the brazier so that it gave off a sickly odour and the room began to fill with smoke. Then he stood over the corpse, his body rigid, and began to sing an incantation in the old language of his forefathers, the Sorcerer Emperors of Melniboné. The song seemed scarcely akin to human speech, rising and falling from a deep groan to a high-pitched shriek.

The brazier speared flaring red light over Elric's face and grotesque shadows skipped about the room. On the floor the dead corpse began to stir, its ruined head moving from side to side. Elric drew his runesword and placed it before him, his two hands on the hilt. "Arise, soulless one!" he commanded.

Slowly, with jerky movements, the creature raised itself stiffly upright and pointed a clawed finger at Elric, its glazed eyes staring as if beyond him.

"All this," it whispered, "was preordained. Think not that you can escape your fate, Elric of Melniboné. You have tampered with my corpse and I am a creature of Chaos. My masters will avenge me."

"How?"

"Your destiny is already laid down. You will know soon enough."

"Tell me, dead one, why did you come to abduct my wife? Who sent you hither? Where has my wife been taken?"

"Three questions, Lord Elric. Requiring three answers. You know that the dead who have been raised by sorcery can answer nothing directly."

"Aye—that I know. So answer as you can."

"Then listen well for I may recite only once my rede and then must return to the nether regions where my being may peacefully rot to nothing. Listen:

"Beyond the ocean brews a battle;
Beyond the battle blood shall fall.
If Elric's kinsman ventures with him
(Bearing a twin of that he bears)
To a place where, man-forsaken,
Dwells the one who should not live,
Then a bargain shall be entered.
Elric's wife shall be restored."

With this the thing fell to the floor and did not stir thereafter.

Elric went to the window and opened the shutters. Used as he was to enigmatic verse-omens, this one was difficult to unravel. As daylight entered the room, the rushes sputtered and the smoke faded. *Beyond the ocean . . .* There were many oceans.

He resheathed his runesword and climbed onto the disordered bed to lie down and contemplate the rede. At last, after long minutes of this contemplation, he remembered something he had heard from a traveller who had come to Karlaak, from Tarkesh, a nation of the Western Continent, beyond the Pale Sea.

The traveller had told him how there was trouble brewing between the land of Dharijor and the other nations of the West. Dharijor had contravened treaties she had signed with her neighbouring kingdoms and had signed a new one with the Theocrat of Pan Tang. Pan Tang was an unholy island dominated by its dark aristocracy of warrior-wizards. It was from here that Elric's old enemy, Theleb K'aarna, had come. Its capital of Hwamgaarl was called the City of Screaming Statues and until recently its residents had had little contact with the folk of the outside world. Jagreen Lern was the new Theocrat and an ambitious man. His alliance with Dharijor could only mean that he sought more power over the nations of the Young Kingdoms. The traveller had said that strife was sure to break out at any moment since there was ample evidence that Dharijor and Pan Tang had entered a war alliance.

Now, as his memory improved, Elric related this information with the news he had had recently that Queen Yishana of Jharkor, a neighbouring kingdom to Dharijor, had recruited the aid of Dyvim Slorm and his Imrryrian mercenaries. And Dyvim Slorm was Elric's only kinsman. This meant that Jharkor must be preparing for battle against Dharijor. The two facts were too closely linked with the prophecy to be ignored.

Even as he thought upon it, he was gathering his clothes together and preparing for a journey. There was nothing for it but to go to Jharkor and speedily, for there he was sure to meet his kinsman. And there, also, there would soon be a battle if all the evidence were true.

Yet the prospect of the journey, which would take many days, caused a cold ache to grow in his heart as he thought of the weeks to come in which he would not know how his wife fared.

"No time for that," he told himself as he laced up his black quilted jacket. "Action is all that's required of me now—and speedy action."

He held the sheathed runeblade before him, staring beyond it into space. "I swear by Arioch that those who have done this, whether they be man or immortal, shall suffer from their deed. Hear me, Arioch! That is my oath!"

But his words found no answer and he sensed that Arioch, his patron demon, had either not heard him or else heard his oath and was unmoved.

Then he was striding from the death-heavy chamber, yelling for his horse.

2

Where the Sighing Desert gave way to the borders of Ilmiora, between the coasts of the Eastern Continent and the lands of Tarkesh, Dharijor, Jharkor and Shazaar, there lay the Pale Sea.

It was a cold sea, a morose and chilling sea, but ships preferred to cross from Ilmiora to Dharijor by means of it, rather than chance the weirder dangers of the Straits of Chaos which were lashed by eternal storms and inhabited by malevolent sea-creatures.

On the deck of an Ilmioran schooner, Elric of Melniboné stood wrapped in his cloak, shivering and staring gloomily at the cloud-covered sky.

The captain, a stocky man with blue, humorous eyes, came struggling along the deck towards him. He had a cup of hot wine in his hands. He steadied himself by clinging to a piece of rigging and gave the cup to Elric.

"Thanks," said the albino gratefully. He sipped the wine. "How soon before we make the port of Banarva, captain?"

The captain pulled the collar of his leather jerkin about his unshaven face. "We're sailing slow, but we should sight the Tarkesh peninsula well before sunset." Banarva was in Tarkesh, one of its chief trading posts. The captain leaned on the rail. "I wonder how long these waters will be free for ships now that war's broken out between the kingdoms of the West. Both Dharijor and Pan Tang have been notorious in the past for their piratical activities. They'll soon extend them under the guise of war, I'll warrant."

Elric nodded vaguely, his mind on other things than the prospect of piracy.

Disembarking in the chilly evening at the port of Banarva, Elric soon saw ample evidence that war darkened the lands of the Young Kingdoms. There were rumours rife, talk of nothing but battles gained and warriors lost. From the confused gossip, he could get no clear impression of how the war went, save that the decisive battle was yet to be fought.

Loquacious Banarvans told him that all over the Western Continent men were marching. From Myyrrhn, he heard, the winged men were flying. From Jharkor, the White Leopards, Queen Yishana's personal guard, ran towards Dharijor, while Dyvim Slorm and his mercenaries pressed northwards to meet them.

Dharijor was the strongest nation of the West and Pan Tang was a formidable ally, more for her people's occult knowledge than for her numbers. Next in power to Dharijor came Jharkor, who, with her allies Tarkesh, Myyrrhn and Shazaar, was still not as strong as those who threatened the security of the Young Kingdoms.

For some years Dharijor had sought an opportunity for conquest and the hasty alliance against her had been made in an effort to stop her before she had fully prepared for conquest. Whether this effort would succeed, Elric did not know, and those who spoke to him were equally uncertain.

The streets of Banarva were packed with soldiers and supply trains of horses and oxen. The harbour was filled with warships and it was difficult to find lodgings since most inns and many private houses had been requisitioned by the army. And it was the same all over the Western Continent. Everywhere, men strapped metal about them, bestrode heavy chargers, sharpened their arms, and rode beneath bright silken banners to slay and to despoil.

Here, without doubt, Elric reflected, he would find the battle of the prophecy. He tried to forget his tormented longing for news of Zarozinia and turned his moody eyes towards the west. Stormbringer hung like an anchor at his side and he fingered it constantly, hating it even as it fed him his vitality.

He spent the night in Banarva and by morning had hired a good horse and was riding through the sparse grassland towards Jharkor.

STORMBRINGER

Across a war-torn world rode Elric, his crimson eyes burning with a fierce anger at the sights of wanton destruction he witnessed. Although he had himself lived by his sword for many years and had committed acts of murder, robbery and urbicide, he disliked the senselessness of wars such as this, of men who killed one another for only the vaguest of reasons. It was not that he pitied the slain or hated the slayers; he was too remote from ordinary men to care greatly about what they did. Yet, in his own tortured way, he was an idealist who, because he lacked peace and security himself, resented the sights of strife which the war brought to him. His ancestors, he knew, had also been remote, yet they had delighted in the conflicts of the men of the Young Kingdoms, observing them from a distance and judging themselves above such activities; above the morass of sentiment and emotion in which these new men struggled. For ten thousand years the Sorcerer Emperors of Melniboné had ruled this world, a race without conscience or moral creed, unneedful of reasons for their acts of conquest, seeking no excuses for their natural malicious tendencies. But Elric, the last in the direct line of emperors, was not like them. He was capable of cruelty and malevolent sorcery, had little pity, yet could love and hate more violently than ever his ancestors. And these strong passions, perhaps, had been the cause of his breaking with his homeland and travelling the world to compare himself against these new men since he could find none in Melniboné who shared his feelings. And it was because of these twin forces of love and hate that he had returned to have vengeance on his cousin Yyrkoon who had put Cymoril, Elric's betrothed, into a magic slumber and usurped the kingship of Melniboné, the Dragon Isle, the last territory of the fallen Bright Empire. With the aid of a fleet of reavers, Elric had razed Imrryr in his vengeance-taking, destroyed the Dreaming City and scattered for ever the race who had founded it so that the last survivors were now mercenaries roaming the world to sell their arms to whoever bid highest. Love and hate; they had led him to kill Yyrkoon who deserved death and, inadvertently, Cymoril, who did not. Love and hate. They welled in him now as bitter smoke stung his throat and he passed a straggling group of townspeople who were fleeing, without knowledge of their direction, from the latest depredation of the roving Dharijorian troops who had struck far into this part of Tarkesh and had met little hindrance from the armies of King Hilran of Tarkesh whose main force was concentrated further north, readying itself for the major battle.

Now Elric rode close to the Western Marches, near the Jharkorian border. Here lived sturdy foresters and harvesters in better times. But now the forests were blackened and burned and the crops of the fields were ruined.

His journey, which was speedy for he wasted no time, took him through one of the stark forests where remnants of trees cast cold silhouettes against the grey, seething sky. He raised the hood of his cloak over his head so that the heavy black fabric completely hid his face, and rode on as rain rushed suddenly down and beat through the skeleton trees, sweeping across the distant plains beyond so that all the world seemed grey and black with the hiss of the rain a constant and depressing sound.

Then, as he passed a ruined hovel which was half cottage and half hole in the earth, a cawing voice called out:

"*Lord Elric!*"

Astonished that he should be recognised, he turned his bleak face in the direction of the voice, pushing his hood back as he did so. A ragged figure appeared in the hole's opening. It beckoned him closer. Puzzled, he walked his horse towards the figure and saw that it was an old man, or perhaps a woman, he couldn't tell.

"You know my name. How?"

"Thou art a legend throughout the Young Kingdoms. Who could not recognise that white face and heavy blade thou art carrying?"

"True, perhaps, but I have a notion there is more to this than chance recognition. Who are you and how do you know the High Speech of Melniboné?" Elric deliberately used the coarse common speech.

"Thou shouldst know that all who practise dark sorcery use the High Tongue of those who are past masters in its arts. Wouldst thou guest with me a while?"

STORMBRINGER

Elric looked at the hovel and shook his head. He was fastidious at the best of times. The wretch smiled and made a mock bow, resorting to the common speech and saying: "So the mighty lord disdains to grace my poor home. But does he not perhaps wonder why the fire which raged through this forest a while ago did not, in fact, harm me?"

"Aye," said Elric thoughtfully, "that is an interesting riddle."

The hag took a step towards him. "Soldiers came not a month gone— from Pan Tang they were. Devil Riders with their hunting tigers running with them. They despoiled the harvest and burned even the forests that those who fled them might not eat game or berries here. I lived in this forest all my life, doing a little simple magic and prophecy for my needs. But when I saw the walls of flame soon to engulf me, I cried the name of a demon I knew—a thing from Chaos which, latterly, I had dared not summon. It came.

"'Save me,' I cried, 'And what would ye do in return?' said the demon. 'Anything,' I quoth. 'Then bear this message for my masters,' it said. 'When the kinslayer known as Elric of Melniboné shall pass this way, tell him that there is one kinsman he shall not slay and he will be found in Sequaloris. If Elric loves his wife, he will play his role. If he plays it well, his wife shall be returned.' So I fixed the message in my mind and now give it thee as I swore."

"Thanks," said Elric, "and what did you give in the first place for the power to summon such a demon?"

"Why, my soul, of course. But it was an old one and not of much worth. Hell could be no worse than this existence."

"Then why did you not let yourself burn, your soul unbartered?"

"I wish to live," said the wretch, smiling again. "Oh, life is good. My own life, perhaps, is squalid, yet the life around me, that is what I love. But let me not keep you, my lord, for you have weightier matters on your mind." Once more the wretch gave a mock bow as Elric rode off, puzzled, but encouraged. His wife still lived and was safe. But what bargain must he strike before he could get her back?

Savagely he goaded his horse into a gallop, heading for Sequaloris in Jharkor. Behind him, faintly through the beating rain, he heard a cackling at once mocking and miserable.

Now his direction was not so vague, and he rode at great speed, but cautiously, avoiding the roving bands of invaders, until at length the arid plains gave way to the lusher wheatlands of the Sequa province of Jharkor. Another day's ride and Elric entered the small walled city of Sequaloris which had so far not suffered attack. Here, he discovered preparations for war and learned news that was of greater interest to him.

The Imrryrian mercenaries, led by Dyvim Slorm, Elric's cousin and son of Dyvim Tvar, Elric's old friend, were due to arrive next day in Sequaloris.

There had been a certain enmity between Elric and the Imrryrians since the albino had been the direct cause of their need to leave the ruins of the Dreaming City and live as mercenaries. But those times were past, long since, and on two previous occasions he and the Imrryrians had fought on the same side. He was their leader by right and the ties of tradition were strong in the elder race. Elric prayed to Arioch that Dyvim Slorm would have some clue to his wife's whereabouts.

At noon of the next day the mercenary army rode swaggering into the city. Elric met them close to the city gate. The Imrryrian warriors were obviously weary from the long ride and were loaded with booty since, before Yishana sent for them, they had been raiding in Shazaar close to the Marshes of the Mist. They were different from any other race, these Imrryrians, with their tapering faces, slanting eyes and high cheekbones. They were pale and slim with long, soft hair drifting to their shoulders. The finery they wore was not stolen, but definitely Melnibonéan in design; shimmering cloths of gold, blue and green, metals of delicate workmanship and intricately patterned. They carried lances with long, sweeping heads and there were slender swords at their sides. They sat arrogantly in their saddles, convinced of their superiority over other mortals, and were, as Elric, not quite human in their unearthly beauty.

He rode up to meet Dyvim Slorm, his own sombre clothes contrasting with theirs. He wore a tall-collared jacket of quilted leather, black and buckled in by a broad, plain belt at which hung a poignard and Stormbringer. His milk-white hair was held from his eyes by a fillet of black bronze and his breeks and boots were also black. All this black set off sharply his white skin and crimson, glowing eyes.

Dyvim Slorm bowed in his saddle, showing only slight surprise.

"Cousin Elric. So the omen was true."

"What omen, Dyvim Slorm?"

"A raven's—your name bird if I remember."

It had been customary for Melnibonéans to identify newborn children with birds of their choice; thus Elric's was a raven, a wise, if unpopular, bird.

"What did it tell you, cousin?" Elric asked eagerly.

"It gave a puzzling message. While we had barely gone from the Marshes of the Mist, it came and perched on my shoulder and spoke in human tongue. It told me to come to Sequaloris and there I would meet my king. From Sequaloris we were to journey together to join Yishana's army and the battle, whether won or lost, would resolve the direction of our linked destinies thereafter. Do you make sense of that, cousin?"

"Some," Elric frowned. "But come—I have a place reserved for you at the inn. I will tell you all I know over wine—if we can find decent wine in this forsaken hamlet. I need help, cousin; as much help as I can obtain, for Zarozinia has been abducted by supernatural agents and I have a feeling that this and the wars are but two elements in a greater play."

"Then quickly, to the inn. My curiosity is further piqued. This matter increases in interest for me. First ravens and omens, now abductions and strife! What else, I wonder, are we to meet!"

With the Imrryrians straggling after them through the cobbled streets, scarcely a hundred warriors but hardened by their outlawed life, Elric and Dyvim Slorm made their way to the inn and there, in haste, Elric outlined all he had learned.

Before replying, his cousin sipped his wine and carefully placed the cup upon the board, pursing his lips. "I have a feeling in my bones that we are puppets in some struggle between the gods. For all our blood and flesh and will, we can see none of the bigger conflict save for a few scarcely related details."

"That may be so," said Elric impatiently, "but I'm greatly angered at being involved and require my wife's release. I have no notion why we, together, must make the bargain for her return, neither can I guess what it is we have that those who captured her want. But, if the omens are sent by the same agents, then we had best do as we are told, for the meantime, until we can see matters more clearly. Then, perhaps, we can act upon our *own* volition."

"That's wise," Dyvim Slorm nodded, "and I'm with you in it." He smiled slightly and added: "Whether I like it or not, I fancy."

Elric said: "Where lies the main army of Dharijor and Pan Tang? I heard it was gathering."

"It has gathered—and marches closer. The impending battle will decide who rules the Western lands. I'm committed to Yishana's side, not only because she has employed us to aid her, but because I felt that if the warped lords of Pan Tang dominate these nations, then tyranny will come upon them and they will threaten the security of the whole world. It is a sad thing when a Melnibonéan has to consider such problems." He smiled ironically. "Aside from that, I like them not, these sorcerous upstarts—they seek to emulate the Bright Empire."

"Aye," Elric said. "They are an island culture, as ours was. They are sorcerers and warriors as our ancestors were. But their sorcery is less healthy than ever ours was. Our ancestors committed frightful deeds, yet it was *natural* to them. These newcomers, more human than we, have perverted their humanity whereas we never possessed it in the same degree. There will never be another Bright Empire, nor can their power last more than ten thousand years. This is a fresh age, Dyvim Slorm, in more than one way. The time of subtle sorcery is on the wane. Men are finding new means of harnessing natural power."

"Our knowledge is ancient," Dyvim Slorm agreed, "yet, so old is it that it has little relation to present events, I think. Our logic and learning are suited to the past . . ."

"I think you are right," said Elric, whose mingled emotions were suited neither to past, present nor future. "Aye, it is fitting that we should be wanderers, for we have no place in this world."

They drank in silence, moodily, their minds on matters of philosophy. Yet, for all this, Elric's thoughts were forever turning to Zarozinia and the fear of what might have befallen her. The very innocence of this girl, her vulnerability and her youth had been, to some degree at least, his salvation. His protective love for her had helped to keep him from brooding too deeply on his own doom-filled life and her company had eased his melancholy. The strange rede of the dead creature lingered in his memory. Undoubtedly the rede had referred to a battle, and the raven which Dyvim Slorm had seen had spoken of one also. The battle was sure to be the forthcoming one between Yishana's forces and those of Sarosto of Dharijor and Jagreen Lern of Pan Tang. If he was to find Zarozinia then he must go with Dyvim Slorm and there take part in the conflict. Though he might perish, he reasoned that he had best do as the omens ordered—otherwise he could lose even the slight chance of ever seeing Zarozinia again. He turned to his cousin.

"I'll make my way with you tomorrow, and use my blade in the battle. Whatever else, I have the feeling that Yishana will need every warrior against the Theocrat and his allies."

Dyvim Slorm agreed. "Not only *our* doom but the doom of nations will be at stake in this . . ."

3

Ten terrible men drove their yellow chariots down a black mountain which vomited blue and scarlet fire and shook in a spasm of destruction.

In such a manner, all over the globe, the forces of nature were disrupted and rebellious. Though few realised it, the Earth was changing. The Ten knew why, and they knew of Elric and how their knowledge linked with him.

The night was pale purple and the sun hung a bloody globe over the mountains, for it was late summer. In the valleys, cottages were burning as smoking lava smacked against the straw roofs.

Sepiriz, in the leading chariot, saw the villagers running, a confused rabble—like ants whose hills had been scattered. He turned to the blue-armoured man behind him and he smiled almost gaily.

"See them run," he said. "See them run, brother. Oh, the joy of it—such forces there are at work!"

"'Tis good to have woken at this time," his brother agreed, shouting over the rumbling noise of the volcano.

Then the smile left Sepiriz and his eyes narrowed. He lashed at his twin horses with a bull-hide whip, so that blood laced the flanks of the great black steeds as they galloped even faster down the steep mountain.

In the village, one man saw the Ten in the distance. He shrieked, voicing his fear in a warning:

"The fire has driven them out of the mountain. Hide—escape! The men from the volcano have awakened—they are coming. The Ten have awakened according to the prophecy—it is the end of the world!" Then the mountain gushed a fresh spewing of hot rock and flaming lava and the man was struck down, screamed as he burned, and died. He died needlessly, for the Ten had no interest in him or his fellows.

Sepiriz and his brothers rode straight through the village, their chariot wheels rattling on the coarse street, the hoofs of their horses pounding.

Behind them, the mountain bellowed.

"To Nihrain!" cried Sepiriz. "Speedily, brethren, for there is much work to do. A blade must be brought from limbo and a pair of men must be found to carry it to Xanyaw!"

Joy filled him as he saw the earth shuddering about him and heard the gushing of fire and rock behind him. His black body glistened, reflecting the flames of the burning houses. The horses leaned in their harness, dragging the bucking chariot at wild speed, their hoofs blurred movement over the ground so that it often seemed they flew.

Perhaps they did, for the steeds of Nihrain were known to be different from ordinary beasts.

Now they flung themselves along a gorge, now up a mountain path, making their speedy way towards the Chasm of Nihrain, the ancient home of the Ten who had not returned there for two thousand years.

Again, Sepiriz laughed. He and his brothers bore a terrible responsibility, for though they had no loyalty to men or gods, they were Fate's spokesmen and thus bore an awful knowledge within their immortal skulls.

For centuries they had slept in their mountain chamber, dwelling close to the dormant heart of the volcano since extremes of heat and cold bothered them little. Now the spewing rock had awakened them and they knew that their time had come—the time for which they had been waiting for millennia.

This was why Sepiriz sang in joy. At last he and his brothers were to be allowed to perform their ultimate function. And this involved two Melnibonéans, the two surviving members of the royal line of the Bright Empire.

Sepiriz knew they lived—they had to be alive, for without them Fate's scheme was impossible. But there were those upon the Earth, Sepiriz knew, who were capable of cheating Fate, so powerful were they. Their minions lay everywhere, particularly among the new race of men, but ghouls and demons were also their tools.

This made his chosen task the harder.

But now—to Nihrain! To the hewn city and there to draw the threads of destiny into a finer net. There was still a little time, but it was running short; and Time the Unknown was master of all . . .

The pavilions of Queen Yishana and her allies were grouped thickly about a series of small, wooded hills. The trees afforded cover from a distance and no campfires burned to give away their position. Also the sounds of the great army were as muted as possible. Outriders went to and fro, reporting the enemy's positions and keeping wary eyes open for spies.

But Elric and his Imrryrians were unchallenged as they rode in, for the albino and his men were easily recognisable and it was well-known that the feared Melnibonéan mercenaries had elected to aid Yishana.

Elric said to Dyvim Slorm: "I had best pay my respects to Queen Yishana, on account of our old bond, but I do not want her to know of my wife's disappearance—otherwise she may try to hinder me. We shall just say that I have come to aid her, out of friendship."

Dyvim Slorm nodded, and Elric left his cousin to tend to making camp, while he went at once to Yishana's tent where the tall queen awaited him impatiently.

The look in her eyes was shielded as he entered. She had a heavy, sensuous face that was beginning to show signs of ageing. Her long hair was black and shone around her head. Her breasts were large and her hips broader than Elric remembered. She was sitting in a padded chair and the table before her was scattered with battle-maps and writing materials, parchment, ink and quills.

"Good morning, wolf," said she with a half-smile that was at once sardonic and provocative. "My scouts reported that you were riding with your countrymen. This is pleasant. Have you forsaken your new wife to return to subtler pleasures?"

"No," he said.

He stripped off his heavy riding cloak and flung it on a bench. "Good morning, Yishana. You do not change. I've half a suspicion that Theleb K'aarna gave you a draught of the waters of Eternal Life before I killed him."

"Perhaps he did. How goes your marriage?"

"Well," he said as she moved closer and he felt the warmth of her body.

"And now I'm disappointed," she smiled ironically and shrugged. They had been lovers on different occasions, in spite of the fact that Elric had been partially responsible for her brother's death during the raid on Imrryr. Dharmit of Jharkor's death had put her on the throne and, being an ambitious woman, she had not taken the news with too much sadness. Elric had no wish to resume the relationship, however.

He turned immediately to the matter of the forthcoming battle.

"I see you're preparing for more than a skirmish," he said. "What forces have you and what are your chances of winning?"

"There are my own White Leopards," she told him, "five hundred picked warriors who run as swiftly as horses, are as strong as mountain cats and as ferocious as blood-mad sharks—they are trained to kill and killing is all they know. Then there are my other troops—infantry and cavalry, some eighty lords in command. The best cavalry are from Shazaar, wild riders but clever fighters and well-disciplined. Tarkesh has sent fewer men since I understand King Hilran needed to defend his southern borders against a heavy attack. However, there are almost a thousand and fifty foot soldiers and some two hundred mounted men from Tarkesh. In all we can put perhaps six thousand trained warriors on the field. Serfs, slaves and the like are also fighting, but they will of course serve only to meet the initial onslaught and will die in the early part of the battle."

Elric nodded. These were standard military tactics. "And what of the enemy?"

"We have more numbers—but they have Devil Riders and hunting tigers. There are also some beasts they keep in cages—but we cannot guess what they are since the cages are covered."

"I heard that the men of Myyrrhn are flying hither. The import must be great for them to leave their eyries."

"If we lose this battle," she said gravely, "Chaos could easily engulf the Earth and rule over it. Every oracle from here to Shazaar says the same thing, that Jagreen Lern is but the tool of less natural masters, that he is aided by the Lords of Chaos. We are not only fighting for our lands, Elric, we are fighting for the human race!"

"Then let us hope we win," he said.

Elric stood among the captains as they surveyed the mobilising army. Tall Dyvim Slorm was by his side, his golden shirt loose on his slim body and his manner confident, arrogant. Also here were hardened soldiers of many smaller campaigns; short, dark-faced men from Tarkesh with thick armour and black, oiled hair and beards. The half-naked winged men from Myyrrhn had arrived, with their brooding eyes, hawklike faces, their great wings folded on their backs, quiet, dignified, seldom speaking. The Shazaarian commanders were there also, in jackets of grey, brown and black, in rust-coloured bronze armour. With them stood the captain of Yishana's White Leopards, a long-legged, thick-bodied man with blond hair tied in a knot at the back of his bull-necked head, silver armour bearing the emblazon of a leopard, albino like Elric, rampant and snarling.

The time of the battle was drawing close . . .

Now, in the grey dawn, the two armies advanced upon each other, coming from opposite ends of a wide valley, flanked by low, wooded, hills.

The army of Pan Tang and Dharijor moved, a tide of dark metal, up the shallow valley to meet them. Elric, still unarmoured, watched as they approached, his horse stamping the turf. Dyvim Slorm, beside him, pointed and said: "Look—there are the plotters—Sarosto on the left and Jagreen Lern on the right!"

The leaders headed their army, banners of dark silk rustling above their helms. King Sarosto and his thin ally, aquiline Jagreen Lern in glowing scarlet armour that seemed to be red-hot and may have been. On his helm was the Merman Crest of Pan Tang, for he claimed kinship with the sea-people. Sarosto's armour was dull, murky yellow, emblazoned with the Star of Dharijor upon which was the Cleft Sword which history said was borne by Sarosto's ancestor Atarn the City-Builder.

Behind them, instantly observable, came the Devil Riders of Pan Tang on their six-legged reptilian mounts, bred by sorcery it was said. Swarthy and with introspective expressions on their sharp faces, they carried long, curved sabres, naked at their belts. Prowling among them came over a hundred hunting tigers, trained like dogs, with tusklike teeth and claws that could rend a man to the bone with a single sweep. Beyond the rolling army as it moved towards them, Elric could just see the tops of the mysterious cage-wagons. What weird beasts did *they* contain? he wondered.

Then Yishana shouted a command.

The archers' arrows spread a rattling black cloud above them as Elric led the first wave of infantry down the hill to meet the van of the enemy army. That he should be forced to risk his life embittered him, but if he was ever to discover Zarozinia's whereabouts he had to play out his ordered part and pray that he lived.

The main force of cavalry followed the infantry, flanking it with orders to encircle the enemy if possible. Brightly clad Imrryrians and bronze-armoured Shazaarians were to one side. Blue-armoured Tarkeshites with brilliant plumes of red, purple and white, long lances levelled, and gold-armoured Jharkorians, longswords already unscabbarded, galloped on the other side. In the centre of Elric's advance phalanx loped Yishana's White Leopards and the queen herself rode beneath her banner, behind the first phalanx, leading a battalion of knights.

Down they rushed towards the enemy whose own arrows rose upwards and then swept down to clash against helmets or thud into flesh.

Now the sound of war-shouts smashed through the still dawn as they streaked down the slopes and clashed.

Elric found himself confronting lean Jagreen Lern, and the snarling Theocrat met Stormbringer's swing with a flame-red buckler which successfully protected him—proving the shield to be treated against sorcerous weapons.

Jagreen Lern's features wrinkled into a malicious smile as he recognised Elric. "I was told you'd be here, Whiteface. I know you Elric and I know your doom!"

"Too many men appear to know my destiny better than I," said the albino. "But perhaps if I slay you, Theocrat, I may force the secret from you before you die?"

"Oh, no! That is not my masters' plan at all."

"Well, mayhap 'tis mine!"

He struck again at Jagreen Lern, but again the blade was turned, screaming its anger. He felt it move in his hand, felt it throb with chagrin, for normally the hell-forged blade could slice through metal however finely tempered.

In Jagreen Lern's gauntleted right hand was a huge war-axe which he now swung at the unprotected head of Elric's horse. This was odd since he was in a position to strike at Elric himself. The albino jerked his steed's head to one side, avoided the blow and drove again point first at Jagreen Lern's midriff. The runeblade shrieked as it failed to pierce the armour. The war-axe swung again and Elric brought up his sword as protection but, in astonishment, was driven back in his saddle by the force of the blow, barely able to control his horse, one foot slipping from the stirrup.

Jagreen Lern struck again and successfully split the skull of Elric's horse which crumpled to its knees, blood and brains gushing, great eyes rolling as it died.

Flung from the beast, Elric rose painfully and readied himself for Jagreen Lern's next blow. But to his surprise, the sorcerer-king turned away and moved into the thick of the battle.

"Sadly your life is not mine to take, Whiteface! That is the prerogative of other powers. If you live and we are the victors—I will seek you out, perhaps."

Unable, in his dazed condition, to make sense of this, Elric looked desperately around for another horse and saw a Dharijorian mount, its head and foreparts well protected by dented black armour, running loose and away from the fight.

Swiftly, he leapt for its harness and caught a dangling rein, steadied the beast, got a foot into a stirrup and swung himself up in the saddle which was uncomfortable for an unarmoured man. Standing in the stirrups, Elric rode it back into the battle.

He hewed his way through the enemy knights, slaying now a Devil Rider, now a hunting tiger that lashed at him with bared fangs, now a gorgeously armoured Dharijorian commander, now two foot soldiers who struck at him with halberds. His horse reared like a monster and, desperately, he forced it closer to the standard of Yishana until he could see one of the heralds.

Yishana's army was fighting bravely, but its discipline was lost. It must regroup if it was to be most effective.

"*Recall the cavalry!*" Elric yelled. "*Recall the cavalry!*"

The young herald looked up. He was badly pressed by two Devil Riders. His attention diverted, he was skewered on a Devil Rider's blade and shrieked as the two men butchered him.

Cursing, Elric rode closer and struck one of the attackers in the side of the head. The man toppled and fell into the churned mud of the field. The other Rider turned, only to meet howling Stormbringer's point, and he died yelling, as the runeblade drank his soul.

The herald, still mounted, was dead in the saddle, his body a mass of cuts. Elric leaned forward, tearing the bloody horn from around the corpse's neck. Placing it to his lips, he sounded the Cavalry Recall and caught a glimpse of horsemen turning. Now he saw the standard itself begin to fall and realised that the standard-bearer was slain. He rose in the saddle and grasped the pole which bore the bright flag of Jharkor and, with this in one hand, the horn at his lips, attempted to rally his forces.

Slowly, the remnants of the battered army gathered around him. Then Elric, taking control of the battle, did the only thing he could—took the sole course of action which might save the day.

He sounded a long, wailing note on the horn. In response to this he heard the beating of heavy wings as the men of Myyrrhn rose into the air.

Observing this, the enemy released the traps of the mysterious cages.

Elric groaned with despair.

A weird hooting preceded the sight of giant owls, thought extinct even in Myyrrhn the land of their origin, circling skyward.

The enemy had prepared against a threat from the air and, by some means, had produced the age-old enemies of the men of Myyrrhn.

Only slightly daunted by this unexpected sight, the men of Myyrrhn, armed with long spears, attacked the great birds. The embattled warriors on the ground were showered with blood and feathers. Corpses of men and birds began to flop downwards, crushing infantry and cavalry beneath them.

Through this confusion, Elric and the White Leopards of Yishana cut their way into the enemy to join up with Dyvim Slorm and his Imrryrians, the remnants of the Tarkeshite cavalry, and about a hundred Shazaarians, who had survived. Looking upwards, Elric saw that most of the great owls were destroyed, but only a handful of the men of Myyrrhn had survived the fight in the air. These, having done what they could against the owls, were themselves circling about preparing to leave the battle. Obviously they realised the hopelessness of it all.

Elric called to Dyvim Slorm as their forces joined: "The battle's lost—Sarosto and Jagreen Lern rule here now!"

Dyvim Slorm hefted his longsword in his hand and gave Elric a look of assent. "If we're to live to keep our destiny, we'd best make speed away from here!" he cried.

There was little more they could do.

"Zarozinia's life is more important to me than anything else!" Elric yelled. "Let's look to our own predicament!"

But the weight of the enemy forces was like a vice, crushing Elric and his men. Blood covered Elric's face from a blow he had received on the forehead. It clogged his eyes so that he had to keep raising his left hand to his face to get rid of the stuff.

His right arm ached as he lifted Stormbringer again and again, hacking and stabbing about him, desperate now, for although the dreadful blade had a life, almost an intelligence, of its own, even it could not supply the vitality which Elric needed to remain entirely fresh. In a way he was glad, for he hated the runesword, though he had to depend on the force which flowed from it to him.

Stormbringer more than slew Elric's attackers—it drank their souls, and some of that life-force was passed on to the Melnibonéan monarch . . .

Now the ranks of the enemy fell back and seemed to open. Through this self-made breach, animals came running. Animals with gleaming eyes and red, fang-filled jaws. Animals with claws.

The hunting tigers of Pan Tang.

Horses screamed as the tigers leapt and rent them, tearing down mount and man and slashing at the throats of their victims. The tigers raised bloody snouts and stared around for a new prey. Terrified, many of Elric's small force fell back shouting. Most of the Tarkeshite knights broke and fled the field, precipitating the flight of the Jharkorians whose maddened horses bore them away and were soon followed by the few remaining Shazaarians still mounted. Soon only Elric, his Imrryrians and about forty White Leopards stood against the might of Dharijor and Pan Tang.

Elric raised his horn and sounded the Retreat, wheeled his black steed about and raced up the valley, Imrryrians behind him. But the White Leopards fought on to the last. Yishana had said that they knew nothing but how to kill. Evidently they also knew how to die.

Elric and Dyvim Slorm led the Imrryrians up the valley, half-thankful that the White Leopards covered their retreat. The Melnibonéan had seen nothing of Yishana since he had clashed with Jagreen Lern. He wondered what had become of her.

As they turned a bend in the valley, Elric understood the full battle plan of Jagreen Lern and his ally—for a strong, fresh force of foot soldiers and cavalry had assembled at the other end of the valley, for the purpose of cutting off any retreat made by his army.

Scarcely thinking, Elric urged his horse up the slopes of the hills, his men following, ducking beneath the low branches of the birch trees as the Dharijorians rushed towards them, spreading out to cut off their escape.

Elric turned his horse about and saw that the White Leopards were still fighting around the standard of Jharkor and he headed back in that direction, keeping to the hills. Over the crest of the hills he rode, Dyvim Slorm and a handful of Imrryrians with him, and then they were galloping for open countryside while the knights of Dharijor and Pan Tang gave chase. They had obviously recognised Elric and wished either to kill or to capture him.

Ahead Elric could see that the Tarkeshites, Shazaarians and Jharkorians who had earlier fled had taken the same route out as he had. But they no longer rode together, were scattering away.

Elric and Dyvim Slorm fled westwards across unknown country while the other Imrryrians, to take attention off their leaders, rode to the north-east towards Tarkesh and perhaps a few days of safety.

The battle was won. The minions of evil were the victors and an age of terror had settled on the lands of the Young Kingdoms in the west.

Some days later, Elric, Dyvim Slorm, two Imrryrians, a Tarkeshite commander called Yedn-pad-Juizev, badly wounded in the side, and a Shazaarian foot soldier, Orozn, who had taken a horse away from the battle, were temporarily safe from pursuit and were trudging their horses wearily towards a range of slim-peaked mountains which loomed black against the red evening sky.

They had not spoken for some hours. Yedn-pad-Juizev was obviously dying and they could do nothing for him. He knew this also and expected nothing, merely rode with them for company. He was very tall for a Tarkeshite, his scarlet plume still bobbing on his dented blue-metal helmet, his breastplate scarred and smeared with his own blood and others'. His beard was black and shiny with oil, his nose a jutting crag on the rock of his soldier's face, his eyes half-glazed. He was bearing the pain well. Though they were impatient to reach the comparative safety of the mountain range, the others matched their pace to his, half in respect and half in fascination that a man could cling to life for so long.

Night came and a great yellow moon hung in the sky over the mountains. The sky was completely clear of cloud and stars shone brightly. The warriors wished that the night had been dark, storm-covered, for they could have then sought more security in the shadows. As it was the night was lighted and they could only hope that they reached the mountains soon—before the hunting tigers of Pan Tang discovered their tracks and they died under the rending claws of those dreadful beasts.

Elric was in a grim and thoughtful mood. For a while the Dharijorian and Pan Tang conquerors would be busy consolidating their new-won empire. Perhaps there would be quarrels between them when this was done, perhaps not. But soon, anyway, they would be very powerful and threatening the security of other nations on the Southern and Eastern Continents.

But all this, however much it overshadowed the fate of the whole world, meant little to Elric for he still could not clearly see his way to Zarozinia. He remembered the dead creature's prophecy, part of which had now come about. But still it meant little. He felt as if he were being driven constantly westwards, as if he must go further and further into the sparsely settled lands beyond Jharkor. Was it here his destiny lay? Was it here that Zarozinia's captors were? *Beyond the ocean brews a battle; Beyond the battle blood shall fall . . .*

Well, had the blood fallen, or was it yet to fall? What was the "twin" that Elric's kinsman, Dyvim Slorm, bore? Who was the one who should not live?

Perhaps the secret lay in the mountains ahead of them?

Beneath the moon they rode, and at last came to a gorge. Halfway along it they located a cave and lay down inside to rest.

In the morning, Elric was awakened by a sound outside the cave. Instantly he drew Stormbringer and crept to the mouth of the cave. What he saw caused him to sheathe the blade and call in a soft voice to the battered man who was riding up the gorge towards the cave. "Here, herald! We are friends!"

The man was one of Yishana's heralds. His surcoat was in ribbons, his armour crumpled on his body. He was swordless and without a helmet, a young man with his face made gaunt by weariness and despair. He looked up and relief came when he recognised Elric.

"My lord Elric—they said you were slain on the field."

"I'm glad they did, since that makes pursuit less likely. Come inside."

The others were awake now—all but one. Yedn-pad-Juizev had died, sleeping, in the night. Orozn yawned and jerked a thumb at the corpse. "If we do not find food soon, I'll be tempted to eat our dead friend."

The man looked at Elric for response to this jest, but seeing the albino's expression he was abashed and retreated to the depths of the cave grumbling and kicking at loose stones.

Elric leaned against the wall of the cave near the opening. "What news have you?" he asked.

"Dark news, my lord. From Shazaar to Tarkesh black misery prevails and iron and fire beat across nations like an unholy storm. We are fully conquered. Only small bands of men carry on a hopeless struggle against the enemy. Some of our folk are already talking of turning bandit and preying on each other, so desperate have times become."

Elric nodded. "Such is what happens when foreign allies are beaten on friendly soil. What of Queen Yishana?"

"She fared ill, my lord. Clad in metal, she battled against a score of men before expiring—her body torn asunder by the force of their attack. Sarosto took her head for a keepsake and added it to other trophies including the hands of Karnarl, his half-brother who opposed him over the Pan Tang alliance, the eyes of Penik of Nargesser, who raised an army against him in that province. Theocrat Jagreen Lern ordered that all other prisoners be tortured to death and hanged in chains through the lands as warning against insurrection. They are an unholy pair, my lord!"

Elric's mouth grew tight when he heard this. Already it was becoming clear to him that his only route was westwards, for the conquerors would soon search him out if he went back. He turned to Dyvim Slorm. The Imrryrian's shirt was in rags and his left arm covered in dried blood.

"Our destiny appears to lie in the west," he said quietly.

"Then let us make speed," said his cousin, "for I am impatient to get it over and at least learn whether we live or perish in this enterprise. We gained nothing by our encounter with the enemy, but wasted time."

"I gained something," Elric said, remembering his fight with Jagreen Lern. "I gained the knowledge that Jagreen Lern *is* connected in some way with the kidnapping of my wife—and if he had aught to do with it, I'll claim my vengeance no matter what."

"Now," said Dyvim Slorm. "Let us make haste to the west."

4

They drove deeper into the mountains that day, avoiding the few hunting parties sent out by the conquerors, but the two Imrryrians, recognising that their leaders were on a special journey, left to go in another direction. The herald was gone southward to spread his gloomy news so that only Elric, Dyvim Slorm and Orozn were left. They did not welcome Orozn's company, but bore with it for the meanwhile.

Then, after a day, Orozn disappeared and Elric and Dyvim Slorm ranged deeper into the black crags, riding through towering, oppressive canyons or along narrow paths.

Snow lay on the mountains, bright white against sharp black, filling gorges, making paths slippery and dangerous. Then one evening they came to a place where the mountains opened out into a wide valley and they rode with difficulty down the foothills of the mountains, their tracks making great black scars in the snow and their horses steaming, their breath billowing white in the cold air.

They observed a rider coming across the valley floor towards them. One rider they did not fear, so they waited for him to approach. To their surprise it was Orozn, clad in fresh garments of wolfskin and deer hide. He greeted them in a friendly manner.

"I have come seeking you both. You must have taken a more difficult route than mine."

"From where have you come?" Elric asked; his face was drawn, his cheekbones emphasised by the sunken skin. He looked more like a wolf than ever with his red eyes gleaming. Zarozinia's fate weighed heavily on his mind.

"There is a settlement nearby. Come, I will take you to it."

They followed Orozn for some way and it was getting near nightfall, the setting sun staining the mountains scarlet, when they reached the opposite side of the valley, dotted with a few birch trees and, further up, a cluster of firs.

Orozn led them into this grove.

They came screaming out of the dark, a dozen swarthy men, possessed by hatred—and something else. Weapons were raised in mailed hands. By their armour, these men were from Pan Tang. Orozn must have been captured and persuaded to lead Elric and his cousin into ambush.

Elric turned his horse, rearing.

"Orozn! You betrayed us!"

But Orozn was riding. He looked back once, his pale face tortured with guilt. Then his eyes darted away from Elric and Dyvim Slorm and he frowned, rode down the moss-wet hill back into the howling darkness of the night.

Elric lifted Stormbringer from his belt, gripped the hilt, blocked a blow from a brass-studded mace, slid his sword down the handle and sheared off his attacker's fingers. He and Dyvim Slorm were soon surrounded, yet he fought on, Stormbringer shrilling a wild, lawless song of death.

But Elric and Dyvim Slorm were still weak from the rigours of their past adventures. Not even Stormbringer's evil strength was sufficient fully to revitalise Elric's deficient veins and he was filled with fear—not of the attackers, but of the fact that he was doomed to die or be captured. And he had the feeling that these warriors had no knowledge of their master's part in the matter of the prophecy, did not realise that, perhaps, he was not meant to die at that moment.

In fact, he decided, as he battled, a great mistake was about to be perpetrated . . .

"Arioch!" he cried in his fear to the demon-god of Melniboné. "Arioch! Aid me! Blood and souls for thine aid!"

But that intractable entity sent no aid.

Dyvim Slorm's long blade caught a man just below his gorget and pierced him through the throat. The other Pan Tang horsemen threw themselves at him but were driven back by his sweeping sword. Dyvim Slorm shouted: "Why do we worship such a god when whim decides him so often?"

"Perhaps he thinks our time has come!" Elric yelled back as his runeblade drank another foe's life-force.

Tiring fast, they fought on until a new sound broke above the clash of arms—the sound of chariots and low, moaning cries.

Then they were sweeping into the mêlée, black men with handsome features and thin, proud mouths, their magnificent bodies half-naked as their cloaks of white fox fur streamed behind them and their javelins were flung with terrible accuracy at the bewildered men of Pan Tang.

Elric sheathed his sword and remained ready to fight or flee. "This is the one—the white-faced one!" cried a black charioteer as he saw Elric. The chariots rolled to a halt, tall horses stamping and snorting. Elric rode up to the leader.

"I am grateful," he said, half falling from his saddle in weariness. He turned the droop of his shoulders into a bow. "You appear to know me—you are the third I've met while on this quest who recognises me without my being able to return the compliment."

The leader tugged the fox cape about his naked chest and smiled with his thin lips. "I'm named Sepiriz and you will know me soon enough. As for you, we have known of you for thousands of years. Elric are you not—last king of Melniboné?"

"That is true."

"And you," Sepiriz addressed Dyvim Slorm, "are Elric's cousin. Together you represent the last of the pure line of Melniboné."

"Aye," Dyvim Slorm agreed, curiosity in his eyes.

"Then we have been waiting for you to pass this way. There was a prophecy . . ."

"*You* are the captors of Zarozinia?" Elric reached for his sword.

Sepiriz shook his head. "No, but we can tell you where she is. Calm your-self. Though I realise the agony of mind you must be suffering, I will be better able to explain all I know back in our own domain."

"First tell us who you are," Elric demanded.

Sepiriz smiled slightly. "You know us, I think—or at least you know of us. There was a certain friendship between your ancestors and our folk in the early years of the Bright Empire." He paused a moment before continuing: "Have you ever heard legends, in Imrryr perhaps, of the Ten from the moun-tain? The Ten who sleep in the mountain of fire?"

"Many times." Elric drew in his breath. "Now I recognise you by descrip-tion. But it is said that you sleep for centuries in the mountain of fire. Why are you roaming abroad in this manner?"

"We were driven by an eruption from our volcano home which had been dormant for two thousand years. Such movements of nature have been taking place all over the Earth of late. Our time, we knew, had come to awaken again. We are servants of Fate—and our mission is strongly bound up with your des-tiny. We bear a message for you from Zarozinia's captor—and another from a different source. Would you return now, with us, to the Chasm of Nihrain and learn all we can tell you?"

Elric pondered for a moment, then he lifted his white face and said: "I am in haste to claim vengeance, Sepiriz. But if what you can tell me will lead me closer to claiming it, I'll come."

"Then come!" The black giant jerked the reins of his horse and turned the chariot about.

It was a journey of a day and a night to the Chasm of Nihrain, a huge gaping fissure high in the mountains, a place avoided by all; it had supernatural sig-nificance for those who dwelt near the mountains.

The lordly Nihrain conversed little on the journey and at last they were above the chasm, driving their chariots down the steep path which wound into its dark depths.

About half a mile down no light penetrated, but they saw ahead of them flickering torches that illuminated part of the carved outline of an unearthly mural or betrayed a gaping opening in the solid rock. Then, as they guided their horses down further, they saw, in detail, the awe-inspiring city of Nihrain which outsiders had not glimpsed for many centuries. The last of the Nihrain now lived here; ten immortal men of a race older even than that of Melniboné which had a history of twenty thousand years.

Huge columns rose above them, hewn ages before from the living rock, giant statues and wide balconies, many-tiered. Windows a hundred feet high and sweeping steps cut into the face of the chasm. The Ten drove their yellow chariots through a mighty gate and into the caverns of Nihrain, carved to their entire extent with strange symbols and stranger murals. Here slaves, wakened from a sleep of centuries to tend their masters, ran forward. Even these did not fully bear resemblance to the men that Elric knew.

Sepiriz gave the reins to a slave as Elric and Dyvim Slorm dismounted, staring about them in awe.

He said: "Now—to my own chambers and there I'll inform you of what you wish to know—and what you must do."

Led by Sepiriz, the kinsmen stalked impatiently through galleries and into a large chamber full of dark sculpture. A number of fires burned behind this hall, in big grates. Sepiriz folded his great body in a chair and bade them sit in two similar chairs, carved from solid blocks of ebony. When they were all seated before one of the fires, Sepiriz took a long breath, staring around the hall, perhaps remembering its earlier history.

Somewhat angered by this show of casualness, Elric said impatiently: "Forgive me, Sepiriz—but you promised to pass on your message to us."

"Yes," Sepiriz said, "but so much do I have to tell you that I must pause one moment to collect my thoughts." He settled himself in the chair before continuing.

"We know where your wife is," he said at last, "and know also that she is safe. She will not be harmed since she is to be bargained for something which you possess."

"Then tell me the *whole* story," Elric demanded bleakly.

"We were friendly with your ancestors, Elric. And we were friendly with those they superseded, the ones who forged that blade you bear."

Elric was interested in spite of his anxiety. For years he had attempted to rid himself of the runesword, but had never succeeded. All his efforts had failed and he still needed to carry it, although drugs now gave him most of his strength.

"Would you be rid of your sword, Elric?" Sepiriz said.

"Aye—it's well known."

"Then listen to this tale.

"We know for whom and for what the blade—and its twin—were forged. They were made for a special purpose and for special men. Only Melnibonéans may carry them, and of those only the blood of the royal line."

"There is no hint of any special purpose for the swords in Melnibonéan history or legend," Elric said leaning forward.

"Some secrets are best kept fully guarded," Sepiriz said calmly. "Those blades were forged to destroy a group of very powerful beings. Among them are the Dead Gods."

"The Dead Gods—but, by their very name, *you* must know that they perished long ages ago."

"They 'perished' as you say. In human terms they are dead. But they *chose* to die, chose to rid themselves of material shape and hurled their lifestuff into the blackness of eternity, for in those days they were full of fear."

Elric had no real conception of what Sepiriz described but he accepted what the Nihrainian said and listened on.

"One of them has returned," Sepiriz said.

"Why?"

"To get, at any cost, two things which endanger him and his fellow gods—wherever they may be they can still be harmed by these things."

"They are . . . ?"

"They have the earthly appearance of two swords, runecarved and sorcerous—Mournblade and Stormbringer."

"This!" Elric touched his blade. "Why should the gods fear this? And the other went to limbo with my cousin Yyrkoon whom I killed many years ago. It is lost."

"That is not true. We recovered it—that was part of Fate's purpose for us. We have it here in Nihrain. The blades were forged for your ancestors who drove the Dead Gods away by means of them. They were made by other unhuman smiths who were also enemies of the Dead Gods. These smiths were compelled to combat evil *with* evil, although they, themselves, were not pledged to Chaos, but to Law. They forged the swords for several reasons—ridding the world of the Dead Gods was but one!"

"The other reasons?"

"Those you shall learn in times to come—for our relationship will not be ended until the whole destiny has been worked out. We are obliged not to reveal the other reasons until the proper time. You have a dangerous destiny, Elric, and I do not envy it."

"But what is the message you have?" Elric said impatiently.

"Due to the disturbance created by Jagreen Lern, one of the Dead Gods has been enabled to return to Earth, as I told you. He has gathered acolytes about him. They kidnapped your wife."

Elric felt a mood of deep despair creep over him. Must he defy such power as this?

"Why . . . ?" he whispered.

"Darnizhaan is aware that Zarozinia is important to you. He wishes to barter her for the two swords. We, in this matter, are merely messengers. We must give up the sword we keep, at the request of you or Dyvim Slorm, for they rightfully belong to any of the royal line. Darnizhaan's terms are simple. He will dispatch Zarozinia to limbo unless you give him the blades which threaten his existence. Her death, it would not be death as we know it, would be unpleasant and eternal."

"And if I agreed to do that, what would happen?"

"All the Dead Gods would return. Only the power of the swords keeps them from doing so now!"

"And what would happen if the Dead Gods came back?"

"Even without the Dead Gods, Chaos threatens to conquer the planet, but with them it would be utterly invincible, its effect immediate. Evil would sweep the world. Chaos would plunge this Earth into a stinking inferno of terror and destruction. You have already had a taste of what is happening, and Darnizhaan has only been back for a short time."

"You mean the defeat of Yishana's armies and the conquest by Sarosto and Jagreen Lern?"

"Exactly. Jagreen Lern has a pact with Chaos—all the Lords of Chaos, not merely the Dead Gods—for Chaos fears Fate's plan for Earth's future and would attempt to tamper with it by gaining domination of our planet. The Lords of Chaos are strong enough without the help of the Dead Gods. Darnizhaan must be destroyed."

"I have an impossible choice, Sepiriz. If I give up Stormbringer I can probably survive on herbs and the like. But if I do give it up for Zarozinia, then Chaos will be unleashed to its full extent and I will have a monstrous crime upon my conscience."

"The choice is yours alone to make."

Elric deliberated but could think of no way of solving the problem.

"Bring the other blade," he said at last.

Sepiriz rejoined them a while later, with a scabbarded sword that seemed little different from Stormbringer.

"So, Elric—is the prophecy explained?" he asked, still keeping hold of Mournblade.

"Aye—here is the twin of that I bear. But the last part—where are we to go?"

"I will tell you in a moment. Though the Dead Gods, and the powers of Chaos, are aware that we possess the sister blade, they do not know whom we really serve. Fate, as I told you, is our master, and Fate has wrought a fabric for this Earth which would be hard to alter. But it *could* be altered and we are entrusted to see that Fate is not cheated. You are about to undergo a test. How you fare in it, what your decision is, will decide what we must tell you upon your return to Nihrain."

"You wish me to return here?"

"Yes."

"Give me Mournblade," Elric said quickly.

Sepiriz handed him the sword and Elric stood there with one twin blade in each hand, as if weighing something between them.

Both blades seemed to moan in recognition and the powers swam through his body so that he seemed to be built of steel-hard fire.

"I remember now that I hold them both that their powers are greater than I realise. There is one quality they possess when paired, a quality we may be able to use against this Dead God." He frowned. "But more of that in a moment." He stared sharply at Sepiriz. "Now tell me, where is Darnizhaan?"

"The Vale of Xanyaw in Myyrrhn!"

Elric handed Mournblade to Dyvim Slorm who accepted it gingerly.

"What will your choice be?" Sepiriz asked.

"Who knows?" Elric said with bitter gaiety. "Perhaps there is a way to beat this Dead God . . .

"But I tell you this, Sepiriz—given the opportunity I shall make that god rue his homecoming, for he has done the one thing that can move me to real anger. And the anger of Elric of Melniboné and his sword Stormbringer can destroy the world!"

Sepiriz rose from his chair, his eyebrows lifting.

"And gods, Elric, can it destroy gods?"

5

Elric rode like a giant scarecrow, gaunt and rigid on the massive back of the Nihrainian steed. His grim face was set fast in a mask that hid emotion and his crimson eyes burned like coals in their sunken sockets. The wind whipped his hair this way and that, but he sat straight, staring ahead, one long-fingered hand gripping Stormbringer's hilt.

Occasionally Dyvim Slorm, who bore Mournblade both proudly and warily, heard the blade moan to its sister and felt it shudder at his side. Only later did he begin to ask himself what the blade might make him, what it would give him and demand of him. After that, he kept his hand away from it as much as possible.

Close to the borders of Myyrrhn, a pack of Dharijorian hirelings—native Jharkorians in the livery of the conquerors—came upon them. Unsavoury louts they were, who should have known better than to ride across Elric's path. They steered their horses towards the pair, grinning. The black plumes of their helmets nodded, armour straps creaked and metal clanked. The leader, a squint-eyed bully with an axe at his belt, pulled his mount short in front of Elric.

At a direction from its master, the albino's horse came to a stop. His expression unchanged, Elric drew Stormbringer in an economic, catlike gesture. Dyvim Slorm copied him, eyeing the silently laughing men. He was surprised at how easily the blade sprang from its scabbard.

Then, with no challenges, Elric began to fight.

He fought like an automaton, quickly, efficiently, expressionlessly, cleaving the leader's shoulder plate in a stroke that cut through the man from shoulder to stomach in one raking movement which peeled back armour and flesh, rupturing the body so that a great scarlet gash appeared in the black metal and the leader wept as he slowly died, sprawling for a moment over his horse before slumping from the mount, one leg high, caught in a stirrup strap.

Stormbringer let out a great metallic purr of pleasure and Elric directed arm and blade about him, emotionlessly slaying the horsemen as if they were unarmed and chained, so little chance did they have.

Dyvim Slorm, unused to the semi-sentient Mournblade, tried to wield her like an ordinary sword but she moved in his hand, making cleverer strokes than he. A peculiar sense of power, at once sensual and cool, poured into him and he heard his voice yelling exultantly, realised what his ancestors must have been like in war.

The fight was quickly done with and leaving the soul-drained corpses on the ground behind them, they were soon in the land of Myyrrhn. Both blades had now been commonly blooded.

Elric was now better able to think and act coherently, but he could spare nothing for Dyvim Slorm while intratemporally asking nothing of his cousin who rode at his side, frustrated in that he was not called upon for his help.

Elric let his mind drift about in time, encompassing past, present and future and forming it into a whole—a pattern. He was suspicious of pattern, disliking shape, for he did not trust it. To him, life was chaotic, chance-dominated, unpredictable. It was a trick, an illusion of the mind, to be able to see a pattern to it.

He knew a few things, judged nothing.

He knew he bore a sword which physically and psychologically he needed to bear. It was an unalterable admission of a weakness in him, a lack of confidence in either himself or the philosophy of cause and effect. He believed himself a realist.

He knew that he loved, obscurely at times, his wife Zarozinia and would die if it meant she would not be harmed.

He knew that, if he were to survive and keep the freedom he had won and fought to hold, he must journey to the Dead God's lair and do what he saw fit to do when he had managed to assess the situation. He knew that for all his admission of Chaos he would be better able to do what he wished in a world ordered by some degree of Law.

The wind had been warm but now, nearing dusk, it grew colder. A low, cloudy sky with the heavy banks of grey picked out against the lighter shades of grey like islands in a cold sea. And there was a smell of smoke in Elric's nostrils, the frantic chirruping of birds in his ears and the sound of a whistling boy heard over the droning wind.

Dyvim Slorm turned his horse in the direction of the whistling, rode into scrub, leaned down in the saddle and hauled himself up with a wriggling youngster gripped by the slack of his shirt.

"Where are you from, lad?" Dyvim Slorm asked.

"From a village a mile or two away, sir," the boy replied, out of breath and scared.

He looked with wide eyes at Elric, fascinated by the tall albino's stern and pitiless mien.

He turned his head sharply to stare up at Dyvim Slorm. "Is that not Elric Friendslayer?" he said.

Dyvim Storm released the boy and said, "Where lies the Vale of Xanyaw?"

"North-west of here—it is no place for mortals. Is that not Elric Friend-slayer, sir, tell me?"

Dyvim Slorm glanced miserably at his cousin and did not reply to the boy. To-gether they urged their horses north-west and Elric's pace was even more urgent.

Through the bleak night they rode, buffeted by a vicious wind.

And as they came closer to the Vale of Xanyaw, the whole sky, the earth, the air became filled with heavy, throbbing music. Melodious, sensual, great chords of sound, on and on it rose and fell, and following it came the white-faced ones.

Each had a black cowl and a sword which split at the end into three curved barbs. Each grinned a fixed grin. The music followed them as they came running like mad things at the two men who reined in their horses, restraining the urge to turn and flee. Elric had seen horrors in his life, had seen much that would make others insane, but for some reason these shocked him more deeply than any. They were men, ordinary men by the look of them—but men possessed by an unholy spirit.

Prepared to defend themselves, Elric and Dyvim Slorm drew their blades and waited for the encounter, but none came. The music and the men rushed past them and away beyond them in the direction from which they had come.

Overhead, suddenly, they heard the beat of wings, a shriek from out of the sky and a ghastly wail. Fleeing, two women rushed by and Elric was disturbed to see that the women were from the winged race of Myyrrhn, but were wingless. These, unlike a woman Elric remembered, had had their wings deliberately hacked off. They paid no attention to the two riders, but disappeared, running into the night, their eyes blank and their faces insane.

"What is happening, Elric?" cried Dyvim Slorm, resheathing his runeblade, his other hand striving to control the prancing horse.

"I know not. What *does* happen in a place where the Dead Gods' rule has come back?"

All was rushing noise and confusion; the night was full of movement and terror.

"Come!" Elric slapped his sword against his mount's rump and sent the beast into a jerking gallop, forcing himself and the steed forward into the terrible night.

Then mighty laughter greeted them as they rode between hills into the Vale of Xanyaw. The valley was pitch-black and alive with menace, the very hills seeming sentient. They slowed their pace as they lost their sense of direction, and Elric had to call to his unseen cousin, to make sure he was still close. The echoing laughter sounded again, roaring from out of the dark, so that the earth shook. It was as if the whole planet laughed in ironic mirth at their efforts to control their fears and push on through the valley.

Elric wondered if he had been betrayed and this was a trap set by the

Dead Gods. What proof had he that Zarozinia was here? Why had he trusted Sepiriz? Something slithered against his leg as it passed him and he put his hand on the hilt of his sword, ready to draw it.

But then, shooting upwards into the dark sky, there arose, seemingly from the very earth, a huge figure which barred their way. Hands on hips, wreathed in golden light, a face of an ape, somehow blended with another shape to give it dignity and wild grandeur, its body alive and dancing with colour and light, its lips grinning with delight and knowledge—Darnizhaan, the Dead God!

"*Elric!*"

"Darnizhaan!" cried Elric fiercely, craning his head to stare up at the Dead God's face. He felt no fear now. "I have come for my wife!"

Around the Dead God's heels appeared acolytes with wide lips and pale, triangular faces, conical caps on their heads and madness in their eyes. They giggled and shrilled and shivered in the light of Darnizhaan's grotesque and beautiful body. They gibbered at the two riders and mocked them, but they did not move away from the Dead God's heels.

Elric sneered. "Degenerate and pitiful minions," he said.

"Not so pitiful as you, Elric of Melniboné," laughed the Dead God. "Have you come to bargain, or to give your wife's soul into my custody, so that she may spend eternity dying?"

Elric did not let his hate show on his face.

"I would destroy you; it is instinctive for me to do so. But—"

The Dead God smiled, almost with pity. "*You* must be destroyed, Elric. You are an anachronism. Your time is gone."

"Speak for yourself, Darnizhaan!"

"I *could* destroy you."

"But you will not." Though passionately hating the being, Elric also felt a disturbing sense of comradeship for the Dead God. Both of them represented an age that was gone; neither was really part of the new Earth.

"Then I will destroy her," the Dead God said. "That I could do with impunity."

"Zarozinia! Where is she?"

Once again Darnizhaan's mighty laughter shook the Vale of Xanyaw. "Oh, what have the old folk come to? There was a time when no man of Melniboné, particularly of the royal line, would admit to caring for another mortal soul, especially if they belonged to the beast-race, the new race of the age you call that of the Young Kingdoms. What? Are you mating with animals, King of Melniboné? Where is your blood, your cruel and brilliant blood? Where the glorious malice? Where the evil, Elric?"

Peculiar emotions stirred in Elric as he remembered his ancestors, the Sorcerer Emperors of the Dragon Isle. He realised that the Dead God was deliberately awakening these emotions and, with an effort, he refused to let them dominate him.

"That is past," he shouted, "a new time has come upon the Earth. Our time will soon be gone—and yours is *over*!"

"No, Elric. Mark my words, whatever happens. The dawn is over and will soon be swept away like dead leaves before the wind of morning. The Earth's history has not even begun. You, your ancestors, these men of the new races even, you are nothing but a *prelude to history*. You will all be forgotten if the real history of the world begins. But we can avert that—we can survive, conquer the Earth and hold it against the Lords of Law, against Fate herself, against the Cosmic Balance—we *can* continue to live, but you *must* give me the swords!"

"I fail to understand you," Elric said, his lips thin and his teeth tight in his skull. "I am here to bargain or do battle for my wife."

"You do not understand," the Dead God guffawed, "because we are all of us, gods and men, but shadows playing puppet parts before the true play begins. You would best not fight me—rather side with me, for I know the truth. We share a common destiny. We do not, any of us, exist. The old folk are doomed, you, myself and my brothers, unless you give me the swords. We must not fight one another. Share our frightful knowledge—the knowledge that turned us insane. There is nothing, Elric—no past, present, or future. *We do not exist, any of us!*"

Elric shook his head quickly. "I do not understand you, still. I would not understand you if I could. I desire only the return of my wife—not baffling conundrums!"

Darnizhaan laughed again. "No! You shall not have the woman unless we are given control of the swords. You do not realise their properties. They were not only designed to destroy us or exile us—their destiny is to destroy the world as we know it. If you retain them, Elric, you will be responsible for wiping out your own memory for those who come after you."

"I'd welcome that," Elric said.

Dyvim Slorm remained silent, not altogether in sympathy with Elric. The Dead God's argument seemed to contain truth.

Darnizhaan shook his body so that the golden light danced and its area widened momentarily. "Keep the swords and all of us will be as if we had *never* existed," he said impatiently.

"So be it," Elric's tone was stubborn, "do you think I wish the memory to live on—the memory of evil, ruin and destruction? The memory of a man with deficient blood in his veins—a man called Friendslayer, Womanslayer and many other such names?"

Darnizhaan spoke urgently, almost in terror. "Elric, you have been duped! Somewhere you have been given a conscience. You must join with us. Only if the Lords of Chaos can establish their reign will we survive. If they fail, we shall be obliterated!"

"*Good!*"

"Limbo, Elric. *Limbo!* Do you understand what that means?"

"I do not care. Where is my wife?"

Elric blocked the truth from his mind, blocked out the terror in the meaning of the Dead God's words. He could not afford to listen or fully to comprehend. He must save Zarozinia.

"I have brought the swords," said he, "and wish my wife to be returned to me."

"Very well," the Dead God smiled hugely in his relief. "At least if we keep the blades, in their true shape, beyond the Earth, we may be able to retain control of the world. In your hands they could destroy not only us but you, your world, all that you represent. Beasts would rule the Earth for millions of years before the age of intelligence began again. And it would be a duller age than this. We do not wish it to occur. But if you had *kept* the swords, it would have come about almost inevitably!"

"Oh, be silent!" Elric cried. "For a god, you talk too much. Take the swords—and give me back my wife!"

At the Dead God's command, some of the acolytes scampered away. Elric saw their gleaming bodies disappear into the darkness. He waited nervously until they returned, carrying the struggling body of Zarozinia. They set her on the ground and Elric saw that her face bore the blank look of shock.

"Zarozinia!"

The girl's eyes roamed about before they saw Elric. She began to move towards him, but the acolytes held her back, giggling.

Darnizhaan stretched forward two gigantic, glowing hands.

"The swords first."

Elric and Dyvim Slorm put them into his hands. The Dead God straightened up, clutching his prizes and roaring his mirth. Zarozinia was now released and she ran forward to grasp her husband's hand, weeping and trembling. Elric leaned down and stroked her hair, too disturbed to say anything.

Then he turned to Dyvim Slorm, shouting: "Let us see if our plan will work, cousin!"

Elric stared up at Stormbringer writhing in Darnizhaan's grasp. "Stormbringer! *Kerana soliem, o'glara . . .*"

Dyvim Slorm also called to Mournblade in the High Tongue of Melniboné, the mystic, sorcerous tongue which had been used for rune-casting and demon-raising all through Melniboné's twenty thousand years of history.

Together, they commanded the blades, as if they were actually wielding them in their hands, so that merely by shouting orders, Elric and Dyvim Slorm began their work. This was the remembered quality of both blades when paired in a common fight. The blades twisted in Darnizhaan's glowing hands. He started backwards, his shape faltering, sometimes manlike, sometimes beastlike, sometimes totally alien. But he was evidently horrified, this god.

Now the swords wrenched themselves from the clutching hands and turned on him. He fought against them, fending them off as they wove about in the air, whining malevolently, triumphantly, attacking him with vicious power. At Elric's command, Stormbringer slashed at the supernatural being and Dyvim Slorm's Mournblade followed its example. Because the runeblades were also supernatural, Darnizhaan was harmed dreadfully whenever they struck his form.

"Elric!" he raved, "Elric—you do not know what you are doing! Stop them! Stop them! You should have listened more carefully to what I told you. Stop them!"

But Elric in his hate and malice urged on the blades, made them plunge into the Dead God's being time after time so that his shape sometimes faltered, faded, the colours of its bright beauty dulling. The acolytes fled upwards into the vale, convinced that their lord was doomed. Their lord, also, was so convinced. He made one lunge towards the mounted men and then the fabric of his being began to shred before the blades' attack; wisps of his body-stuff seemed to break away and drift into the air to be swallowed by the black night.

Viciously and ferociously, Elric goaded the blades while Dyvim Slorm's voice blended with his in a cruel joy to see the bright being destroyed.

"*Fools!*" he screamed, "*in destroying me, you destroy yourselves!*"

But Elric did not listen and at last there was nothing left of the Dead God and the swords crept back to lie contentedly in their masters' hands.

Quickly, with a sudden shudder, Elric scabbarded Stormbringer.

He dismounted and helped his girl-wife onto the back of his great stallion and then swung up into the saddle again. It was very quiet in the Vale of Xanyaw.

6

Three people, bent in their saddles with weariness, reached the Chasm of Nihrain days later. They rode down the twisting paths into the black depths of the mountain city and were there welcomed by Sepiriz whose face was grave, though his words were encouraging.

"So you were successful, Elric," he said with a small smile.

Elric paused while he dismounted and aided Zarozinia down. He turned to Sepiriz. "I am not altogether satisfied with this adventure," he said grimly, "though I did what I had to in order to save my wife. I would speak with you privately, Sepiriz."

The black Nihrainian nodded gravely. "When we have eaten," he said, "we will talk alone."

They walked wearily through the galleries, noting that there was considerably more activity in the city now, but there was no sign of Sepiriz's nine brothers. He explained their absence as he led Elric and his companions towards his own chamber. "As servants of Fate they have been called to another plane where they can observe something of the several different possible futures of the Earth and thus keep me informed of what I must do here."

They entered the chamber and found food ready and, when they had satisfied their hunger, Dyvim Slorm and Zarozinia left the other two.

The fire from the great hearth blazed. Elric and Sepiriz sat together, unspeaking, hunched in their chairs.

At last, without preamble, Elric told Sepiriz the story of what had happened, what he remembered of the Dead God's words, how they had disturbed him—even struck him as being true.

When he had finished, Sepiriz nodded. "It is so," he said. "Darnizhaan spoke the truth. Or, at least, he spoke most of the truth, as he understood it."

"You mean we will all soon cease to exist? That it will be as if we had never breathed, or thought, or fought?"

"That is likely."

"But why? It seems unjust."

"Who told you that the world was just?"

Elric smiled, his own suspicions confirmed. "Aye, as I expected, there is no justice."

"But there *is*," Sepiriz said, "justice of a kind—justice which must be carved from the chaos of existence. Man was not born to a world of justice. But he can *create* such a world!"

"I'd agree to that," Elric said, "but what are all our strivings for if we are doomed to die and the results of our actions with us?"

"That is not absolutely the case. Something will continue. Those who come after us will inherit something from us."

"What is that?"

"An Earth free of the major forces of Chaos."

"You mean a world free of sorcery, I presume . . . ?"

"Not entirely free of sorcery, but Chaos and sorcery will not dominate the world of the future as it does this world."

"Then that *is* worth striving for, Sepiriz," Elric said almost with relief. "But what part do the runeblades play in the scheme of things?"

"They have two functions. One, to rid this world of the great dominating sources of evil—"

"But they *are* evil, themselves!"

"Just so. It takes a strong evil to battle a strong evil. The days that will come will be when the forces of good can overcome those of evil. They are not yet strong enough. That, as I told you, is what we must strive for."

"And what is the other purpose of the blades?"

"That is their final purpose—your destiny. I can tell you now. I *must* tell you now, or let you live out your destiny unknowing."

"Then tell me," Elric said impatiently.

"Their ultimate purpose is to destroy this world!"

Elric stood up. "Ah, no, Sepiriz. That I cannot believe. Shall I have such a crime on my conscience?"

"It is not a crime, it is in the nature of things. The era of the Bright Empire, even that of the Young Kingdoms, is drawing to a close. Chaos formed this Earth and, for aeons, Chaos ruled. Men were created to put an end to that rule."

"But my ancestors worshipped the powers of Chaos. My patron demon, Arioch, is a Duke of Hell, one of the prime Lords of Chaos!"

"Just so. You, and your ancestors, were not true men at all, but an intermediary type created for a purpose. You understand Chaos as no true men ever could understand it. You can control the forces of Chaos as no true men ever could. And, as a manifestation of the Champion Eternal, you can weaken the forces of Chaos—for you know the qualities of Chaos. Weaken them is what you *have* done. Though worshipping the Lords of Chance, your race was the first to bring some kind of order to the Earth. The people of the Young Kingdoms have inherited this from you—and have consolidated it. But, as yet, Chaos is still that much stronger. The runeblades, Stormbringer and Mournblade, this more orderly age, the wisdom your race and mine have gained, all will go towards creating the basis for the true beginnings of mankind's history. That history will not begin for many thousands of years, the type may take on a lowlier form, become more beastlike before it re-evolves, but when it does, it will re-evolve into a world bereft of the stronger forces of Chaos. It will have a fighting chance. We are all doomed, but *they* need not be."

"So that is what Darnizhaan meant when he said we were just puppets, acting out our parts before the true play began . . ." Elric sighed deeply, the weight of his mighty responsibility was heavy on his soul. He did not welcome it; but he accepted it.

Sepiriz said gently: "It is your purpose, Elric of Melniboné. Hitherto, your life has appeared comparatively meaningless. All through it you have been searching for some purpose for living, is that not true?"

"Aye," Elric agreed with a slight smile, "I've been restless for many a year since my birth; restless the more between the time when Zarozinia was abducted and now."

"It is fitting that you should have been," Sepiriz said, "for there *is* a purpose for you—Fate's purpose. It is this destiny that you have sensed all your mortal days. You, the last of the royal line of Melniboné, must complete your destiny in the times which are to follow closely upon these. The world is darkening—nature revolts and rebels against the abuses to which the Lords of Chaos put it. Oceans seethe and forests sway, hot lava spills from a thousand mountains, winds shriek their angry torment and the skies are full of awful movement. Upon the face of the Earth, warriors are embattled in a struggle which will decide the fate of the world, linked as the struggle is, with greater conflicts among gods. Women and little children die on a million funeral pyres upon this continent alone. And soon the conflict will spread to the next continent and the next. Soon all the men of the Earth will have chosen sides and Chaos might easily win. It would win but for one thing: you and your sword Stormbringer."

"Stormbringer. It has brought enough storms for me. Perhaps this time it can calm one. And what if Law should win?"

"And if Law should win—then that, too, will mean the decline and death of this world—we shall all be forgotten. But if Chaos should win—then doom will cloud the very air, agony will sound in the wind and foul misery will dominate a plunging, unsettled world of sorcery and evil hatred. But you, Elric, with your sword and our aid, could stop this. It must be done."

"Then let it be done," Elric said quietly, "and if it must be done—then let it be done well."

Sepiriz said: "Armies will soon be marshalled to drive against Pan Tang's might. These must be our first defence. Thereafter, we shall call upon you to fulfil the rest of your destiny."

"I'll play my part, willingly," Elric replied, "for, whatever else, I have a mind to pay the Theocrat back for his insults and the inconvenience he has caused me. Though perhaps he didn't instigate Zarozinia's abduction, he aided those who did, and he shall die slowly for that."

"Go then, speedily, for each moment wasted allows the Theocrat to consolidate further his new-won empire."

"Farewell," said Elric, now more than ever anxious to leave Nihrain and return to familiar lands. "I know we'll meet again, Sepiriz, but I pray it be in calmer times than these."

Now the three of them rode eastwards, towards the coast of Tarkesh where they hoped to find a secret ship to take them across the Pale Sea to Ilmiora and thence to Karlaak by the Weeping Waste. They rode their magical Nihrain horses, careless of danger, through a war-wasted world, strife-ruined and miserable under the heel of the Theocrat.

Elric and Zarozinia exchanged many glances, but they did not speak much, for they were both moved by a knowledge of something which they could not speak of, which they dared not admit. She knew they would not have much time together even when they returned to Karlaak, she saw that he grieved and she grieved also, unable to understand the change that had come upon her husband, only aware that the black sword at his side would never, now, hang in the armoury again. She felt she had failed him, though this was not the case.

As they topped a hill and saw smoke drifting, black and thick across the plains of Toraunz, once beautiful, now ruined, Dyvim Slorm shouted from behind Elric and his bride: "One thing, cousin—whatever happens, we must have vengeance on the Theocrat and his ally."

Elric pursed his lips.

"Aye," he said, and glanced again at Zarozinia whose eyes were downcast.

Now the Western lands from Tarkesh to Myyrrhn were sundered by the servitors of Chaos. Was this truly to be the final conflict that would decide whether

Law or Chaos would dominate the future? The forces of Law were weak and scattered. Could this possibly be the final paroxysm on Earth of the great Lords of Evil? Now, between armies, one part of the world's fate was being decided. The lands groaned in the torment of bloody conflict.

What other forces must Elric fight before he accomplished his final destiny and destroyed the world he knew? What else before the Horn of Fate was blown—to herald in the night?

Sepiriz, no doubt, would tell him when the time came.

But meanwhile more material scores had to be settled. The lands to the east must be made ready for war. The sea-lords of the Purple Towns must be approached for aid, the kings of the South marshalled for attack on the Western Continent. It would take time to do all this.

Part of Elric's mind welcomed the time it would take.

Part of him was reluctant to continue his heavy destiny, for it would mean the end of the Age of the Young Kingdoms, the death of the memory of the Age of the Bright Empire which his ancestors had dominated for ten thousand years.

The sea was at last in sight, rolling its troubled way towards the horizon to meet a seething sky. He heard the cry of gulls and smelled the tang of the salt air in his nostrils.

With a wild shout he clapped his steed's flanks and raced down towards the sea . . .

BOOK TWO

BLACK SWORD'S BROTHERS

In which a million blades decide an issue between
Elric and the Lords of Chaos . . .

I

One day there came a gathering of kings, captains, and warlords to the peaceful city of Karlaak in Ilmiora by the Weeping Waste.

They did not come in great pomp or with grandiose gestures. They came grim-faced and hurriedly to answer the summons of Elric, who dwelt again in Karlaak with his lately-rescued wife Zarozinia. And they gathered in a great chamber which had once been used by the old rulers of Karlaak for the planning of wars. To this same purpose Elric now put it.

Illuminated by flaring torches, a great coloured map of the world was spread behind the dais on which Elric stood. It showed the three major continents of the East, West and South. That of the West, comprising Jharkor, Dharijor, Shazaar, Tarkesh, Myyrrhn and the Isle of Pan Tang, was shaded black, for all these lands were now the conquered Empire of the Pan Tang–Dharijor alliance which threatened the security of the assembled nobles.

Some of the men who stood armoured before Elric were exiles from the conquered lands—but there were few. Few also were Elric's Imrryrian kinsmen who had fought at the Battle of Sequa and had been defeated with the massed army that had sought to resist the combined might of the evil alliance. At the head of the eldritch Imrryrians stood Dyvim Slorm, Elric's cousin. At his belt, encased in a sturdy scabbard, was the runesword Mournblade, twin to the one Elric wore.

Here also was Montan, Lord of Lormyr, standing with fellow rulers from the Southlands—Jerned of Filkhar, Hozel of Argimiliar, and Kolthak of Pikarayd, adorned in painted iron, velvet, silk and wool.

The sea-lords from the Isle of the Purple Towns were less gaudily clad with helms and breastplates of plain bronze, jerkins, breeks and boots of unstained leather and great broadswords at their hips. Their faces were all but hidden by their long shaggy hair and thick, curling beards.

All these, kings and sea-lords alike, were inclined to stare at Elric suspiciously, since years before he had led their royal predecessors on the raid of Imrryr—though it had left many thrones clear for those who now sat on them.

In another group stood the nobles of that part of the Eastern Continent lying to the east of the Sighing Desert and the Weeping Waste. Beyond these two barren stretches of land were the kingdoms of Eshmir, Chang Shai and Okara, but there was no contact between Elric's part of the world and theirs—save for the small, red-headed man beside him—his friend Moonglum of Elwher, an Eastern adventurer.

The Regent of Vilmir, uncle of the ten-month-old king, headed this last group made up of senators from the city-states comprising Ilmiora; the red-clothed archer Rackhir representing the city of Tanelorn; and various merchant princes from towns coming under the indirect rule of Vilmir as protectorates.

A mighty gathering, representing the massed power of the world.

But would even this be sufficient, Elric wondered, to wipe out the growing menace from the Westlands?

His white albino's face was stern, his red eyes troubled as he addressed the men he had caused to come here.

"As you know, my lords, the threat of Pan Tang and Dharijor is not likely to remain confined to the Western Continent for much longer. Though barely two months have passed since their victory was achieved, they are already marshalling a great fleet aimed at crushing the power of those kings dependent, largely, on their ships for livelihood and defence."

He glanced at the sea-lords of the Purple Towns and the kings of the Southern Continent.

"We of the East, it seems, are not regarded as so much of a danger to their immediate plans and, if we did not unite now, they would have a greater chance of success by conquering first the Southern sea power and then the scattered cities of the East. We must form an alliance which can match their strength."

"How do you know this is their plan, Elric?"

The voice was that of Hozel of Argimiliar, a proud-faced man inclined it was said to fits of insanity, the inbred offspring of a dozen incestuous unions.

"Spies, refugees—and supernatural sources. They have all reported it."

"Even without these reports, we could be sure that this is, indeed, their plan," growled Kargan Sharpeyes, spokesman for the sea-lords. He looked directly at Hozel with something akin to contempt. "And Jagreen Lern of Pan Tang might also seek allies amongst the Southerners. There are some who would rather capitulate to a foreign conqueror than lose their soft lives and easily earned treasure."

Hozel smiled coldly at Kargan. "There are some, too, whose animal suspicions might cause them to make no move against the Theocrat until it was too late."

Elric said hastily, aware of age-old bitternesses between the hardy sea-lords and their softer neighbours: "But worst of all they would be best aided by internal feuds in our ranks, brothers. Hozel—take it for granted that I speak truly and that my information is exact."

Montan, Lord of Lormyr, his face, beard and hair all shaded grey, said haughtily: "You of the North and East are weak. We of the South are strong. Why should we lend you our ships to defend your coasts? I do not agree with your logic, Elric. It will not be the first time it has led good men astray—to their deaths!"

"I thought we had agreed to bury old disputes!" Elric said, close to anger, for the guilt of what he had done was still in him.

"Aye," nodded Kargan. "A man who can't forget the past is a man who cannot plan for the future. I say Elric's logic is good!"

"You traders were always too reckless with your ships and too gullible when you heard a smooth tongue. That's why you now envy our riches." Young Jerned of Filkhar smiled in his thin beard, his eyes on the floor.

Kargan fumed. "Too honest, perhaps, is the word you should have used, Southerner! Belatedly our forefathers learned how the fat Southlands were cheating them. Their forefathers raided your coasts, remember? Maybe we should have continued their practice! Instead, we settled, traded—and your bellies swelled from the profits of our sweat! Gods! I'd not trust the word of a Southern—"

Elric leaned forward to interrupt, but was interrupted himself by Hozel who said impatiently: "The fact is this. The Theocrat is more likely to concentrate his first attacks on the East. For these reasons: The Eastlands are weak. The Eastlands are poorly defended. The Eastlands are closer to his shores and therefore more accessible. Why should he risk his recently united strength on the stronger Southlands, or risk a more hazardous sea-crossing?"

"Because," Elric said levelly, "his ships will be magic-aided and distance will not count. Because the South is richer and will supply him with metals, food—"

"Ships and men!" spat Kargan.

"So! You think we already plan treachery!" Hozel glanced first at Elric and then at Kargan. "Then why summon us here in the first place?"

"I did not say that," Elric said hastily. "Kargan spoke his own thoughts, not mine. Calm yourselves—we *must* be united—or perish before superior armies and supernatural might!"

"Oh, no!" Hozel turned to the other Southern monarchs. "What say you, my peers? Shall we lend them our ships and warriors to protect their shores as well as ours?"

"Not when they are so ungratefully spurned," Jerned murmured. "Let Jagreen Lern expend his energies upon them. When he looks towards the South he will be weakened, and we shall be ready for him!"

"You are fools!" Elric cried urgently. "Stand with us or we'll all perish! The Lords of Chaos are behind the Theocrat. If he succeeds in his ambitions it will mean more than conquest by a human schemer—it will mean that we shall all be subjected to the horror of total anarchy, on the Earth and above it. The human race is threatened!"

Hozel stared hard at Elric and smiled. "Then let the human race protect itself and not fight under an unhuman leader. 'Tis well-known that the men of Melniboné are not true men at all."

"Be that as it may." Elric lowered his head and lifted a thin, white hand to point at Hozel. The king shivered and held his ground with obvious effort. "But I know more than that, Hozel of Argimiliar. I know that the men of the Young Kingdoms are only the gods' first mouldings—shadow-things who precede the race of real men, even as we preceded you. And I know more! I know that if we do not vanquish both Jagreen Lern and his supernatural allies, then men will be swept from the boiling face of a maddened planet, their destiny unfulfilled!"

Hozel swallowed and spoke, his voice trembling.

"I've seen your muttering kind in the market places, Elric. Men who prophesy all kinds of dooms that never take place—mad-eyed men such as you. But we do not let them live in Argimiliar. We fry them slowly, finger by finger, inch by inch until they admit their omens are fallacious! Perhaps we'll have that opportunity, yet!"

He swung about and half-ran from the hall. For a moment the other Southern monarchs stood staring irresolutely after him.

Elric said urgently: "Heed him not, my lords. I swear on my life that my words are true!"

Jerned said softly, half to himself: "That could mean little. There are rumours you're immortal."

Moonglum came close to his friend and whispered: "They are unconvinced, Elric. 'Tis plain they're not our men."

Elric nodded. To the Southern nobles he said: "Know this: Though you foolishly reject my offer of an alliance, the day will come when you will regret your decision. I have been insulted in my own palace, my friends have been insulted and I curse you for the upstart fools you are. But when the time comes for you to learn the error of this decision I swear that we shall aid you, if it is in our power. Now go!"

Disconcerted, the Southerners straggled from the hall in silence.

Elric turned to Kargan Sharpeyes. "What have you decided, sea-lord?"

"We stand with you," Kargan said simply. "My brother Smiorgan Baldhead always spoke well of you and I remember his words rather than the rumours which followed his death under your leadership. Moreover," he smiled broadly, "it is in our nature to believe that whatever a Southern weakling decides must therefore be wrong. You have the Purple Towns as allies—and our ships, though fewer than the combined fleets of the South, are smooth-sailing fighting ships and well-equipped for war."

"I must warn you that we stand little chance without Southern aid," Elric said gravely.

"I'm doubtful if they'd have been more than an encumbrance with their guile and squabblings," Kargan replied. "Besides—have you no sorcery to help us in this?"

"I plan to seek some tomorrow," Elric told him. "Moonglum and myself will be leaving my cousin Dyvim Slorm in charge here while we go to Sorcerers' Isle, beyond Melniboné. There, among the hermit practitioners of the White Arts, I might find means of contacting the Lords of Law. I, as you know, am half-sworn to Chaos, though I fight it, and am finding increasingly that my own demon-god is somewhat loath to aid me these days. At present, the White Lords are weak, beaten back, just as we are on Earth, by the increasing power of the Dark Ones. It is hard to contact them. The hermits can likely help me."

Kargan nodded. "'Twould be a relief to us of the Purple Towns to know that we were not too strongly leagued with dark spirits, I must admit."

Elric frowned. "I agree, of course. But our position is so weak that we must accept *any* help—be it black or white. I presume that there is dispute among the Masters of Chaos as to how far they should go—that is why some of my own help still comes from Chaos. This blade that hangs at my side, and the twin which Dyvim Slorm bears, are both evil. Yet they were forged by creatures of Chaos to bring an end, on Earth at least, to the Masters' rule here. Just as my blood-loyalties are divided, so are the swords' loyalties. We have no supernatural allies we can wholly rely upon."

"I feel for you," Kargan said gruffly, and it was obvious that he did. No man could envy Elric's position or Elric's destiny.

Orgon, Kargan's cousin-in-law, said bluntly: "We'll to bed now. Has your kinsman your full confidence?"

Elric glanced at Dyvim Slorm and smiled. "My full confidence—he knows as much as I about this business. He shall speak for me since he knows my basic plans."

"Very well. We'll confer with him tomorrow and, if we do not see you before we leave, do well for us on Sorcerers' Isle."

The sea-lords left.

Now, for the first time, the Regent of Vilmir spoke. His voice was clear and cool. "We, too, have confidence in you and your kinsman, Elric. Already we know you both for clever warriors and cunning planners. Vilmir has good cause to know it from your exploits in Bakshaan and elsewhere throughout our territories. We, I feel, have the good sense to bury old scores." He turned to the merchant princes for confirmation and they nodded their agreement.

"Good," Elric said. He addressed the gaunt-faced archer, Rackhir, his friend, whose legend almost equalled his own.

"You come as a spokesman of Tanelorn, Rackhir. This will not be the first time we have fought the Lords of Chaos."

"True," Rackhir nodded. "Most recently we averted a threat with certain aid from the Grey Lords—but Chaos had caused the gateways to the Grey Lords to be closed to mortals. We can offer you only our warriors' loyalty."

"We shall be grateful for that." Elric paced the dais. There was no need to ask the senators of Karlaak and the other cities of Ilmiora, for they had agreed to support him, come what may, long before the other rulers were called.

The same was true of the bleak-faced band who made up the refugees from the West, headed by Viri-Sek, the winged youth from Myyrrhn, last of his line since all the other members of the ruling family had been slain by Jagreen Lern's minions.

Just beyond the walls of Karlaak was a sea of tents and pavilions over which the banners of many nations waved sluggishly in the hot, moist wind. At this moment, Elric knew, the proud lords of the South were uprooting their standards and packing their tents, not looking at the war-battered warriors of Shazaar, Jharkor and Tarkesh who stared at them in puzzlement. Sight of those dull-eyed veterans should have decided the Southern nobles to ally themselves with the East, but evidently it had not.

Elric sighed and turned his back on the others to contemplate the great map of the world with its shaded dark areas.

"Now only a quarter is black," he said softly to Moonglum. "But the dark tide spreads farther and faster and soon we may all be engulfed."

"We'll dam the flow—or try to—when it comes," Moonglum said with attempted jauntiness. "But meanwhile your wife would spend some time with you before we leave. Let's both to bed and trust our dreams are light!"

2

Two nights later they stood on the quayside in the city of Jadmar while a cold wind sliced its way inland.

"There she is," Elric said, pointing down at the small boat rocking and bumping in the water below.

"A small craft," Moonglum said dubiously. "She scarcely looks seaworthy."

"She'll stay afloat longer than a larger vessel in a heavy storm." Elric clambered down the iron steps. "Also," he added, as Moonglum put a cautious foot on the rung above him, "she'll be less noticeable and won't draw the attention of any enemy vessels which might be scouting in these waters."

He jumped and the boat rocked crazily. He leaned over, grasped a rung and steadied the boat so that Moonglum could climb aboard.

The cocky little Eastlander pushed a hand through his shock of red hair and stared up at the troubled sky.

"Bad weather for this time of year," he noted. "It's hard to understand. All the way from Karlaak we've had every sort of weather, freak snowstorms, thunderstorms, hail and winds as hot as a furnace blast. Those rumours were disturbing, too—a rain of blood in Bakshaan, balls of fiery metal falling in the west of Vilmir, unprecedented earthquakes in Jadmar a few hours before we arrived. It seems nature has gone insane."

"Not far from the truth," Elric said grimly, untying the mooring line. "Lift the sail will you, and tack into the wind?"

"What do you mean?" Moonglum began to loosen the sail. It billowed into his face and his voice was muffled. "Jagreen Lern's hordes haven't reached this part of the world yet."

"They haven't needed to. I told you the forces of nature were being disrupted by Chaos. We have only experienced the backwash of what is going on in the West. If you think these weather conditions are peculiar, you would be horrified by the effect which Chaos has on those parts of the world where its rule is almost total!"

"I wonder if you haven't taken on too much in this fight." Moonglum adjusted the sail and it filled to send the little boat scudding between the two long harbour walls towards the open sea.

As they passed the beacons, guttering in the cold wind, Elric gripped the tiller tighter, taking a south-westerly course past the Vilmirian peninsula. Overhead the stars were sometimes obscured by the tattered shreds of clouds streaming before the cold, unnatural blast of the wind. Spray splashed in his face, stinging it in a thousand places, but he ignored it. He had not answered Moonglum, for he also had doubts about his ability to save the world from Chaos.

Moonglum had learned to judge his friend's moods. For some years before they had travelled the world together and had learned to respect one another. Lately, since Elric had near-permanent residence in his wife's city of Karlaak, Moonglum had continued to travel and had been in command of a small mercenary army patrolling the Southern Marches of Pikarayd, driving back the barbarians inhabiting the hinterland of that country. He had immediately relinquished this command when Elric's news reached him and now, as the tiny ship bore them towards a hazy and peril-fraught destiny, savoured the familiar mixture of excitement and perturbation which he had felt a dozen times before when their escapades had led them into conflict with the unknown supernatural forces so closely linked with Elric's destiny. He had come to accept as a fact that his destiny was bound to Elric's and felt, in the deepest places of his being, that when the time came they would both die together in some mighty adventure.

Is this death imminent? he wondered, as he concentrated on the sail and shivered in the blasting wind. Not yet, perhaps, but he felt, fatalistically, that it was not far away, for the time was looming when the only deeds of men would be dark, desperate and great and even these might not serve to form a bastion against the inrush of the creatures of Chaos.

Elric, himself, contemplated nothing, kept his mind clear and relaxed as much as he could. His quest for the aid of the White Lords was one which could well prove fruitless, but he chose not to dwell on this until he knew for certain whether their help could be invoked or not.

Dawn came swimming over the horizon, showing a heaving waste of grey water with no land in sight. The wind had dropped and the air was warmer. Banks of purple clouds bearing veins of saffron and scarlet poured into the sky, like the smoke of some monstrous pyre. Soon they were sweating beneath a moody sun and the wind had dropped so that the sail hardly moved and yet, at the same time, the sea began to heave as if lashed by a storm.

The sea was moving like a living entity thrashing in nightmare-filled sleep. Moonglum glanced at Elric from where he lay sprawled in the prow of the boat. Elric returned the gaze, shaking his head and releasing his half-conscious grip of the tiller. It was useless to attempt steering the boat in conditions like these. The boat was being swept about by the wild waves, yet no water seemed to enter it, no spray wet them. Everything had become unreal, dreamlike and for a while Elric felt that even if he had wished to speak, he would not have been able to.

Then, in the distance at first, they heard a low droning which grew to a whining shriek and suddenly the boat was sent half-flying over the rolling waves and driven down into a trench. Above them, the blue and silver water seemed for a moment to be a wall of metal—and then it came crashing down towards them.

His mood broken, Elric clung to the tiller, yelling: "Hang on to the boat, Moonglum! Hang on, or you're lost!"

Tepid water groaned down and they were flattened beneath it as if swatted by a gigantic palm. The boat dropped deeper and deeper until it seemed they would be crushed on the bottom by the surging blow. Then, they were flung upwards again, and down, and as he glimpsed the boiling surface, Elric saw three mountains pushing themselves upwards, gouting flame and lava. The boat wallowed, half-full of water, and they set to frantically baling it out as the boat was swirled back and forth, being driven nearer and nearer to the new-formed volcanoes.

Elric dropped his baling pan and flung his weight against the tiller, forcing the boat away from the mountains of fire. It responded sluggishly, but began to drift in the opposite direction.

Elric saw Moonglum, pale-faced, attempting to shake out the sodden sail. The heat from the volcanoes was hardly bearable. He glanced upwards to try and get some kind of bearing, but the sun seemed to have swollen and broken so that he saw a million fragments of flame.

"This is the work of Chaos, Moonglum!" he shouted. "And only a taste, I fancy, of what it can become!"

"They must know we are here and seek to destroy us!" Moonglum swept sweat from his eyes with the back of his hand.

"Perhaps, but I think not." Now he looked up again and the sun seemed almost normal. He took a bearing and began to steer the boat away from the mountains of fire, but they were many miles off their original course.

He had planned to sail to the south of Melniboné, Isle of the Dragon, and avoid the Dragon Sea lying to the north, for it was well-known that the last great sea-monsters still roamed this stretch. But now it was obvious that they were, in fact, north of Melniboné and being driven further north all the time—towards Pan Tang!

There was a no chance of heading for Melniboné itself—he wondered if the Isle of the Dragon had even survived the monstrous upheavals. He would have to make straight for Sorcerers' Isle if he could.

The ocean was calmer now, but the water had almost reached boiling point so that every drop that fell on his skin seemed to scald him. Bubbles formed on the surface and it was as if they sailed in a gigantic witch's cauldron. Dead fish and half-reptilian forms drifted about, as thick as seaweed, threatening to clog the boat's passage. But the wind, though strong, had begun to blow in one direction and Moonglum grinned in relief as it filled the sail.

Slowly, through the death-thick waters, they managed to steer a southwesterly course towards Sorcerers' Isle as clouds of steam formed on the ocean and obscured their view.

Hours later, they had left the heated waters behind and were sailing beneath clear skies on a calm sea. They allowed themselves to doze. In less than a day they would reach Sorcerers' Isle, but now they were overcome by the reaction to their experience and wondered, dazedly, how they had lived through the awful storm.

Elric jerked his eyes open with a shock. He was certain he had not slept long, yet the sky was dark and a cold drizzle was falling. As the drops touched his head and face, they oozed down it like viscous jelly. Some of it entered his mouth and he hastily spat out the bitter-tasting stuff.

"Moonglum," he called through the gloom, "what's the hour, do you know?"

The Eastlander's sleep-heavy voice answered dazedly. "I know not. I'd swear it is not night already."

Elric gave the tiller a tentative push. The boat did not respond. He looked over the side.

It seemed they were sailing through the sky itself. A dully luminous gas seemed to swirl about the hull, but he could see no water. He shuddered. Had they left the plane of Earth? Were they sailing through some frightful, supernatural sea? He cursed himself for sleeping, feeling helpless; more helpless than when he had fought the storm. The heavy, gelatinous rain beat down strongly and he pulled the hood of his cloak over his white hair. From his belt pouch he took flint and tinder and the tiny light was just sufficient to show him Moonglum's half-mad eyes. The little Eastlander's face was taut with fear. Elric had never seen such fear on his friend's face, and knew that with a little less self-control, his own face would assume a similar expression.

"Our time has ended," Moonglum trembled. "I fear that we're dead, at last, Elric."

"Don't prattle such emptiness, Moonglum. I have heard of no afterlife such as this." But secretly, Elric wondered if Moonglum's words were true. The ship seemed to be moving rapidly through the gaseous sea, being driven or drawn to some unknown destination. Yet Elric could swear that the Lords of Chaos had no knowledge of his boat.

Faster and faster the little craft moved and then, with relief, they heard the familiar splash of water about its keel and it was surging through the salt-sea again. For a short while longer the viscous rain continued to fall and then even that was gone.

Moonglum sighed as the blackness slowly gave way to light and they saw again a normal ocean about them.

"What was it, then?" he ventured, finally.

"Another manifestation of ruptured nature," Elric attempted to keep his voice calm. "Some warp in the barrier between the realm of men and the realm of Chaos, perhaps? Don't question our luck in surviving it. We are again off course, and," he pointed to the horizon, "a natural storm seems to be brewing yonder."

"A natural storm I can accept, no matter how dangerous," Moonglum murmured, and made swift preparations, furling the sail as the wind increased and the sea churned.

In a way, Elric welcomed the storm when it finally struck them. At least it obeyed natural laws and could be fought by natural means. The rain refreshed their faces, the wind swept through their hair and they battled the storm with fierce enjoyment, the plucky boat riding the waves.

But, in spite of this, they were being driven further and further north-east, towards the conquered coasts of Shazaar, in the opposite direction to their goal.

The healthy storm raged on until all thoughts of destiny and supernatural danger were driven from their minds and their muscles ached and they gasped with the shock of cold waves on their drenched bodies.

The boat reeled and rocked, their hands were sore from the tightness of their grip on wood and rope, but it was as if Fate had singled them out to live, or perhaps for a death that would be less clean, for they continued to ride the heaving waters.

Then, with a shock, Elric saw rocks rearing and Moonglum shouted in recognition: "*The Serpent's Teeth!*"

The Serpent's Teeth lay close to Shazaar and were one of the most feared hazards of the shore-hugging traders of the West. Elric and Moonglum had seen them before, from a distance, but now the storm was driving them nearer and nearer, and though they struggled to keep the boat away, they seemed bound to be smashed to their deaths on the jagged rocks.

A wave surged under the boat, lifted them and bore them down. Elric clung to the side of the boat and thought he heard Moonglum's wild shout above the noise of the storm before they were flung towards the Serpent's Teeth.

"*Farewell!*"

And then there was a terrifying sound of smashing timbers, the feel of sharp rock lacerating his rolling body, and he was beneath the waves, fighting his way to the surface to gasp in air before another wave tossed him and grazed his arm against the rocks.

Desperately, encumbered by the life-giving runesword at his belt, he attempted to swim for the looming cliffs of Shazaar, conscious that even if he lived, he had returned to enemy soil and his chances of reaching the White Lords were now almost non-existent.

3

Elric lay exhausted on the cold shingle, listening to the musical sound that the tide made as it drew back over the stones. Another sound joined that of the surf, and he recognised it as the crunch of boots. Someone was coming towards him. In Shazaar it was most likely to be an enemy. He rolled over and began scrambling to his feet, drawing the last reserves from his worn-out body. His right hand had half-drawn Stormbringer from its scabbard before he realised that it was Moonglum, bent with weariness, standing grinning before him.

"Thank the gods, you live!" Moonglum lowered himself to the shingle and leaned back with his arms supporting his weight, regarding the now calm sea and the towering Serpent's Teeth in the distance.

"Aye, we live," Elric squatted down, moodily, "but for how long in this ruined land, I cannot guess. Somewhere, perhaps, we can find a ship—but it will mean seeking a town or city and we're a marked pair, easily recognised by our physical appearance."

Moonglum shook his head and laughed lightly. "You're still the gloomy one, friend. Be thankful for your life, say I."

"Small mercies are all but useless in this conflict," Elric said. "Rest, now, Moonglum, while I watch, then you can take my place. There was no time to lose when we began this adventure, and now we've lost days."

Moonglum gave no argument, but allowed himself immediately to sleep and when he awoke, much refreshed though aching still, Elric slept until the moon was high and shining brightly in the clear sky.

They trudged through the night, the sparse grass of the coast region giving

way to wet, blackened ground. It was as if a holocaust had raged over the countryside, followed by a rainstorm which had left behind it a marsh of ashes. Remembering the grassy plains of this part of Shazaar, Elric was horrified, unable
to tell whether men or the creatures of Chaos had caused such wanton ruin.

Noon was approaching, with a hint of weird disturbances in the bright-
clouded sky, when they saw a long line of people coming towards them. They
flattened themselves behind a small rise and peered cautiously over it as the
party drew nearer. These were no enemy soldiers, but gaunt women and starving children, men who staggered in rags, and a few battered riders, obviously
the remnants of some defeated band of partisans who had held out against
Jagreen Lern.

"I think we'll find friends, of sorts, here," Elric muttered thankfully, "and
perhaps some information which will help us."

They arose and walked towards the wretched herd. The riders quickly
grouped around the civilians and drew their weapons, but before any challenges could be given, someone cried from the enclosed ranks:

"Elric of Melniboné! Elric—have you returned with news of rescue?"

Elric didn't recognise the voice, but he knew his face was a legend, with its
dead white skin and glowing crimson eyes.

"I'm seeking rescue myself, friend," he said with poorly assumed cheer-
fulness. "We were shipwrecked on your coasts while on a journey which we
hoped would help us lift the yoke of Jagreen Lern from off the Westlands, but
unless we find another ship, our chances are poor."

"Which way did you sail, Elric?" said the unseen spokesman.

"We sailed to Sorcerers' Isle in the south-west, there to invoke the aid, if
we could, of the White Lords," Moonglum replied.

"Then you were going in the wrong direction!"

Elric straightened his back and tried to peer into the throng. "Who are
you to tell us that?"

There was a disturbance in the crowd and a bent, middle-aged man with
long, curling moustachios adorning his fair-skinned face broke from the ranks

and stood leaning on a staff. The riders drew back their horses so that Elric could see him properly.

"I am named Ohada the Seer, once famous in Aflitain as an oracle. But Aflitain was razed in the sack of Shazaar and I was lucky enough to escape with these few people who are all from Aflitain, one of the last cities to fall before Pan Tang's sorcerous might. I have a message of great import for you, Elric. It is for your ears only and I received it from one you know—one who may help you and, indirectly, us."

"You have piqued my curiosity and raised my hopes," Elric beckoned with his hand. "Come, seer, tell me your news and let's all trust it is as good as you hint."

Moonglum took a step back as the seer approached. Both he and the Aflitainians watched with curiosity as Ohada whispered to Elric. Elric himself had to strain to catch the words. "I bear a message from a strange man called Sepiriz. He says that what you have failed to do, he has done, but there is something which you must do that he cannot. He says to go to the carved city and there he will enlighten you further."

"Sepiriz! How did he contact you?"

"I am clairvoyant. He came to me in a dream."

"Your words could be treacherous, designed to lead me into Jagreen Lern's hands."

"Sepiriz added one thing to me—he told me that we should meet on this very spot. Could Jagreen Lern know that?"

"Unlikely—but, by the same reckoning, could *anyone* know that?" He nodded. "Thanks, seer." Then he shouted to the riders. "We need a pair of horses—your best!"

"Our horses are valuable to us," grumbled a knight in torn armour, "they are all we have."

"My companion and I need to move swiftly if we are to save the world from Chaos. Come, risk a pair of horses against the chance of vengeance on your conquerors."

"Aye, very well." The knight dismounted and so did the man beside him. They led their steeds up to Elric and Moonglum.

"Use them with care, Elric."

Elric took the reins and swung himself into the saddle, the huge runesword slapping at his side. "I will," said he. "What are your plans now?"

"We'll fight on, as best we can."

"Would it not be wiser to hide in the mountains or the Marshes of the Mist?"

"If you had witnessed the depravity and terror of Jagreen Lern's rule, you would not make such an enquiry," the knight said bleakly. "Though we cannot hope to win against a warlock whose servants can command the very earth to heave like the ocean, pull down floods of salt water from the sky, and send green clouds scudding down to destroy helpless children in nameless ways, we shall take what vengeance we can. This part of the continent is calm beside what is going on elsewhere. Dreadful geological changes are taking place. You would not recognise a hill or forest ten miles north. And those that you passed one day might well have changed or disappeared the next."

"We have witnessed something of the like on our sea journey," Elric nodded. "I wish you a long life of revenge, friend. I myself have scores to settle with Jagreen Lern and his accomplice."

"His accomplice? You mean King Sarosto of Dharijor?" A thin smile crossed the knight's haggard face. "You'll take no vengeance on Sarosto. He was assassinated soon after our forces were vanquished at the Battle of Sequa. Though nothing was proved, it is common knowledge that he was killed at the orders of the Theocrat who now rules unchallenged." The knight shrugged. "And who can stand for long against Jagreen Lern, let alone his captains?"

"Who are these captains?"

"Why, he has summoned all the Dukes of Hell to him. Whether they will accept his mastery much longer, I do not know. It is our belief that Jagreen Lern will be the next to die—and hell unchecked will rule in his place!"

"I hope not," Elric said softly, "for I won't be cheated of my vengeance."

The knight sighed. "With the Dukes of Hell as his allies, Jagreen Lern will soon rule the world."

"Let us hope I can find a means of disposing of that dark aristocracy, and keeping my vow to slay Jagreen Lern," Elric said and, with a wave of thanks to the seer and the two knights, turned his horse towards the mountains of Jharkor, Moonglum in his wake.

They got little rest on their perilous ride to the mountain home of Sepiriz, for, as the knight had told them, the ground itself seemed alive and anarchy ruled everywhere. Afterwards, Elric remembered little, save a feeling of utter horror and the noise of unholy screechings in his ear, dark colours, gold, reds, blues, black, and the flaring orange that was everywhere the sign of Chaos on Earth.

In the mountain regions close to Nihrain, they found that the rule of Chaos was not so complete as in other parts. This proved that Sepiriz and his nine black brothers were exerting at least some control against the forces threatening to engulf them.

Through steep gorges of towering black rock, along treacherous mountain paths, down slopes that rattled with loose stones and seemed likely to start an avalanche, they pressed deeper and deeper into the heart of the ancient mountains. These were the oldest mountains in the world, and they held one of the Earth's most ancient secrets—the domain of the immortal Nihrain who had ruled for centuries even before the coming of the Melnibonéans. At last, they came to the Hewn City of Nihrain, its towering palaces, temples and fortresses carved into the living black granite, hidden in the depths of the chasm that might have been bottomless. Virtually cut off from all but the faintest filterings of sunlight, it had brooded here since earliest times.

Down the narrow paths they guided their reluctant steeds until they had reached a huge gateway, its pillars carved with the figures of titans and half-men looming above them, so that Moonglum gasped and immediately fell silent, overawed by the genius which could accomplish the twin feats of gigantic engineering and powerful art.

In the caverns, also carved to represent scenes from the legends of the Nihrain, Sepiriz awaited them, a welcoming smile on his thin-lipped ebony face.

"Greetings, Sepiriz," Elric dismounted and allowed slaves to lead his horse away. Moonglum did likewise, a trifle warily.

"I was informed correctly," Sepiriz clasped Elric's shoulders in his hands. "I am glad for I learned you were bound to Sorcerers' Isle to seek the White Lords' help."

"True. Is their help, then, unobtainable?"

"Not yet. We ourselves are trying to contact them, with the aid of the hermit magicians of the island, but so far Chaos has blocked our attempts. But there is work for you and your sword closer to home. Come to my chamber and refresh yourselves. We have some wine which will revitalise you and when you have drunk your fill I'll tell you what task Fate has decided for you now."

Sitting in his chair, sipping his wine and glancing around Sepiriz's dark chamber, lighted only by the fires which burned in its several grates, Elric searched his mind for some clue to the unidentifiable impressions which seemed to drift just below the surface of his conscious brain. There was something mysterious about the chamber, a mystery that was not solely created by its vastness and the shadows that filled it. Without knowing why, Elric thought that though it was bounded by miles of solid rock in all directions, it had no proper dimensions that could be measured by the means normally employed; it was as if it extended into planes that did not conform to the Earth's space and time—planes that were, in fact, timeless and spaceless. He felt that he might attempt to cross the chamber from one wall to the other—but could walk for ever without ever reaching the far wall. He made an attempt to dismiss these thoughts and put down his cup, breathing in deeply. There was no doubt that the wine relaxed and invigorated him. He pointed to the wine jar on the stone table and said to Sepiriz: "A man might easily become addicted to such a brew!"

"I'm addicted already," Moonglum grinned, pouring himself another cup.

Sepiriz shook his head. "It has a strange quality, our Nihrain wine. It tastes pleasant and refreshes the weary, yet once his strength is regained, the man who drinks it then is nauseated. That is why we still have some of it left. But our stocks are low—the vines from which it was made have long since passed from the Earth."

"A magic potion," Moonglum said, replacing his cup on the table.

"If you like so to designate it. Elric and I are of an earlier age when what you call magic was part of normal life and Chaos ruled entirely, if more quietly than now. You men of the Young Kingdoms are perhaps right to be suspicious of sorcery, for we hope to ready the world for Law soon and then, perhaps, you'll find similar brews by more painstaking methods, methods you can understand better."

"I doubt it," Moonglum laughed.

Elric sighed. "If we are not luckier than we have been, we'll see Chaos unleashed on the globe and Law forever vanquished," he said gloomily.

"And no luck for us if Law is triumphant, eh?" Sepiriz poured himself a cup of the wine.

Moonglum looked sharply at Elric, understanding that much more of his friend's unenviable predicament.

"You said there was work for me and my sword, Sepiriz," Elric said. "What's its nature?"

"You have already learned that Jagreen Lern has summoned some of the Dukes of Hell to captain his men and keep his conquered lands under control?"

"Yes."

"You understand the import of this? Jagreen Lern has succeeded in making a sizeable breach in the Law-constructed barrier which once kept the creatures of Chaos from wholly ruling the planet. He is forever widening this breach as his power increases. This explains how he could summon such a mighty assembly of hell's nobility where, in the past, it was hard to bring one to our plane. Arioch is among them . . ."

"Arioch!" Arioch had always been Elric's patron demon, the principal god worshipped by his ancestors. That matters had reached such a stage conveyed to him, deeper than anything else, that he was now a total outcast, unprotected either by Law or Chaos.

"Your only close supernatural ally is your sword," Sepiriz said grimly. "And, perhaps, its brothers."

"What brothers? There is only the sister sword Mournblade, which Dyvim Slorm has!"

"Do you remember that I told you how the twin swords were actually only an earthly manifestation of their supernatural selves?" Sepiriz said calmly.

"I do."

"Well, I can tell you now that Stormbringer's 'real' being is related to other supernatural forces on another plane. I know how to summon them, but these entities are also creatures of Chaos and therefore, as far as you're concerned, somewhat hard to control. They could well get out of hand—perhaps even turn against you. Stormbringer, as you have discovered in the past, is bound to you by ties even stronger than those which bind it to its brothers who are lesser beings altogether, but its brothers outnumber it, and Stormbringer might not be able to protect you against them."

"Why have I never known this?"

"You *have* known it, in a way. Do you remember times when you have called to the Dark Ones for help and help has come?"

"Yes. You mean that this help has been supplied by Stormbringer's brethren?"

"Much of the time, yes. Already they are used to coming to your help. They are not what you and I would call intelligent, though sentient, and are therefore not so strongly bound to Chaos as its reasoning servants. They can be controlled, to a degree, by anyone who has power such as you have over one of their brothers. If you need their help, you will need to remember a rune which I shall tell you later."

"And what is my task?"

"To destroy the Dukes of Hell."

"Destroy the—Sepiriz, that's *impossible*. They are Lords of Chaos, one of the most powerful groups in the whole Realm of Chance. Sepiriz, I could not do it!"

"True. But you control one of the mightiest weapons. Of course, no mortal can destroy the dukes entirely—all he can hope to do is banish them to their own plane by wrecking the substance which they use for bodies on Earth. That is your task. Already there are hints that the Dukes of Hell—namely Arioch, and Balan, and Maluk—have taken some of Jagreen Lern's power from him. The fool still thinks he can rule over such supernatural might as they represent. It suits them, perhaps, to let him think so, but it is certain that with these friends Jagreen Lern can defeat the Southlands with a minimum of expenditure in arms, ships or men. Without them, he could do it—but it would take more time and effort and therefore give us a slight advantage to prepare against him while he subdues the Southlands."

Elric did not bother to ask Sepiriz how he knew of the Southerners' decision to fight Jagreen Lern alone. Sepiriz obviously had many powers as was proved by his ability to contact Elric through the seer. "I have sworn to help the Southlands in spite of their refusal to side with us against the Theocrat," he said calmly.

"And you'll keep your oath—by destroying the dukes if you can."

"Destroying Arioch, and Balan, and Maluk . . ." Elric whispered the names, fearful that even here he might invoke them.

"Arioch has always been an unhelpful demon," Moonglum pointed out. "Many's the time in the past he has refused to aid you, Elric."

"Because," Sepiriz said, "he already had some knowledge that you and he were to fight in the future."

Though the wine had refreshed his body, Elric's mind was close to snapping. The strain on his soul was almost at breaking point. To fight the demon-god of his ancestors . . . The old blood was still strong in him, the old loyalties still present.

Sepiriz rose and gripped Elric's shoulder, staring with black eyes into the dazed and smouldering crimson ones.

"You have pledged yourself to this mission, remember?"

"Aye, pledged—but Sepiriz—the Dukes of Hell—Arioch—I—oh, I wish that I were dead now . . ."

"You have much to do before you'll be allowed to die, Elric," Sepiriz said quietly. "You must realise how important you and your great sword are to Fate's cause. Remember your pledge!"

Elric drew himself upright, nodded vaguely. "Even had I been given this knowledge before I made that pledge, I would still have made it. But . . ."

"What?"

"Do not place too much faith on my ability to fulfil this part, Sepiriz."

The black Nihrain said nothing. Moonglum's normally animated face was grave and miserable as he looked at Elric standing in the mighty hall, the firelight writhing around him, his arms folded on his chest, the huge broadsword hanging straight at his side, and a look of stunned shock on his white face. Sepiriz walked away into the darkness and returned later with a white tablet on which old runes were engraved. He handed it to the albino.

"Memorise the spell," Sepiriz said softly, "and then destroy the tablet. But remember, only use it in extreme adversity for, as I warned you, Stormbringer's brethren may refuse to aid you."

Elric made an effort and controlled his emotions. Long after Moonglum had gone to rest, he studied the rune under the guidance of the Nihrainian, learning not only how to vocalise it, but also the twists of logic which he would have to understand, and the state of mind into which he must put himself if it were to be effective.

When both he and Sepiriz were satisfied, Elric allowed a slave to take him to his sleeping chamber, but slumber came hard to him and he spent the night in restless torment until the slave came to wake him the next morning and found him fully dressed and ready to ride for Pan Tang where the Dukes of Hell were assembled.

4

Through the stricken lands of the West rode Elric and Moonglum, astride
sturdy Nihrain steeds that seemed to need no rest and contained no fear. The
Nihrain horses were a special gift, for they had certain additional powers to
their unnatural strength and endurance. Sepiriz had told them how, in fact, the
steeds did not have full existence on the earthly plane and that their hoofs did
not touch the ground in the strict sense, but touched the stuff of their other
plane. This gave them the ability to appear to gallop on air—or water.

Scenes of terror were everywhere to be found. At one time they saw a
frightful sight; a wild and hellish mob destroying a village built around a
castle. The castle itself was in flames and on the horizon a mountain gouted
smoke and fire—yet another volcano in lands previously free of them. Though
the looters had human shape, they were degenerate creatures, spilling blood
and drinking it with equal abandon. And directing them without joining their
orgy, Elric and Moonglum saw what seemed to be a corpse astride the living
skeleton of a horse, bedecked in bright trappings, a flaming sword in its hand
and a golden helm on its head.

They skirted the scene and rode fast away from it, through mists that
looked and smelled like blood, over steaming rivers dammed with death, past
rustling forests that seemed to follow them, beneath skies often filled with
ghastly, winged shapes bearing even ghastlier burdens.

At other times, they met groups of warriors, many of them in the armour
and trappings of the conquered nations, but depraved and obviously sold to
Chaos. These they fought or avoided, depending on circumstance and, when

at last they reached the cliffs of Jharkor and saw the sea which would take them to the Isle of Pan Tang, they knew they had ridden through a land to which hell had come.

Along the cliffs they galloped, high above the churning, grey sea, the lowering sky dark and cold; down to the beaches to pause for a second time on the water's edge.

"Come!" Elric cried, urging his horse forward. "To Pan Tang!"

Scarcely stopping, they rode their magical steeds over the water towards the evil-heavy island of Pan Tang, where Jagreen Lern and his terrible allies prepared to sail with their giant fleet and smash the sea power of the South before conquering the Southlands themselves.

"Elric!" Moonglum called above the whining wind. "Should we not proceed with more caution?"

"Caution? What need of that when the Dukes of Hell must surely know their turncoat servant comes to fight them!"

Moonglum pursed his long lips, disturbed, for Elric was in a wild, maddened mood. He got little comfort, also, from the knowledge that Sepiriz had charmed his shortsword and his sabre both, with one of the few white spells he had at his command.

Now the bleak cliffs of Pan Tang rose into sight, spray-lashed and ominous, the sea moaning about them as if in some special torture which Chaos could inflict on nature itself.

And also around the island a peculiar darkness hovered, shifting and changing.

They entered the darkness as the Nihrain steeds pounded up the steep, rocky beach of Pan Tang, a place that had always been ruled by its black priesthood, a grim theocracy that had sought to emulate the legendary Sorcerer Emperors of the Bright Empire of Melniboné. But Elric, last of those emperors, and landless now, with few subjects, knew that the dark arts had been natural and lawful to his ancestors, whereas these human beings had perverted themselves to worship an unholy hierarchy they barely understood.

Sepiriz had given them their route and they galloped across the turbulent land towards the capital—Hwamgaarl, City of Screaming Statues.

Pan Tang was an island of green, obsidian rock that gave off bizarre reflections; rock that seemed alive.

Soon they could see the looming walls of Hwamgaarl in the distance. As they drew nearer, an army of black-cowled swordsmen, chanting a particularly horrible litany, seemed to rise from the ground ahead and block their way.

Elric had no time to spare for these, recognisable as a detachment of Jagreen Lern's warrior-priests.

"Up, steed!" he cried, and the Nihrain horse leapt skywards, passing over the disconcerted priests with a fantastic bound. Moonglum did likewise, his laughter mocking the swordsmen as he and his friend thundered on towards Hwamgaarl. Their way was clear for some distance, since Jagreen Lern had evidently expected the detachment to hold the pair for a long time. But, when the City of Screaming Statues was barely a mile away, the ground began to grumble and gaping cracks split its surface. This did not overly disturb them, for the Nihrain horses had no use for earthly terrain in any case.

The sky above heaved and shook itself, the darkness became flushed with streaks of luminous ebony, and from the fissures in the ground, monstrous shapes sprang up!

Vulture-headed lions, fifteen feet high, prowled in hungry anticipation towards them, their feathered manes rustling as they approached.

To Moonglum's frightened astonishment, Elric laughed and the Eastlander knew his friend had gone mad. But Elric was familiar with this ghoulish pack, since his ancestors had formed it for their own purposes a dozen centuries before. Evidently, Jagreen Lern had discovered the pack lurking on the borders between Chaos and Earth and had utilised it without being aware of how it had been created.

Old words formed on Elric's pale lips, and he spoke affectionately to the towering bird-beasts. They ceased their progress towards him, and glanced uncertainly around them, their loyalties evidently divided. Feathered tails lashed, claws worked in and out of pads, scraping great gashes in the obsidian rock. And, taking advantage of this, Elric and Moonglum walked their horses through them, and emerged just as a droning but angry voice rapped from the heavens, ordering, in the High Tongue of Melniboné: "*Destroy them!*"

One lion-vulture bounded uncertainly towards the pair. Another followed it, and another, till the whole pack raced to catch them.

"Faster!" Elric whispered to the Nihrain horse, but the steed could hardly keep the distance separating them. There was nothing for it but to turn. Deep in the recesses of his memory, he recalled a certain spell he had learned as a child. All the old spells of Melniboné had been passed on to him by his father, with the warning that, in these times, many of them were virtually useless. But there had been one—the spell for calling the vulture-headed lions, and another spell . . . Now he remembered it! The spell for sending them back to the domain of Chaos. Would it work?

He adjusted his mind, sought the words he needed as the beasts plunged on towards him.

> *"Creatures! Matik of Melniboné made thee*
> *From stuff of unformed madness!*
> *If thou wouldst live as thou art now,*
> *Get hence, or Matik's brew again shall be!"*

The creatures paused and, desperately, Elric repeated the spell, afraid that he had made a small mistake, either within his mind, or in the words.

Moonglum, who had drawn his horse up beside Elric, did not dare speak his fears, for he knew the albino sorcerer must not be hindered whilst spell-making. He watched in trepidation as the leading beast gave voice to a cawing roar.

But Elric heard the sound with relief, for it meant the beasts had understood his threat and were still bound to obey the spell. Slowly, half-reluctantly, they crawled down into the fissures, and vanished.

Sweating, Elric said triumphantly: "Luck is with us so far! Jagreen Lern either underestimated my powers, or else this is all he could summon with his own! More proof, perhaps, that Chaos uses him, and not the other way about!"

"Tempt not such luck by speaking of it," Moonglum warned. "From what you'd told me, these are puny things compared with what we must soon face."

Elric shot an angry look at his friend. He did not like to think of his coming task.

Now they neared the huge walls of Hwamgaarl. At intervals along these walls, which slanted outwards at an angle to encumber potential besiegers, they saw the screaming statues—once men and women whom Jagreen Lern and his forefathers had turned to rock but allowed them to retain their life and ability to speak. They spoke little, but screamed much, their ghastly shouts rolling over the disgusting city like the tormented voices of the damned—and damned they were. These sobbing waves of sound were horrifying, even to Elric's ears, familiar with such sounds. Then another noise blended with this as the mighty portcullis of Hwamgaarl's main gate squealed upwards and from it poured a host of well-armed men.

"Evidently, Jagreen Lern's powers of sorcery have been exhausted for the meantime and the Dukes of Hell disdain to join him in a fight against a pair of mere mortals!" Elric said, reaching for the hilt of the black runesword.

Moonglum was beyond speech. Wordlessly, he drew both his own charmed blades, knowing he must fight and vanquish his own fears before he could encounter the men who ran at him.

With a wild howl that drowned out the screams from the statues, Stormbringer climbed from the scabbard and stood in Elric's hand, waiting in anticipation for the new souls it might drink, for the lifestuff which it could pass on to Elric and fill him with dark and stolen vitality.

Elric half-cringed at the feel of his blade in his damp hand. But he shouted to the advancing soldiers: "See, jackals! See the sword! Forged by Chaos to vanquish Chaos! Come, let it drink your souls and spill your blood! We are ready for you!"

He did not wait but, with Moonglum behind him, spurred the Nihrain horse into their ranks, hewing about him with something of the old delight.

Now, so symbiotically linked with the hellblade was he that a hungry joy of killing swept through him, the joy of soul-stealing which drew a surging, unholy vitality into his deficient veins.

Though there were over a hundred warriors blocking his path, he smashed a bloody trail through them and Moonglum, seized by something akin to his friend's mood, was equally successful in dispatching all who came against him. Familiar with horror as they were, the soldiers soon became loath to approach the screaming runesword as it shone with a peculiarly brilliant light—a black light that pierced the blackness itself.

Laughing in his half-insane triumph, Elric felt the callous joy that his ancestors must have felt long ago, when they conquered the world and made it kneel to the Bright Empire. Chaos was, indeed, fighting Chaos—but Chaos of an older, cleaner sort, come to destroy the perverted upstarts who thought themselves as mighty as the wild Dragon Lords of Melniboné! Through the red ruin they had made of the enemy's ranks the pair plunged until the gateway gaped like a monster's maw before them. Without pausing, Elric rode laughing through it and people scuttled to hiding as he entered, in bizarre triumph, the City of Screaming Statues.

"Where now?" gasped Moonglum, all fear driven from him.

"To the Theocrat's Temple-Palace, of course. There Arioch and his fellow dukes no doubt await us!"

Through the echoing streets of the city they rode, proud and terrible, as if with an army at their backs. Dark buildings towered above them, but not a face dared peep from a window. Pan Tang had planned to rule the world—and it might yet—but, for the moment, its denizens were fully demoralised by the sight of two men taking their huge city by storm.

As they reached the wide plaza, Elric and Moonglum pulled their horses to a halt and observed the huge bronze shrine swinging on its chains in the centre. Beyond it rose Jagreen Lern's palace, all columns and towers, ominously quiet. Even the statues had ceased to scream, and the horses' hoofs made no sound as Elric and Moonglum approached the shrine. The blood-reddened runesword was still in Elric's two hands and he raised it upwards and to one side as he reached the brazen shrine. Then he took a mighty sweep at the chains supporting it. The supernatural blade bit into the metal and severed the links. The crash as the shrine dropped and smashed, scattering the bones of Jagreen Lern's ancestors, was magnified a thousand times by the silence. The noise echoed throughout Hwamgaarl and every inhabitant left alive knew what it signified.

"Thus I challenge thee, Jagreen Lern!" Elric shouted, aware that these words would also be heard by everyone. "I have come to pay the debt I promised! Come, puppet!" He paused, even his triumph not sufficient fully to quench his hesitation at what he must do now. "Come! Bring hell's dukes with you—"

Moonglum swallowed, his eyes rolling as he studied Elric's twisted face, but the albino continued:

"Bring Arioch. Bring Balan. Bring Maluk! Bring the proud princes of Chaos with you, for I have come to send them back to their own realm for ever!"

The silence again enfolded his high challenge, and he heard its echoes die away in the far places of the city.

Then, from somewhere inside the palace, he heard a movement. His heart pounded against his rib cage, threatening to break through the bones and hang throbbing on his chest as proof of his mortality. He heard a sound like the clopping of monstrous hoofs and, ahead of this noise, the measured steps that must be those of a man.

His eyes fixed themselves on the great, golden doors of the palace, half-hidden in the shadows that the columns threw. The doors silently began to open. Then a high-shouldered figure, dwarfed by the size of the doors, stepped forth and stood there, regarding Elric with a horrible anger smouldering in its face.

On his body, scarlet armour glowed as if red-hot. On his left arm was a shield of the same stuff and in his hand a steel sword. He had a narrow, aquiline head with a closely trimmed black beard and moustache. On his elaborate helm was the Merman Crest of Pan Tang. Jagreen Lern said, in a voice that trembled with rage: "So, Elric, you have kept part of your word, after all. How I wish I'd been able to kill you at Sequa when I had the chance, but then I had a bargain with Darnizhaan . . ."

"Step forward, Theocrat," Elric said with sudden calm. "I'll give you the chance again and meet you fairly in single combat."

Jagreen Lern sneered. "Fairly? With that blade in your hands? Once I met it and did not perish, but now it burns with the souls of my best warrior-priests. I know its power. I would not be so foolish as to stand against it. No—let those you have challenged meet you."

He stepped to one side. The doors gaped wider and, if Elric expected to see giant figures to emerge, he was disappointed. The dukes had assumed human proportions and the forms of men. But there was a power about them that filled the air as they moved to stand, disdainful of Jagreen Lern, upon the topmost step of the palace.

Elric looked upon their beautiful, smiling faces and shuddered again, for there was a kind of love on their faces, love mingled with pride and confidence, so that, for a moment, he was filled with the wish to jump from his horse and fling himself at their feet to plead forgiveness for what he had become. All the longing and the loneliness within him seemed to well up and he knew that these lovely beings would claim him, protect him, care for him . . .

"Well, Elric," said Arioch, the leader, softly. "Would you repent and return to us?"

The voice was silvery in its beauty, and Elric half-made to dismount, but then he clapped his hands to his ears, the runesword hanging by its wrist-throng, and cried: "*No! No! I must do what I must! Your time, like mine, is over!*"

"Do not speak thus, Elric," Balan said persuasively, "our rule has hardly begun. Soon the Earth and all its creatures will be part of the Realm of Chaos and a wild and splendid era will begin!" His words passed Elric's hands and whispered in his skull. "Chaos has never been so powerful on Earth—not even in earliest days. We shall make you great. We shall make you a Lord of Chaos, equal to ourselves! We give you immortality, Elric. If you behave so foolishly, you will bring yourself only death, and none shall remember you."

"I know that! I would not wish to be remembered in a world ruled by Law!"

Maluk laughed softly. "That will never come to pass. We block every move that Law makes to try to bring help to Earth."

"And this is why you must be destroyed!" Elric cried.

"We are immortal—we can never be slain!" Arioch said, and there was a tinge of impatience in his voice.

"Then I shall send you back to Chaos in such a way that you shall never have power on the Earth again!"

Elric swung his runeblade into his hand and it trembled there, moaning quietly, as if unsure of itself, just as he was.

"See!" Balan walked part-way down the steps. "See—even your trusted sword knows that we speak truth!"

"You speak a sort of truth," Moonglum said in a quavering tone, astonished at his own bravery. "But I remember something of a greater truth—a law that should bind both Chaos and Law—the Law of the Balance. That balance is held over the Earth and it has been ordained that Chaos and Law must keep it straight. Sometimes the Balance tips one way, sometimes another—and thus are the ages of the Earth created. But an unequal balance of this magnitude is *wrong*. In your struggling, you of Chaos may have forgotten this!"

"We have forgotten it for good reason, mortal. The Balance has tipped to such an extent in our favour that it is no longer adjustable. We triumph!"

Elric used this pause to collect himself. Sensing his renewed strength, Stormbringer responded with a confident purr.

The dukes also sensed it and glanced at one another.

Arioch's beautiful face seemed to flare with anger and his pseudo-body glided down the steps towards Elric, his fellow dukes following.

Elric's steed backed away a few paces.

A blot of living fire appeared in Arioch's hand and it shot towards the albino. He felt cold pain in his chest and he staggered in the saddle.

"Your body is unimportant, Elric. But think of a similar blow to your soul!" The façade of patience was dropping from Arioch.

Elric flung back his head and laughed. Arioch had betrayed himself. If he had remained calm, he would have had a greater advantage, but now he showed himself perturbed, whatever he had said to the contrary.

"Arioch, you aided me in the past, aided me to live. You will regret that!"

"There's still time to undo my folly, upstart man!" Another bolt came streaking towards him, but he passed Stormbringer before it and, in relief, saw that it deflected the unholy weapon.

But against such might they were surely doomed, unless they could invoke some supernatural aid. But Elric dared not risk summoning his runesword's brothers. Not yet. He must think of some other means. As he retreated before the searing bolts, Moonglum behind him whispering almost impotent charms, he thought of the vulture-lions he had sent back to Chaos. Perhaps he could recall them—for a different purpose.

The spell was fresh in his mind, requiring a slightly changed mental state and scarcely changed wording. Calmly, mechanically deflecting the bolts of the dukes, whose features had changed hideously to retain their previous beauty but take on an increasingly malevolent look, he uttered the spell.

Creatures! Matik of Melniboné made thee,
From stuff of unformed madness!
If thou wouldst live, then aid me now.
Come hither, or Matik's brew again shall be!

From out of the rolling darks of the plaza, the beaked beasts prowled. Elric yelled at the dukes. "Mortal weapons cannot harm you! But these are beasts of your own plane! Sample their ferocity!" In the bizarre tongue of Melniboné, he ordered the vulture-lions upon the dukes.

Apprehensively, Arioch and his fellows backed towards the steps again, calling their own commands to the giant animals, but the things advanced, gathering speed.

Elric saw Arioch shout, rave, and then his body seemed to split asunder and rise in a new, less recognisable shape as the beasts attacked. All was suddenly ragged colour, shrill sound and disordered matter. Behind the embattled demons, Elric saw Jagreen Lern running back into his palace. Hoping that the creatures he had summoned would hold the dukes, Elric rode his horse around the boiling mass and galloped up the steps.

Through the doors the two men rode, catching a glimpse of the terrified Theocrat running before them.

"Your allies were not so strong as you believed, Jagreen Lern!" Elric yelled as he bore down upon his enemy. "Why, you foolish latecomer, did you think your knowledge matched that of a Melnibonéan!"

Jagreen Lern began to climb a winding staircase, labouring up the steps, too afraid to look back. Elric laughed again and pulled his horse to a stop, watching the running man.

"Dukes! Dukes!" sobbed Jagreen Lern as he climbed. "Do not desert me now!"

Moonglum whispered. "Surely those creatures will not defeat the aristocracy of hell?"

Elric shook his head. "I do not expect them to, but if I finish Jagreen Lern, at least it could put an end to his conquests and demon-summoning." He spurred the Nihrain steed up the steps after the Theocrat who heard him coming and flung himself into a room. Elric heard a bar fall and bolts squeal.

When he reached the door, it fell in at a blow of his sword and he was in a small chamber. Jagreen Lern had disappeared.

Dismounting, Elric went to a small door in the farthest corner of the room and again demolished it. A narrow stair led upwards, obviously into a tower. Now he could take his vengeance, he thought, as he reached yet another door at the top of the stair and drew back his sword to smite it. The blow fell, but the door held.

"Curse the thing, it is protected by charms!"

He was just about to aim another blow, when he heard Moonglum's urgent calling from below.

"Elric! Elric—they've defeated the creatures. They are returning to the palace!"

He would have to leave Jagreen Lern for the meantime. He sprang down the steps, into the chamber and out onto the stair. In the hall he saw the flowing shapes of the unholy trinity. Halfway up the stair, Moonglum was quaking.

"Stormbringer," said Elric, "it is time to summon your brothers."

The sword moved in his hand, as if in assent. He began to chant the difficult rune that Sepiriz had taught him. Stormbringer moaned a counterpoint to the dirge as the battle-worn dukes assumed different shapes and began to rise menacingly towards Elric.

Then, in the air all about him, he saw shapes appear, shadowy shapes half on his own plane, half on the plane of Chaos. He saw them stir and suddenly it seemed as if the air was filled with a million swords, each a twin to Stormbringer!

Acting on instinct, Elric released his grip on his blade and flung it towards the rest. It hung in the air before them and they seemed to acknowledge it. "Lead them, Stormbringer! Lead them against the dukes—or your master perishes and you'll not drink another human soul again!"

The sea of swords rustled and a dreadful moaning emanated from them. The dukes flung themselves upwards towards the albino and he recoiled before the evil hatred that poured from the twisting shapes.

Glancing down, he saw Moonglum slumped in his saddle and did not know if he had perished or fainted.

Then the swords rushed upon the reaching dukes and Elric's head swam with the sight of a million blades plunging into the stuff of their beings.

The ululating noise of the battle filled his ears, the dreadful sight of the toiling conflict clouded his vision. Without Stormbringer's vitality, he felt weak and limp. He felt his knees shake and crumple and he could do nothing to aid the Black Sword's brothers as they clashed with the Dukes of Hell.

He collapsed, aware that if he witnessed further horror he would become totally insane. Thankfully, he felt his mind go blank and then, at last, he was unconscious, unable to know which would win.

5

His body itched. His arms and back ached. His wrists pounded with agony.
Elric opened his eyes.

Immediately opposite him, spreadeagled in chains against the wall he saw
Moonglum. Dull flame flickered in the centre of the place and he felt pain on
his naked knee, looked down and saw Jagreen Lern.

The Theocrat spat at him.

"So," Elric said thickly, "I failed. You triumph after all."

Jagreen Lern did not look triumphant. Rage still burned in his eyes.

"Oh, how shall I punish you?" he whispered.

"Punish me? Then—?" Elric's heartbeat increased.

"Your final spell succeeded," the Theocrat said flatly, turning away to contemplate the brazier. "Both your allies and mine vanished and all my attempts
to contact the dukes have proved fruitless. You achieved your threat—or your
minions did—you sent them back to Chaos for ever!"

"My sword—what of that?"

The Theocrat smiled bitterly. "That's my only pleasure. Your sword vanished with the others. You are weak and helpless now, Elric. You are mine to
maim and torture until the end of my life."

Elric was dumbfounded. Part of him rejoiced that the dukes had been
beaten. Part of him lamented the loss of his sword. As Jagreen Lern had emphasised, without the blade, he was less than half a man, for his albinism
weakened him. Already, his eyesight was dimmer and he felt no response in
his limbs.

Jagreen Lern looked up at him.

"Enjoy the comparatively painless days left you, Elric. I leave you to anticipate what I have in store for you. I must away and instruct my men in the final preparations for the war-fleet soon to sail against the South. I won't waste time with crude torture now, for all the while I shall be scheming the most exquisite tortures conceivable. You shall take long years to die, I swear."

He left the cell and, as the door slammed, Elric heard Jagreen Lern instructing the guard.

"Keep the brazier at full blast. Let them sweat like damned souls. Feed them enough to keep them alive, once every three days. They will soon be crying for water. Give them only sufficient to sustain their lives. They deserve far worse than this and they'll get their deserts when my mind has had time to work on the problem."

A day later, the real agony began. Their bodies gave out the last of their sweat. Their tongues were swollen in their heads and all the time as they groaned in their torment they were aware that this terrible torture would be nothing to what they might expect. Elric's weakened body would not respond to his desperate struggling and at length his mind dulled, the agony became constant and familiar, and time was non-existent.

Finally, through a pain-thick daze, he recognised a voice. It was the hate-filled voice of Jagreen Lern.

Others were in the chamber. He felt their hands seize him and his body was suddenly light as he was borne, moaning, from the cell.

Though he heard disjointed phrases, he could make no sense of Jagreen Lern's words. He was taken to a dark place that rolled about, hurting his scorched chest.

Later, he heard Moonglum's voice and strained to hear the words.

"Elric! What's happening? We're aboard a ship at sea, I'd swear!"

But Elric mumbled without interest. His deficient body was weakening faster than would a normal man's. He thought of Zarozinia, whom he would never see again. He knew he would not live to know whether Law or Chaos finally won, or even if the Southlands would stand against the Theocrat.

And these problems were fading in his mind again.

Then the food started to come and the water and it revived him somewhat. At one stage, he opened his eyes and stared upwards into the thinly smiling face of Jagreen Lern.

"Thank the gods," said the Theocrat. "I feared we'd lost you. You're a delicate case to be sure, my friend. You must stay alive longer than this. To begin my entertainment, I have arranged for you to sail on my own flagship. We are now crossing the Dragon Sea, our fleet well-protected by charms against the monsters roaming these parts." He frowned. "Thanks to you, we haven't the same call for the charms which would have borne us safely through the Chaos-torn waters. The seas are almost normal for the moment. But that will soon be changed."

Elric's old spirit returned for a moment and he glared at his enemy, too weak to voice the loathing he felt.

Jagreen Lern laughed softly and stirred Elric's gaunt white head with the toe of his boot. "I think I can brew a drug which will give you a little more vitality."

The food, when it came, was foul-tasting, and had to be forced between Elric's mumbling lips, but after a while he was able to sit up and observe the huddled body of Moonglum. Evidently, the little man had totally succumbed to his torture. To his surprise, Elric discovered he was unfettered and he crawled the agonising distance between himself and the Eastlander, shaking Moonglum's shoulder. He groaned, but did not otherwise respond.

A shaft of light suddenly struck through the darkness of the hold and Elric blinked, looking up to see that the hatch cover had been prised aside and Jagreen Lern's bearded face stared down at him.

"Good, good. I see the brew had its effect. Come, Elric, smell the invigorating sea and feel the warm sun on your body. We are not many miles from the coasts of Argimiliar and our scout ships report quite a sizeable fleet sailing hence."

Elric cursed. "By Arioch, I hope they send you all to the bottom!"

Jagreen Lern pursed his lips, mockingly. "By whom? Arioch? Do you not remember what ensued in my own palace? Arioch cannot be invoked. Not by you—not by me. Your stinking spells saw to that."

He turned to an unseen lieutenant. "Bind him and bring him on deck. You know what to do with him."

Two warriors dropped into the hold and grasped the still-weak Elric, tying his arms and legs and manhandling him onto the deck. He gasped as the sun's glare struck his eyes.

"Prop him up so he may see all," Jagreen Lern ordered.

The warriors obeyed, and Elric was lifted to a standing position, seeing Jagreen Lern's huge, black flagship with its silken deck canopies flapping in a steady westerly breeze, its three banks of straining oarsmen and its tall ebony mast, bearing a sail of dark red.

Beyond the ship's rails, Elric saw a massive fleet surging in the flagship's wake. As well as the vessels of Pan Tang and Dharijor, there were many from Jharkor, Shazaar and Tarkesh, but on every scarlet sail the Merman blazon of Pan Tang was painted.

Despair filled Elric, for he knew that the Southlands, however strong, could not match a fleet like this.

"We have been at sea for only three days," said Jagreen Lern, "but thanks to a witch-wind, we're almost at our destination. A scout ship has recently reported that the Lormyrian navy, hearing rumours of our superior sea power, is sailing to join with us. A wise move of King Montan—for the moment, at any rate. I'll make use of him for the time being and, when his usefulness is over, I'll kill him for a treacherous turncoat."

"Why do you tell me all this?" Elric whispered, his teeth gritted against the pain that came with any slight movement of his face or body.

"Because I want you to witness for yourself the defeat of the South. The merchant princes sail against us—and we shall easily crush them. I want you to know that what you sought to avert will come to pass. After we have subdued the South and sucked her of her treasures, we'll vanquish the Isle of the

Purple Towns and press forward to sack Vilmir and Ilmiora. That will be an easy matter, don't you agree? We have allies other than those you defeated."

When Elric did not reply, Jagreen Lern gestured impatiently to his men.

"Tie him to the mast so that he may get a good view of the battle. I'll put a protective charm around his body, for I do not want him to be killed by a stray arrow and cheat me of my full vengeance."

Elric was borne up and roped to the mast, but he was scarcely aware of it, for his head lolled on his right shoulder, only semi-conscious.

The massive fleet plunged onwards, certain of victory.

By mid-afternoon, Elric was aroused from his stupor by the shout of the helmsman.

"Sail to the south-east! Lormyrian fleet approaches!"

With impotent anger, Elric saw the fifty two-masted ships, their bright sails contrasting with the sombre scarlet of Jagreen Lern's vessels, come into line with the others.

Lormyr, though a smaller power than Argimiliar, had a larger navy. Elric judged that King Montan's treachery had cost the South more than a quarter of its strength.

Now he knew there was absolutely no hope for the South and that Jagreen Lern's certainty of victory was well-founded.

Night fell and the huge fleet lay at anchor. A guard came to feed Elric a mushy porridge containing another dose of the drug. As he revived, his anger increased, and Jagreen Lern paused by the mast on two occasions, taunting him savagely.

"Soon after dawn we shall meet the Southern fleet," Jagreen Lern smiled, "and by noon what is left of it will float as bloody driftwood behind us as we press on to establish our reign over those nations who so foolishly relied on their sea power as defence."

Elric remembered how he had warned the kings of the Southlands that this was likely to happen if they stood alone against the Theocrat. But he wished that he had been wrong. With the defeat of the South, the conquest of the East seemed bound to follow and, when Jagreen Lern ruled the world, Chaos would dominate and the Earth revert to the stuff from which it had been formed millions of years before.

All through that moonless night, he brooded. He pulled his thoughts together, summoning all his strength for a plan that was, as yet, only a shadow in the back of his mind.

6

The rattle of anchors woke him.

Blinking in the light of the watery sun, he saw the Southern fleet on the horizon, riding gracefully in hollow pomp towards the ships of Jagreen Lern. Either, he thought, the Southern kings were very brave, or else they did not understand the strength of their enemies.

Beneath him, on Jagreen Lern's foredeck, a great catapult rested, and slaves had already filled its cup with a large ball of flaming pitch. Normally, Elric knew, such catapults were an encumbrance, since when they reached that size they were difficult to rewind and gave lighter war-engines the advantage. Yet obviously Jagreen Lern's engineers were not fools. Elric noted extra mechanisms on the big catapult and realised they were equipped to rewind rapidly.

The wind had dropped and five hundred pairs of muscles strove to row Jagreen Lern's galley along. On the deck, in disciplined order, his warriors took their posts beside the great boarding platforms that would drop down on the opponent's ships and grapple them at the same time as they formed a bridge between the vessels.

Elric was forced to admit that Jagreen Lern had used foresight. He had not relied wholly on supernatural aid. His ships were the best equipped he had ever seen. The Southern fleet, he decided, was doomed. To fight Jagreen Lern was insanity.

But the Theocrat had made one mistake. He had, in his gnawing desire for vengeance, ensured that Elric's vitality was restored for a few hours and this vitality extended to his mind as well as his body.

Stormbringer had vanished. With the sword he was, among men, all but invincible. Without it, he was helpless. These were facts. Therefore he must somehow regain the blade. But how? It had returned to the plane of Chaos with its brothers, presumably drawn back there by the overwhelming power of the rest.

He must contact it.

He dare not summon the entire horde of blades with the spell, that would be tempting providence too far.

He heard the sudden *thwack* and roar as the giant catapult discharged its first shot. The flame-shrouded pitch went arching over the ocean and landed short, boiling the sea around it as it guttered and sank. Swiftly the war-engine was rewound, and Elric marvelled at the speed as another ball of flaring pitch was forked into its cup. Jagreen Lern looked up at him and laughed.

"My pleasure will be short. There are not enough of them to put up a long fight. Watch them perish, Elric!"

Elric said nothing, pretended to be dazed and frightened.

The next fireball struck one of the leading ships directly and Elric saw tiny figures scampering about, striving desperately to quench the spreading pitch, but within a minute the whole ship was ablaze, a gouting mass of flame as the figures now jumped overboard, unable to save their vessel.

The air around him sounded to the rushing heat of the fireballs and, within range now, the Southerners retaliated with their lighter machines until it seemed the sky was filled with a thousand comets and the heat almost equalled that which Elric had experienced in the torture chamber. Black smoke began to drift as the brass beaks of the ships' rams ground through timbers, impaling ships like skewered fish. The hoarse yells of fighting men began to be heard, and the clash of iron as the first few opposing warriors met.

But now he only vaguely heard the sounds, for he was thinking deeply.

Then, when at last his mind was ready, he called in a desperate and agonised voice that human ears could not hear above the noise of war: "Stormbringer!"

His straining mind echoed the shout and he seemed to look beyond the turbulent battle, beyond the ocean, beyond the very Earth to a place of shadows and terror. Something moved there. Many things moved there.

"*Stormbringer!*"

He heard a curse from beneath him and saw Jagreen Lern pointing up at him. "Gag the white-faced sorcerer," Jagreen Lern's eyes met Elric's and the Theocrat sucked in his lips, deliberating a bare moment before adding: "And if that doesn't put an end to his babbling—best slay him!"

The lieutenant began to climb the mast towards Elric.

"Stormbringer! Your master perishes!"

He struggled in the biting ropes, but could hardly move.

"*Stormbringer!*"

All his life he had hated the sword he relied on so much; which he was relying on more and more, but now he called for it as a lover calls for his betrothed.

The warrior grasped his foot and shook it. "Silence! You heard my master!"

With insane eyes, Elric looked down at the warrior who shuddered and drew his sword, hanging to the mast with one hand and readying himself to make a stab at Elric's vitals.

"*Stormbringer!*" Elric sobbed the name. He *must* live. Without him, Chaos would surely rule the world.

The man lunged at Elric's body—yet the blade did not reach the albino. Then Elric remembered, with sudden humour, that Jagreen Lern had placed a protective spell about him! The Theocrat's own magic had saved his enemy!

"*Stormbringer!*"

Now the warrior gasped and the sword dropped from his fingers. He seemed to grapple with something invisible at his throat and Elric saw the man's fingers sliced off and blood spurt from the stumps. Then, slowly, a shape materialised and, with bounding relief, the albino saw that it was a sword— his own runesword impaling the warrior and sucking out his soul!

The warrior dropped, but Stormbringer hung in the air and then turned to slash the ropes restraining Elric's hands and then nestled firmly, with horrid affection, in its master's right fist.

At once the stolen lifestuff of the warrior began to pour through Elric's being and the pain of his body vanished. Quickly he grasped a piece of the sail's rigging and cut away the rest of his bonds until he was swinging by one hand on the rope.

"Now, Jagreen Lern, we'll see who takes vengeance, finally," he grimaced as he swung towards the deck and dropped lightly upon it, the unholy vitality from the sword surging through him to fill him with a godlike ecstasy. He had never known it so strong before.

But then he noted that the boarding platforms had been lowered and only a skeleton crew remained on the flagship. Jagreen Lern must have led his main strength onto the ship which was now held fast by grapples.

Close by was a great barrel of pitch, used to form the fireballs. Close to that was a flaring torch used to ignite them. Elric seized the brand and flung it into the pitch.

"Though Jagreen Lern may win this battle, his flagship shall go to the bottom with the Southern fleet," he said grimly, and dashed for the hold where he had been imprisoned, aware that Moonglum lay helpless there.

He wrenched up the hatch cover and stared down at the pitiful figure of his friend. Evidently, he had been left to starve to death. A rat chittered away as the light shone down.

Elric jumped into the hold and saw, with horror, that part of Moonglum's right arm had been gnawed already. He heaved the body onto his shoulder, aware that the heart still beat, though faintly, and clambered back up to the deck. How to ensure his friend's safety and still take vengeance on Jagreen Lern was a problem. But Elric moved towards the boarding platform which he guessed the Theocrat to have crossed. As he did so, three warriors leapt towards him. One of them cried: "The albino! The reaver escapes!"

Elric struck him down with a blow that required only a slight movement of his wrist. The Black Sword did the rest. The others retreated, remembering how Elric had entered Hwamgaarl.

New energy flowed through him. For every corpse he created, his strength increased—a stolen strength, but necessary if he was to survive and win the day for Law.

He ran, untroubled by his burden, over the boarding platform and onto the deck of the Southern ship. Up ahead he saw the standard of Argimiliar and a little group of men around it, headed by King Hozel himself, his face gaunt as he stared at the knowledge of his own death. A deserved death thought Elric grimly, but nonetheless when Hozel died it would mean another victory for Chaos.

Then he heard a shout of a different quality, thought for a moment that he had been observed, but one of Hozel's men was pointing to the north and mouthing something.

Elric looked in that direction and saw the brave sails of the Purple Towns. They were fighting ships, better equipped for battle than those of the merchant princes. Their brightly painted sails caught the light. The only rich decoration the austere sea-lords allowed themselves was upon their sails. Elric's ally Kargan must command them.

But they had arrived belatedly. Even if they had sailed with the other Southern vessels it would have been unlikely that they could have turned the day against Pan Tang.

At that moment, staring around him, Jagreen Lern saw Elric and bellowed at his men who moved forward warily and reluctantly, approaching the albino in a wide semicircle.

Elric cursed the brave sea-lords who had added a further factor to his indecision.

Menacingly he swung the moaning runeblade about him as he advanced to meet the half-terrified Pan Tang warriors. They dropped back, some of them groaning as the blade touched them. The way was now clear to Jagreen Lern.

But the ships of the Purple Towns were drawing closer, almost within catapult range.

Elric looked directly into Jagreen Lern's frightened face and snarled: "I doubt if my blade has the strength to pierce your burning armour with one blow, and one blow is all I have time for. I leave you now, Theocrat, but re-member that even if you conquer all the world including the unmapped lands of the East, I'll have my sword drink your black soul at length."

With that he dropped Moonglum's unconscious body overboard and dived after it into the choppy sea.

The blade gave him superhuman strength and he swam towards the lead-ing ship of the sea-lords, which he recognised as Kargan's, dragging Moon-glum's body after him.

Now, behind him, Jagreen Lern and his men saw their own flagship blaz-ing. Elric had done his work well.

That, too, would serve to divert attention from Kargan's fleet.

Trusting to the sea-lords' famed seamanship, he swam directly in the path of the leading galleon, shouting Kargan's name.

The ship veered slightly and he saw bearded faces at the rail, saw ropes flicker towards him and grasped one, letting them haul him upwards with his burden.

As the seamen pulled them both over the rail, Elric saw Kargan staring at him with shocked eyes. The sea-lord was dressed in the tough brown leather armour of his folk. He had an iron cap on his massive head and his black beard bristled. "Elric! We thought you dead—lost on your voyage south!"

Elric spat salt water from his mouth and said urgently: "Turn your fleet, Kar-gan! Turn it back the way it has come, there is no hope of saving the Southlanders—they are doomed. We must preserve our forces for a later struggle."

Hesitating momentarily, Kargan gave the order which was swiftly relayed to the rest of his sixty-strong fleet.

As the ships turned away, Elric noted that hardly a Southern ship remained afloat. For more than a mile the water burned and the sputtering of the flam-ing, sinking ships was blended with the screams of the maimed and drowning.

"With the Southern sea power crushed so decisively," Kargan said, watch-ing the physician who was tending to Moonglum, "the lands will not last long before Pan Tang's marching hordes. Like us, the South relied too much on its ships. It has taught me that we must strengthen our land defences if we are to have any chance at all."

"From now on we'll use your island as our main headquarters," Elric said. "We'll fortify the whole place and from there keep in close touch with what is happening in the South. How is my friend, physician?"

The physician looked up. "These are no battle-made wounds. He's been hurt sorely, but he'll live. He should recover to perfect fitness given a month or so of rest."

"He'll have it," Elric promised. He gripped the runesword at his belt and wondered what other tasks lay in store for them before the last great battle between Law and Chaos was joined.

Chaos would soon rule more than half the world, in spite of the powerful blow he had dealt it in forever sentencing the Dukes of Hell to their own plane; the more power that Jagreen Lern gathered, the more the threat from Chaos would increase.

He sighed and looked northwards.

Two days later they returned to the Isle of the Purple Towns, the fleet remaining in the largest harbour of Utkel since it was thought wise to have it at hand and not disperse it.

All that following night, Elric talked with the sea-lords, ordered messengers to Vilmir and Ilmiora and, towards morning, there came a polite knock on the door of the room.

Kargan got up to open it and stared in astonishment at the tall, black-faced man who stood there.

"Sepiriz!" Elric cried. "How did you come here?"

"On horseback," smiled the giant, "and you know the power of the Nihrain steeds. I had come to warn you. We have, at last, managed to contact the White Lords but they can do little as yet. Somehow a path to their plane must be made through the barricades which Chaos has constructed against them. Jagreen Lern's ships have vomited their contents on the Southern shores and his warriors swarm inland. There is nothing we can do now to stop his conquests there. Once consolidated, his earthly power increased, he will be able to summon more and more allies from Chaos."

"Then where does my next task lie?" Elric asked softly.

"I am not sure yet. But that is not what I came for. Your blade's sojourn with its brothers has strengthened it. You notice how swiftly it pours power into your body now?"

"True. Yet I seem ever more reliant upon that power." He spoke flatly. "The power is stronger, but I am weaker, it seems."

Sepiriz said gravely: "That power is evilly gained and evil in itself. The blade's strength will continue to increase but as Chaos-begotten power fills your being, you will have to fight yet more strongly to control the force within you. That also will take strength. So, you see, you must use part of the strength to fight the strength itself."

Elric sighed and grasped Sepiriz's arm.

"Thanks for the warning, friend, but when I beat the Dukes of Hell, to whom I formerly pledged allegiance, I did not expect to escape with a mere scratch or a flesh wound. Know this, Sepiriz," he turned to the watching sea-lords, "and know this all of you."

He drew the groaning runeblade from its scabbard and held it aloft so that it shone and flared in its awful power.

"This blade was forged by Chaos to conquer Chaos and that is my destiny, too. Though the world crumbles and turns to boiling gas, I shall live now. I swear by the Cosmic Balance that Law shall triumph and the New Age come to this Earth."

Taken aback by this grim vow, the sea-lords glanced at one another and Sepiriz smiled.

"Let us hope so, Elric," he said. "Let us hope so."

BOOK THREE

SAD GIANT'S SHIELD

Thirteen times thirteen, the steps to the sad giant's lair;
And the Chaos Shield lies there.
Seven times seven are the elder trees
Twelve times twelve warriors he sees
But the Chaos Shield lies there.
And the hero fair will the sad giant dare
And a red sword wield for the sad giant's shield
On a mournful victory day.

—The Chronicle of the Black Sword

I

Across the whole world the shadow of anarchy had fallen. Neither god, nor man, nor that which ruled both could clearly read the future and see the fate of Earth as the forces of Chaos increased their strength both personally and through their human minions.

From Westland mountain, over the agitated ocean to Southland plain, Chaos now held its monstrous sway. Tormented, miserable, unable to hope any longer for liberation from the corroding, warping influence of Chaos, the remnants of races fled over the two continents already fallen to the human minions of Disorder, led by their warped Theocrat Jagreen Lern of Pan Tang, aquiline, high-shouldered and greedy for power, in his glowing scarlet armour, controlling human vultures and supernatural creatures alike as he widened his black boundaries.

Upon the face of the Earth all was disruption and roaring anguish, save for the thinly populated, already threatened Eastern Continent and the Isle of the Purple Towns, which now readied itself to withstand Jagreen Lern's initial onslaught. The onrushing tide of Chaos must soon sweep the world unless some great force could be summoned to halt it.

Bleakly, bitterly, the few who still resisted Jagreen Lern, under the command of Elric of Melniboné, talked of strategy and tactics in the full knowledge that more than these were needed to beat back Jagreen Lern's unholy horde.

Desperately, Elric attempted to utilise the ancient sorcery of his emperor forefathers to contact the White Lords of Law; but he was unused to seeking such aid and, as well, the forces of Chaos were now so strong that those of Law could no longer gain easy access to the Earth as they had contrived to do in earlier times.

As they prepared for the coming fight, Elric and his allies went about the preparation with heavy souls and a sense of the futility of such action. And in the back of Elric's mind was the constant knowledge that even if he won against Chaos, the very act of winning would destroy the world he knew and leave it ripe for the forces of Law to rule—and there would be no place in such a world for the wild albino sorcerer.

Beyond the earthly plane, in their bordering realms, the Lords of the Higher Worlds watched the struggle, and even they did not realise Elric's entire destiny.

Chaos triumphed. Chaos blocked the efforts of Law on each occasion they tried to pass through the domain of Chaos, now the only road to Earth. And the Lords of Law shared Elric's frustration.

And, if Chaos and Law were observing the Earth and her struggle, who watched these? For Chaos and Law were but the twin weights in a balance and the hand that held the Balance, though it rarely deigned to interfere in their struggle, still less in the affairs of men, had reached the rare state of a decision to alter the status quo. Which weight would drop? Which rise? Could men decide? Could the lords decide? Or could only the Cosmic Hand remould the pattern of the Earth, reforming her stuff, changing her spiritual constituents and placing her on a different path, a fresh course of destiny?

Perhaps all would play some part before the outcome was decided.

The great zodiac influencing the universe and its Ages had completed its twelve cycles and the cycles would soon begin again. The wheel would spin and, when it stopped its spinning, which symbol would dominate, how changed would it be?

Great movements on the Earth and beyond it; great destinies being shaped, great deeds being planned and, marvellously, could it just be possible that in spite of the Lords of the Higher Worlds, in spite of the Cosmic Hand, in spite of the myriad supernatural denizens that swarmed the multiverse, that Man might decide the issue?

Even one man?

One man, one sword, one destiny?

Elric of Melniboné sat hunched in his saddle, watching the warriors bustle to and fro around him in the city square of Bakshaan. Here, years before, he had conducted a siege against the city's leading merchant, tricked others and left rich, but such scores that they held against him were now forgotten, pushed from their minds by the threat of war and the knowledge that if Elric's command could not save them, nothing could. The walls of the city were being widened and heightened, warriors being trained in the use of unfamiliar war-engines. From being a lazy merchant city, Bakshaan had become a functional place, ready for battle when it came.

For a month, Elric had been riding the length and breadth of the Eastern kingdoms of Ilmiora and Vilmir, overseeing preparations, building the strength of the two nations into an efficient war machine.

Now he studied parchments handed him by his lieutenants and, recalling all the old tactical skill of his ancestors, gave them his decisions.

The sun was setting and heavy black clouds hung against a sharp, metallic blue sky, stretching over the horizon. Elric loosened his cloak strings and allowed the folds of the garment to enclose him, for a chill had come.

Then, as he silently regarded the sky to the west, he frowned as he noticed something like a flashing golden star appear, moving swiftly towards him.

Ever wary for signs of the coming of Chaos, he turned in his saddle shouting:

"Every man to his position! 'Ware the golden globe!"

The thing approached rapidly until soon it was hanging over the city, all men looking up at it in astonishment, their hands on their weapons. As black night fell, the clouds admitting no moonlight, the globe began to fall towards the spires of Bakshaan, a strange luminescence pulsing from it. Elric tugged Stormbringer from its scabbard and black fire flickered along the blade as it gave out a low moaning sound. The globe touched the cobbles of the city square—broke into a million fragments that glowed for a moment before vanishing.

Elric laughed in relief, resheathing Stormbringer as he saw who now stood in the place of the golden globe.

"Sepiriz, my friend. You choose strange means of transport to carry you from the Chasm of Nihrain."

The tall, black-faced seer smiled, his white pointed teeth gleaming. "I have so few carriages of that type that I must only use them when pressed. I come with news for you—much news."

"I hope it is good, for we have enough bad to last us for ever."

"It is mixed. Where can we converse in private?"

"My headquarters are in yonder mansion," Elric pointed at a richly decorated house on the far side of the square.

Inside, Elric poured yellow wine for his guest. Kelos the merchant, whose house this was, had not accepted the requisitioning altogether willingly and, partly because of this, Elric maliciously made free with all Kelos's best.

Sepiriz took the goblet and sipped the strong wine.

"Have you succeeded in contacting the White Lords again, Sepiriz?" Elric asked.

"We have."

"Thank the gods. Are they willing to give their aid to us?"

"They have always been so willing—but they have not yet made a sufficient breach in the defences that Chaos has set up around this planet. However, the fact that I have at last managed to contact them is a better sign than we've had these past months."

"So—the news *is* good," Elric said cheerfully.

"Not altogether. Jagreen Lern's fleet has set sail again—and they head towards the Eastern Continent, with thousands of ships—and supernatural allies, too."

"It was only what I expected, Sepiriz. My work's done here, anyway. I'll ride for the Isle of the Purple Towns at once, for I must lead the fleet against Jagreen Lern."

"Your chances of winning will be all but non-existent, Elric," Sepiriz warned him gravely. "Have you heard of the Ships of Hell?"

"I've heard of them—do they not sail the depths of the sea, taking on board dead mariners as crews?"

"They do—they're things of Chaos and far larger than even the largest mortal warship. You'd never withstand them, even if you did not have the Theocrat's fleet to fight as well."

"I'm aware the fight will be hard, Sepiriz—but what else can we do? I have a weapon against Chaos in my blade here—or so you tell me."

"Not enough, that bodkin—you still have no *protection* against the Dark Lords. That is what I have to tell you of—a personal armament for yourself to help you in your struggle, though you'll have to win it from its present possessor."

"Who owns it?"

"A giant who broods in eternal misery in a great castle on the edge of the world, beyond the Sighing Desert. Mordaga is his name and he was once a god, but is now made mortal for sins he committed against his fellow gods long ages ago."

"Mortal? Yet he has lived so long?"

"Aye. Mordaga is mortal—though his life-span's considerably greater than an ordinary man's. He is obsessed with the knowledge that he must one day die. That is what saddens him."

"And the weapon?"

"Not a weapon exactly—a shield. A shield with a purpose—one that Mordaga had made for himself when he raised a rebellion in the domain of the gods and sought to make himself greatest of them, and even wrest the Eternal Balance from He who holds it. For this he was banished to Earth and informed that he would one day die—slain by a mortal's blade. The shield, as you might guess, is proof against the workings of Chaos."

"How so?"

"The chaotic forces, if powerful enough, can disrupt any defence made of lawful matter; no construction based on the principles of order can withstand for long the ravages of sheer chaos, as we know." Sepiriz leaned forward a little. "Stormbringer has shown you that the only weapon effective against Chaos is something of Chaos-manufacture. The same can be said for the Chaos Shield. This itself is chaotic in nature and therefore there is nothing organised in it on which the random forces can act and destroy. It meets Chaos with Chaos, and so the hostile powers are subverted."

"If I had only had such a shield of late—things might have gone better for us all!"

"I could not tell you of it. I am merely the servant of Fate and cannot act unless it is sanctioned by that which I serve. Perhaps, as I have guessed, it is willing to see Chaos sweep the world before it is defeated—if indeed it *is* defeated—so that it can completely change the nature of our planet before the new cycle begins. Change it will—but whether it will be ruled in the future primarily by Law or Chaos, that is in your hands, Elric!"

"How would I recognise this shield?"

"By the eight-arrowed Sign of Chaos which radiates from its boss. It is a heavy, round shield, made as a buckler for a giant. But, with the vitality you receive from your runesword, you will have the strength to carry it, have no fear. But first you must have the courage to win it from its current holder. Mordaga is aware of the prophecy, told him by his fellow gods before they cast him forth."

"Are you, too, aware of it?"

"I am. In our language it forms a simple rhyme:

"Mordaga's pride; Mordaga's doom,
Mordaga's fate shall be
To die as men when slain by men,
Four men of destiny."

"Four men? Who are the other three?"

"Those you will know of when the time comes for you to seek the Chaos Shield. Which will you do? Go to the Purple Towns—or will you go to find the shield?"

"I wish that I had the time to embark on a quest of that kind, but I have not. I must go to rally my men, shield or no."

"You will be defeated."

"We shall see, Sepiriz."

"Very well, Elric. Since so little of your destiny is in your own hands, we should allow you to take just one decision at times," Sepiriz said sympathetically.

"Fate is kind," Elric commented ironically. He rose from his seat. "I'll begin the journey straightway, for there's no time to lose."

2

With his milk-white hair streaming behind him and his red eyes blazing with purpose, Elric lashed his stallion through the cold darkness of the night, through a disturbed land which awaited Jagreen Lern's attack in trepidation, for it could mean not only their deaths, but the drawing of their souls into the servitude of Chaos.

Already the standards of a dozen Western and Southern monarchs fluttered with Jagreen Lern's as the kings of the conquered lands chose his command rather than death—and placed their peoples under his dominance so that they became marching, blank-faced creatures with enslaved souls, their wives and children dead, tormented or feeding the blood-washed altars of Pan Tang where the priests send up invocations to the Chaos Lords, and, ever-willing to further their power on Earth, the lords answered with support.

And not only the entities themselves, but the stuff of their own weird cosmos was entering the Earth, so that where their power was the land heaved like the sea, or the sea flowed like lava, mountains changed shape and trees sprouted ghastly blossoms never seen on Earth before—all nature was unstable and it could not be long until Earth was wholly one with the Realm of Chaos.

Wherever Jagreen Lern conquered, the warping influence of Chaos was manifest. The very spirits of nature were tortured into becoming what they should not be—air, fire, water and earth, all became unstable, for Jagreen Lern and his allies were tampering not only with the lives and souls of men, but the very constituents of the planet itself. And there was none of sufficient power to punish them for these crimes. None.

With this knowledge within him, Elric's progress was swift and wild, as he strove to reach the Isle of the Purple Towns before his pitifully inadequate fleet sailed to do battle with Chaos.

Two days later he arrived in the port of Uhaio, at the tip of the smallest of the three Vilmirian peninsulas, and took ship at once to the Isle of the Purple Towns, where he disembarked and rode into the interior towards the ancient fortress *Ma-ha-kil-agra*, which had withstood every siege ever made against it, and was regarded as the most impregnable construction in the whole of the lands still free from Chaos. Its name was in an older language than any known to those who lived in the current Age of the Young Kingdoms. Only Elric knew what the name signified. The fortress had been there long before the present races came to dominance, even before Elric's ancestors had begun their conquerings. *Ma-ha-kil-agra*—the Fortress of Evening, where long ago, a lonely race had come to die.

As he arrived in the courtyard, Moonglum, the Eastlander, came rushing from the entrance of a tower.

"Elric! We have been awaiting your arrival, for time grows scarce before we must embark against the enemy. We have sent out ship-borne spies to estimate the size and power of Jagreen Lern's fleet. Only four returned and all were uselessly insane. The fifth has just come back, but—"

"But what?"

"See for yourself. He has been—altered, Elric."

"Altered! Altered! Let me see him. Take me to him." Elric nodded curtly to the other captains who had come out to greet him. He passed them and followed behind Moonglum through the stone corridors of the fortress, lit badly by sputtering rushes.

Leading Elric to an antechamber, Moonglum stopped outside, running his fingers through his thick, red hair. "He is therein. Would you care to interview him alone? I'd rather not set eyes on him again!"

"Very well," Elric opened the door, wondering how this spy would be changed. Sitting at the plain wooden table was the remains of a man. It looked up. As Moonglum had warned him—it had been altered.

Elric felt pity for the man, but he was not nauseated or horrified like Moonglum, for in his sorcery-working he had seen far worse creatures. It was as if the whole of one side of the spy's body had become at one stage viscous, had flowed, and then coiled in a random shape. Side of head, shoulder, arm, torso, leg, all were replaced by streamers of flesh like rat's tails, lumps of matter like swollen boils, weirdly mottled. The spy spread his good hand and some of the streamers seemed to jerk and wave in unison.

Elric spoke quietly. "What magic wrought this drastic change?"

A kind of chuckle came from the lopsided face.

"I entered the Realm of Chaos, lord. And Chaos did this, it changed me as you see. The boundaries are being extended. I did not know it. I was inside before I realised what had happened. *The area of Chaos is being widened!*" He leaned forward, his shaking voice almost screaming. "With it sail the massed fleets of Jagreen Lern—great waves of warships, squadrons of invasion craft, thousands of transports, ships mounting great war-engines, fire-ships—ships of all kinds, bearing a multitude of standards—the kings of the South left alive have sworn loyalty to Jagreen Lern and he has used all their resources and his own to marshal this sea-horde! As he sails, he extends the area of Chaos, so whereas his sailing is slower than normal, when he reaches us here—Chaos will be with him. I saw such ships that could be of no earthly contriving—the size of castles—each one seeming to be a dazzling combination of all colours!"

"So he *has* managed to bring more supernatural allies to his standard," Elric mused. "Those are the Ships of Hell, Sepiriz mentioned . . ."

"Aye—and even if we beat the natural craft," the messenger said, hysterically, "we could not beat both the ships of Chaos and the stuff of Chaos which boils around them and did to me what you observe! It boils, it warps, it changes constantly. That is all I know, save that Jagreen Lern and his human allies are unharmed by it as I was harmed. When this change began to take place in my body, I fled to the Dragon Isle of Melniboné, which seems to have withstood the process and is the only safe land in all the waters of the world. My body—healed—swiftly, and I chanced another sailing to bring me here."

"You were courageous," Elric said hollowly. "You will be well rewarded, I promise."

"I want only one reward, my lord."

"What is that?"

"Death. I can no longer live with the horror of my body mirroring the horror in my brains!"

"I will see to it," Elric promised. He remained brooding for a few seconds before nodding farewell to the spy and leaving the room.

Moonglum met him outside.

"It looks black for us, Elric," he said softly.

Elric sighed. "Aye—perhaps I should have gone to seek the Chaos Shield *first*."

"What's that?"

Elric explained all Sepiriz had told him.

"We could do with such a defence," Moonglum agreed. "But there it is— the priority is tomorrow's sailing. Your captains await you in the conference chamber."

"I will see them in a short while," Elric promised. "First I wish to go to my own room to collect my thoughts. Tell them I'll join them when that's done."

When he reached his room, Elric locked the door behind him, still thinking of the spy's information. He knew that without supernatural aid no ordinary fleet, no matter how large or how courageously manned, could possibly withstand Jagreen Lern. And the fact was that he had only a comparatively small fleet, no supernatural entities for allies, no means of combatting the disrupting chaotic forces. If only he had the Chaos Shield beside him now . . . But it was useless to regret a decision of the kind he'd made. If he sought the shield now, he couldn't fight the battle in any case.

For weeks he had consulted the grimoires that, in the form of scrolls, tablets, books and sheets of precious metals engraved with ancient symbols, littered his room. The elementals had helped him in the past, but so disrupted were they by Chaos that they were weak for the most part.

He unstrapped his hellsword and flung it on the bed of tumbled silks and furs. Wryly he thought back to earlier times when he had given in to despair and how those incidents which had engendered the mood seemed merely gay escapades in comparison to the task which now weighed on his mind. Though weary, he chose not to draw Stormbringer's stolen energy into himself, for the feeling that was so close to ecstasy was leavened by the guilt—the guilt which had possessed him since a child when he had first realised that the expression on his remote father's face had not been one of love, but of disappointment that he should have spawned a deficient weakling—a pale albino, good for nothing without the aid of drugs or sorcery.

Elric sighed and went to the window to stare out over the low hills and beyond them to the sea. He spoke aloud, perhaps subconsciously, hoping that the release of the words would relieve some of the tension within him.

"I do not care for this responsibility," he said. "When I fought the Dead God he spoke of both gods and men as shadow-things, playing puppet parts before the true history of Earth began and men found their fate in their own hands. Then Sepiriz tells me I must turn against Chaos and help destroy the whole nature of the world I know or history might never begin again, and Fate's great purpose would be thwarted. Therefore *I* am the one who must be split and tempered to fulfil my destiny—*I* must know no peace of mind, must fight men and gods and the stuff of Chaos without surcease, must bring about the death of this age so that, in some far dawn-age, men who know little of sorcery or the Lords of the Higher Worlds may move about a world where the major forces of Chaos can no longer enter, where justice may actually exist as a reality, and not as a mere concept in the minds of all philosophers."

He rubbed his red eyes with his fingers.

"So fate makes Elric a martyr that Law might rule the world. It gives him a sword of ugly evil that destroys friends and enemies alike and sucks their soul-stuff out to feed him the strength he needs. It binds me to evil and to

Chaos, in order that I may *destroy* evil and Chaos—but it does not make me some senseless dolt easily convinced and a willing sacrifice. No, it makes me Elric of Melniboné and floods me with a mighty misery . . ."

"My lord speaks aloud to himself—and his thoughts are gloomy. Speak them to me, instead, so that I might help you bear them, Elric."

Recognising the soft voice, but astonished nonetheless, Elric turned quickly towards the source and saw his wife Zarozinia standing there, her arms outstretched and a look of deep sympathy on her young face.

He took a step towards her before stopping and saying angrily: "When did you come here? Why? I told you to remain in your father's palace at Karlaak until this business is done, if ever!"

"If ever . . ." she repeated, dropping her arms to her sides with a little shrug. Though scarcely more than a girl, with her full red lips and long black hair, she bore herself as a princess must and seemed more than her age.

"Ask not *that* question," he said cynically. "It is not one we ask ourselves here. But answer mine. How did you come here and why?" He knew what her reply would be, but he spoke only to emphasise his anger which in turn was a result of his horror that she should have come so close to danger—danger which he had already rescued her from once.

"I came with my cousin Opluk's two thousand," she said, lifting her head defiantly, "when he joined the defenders of Uhaio. I came to be near my husband at a time when he may need my comforting. The gods know I've had little opportunity to discover if he does!"

Elric paced the room in agitation. "As I love you, Zarozinia, believe that I would be in Karlaak now with you had I any excuse at all. But I have not—you know my role, my destiny, my doom. You bring sorrow with your presence, not help. If this business has a satisfactory end, then we'll meet again in joy—not in misery as we now must!"

He crossed to her and took her in his arms. "Oh, Zarozinia, we should never have met, never have married. We can only hurt one another at this time. Our happiness was so brief . . ."

"If you would be hurt by me, then hurt you shall be," she said softly, "but if you would be comforted, then I am here to comfort my lord."

He relented with a sigh. "These are loving words, my dear—but they are not spoken in loving times. I have put love aside for the nonce. Try to do likewise and thus we'll both dispense with added complication."

Without anger, she drew slowly away from him and with a slight smile that had something of irony in it, pointed to the bed, where Stormbringer lay.

"I see your other mistress still shares your bed," she said. "And now you need never try to dismiss her again, for that black lord of Nihrain has given you an excuse to forever keep her by your side. Destiny—is that the word? Destiny! Ah, the deeds men have done in destiny's name. And what is destiny, Elric, can you answer?"

He shook his head. "Since you ask the question in malice, I'll not make the attempt to answer it."

She cried suddenly: "Oh, Elric! I have travelled for many days to see you, thinking you would welcome me. And now we speak in anger!"

"*Fear!*" he said urgently. "It is fear, not anger. I fear for you as I fear for the fate of the world! See me to my ship in the morning and then make speed back to Karlaak, I beg you."

"If you wish it."

She walked back into the small chamber which joined the main one.

3

"We talk only of defeat!" roared Kargan of the Purple Towns, beating upon the table with his fist. His beard seemed to bristle with rage.

Dawn had found all but a few of the captains retiring through weariness. Kargan, Moonglum, Elric's cousin Dyvim Slorm and moon-faced Dralab of Tarkesh, remained in the chamber, pondering tactics.

Elric answered him calmly: "We talk of defeat, Kargan, because we must be prepared for that eventuality. It seems likely, does it not? We must, if defeat seems imminent, flee our enemies, conserving our force for another attack on Jagreen Lern. We shall not have the forces to fight another major battle, so we must use our better knowledge of currents, winds and terrain to fight him from ambush on sea or land. Thus we can perhaps demoralise his warriors and take considerably more of them than they can of us."

"Aye—I see the logic," Kargan rumbled unwillingly, evidently disturbed by this talk for, if the major battle was lost, then lost also would be the Isle of the Purple Towns, bastion against Chaos for the mainland nations of Vilmir and Ilmiora.

Moonglum shifted his position, grunting slightly. "And if they drive us back, then back we must go, bending rather than breaking, and returning from other directions to attack and confuse them. It's in my mind that we'll have to move more rapidly than we'll be able to, since we'd be tired and with few provisions . . ." He grinned faintly. "Ah, forgive me for my pessimism. Ill-placed, I fear."

"No," Elric said. "We must face all this or be caught unawares. You are right. And to allow for ordered retreat, I have already sent detachments to the Sighing Desert and the Weeping Waste to bury large quantities of food and such things as extra arrows, lances and so forth. If we are forced back as far as the barrens, we'll likely fare better than Jagreen Lern, assuming that it takes him time to extend the area of Chaos and that his allies from the Higher Worlds are not overwhelmingly powerful."

"You spoke of realism . . ." said Dyvim Slorm, pursing his curving lips and raising a slanting eyebrow.

"Aye—but some things cannot be faced or considered—for if we are totally engulfed by Chaos at the outset, then we'll have no need of plans. So we plan for the other eventuality, you see."

Kargan let out his breath and rose from the table. "There's no more to discuss," he said. "I'll to bed. We must be ready to sail with the noon tide tomorrow."

They all gave signs of assent and chairs scraped as they pushed them back and left the chamber.

Bereft of human occupants, the chamber was silent save for the sputtering of the lamps and the rustle of the maps and papers as they were stirred by a warm wind.

It was late in the morning when Elric arose and found Zarozinia already up and dressed in a skirt and bodice of cloth-of-gold with a long, black-trimmed cloak of silver spreading to the floor.

He washed, shaved and ate the dish of herb-flavoured fruit she handed him.

"Why have you arrayed yourself in such finery?" he asked.

"To bid you goodbye from the harbour," she said.

"If you spoke truth last night, then you'd best be dressed in funeral red," he smiled and then, relenting, clasped her to him. He gripped her tightly, desperately, before standing back from her and taking her chin in his hand raised her face to stare down into it. "In these tragic times," he said, "there's little room for love-play and kind words. Love must be deep and strong, manifesting itself in our actions. Seek no courtly words from me, Zarozinia, but remember earlier nights when the only turbulence was our pulse-beats blending."

He was clad, himself, in Melnibonéan war regalia; with a breastplate of shiny black metal, a high-collared jerkin of black velvet, black leather breeks covered to the knee by his boots, also of black leather. Over his back was pushed a cloak of deep red, and on one thin, white finger was the Ring of Kings, the single rare Actorios stone, set in silver. His long white hair hung loose down to his shoulders, held by a bronze circlet. Stormbringer was at his hip and upon the table among the open books was a tapering black helm, engraved with old runes, its crown gradually rising into a spoke standing almost two feet from the base. At this base, dominating the eye slits was a replica of a spread-winged dragon with gaping snout, a reminder that, as emperors of the Bright Empire, his ancestors had been Dragon Masters and that perhaps the Phoorn dragons of Melniboné still slept in their underground caverns. Now he picked up this helm and fitted it over his head so that it covered the top half of his face, only his red eyes gleaming from its shadows. He refrained from pulling the side wings about his lower face but for the meantime, left them sweeping back from the bottom of the helmet.

Noting her silence, he said, with a heart already heavy, "Come, my love, let's to the harbour to astound these under-civilised allies of ours with our elegance. Have no fear that I shall not live to survive this day's battle—for Fate has not finished with me yet and protects me as a mother would her son—so that I might witness further misery until such a day when it's over for all time."

Together, they left the Fortress of Evening, riding on magical Nihrain horses, down to the harbour where the other sea-lords and captains were already assembled beneath the bright sun.

All were dressed in their finest martial glory, though none could match Elric. Old racial memories were awakened in many when they saw him and they were troubled, fearing him without knowing why, for their ancestors had had great cause to fear the Bright Emperors in the days when Melniboné ruled the world and a man accoutred as Elric commanded a million eldritch warriors. Now a bare handful of Imrryrians greeted him as he rode along the quayside, noting the ships riding at anchor with their coloured banners and heraldic devices lifting proudly in the breeze.

Dyvim Slorm was equipped in a close-fitting dragon helm, its protecting pieces fashioned to represent the entire head of a dragon, scaled in red and green and silver. His armour was lacquered yellow, though the rest of his dress was black, like Elric's. At his side was Stormbringer's sister sword Mournblade.

As Elric rode up to the group, Dyvim Slorm turned his heavily armoured head towards the open sea. There was little inkling of encroaching Chaos on the calm water or in the clear sky.

"At least we'll have good weather on our way to meet Jagreen Lern," Dyvim Slorm said.

"A small mercy," Elric smiled faintly. "Is there any more news of their numbers?"

"Before the spy who returned yesterday died he said there were at least four thousand warships, ten thousand transports—and perhaps twenty of the Chaos ships. They'll be the ones to watch since we've no idea what powers they have."

Elric nodded. Their own fleet comprised some five thousand warships, many equipped with catapults and other heavy war-engines. The transports, though they turned the odds, in numbers, to a far superior figure, would be slow, unwieldy, and of not much use in a pitched sea-battle. Also, if the battle were won, they could be dealt with later, for they would obviously follow in the rear of Jagreen Lern's war-fleet.

So, for all Jagreen Lern's numerical strength, there would be a good chance of winning a sea-fight under ordinary conditions. The disturbing factor was the presence of the supernatural ships. The spy's description had been vague. Elric needed more objective information—information he would be unlikely to receive now, until the fleets joined in battle.

In his shirt was tucked the beast-hide manuscript of an extraordinarily strong invocation used in summoning Straasha the Sea-King. He had already attempted to use it, without success, but hoped that on open sea his chances would be better, particularly since the sea-king would be angered at the disruption Jagreen Lern and his occult allies were causing in the balance of nature. Once before, long ago, the sea-king had aided him and had, Elric recalled, predicted that Elric would summon him again.

Kargan, in the thick but light sea-armour of his people which gave him the appearance of a hairy-faced armadillo, pointed as several small boats detached themselves from the fleet and sailed towards the quay.

"Here come the boats to take us to our ships, my lords!"

The gathered captains stirred, all of them with serious expressions, seeming, each and every one, to be pondering some personal problem, staring into the depths of their own hearts—perhaps trying to reach the fear which lay there; trying to reach it and tear it out and fling it from them. They all had more than the usual trepidation experienced when facing a fight—for, like Elric, they could not guess what the Chaos ships were capable of.

They were a desperate company, understanding that something less palatable than death might await them beyond the horizon.

Elric squeezed Zarozinia's arm.

"Goodbye."

"Farewell, Elric—may whatever benevolent gods there are left on the Earth protect you."

"Save your prayers for my companions," he said quietly, "for they will be less able than I to face what lies out there."

Moonglum called to him and Zarozinia: "Give her a kiss, Elric, and come to the boat. Tell her we'll be back with victory tidings!"

Elric would never have admitted such familiarity, not even with his kinsman Dyvim Slorm, from anyone but Moonglum. But he took it in good part saying softly to her: "There, you see, little Moonglum is confident—and he's usually the one with warnings of ominous portent!"

She said nothing, but kissed him lightly on the mouth, grasped his hand for a moment and then watched him as he strode down the quay and clambered into the boat which Moonglum and Kargan were steadying for him.

The oars splashed and bore the captains towards the flagship, *Timbertearer*, Elric standing in the bow staring ahead, looking back only once when the boat drew alongside the ship and he began to climb the rope ladder up to the deck, his black helm bobbing.

Bracing himself on the deck, Elric watched the backs of the warrior-rowers as they bent to the oars, supplementing the light wind which filled the great purple sail, making it curve out in a graceful billow.

The Isle of the Purple Towns was now out of sight and green, glinting water was all that was visible around the fleet, which stretched behind the flagship, its furthest ships tiny shapes in the distance. Already the fleet was moving into battle order, forming into five squadrons, each under the command of an experienced sea-lord from the Purple Towns, for most of the other captains were landsmen who, though quick to learn, had little experience of sea tactics.

Moonglum came stumbling along the swaying deck to stand beside his friend.

"How did you sleep last night?" he asked Elric.

"Well enough, save for a few nightmares."

"Ah, then you shared something with us all. Sleep was hard won for everyone, and when it came it was troubled. Visions of pits of monsters and demons, of horrifying shapes, of unearthly powers, they crowded our dreams."

Elric nodded, paying little attention to Moonglum. The elements of chaos in their own beings were evidently awakening in response to the approach of the Chaos horde itself. He hoped they would be strong enough to withstand the actuality as they had survived their dreams.

"*Disturbance to forward!*"

It was the lookout's cry, baffled and perturbed. Elric cupped his hands around his mouth and tilted his head back.

"What sort of disturbance?"

"It's like nothing I've ever seen, my lord—I can't describe it."

Elric turned to Moonglum. "Relay the order through the fleet—slow the pace to one drumbeat in four, squadron commanders stand by to receive final battle orders." He strode towards the mast and began to climb up it towards the lookout's post. He climbed until he was high above the deck. The lookout swung out of his cradle, since there was only room for one.

"Is it the enemy, my lord?" he said as Elric clambered into his place. Elric stared hard towards the horizon, making out a kind of dazzling blackness that from time to time sent up sprawling gouts of stuff into the air where it hung for some moments before sinking back into the main mass. Smoky, hard to define, it crept gradually nearer, crawling over the sea towards them.

"It's the enemy," said Elric quietly.

He remained for some while in the lookout's cradle, studying the Chaos-stuff as it flung itself about in the distance, like some amorphous monster in its death-agonies. But these were not death-agonies. Chaos was far from dead.

From this vantage point, Elric also had a clear view of the fleet as it formed itself into its respective squadrons, making up a black wedge nearly a mile across at its longest point and nearly two miles deep. His own ship was a short distance in front of the rest, well in sight of the squadron commanders. Elric shouted down to Kargan whom he saw passing the mast: "Stand by to move ahead, Kargan!"

The sea-lord nodded without pausing in his stride. He was fully aware of the battle plan, as they all were for they had discussed it long enough. The leading squadron, under the command of Elric, was comprised of their heaviest warships which would smash into the centre of the enemy fleet and seek to break its order, aiming particularly at whichever ship Jagreen Lern now used. If Jagreen Lern could be slain or captured, their victory would be more likely.

Now the dark stuff was closer and Elric could just make out the sails of the first vessels, spread out one behind the other. Then, as they came even closer, he was aware that to each side of this leading formation were great glinting shapes that dwarfed even the huge battlecraft of Jagreen Lern.

The Chaos Ships.

Elric recognised them, now, from his own knowledge of occult lore. These were the ships said normally to sail the deeps of the oceans, taking on drowned sailors as crews, captained by creatures that had never been human. It was a fleet from the deepest, gloomiest parts of the vast underwater domain which had, since the beginning of time, been disputed territory—disputed between water elementals under their king Straasha, and the Lords of Chaos, who claimed the sea-depths as their main territory on Earth, by right. Legends said that at one time Chaos had ruled the sea and Law the land. This, perhaps, explained the fear of the sea that many human beings had to this day, and the pull the sea had for others.

But the fact was that, although the elementals had succeeded in winning the shallower portions of the sea, the Chaos Lords had retained the deeper parts by means of this, their fleet of the dead. The ships themselves were not of earthly manufacture, neither were their captains originally from Earth, but their crews had once been human, and were now indestructible in any ordinary sense.

As they approached, Elric was soon in no doubt that they were, indeed, those ships. The Sign of Chaos flashed on their sails, eight amber arrows radiating from a central hub—signifying the boast of Chaos, that it contained all possibilities whereas Law was supposed, in time, to destroy possibility and result in eternal stagnation. The Sign of Law was a single arrow pointing upwards, symbolising dynamic growth.

Elric knew that in reality Chaos was the harbinger of stagnation, for though it changed constantly, it never progressed. But, in his heart, he still felt a yearning for this state, for his past loyalties to the Lords of Chaos had suited him better to wild destruction than to stable progress.

But now Chaos must make war on Chaos; Elric must turn against those he had once been loyal to, using weapons formed by chaotic forces to defeat those self-same forces in these ironic times.

He clambered from the cradle and began to shin down the mast, leaping the last few feet to land on the deck as Dyvim Slorm came up. Quickly he told his cousin what he had seen.

Dyvim Slorm was astounded. "But the fleet of the dead never comes to the surface—save for . . ." His eyes widened.

Elric shrugged. "That's the legend—the fleet of the dead will rise from the depths when the final struggle comes, when Chaos shall be divided against itself, when Law shall be weak and mankind shall choose sides in the battle that will result in a new Earth dominated either by total Chaos or by almost-total Law. When Sepiriz told us this was the case, I felt a response. Since then, in studying my manuscripts, I have been fully reminded."

"Is this, then, to be the final battle?"

"It might be," Elric answered. "It is certain to be one of the last when it will be decided for all time whether Law or Chaos shall rule here."

"If we're defeated, then Chaos will undoubtedly rule."

"Perhaps, but remember that the struggle need not be decided by battles alone."

"So Sepiriz said, but if we're defeated this day, we'll have little chance to discover the truth of that." Dyvim Slorm gripped Mournblade's hilt. "Someone must wield these blades—these destiny-swords—when the time comes for the deciding duel. Our allies diminish, Elric."

"Aye. But I've a hope that we can summon a few others. Straasha, King of the Water Elementals, has ever fought against the death fleet—and he is brother to Graoll and Misha, the Wind Lords. Perhaps through Straasha, I can summon his unearthly kin. In this way we will be better matched, at least."

"I know only a fragment of the spell for summoning the water-king," Dyvim Slorm said.

"I know the whole rune. I had best make haste to meditate upon it, for our fleets will clash in two hours or less and then I'll have no time for the summoning of spirits but will have to keep tight hold on my own lest some Chaos creature releases it."

Elric moved towards the prow of the ship, and, leaning over, stared into the ocean depths, turning his mind inward and contemplating the strange and ancient knowledge which lay there. He became almost hypnotised as he lost contact with his own personality and began to identify with the swirling ocean below.

Involuntarily, old words began to form in his throat and his lips began to move in the rune which his ancestors had known when they and all the elementals of the Earth had been allies and sworn to aid one another long ago in the dawn of the Bright Empire, more than ten thousand years before.

"Waters of the sea, thou gave us birth
And were our milk and mother both
In days when skies were overcast
You who were first shall be the last.

"Sea-rulers, fathers of our blood,
Thine aid is sought, thine aid is sought,
Your salt is blood, our blood your salt,
Your blood the blood of Man.

"Straasha, eternal king, eternal sea
Thine aid is sought by me;
For enemies of thine and mine
Seek to defeat our destiny, and drain away our sea."

The spoken rune was merely a vocalisation of the actual invocation which was produced mentally and went plunging into the depths, through the dark green corridors of the sea until it finally found Straasha in his domain of curving, coral-coloured, womblike constructions which were only partially in the natural sea and partially in the plane where the elementals spent a large part of their immortal existence.

Straasha knew of the Ships of Hell rising to the surface and had been pleased that his domain was now cleared of them, but Elric's summons awakened his memory and he remembered the folk of Melniboné upon whom all the elementals had once looked with a sense of comradeship; he remembered the ancient invocation, and felt bound to answer it, though he knew his people were badly weakened by the effect Chaos had had in other parts of the world. Not only humans had suffered; the elemental spirits of nature had been sorely pressed as well.

But he stirred so that water and the stuff of his other plane were both disturbed. He summoned some of his followers and began to glide upwards into the domain of the Air.

Semi-conscious now, Elric knew that his invocation had met with success. Sprawled in the prow, he waited.

At last the waters heaved and broke and revealed a great green figure, with turquoise beard and hair, pale green skin that seemed made of the sea itself, and a voice that was like a rushing tide.

"*Once more Straasha answers thy summons, mortal. Our destinies are bound together. How may I aid thee, and, in aiding thee, aid myself?*"

In the throat-torturing speech of the elemental, Elric answered, telling the sea-king of the forthcoming battle and what it implied.

"*So at long last it has come to pass! I fear I cannot aid you much, for my folk are already suffering terribly from the depredations of our mutual enemy. We shall attempt to aid you if we can. That's all I promise.*"

The sea-king sank back into the waters and Elric watched him depart with a feeling of acute disappointment. It was with a brooding mind that he left the prow and went to the main cabin to tell his captains the news.

They received it with mixed feelings, for only Dyvim Slorm was used to dealing with supernaturals. Moonglum had always been dubious of Elric's powers to control his wild, elemental friends, while Kargan growled that Straasha may have been an ally of Elric's folk but had been more of an enemy to his. The four of them, however, could plan with slightly more optimism and face the coming ordeal with better confidence.

4

The fleet of Jagreen Lern bore towards them and, in its wake, the boiling stuff of Chaos hovered.

Elric gave the command and the rowers hauled at their oars, sending *Timber-tearer* rushing towards the enemy. So far his elemental allies had not appeared, but he could not afford to wait for them.

As *Timber-tearer* rode the foaming waves, Elric hauled his sword from its scabbard, brought the side wings of his helmet round to cover his face and cried the age-old ululating war-shout of Melniboné, a shout full of joyous evil. Stormbringer's eery voice joined with his, giving vent to a thrumming song, anticipating the blood and the souls it would soon feast upon.

Jagreen Lern's new flagship now lay behind three rows of men-o'-war and behind the flagship were the Chaos ships.

Timber-tearer's iron ram ripped into the first enemy ship and the rowers leaned on their oars, backing away and turning to pierce another ship below the waterline. Showers of arrows sprayed from the holed ship and clattered on deck and armour. Several rowers went down.

Elric and his three companions directed their men from the main deck, standing so that between them they had an overall view of what was going on around them. Elric looked up suddenly, warned by some sixth sense, and saw streaking balls of green fire come curving out of the sky.

"Prepare to quench fires!" Kargan yelled and the group of men already primed for this leapt for the tubs containing a special brew which Elric had told them how to make earlier. This was spread on decks and splashed on canvas and, when the fireballs landed, they were swiftly quenched. "Don't engage unless forced to," Elric called to the seamen, "keep aiming for the flagship. If we take that, our advantage will be good!"

"Where are your allies, Elric?" Kargan asked sardonically, shuddering a little as he saw the Chaos-stuff in the distance suddenly move and erupt tendrils of black matter into the sky.

"They'll come, never fear," Elric answered, but he was unsure.

Now they were in the thick of the enemy fleet, the ships of their squadron following behind, their great oars slicing through the ocean's foam. The war-engines of their own fleet sent up a constant barrage of fire and heavy stones. Only a few of Elric's craft broke through the enemy's first rank and reached the open sea, sailing towards Jagreen Lern's flagship.

As they were observed, the enemy ships sailed to protect the flagship and the scintillating ships of death, moving with fantastic speed for their size, surrounded the Theocrat's vessel.

Shouting over the waters, Kargan ordered their diminished squadron into a new formation. Moonglum shook his head in astonishment. "How can things of that size support themselves on the water?" he said to Elric.

"It's unlikely that they actually do." As their ship manoeuvred into its new position, he stared at the huge craft, twenty of them, dwarfing everything else on the sea. They seemed covered with a kind of shining fluid which flashed all the colours of the spectrum so that their outlines were hard to see and the shadowy figures moving about on their gigantic decks could not easily be observed. Wisps of dark stuff began to drift across the scene, close to the water, and Dyvim Slorm, from the lower deck, pointed and shouted: "See! Chaos comes! Where is Straasha and his folk?"

Elric shook his head, perturbed. He had expected aid by now.

"We cannot wait. We must attack!" Kargan's voice was pitched higher than usual.

A mood of bitter recklessness came upon Elric, as he gripped the rigging to steady himself on the swaying deck, then he smiled. "Come then. Let's do so!"

Speedily the squadron coursed towards the disturbing ships of death. Moonglum muttered: "We are going to our doom, Elric. No man would willingly get close to those ships. Only the dead are drawn to them, and they do not go with joy!"

But Elric ignored his friend.

A strange silence descended over the waters and the rhythmic sound of the splashing oars was sharp. The death fleet waited for them, impassively, as if they did not need to prepare for battle. He tightened his grip on Stormbringer. The blade responded to the pounding of his pulse-beat, moving in his hand with each thud of his heart, as if linked to it by veins and arteries. Now they were so close to the Chaos ships that they could make out better the figures crowding the great decks. Horribly, Elric thought he recognised some of the gaunt faces of the dead and, involuntarily, he called to the sea-folk's king.

"*Straasha!*"

The waters heaved, foamed and seemed to be attempting to rise but then subsided again. Straasha heard—but he was finding it difficult to fight against the forces of Chaos.

"*Straasha!*"

It was no good, the waters hardly moved.

In his wild despair Elric screamed to Kargan: "We cannot wait for aid. Swing the ship round the Chaos fleet and we'll attempt to reach Jagreen Lern's flagship from the rear!"

Under Kargan's expert direction, the ship swung to avoid the Ships of Hell in a wide semicircle. Spray cascaded against Elric's face, flooding the decks with white foam. He could hardly see through it as they cleared the Chaos ships which had now engaged other craft and were altering the nature of their timbers so that they fell apart and the unfortunate crews were drowned or warped into alien shapes.

To his ears came the miserable cries of the defeated and the triumphantly surging thunder of the Chaos fleet's music as it pushed forward to destroy the Eastern ships. *Timber-tearer* was rocking badly and was hard to control, but at last they were around the hell fleet and bearing down on Jagreen Lern's vessel from behind.

Now they nearly struck the Theocrat's vessel with their ram, but were swept off course and had to manoeuvre again. Arrows rose from the enemy's decks and thudded and rattled on their own. They retaliated as, riding a huge wave, they slid alongside the flagship and flung out grappling irons. A few held, dragging them towards the Theocrat's vessel as the men of Pan Tang strove to cut the grappling ropes. More ropes followed and then a boarding platform fell from its harness and landed squarely on Jagreen Lern's deck. Another followed it. Elric ran for the nearest platform, Kargan behind him, and they led a body of warriors over it, searching for Jagreen Lern. Stormbringer took a dozen lives and a dozen souls before Elric had gained the main deck. There a resplendent commander stood, surrounded by a group of officers. But he was not Jagreen Lern. Elric clambered up the gangway, slicing through a warrior's waist as the man sought to block his path. He yelled at the group: "Where's your cursed leader? Where's Jagreen Lern!"

The commander's face was pale for he had seen in the past what Elric and his hellblade could do.

"He's not here, Elric, I swear."

"What? Am I to be thwarted again? I know you are lying!" Elric advanced on the group who backed away, their swords ready.

"Our Theocrat does not need to protect himself by means of lies, doom-fostered one!" sneered a young officer, braver than the rest.

"Perhaps not," Elric's voice was low and menacing as he rushed towards the youth, swinging Stormbringer in a shrieking arc, "but at least I'll have your life before I put the truth of your words to the test."

The man put up his blade to block Stormbringer's swing. The runesword cut through the metal with a triumphant cry, swung back again and plunged itself into the officer's side. He gasped, but remained standing with his hands clenched.

Elric laughed. "My sword and I need revitalising—and your soul should make an appetiser before I take Jagreen Lern's!"

"No!" the youth groaned. "Oh, no, not my soul!" His eyes widened, tears streamed from them and madness came into them for a second before Stormbringer satiated itself and Elric drew it out, replenished. He had no sympathy for the man. "Your soul would have gone to the depths of hell in any case," he said lightly. "But now I've put it to some use, at least."

Two other officers scrambled over the rail, seeking to escape their comrade's fate.

Elric hacked at the hand of one. He fell, screaming, to the deck, his hand still grasping the rail. The other he skewered in the bowels and, as Stormbringer sucked out his soul, he hung there, pleading incoherently in an effort to avert the inevitable.

So much vitality flowed into Elric that, as he rushed at the remaining group around the commander, he seemed to fly over the deck and rip into them, slicing away limbs as if they were flower-stalks, until he encountered the commander himself. The commander said weakly: "I surrender. Do not take my soul."

"Where is Jagreen Lern?"

The commander pointed into the distance, where the Chaos fleet could be seen creating havoc amongst the Eastern ships. "There! He sails with Pyaray of Chaos whose fleet that is. You cannot reach him there for any man not protected—or not already dead—would turn to flowing flesh once he neared the fleet."

"That cursed hellspawn still cheats me," Elric grimaced. "Here's payment for your information—" Without mercy for one of the men who had wasted and enslaved two continents, Elric stuck his blade through the ornate armour and, delicately, with all the old malevolence of his sorcerer ancestors, tickled the man's heart before finishing him.

He looked around for Kargan, but couldn't see him. Then he noted that the Chaos fleet had turned back. At first he thought it was because Straasha had at last brought aid, but then he saw that the remnants of his fleet were fleeing. Jagreen Lern was victorious. Their plans, their formations, their courage—none of these had been capable of withstanding the horrible warpings of Chaos. And now the dreadful fleet was bearing down on the two flagships, locked together by their grapples. There was no chance of cutting one of them free before the fleet arrived. Elric yelled to Dyvim Slorm and Moonglum whom he saw running towards him from the other side of the deck.

"Over the side! Over, for your lives—and swim as far as you can away from here!"

They looked at him, startled, then realised the truth of his words. Others, from both sides, were already leaping into the bloody water. Elric sheathed his sword and dived. The sea was cold, for all the warm blood in it, and he gasped as he swam in the direction of Moonglum's red head, which he could see ahead and, close to it, Dyvim Slorm's honey-coloured hair. He turned once and saw the very timbers of the two ships begin to melt, to twist and curl in strange patterns as the Ships of Hell arrived. He felt very relieved he had not been aboard. He reached his companions.

"A short-term escape this," said Moonglum, spitting water from his mouth. "What now, Elric? Shall we strike for the Purple Towns?" Moonglum's capacity for facetiousness had not, it seemed, been limited by witnessing the defeat of their fleet and the advance of Chaos. The Isle was too far away.

Everywhere, the Chaos ships were disrupting nature. Soon their influence would engulf them, too.

Then, to their left they saw the water froth and form itself into what was to Elric a familiar shape.

"Straasha!"

"*I could not aid thee, I could not aid thee. Though I tried, my ancient enemy was too strong for me. Forgive me. In recompense let me take you and your friends back with me to my own land and save you, at least from Chaos.*"

"But we cannot breathe beneath the sea!"

"*You will not need to.*"

"Very well."

Trusting to the elemental's words, they allowed themselves to be dragged beneath the waters and down into the cool, green depths of the sea, deeper and deeper until no sunlight filtered there and all was wet darkness and they lived, though at normal times the pressure would have crushed them.

They seemed to travel for miles through the mysterious underwater grottoes until at last they came to a place of coral-coloured rounded constructions that seemed to drift slowly in a sluggish current. Elric knew it. The domain of Straasha the Sea-King.

The elemental bore them to the largest construction and one section of it seemed to fade away to admit them. They moved now through twisting corridors of a delicate pink texture, slightly shadowed, no longer in water. They were now on the plane of the elemental folk. In a huge circular cave, they came to rest.

With a peculiar rushing sound, the sea-king walked to a large throne of milky jade and sat upon it, his green head on his green fist.

"*Elric, once again I regret I was unable, after all, to aid you. All I can do now is have some of my folk carry you back to your own land when you have rested here for a while. We are all, it seems, helpless against this new strength which Chaos has of late.*"

Elric nodded. "Nothing can stand against its warping influence—unless it is the Chaos Shield."

Straasha straightened his back. "*The Chaos Shield. Ah, yes. It belongs to an exiled god, does it not? But his castle is virtually impregnable.*"

"Why is that?"

"*It lies upon the topmost crag of a tall and lonely mountain, reached by a hundred and sixty-nine steps. Lining these steps are forty-nine elder trees, and of these you would have to be especially wary. Also Mordaga has a guard of a hundred and forty-four warriors. I'm explicit in giving numbers, for they have a mystic value.*"

"Of the warriors I would certainly be wary. But why the elders?"

"*Each elder contains the soul of one of Mordaga's followers who was punished thus. They are vengeful trees—ever ready to take the life of anyone that comes into their domain.*"

"A hard task, to get that shield for myself," Elric mused. "But get it I must, for without it Fate's purpose would be forever thwarted—and with it I might have vengeance on the one who commands the Chaos fleet—and Jagreen Lern who sails with him."

"*Slay Pyaray, Lord of the Fleet of Hell, and, lacking his direction, the fleet itself would perish. His life-force is contained in a blue crystal set in the top of his head and striking at that with a special weapon is the only means of killing him.*"

"Thanks for that information," Elric said gratefully. "For when the time comes, I shall need it."

"What do you plan to do, Elric?" Dyvim Slorm asked.

"Put all else aside for the moment and seek the sad giant's shield. I *must*—for if I do not have it, every battle fought will be a repetition of the one we have just lost."

"I will come with you, Elric," Moonglum promised.

"I also," said Dyvim Slorm.

"We shall require a fourth if we are to carry out the prophecy," Elric said. "I wonder what became of Kargan."

Moonglum looked at the ground. "Did you not notice?"

"Notice what?"

"On board Jagreen Lern's flagship when you were hewing about you in an effort to reach the main deck. Did you not know, then, what you had done—or rather what your cursed sword did?"

Elric felt suddenly exhausted. "No. Did I—did it—*kill* him?"

"Aye."

"Gods!" He wheeled and paced the chamber, slapping his fist in his palm. "Still this hell-made blade exacts its tribute for the service it gives me. Still it drinks the souls of friends. 'Tis a wonder you two are still with me!"

"I agree it's extraordinary," Moonglum said feelingly.

"I grieve for Kargan. He was a good friend."

"Elric," Moonglum said urgently. "You know that Kargan's death was not your responsibility. It was fated."

"Aye, but why must I always be the executioner of fate? I hesitate to list the names of the good friends and useful allies whose souls my sword has stolen. I hate it enough that it must suck souls out to give me my vitality—but that it should be most partial to my friends, that is what I cannot bear. I've half a mind to venture into the heart of Chaos and there sacrifice us both! The guilt is indirectly mine, for if I was not so weak I *must* bear such a blade, many of those who have befriended me might be alive now."

"Yet the blade's major purpose seems a noble one," Moonglum said in a baffled voice. "Oh, I fail to understand all this—paradox, paradox upon paradox. Are the gods mad or are they so subtle we cannot fathom the workings of their minds?"

"It's hard enough at times like these to remember any greater purpose," Dyvim Slorm agreed. "We are pressed so sorely that we haven't a moment for thought, but must fight the next battle and the next, forgetting often why it is we fight."

"Is the purpose, indeed, greater and not lesser," Elric smiled bitterly. "If we are the toys of the gods—are not perhaps the gods themselves mere children?"

"*These questions are of no present importance*," said Straasha from his throne.

"And at least," Moonglum told Elric, "future generations will thank Stormbringer if she fulfils her destiny."

"If Sepiriz is right," Elric said, "future generations will know nothing of any of us—blades or men!"

"Perhaps not consciously—but in the depths of their souls they will remember us. Our deeds will be spoken of as belonging to heroes with other names, that is all."

"That the world forgets me is all I ask," Elric sighed.

As if growing impatient with this fruitless discussion, the sea-king rose from his throne and said: "*Come, I will make certain that you are transported to land, if you have no objection to travelling back in the same manner as you came here?*"

"None," said Elric.

5

They staggered wearily onto the beach of the Isle of the Purple Towns and Elric turned back to address the sea-king, who remained in the shallows.

"Again I thank you for saving us, Lord of the Sea," he said respectfully. "And thanks also for telling me more of the sad giant's shield. By this action you have perhaps given us the opportunity to make certain that Chaos will be swept away from the ocean—and the land, also."

"*Aahh*," the sea-king nodded, "*yet even if you are successful and the sea is unspoiled, it will mean the passing of us both, will it not?*"

"True."

"*Then let it be so, for I at least am weary of my long existence. But come—now I must return to my folk and hope to withstand Chaos for a little longer. Farewell!*"

And the sea-king sank into the waves again and vanished.

When they eventually reached the Fortress of Evening, heralds ran out to assist them.

"How went the battle? Where is the fleet?" one asked Moonglum.

"Have the survivors not yet returned?"

"Survivors? Then . . . ?"

"We were defeated," Elric said hollowly. "Is my wife still here?"

"No, she left soon after the fleet sailed, riding for Karlaak."

"Good. At least we shall have time to erect new defences against Chaos before they reach that far. Now, we must have food and wine. We must devise a fresh plan of battle."

"Battle, my lord? With what shall we fight?"

"We shall see," Elric said, "we shall see."

Later they watched the battered survivors of the fleet sailing into the harbour. Moonglum counted despairingly. "Too few," he said. "This is a black day."

From behind them in the courtyard a trumpet sounded.

"An arrival from the mainland," Dyvim Slorm said.

They strode together down to the courtyard in time to see a scarlet-clad archer dismounting from his horse. His near-fleshless face might have been carved from bone. He stooped with weariness.

Elric was surprised. "Rackhir! You command the Ilmioran coast. Why are you here?"

"We were driven back. The Theocrat launched not one fleet but two. The other came in from the Pale Sea and took us by surprise. Our defences were crushed, Chaos swept in and we were forced to flee. The enemy has established itself less than a hundred miles from Bakshaan and marches across country—if march is the word, rather it *flows*. Presumably it expects to meet up with the army the Theocrat intends to land here."

"Aaahh, we are surely defeated . . ." Moonglum's voice was little more than a sigh.

"We must have that shield, Elric," Dyvim Slorm said.

Elric frowned, his heart sinking. "Any further steps we take against Chaos will be doomed unless we have its protection. You, Rackhir, will be the fourth man in the prophecy."

"What prophecy?"

"I'll explain later. Are you fit enough to ride back with us now?"

"Give me two hours to sleep and then I will be."

"Good. Two hours. Make your preparations, my friends, for we go to claim the sad giant's shield!"

From two sides now, Chaos enclosed the East and the four men left the Fortress of Evening knowing it was unlikely it would survive. They rode across the waters to the mainland to discover that garrisons were abandoned as men fled away from the dreadful threat of Chaos. It was not until a day later that they came upon the first survivors of the land-fighting, many of them with bodies twisted into terrible shapes by Chaos, struggling along a white road leading towards Jadmar, a city still free. From them they learned that half Ilmiora, parts of Vilmir and the tiny independent kingdom of Org had all fallen. Chaos was closing in, its shadow spreading more and more swiftly as its conquests increased.

It was with relief that Elric and his companions finally reached Karlaak to find it still free from attack. But reports placed the Chaos army less than two hundred miles away and coming nearer.

Zarozinia greeted Elric with troubled joy. "There were rumours you were dead—killed in the sea-battle."

"I cannot stay long. I have to go beyond the Sighing Desert."

"I know."

"You know? How?"

"Sepiriz was here. He left a gift in our stables for you. Four Nihrain horses."

"A useful gift. They will carry us far more swiftly than any other beasts. But will that be swift enough? I hesitate to leave you here with Chaos encroaching at such a rate."

"You must leave me, Elric. If all seems lost here, we shall flee to the Weeping Waste. Even Jagreen Lern can have scant interest in those barrens."

"Promise me that you will."

"I promise."

Feeling a little more relieved, Elric took her by the hand. "I spent the most restful period of my life in this palace," he said. "Let me spend this last night with you and perhaps we shall find a little of the old peace we once had—before I ride on to the sad giant's lair."

So they made love, but when they slept, their dreams were so full of dark portent that each wakened the other with their groans so that they lay side by side, clinging to one another until the dawn, when Elric rose, kissed her lightly, clasped her hand and then went to the stables where he found his friends waiting—around a fourth figure. It was Sepiriz.

"Sepiriz, thanks for your gift. They will probably make the difference between our being too late or not," Elric said sincerely. "But why are you here now?"

"Because I can perform another small service before your main journey begins," said the black seer. "All of you save Moonglum have retained weapons endowed with some special power. Elric and Dyvim Slorm have their runeblades, Rackhir, the Arrows of Law, which the sorcerer Lamsar gave him at the time of the Siege of Tanelorn—but Moonglum's weapon has nothing save the skill of its bearer."

"I think I prefer it thus," retorted Moonglum. "I've seen what a charmed blade can take from a man."

"I can give you nothing so strong—nor so evil—as Stormbringer," Sepiriz said. "But I have a charm for your sword, a slight one that my contact with the White Lords has enabled me to use. Give me your sword, Moonglum."

A trifle unwillingly, Moonglum unsheathed his curved steel blade and handed it to the Nihrain who took a small engraving tool from his robe and, whispering a rune, scratched several symbols on the sword near its hilt. Then he gave it back to the Eastlander.

"There. Now the sword has the blessing of Law and you will find it more able to withstand Law's enemies."

Elric said impatiently, "We must ride now, Sepiriz, for time grows desperately short."

"Ride, then. But be wary for patrolling bands of Jagreen Lern's warriors. I do not think they will be anywhere along your route when you journey there—but watch for them coming back."

They mounted the magical Nihrain steeds which had helped Elric more than once, and rode away from Karlaak by the Weeping Waste. Rode away perhaps for ever.

In a short while they had entered the Weeping Waste, for this was the quickest route to the Sighing Desert. Rackhir alone knew this country well, and he guided them.

The Nihrain steeds, treading the ground of their own strange plane, seemed literally to fly for it could be observed that their hoofs did not touch the damp grasses of the Weeping Waste. They moved at incredible speed and Rackhir, until he became used to the pace, gripped his reins tightly. In this place of eternal rain, the land was difficult to see far ahead, and the drizzle spread down their faces and into their eyes as they peered through it, trying to make out the high mountain range, which ran along the edge of the Weeping Waste, separating it from the Sighing Desert.

Then at last, after two days, they could observe tall crags and knew they were near the borders of the desert. Soon they were riding through the deep gorges and the rain ceased until, on the third day, the breeze became warm and then harsh and hot as they left the mountains and entered the desert. The sun blazed down and the wind soughed constantly over the barren sand and rocks, its continuous sighing giving the desert its name. They protected their faces, particularly their eyes, with their hoods as best they could, for the stinging sand was ever present.

Resting only for a few hours at a time, Rackhir directing them, they sped further and further into the depths of the vast desert, speaking little, for it was difficult to be heard over the wind.

Elric had long since fallen into what was virtually a mindless trance, letting the horse carry him over the desert. He had fought against his own churning thoughts and emotions, finding it hard, as he often did, to retain any objective impression of his predicament. His past had been too troubled, his background too morbid for him to do much now to see clearly.

He had always been a slave to his melancholic emotions, his physical failings and to the very blood flowing in his veins. He saw life not as a consistent pattern, but as a series of random events. Unlike others, he had fought all his life to assemble his thoughts and, if necessary, accept the chaotic nature of things, learn to live with it, but, except in moments of extreme personal crisis, had rarely managed to think coherently for any length of time. He was, perhaps, because of his outlawed life, his albinism, his very reliance on his runesword for strength, obsessed with the knowledge of his own doom.

What was thought, he asked himself, what was emotion? What was control and was it worth achieving? Better to live by instinct than to theorise and be wrong; better to remain the puppet, letting the gods move him at their pleasure, than to seek control of his own fate, clash with the will of the Higher Worlds and perish for his pains.

So he considered as he rode into the searing lash of the wind, already striving against natural hazard. And what was the difference between an earthly hazard and the hazard of uncontrolled thought and emotion? Both held something of the same qualities.

But his race, though they had ruled the world for ten thousand years, had lived under the dominance of a different star. They had been neither true men nor true members of the ancient races who had come before men. They were an intermediary type and Elric was half-consciously aware of this; aware that he was the last of an inbred line who had, without effort, used Chaos-given sorcery for convenience and for no other purpose. His race had been of Chaos, having no need of self-control or the self-restrictions of the new races who had emerged with the Age of the Young Kingdoms, and even these, according to the seer Sepiriz, were not the true men who would one day walk an Earth where order and progress might become the rule and Chaos rarely exert influence—if Elric triumphed, destroying the world he knew.

This thought added to his gloom, for he had no destiny but death, no purpose save what fate willed. Why fight against it, why bother to sharpen his wits or put his mind in order? He was little more than a sacrifice on the altar of destiny. He breathed deeply of the hot, dry air and expelled it from his stinging lungs, spitting out the clogging sand which had entered his mouth and nostrils.

Dyvim Slorm shared something of Elric's mood, though his feelings were not so strong. He had a more ordered life than had Elric, though they were of the same blood. Whereas Elric had questioned the custom of his folk, even renounced kingship that he might explore the new lands of the Young Kingdoms and compare their way of life with his own, Dyvim Slorm had never indulged in such questioning. He had suffered bitterness when through Elric's renegade activities, the Dreaming City of Imrryr, last stronghold of the old race of Melniboné, had been razed; shock, too, of a kind, when he and what remained of the Imrryrians had been forced out into the world, also, to make their living as mercenaries of those they considered upstart kings of lowly and contemptible peoples. Dyvim Slorm, who had never questioned, did not question now, though he was disturbed.

Moonglum was less self-absorbed. Since the time, many years before, when he and Elric had met and fought against the Dharzi together, he had felt a peculiar sympathy, even empathy, with his friend. When Elric sank into such moods as the one he was in now, Moonglum felt tormented only because he could not help him. Many times he had sought the means of pulling Elric out of his gloomy depression, but these days he had learned that it was impossible. By nature cheerful and optimistic, even he felt dominated by the doom which was on them.

Rackhir, too, who was of a calmer and more philosophical frame of mind than his fellows, did not feel capable of fully grasping the implications of their mission. He had thought to spend the rest of his days in contemplation and meditation in the peaceful city of Tanelorn, which exerted a strange calming influence on all who lived there. But this call to aid in the fight against Chaos had been impossible to ignore and he had unwillingly strapped on his quiver of Arrows of Law and taken up his bow again to ride from Tanelorn with a small party of those who wished to accompany him and offer their services to Elric.

Peering through the sand-filled air, he saw something looming ahead—a single mountain rising from the wastes of the desert as if placed there by unnatural means.

He called, pointing: "Elric! There! That must be Mordaga's castle!"

Elric roused himself and let his eyes follow Rackhir's pointing hand. "Aye," he sighed. "We are there. Let us rest here before we ride the final distance!"

They reined in their steeds and dismounted, easing their aching limbs and stretching their legs to allow the blood to flow freely again.

They raised their tent against the wind-blown sand and ate their meal in a mood of companionship, created by the knowledge that after they reached the mountain, they might never see one another alive again.

6

The steps wound up around the mountain. High above they could see the gleam of masonry and, just where the steps curved and disappeared for the first time, they saw an elder tree. It looked like any ordinary tree but it became a symbol for them—there was their initial antagonist. How would it fight? Elric placed a booted foot on the first step. It was high, built for the feet of a giant. He began to climb, the other three following behind him. Now, as he reached the tenth step, he unsheathed Stormbringer, felt it quiver and send energy into him. The climbing instantly became easier. As he came close to the elder, he heard it rustle, saw that there was an agitation in its branches. Yes, it was certainly sentient. He was only a few steps from the tree when he heard Dyvim Slorm shout: "Gods! *The leaves*—look at the leaves!"

The green leaves, their veins seeming to throb in the sunlight, were beginning to detach themselves from the branches and drift purposefully towards the group. One settled on Elric's bare hand. He attempted to brush it off, but it clung. Others began to settle on different parts of his body. They were coming in a green wave now and he felt a peculiar stinging sensation in his hand. With a curse he peeled it off and to his horror saw that tiny pinpricks of blood were left where it had been. His body twitched in nausea and he ripped the rest from his face, slashing at others with his runesword. As they were touched by the blade, so they shrivelled, but they were swiftly replaced. He knew instinctively that they were sucking not only blood from his veins, but the soul-force from his being.

With yells of terror, his companions discovered the same thing. These leaves were being directed and he knew where the direction came from—the tree itself. He clambered up the remaining steps, fighting off the leaves which swarmed like locusts around him. With grim intention he began hacking at the trunk which gave out an angry groaning and the branches sought to reach him. He slashed them away and then plunged Stormbringer deep into the tree. Sods of earth spattered upwards as the roots threshed. The tree screamed and began to heel over towards him as if, in death, it sought to kill him also. He wrenched at Stormbringer which sucked greedily at the sentient tree's lifestuff, failed to tug the sword out and leapt aside as the tree crashed down over the steps, barely missing him. One branch slashed his face and drew blood. He gasped and staggered, feeling the life draining from him.

He stumbled to the fallen tree and saw that the wood was suddenly dead and the remaining leaves brown and shrivelled. "Quickly," he gasped as the three came up, "shift this thing. My sword's beneath and without it I'm dead!"

Swiftly they set to work and rolled the tree over so that Elric could weakly grasp the hilt of Stormbringer still imbedded therein. As he did so he almost screamed, experiencing a sensation of ecstatic power as the tree's energy filled him, pulsed through him so that he felt like a god himself. He laughed, as if possessed by a demon, and the others looked at him in astonishment. "Come, my friends, follow me. I can deal with a million such trees now!"

He leapt up the steps as another shoal of leaves came towards him. Ignoring their bites, he went straight for the second elder and drove his sword at its centre. Again, this tree screamed.

"Dyvim Slorm!" he shouted, drunk on its life-force. "Do as I do—let your sword drink a few such souls and we're invincible!"

"Such power is scarcely palatable," Rackhir said, brushing dead leaves from his body as Elric withdrew his sword again and ran towards the next. The elders grew thicker here and they bent their branches to reach him, looming over him, their branches like fingers seeking to pluck him apart.

Dyvim Slorm, a trifle less spontaneously, imitated Elric's method of dispatching the tree-creatures and soon he too became filled with the stolen souls of the demons imprisoned within the elders and his wild laugh joined Elric's as, like fiendish woodsmen, they attacked again and again, each victory lending them more strength so that Moonglum and Rackhir looked at each other in wonder and fear to see such a terrible change come over their friends.

But there was no denying that their methods were effective against the elders. Soon they looked back at a waste of fallen, blackened trees spreading down the mountain side.

All the old, unholy fervour of the dead kings of Melniboné was in the faces of the two kinsmen as they sang old battle-songs, their twin blades joining the harmony to send up a disturbing melody of doom and malevolence. His lips parted to reveal his white teeth, his red eyes blazing with dreadful fire, his milk-white hair streaming in the burning wind, Elric flung up his sword to the sky and turned to confront his companions.

"Now, friends, see how the ancient ones of Melniboné conquered man and demon to rule the world for ten thousand years!"

Moonglum thought that he merited the name of Wolf, gained in the West long since. All the chaos-force that was now within him had gained complete control over every other part of him. He realised that Elric was no longer split in his loyalties, there was no conflict in him now. His ancestors' blood dominated him and he appeared as they must have done ages since when all other races of mankind fled before them, fearing their magnificence, their malice and their evil. Dyvim Slorm seemed equally as possessed. Moonglum sent up a heartfelt prayer to whatever kindly gods remained in the universe that Elric was his ally and not his enemy.

They were close to the top now, Elric and his cousin springing ahead with superhuman bounds. The steps terminated at the mouth of a gloomy tunnel and into the darkness rushed the pair, laughing and calling to one another. Less speedily, Moonglum and Rackhir followed, the Red Archer nocking an arrow to his bow.

Elric peered into the gloom, his head swimming with the power that seemed to burst from every pore of his body. He heard the clatter of armoured feet coming towards him and, as they approached, he realised that these warriors were mere human beings. Though nearly a hundred and fifty, they did not daunt him. As the first group rushed at him, he blocked blows easily and struck them down, each soul taken making only a fraction of difference to the vitality already in him. Shoulder to shoulder stood the kinsmen, butchering the soldiers like so many unarmed children. It was dreadful to the eyes of Moonglum and Rackhir as they came up to witness the flood of blood which soon made the tunnel slippery. The stench of death in the close confines became too much as Elric and Dyvim Slorm moved past the first of the fallen and carried the attack to the rest.

Rackhir groaned: "Though they be enemies and the servants of those we fight, I cannot bear to witness such slaughter. We are not needed here, friend Moonglum. These are demons waging war, not men!"

"Aye," agreed Moonglum, disquieted. They broke out into sunlight again and saw the castle ahead, the remaining warriors reassembling as Elric and Dyvim Slorm advanced menacingly with malevolent joy towards them.

The air rang with the sounds of shouting and steel clashing. Rackhir aimed an arrow at one of the warriors and launched it to take the man in the left eye. "I'll see that a few of them get a cleaner death," he muttered, nocking another arrow to the string.

As Elric and his cousin disappeared into the enemy ranks, others, sensing perhaps that Rackhir and Moonglum were less of a danger, rushed at the two. Moonglum found himself engaging three warriors and discovered that his sword seemed extraordinarily light and gave off a sweet, clear tone as it met the warriors' weapons, turning them aside readily. The sword supplied him with no energy, but it did not blunt as it might have and the heavier swords could not force it down so easily. Rackhir had expended all his arrows in what had been an act of mercy. He engaged the enemy with his sword and killed two, taking Moonglum's third opponent from behind with an upward thrust into the man's side and through to his heart.

Then they went with little stomach into the main fray and saw that already the turf was littered with a great many corpses. Rackhir cried to Elric: "Stop! Elric—let *us* finish these. You have no need to take their souls. We can kill them with more natural methods!"

But Elric laughed and carried on his work. As he finished another warrior and there were no others in the immediate area, Rackhir seized him by the arm. "Elric—"

Stormbringer turned in Elric's hand, howling its satiated glee and clove down at Rackhir. Seeing his fate, the Red Archer sobbed and sought to avoid the blow. But it landed in his shoulder blade and sheared down to his breastbone. "Elric!" he cried. "Not *my* soul, too!"

And so died the hero Rackhir the Red Archer, famous in the Eastlands as the saviour of Tanelorn. Cloven by a treacherous blade. By the friend whose life he had saved, long ago when they had first met near the city of Ameeron.

And Elric laughed until realisation came and he tugged his sword away though it was too late. The stolen energy still pulsed in him, but his great grief no longer gave it the same control over him. Tears streamed down Elric's tortured face and a great, racking groan came from him.

"Ah, Rackhir—will it ever cease?"

On opposite sides of the slain-strewed field, his two remaining companions stood regarding him. Dyvim Slorm had done with killing, but only because there was none left to kill. He gasped, staring around him half in bewilderment. Moonglum glared at Elric with horrified eyes which yet held a gleam of sympathy for his friend, for he knew well Elric's doom and knew that the life of one close to Elric was coveted by Stormbringer.

"There was no gentler hero than Rackhir," he said, "no man more desirous of peace and order than him." Then he shuddered.

Elric raised himself to his feet and turned to look at the huge castle of granite and bluestone which waited in enigmatic silence as if for his next action. On the battlements of the topmost turret he could make out a figure which could only be the giant.

"I swear by your stolen soul, Rackhir, that what you wished to come to pass *shall* come to pass, though I, a thing of Chaos, achieve it. Law will triumph and Chaos will be driven back! Armed with sword and shield of Chaos forging I shall do battle with every fiend of hell if needs be. Chaos was the indirect cause of your death. And Chaos will be punished for it. But first, we must take the shield."

Dyvim Slorm, not realising quite what had happened, shouted in exultation to his kinsman. "Elric—let's visit the sad giant now!"

But Moonglum, coming up to gaze down on the ruined body of Rackhir, murmured: "Aye, Chaos is the cause, Elric. I'll join in your vengeance with a will so long as," he shuddered, "I'm spared from the attentions of your hell-blade."

Together, three abreast, they marched through the open portal of Mordaga's castle and were immediately in a rich and barbarically furnished hall.

"Mordaga!" Elric cried. "We have come to fulfil a prophecy!"

They waited impatiently, until at last a bulky figure came through a great arch at the end of the vast hall. Mordaga was as tall as two men, but his back was bent. He had long, curling black hair and was clad in a deep blue smock belted at the waist. Upon his great feet were simple leather sandals. His black eyes were full of a sorrow such as Moonglum had only seen before in Elric's eyes.

Upon the sad giant's arm was a round shield which bore upon it the eight amber arrows of Chaos. It was of a silvery green colour and very beautiful. He had no other weapons.

"I know the prophecy," he said in a voice that was like a lonely, roaring wind. "But still I must seek to avert it. Will you take the shield and leave me in peace, human? I do not want death."

Elric felt a kind of sympathy for sad Mordaga and he knew something of what the fallen god must feel at this moment. "The prophecy says death," he said softly.

"Take the shield," Mordaga lifted it off his mighty arm and held it towards Elric. "Take the shield and change fate this once."

Elric nodded. "I will."

With a tremendous sigh, the giant deposited the Chaos Shield upon the floor.

"For thousands of years I have lived in the shadow of that prophecy," he said, straightening his back. "Now, though I die in old age, I shall die in peace and, though once I did not think so, I shall welcome such a death after all this time, I think."

"The whole world seems to sigh for death," Elric replied, "but you may not die naturally, for Chaos comes and will engulf you as it will engulf everything unless I can stop it. But at least, it seems, you'll be in a more philosophical frame of mind to meet it."

"Farewell and I thank you," said the giant, turning, and he plodded back towards the entrance through which he had come.

As Mordaga disappeared, Moonglum dashed forward on fleet feet and followed him through the entrance before either Elric or Dyvim Slorm could cry out or stop him.

Then they heard a single shriek that seemed to echo away into eternity, a crash which shook the hall and then the footfall returning.

Moonglum reappeared in the entrance, a bloody sword in his hand.

"It was murder," he said simply. "I admit it. I took him in the back before he was aware of it. It was a good, quick death and he died whilst happy. Moreover, it was a better death than any his minions tried to mete to us. It was murder, but it was necessary in my eyes."

"Why?" said Elric, still mystified.

Grimly, Moonglum continued: "He had to perish as Fate decreed. We are servants of Fate, now, Elric, and to divert it in any small way is to hamper its aims. But more than that, it was the beginning of my own vengeance-taking. If Mordaga had not surrounded himself with such a host, Rackhir would not have died."

Elric shook his head. "Blame me for that, Moonglum. The giant should not have perished for my own sword's crime."

"Someone had to perish," said Moonglum steadfastly, "and since the prophecy contained Mordaga's death, he was the one. Who else, here, could I kill, Elric?"

Elric turned away. "I wish it were I," he sighed. He looked down at the great, round shield with its shifting amber arrows and its mysterious silver-green colour. He picked it up easily enough and placed it on his arm. It virtually covered his body from chin to ankles.

"Let's make haste and leave this place of death and misery. The lands of Ilmiora and Vilmir await our aid—if they have not already wholly fallen to Chaos!"

7

It was in the mountains separating the Sighing Desert from the Weeping Waste that they first learned of the fate of the last of the Young Kingdoms. They came upon a party of six tired warriors led by Lord Voashoon, Zarozinia's father.

"What has happened?" Elric asked anxiously. "Where is Zarozinia?"

"I know not if she's lost, dead or captured, Elric. Our continent has fallen to Chaos."

"Did you not seek for her?" Elric accused.

The old man shrugged. "My son, I have looked upon so much horror these past days that I am now bereft of emotion. I care for nothing but a quick release from all this. The day of mankind is over on the Earth. Go no further than here, for even the Weeping Waste is beginning to change before the crawling tide of Chaos. It is hopeless."

"Hopeless! No! We still live—perhaps Zarozinia still lives. Did you hear nothing of her fate?"

"Only a rumour that Jagreen Lern had taken her aboard the leading Chaos ship."

"She is on the seas?"

"No—those cursed craft sail land as well as sea, if it can be told apart these days. It was they who attacked Karlaak, with a vast horde of mounted men and infantry following behind. Confusion prevails—you'll find nothing but your death back there, my son."

"We shall see. I have some protection against Chaos at long last, plus my sword and my Nihrain steed." He turned in the saddle to address his companions. "Well, will you stay here with Lord Voashoon or accompany me into the heart of Chaos?"

"We'll come with you," Moonglum said quietly, speaking for them both. "We've followed you until now and our fates are linked with yours in any case. We can do nought else."

"Good. Farewell, Lord Voashoon. If you would do a service, ride over the Weeping Waste to Eshmir and the Unmapped East where Moonglum's homeland lies. Tell them what to expect, though they're probably beyond rescue now."

"I will try," said Voashoon wearily, "and hope to arrive there before Chaos."

Then Elric and his companions rode away, towards the massed hordes of Chaos—three men against the unleashed forces of darkness. Three foolhardy men who had pursued their course so faithfully that it was inconceivable for them to flee now. The last acts must be played out whether howling night or calm day followed.

The first signs of Chaos were soon apparent as they saw the place where lush grassland once had been. It was now a yellow morass of molten rock that, though cool, rolled about with a purposeful air. The Nihrain horses, since they did not gallop on the plane of Earth, crossed it with comparative ease and here the Chaos Shield was first shown to work, for, as they passed, the yellow liquid rock changed and became grass again for a short time.

They met once a shambling thing that still had limbs of sorts and a mouth that could speak. From this poor creature they learned that Karlaak was no more, that it had been churned into broiling nothingness and where it had been the forces of Chaos, both human and supernatural, had set up their camp, their work done. The thing also spoke of something that was of particular interest to Elric. Rumour was that the Dragon Isle of Melniboné was the only place where Chaos had been unable to exert its influence.

"If, when our business is done, we can reach Melniboné," Elric said to his friends as they rode on, "we might be able to abide until such a time that the White Lords can help us. Also there are dragons slumbering in the caves—and these would be useful against Jagreen Lern if we could waken them."

"What use is it to fight them now?" Dyvim Slorm said defeatedly. "Jagreen Lern has won, Elric. We have not fulfilled our destiny. Our role is over and Chaos rules."

"Does it? But we have yet to fight it and test its strength against ours. Let us decide then what the outcome has been."

Dyvim Slorm looked dubious, but he said nothing.

And then, at last, they came to the Camp of Chaos.

No mortal nightmare could encompass such a terrible vision. The towering Ships of Hell dominated the place as they observed it from a distance, utterly horrified by the sight. Shooting flames of all colours seemed to flicker everywhere over the camp, fiends of all kinds mingled with the men, hell's evilly beautiful nobles conferred with the gaunt-faced kings who had allied themselves to Jagreen Lern and perhaps now regretted it. Every so often the ground heaved and erupted and any human beings unfortunate enough to be in the area were either engulfed and totally transformed, or else had their bodies warped in indescribable ways. The noise was a dreadful blending of human voices and roaring Chaos sounds, devils' wailing laughter and, quite often, the tortured shout of a human soul who had perhaps regretted his choice of loyalty and now suffered madness. The stench was disgusting, of corruption, of blood and of evil. The Ships of Hell moved slowly about through the horde which stretched for miles, dotted with great pavilions of kings, their silk banners fluttering; hollow pride compared to the might of Chaos. Many of the human beings could scarcely be told from the Chaos creatures, their forms were so changed under the influence of Chaos.

Elric muttered to his friends as they sat in their saddles watching. "It is obvious that the warping influence of Chaos grows even stronger among the human ranks. This will continue until even Jagreen Lern and the traitor kings will lose every semblance of humanity and become just a fraction of the churning stuff of Chaos. This will mean the end of the human race—mankind will pass away for ever, taken into the maw of Chaos.

"You look upon the last of mankind, my friends, save for ourselves. Soon it will be indistinguishable from anything else. All this unstable Earth is beneath the heel of the Lords of Chaos, and they are gradually absorbing it into their realm, into their own plane. They will first remould and then steal the Earth altogether; it will become just another lump of clay for them to mould into whatever grotesque shapes take their fancy."

"And we seek to stop *that*," Moonglum said hopelessly. "We cannot, Elric!"

"We must continue to strive, until we are conquered. I remember that Straasha the Sea-King said if Pyaray, commander of the Chaos fleet, is slain, the ships themselves will no longer be able to exist. I have a mind to put that to the test. Also, I have not forgotten that my wife may be prisoner aboard his ship, or that Jagreen Lern is there. I have three good reasons for venturing there."

"No, Elric! It would be more than suicide!"

"I do not ask you to accompany me."

"If you go, we shall come, but I like it not."

"If one man cannot succeed, neither can three. I shall go alone. Wait for me. If I do not return, then try to get to Melniboné."

"Elric—!" Moonglum cried and then watched as, his Chaos Shield pulsing, Elric spurred the Nihrain steed towards the camp.

Protected against the influence of Chaos, Elric was sighted by a detachment of warriors as he neared the ship which was his destination. They recognised him and rode towards him, shouting.

He laughed in their faces. "Just the fodder my blade needs before we banquet on yonder ship!" he cried as he slashed off the first man's head as if it were a buttercup. Secure behind his great round shield, he hewed about him with a will. Since Stormbringer had slain the demons imprisoned in the elder trees, the vitality which the sword passed into him was almost without limit, yet every soul that Elric stole from Jagreen Lern's warriors was another fraction of vengeance reaped. Against men, he was invincible. He split one heavily armoured warrior from head to crotch, sheared through the saddle and smashed the horse's backbone apart.

Then the remaining warriors dropped back suddenly and Elric felt his body tingle with peculiar sensations, knew he was in the area of influence exerted by the Chaos ship and knew also that he was being protected against them by his shield. He was now partially out of his own earthly plane and existed between his world and the world of Chaos. He dismounted from his Nihrain steed and ordered it to wait for him. There were ropes trailing from the huge sides of the foremost ship and Elric saw with horror that other figures were climbing up them—and he recognised several as men he had known in Karlaak. But before he could reach the ship he was surrounded by all manner of horrifying shapes, things that flew at him cawing, with heads of men and beaks of birds, things that writhed from out of the seething ground and struck at him, things that groped and mewled and screamed, attempting to pull him down to join them. Frantically, he swung Stormbringer this way and that, cutting his way through the Chaos creatures, protected from becoming like them by the pulsing Chaos Shield on his left arm, until at length he joined the ghastly ranks of the dead and swarmed with them up the sides of the great, gleaming ship, grateful at least for the cover they gave him.

He reached the ship's rail and hauled himself over it, spitting bile from his throat as he entered a peculiar region of darkness and came to the first of a series of decks that rose like steps to the topmost one where he could see the occupants—a manlike figure and something like a huge, blood-red octopus. The first was probably Jagreen Lern, the second was obviously Pyaray, for this, Elric knew, was the guise he took when he manifested himself on Earth.

Contrasting with the ships seen from the distance, once aboard Elric became conscious of the dark, shadowy nature of the light, filled with moving threads, a network of dark reds, blues, yellows, greens and purples which, as he moved through it, gave and re-formed itself behind him. He was constantly being blundered against by the moving cadavers and he made a point of not looking at their faces too closely, for he had already recognised several of the sea-raiders whom he had abandoned, years before, during the escape from Imrryr.

Slowly he was gaining the top deck, noting that so far both Jagreen Lern and Lord Pyaray seemed unaware of his presence. Presumably they considered themselves entirely free from any kind of attack now they had conquered all the known world. He grinned maliciously to himself as he continued climbing, gripping the shield tightly, knowing that if once he lost hold of it, his body would become transformed either into some shambling alien shape or else flow away altogether to become absorbed into the Chaos-stuff. By now Elric had forgotten everything but his main object, which was to destroy Lord Pyaray's earthly manifestation. He must gain the topmost deck and deal first with the Lord of Chaos. Then he would kill Jagreen Lern and, if she were really there, rescue Zarozinia and bear her to safety.

Up the dark decks, through the nets of strange colours, Elric went, his milk-white hair flowing in contrast to the moody darkness around him. As he came to the last deck but one, he felt a gentle touch on his shoulder and, looking in that direction, saw with heart-lurching horror that one of Pyaray's blood-red tentacles had found him. He stumbled back, putting up his shield.

The tentacle tip touched the shield and rebounded suddenly, the entire tentacle shrivelling. From above, where the Chaos Lord's main bulk was, there came a terrible screaming and roaring.

"*What's this? What's this? What's this?*"

Elric shouted in impudent triumph at seeing his shield work with such effect: "'Tis Elric of Melniboné, great lord. Come to destroy thee!"

Another tentacle dropped towards him, seeking to curl around the shield and seize him. Then another followed it and another. Elric hacked at one, severed its sensitive tip, saw another touch the shield, recoil and shrivel and then avoided the third in order to run round the deck and ascend, as swiftly as he could, the ladder leading to the deck above. Here he saw Jagreen Lern, his eyes wide. The Theocrat was clad in his familiar scarlet armour. On his arm was his buckler and in the same hand an axe, while his right hand held a broadsword. He glanced down at these weapons, obviously aware of their inadequacy against Elric's.

"You later, Theocrat," Elric promised.

"You're a fool, Elric! You're doomed now, whatever you do!"

It was probably true, but he did not care. "Aside, upstart," he said as, shield up, he moved warily towards the many-tentacled Lord of Chaos.

"You are the killer of many cousins of mine, Elric," the creature said in a low, whispering voice. "And you've banished several Dukes of Chaos to their own domain so that they cannot reach Earth again. For that you must pay. I at least do not underestimate you, as, in likelihood, they did." A tentacle reared above him and tried to come down from over the shield's rim and seize his throat. He took a step backwards and blocked the attempt with the shield.

Then a whole web of tentacles began to come from all sides, each one curling around the shield, knowing its touch to be death. He skipped aside, avoiding them with difficulty, slicing about him with Stormbringer. As he fought, he remembered Straasha's last message: *Strike for the crystal atop his head. There is his life and his soul.* Elric saw the blue, radiating crystal which he had originally taken to be one of Lord Pyaray's several eyes. He moved in towards the roots of the tentacles, leaving his back poorly protected, but there was nothing else for it. As he did so, a huge maw gaped in the thing's head and tentacles began to draw him towards it. He extended his shield towards the maw until it touched the lips. Yellow, jellylike stuff spurted from the mouth as the Lord of Chaos screamed in pain. He got his foot on one tentacle stump and clambered up the slippery hide of the Chaos Lord, shuddering beneath his feet. Every time his shield touched Pyaray, it created some sort of wound so that the Chaos Lord began to thresh about dreadfully. Then he stood unsteadily over the glowing soul-crystal. For an instant he paused, then plunged Stormbringer point first into the crystal!

There came a mighty throbbing from the heart of the entity's body. It gave vent to a monstrous shriek and then Elric yelled as Stormbringer took the soul of a Lord of Hell and channelled this surging vitality through to him. It was too much. He was hurled backwards. He lost his footing on the slippery back, stumbled off the deck itself and fell to another, nearly a hundred feet below. He landed with bone-cracking force, but, thanks to the stolen vitality, was completely unhurt. He got up, ready to clamber again towards Jagreen Lern. The Theocrat's anxious face peered down at him and he yelled: "You'll find a present for you in yonder cabin, Elric!"

Torn between pursuing the Theocrat and investigating the cabin, Elric turned and opened the door. From inside came a dreadful sobbing.

"Zarozinia!" He ducked into the dark place and there he saw her.

Chaos had warped her. Only her head, the same beautiful head was left.

But her lovely body was dreadfully changed. Now it resembled the body of a huge white worm.

"Did Jagreen Lern do this?"

"He and his ally."

"How have you retained your sanity?"

"By waiting for you. I have something to do that required me to keep my wits." The worm-body undulated towards him.

"No—stand back," he cried, disgusted against his will. He could hardly bear to look at her. But she did not heed him. The worm-body threshed forward and impaled itself on his sword. "There," cried her head. "Take my soul into you, Elric, for I am useless to myself and you now! Carry my soul with yours and we shall be forever together."

"No! You are wrong!" He tried to withdraw the thirsty runeblade, but it was impossible. And, unlike any other sensation he had ever received from it, this was almost gentle. Warm and pleasant, bringing with it her youth and innocence, his wife's soul flowed into his and he wept. "Oh, Zarozinia. Oh, my love!"

So she died, her soul blending with his as, years earlier, the soul of his first love, Cymoril, had been taken. He did not look at the grotesque worm-body, did not glance at her face, but walked slowly from the cabin.

Though he was moved to an aching sadness, his sword seemed to chuckle as he resheathed it.

As he left the cabin, it appeared to him that the deck was disintegrating, flowing apart. Straasha had been right. The destruction of Pyaray also meant the destruction of his ghastly fleet. Jagreen Lern had evidently made good his escape and Elric, in his present mood, did not feel ready to pursue him. He was only regretful that the fleet had achieved its purpose before he had been able to destroy it. Sword and shield both aiding him in their ways, he leapt from the ship to the pulsating ground and ran for the Nihrain steed which was rearing up and flailing with its hoofs to protect itself from a group of gibbering Chaos creatures. He drew his runesword again and drove into them, quickly dispersing them and mounting the Nihrain stallion. Then, the tears still flowing down his white face, he rode wildly from the Camp of Chaos, leaving the Ships of Hell breaking apart behind him. At least these would threaten the world no more and a blow had been struck against Chaos. Now only the horde itself remained to be dealt with—and the dealing would not be so easy.

Fighting off the warped things which clawed at him, he finally rejoined his friends, said nothing to them but wheeled his horse to lead the way over the shaking earth towards Melniboné, where the last stand against Chaos could be prepared, the last battle fought and his destiny completed.

And in his dark, tormented mind he seemed to hear Zarozinia's youthful voice whispering comfort as, still sobbing, he rode away from that Camp of Chaos.

BOOK FOUR

DOOMED LORD'S PASSING

*For the mind of Man alone is free to explore the lofty vastness
of the cosmic infinite, to transcend ordinary consciousness, to
roam the secret corridors of the brain where past and future
melt into one . . . And universe and individual are linked, the
one mirrored in the other, and each contains the other.*

—The Chronicle of the Black Sword

I

The Dreaming City no longer dreamed in splendour. The tattered towers of Imrryr were blackened husks, tumbled rags of masonry standing sharp and dark against a sullen sky. Once, Elric's vengeance had brought fire to the city, and the fire had brought ruin.

Streaks of cloud, like sooty smoke, whispered across the pulsing sun so that the shouting, red-stained waters beyond Imrryr were soiled by shadow, and they seemed to become quieter as if hushed by the black scars that rode across their ominous turbulence.

Upon a confusion of fallen masonry, a man stood watching the waves. A tall man, broad-shouldered, slender at hip, a man with slanting brows, pointed, lobeless ears, high cheekbones and crimson, moody eyes in a dead white ascetic face. He was dressed in black quilted doublet and heavy cloak, both high-collared, emphasising the pallor of his albino skin. The wind, erratic and warm, played with his cloak, fingered it and passed mindlessly on to howl through the broken towers.

Elric heard the howling and his memory was filled by the sweet, the malicious and melancholy melodies of old Melniboné. He remembered, too, the other music his ancestors had created when they had elegantly tortured their slaves, choosing them for the pitch of their screams and forming them into the instruments of unholy symphonies. Lost in this nostalgia for a while, he found something close to forgetfulness and he wished that he had never doubted the code of Melniboné, wished that he had accepted it without question and thus left his mind unsundered. Bitterly, he smiled.

A figure appeared below him and climbed the tumbled stones to stand by his side. He was a small, red-haired man with a wide mouth and eyes that had once been bright and amused.

"You look to the East, Elric," Moonglum murmured. "You look back towards something irremediable."

Elric put his long-fingered hand on his friend's shoulder. "Where else is there to look, Moonglum, when the world lies beneath the heel of Chaos? What would you have me do? Look forward to days of hope and laughter, to an old age lived in peace, with children playing around my feet?" He laughed softly. It was not a laugh that Moonglum liked to hear.

"Sepiriz spoke of help from the White Lords. It must come soon. We must wait patiently." Moonglum turned to squint into the glowering and motionless sun and then, his face set in an introspective look, cast his eyes down to the rubble on which he stood.

Elric was silent for a moment, watching the waves. Then he shrugged. "Why complain? It does me no good. I cannot act on my own volition. Whatever fate is before me cannot be changed. I pray that the men who follow us will make use of their ability to control their own destinies. I have no such ability." He touched his jawbone with his fingers and then looked at the hand, noting nails, knuckles, muscles and veins standing out on the pale skin. He ran this hand through the silky strands of his white hair, drew a long breath and let it out in a sigh. "Logic! The world cries for logic. I have none, yet here I am, formed as a man with mind, heart and vitals, yet formed by a chance coming together of certain elements. The world needs logic. Yet all the logic in the world is worth as much as one lucky guess. Men take pains to weave a web of careful thoughts—yet others thoughtlessly weave a random pattern and achieve the same result. So much for the thoughts of the sage."

"Ah," Moonglum winked with attempted levity, "thus speaks the wild adventurer, the cynic. But we are not all wild and cynical, Elric. Other men tread other paths—and reach other conclusions than yours."

"I tread one that's preordained. Come, let's to the Dragon Caves and see what Cousin Slorm has done to rouse our reptilian friends."

They stumbled together down the ruins and walked the shattered canyons that had once been the lovely streets of Imrryr, out of the city and along a grassy track that wound through the gorse, disturbing a flock of large ravens that fled into the air, cawing, all save one, the king, who balanced himself on a bush, his cloak of ruffled feathers drawn up in dignity, his black eyes regarding them with wary contempt.

Down through sharp rocks to the gaping entrance of the Dragon Caves, down the steep steps into torchlit darkness with its damp warmth and smell of scaly reptilian bodies. Into the first cave where the great recumbent forms of the sleeping so-called "Black Phoorn" lay, their folded leathery wings rising into the shadows, their green and black scales glowing faintly, their clawed feet folded and their slender snouts curled back, even in sleep, to display the long, ivory teeth that seemed like so many white stalactites. Their dilating red nostrils groaned in torpid slumber. The smell of their hides and their breath was unmistakeable, rousing in Moonglum some memory inherited from his ancestors, some shadowy impression of a time when these dragons and their masters swept across a world they ruled, their inflammable venom dripping from their fangs and heedlessly setting fire to the countryside across which they flew. Elric, used to it, hardly noticed the smell, but passed on through the first cave and the second until he found Dyvim Slorm, striding about with a torch in one hand and a scroll in the other, swearing to himself.

He looked up as he heard their booted feet approach. He spread out his arms and shouted, his voice echoing through the caverns, "Nothing! Not a stir, not an eyelid flickering! There is no way of rousing them. They'll not wake until they have slept their necessary number of years. Oh, that we had not used them on the last two occasions, for we have greater need of them today!"

"Neither you nor I had the knowledge we have now. Regret is useless since it can achieve nothing." Elric stared around him at the huge, shadowy forms. Here, slightly apart from the rest, lay the leader-dragon, one he recognised and felt affection for: Flamefang, the eldest, who was five thousand years old and still young for a Phoorn. But Flamefang, like the rest, slept on.

He went up to the beast and stroked its metal-like scales, ran his hand down the ivory smoothness of its great front fangs, felt its warm breath on his body and smiled. Beside him, on his hip, he heard Stormbringer murmur. He patted the blade. "Here's one soul you cannot have. The dragons are indestructible. They will survive, even though all the world collapses into nothing."

Dyvim Slorm said from another part of the cavern: "I can't think of further action to take for the meantime, Elric. Let's go back to the Tower of D'a'rputna and refresh ourselves."

Elric nodded assent and, together, the three men returned through the caverns and ascended the steps into the sunlight.

"So," Dyvim Slorm remarked, "still no nightfall. The sun has remained in that position for thirteen days, ever since we left the Camp of Chaos and made our perilous way to Melniboné. How much power must Chaos wield if it can stop the sun in its course?"

"Chaos might not have done this for all we know," Moonglum pointed out. "Though it's likely, of course, that it did. Time has stopped. Time waits. But waits for what? More confusion, further disorder? Or the influence of the Great Balance which will restore order and take vengeance against those forces who have gone against its will? Or does time wait for us—three mortal men adrift, cut off from what is happening to all other men, waiting on time as it waits on us?"

"Perhaps the sun waits on us," Elric agreed. "For is it not our destiny to prepare the world for its fresh course? It makes me feel a little more than a mere pawn if that's the case. What if we do nothing? Will the sun remain where it is for ever?"

They paused in their progress for a moment and stood staring up at the pulsating red disc which flooded the streets with scarlet light, at the black clouds which fled across the sky before it. Where were the clouds going? Where did they come from? They seemed instilled with purpose. It was possible that they were not even clouds at all, but spirits of Chaos bent on dark errands.

Elric grunted to himself, aware of the uselessness of such speculation. He led the way back to the Tower of D'a'rputna where years before he had sought his love, his cousin Cymoril, and later lost her to the ravening thirst of the blade by his side.

The tower had survived the flames, though the colours that had once adorned it were blackened by fire. Here he left his friends and went to his own room to fling himself, fully clad, upon the soft Melnibonéan bed and, almost immediately, fall asleep.

2

Elric slept and Elric dreamed and, though he was aware of the unreality of his visions, his attempts to rouse himself to wakefulness were entirely futile. Soon he ceased trying and merely let his dream form itself and draw him into its bright landscapes . . .

He saw Imrryr as it had been many centuries ago. Imrryr, the same city he had known before he led the raid on it and caused its destruction. The same, yet with a different, brighter appearance as if it were newly built. As well, the colours of the surrounding countryside were richer, the sun darker orange, the sky deep blue and sultry. Since then, he realised, the very tints of the world had faded with the planet's ageing . . .

People and beasts moved in the shining streets; tall, eldritch Melnibonéans, men and women walking with grace, like proud tigers; hard-faced slaves with hopeless, stoic eyes, long-legged horses of a type now extinct, small mastodons drawing gaudy cars. Clearly on the breeze came the mysterious scents of the place, the muted sounds of activity—all hushed, for the Melnibonéans hated noise as much as they loved harmony. Heavy silk banners flapped from the scintillating towers of bluestone, jade, ivory, crystal and polished red granite. And Elric moved in his sleep and ached to be there amongst his own ancestors, the golden folk who had dominated the old world.

Monstrous galleys passed through the water-maze which led to Imrryr's inner harbour, bringing the best of the world's booty, tax gathered from all parts of the Bright Empire. And across the azure sky lazy dragons flapped their way towards the caves where thousands of the beasts were stabled, unlike the present where scarcely a hundred remained. In the tallest tower—the Tower of B'aal'nezbett, the Tower of Kings—his ancestors had studied sorcerous lore, conducted their malicious experiments, indulged their sensuous appetites— not decadently as men of the Young Kingdoms might behave, but according to their native instincts.

Elric knew that he looked upon the ghost of a now-dead city. And he seemed to pass beyond the tower's gleaming walls and see his emperor-ancestors indulging in drug-sharpened conversation, lazily sadistic, sporting with demon-women, torturing, investigating the peculiar metabolism and psychology of the enslaved races, delving into mystic lore, absorbing a knowledge which few men of the later period could experience without falling insane.

But it was clear that this must either be a dream or vision of a netherworld which the dead of all ages inhabited, for here were emperors of many different generations. Elric knew them from their portraits: Black-ringleted Rondar IV, twelfth emperor; sharp-eyed, imperious Elric I, eightieth emperor; horror-burdened Kahan VII, three-hundred-and-twenty-ninth emperor. A dozen or more of the mightiest and wisest of his four-hundred-and-twenty-seven ancestors, including Terhali, the Green Empress, who had ruled the Bright Empire from the year 8406 after its foundation until 9011. Her longevity and green-tinged skin and hair had marked her out. She had been a powerful sorceress, even by Melnibonéan standards. She was also reputed the daughter of a union between Emperor Iuntric X and a demon.

Elric, who saw all these as if from a darkened corner of the great main chamber, observed the shimmering door of black crystal open and a newcomer enter. He started and again attempted to wake himself, without success. The man was his father, Sadric the Eighty-Sixth, a tall man with heavy-lidded eyes and a misery in him. He passed through the throng as if it did not exist. He walked directly towards Elric and stopped two paces from him. He stood looking at him, the eyes peering upwards from beneath the heavy lids and prominent brow. He was a gaunt-faced man who had been disappointed in his albino son. He had a sharp, long nose, sweeping cheekbones and a slight stoop because of his unusual height. He fingered the thin, red velvet of his robe with his delicate, beringed hands. Then he spoke in a clear whisper which, Elric remembered, it had always been his habit to employ.

"My son, are you, too, dead? I thought I'd been here but a fleeting moment and yet I see you changed in years and with a burden on you that time and fate have placed there. How did you die? In reckless combat on some upstart's foreign blade? Or in this very tower in your ivory bed? And what of Imrryr now? Does she fare well or ill, dreaming in her decline of past splendour? The line continues, as it must—I will not ask you if that part of your trust was kept. A son, of course, born of Cymoril whom you loved, for which your cousin Yyrkoon hated you."

"Father—"

The old man raised a hand that was almost transparent with age. "There is another question I must ask of you. One that has troubled all who spend their immortality in the Forest of Souls, which surrounds this shade of a city. Some of us have noticed that the city itself fades at times and its colours dim, quivering as if about to vanish. Companions of ours have passed even beyond death and, perhaps, I shudder to contemplate it, into non-existence. Even here, in the timeless region of death, unprecedented changes manifest themselves, and those of us who've dared ask the question and also give its answer fear that some tumultuous event has taken place in the world of the living. Some event, so great is it, that even here we feel our souls' extinction threatened. A legend says that until the Dreaming City dies, we ghosts may inhabit its earlier glory. Is that the news you bear to us? Is this your message? For I note on clearer observation that your body lives still and this is merely your astral body, released for a while to wander the realms of the dead."

"Father—" but already the vision was fading; already he was withdrawing back down the bellowing corridors of the cosmos, through planes of existence unknown to living men, away, away . . .

"Father!" he called, and his own voice echoed, but there was none there to make reply. And in some sense at least he was glad, for how could he answer the poor spirit and reveal to him the truth of his guesses, admit the crimes he himself was guilty of against his ancestral city, against the very blood of his forefathers? All was mist and groaning sorrow as his echoes boomed into his ears, seeming to take on their own independence and warp the word into weirder words: "F-a-a-a-ath-e-er-r-r . . . A-a-a-a-a-v-a-a-a . . . A-a-a-a-h-a-a-a-a-a . . . R-a-a-a . . . D-a-ra-va-ar-a-a . . . !"

Still, though he strove with all his being, he could not rouse himself from slumber, but felt his spirit drawn through other regions of smoky indeterminacy, through patterns of colour beyond his earthly spectrum, beyond his mind's conception.

A huge face began to take form in the mist.

"Sepiriz!" Elric recognised the face of his mentor. But the black Nihrainian, disembodied, did not appear to hear him. "Sepiriz—are *you* dead?"

The face faded, then reappeared almost at once upon the rest of the man's tall frame.

"Elric, I have discovered you at last, robed in your astral body, I see. Thank Fate, for I thought I had failed to summon you. Now we must make haste. A breach has been made in the defences of Chaos and we go to confer with the Lords of Law!"

"Where are we?"

"Nowhere as yet. We travel to the Higher Worlds. Come, hurry, I'll be your guide."

Down, down, through pits of softest wool that engulfed and comforted, through canyons that were cut between blazing mountains of light which utterly dwarfed them, through caverns of infinite blackness wherein their bodies shone and Elric knew that the dark nothingness went away in all directions for ever.

And then they seemed to stand upon an horizonless plateau, perfectly flat with occasional green and blue geometric constructions rising from it. The iridescent air was alive with shimmering patterns of energy, weaving intricate shapes that seemed very formal. And there, too, were things in human form—

things which had assumed such shape for the benefit of the men who now encountered them.

The White Lords of the Higher Worlds, enemies of Chaos, were marvellously beautiful, with bodies of such symmetry that they could not be earthly. Only Law could create such perfection and, Elric thought, such perfection defeated progress. That the twin forces complemented one another was now plainer than ever before, and for either to gain complete ascendancy over the other meant entropy or stagnation for the cosmos. Even though Law might dominate the Earth, Chaos *must* be present, and vice versa.

The Lords of Law were accoutred for war. They had made this apparent in their choice of Earthlike garb. Fine metals and silks—or their like on this plane—gleamed on their perfect bodies. Slender weapons were at their sides and their overpoweringly beautiful faces seemed to glow with purpose. The tallest stepped forward.

"So, Sepiriz, you have brought the one whose destiny it is to aid us. Greetings, Elric of Melniboné. Though spawn of Chaos you be, we have cause to welcome you. Do you recognise me? The one whom your earthly mythology calls Donblas the Justice Maker."

Immobile, Elric said: "I remember you, Lord Donblas. You are misnamed, I fear, for justice is nowhere present in the world."

"You speak of your realm as if it were all realms." Donblas smiled without rancour, though it appeared that he was unused to such impudence from a mortal. Elric remained insouciant. His ancestors had been opposed to Donblas and all his brethren, and it was still hard to consider the White Lord an ally. "I see now how you have managed to defy our opponents," Lord Donblas continued with approval. "And I grant you that justice cannot be found on Earth at this time. But I am named the Justice *Maker* and have still the will to make it when conditions change on your plane."

Elric did not look directly at Donblas, for the sight of his beauty was disturbing. "Then let's to work, my lord, and change the world as soon we may. Let's bring the novelty of justice to our sobbing realm."

"Haste, mortal, is impossible here!" It was another White Lord speaking, his pale yellow surcoat rippling over the clear steel of breastplate and greaves, the single Arrow of Law emblazoned on it.

"I'd thought the breach to Earth made," Elric frowned. "I'd thought this martial sight a sign that you prepared war against Chaos!"

"War *is* prepared—but not possible until the summons comes from your realm."

"From us! Has not Earth screamed for your aid? Have we not worked sorceries and incantations to bring you to us? What further summons do you need?"

"The ordained one," said Lord Donblas firmly.

"The ordained one? Gods! (You'll pardon me, my lords.) Is further work required of me, then?"

"One last great task, Elric," said Sepiriz softly. "As I have told you, Chaos blocks the attempts of the White Lords to gain access to our world. The Horn of Fate must be blown thrice before this business is fully terminated. The first blast will wake the Dragons of Imrryr, the second will allow the White Lords entrance to the earthly plane, the third—" he paused.

"Yes, the third?" Elric was impatient.

"The third will herald the death of our world!"

"Where lies this mighty horn?"

"In one of several realms," said Sepiriz. "A device of this kind cannot be made on our plane, therefore it has had to be constructed on a plane where logic rules over sorcery. You must journey there to locate the Horn of Fate."

"And how can I accomplish such a journey?"

Once again Lord Donblas spoke levelly. "We will give you the means. Equip yourself with sword and shield of Chaos, for they will be of some use to you, though not so powerful as in your world. Go you then to the highest point on the ruined Tower of B'aal'nezbett in Imrryr and step off into space. You will not fall—unless what little power we retain on Earth fails us."

"Comforting words, my Lord Donblas. Very well, I shall do as you decree, to satisfy my own curiosity if nought else."

Donblas shrugged. "This is only one of many worlds—almost as much a shadow as your own—but you may not approve of it. You will notice its sharpness, its clearness of outline—that will indicate that time has exerted no real influence upon it, that its structure has not been mellowed by many events. However, let me wish you safe passage, mortal, for I like you—and I have cause to thank you, too. Though you be of Chaos, you have within you several of the qualities we of Law admire. Go now—return to your mortal body and prepare yourself for the venture ahead of you."

Elric glanced at Sepiriz. The black Nihrainian stepped back three paces and disappeared into the gleaming air. Elric followed him.

Once again their astral bodies ranged the myriad planes of the supernatural universe, experiencing sensations unfamiliar to the physical mind, before, quite without warning, Elric felt suddenly heavy and opened his eyes to discover that he was in his own bed in the Tower of D'a'rputna. Through the faint light filtering between chinks in the heavy curtain thrown over the window slit, he saw the round Chaos Shield, its eight-arrowed symbol pulsing slowly as if in concert with the sun, and beside it his unholy runeblade, Stormbringer, lying against the wall as if already prepared for their journey into the might-be world of a possible future.

Then Elric slept again, more naturally, and was tormented, also, by more natural nightmares so that at last he screamed in his sleep and woke himself to find Moonglum standing by the bed. There was an expression of sad concern upon his narrow face. "What is it, Elric? What ails your slumber?"

He shuddered. "Nothing. Leave me, Moonglum, and I'll join you when I rise."

"There must be reason for such shouting. Some prophetic dream, perhaps?"

"Aye, prophetic sure enough. I thought I saw a vision of my thin blood spilt by a hand that was my own. What import has this dream, what moment? Answer that, my friend, and, if you can't, then leave me to my morbid bed until these thoughts are gone."

"Come, rouse yourself, Elric. Find forgetfulness in action. The candle of the fourteenth day burns low and Dyvim Slorm awaits your good advice."

The albino pulled himself upright and swung his trembling legs over the bed. He felt enfeebled, bereft of energy, Moonglum helped him rise. "Throw off this troubled mood and help us in our quandary," he said with a hollow levity that made his fears more plain.

"Aye," Elric straightened himself. "Hand me my sword. I need its stolen strength."

Unwillingly, Moonglum went to the wall where stood the evil weapon, took the runeblade by its scabbard and lifted it with difficulty, for it was an over-heavy sword. He shuddered as it seemed to titter faintly at him, and he presented it hilt first to his friend. Gratefully, Elric seized it, was about to pull it from the sheath when he paused. "Best leave the room before I free the blade."

Moonglum understood at once and left, not anxious to trust his life to the whim of the hellsword—or his friend.

When he was gone, Elric unsheathed the great sword and at once felt a faint tingle as its supernatural vitality began to stream into his nerves. Yet it was scarcely adequate and he knew that if the blade did not feed soon upon the lifestuff of another it would seek the souls of his two remaining friends. He replaced it thoughtfully in the scabbard, buckled it around his waist and strode to join Moonglum in the high-ceilinged corridor.

In silence, they proceeded down the twisting marble steps of the tower, until they reached the centre level where the main chamber was. Here, Dyvim Slorm was seated, a bottle of old Melnibonéan wine on the table before him, a large silver bowl in his hands. His sword Mournblade was on the table beside the bottle. They had found the store of wine in the secret cellars of the place, missed by the sea-reavers whom Elric had led upon Imrryr when he and his cousin had fought on opposite sides. The bowl was full of the congealed mixture of herbs, honey and barley which their ancestors had used to sustain themselves in times of need. Dyvim Slorm was brooding over it, but looked up when they came close and sat themselves on chairs opposite him. He smiled hopelessly.

"I fear, Elric, that I have done all I can to rouse our sleeping friends. No more is possible—and they still slumber."

Elric remembered the details of his vision and, half-afraid that it had been merely a figment of his own imaginings, supplying the fantasy of hope where, in reality, no hope was, said: "Forget the dragons, for a while at least. Last night I left my body, so I thought, and journeyed to places beyond the Earth, eventually to the White Lords' plane where they told me how I might rouse the dragons by blowing upon a horn. I intend to follow their directions and seek that horn."

Dyvim Slorm replaced his bowl upon the table. "We'll accompany you, of course."

"No need—and anyway impossible—I'll have to go alone. Wait for me until I return and if I do not—well, you must do what you decide, spending your remaining years imprisoned on this isle, or going to battle with Chaos."

"I have the idea that time has stopped in truth and if we stay here we shall live on for ever and shall be forced to face the resulting boredom," Moonglum put in. "If you don't return, I for one will ride into the conquered realms to take a few of our enemies with me to limbo."

"As you will," Elric said. "But wait for me until all your patience is ended, for I know not how long I'll be."

He stood up and they seemed a trifle startled, as if they had not until then understood the import of his words.

"Fare you well, then, my friend," said Moonglum.

"How well I fare depends on what I meet where I go," Elric smiled. "But thanks, Moonglum. Fare *you* well, good cousin, do not fret. Perhaps we'll wake the dragons yet!"

"Aye," Dyvim Slorm said with a sudden resurgence of vitality. "We shall, we shall! And their fiery venom will spread across the filth that Chaos brings, burning it clean! That day *must* come or I'm no prophet at all!"

Infected by this unexpected enthusiasm, Elric felt an increase of confidence, saluted his friends, smiled, and walked upright from the chamber, ascending the marble stairs to take the Chaos Shield from its place and go down to the gateway of the tower and pass through it, walking the jagged streets towards the magic-sundered ruin that had once been the scene of his dreadful vengeance and unwitting murder—the Tower of B'aal'nezbett.

3

Now, as Elric stood before the broken entrance of the tower, his mind was beset with bursting thoughts which fled about his skull, made overtures to his convictions and threatened to send him hopelessly to rejoin his companions. But he fought them, forced them down, forgot them, clung to his remembrance of the White Lord's assurance and passed into the shadowed shell which still had the smell of burned wood and fabric about its blackened interior.

This tower, which had formed a funeral pyre for the murdered corpse of his first love Cymoril and his warped cousin, her brother Yyrkoon, had been gutted of innards. Only the stone stairway remained and that, he noted, peering into the gloom through which rays of sunlight slanted, had collapsed before it reached the roof.

He dare not think, for thought might rob him of action. Instead, he placed a foot upon the first stair and began to climb. As he did so, a faint sound entered his ears, or it may have been that it came from within his mind. However it reached his consciousness, it sounded like a faraway orchestra tuning itself. As he climbed higher, the sound mounted, rhythmic yet discordant until, by the time he reached the final step still left intact, it thundered through his skull, pounded through his body producing a sensation of dull pain.

He paused and stared downward to the tower's floor far below. Fears beset him. He wondered whether Lord Donblas had intended him to climb to the highest point he could easily reach, or the actual point which was still some twenty feet above him. He decided it was best to take the White Lord literally and swinging the great Chaos Shield upon his back, reached above him and got his fingers into a crack in the wall, which now sloped gently inwards. He heaved himself up, his legs dangling and his feet seeking a hold. He had always been troubled by heights and disliked the sensation that came to him as he glanced down to the rubble-laden floor, eighty feet below, but he continued to climb and the climbing was made easier by the fissures in the tower's wall. Though he expected to fall, he did not, and at last reached the unsafe roof, easing himself through a hole and onto the sloping exterior. Bit by bit he climbed until he was on the highest part of the tower. Then, fearing hesitation still, he stepped outwards, over the festering streets of Imrryr far below.

The discordant music stopped. A roaring note replaced it. Swirling waves of red and black rushed towards him and then he had burst through them to find he was standing on firm turf beneath a small, pale sun, the smell of grass in his nostrils. He noted that, whereas the ancient world seen in his dream had seemed more colourful than his own, this world, in turn, contained even less colour, though it seemed to be cleaner in its outlines, in sharper focus. And the breeze that blew against his face was colder. He began to walk over the grass towards a thick forest of low, solid foliage which lay ahead. He reached the perimeter of the forest but did not enter, circumnavigating it until he came to a stream that went off into the distance, away from the forest.

He noticed with curiosity that the bright clear water appeared not to move. It was frozen, though not by any natural process that he recognised. It had all the attributes of a summer stream—yet it did not flow. Feeling that this phenomenon contrasted strangely with the rest of the scenery, he swung the round Chaos Shield onto his arm, drew his throbbing sword and began to follow the stream.

The grass gave way to gorse and rocks with the occasional clump of waving ferns of a variety he didn't recognise. Ahead, he thought he heard the tinkle of water, but here the stream was still frozen. As he passed a rock taller than the rest, he heard a voice above him.

"Elric!"

He looked up.

There, on the rock, stood a young dwarf with a long, brown beard that reached below his waist. He clutched a spear, his only weapon, and he was clad in russet breeks and jerkin with a green cap on his head and no shoes on his broad, naked feet. He had eyes like quartz that were at once hard, harsh and humorous.

"That's my name," Elric said quizzically. "Yet how is it you know me?"

"I am not of this world myself—at least, not exactly. I have no existence in time as you know it, but move here and there in the shadow worlds that the gods make. It is my nature to do so. In return for allowing me to exist, the gods sometimes use me as a messenger. My name is Jermays the Crooked, as unfinished as these worlds themselves." He clambered down the rock and stood looking up at Elric.

"What's your purpose here?" asked the albino.

"Methought you sought the Horn of Fate?"

"True. Know you where it lies?"

"Aye," smiled the young dwarf sardonically. "It's buried with the still-living corpse of a hero of this realm—a warrior they call Roland. Possibly yet another incarnation of the Champion Eternal."

"An outlandish name."

"No more than yours to other ears. Roland, save that his life was not so doom-beset, is your counterpart in his own realm. He met his death in a valley not far from here, trapped and betrayed by a fellow warrior. The horn was with him then and he blew it once before he died. Some say that the echoes still resound through the valley, and will resound for ever, though Roland perished many years ago. The horn's full purpose is unknown here—and was unknown even to Roland. It is called Olifant and, with his magic sword Durandana, was buried with him in the monstrous grave mound that you see yonder."

The dwarf pointed into the distance and Elric saw that he indicated something he had earlier taken to be a large hillock.

"And what must I do to gain this horn?" he asked.

The dwarf grinned with a hint of malice in his voice. "You must match that bodkin there 'gainst Roland's Durandana. His was consecrated by the Forces of Light whereas yours was forged by the Forces of Darkness. It should be an interesting conflict."

"You say he's dead—then how can he fight me?"

"He wears the horn by a thong about his neck. If you attempt to remove it, he will defend his ownership, waking from the deathless sleep that seems to be the lot of most heroes in this world."

Elric smiled. "It seems to me they must be short of heroes if they have to preserve them in that manner."

"Perhaps," the dwarf answered carelessly, "for there are a dozen or more who lie sleeping somewhere in this land alone. They are supposed to awaken only when a desperate need arises, yet I've known unpleasant things to happen and still they have slept. It could be they await the end of their world, which the gods may destroy if it proves unsuitable, in which case they will fight to prevent such a happening. It is merely a poorly conceived theory of my own and of little weight. Perhaps the legends arise from some dim knowledge of the fate of the Champion Eternal."

The dwarf bobbed a cynical bow and, hefting his spear, saluted Elric. "Farewell, Elric of Melniboné. When you wish to return I will be here to lead you—and return you must, whether alive or dead, for, as you are probably aware, your very presence, your physical appearance itself, contradicts this environment. Only one thing fits here . . ."

"What's that?"

"Your sword."

"My sword! Strange, I should have thought that would be the last thing." He shook a growing idea out of his mind. He did not have time to speculate. "I've no liking to be here," he commented as the dwarf clambered over the rocks. He glanced in the direction of the great burial mound and began to advance towards it. Beside him he saw that the stream was moving naturally and he had the impression that though Law influenced this world, it was to some extent still forced to deal with the disrupting influence of Chaos.

The grave barrow, he could now see, was fenced about with giant slabs of unadorned stone. Beyond the stones were olive trees that had dull jewels hanging from their branches, and beyond them, through the leafy apertures, Elric saw a tall, curved entrance blocked by gates of brass embossed with gold.

"Though strong, Stormbringer," he said to his sword, "I wonder if you'll be strong enough to war in this world as well as giving my body vitality. Let's test you."

He advanced to the gate and drawing back his arm delivered a mighty blow upon it with the runesword. The metal rang and a dent appeared. Again he struck, this time holding the sword with both hands, but then a voice cried from his right.

"What demon would disturb dead Roland's rest?"

"Who speaks the language of Melniboné?" Elric retorted boldly.

"I speak the language of demons, for I perceive that is what you are. I know of no Mulnebooney and am well-versed in the ancient mysteries."

"A proud boast," said Elric, who had not yet seen the speaker. She emerged, then, from around the barrow, and stood staring at him from out of her glowing green eyes. She had a long, beautiful face and was almost as pale as himself, though her hair was jet-black. "What's your name?" he asked. "And are you a native of this world?"

"I am named Vivian, an enchantress, but earthly enough. Your Master knows the name of Vivian who once loved Roland, though he was too upright to indulge her, for she is immortal and a witch." She laughed good-humouredly. "Therefore I am familiar with demons of your like and do not fear you. Aroint thee! Aroint thee—or shall I call Bishop Turpin to exorcise thee?"

"Some of your words," said Elric courteously, "are unfamiliar and the speech of my folk much garbled. Are you some guardian of this hero's tomb?"

"Self-made guardian, aye. Now go!" She pointed towards the stone slabs.

"That is not possible. The corpse within has something of value to me. The Horn of Fate we call it, but you know it by another name."

"Olifant! But that's a blessed instrument. No demon would dare touch it. Even I . . ."

"I am no demon. I'm sufficiently human, I swear. Now stand aside. This cursed door resists my efforts too well."

"Aye," she said thoughtfully. "You could be a man—though an unlikely one. But the white face and hair, the red eyes, the tongue you speak . . ."

"Sorcerer I be, but no demon. Please—stand aside."

She looked carefully into his face and her look disturbed him. He took her by her shoulder. She felt real enough, yet somehow she had little real *presence*. It was as if she were far away rather than close to him. They stared at one another, both curious, both troubled. He whispered: "What knowledge could you have of my language? Is this world a dream of mine or of the gods? It seems scarcely tangible. Why?"

She heard him. "Say you so of us? What of your ghostly self? You seem an apparition from the dead past!"

"From the past! Aha—and *you* are of the future, as yet unformed. Perhaps that brings us to a conclusion?"

She did not pursue the topic but said suddenly: "Stranger, you will never break this door down. If you can touch Olifant, that speaks of you as mortal, despite your appearance. You must need the horn for an important task."

Elric smiled. "Aye—for if I do not take it back whence it came, you will never exist!"

She frowned. "Hints! Hints! I feel close to a discovery yet cannot grasp why, and that's unusual for Vivian. Here—" she took a big key from her gown and offered it to him—"this is the key to open Roland's tomb. It is the only one. I had to kill to get it, but oftimes I venture into the gloom of his grave to stare down at his face and pine that I might revive him and keep him living for ever on my island home. Take the horn! Rouse him—and when he has slain you, he will come to me and my warmth, my offer of everlasting life, rather than lie in that cold place again. Go—be slain by Roland!"

He took the key.

"Thanks, Lady Vivian. If it were possible to convince one who in truth did not yet exist, I would tell you that Roland's slaying of me would be worse for you than if I am successful."

He put the large key in the lock and it turned easily. The doors swung open and he saw that a long, low-roofed corridor twisted before him. Unhesitatingly, he advanced down it towards a flickering light that he could see through the cold and misty gloom. Yet, as he walked, it was as if he glided in a dream less real than that he had experienced the previous night. Now he entered the funeral chamber, illuminated by tall candles surrounding the bier of a man who lay upon it dressed in armour of a crude and unfamiliar design, a huge broadsword, almost as large as Stormbringer gripped to his chest and, upon the hilt, attached to his neck by a silver chain—the Horn of Fate, Olifant!

The man's face, seen in the candlelight, was strange; old and yet with a youthful appearance, the brow smooth and the features unlined.

Elric took Stormbringer in his left hand and reached out to grasp the horn. He made no attempt at caution, but wrenched it off Roland's neck.

A great roar came from the hero's throat. Immediately he had raised himself to a sitting position, the sword shifting into his two hands, his legs swinging off the bier. His eyes widened as he saw Elric with the horn in his hands, and he jumped at the albino, the sword Durandana whistling downwards towards Elric's head. He raised the shield and blocked the blow, slipped the horn into his jerkin and, backing away, returned Stormbringer to his right hand. Roland was now shouting something in a language completely unfamiliar to Elric. He did not bother trying to understand, since the angry tones were sufficient to tell him the knight was not suggesting a peaceful negotiation. He continued defending himself without once carrying the offensive to Roland, backing inch by inch down the long tunnel towards the barrow's mouth. Every time Durandana struck the Chaos Shield, both sword and shield gave out wild notes of great intensity. Implacably the hero continued to press Elric backwards, his broadsword whirling and striking the shield, sometimes the blade, with fantastic strength. Then they had broken into daylight and Roland seemed momentarily blinded. Elric glimpsed Vivian watching them eagerly for it appeared Roland was winning.

However, in daylight and with no chance of avoiding the angered knight, Elric retaliated with all the energy he had been saving until this moment. Shield high, sword swinging, he now took the attack, surprising Roland who was evidently unused to this behaviour on the part of an opponent. Stormbringer snarled as it bit into Roland's poorly forged armour of iron, riveted with big unsightly nails, painted on the front with a dull red cross that was a scarcely adequate insignia for so famous a hero. But there was no mistaking Durandana's powers for, though seemingly as crudely forged as the armour, it did not lose its edge and threatened to bite through the Chaos Shield with every stroke. Elric's left arm was numb from the blows and his right arm ached. Lord Donblas had not lied to him when he had said that the strength of his weapons would be diminished on this world.

Roland paused, shouting something, but Elric did not heed him, seized his opportunity and rushed in to crush his shield against Roland's body. The knight reeled and staggered, his sword giving off a keening note. Elric struck at a gap between Roland's helmet and gorget. The head sprang off the shoulders and rolled grotesquely away, but no blood pumped from the jugular. The eyes of the head remained open, staring at Elric.

Vivian screamed and shouted something in the same language which Roland had used. Elric stepped back, his face grim.

"Oh, his legend, his legend!" she cried. "The only hope the people have is that Roland will some day ride once more to their aid. Now you have slain him! Fiend!"

"Possessed I may be," he said quietly as she sobbed by the headless corpse, "but I was ordained by the gods to do this work. I'll take my leave of your drab world, now."

"Have you no sorrow for the crime you've done?"

"None, madam, for this is only one of many such acts which, I'm told, serve some greater purpose. That I sometimes doubt the truth of this consolation need not concern you. Know you this, though, I have been told that it is the fate of such as your Roland and myself never to die—always to be reborn. Farewell."

And he walked away from there; passed through the olive grove and the tall stones, the Horn of Fate cold against his heart.

He followed the river towards the high rock where he saw a small figure poised and, when he reached it, looked up at the young dwarf Jermays the Crooked, took the horn from his jerkin and displayed it.

Jermays chuckled. "So Roland is dead, and you, Elric, have left a fragment of a legend in this world, if it survives. Well, shall I escort you back to your own place?"

"Aye, and hurry."

Jermays skipped down the rocks and stood beside the tall albino. "Hmm," he mused, "that horn could prove troublesome to us. Best replace it in your jerkin and keep it covered by your shield."

Elric obeyed the dwarf and followed him down to the banks of the strangely frozen river. It looked as if it should have been moving, but it evidently was not. Jermays leapt into it and, incredibly, began to sink. "Quickly! Follow!"

Elric stepped in after him and for a moment stood on the frozen water before he, also, began to sink.

Though the stream was shallow, they continued to sink until all similarity to water was gone and they were passing down into rich darkness that became warm and heavy-scented. Jermays pulled at his sleeve. "This way!" And they shot off at right angles, darting from side to side, up and down, through a maze that apparently only Jermays could see. Against his chest, the horn seemed to heave and he pressed his shield to it. Then he blinked as he found himself in the light again, staring at the great red sun throbbing in the dark blue sky. His feet were on something solid. He looked and saw that it was the Tower of B'aal'nezbett. For a while longer the horn heaved as if alive, like a trapped bird but, after some moments, it became quiescent.

Elric lowered himself to the roof and began to edge down it until he came to the gap through which he had passed earlier.

Then suddenly he looked up as he heard a noise in the sky. There, his feet planted on air, stood grinning Jermays the Crooked. "I'll be passing on, for I like not this world at all." He chuckled. "It has been a pleasure to have had a part in this. Goodbye, Sir Champion. Remember me, the unfinished one, to the Lords of the Higher Worlds—and perhaps you could hint to them that the sooner they improve their memories or else their creative powers, the sooner I shall be happy."

Elric said: "Perhaps you'd best be content with your lot, Jermays. There are disadvantages to stability, too."

Jermays shrugged and vanished.

Slowly, all but spent, Elric descended the fractured wall and, with great relief, reached the first stair to stumble down the rest and run back to the Tower of D'a'rputna with the news of his success.

4

The three thoughtful men left the city and went down to the Dragon Caves. On a new silver chain, the Horn of Fate was slung around Elric's neck. He was dressed in black leather, with his head unprotected save for a golden circlet that kept his hair from his eyes. Stormbringer scabbarded at his side, the Chaos Shield on his back, he led his companions into the grottoes, to come eventually to the slumbering bulk of Flamefang the Phoorn Leader. His lungs seemed to have insufficient capacity as he drew air into them and grasped the horn. Then he glanced at his friends, who regarded him expectantly, straddled his legs slightly and blew with all his strength into the horn.

The note sounded, deep and sonorous, and as it reverberated through the caverns, he felt all his vitality draining from him. Weaker and weaker he became until he sank to his knees, the horn still at his lips, the note failing, his vision dimming, his limbs shaking, and then he sprawled face down on the rock, the horn clattering beside him.

Moonglum dashed towards him and gasped as he saw the bulk of the leading dragon stir and one huge, unblinking eye, as cold as the Northern wastes, stare at him.

Dyvim Slorm yelled jubilantly: "Flamefang! Brother Flamefang, you wake!"

All about him he saw the other Phoorn stirring also, shaking their wings and straightening their slender necks, ruffling their horny crests. Moonglum felt smaller than usual as the dragons wakened. He began to feel nervous of the huge beasts, wondering how they would respond to the presence of one who was not a Dragon Master. Then he remembered the enervated albino and knelt beside Elric, touching his leathern-covered shoulder.

"Elric! D'you live?"

Elric groaned and tried to turn over onto his back. Moonglum helped him sit upright. "I'm weak, Moonglum—so weak I can't rise. The horn took all my energy!"

"Draw your sword—it will supply what you need."

Elric shook his head. "I'll take your advice, though I doubt whether you're right this time. That hero I slew must have been soulless, or else his soul was well-protected, for I gained nothing from him."

His hand fumbled towards his hip and grasped Stormbringer's hilt. With a tremendous effort, he drew it from the scabbard and felt a faint flowing leave it and enter him, but not enough to allow him any great exertion. He got up and staggered towards Flamefang. The monster recognised him and rustled its wings by way of welcome, its hard, solemn eyes seeming to warm slightly. As he moved round to pat its neck, he staggered and fell to one knee, rising with effort.

In earlier times there had been slaves to saddle the dragons but now they would have to saddle their beasts themselves. They went to the saddle-store and chose the *skeffla'an* they needed, for each was designed for an individual beast. Elric could scarcely bear the weight of Flamefang's elaborately carved saddle of membraneous wood, steel, jewels and precious metals. He was forced to drag it across the cavern floor. Not wishing to embarrass him with their glances, the other two ignored his impotent struggling and busied themselves with their own *skeffla'an*. The dragons must have understood that Moonglum was a friend, for they did not demur when he cautiously approached to dress his dragon with its high wooden saddle with silver stirrups and sheathed, lancelike goad from which was draped the pennant of a noble family of Melniboné, now all dead.

When they had finished saddling their own beasts, they went to help Elric who was half-falling with weariness, his back leaning against Flamefang's scaly body. While they tied the girths, Dyvim Slorm said: "Will you have strength enough to lead us?"

Elric sighed. "Aye—enough, I think, for that. But I know I'll have none for the ensuing battle. There must be *some* means of gaining vitality."

"What of the herbs you once used?"

"Those I had have lost their properties, and there are no fresh ones to be found now that Chaos has warped plant, rock and ocean with its dreadful stamp."

Leaving Moonglum to finish Flamefang's saddling, Dyvim Slorm went away to return with a cup of liquid which he hoped would help revivify Elric. Elric drank it, gave the cup back to Dyvim Slorm and reached up to grasp the saddle-pommel, hauling himself into the saddle. "Bring straps," he ordered.

"Straps?" Dyvim Slorm frowned.

"Aye. If I'm not secured in my *skeffla'a*, I'll likely fall to the ground before we've flown a mile."

So he sat in the tall saddle and gripped the goad which bore his blue, green and silver pennant, gripped it in his gauntleted hand and waited until they came with the straps and bound him firmly into place. He gave a slight smile and shook the dragon's halter. "Forward, Flamefang, lead the way for your brothers and sisters."

With folded wings and lowered head, the dragon began to walk its slithering way to the exit. Behind it, on two dragons almost as large, sat Dyvim Slorm and Moonglum, their faces grimly concerned, watchful for Elric's safety. As Flamefang moved with rolling gait through the series of caverns, its fellow beasts fell in behind it until all of them had reached the great mouth of the last cave which overlooked the threshing sea. The sun was still in its position overhead, scarlet and swollen, seeming to swell in rhythm with the movement of the sea. Voicing a shout that was half-hiss, half-yell, Elric slapped at Flamefang's neck with his goad.

"Up, Flamefang! Up for Melniboné and vengeance!"

As if sensing the strangeness of the world, Flamefang paused on the brink of the ledge, shaking his head and snorting to himself. Then, as he launched into the air, his wings began to beat, their fantastic spread flapping with slow grace but bearing the beast along with marvellous speed.

Up, up, beneath the swollen sun, up into the hot, turbulent air, up towards the East where the camps of hell were waiting. And in Flamefang's wake came its two Phoorn brothers, bearing Moonglum and Dyvim Slorm who had a horn of his own, the one used to direct the dragons. Ninety-five other dragons, males and females, darkened the deep blue sky, all green, red and gold, scales clashing and flashing, wings beating and, in concert, sounding like the throbbing of a million drums as they flew over the unclean waters with gaping jaws and cold, cold eyes.

Though beneath him now Elric saw with blurring eyes many colours of immense richness, they were all dark and changing constantly, shifting from one extreme of a dark spectrum to the other. It was not water down there now—it was a fluid composed of materials both natural and supernatural, real and abstract. Pain, longing, misery and laughter could be seen as tangible fragments of the tossing tide, passions and frustrations lay in it also, as well as stuff made of living flesh that bubbled on occasions to the surface.

In his weakened condition, the sight of the fluid sickened Elric and he turned his red eyes upwards and towards the East as the dragons moved swiftly on their course.

Soon they were flying across what had once been the mainland of the Eastern Continent, the major Vilmirian peninsula. But now it was bereft of its earlier qualities and huge columns of dark mist rose into the air so that they were forced to guide their reptilian steeds among them. Lava streamed, bubbling, on the faraway ground, disgusting shapes flitted over land and air, monstrous beasts and the occasional group of weird riders on skeletal horses who looked up when they heard the beat of the dragon wings and rode in frantic fear towards their camps.

The world seemed a corpse, given life in corruption by virtue of the vermin which fed upon it.

MICHAEL MOORCOCK

Of mankind nothing was left, save for the three mounted on the dragons.

Elric knew that Jagreen Lern and his human allies had long since forsaken their humanity and could no longer claim kinship with the species their hordes had swept from the world. The leaders alone might retain their human shape, the Dark Lords don it, but their souls were warped just as the bodies of their followers had become warped into hell-shapes due to the transmuting influence of Chaos. All the dark powers of Chaos lay upon the world, yet deeper and deeper into its heart went the dragon flight, with Elric swaying in his saddle and only stopped from falling by the straps that bound his body. From the lands below there seemed to rise an aching shriek as tortured nature was defied and its components forced into alien forms.

Onward they sped, towards what had once been Karlaak by the Weeping Waste and which was now the Camp of Chaos. Then, from above, they heard a cawing yell and saw black shapes dropping down on them. Elric had not even strength to cry out, but weakly tapped Flamefang's neck and made the beast veer away from the danger. Moonglum and Dyvim Slorm followed his example and Dyvim Slorm sounded his horn, ordering the dragons not to engage the attackers, but some of the Phoorn in the rear were too late and were forced to turn and battle with the black phantoms.

Elric looked behind him and, for a few seconds, saw them outlined against the sky, rending things with the jaws of whales, locked in combat with the Phoorn that shot their flaming venom at them and tore at them with teeth and claws, wings flapping as they strove to hold their height, but then another wave of dark green mist spread across his field of vision and he did not see the fate that befell the dozen dragons.

Now Elric signalled Flamefang to fly low over a small army of riders fleeing through the tormented land, the eight-arrowed standard of Chaos flapping from their leader's encrusted lance. Down they went and loosed their venom, having the satisfaction of seeing the beasts and riders scream, burn and perish, their ashes absorbed into the shifting ground.

Here and there, now, they saw a gigantic castle, newly raised by sorcery, perhaps as a reward to some traitor king who had aided Jagreen Lern, perhaps as the keeps of the Captains of Chaos who, now that Chaos ruled, were establishing themselves on Earth. They swept down on them, released their venom and left them burning with unnatural fires, the gouting smoke blending with the shredding mist. And at last Elric saw the Camp of Chaos—a city but recently made in the same manner as the castles, the flaring Sign of Chaos hanging amber in the sky overhead. Yet he felt no elation, only despair that he was so weak he would not have the strength to meet his enemy Jagreen Lern in combat. What could he do? How could strength be found—for, even if he took no part in the fighting, he must have sufficient vitality to blow the horn a second time and summon the White Lords to Earth.

The city seemed peculiarly silent as if it waited or prepared for something. It had an ominous atmosphere and Elric, before Flamefang crossed the perimeter, made his dragon steed turn and circle.

Dyvim Slorm and Moonglum and the rest of the Phoorn flight followed his example and Dyvim Slorm called across the air to him. "What now, Elric? I had not expected a *city* to be here so soon!"

"Neither had I. But look—" he pointed with a trembling hand he could hardly lift, "there's Jagreen Lern's Merman standard. And there—" now he pointed to the left and right, "the standards of a score of the Dukes of Hell! Yet I see no other human standards."

Moonglum shouted: "Those castles we destroyed. I suspect that Jagreen Lern has already divided up these sundered lands and given them to his hirelings. How can we tell how much time has really passed—time in which all this could have been brought about?"

"True," Elric nodded, looking up at the still sun. He lurched forward in his saddle, half-swooning, pulled himself upright, breathing heavily. The Chaos Shield seemed like a huge weight on his arm, but he held it warily before him.

Then he acted on impulse and goaded Flamefang into speed so that the Phoorn rushed towards the city, diving down towards the castle of Jagreen Lern.

Nothing sought to stop him and he landed the beast among the turrets of the castle. Silence was dominant. He looked around, puzzled, but could see nothing save the towering buildings of dark stone that seemed to ooze beneath Flamefang's feet.

The straps stopped him from dismounting, but he saw enough to be sure the city was deserted. Where was the horde of hell? Where was Jagreen Lern?

Dyvim Slorm and Moonglum came to join him, while the rest of the dragons circled above. Claws scratched on rock, wings slashed the air and they settled, turning their mighty heads this way and that, ruffling their scales restlessly for, once aroused from their slumber, the dragons preferred the air to the land.

Dyvim Slorm stayed but long enough to mutter: "I'll scout the city," and then was flying away again, low amongst the castles until they heard him cry out and saw him swoop out of sight. There came a yell, but they could not see what caused it, a pause, and then Dyvim Slorm's dragon was flapping up again and they saw he had a writhing prisoner slung over the front of his saddle. He landed. The thing he had captured bore resemblance to a human being, but was misshapen and ugly with a jutting underlip, low forehead and no chin; huge, square, uneven teeth bristled in its mouth and its bare arms were covered in waving hairs.

"Where are your masters?" Dyvim Slorm demanded.

The thing seemed to possess no fear, but chuckled: "They predicted your coming and, since the city limits movement, have assembled their armies on a plateau they have made five miles to the north-east." It turned its dilated eyes to Elric. "Jagreen Lern sent greetings and said he anticipated your foolish downfall."

Elric shrugged.

Dyvim Slorm drew his own runeblade and hacked the creature down. It cackled as it died, for its sanity had fled with its fear. He shivered as the thing's soul-stuff blended with his own and passed extra energy to him. Then he cursed and looked at Elric with pain in his eyes.

"I acted in haste—I should have given him to you."

Elric said nothing to this but whispered in his failing voice: "Let's to their battlefield. Hurry!"

Up to join their flight they went again, into the rushing, populated air and towards the north-east.

It was with astonishment that they sighted Jagreen Lern's horde, for they could not understand how it could have managed to regroup itself so swiftly. Every fiend and warrior on Earth seemed to have come to fight under the Theocrat's standard. It clung like a vile disease to the undulating plain. And around it, clouds grew darker, even though lightning, obviously of supernatural origin, blossomed and shouted, criss-crossing the plain.

Into this noisy agitation swept the dragon flight and they recognised the force commanded by Jagreen Lern himself for his banner flew above it. Other divisions were commanded by Dukes of Hell—Malohin, Zhortra, Xiombarg and others. Also Elric noted the three oldest and wisest Lords of Chaos, dwarfing the rest. Chardros the Reaper with his great head and his curving scythe, Mabelode the Faceless with his face always in shadow no matter which way you looked at it, and Slortar the Old, slim and beautiful, reputed the oldest of the gods. This was a force which a thousand powerful sorcerers would find it hard to defend against, and the thought of attacking them seemed folly.

Elric did not bother to consider this for he had embarked on his plan and was committed to carrying it through even though, in his present condition, he was bound to destroy himself if he continued.

They had the advantage of attacking from the air, but this would only be of value while the dragons' venom lasted. When it gave out, they must go in closer. At that moment Elric would need much energy—and he had none.

Down swept the dragons, shooting their incendiary venom into the ranks of Chaos.

Normally, no army could stand against such an attack but, protected by sorcery, Chaos was able to turn much of the fiery venom aside. The venom seemed to spread against an invisible shield and dissipate. Some of it struck its target, however, and hundreds of warriors were engulfed in flame and died blazing.

Again and again the dragons rose and dived upon their enemies, Elric swaying almost unconscious in his saddle, his awareness of what was going on diminishing with every attack.

His dimming vision was further encumbered by the stinking smoke that had begun to rise off the battlefield. From the horde, huge lances were rising with seeming slowness, lances of Chaos like streaks of amber lightning striking at the Phoorn so that the beasts hit bellowed and hurtled dead to the ground. Closer and closer Elric's steed bore him until he was flying over the division commanded by Jagreen Lern himself. He caught a misty glimpse of the Theocrat sitting a repulsive, hairless horse and waving his sword, convulsed with mocking mirth. He faintly heard his enemy's voice drift up to him.

"Farewell, Elric—this is our last encounter, for today you go to limbo!"

Elric turned Flamefang about and whispered into his ear: "That one, brother—that one!"

With a roar, Flamefang loosed his venom at the laughing Theocrat. It seemed to Elric that Jagreen Lern must surely be burned to ashes, but just as the venom seemed to touch him, it was hurled back and only a few drops struck some of the Theocrat's retainers, igniting their flesh and clothing.

Still Jagreen Lern laughed and now he released an amber spear which had appeared in his hand. Straight towards Elric it went and, with difficulty, the albino put up his Chaos Shield to deflect it.

So great was the force of the bolt striking his shield that he was hurled backwards in his saddle and one of the straps securing him snapped so that he fell to the left and was only saved by the other strap that had held. Now he crouched behind the shield's protection as it was battered with supernatural weapons. Flamefang, too, was encompassed by the shield's great power; but how long would even the Chaos Shield resist such an attack?

It seemed that he was forced to use the shield for an infinite time before Flamefang's wings cracked the air like a ship's sail and he was rushing high above the horde.

He was dying.

Minute by minute the vitality was leaving him as if he were an old man ready for death. "I cannot die," he muttered, "I must not die. Is there no escape from this dilemma?"

Flamefang seemed to hear him. The dragon descended towards the ground again and dropped until its scaly belly was scraping the lances of the horde. Then the Phoorn had landed on the unstable ground and waited with folded wings as a group of warriors goaded their beasts towards him.

Elric gasped: "What have you done, Flamefang? Is nothing dependable? You have delivered me into the hands of the enemy!"

With great effort he drew his sword as the first lance struck his shield and the rider passed, grinning, sensing Elric's weakness. Others came on both sides. Weakly, he slashed at one and Stormbringer suddenly took control to make his aim true. The rider's arm was pierced and he was locked to the blade as it fed, greedily, upon his lifestuff. Immediately, Elric felt some slight return of strength and realised that between them dragon and sword were helping him gain the energy he needed. But the blade kept the most part to itself. There was a reason for this, as Elric found out at once, for the sword continued to direct his arm. Several more riders were slain in this manner and Elric grinned as he felt the vitality flowing back into his body. His vision cleared, his reactions became normal, his spirits rose. Now he carried the attack to the rest of the division, Flamefang moving over the ground with a speed belying his bulk. The warriors scattered and fled back to rejoin the main force, but Elric no longer cared, he had the souls of a dozen of them and it was enough. "Now up, Flamefang! Rise and let us seek out more powerful enemies!"

Obediently Flamefang spread his wings. They began to flap and bear him off the ground until he was gliding low over the horde.

In the midst of Lord Xiombarg's division, Elric landed again, dismounted from Flamefang and, possessed of his supernatural energy, rushed into the ranks of fiendish warriors, hewing about him, invulnerable to all but the strongest attack of Chaos. Vitality mounted and a kind of battle madness with it. Further and further into the ranks he sliced his way, until he saw Lord

Xiombarg in his earthly guise of a slender, dark-haired woman. Elric knew that the woman's shape was no indication of Xiombarg's mighty strength but, without fear, he leapt towards the Duke of Hell and stood before him, looking up at where he sat on his lion-headed, bull-bodied mount.

Xiombarg's girl's voice came sweetly to Elric's ears. "Mortal, you have defied many Dukes of Hell and banished others back to the Higher Worlds. They call you godslayer now, so I've heard. Can you slay me?"

"You know that no mortal can slay one of the Lords of the Higher Worlds whether they be of Law or Chaos, Xiombarg—but he can, if equipped with sufficient power, destroy their earthly semblance and send them back to their own plane, never to return!"

"Can you do this to me?"

"Let us see!" Elric flung himself towards the Dark Lord.

Xiombarg was armed with a long-shafted battle-axe that gave off a night-blue radiance. As his steed reared, he swung the axe down at Elric's unprotected head. The albino flung up his shield and the axe struck it. A kind of metallic shout came from the weapons and huge sparks flew away. Elric moved in close and hacked at one of Xiombarg's feminine legs. A light moved down from his hips and protected the leg so that Stormbringer was brought to a stop, jarring Elric's arm. Again the axe struck the shield with the same effect as before. Again Elric tried to pierce Xiombarg's unholy defence. And all the while he heard the Dark Lord's laughter, sweetly modulated, yet as horrible as a hag's.

"Your mockery of human shape and human beauty begins to fail, my lord!" cried Elric, standing back for a moment to gather his strength.

Already the girl's face was writhing and changing as, disconcerted by Elric's power, the Duke of Hell spurred his beast down on the albino.

Elric dodged aside and struck again. This time Stormbringer throbbed in his hand as it pierced Xiombarg's defence and the Dark Lord moaned, retaliating with another axe-blow which Elric barely succeeded in blocking. He turned his beast, the axe rushing about his head as he whirled it and flung it at Elric with the intention of striking him in the head.

Elric ducked and put up his shield, the axe clipping it and falling to the shifting ground. He ran after Xiombarg who was once again turning his steed. From nowhere he had produced another weapon, a huge double-handed broadsword, the breadth of its blade triple that of even Stormbringer's. It seemed incongruous in the small, delicate hands of the girl-shape. And its size, Elric guessed, told something of its power. He backed away warily, noting absently that one of the Dark Lord's legs was missing and replaced by an insect's claw. If he could only destroy the rest of Xiombarg's disguise, he would have succeeded in banishing him.

Now Xiombarg's laughter was no longer sweet, but had an unhinged note. The lion-head roared in unison with its master's voice as it rushed towards Elric. The monstrous sword went up and crashed upon the Chaos Shield. Elric fell on his back, feeling the ground itch and crawl beneath him, but the shield was still in one piece. He caught sight of the bull-hoofs pounding down on him, drew himself beneath the shield, leaving only his sword-arm free. As the beast thundered above, seeking to crush him with its hoofs, he thrust upwards into its belly. The sword was initially halted and then seemed to pierce through whatever obstructed it and draw out the life-force. The vitality of the unholy beast passed from sword to man and Elric was taken aback by its strange, insensate quality, for the soul-stuff of an animal was different from that of an intelligent protagonist. He rolled from under the beast's bulk and sprang to his feet as the lion-bull collapsed, hurling Xiombarg's still-earthly shape to the ground.

Instantly the Dark Lord was up, standing with a peculiarly unbalanced stance with one leg human and the other alien. It limped swiftly towards Elric, bringing the huge sword round in a sideways movement that would slice Elric in two. But Elric, full of the energy gained from Xiombarg's steed, leapt back from the blow and struck at the sword with Stormbringer. The two blades met, but neither gave. Stormbringer shrieked in anger for it was unused to resistance of this kind. Elric got the rim of his shield under the blade and forced it up. For an instant Xiombarg's guard was open and Elric used that instant with effect, driving Stormbringer into the Dark Lord's breast with all his strength.

Xiombarg whimpered and at once his earthly shape began to dissolve as Elric's sword sucked his energy into itself. Elric knew that this energy was only that fraction constituting Xiombarg's life-force on this plane, that the major part of the Dark Lord's soul was still in the Higher Worlds for not even the most powerful of these godlings could summon the power to transport all of himself to the Earth. If Elric had taken every scrap of Xiombarg's soul, his own body could not have retained it but would have burst. However, so much more powerful than any human soul was the force flowing into him from the wound he had made that he was once again the vessel for a mighty energy.

Xiombarg changed. He became little more than a flickering coil of coloured light which began to drift away and finally vanish as Xiombarg was swept, raging, back to his own plane.

Elric looked upwards. He was horrified to see that only a few of the Phoorn survived. One was fluttering down now and it had a rider on its back. From that distance he could not see which of his friends it was.

He began to run towards the place where it fell.

He heard the crash as it came to ground, heard a weird wailing, a bubbling cry and then nothing.

He battled his way through the milling warriors of Chaos and none could withstand him, until he came at last to the fallen Phoorn. There was a broken body lying on the ground beside it, but of the runeblade there was no sign. It had vanished.

It was the body of his cousin Dyvim Slorm, last of his kinsmen.

There was no time for mourning. Elric and Moonglum and the bare score of remaining dragons could not possibly win against Jagreen Lern's strength, which had been hardly touched by the attack. Standing over the body of his cousin, he placed the Horn of Fate to his lips, took a huge breath and blew. The clear, melancholy note of the horn rang out over the battlefield and seemed to carry in all directions, through all the dimensions of the cosmos, through all the myriad planes and existences, through all eternity to the ends of the multiverse and the ends of time itself.

The note took long moments to fade and, when it had at last died away, there was an absolute hush over the world, the milling millions were still, there was an air of expectancy.

And then the White Lords came.

5

It was as if some enormous sun, thousands of times larger than Earth's, had sent a ray of light pulsing through the cosmos, defying the flimsy barriers of time and space, to strike upon that great black battlefield. And along it, appearing on the pathway that the horn's weird power had created for them, strode the majestic Lords of Law, their earthly forms so beautiful that they challenged Elric's sanity, for his mind could scarcely absorb the sight. They disdained to ride, like the Lords of Chaos, on bizarre beasts, but moved without steeds, a magnificent assembly with their mirror-clear armour and rippling surcoats bearing the single Arrow of Law.

Leading them came Donblas the Justice Maker, a smile upon his perfect lips. He carried a slender sword in his right hand, a sword that was straight and sharp and like a beam of light itself.

Elric moved swiftly then, rushed to where Flamefang awaited him and urged the great reptile into the moaning air.

Flamefang moved with less ease than earlier, but Elric did not know whether it was because the beast was tired or whether the influence of Law was weighing on the Phoorn which was, after all, a likely creation of Chaos.

But at last he flew beside Moonglum and, looking around, saw that the remaining dragons had turned and were flying back to the West. Only their own steeds remained. Perhaps the last of the dragons had sensed their part played and were returning to the Dragon Caves to sleep again.

Elric and Moonglum exchanged glances but said nothing, for the sight below was too awe-inspiring to speak of.

A light, white and dazzling, spread from the midst of the Lords of Law, the beam upon which they had come faded, and they began to move towards the spot where Chardros the Reaper, Mabelode the Faceless, and Slortar the Old and the lesser Lords of Chaos had assembled themselves, ready for the great fight.

As the White Lords passed through the other denizens of hell and the polluted men who were their comrades, these creatures backed away screaming, falling where the radiance touched them. The dross was being cleaned away without effort—but the real strength in the shape of the Dukes of Hell and Jagreen Lern was still to be encountered.

Though at this stage the Lords of Law were scarcely taller than the human beings, they seemed to dwarf them and even Elric, high above, felt as if he were a tiny figure, scarcely larger than a fly. It was not their *size* so much as the implication of vastness which they seemed to carry with them.

Flamefang's wings beat wearily as he circled over the scene. All around him the dark colours were now full of clouds of lighter, softer shades.

The Lords of Law reached the spot where their ancient enemies were assembled and Elric heard Lord Donblas's voice carry up to him.

"You of Chaos have defied the edict of the Cosmic Balance and sought complete dominance of this planet. Destiny denies you this—for the Earth's life is over and it must be resurrected in a new form where your influence will be weak."

A sweet, mocking voice came from the ranks of Chaos. It was the voice of Slortar the Old. "You presume too much, brother. The fate of the Earth has not yet been finally decided. Our meeting will result in that decision—nothing else. If we win, Chaos shall rule. If you succeed in banishing us, then paltry Law bereft of possibility will gain ascendancy. But we shall win—though Fate herself complains!"

"Then let this thing be settled," replied Lord Donblas, and Elric saw the shining Lords of Law advance towards their dark opponents.

The very sky shook as they clashed. The air cried out and the Earth appeared to tilt. Those lesser beings left alive scattered away from the conflict and a sound like a million throbbing harp strings, each of a subtly different pitch, began to emanate from the warring gods.

Elric saw Jagreen Lern leave the ranks of the Dukes of Hell and ride in his flaming scarlet armour, away from them. He realised, perhaps, that his impertinence would be swiftly rewarded by death.

Elric sent Flamefang soaring down and he drew Stormbringer, yelling the Theocrat's name and shouting challenges.

Jagreen Lern looked up, but he did not laugh this time. He increased his speed until, as Elric had already noted, he saw towards what he was riding. Ahead, the earth had turned to black and purple gas that danced frenetically as if seeking to free itself from the rest of the atmosphere. Jagreen Lern halted his hairless horse and drew his war-axe from his belt. He raised his flame-red buckler which, like Elric's, was treated against sorcerous weapons.

The Phoorn hurtled downwards making Elric gasp with the speed of its descent. It flapped to earth a few yards from where Jagreen Lern sat his horrible horse, waiting, philosophically, for Elric to attack. Perhaps he sensed that their fight would mirror the larger fight going on around them, that the outcome of the one would be reflected in the outcome of the other. Whatever it was, he did not indulge in his usual braggadocio, but waited in silence.

Careless whether Jagreen Lern had the advantage or not, Elric dismounted and spoke to Flamefang in a purring murmur.

"Back, Flamefang, now. Back with your brothers. Whatever comes to pass, if I win or lose, the Phoorn's part is over." As Flamefang stirred and turned his huge head to look into Elric's face, another dragon descended and landed a short distance away. Moonglum, too, dismounted, beginning to advance through the black and purple mist. Elric shouted to him: "I want no help in this, Moonglum!"

"I'll give you none. But it will be my pleasure to see you take his life and soul!"

Elric looked at Jagreen Lern whose face was still impassive.

Flamefang's wings beat and he swept up into the sky and was soon gone, the other dragon following. He would not return.

Elric stalked towards the Theocrat, his shield high and his sword ready. Then, with astonishment, he saw Jagreen Lern dismount from his own grotesque mount and slap its hairless rump to send it galloping away. He stood waiting, slightly crouched in a position which emphasised his high-shouldered stance. His long, dark face was taut and his eyes fixed on Elric as the albino came closer. An unstable smile of anticipation quivered on the Theocrat's lips and his eyes flickered.

Elric paused just before he came within sword-reach of his enemy. "Jagreen Lern, are you ready to pay for the crimes you've committed against me and the world?"

"Pay? Crimes? You surprise me, Elric, for I see you have fully absorbed the carping attitude of your new allies. In my conquests I have found it necessary to eliminate a few of your friends who sought to stop me. But that was to be expected. I did what I had to and what I intended—if I have failed now, I have no regret, for regret is a fool's emotion and useless in any capacity. What happened to your wife was no direct fault of mine. Will you have triumph if you slay me?"

Elric shook his head. "My perspectives have, indeed, changed, Jagreen Lern. Yet we of Melniboné were ever a vengeful brood—and vengeance is what I claim!"

"Ah, now I understand you." Jagreen Lern changed his stance and he raised his axe to the defensive position. "I am ready."

Elric leapt at him, Stormbringer shrieking through the air to crash against the scarlet buckler and crash again. Three blows he delivered before Jagreen Lern's axe sought to wriggle through his defence and he halted it by a sideways movement of the Chaos Shield. The axe succeeded only in grazing his arm near the shoulder. Elric's shield clanged against Jagreen Lern's and Elric attempted to exert his weight and push the Theocrat backwards, meanwhile stabbing around the rims of the locked shields and trying to penetrate Jagreen Lern's guard.

For some moments they remained in this position while the music of the battle sounded around them and the ground seemed to fall from under them, columns of blossoming colours erupting, like magical plants, on all sides. Then Jagreen Lern jumped back, slashing at Elric. The albino rushed forward, ducked and struck at the Theocrat's leg near the knee—and missed. From above, the axe dashed down and he flung himself to one side to avoid it. Carried off balance by the force of the blow, Jagreen Lern staggered and Elric leapt up and kicked at the small of the Theocrat's back. The man fell sprawling, losing his grip on both axe and shield as he tried to do many things at once and failed to do anything. Elric put his heel on the Theocrat's neck and held him there, Stormbringer hovering greedily over his prone enemy.

Jagreen Lern heaved his body round so that he looked up at Elric. He was suddenly pale and his eyes were fixed on the black hellblade when he spoke hoarsely to Elric. "Finish me now. There's no place for my soul in all eternity— not any more. I must go to limbo—so finish me!"

Elric was about to allow Stormbringer to plunge itself into the defeated Theocrat when he stayed the weapon, holding it back from its prey with difficulty. The runesword murmured in frustration and tugged in his hand.

"No," he said slowly, "I want nothing of yours, Jagreen Lern. I would not pollute my being by feeding off your soul. Moonglum!" His friend ran up. "Moonglum, hand me your blade."

Silently, the little Eastlander obeyed. Elric sheathed the resisting Stormbringer, saying to it: "There—that's the first time I've stopped you from feeding. What will you do now, I wonder?" Then he took Moonglum's blade and slashed it across Jagreen Lern's cheek, opening it up in a long, deep cut which began slowly to fill with blood.

The Theocrat screamed.

"No, Elric—kill me!"

With an absent smile, Elric slashed the other cheek. His bloody face contorted, Jagreen Lern shouted for death, but Elric continued to smile his vague, half-aware smile, and said softly: "You sought to imitate the emperors of Melniboné, did you not? You mocked Elric of that line, you tortured him and you abducted his wife. You moulded her body into a hell-shape as you moulded the rest of the world. You slew Elric's friends and challenged him in your impertinence. But you are nothing—you are more of a pawn than Elric ever was. Now, little man, know how the folk of Melniboné toyed with such upstarts in the days when they ruled the world!"

Jagreen Lern took an hour to die and only then because Moonglum begged Elric to finish him swiftly.

Elric handed Moonglum's tainted sword back to him after wiping it on a shred of fabric that had been part of the Theocrat's robe. He looked down at the mutilated body and stirred it with his foot, then he looked away to where the Lords of the Higher Worlds were embattled.

He was badly weakened from the fight and also from the energy he had been forced to exert to return the resisting Stormbringer to its sheath, but this was forgotten as he stared in wonder at the gigantic battle.

Both the Lords of Law and those of Chaos had become huge and misty as their earthly mass diminished and they continued to fight in human shape. They were like half-real giants, fighting everywhere now—on the land and above it. Far away on the rim of the horizon, he saw Donblas the Justice Maker engaged with Chardros the Reaper, their outlines flickering and spreading, the slim sword darting and the great scythe sweeping.

Unable to participate, unsure which side was winning, Elric and Moonglum watched as the intensity of the battle increased and, with it, the slow dissolution of the gods' earthly manifestation. The fight was no longer merely on the Earth but seemed to be raging throughout all the planes of the cosmos and, as if in unison with this transformation, the Earth appeared to be losing its form, until Elric and Moonglum drifted in the mingled swirl of air, fire, earth and water.

The Earth dissolved—yet still the Lords of the Higher Worlds battled over it.

The stuff of the Earth alone remained, but unformed. Its components were still in existence, but their new shape was undecided. The fight continued. The victors would have the privilege of re-forming the Earth.

6

At last, though Elric did not know how, the turbulent dark gave way to light, and there came a noise—a cosmic roar of hate and frustration—and he knew that the Lords of Chaos had been defeated and banished. The Lords of Law victorious, Fate's plan had been achieved, though it still required the last note of the horn to bring it to its required conclusion.

And Elric realised he did not have the strength left to blow the horn the third time.

About the two friends, the world was taking on a distinct shape again. They found they were standing on a rocky plain and in the distance were the slender peaks of new-formed mountains, purple against a mellow sky.

Then the Earth began to move. Faster and faster it whirled, day giving way to night with incredible rapidity, and then it began to slow until the sun was again all but motionless in the sky, moving with something like its customary speed.

The change had taken place. Law ruled here now, yet the Lords of Law had departed without thanks.

And though Law ruled, it could not progress until the horn was blown for the last time.

"So it is over," Moonglum murmured. "All gone—Elwher, my birthplace, Karlaak by the Weeping Waste, Bakshaan, even the Dreaming City and the Isle of Melniboné. They no longer exist, they cannot be retrieved. And this is the new world formed by Law. It looks much the same as the old."

Elric, too, was filled with a sense of loss, knowing that all the places that were familiar to him, even the very continents were gone and replaced by different ones. It was like the loss of childhood and perhaps that was what it was—the passing of the Earth's childhood.

He shrugged away the thought and smiled. "I'm supposed to blow the horn for the final time if the Earth's new life is to begin. Yet I haven't the strength. Perhaps Fate is to be thwarted after all?"

Moonglum looked at him strangely. "I hope not, friend."

Elric sighed. "We are the last two left, Moonglum, you and I. It is fitting that even the mighty events that have taken place have not harmed our friendship, have not separated us. You are the only friend whose company has not worn on me, the only one I have trusted."

Moonglum grinned a shadow of his old, cocky grin. "And where we've shared adventures, I've usually profited if you have not. The partnership has been complementary. I shall never know why I chose to share your destiny. Perhaps it was no doing of mine, but Fate's, for there is one final act of friendship I can perform . . ."

Elric was about to question Moonglum when a quiet voice came from behind him.

"I bear two messages. One of thanks from the Lords of Law—and another from a more powerful entity."

"Sepiriz!" Elric turned to face his mentor. "Well, are you satisfied with my work?"

"Aye—greatly." Sepiriz's face was sad and he stared at Elric with a look of profound sympathy. "You have succeeded in everything but the last act which is to blow the Horn of Fate for the third time. Because of you the world shall know progression and its new people shall have the opportunity to advance by degrees to a new state of being."

"But what is the meaning of it all?" Elric said. "That I have never fully understood."

"Who can? Who can know why the Cosmic Balance exists, why Fate exists and the Lords of the Higher Worlds? Why there must always be a champion to fight such battles? There seems to be an infinity of space and time and possibilities. There may be an infinite number of beings, one above the other, who see the final purpose, though, in infinity, there can be no final purpose. Perhaps all is cyclic and this same event will occur again and again until the universe is run down and fades away as the world we knew has faded. Meaning, Elric? Do not seek that, for madness lies in such a course."

"No meaning, no pattern. Then why have I suffered all this?"

"Perhaps even the gods seek meaning and pattern and this is merely one attempt to find it. Look—" he waved his hands to indicate the newly formed Earth. "All this is fresh and moulded by logic. Perhaps the logic will control the newcomers, perhaps a factor will occur to destroy that logic. The gods experiment, the Cosmic Balance guides the destiny of the Earth, men struggle and credit the gods with knowing why they struggle—but do the gods know?"

"You disturb me further when I had hoped to be comforted," he sighed. "I have lost wife and world—and do not know why."

"I am sorry. I have come to wish you farewell, my friend. Do what you must."

"Aye. Shall I see you again?"

"No, for we are both truly dead. Our age has gone."

Sepiriz seemed to twist in the air and disappear.

A cold silence remained.

At length Elric's thoughts were interrupted by Moonglum. "You must blow the horn, Elric. Whether it means nothing or much—you must blow it and finish this business for ever!"

"How? I have scarcely enough strength to stand on my feet."

"I have decided what you must do. Slay me with Stormbringer. Take my soul and vitality into yourself—then you will have sufficient power to blow the last blast."

"Kill you, Moonglum! The only one left—my only true friend? You babble!"

"I mean it. You must, for there is nothing else to do. Further, we have no place here and must die soon at any rate. You told me how Zarozinia gave you her soul—well, take mine, too!"

"I cannot."

Moonglum paced towards him and reached down to grip Stormbringer's hilt, pulling it halfway from the sheath.

"*No*, Moonglum!"

But now the sword sprang from the sheath on its own volition. Elric struck Moonglum's hand away and gripped the hilt. He could not stop it. The sword rose up, dragging his arm with it, poised to deliver a blow.

Moonglum stood with his arms by his side, his face expressionless, though Elric thought he glimpsed a flicker of fear in the eyes. He struggled to control the blade, but knew it was impossible.

"Let it do its work, Elric."

The blade plunged forward and pierced Moonglum's heart. His blood sprang out and covered it. His eyes blurred and filled with horror. "Ah, no—I—had—not—expected *this*!"

Petrified, Elric could not tug the sword from his friend's heart. Moonglum's energy began to flow up its length and course into his body, yet, even when all the little Eastlander's vitality was absorbed, Elric remained staring at the small corpse until the tears flowed from his crimson eyes and a great sob racked him. Then the blade came free.

He flung it away from him and it did not clatter on the rocky ground but landed as a body might land. Then it seemed to move towards him and stop and he had the suspicion that it was watching him.

He took the horn and put it to his lips. He blew the blast to herald in the night of the new Earth. The night that would precede the new dawn. And though the horn's note was triumphant, Elric was not. He stood full of infinite loneliness and infinite sorrow, his head tilted back as the sound rang on. And, when the note faded from triumph to a dying echo that expressed something of Elric's misery, a huge outline began to form in the sky above the Earth, as if summoned by the horn.

It was the outline of a gigantic hand holding a balance and, as he watched, the Balance began to right itself until each side was true.

And somehow this relieved Elric's sorrow as he released his grip on the Horn of Fate.

"There *is* something, at least," he said, "and if it's an illusion, then it's a reassuring one."

He turned his head to one side and saw the blade leave the ground, sweep into the air and then rush down on him.

"Stormbringer!" he cried, and then the hellsword struck his chest, he felt the icy touch of the blade against his heart, reached out his fingers to clutch at it, felt his body constrict, felt it sucking his soul from the very depths of his being, felt his whole personality being drawn into the runesword. He knew, as his life faded to combine with the sword's, that it had always been his destiny to die in this manner. With the blade he had killed friends and lovers, stolen their souls to feed his own waning strength. It was as if the sword had always used him to this end, as if he was merely a manifestation of Stormbringer and was now being taken back into the body of the blade which had never been a true sword. And, as he died, he wept again, for he knew that the fraction of the sword's soul which was his would never know rest but was doomed to immortality, to eternal struggle.

Elric of Melniboné, last of the Bright Emperors, cried out, and then his body collapsed, a sprawled husk beside its comrade, and he lay beneath the mighty balance that still hung in the sky.

Then Stormbringer's shape began to change, writhing and curling above the body of the albino, finally to stand astraddle it.

The entity that was Stormbringer, last manifestation of Chaos which would remain with this new world as it grew, looked down on the corpse of Elric of Melniboné and smiled.

"Farewell, friend. I was a thousand times more evil than thou!"

And then it leapt from the Earth and went spearing upwards, its wild voice laughing mockery at the Cosmic Balance; filling the universe with its unholy joy.

THE ELRIC SAGA: A READER'S GUIDE

BY JOHN DAVEY

Elric of Melniboné—proud prince of ruins, kinslayer—call him what you will. He remains, together with maybe Jerry Cornelius, Michael Moorcock's most enduring, if not always most endearing, character.

This guide attempts to provide a title-by-title breakdown of the novels together with omnibuses in which each appeared, all in a chronological format, listing omnibuses as individual titles rather than including them within the main books' descriptions.

Elric began life sixty years ago, in response to a request from John Carnell, editor of SCIENCE FANTASY magazine, for a series akin to Robert E. Howard's Conan the Barbarian stories. What Carnell received, while steeped in sword-and-sorcery images, was something quite different. All in all, nine Elric novellas appeared in SCIENCE FANTASY between June 1961 and April 1964, the last four "serialising" (in effect) the novel *Stormbringer*, while the first five were collected as **The Stealer of Souls** (**1963**). These five were later split up and re-collected in, or absorbed into, *The Weird of the White Wolf* and *The Bane of the Black Sword* (*q.v.*, both 1977) and were also, as a result of this assimilation, slightly revised. Collectors should note that the true first edition of *The Stealer of Souls* (subtitled by its publishers as "*. . . and Other Stories,*" against Moorcock's wishes) was bound in orange boards; an otherwise identical but less collectable second printing had green boards.

Stormbringer (1965), conceived as a novel, was first published as such when abridged and revised from the four remaining SCIENCE FANTASY novellas. It was later restored to its original length and further revised, in 1977. The original abridgements basically condensed the first two novellas (plus part of the third) into one long section, "The Coming of Chaos."

The Singing Citadel (1970) was a collection of four other novellas originally published in various anthologies and periodicals between 1962 and 1967. They were later split up and all but one were re-collected in, or absorbed into, *The Weird of the White Wolf* and *The Bane of the Black Sword* as their events interconnect with those of *The Stealer of Souls*. They were also, as a result of this assimilation, slightly revised. The unused novella, "The Greater Conqueror" (sometimes erroneously listed as "The Great Conqueror"), was subsequently collected in *Moorcock's Book of Martyrs* (1976, a.k.a. *Dying for Tomorrow*, 1978), *Earl Aubec and Other Stories* (1993), *Elric: To Rescue Tanelorn* (2008) and *Elric: The Sleeping Sorceress* (2013).

The Sleeping Sorceress (1971) was expanded from a novella of the same name, although it was originally commissioned as a serial for Kenneth Bulmer's magazine, SWORD AND SORCERY, which never appeared. One of its sections retells, from Elric's viewpoint, a part of the Corum novel, *The King of the Swords*. In 1977, *The Sleeping Sorceress* was retitled, with minor textual amendments, as *The Vanishing Tower* (*q.v.*).

Elric of Melniboné (1972) is a prequel to all other Elric novels. *The Dreaming City* (1972) was a version of *Elric of Melniboné*, published with unauthorised changes. Collectors should note that, in 1977, *Elric of Melniboné* was one of three Elric books sold as illustrated editions in slip-cases. This first (in a red case) also had a smaller, limited edition (in a brown case) signed by the author, artist (Robert Gould) and publisher. In 2003, *Elric of Melniboné* was the first novel of Moorcock's to become an unabridged audiobook.

Elric: The Return to Melnibone (sic, **1973**) remains, despite its comparative irrelevance to the overall series, one of the scarcest and most sought-after of Elric books. This is the result of its somewhat chequered history, a saga complex enough to rival Elric's own. It is actually little more than a showcase for the exquisite artwork of Philippe Druillet, beginning life in 1966 as double-spread colour illustrations for the only issue of a French magazine, MOI AUSSI, with text by Maxim Jakubowski. In 1969, Druillet illustrated an omnibus called *Elric le Necromancien*, and in 1972 some of this (and new) artwork was put into a twenty-one piece portfolio as *La Saga d'Elric le Necromancien*, this time with text by Michel Demuth. All of this work up until then was unauthorised, but when the portfolio was reprinted and bound (less one piece) in the U.K. as *Elric: The Return to Melnibone* (text by Moorcock), Druillet threatened to sue. Moorcock was forced to step in on behalf of the British publishers, pointing out that permission had never been granted for Druillet to draw Elric in the first place. In order to avoid messy litigation, it was decided to allow the small print run to expire, never to be reprinted. However, a republication was finally agreed, the book made available again in 1997 as *Elric: The Return to Melniboné*, and it was later collected (alongside James Cawthorn's 1976 graphic adaptation of *Stormbringer*) in 2021's *Elric: The Eternal Champion Collection*.

The Jade Man's Eyes (**1973**) was a separate novella which, in order to bring it in line with the developing series, was revised and absorbed into *The Sailor on the Seas of Fate* as "Sailing to the Past."

The Sailor on the Seas of Fate (**1976**) originally slotted, chronologically, between events in *Elric of Melniboné* and *The Weird of the White Wolf*. One of its sections retells, from Elric's viewpoint, a part of the Hawkmoon/Count Brass novel, *The Quest for Tanelorn*. In 2006, *The Sailor on the Seas of Fate* also became an unabridged audiobook.

The Weird of the White Wolf (1977) is a chronological arrangement of selected contents from *The Stealer of Souls* and *The Singing Citadel*, compiled in order to bring them in line with the developing series.

The Vanishing Tower (1977) is a retitling, with minor textual amendments, of *The Sleeping Sorceress*. Collectors should note that, in 1981, *The Vanishing Tower* was the second of three Elric books sold as illustrated editions in slipcases. This edition (in a pictorial red case) also had a smaller, limited edition (in a brown case) signed by the author, artist (Michael Whelan) and publisher.

The Bane of the Black Sword (1977) is a chronological arrangement of selected contents from *The Stealer of Souls* and *The Singing Citadel*, compiled in order to bring them in line with the developing series.

The somewhat misleadingly titled **Six Science Fiction Classics from the Master of Heroic Fantasy** (1979) was a boxed set of six American paperbacks: *Elric of Melniboné*, *The Sailor on the Seas of Fate*, *The Weird of the White Wolf*, *The Vanishing Tower*, *The Bane of the Black Sword* and *Stormbringer*.

Elric at the End of Time (1984) was a collection of short fiction and nonfiction which actually contained only three Elric-related items among its contents of seven (excluding the introduction). The title story was also published separately in 1987 as a large-format novella (*q.v.*) illustrated by Rodney Matthews.

The Elric Saga Part One (1984) was the first Elric omnibus, and contained *Elric of Melniboné*, *The Sailor on the Seas of Fate* and *The Weird of the White Wolf*. *The Elric Saga Part Two* (1984) was the second omnibus, and contained *The Vanishing Tower*, *The Bane of the Black Sword* and *Stormbringer*.

Elric at the End of Time (1987) was a separate, large-format novella illustrated by Rodney Matthews for whom it was originally written some years earlier. Collectors should note that it was published simultaneously in both hardcover and paperback formats.

The Fortress of the Pearl (1989), the first Elric novel for thirteen years, expanded the saga and slots, chronologically, between events in *Elric of Melniboné* and *The Sailor on the Seas of Fate*.

The Revenge Of The Rose (1991) slots between events in *The Sleeping Sorceress/The Vanishing Tower* and the stories from *The Bane of the Black Sword*.

In 1992, Moorcock began an ambitious project of re-ordering, revising and republishing much of his back-catalogue in a large set of omnibuses in the U.K. under the collective title of "The Tale of the Eternal Champion." The first of these to feature the albino prince was *Elric of Melniboné* (1993), containing *Elric of Melniboné*, *The Fortress of the Pearl*, *The Sailor on the Seas of Fate* and selected contents from *The Weird of the White Wolf*. The omnibus was retitled in the U.S.A., when the "Eternal Champion" series began to appear there, as *Elric: Song of the Black Sword* (1995).

The second British omnibus to feature Elric was *Stormbringer* (1993), containing *The Sleeping Sorceress*, *The Revenge of the Rose*, selected contents from *The Bane of the Black Sword*, and *Stormbringer*. This omnibus was retitled in the U.S.A. as *Elric: The Stealer of Souls* (1998), not to be confused with a later volume of the same name (*q.v.*).

Collectors should note that, in the U.K., "The Tale of the Eternal Champion" omnibuses were published simultaneously in both hardcover and matching paperback formats. In the U.S.A., hardcover editions appeared ahead of their paperback versions.

Elric: Tales of the White Wolf (**1994**) was an original anthology of Elric stories by Moorcock and others, edited by Edward E. Kramer & Richard Gilliam.

Michael Moorcock's Multiverse (**1999**) was a graphic novel illustrated by Walter Simonson, Mark Reeve & John Ridgway, originally serialised in twelve parts (1997/'98). It contained three interconnecting tales (each illustrated by a different artist), one of which—Ridgway's—is "Duke Elric."

The Dreamthief's Daughter (**2001**) was the first volume of a new Elric trilogy—in fact the only preconceived Elric trilogy—linking the albino with some of the many and various members of the Family von Bek. (When revising his books for the "Eternal Champion" omnibuses, Moorcock had the opportunity to change several character names in order to bring them in line with the developing "Von Bek" series, which had begun in 1981 with *The War Hound and the World's Pain* although the name's derivation goes back as far as Katinka van Bak in 1973's *The Champion of Garathorm*.) Collectors should note that, also in 2001 (after the true first edition), *The Dreamthief's Daughter* became the last of three Elric books sold as illustrated editions in slip-cases. This limited edition, signed by the author and artists (Randy Broecker, Donato Giancola, Gary Gianni, Robert Gould, Michael Kaluta, Todd Lockwood, Don Maitz & Michael Whelan), was followed two years later—still dated "2001"—by a smaller limited edition which was leather-bound and tray-cased. In 2013, *The Dreamthief's Daughter* was retitled and revised (in the U.K.) as *Daughter of Dreams* (*q.v.*).

Elric (**2001**) was another omnibus, containing *The Stealer of Souls* (or rather its five component novellas) and *Stormbringer*, as part of a "Fantasy Masterworks" series. In 2008, it was repackaged as part of the same publisher's more exclusive "Ultimate Fantasies" sequence.

The Elric Saga Part Three (2002), another omnibus, contained *The Fortress of the Pearl* and *The Revenge of the Rose.*

The Skrayling Tree: The Albino in America (2003) is the second part of the trilogy beginning with *The Dreamthief's Daughter.* In 2013, *The Skrayling Tree* was retitled and revised (in the U.K.) as *Destiny's Brother.*

The White Wolf's Son: The Albino Underground (2005) is the third and last part of the trilogy. Although this Elric sub-series can be read as a standalone adventure (as, indeed, can each volume), brief mention is made of events slotting, chronologically, into those described within *Stormbringer.* In 2013, *The White Wolf's Son* was retitled and revised (in the U.K.) as *Son of the Wolf.*

The Elric Saga Part IV (2005), another omnibus, contained *The Dreamthief's Daughter, The Skrayling Tree* and *The White Wolf's Son.*

Elric: The Making of a Sorcerer (2007) was a graphic novel illustrated by Walter Simonson, originally serialised in four parts (2004–'06), and is a prequel to the novel *Elric of Melniboné.*

Elric: The Stealer of Souls (2008) was the first volume in a series of six Elric omnibuses published (in the order the main novels were written) under the collective title of "Chronicles of the Last Emperor of Melniboné," each containing fiction and non-fiction. The first volume's fiction includes *The Stealer of Souls* and *Stormbringer. Elric: To Rescue Tanelorn* (2008) was the second volume, a collection of Elric (or Elric-related) short fiction. *Elric: The Sleeping Sorceress* (2008) was the third volume, including the novels *The Sleeping Sorceress* and *Elric of Melniboné. Duke Elric* (2009) was the fourth volume, including *The Sailor on the Seas of Fate,* the *Duke Elric* graphic-novel script and a novella, "The Flaneur des Arcades de l'Opera." ***Elric in the Dream Realms***

(2009) was the fifth volume, including *The Fortress of the Pearl*, the *Elric: The Making of a Sorcerer* graphic-novel script and a short story, "A Portrait in Ivory." *Elric: Swords and Roses* (2010), the sixth and final volume, included *The Revenge of the Rose*, a *Stormbringer* (unmade) movie screenplay, and the first of two new novellas, "Black Petals" (2008), the second being "Red Pearls" (2011). At the time of writing, these novellas are being revised and incorporated, with much new material, into a brand-new Elric novel (due 2022).

Elric: Les Buveurs d'Âmes (2011) was an original, collaborative novel (in French) by Moorcock and Fabrice Colin, for which there seems no imminent sign of an English-language edition.

Daughter of Dreams (2013) was a revised retitling of *The Dreamthief's Daughter*; *Destiny's Brother* (2013) was a revised retitling of *The Skrayling Tree*; *Son of the Wolf* (2013) was a revised retitling of *The White Wolf's Son*.

Elric of Melniboné and Other Stories (2013) was the first volume in a set of seven Elric omnibuses published (in narrative-chronology order) as part of a larger series, "The Michael Moorcock Collection," each containing similar long & short fiction and non-fiction to the "Chronicles of the Last Emperor of Melniboné." It was followed by *Elric: The Fortress of the Pearl* (2013), *Elric: The Sailor on the Seas of Fate* (2013), *Elric: The Sleeping Sorceress and Other Stories* (2013), *Elric: The Revenge of the Rose* (2014), *Elric: Stormbringer!* (2014), and *Elric: The Moonbeam Roads* (2014) containing *Daughter of Dreams*, *Destiny's Brother* and *Son of the Wolf*.

In 2019, Centipede Press began publishing limited editions of nine Elric novels—which have all (to date) sold out prior to publication—each accompanied by the relevant shorter fiction required to create an overall narrative chronology. At the time of writing, these volumes have been *Elric of Melniboné*, *The Fortress of the Pearl* and *The Sailor on the Seas of Fate* (all 2019),

The Sleeping Sorceress (2020) and *The Revenge of the Rose* (2021), with *Stormbringer*, *The Dreamthief's Daughter*, *The Skrayling Tree* and *The White Wolf's Son* to follow. The first three volumes have also been produced as out-sized, slip-cased hardcovers offered to subscribers only.

Which brings us at long last to Saga's Elric saga volumes. Unlimited and therefore available to all, Saga Press's three uniform omnibus editions—published from 2022 to commemorate sixty glorious years since the character's very first appearance in print—contain eleven novels in order of narrative chronology: *Elric of Melniboné*, *The Fortress of the Pearl*, *The Sailor on the Seas of Fate* and *The Weird of the White Wolf* in **The Elric Saga Volume One: Elric of Melniboné**, *The Vanishing Tower*, *The Revenge of the Rose*, *The Bane of the Black Sword* and *Stormbringer* in **The Elric Saga Volume Two: Stormbringer**, and *The Dreamthief's Daughter*, *The Skrayling Tree* and *The White Wolf's Son* in **The Elric Saga Volume Three: The White Wolf**.

FIRST EDITIONS AND
FIRST APPEARANCES

The Stealer of Souls:

"The Dreaming City," originally in SCIENCE FANTASY No. 47 (edited
by John Carnell), U.K., June 1961

"While the Gods Laugh," in SCIENCE FANTASY No. 49, Oct. 1961

"The Stealer of Souls," in SCIENCE FANTASY No. 51, Feb. 1962

"Kings in Darkness," in SCIENCE FANTASY No. 54, Aug. 1962

"The Flame Bringers," in SCIENCE FANTASY No. 55, Oct. 1962

Neville Spearman hardcover, U.K., 1963

Lancer paperback, U.S.A., 1967

Stormbringer:

"Dead God's Homecoming," orig. in SCIENCE FANTASY No. 59, June
1963

"Black Sword's Brothers," in SCIENCE FANTASY No. 61, Oct. 1963

"Sad Giant's Shield," in SCIENCE FANTASY No. 63, Feb. 1964

"Doomed Lord's Passing," in SCIENCE FANTASY No. 64, Apr. 1964

Herbert Jenkins h/c (abridged & revised from the "serialised" novellas),
U.K., 1965

Lancer p/b (ditto), U.S.A., 1967

DAW p/b (full length & revised), U.S.A., 1977

Granada p/b (ditto), U.K., 1985

The Singing Citadel:

"The Singing Citadel" (novella), orig. in *The Fantastic Swordsmen*
(anthology edited by L. Sprague de Camp), U.S.A., 1967

"Master of Chaos," in FANTASTIC Vol. 13 No. 5 (ed. Cele Goldsmith),
U.S.A., May 1964

"The Greater Conqueror" (non-Elric), in SCIENCE FANTASY No. 58,
Apr. 1963

"To Rescue Tanelorn . . .," in SCIENCE FANTASY No. 56, Dec. 1962

Mayflower p/b, U.K., 1970

Berkley p/b, U.S.A., 1970

The Sleeping Sorceress:

"The Sleeping Sorceress" (novella), orig. in *Warlocks and Warriors*
(anthol., ed. Douglas Hill), U.K., 1971

New English Library h/c (expanded from the novella), U.K., 1971

Lancer p/b (ditto), U.S.A., 1972

DAW p/b (as *The Vanishing Tower*), U.S.A., 1977

Archival Press h/c (as *The Vanishing Tower*, no dust-wrapper, in pictorial
red slip-case [also limited in brown slip-case]), U.S.A., 1981

Granada p/b (as *The Vanishing Tower*), U.K., 1983

Elric of Melniboné:

Hutchinson h/c, U.K., 1972

Lancer p/b (unauthorised changes, as *The Dreaming City*), U.S.A., 1972

DAW p/b (unchanged, as *Elric of Melniboné*), U.S.A., 1976

Blue Star h/c (ditto, no dust-wrapper, in red slip-case [also limited in
brown slip-case]), U.S.A., 1977

Elric: The Return to Melnibone (illustrated by Philippe Druillet):

Unicorn outsize p/b, U.K., 1973

Jayde Design outsize p/b (as *Elric: The Return to Melniboné*), U.K., 1997

The Jade Man's Eyes:
Unicorn p/b, U.K., 1973

The Sailor on the Seas of Fate:
Quartet h/c, U.K., 1976
DAW p/b, U.S.A., 1976

The Weird of the White Wolf:
DAW p/b, U.S.A., 1977, comprising:
"The Dream of Earl Aubec" (a.k.a. "Master of Chaos")
"The Dreaming City"
"While the Gods Laugh"
"The Singing Citadel"
Granada p/b, U.K., 1984

The Bane of the Black Sword:
DAW p/b, U.S.A., 1977, comprising:
"The Stealer of Souls"
"Kings in Darkness"
"The Flamebringers" (a.k.a. "The Flame Bringers")
"To Rescue Tanelorn . . ."
Granada p/b, U.K., 1984

Six Science Fiction Classics from the Master of Heroic Fantasy:
Six DAW p/bs, boxed, U.S.A., 1979, comprising:
Elric of Melniboné
The Sailor on the Seas of Fate
The Weird of the White Wolf
The Vanishing Tower
The Bane of the Black Sword
Stormbringer

Elric at the End of Time (collection):

NEL h/c, U.K., 1984, comprising the following Elric-related items:

"Elric at the End of Time," orig. in *Elsewhere* (anthol., ed. Terri Windling & Mark Alan Arnold), U.S.A., 1981

"The Last Enchantment," in ARIEL No. 3 (ed. Thomas Durwood), U.S.A., Apr. 1978

"The Secret Life of Elric of Melniboné" (non-fiction), in CAMBER No. 14 (fanzine, ed. Alan Dodd), U.K., June 1964

DAW p/b, U.S.A., 1985

The Elric Saga Part One:

Doubleday (Science Fiction Book Club) h/c, U.S.A., 1984, comprising:

Elric of Melniboné

The Sailor on the Seas of Fate

The Weird of the White Wolf

The Elric Saga Part Two:

Doubleday (SFBC) h/c, U.S.A., 1984, comprising:

The Vanishing Tower

The Bane of the Black Sword

Stormbringer

Elric at the End of Time (novella, illustrated by Rodney Matthews):

Paper Tiger large-format h/c & p/b, U.K., 1987

The Fortress of the Pearl:

Gollancz h/c, U.K., 1989

Ace h/c, U.S.A., 1989

The Revenge of the Rose:
Grafton h/c, U.K., 1991
Ace h/c, U.S.A., 1991

Elric of Melniboné (omnibus):
Orion/Millennium h/c & p/b, U.K., 1993, comprising:
Elric of Melniboné
The Fortress of the Pearl
The Sailor on the Seas of Fate
"The Dreaming City"
"While the Gods Laugh"
"The Singing Citadel"
White Wolf h/c (as *Elric: Song of the Black Sword*), U.S.A., 1995

Stormbringer (omnibus):
Orion/Millennium h/c & p/b, U.K., 1993, comprising:
The Sleeping Sorceress
The Revenge of the Rose
"The Stealer of Souls"
"Kings in Darkness"
"The Caravan of Forgotten Dreams" (a.k.a. "The Flame Bringers")
Stormbringer
"Elric: A Reader's Guide" (non-fiction by John Davey)
White Wolf h/c (as *Elric: The Stealer of Souls*), U.S.A., 1998

Elric: Tales of the White Wolf:
White Wolf h/c, U.S.A., 1994, comprising the following Moorcock items:
"Introduction to *Tales of the White Wolf*" (non-fiction)
"The White Wolf's Song"

plus Elric stories by Tad Williams, David M. Honigsberg, Roland J.
Green & Frieda A. Murray, Richard Lee Byers, Brad Strickland,
Brad Linaweaver & William Alan Ritch, Kevin T. Stein, Scott
Ciencin, Gary Gygax, James S. Dorr, Stewart von Allmen, Paul
W. Cashman, Nancy A. Collins, Doug Murray, Karl Edward
Wagner, Thomas E. Fuller, Jody Lynn Nye, Colin Greenland,
Robert Weinberg, Charles Partington, Peter Crowther & James
Lovegrove, Nancy Holder, Neil Gaiman.

Michael Moorcock's Multiverse:

DC Comics large-format p/b, U.S.A., 1999
> "Moonbeams and Roses" (non-Elric), illustrated by Walter Simonson
> "The Metatemporal Detective" (non-Elric), illustrated by Mark Reeve
> "Duke Elric," illustrated by John Ridgway

The Dreamthief's Daughter:

Earthlight h/c, U.K., 2001
American Fantasy h/c (in slip-case [also limited in tray-case]), U.S.A.,
2001
Gollancz p/b (as *Daughter of Dreams*), U.K., 2013

Elric:

Gollancz p/b, U.K., 2001, comprising:
> "The Dreaming City"
> "While the Gods Laugh"
> "The Stealer of Souls"
> "Kings in Darkness"
> "The Caravan of Forgotten Dreams"
> *Stormbringer*

The Elric Saga Part Three:
SFBC h/c, U.S.A., 2002, comprising:
The Fortress of the Pearl
The Revenge of the Rose

The Skrayling Tree: The Albino in America:
Warner h/c, U.S.A., 2003
Gollancz p/b (as *Destiny's Brother*), U.K., 2013

The White Wolf's Son: The Albino Underground:
Warner h/c, U.S.A., 2005
Gollancz p/b (as *Son of the Wolf*), U.K., 2013

The Elric Saga Part IV:
SFBC h/c, U.S.A., 2005, comprising:
The Dreamthief's Daughter
The Skrayling Tree
The White Wolf's Son

Elric: The Making of a Sorcerer (illustrated by Walter Simonson):
DC Comics large-format p/b, U.S.A., 2007

Elric: The Stealer of Souls: Chronicles of the Last Emperor of Melniboné: Volume 1:
Del Rey p/b, U.S.A., 2008, comprising:
"Putting a Tag on It" (non-fiction), orig. in AMRA Vol. 2 No. 15
(fanzine, ed. George Scithers), U.S.A., May 1961
The Stealer of Souls

"Mission to Asno!" (non-Elric), in TARZAN ADVENTURES Vol. 7 No. 25
   (ed. Moorcock), U.K., Sep. 1957

Stormbringer

"Elric" (non-fiction), in NIEKAS No. 8 (fanzine, ed. Ed Meskys),
   U.S.A., 1964

"The Secret Life of Elric of Melniboné" (non-fiction)

"Final Judgement" (non-fiction by Alan Forrest), in NEW WORLDS No.
   147 (ed. Moorcock, as "Did Elric Die in Vain?"), U.K., Feb. 1965

"The Zenith Letter" (non-fiction by Anthony Skene), in *Monsieur
   Zenith the Albino*, U.K., 2001

Elric: To Rescue Tanelorn:

Del Rey p/b, U.S.A., 2008, comprising:

"The Eternal Champion," orig. in SCIENCE FANTASY No. 53, June
   1962

"To Rescue Tanelorn . . ."

"The Last Enchantment" (a.k.a. "Jesting with Chaos")

"The Greater Conqueror"

"Master of Chaos" (a.k.a. "Earl Aubec")

"Phase 1: A Jerry Cornelius Story," in *The Final Programme*, U.S.A.,
   1968 (U.K., 1969)

"The Singing Citadel"

"The Jade Man's Eyes"

"The Stone Thing," in TRIODE No. 20 (fanzine, ed. Eric Bentcliffe),
   U.K., Oct. 1974

"Elric at the End of Time"

"The Black Blade's Song" (a.k.a. "The White Wolf's Song")

"Crimson Eyes," in NEW STATESMAN & SOCIETY No. 333, U.K., 1994

"Sir Milk-and-Blood," in *Pawn of Chaos: Tales of the Eternal
   Champion* (anthol., ed. Edward E. Kramer), U.S.A., 1996

"The Roaming Forest," in *Cross Plains Universe: Texans Celebrate Robert E. Howard* (anthol., ed. Scott A. Cupp & Joe R. Lansdale), U.S.A., 2006

Elric: The Sleeping Sorceress:

Del Rey p/b, U.S.A., 2008, comprising:

The Sleeping Sorceress

"And So the Great Emperor Received His Education . . .," orig. spoken-word introduction to *Elric of Melniboné* (audiobook), U.S.A., 2003

Elric of Melniboné

"Aspects of Fantasy (1): Introduction" (non-fiction), orig. in SCIENCE FANTASY No. 61, Oct. 1963

"Introduction to *Elric of Melniboné*, Graphic Adaptation" (non-fiction), in *Elric of Melniboné* (by Roy Thomas, P. Craig Russell & Michael T. Gilbert), U.S.A., 1986

"El Cid and Elric: Under the Influence!" (non-fiction), in COMIQUEANDO No. 100, Argentina, Aug./Sep. 2007

Duke Elric:

Del Rey p/b, U.S.A., 2009, comprising:

"Introduction to the AudioRealms version of *The Sailor on the Seas of Fate* (audiobook), U.S.A., 2006

The Sailor on the Seas of Fate

Duke Elric (script)

"Aspects of Fantasy (2): The Floodgates of the Unconscious" (non-fiction), orig. in SCIENCE FANTASY No. 62, Dec. 1963

"The Flaneur des Arcades de l'Opera," in *The Metatemporal Detective*, U.S.A., 2008

"Elric: A Personality at War" (non-fiction by Adrian Snook)

Elric in the Dream Realms:

Del Rey p/b, U.S.A., 2009, comprising:

The Fortress of the Pearl

Elric: The Making of a Sorcerer (script)

"A Portrait in Ivory," orig. in *Logorrhea: Good Words Make Good Stories* (anthol., ed. John Klima), U.S.A., 2007

"Aspects of Fantasy (3): Figures of Faust" (non-fiction), in SCIENCE FANTASY No. 63, Feb. 1964

"Earl Aubec of Malador: Outline for a Series of Four Fantasy Novels"

"Introduction to the Taiwanese Edition of Elric" (non-fiction), in *Elric of Melniboné*, Taiwan, 2007

"One Life, Furnished in Early Moorcock" (by Neil Gaiman), in *Elric: Tales of the White Wolf*, U.S.A., 1994

Elric: Swords and Roses:

Del Rey p/b, U.S.A., 2010, comprising:

The Revenge of the Rose

Stormbringer: First Draft Screenplay

"Black Petals," orig. in WEIRD TALES No. 349 (edited by Stephen H. Segal & Ann VanderMeer), U.S.A., Mar./Apr. 2008

"Aspects of Fantasy (4): Conclusion" (non-fiction), in SCIENCE FANTASY No. 64, Apr. 1964

"Introduction to *The Skrayling Tree*" (non-fiction), written for Borders, Inc., 2003

"Introduction to the French Edition of Elric" (non-fiction), in *Le Cycle d'Elric*, France, 2006

"Elric: A New Reader's Guide" (non-fiction by John Davey)

Elric: Les Buveurs d'Âmes (with Fabrice Colin):

Fleuve Noir p/b, France, 2011

Elric of Melniboné and Other Stories:

Gollancz p/b, U.K., 2013, comprising:

"Putting a Tag on It" (non-fiction)

"Master of Chaos"

Elric: The Making of a Sorcerer (script)

"And So the Great Emperor Received His Education . . ."

Elric of Melniboné

"Aspects of Fantasy (1)" (non-fiction)

"Introduction to *Elric of Melniboné*, Graphic Adaptation" (non-fiction)

"El Cid and Elric: Under the Influence!" (non-fiction)

Elric: The Fortress of the Pearl:

Gollancz p/b, U.K., 2013, comprising:

The Fortress of the Pearl

"Aspects of Fantasy (2)" (non-fiction)

"Introduction to the Taiwanese Edition of Elric" (non-fiction)

"One Life, Furnished in Early Moorcock" (by Neil Gaiman)

Elric: The Sailor on the Seas of Fate:

Gollancz p/b, U.K., 2013, comprising:

"Introduction to the AudioRealms version of *The Sailor on the Seas of Fate* (audiobook)

The Sailor on the Seas of Fate

"The Dreaming City"

"A Portrait In Ivory"

"While the Gods Laugh"

"The Singing Citadel"

"Aspects of Fantasy (3)" (non-fiction)

"Elric: A Personality at War" (non-fiction by Adrian Snook)

Elric: The Sleeping Sorceress and Other Stories:

Gollancz p/b, U.K., 2013, comprising:

"The Eternal Champion"

"The Greater Conqueror"

"Earl Aubec of Malador: Outline for a Series of Four Fantasy Novels"

The Sleeping Sorceress

"The Stone Thing"

"Sir Milk-and-Blood"

"The Roaming Forest"

"The Flaneur des Arcades de l'Opera"

"Aspects of Fantasy (4)" (non-fiction)

Elric: The Revenge of the Rose:

Gollancz p/b, U.K., 2014, comprising:

The Revenge of the Rose

"The Stealer of Souls"

"Kings in Darkness"

"The Caravan of Forgotten Dreams"

"The Last Enchantment"

"To Rescue Tanelorn . . ."

"Introduction to the French Edition of Elric" (non-fiction)

Elric: Stormbringer!:

Gollancz p/b, U.K., 2014, comprising:

Stormbringer

"Elric" (non-fiction)

"The Secret Life of Elric of Melniboné" (non-fiction)

"Final Judgement" (non-fiction by Alan Forrest)

"The Zenith Letter" (non-fiction by Anthony Skene)

"Elric: A New Reader's Guide" (non-fiction by John Davey)

Elric: The Moonbeam Roads:

Gollancz p/b, U.K., 2014, comprising:

Daughter of Dreams

Destiny's Brother

Son of the Wolf

Centipede Press (limited edition h/cs, U.S.A.):

Elric of Melniboné, 2019, comprising:

"Master of Chaos"

"And So the Great Emperor Received His Education . . ."

Elric of Melniboné

The Fortress of the Pearl, 2019, comprising:

The Fortress of the Pearl

"The Black Blade's Song"

The Sailor on the Seas of Fate, 2019, comprising:

"Introduction to the AudioRealms version of *The Sailor on the Seas of Fate* (audiobook)

The Sailor on the Seas of Fate

"The Dreaming City"

"A Portrait In Ivory"

The Sleeping Sorceress, 2020, comprising:

"While the Gods Laugh"

"The Singing Citadel"

The Sleeping Sorceress

The Revenge of the Rose, 2021, comprising:

The Revenge of the Rose

"The Stealer of Souls"

Stormbringer, forthcoming, comprising:

"Kings in Darkness"

"The Caravan of Forgotten Dreams"

"The Last Enchantment"

"To Rescue Tanelorn . . ."

Stormbringer

The Dreamthief's Daughter, The Skrayling Tree, The White Wolfs Son
(all forthcoming)

The Elric Saga Volume One: Elric of Melniboné:

Saga Press h/c, U.S.A., 2022, comprising:

"One Life, Furnished in Early Moorcock" (by Neil Gaiman)

Elric of Melniboné

The Fortress of the Pearl

The Sailor on the Seas of Fate

The Weird of the White Wolf

"The Elric Saga: A Reader's Guide" (non-fiction by John Davey)

The Elric Saga Volume Two: Stormbringer:

Saga Press h/c, U.S.A., 2022, comprising:

The Vanishing Tower

The Revenge of the Rose

The Bane of the Black Sword

Stormbringer

"The Elric Saga: A Reader's Guide" (non-fiction by John Davey)

The Elric Saga Volume Three: The White Wolf:

Saga Press h/c, U.S.A., 2022, comprising:

The Dreamthief's Daughter

The Skrayling Tree

The White Wolf's Son

"The Elric Saga: A Reader's Guide" (non-fiction by John Davey)

MINUTIAE

In both of the variant omnibus editions called *Elric: The Stealer of Souls*, as well as all subsequent appearances, the version of *Stormbringer* is presented in a definitive, re-revised form, retaining its full, four-novella length but also incorporating some of the pertinent changes from its 1965 abridgement which were lost during its 1977 restoration to full length.

Non-Elric items contained within the *Elric at the End of Time* collection include "Sojan the Swordsman" (a composite of short tales featuring Moorcock's first ever fantasy hero), "Jerry Cornelius & Co." (two essays on that character) and the short story "The Stone Thing."

The essay "The Secret Life of Elric of Melniboné"—between its first fanzine appearance (1964) and its collection in *Elric at the End of Time*—was also in *Sojan* (Savoy Books p/b, U.K., 1977). That collection additionally contained another piece of non-fiction, "Elric," which originally appeared in the fanzines NIEKAS No. 8 (ed. Ed Meskys, 1963, as a letter) and CRUCIFIED TOAD No. 4 (ed. David Britton, 1974).

The French omnibus, *Elric le Necromancien* (Éditions Opta h/c, 1969), collected *The Stealer of Souls* and the full version of *Stormbringer*—plus the novellas "The Singing Citadel" and "To Rescue Tanelorn . . ."—all arranged in correct chronological order some eight years before any English-language equivalents. More recently, in France, the mammoth omnibus, *Le Cycle d'Elric*, collected in a single volume *Elric of Melniboné*, *The Fortress of the Pearl*, *The Sailor on the Seas of Fate*, *The Weird of the White Wolf*, *The Sleeping Sorceress*, *The Revenge of the Rose*, *The Bane of the Black Sword*, "The Last Enchantment," *Stormbringer* and "Elric at the End of Time."

Moorcock and Elric are particularly well served in France, where individual and omnibus volumes remain permanently in print, and a two-volume edition of *Elric: Tales of the White Wolf* appeared as well as another anthology of original stories by hands other than Moorcock's (although he introduces it), *Elric et la Porte des Mondes* (2006),which seems unlikely ever to receive an English-language edition (although some stories were translated for the 2017 anthology, *Michael Moorcock's Legends of the Multiverse*).

Many graphic adaptations of the Elric saga have appeared over the years, mostly starting as comics. Moorcock himself, together with James Cawthorn, plotted a two-part strip in 1972, in which Elric and Conan the Barbarian join forces ("A Sword Called Stormbringer!" & "The Green Empress of Melniboné" in CONAN THE BARBARIAN Nos 14 & 15). Cawthorn also produced a one-off graphic adaptation of *Stormbringer* for Savoy Books (1976). Several other Elric one-offs have appeared over the years, drawn by various hands, but the most widely available series for some time were Pacific/First Comics' *Elric of Melniboné* (6 parts), *Elric: Sailor on the Seas of Fate* (7 parts), *Elric: Weird of the White Wolf* (5 parts), *Elric: The Vanishing Tower* (6 parts) and *Elric: The Bane of the Black Sword* (6 parts), all serialised throughout the 1980s. The first three sets were also compiled as bound graphic novels. The sequence was stopped by Moorcock before *Stormbringer*, due to deterioration in the quality of the artwork, although a new graphic version of that novel, adapted by P. Craig Russell, was finally serialised in the U.S.A. for Topps/Dark Horse Comics in 1997 (compiled as a bound graphic novel a year later). All of these and other adaptations have more recently been bound and published by Titan Comics.

The two Moorcock-scripted tales, *Duke Elric* and *Elric: The Making of a Sorcerer*, have of course developed the saga further still, and also more recently there have been both *Elric: The Balance Lost* (2011/'12, an original 12-part graphic series by Chris Roberson & Francesco Biagini) and a French sequence of loose adaptations comprising (to date) *Le Trône de Rubis*, *Stormbringer*, *Le Loup Blanc* and *La Cité Qui Rêve* (2013–'21) by Julien Blondel, with Didier Poli, Robin Recht, Jean-Luc Cano, Julien Telo, and others.

Also heavily and ornately illustrated are the various rule books and supplements for Elric-related role-playing games from the American companies

Chaosium (whose best-known *Stormbringer* has itself been revised and massively expanded several times) and more recently Mongoose Publishing with their *Elric of Melniboné*. There are also French RPGs in existence, and a Swedish video game in development.

Elric ephemera has become quite a major industry and, if a long-awaited Elric movie ever comes to fruition, such things can only be expected to blossom further still. There have already been collectable cards, die-cast miniatures, dolls, jigsaw puzzles, model-kits, posters, T-shirts, "replica" swords and, of course, records.

Moorcock's musical involvement with several rock bands, including his own, is well known. He wrote an Elric-related song, "Black Blade," for Blue Öyster Cult, but it is Hawkwind who have used the albino prince to the best effect. In 1985, they released the album *The Chronicle of the Black Sword*, and went on an accompanying theatrical concert tour—sometimes featuring Moorcock on stage with the band—which also gave rise to a live album, *Live Chronicles*, and video/DVD, some versions of which include Moorcock performances.

Quite what the ever-taciturn Elric would make of all this attention, I am not sure. Sixty years on, he has already endured far more than those first nine SCIENCE FANTASY novellas would have had us believe possible. Only time will tell us where else he goes from here . . .

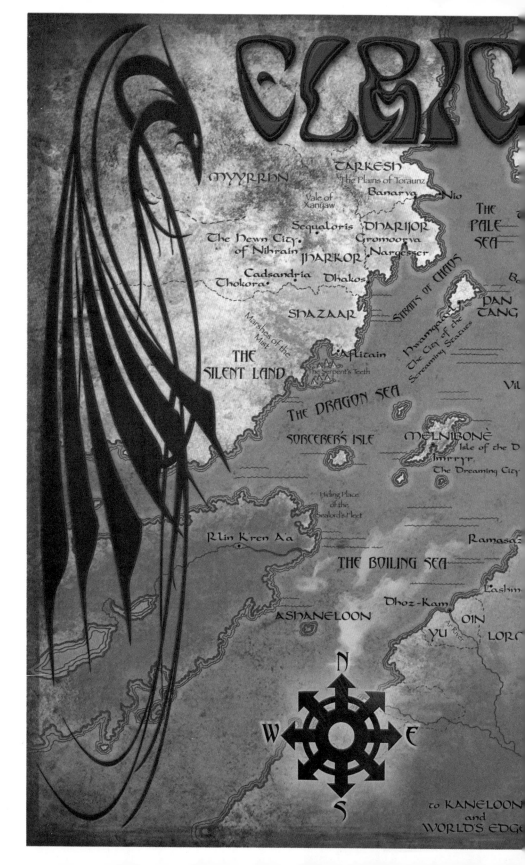